DAVID

"THE FIRST MODERN MAN, THE FIRST TO WRITE REAL LOVE POETRY, THE FIRST TO CONCEIVE OF THE NATION-STATE...MAGNIFICENT, DARING, IMAGINATIVE..."

—Malachi Martin

David lay silent and Lassatha drew close to him, touching, guiding, caressing...He marveled that making love with a woman could be so graceful, so quiet, so gradual. Lassatha waited for him to assimilate each stage while he became more and more hers.

Then, she was all around him, engulfing him, drawing him inexorably upward with some strength superior to his own, through the forms and figures and bodies and faces and desires of hundreds of unknown women....And Lassatha was suddenly all women, a simple profound womb of desire, a single irresistible passage for his seed, a single pair of heavy, fruitful breasts to shelter him.

He heard himself cry out in surprise and wonder as he had never cried before, in tones he had never used but which he recognized as deeply his, fearing that his very fulfillment would undo him, drawing him into a pool of pleasure from which he might never emerge.

KING OF KINGS

MALACHI MARTIN

PUBLISHED BY POCKET BOOKS NEW YORK

I would like to thank Michael Korda for his invaluable direction and editorial wisdom, and John Quinn and Roslyn Siegel for their sharp critical eyes and friendly guidance.

POCKET BOOKS, a Simon & Schuster division of
GULF & WESTERN CORPORATION
1230 Avenue of the Americas, New York, N.Y. 10020

Contents

The Dancer

The place: a walled city called Zion, perched on a fifteen-acre, finger-shaped, 750-foot-high limestone ridge pointing due south, five miles from the Dead Sea, ninety-three miles from the Sinai desert, thirty-five miles from the Mediterranean. Called Jebus by its previous inhabitants, renamed Zion by the Hebrews, it will later be called Jerusalem.

From long wall to long wall on either side, the greatest width of the city is 300 yards. Its length, about half a mile; population, perhaps four thousand. Hardly more than a town by modern standards, but greatly renowned in its day. A warm brown girdle of domed houses punctuated with tall watchtowers runs around the inside of the wall down to the southern tip of the ridge where David's Cedar Palace will be built by quick-witted Phenician craftsmen from Tyre. It will be a tall cube of infinity set within the coronet of those stone bubbles in which David's people will live around him, near him, with him. Beneath the outer courtyard on the site where the palace will stand is the Siloam spring and its pool, the Gichon, which is fed unceasingly by waters that have bubbled since the beginning of time from unknown caverns miles beneath, their source perhaps Sheol, the Great House where all the spirits sleep uneasily.

Clinging to the eastern wall and overhanging the Kidron Valley is the Millo: a long two-storied barracks made of seasoned oak, housing the mercenaries who guard the city's most precious possession, the Siloam.

David and his Hebrews sleep, eat, and work here now. They have possessed the city militarily for slightly less than one year. But it is not their home. The place is still in the control of spirits alien to these invaders from the hills and desert places of Judah. Nothing we know about modern Jerusalem will help us to smell the atmosphere of Zion when David occupied it almost three thousand years ago. Forget the Temple and sacrifice and Bible, Greek and Roman, Crucifixion and Tomb and Mass, Byzantine and Copt and Armenian, Mosque and

1

Prophet's vision, Crusader, Turk, Tommy, Sabra, Palestinian, Zionist. None of that has taken place yet.

On this great day of David's Zion, the city is already more than two thousand years old. It has been home for peoples whose names are strange to us—Hivites, Hittites, Amorites, Jebusites, scores of others. Their houses still stand. Their shrines still brood at street corners. Their divinities are still invoked, still dominate. The very sunlight is still the ruthless smile of the god Shemesh. The night moon is Nana, frigid matriarch of darkness. The winds that freshen are the fickle fairies Tsiptsip, Koreh, Lilithi, Ramram, ferrying good and evil capriciously. Even Siloam's silvery water passes through the hands of Maveth, Lord Death.

David and his Hebrews are relative latecomers, conquering squatters camped where alien spirits are still masters, where nothing is blest, nothing holy, where dogs unaccountably bay at twilight, children groan in their sleep. All are still surrounded by those ancient unseen presences, like the wing beats of invisible birds.

The time: sunrise on the first day of spring in David's eighth year as king. A sacred time in David's land, an immemorial feast day celebrating return of life, fruits of fertility. The night darkness around the eastern sky is now a thin gauze through which the first lights of the sun are piercing. The west is a black purple streaked with dull pinks. The wind from the desert is cool to the skin, like some soothing lotion.

The occasion: a long, slowly moving procession winding its way up between the hills toward the North Gate of Zion. The longest bulk of the procession is composed of armed soldiers, thirty thousand of them, helmeted, swords at their sides, shields on their backs, spears held vertically in hand. In front of them, a hundred and fifty royal court officials, army officers, and priests dressed in bright ceremonial robes, their heads covered by the conical pointed hats of the nomad shepherd. Every man in the procession is wearing woolen padding around each foot. And all are marching in lockstep unison. At the head of the procession: four men carrying a cedar chest. It is slung on staves passed through gold rings at its four corners. It barely sways with the painfully slow motion of the bearers. This is the Ark of the Covenant, the visible sign of God's permanent presence with the Hebrews. It is coming home from its temporary resting place at Obededom's farm to its final shrine in the capital of David's kingdom.

Its polished surface is about three and a half feet long, two feet wide and deep, with a cover of smooth burnished gold without image or drawing. On the cover, two statues of eyeless angels face each other with outstretched wings. Between them a rectangular slab of gold bearing the never-to-be-pronounced name of David's god, YHWH. The Ark had been fashioned some four hundred years before by two Hebrew craftsmen, Aholiab and Bezaleel, according to the precise instructions of Moses, prophet and lawgiver.

As the four bearers enter the North Gate, the morning sun strikes the palace and its watchtowers with shafts of coppery light, suddenly illuminating streets, houses, towers, faces. Within minutes the air is iridescent, as if an unseen hand had scattered diamonds from above.

The spectacle on this occasion: in front of the Ark as it enters the main street of the city, one solitary man is dancing in wild exultation. Totally naked except for a narrow and short bejeweled cloth stole around his neck, every inch of his brown skin bathed in oil, he always keeps about four paces in front of the slowly moving Ark. This man is fleetingly the agile flame at the tip of the candle, a morning spirit from the hidden world, beautifying the ground with a carpet of flowering steps, filling the blue firmament with long, streaking gestures of prayer.

There is almost total silence. No music, no chanting, no sound from the crowds filling the windows and balconies and streets. The regular falls of all those padded feet are muffled in the crisp morning air. In the ripe sunshine the only sounds to hold the ear come from the dancer—the tapping and the slapping and the gliding of his bare feet on the paving stones, his quick gasps of breath, the occasional groan forced from his throat as he flings himself in curving apex to the sky.

Up there, hundreds of feet high, Shibtai, the desert vulture, has been keeping his usual watch for the morning's carrion ever since dawn, hovering almost motionless, his eyes scanning every detail, his instinct poised, ready. Always in the past on this special day, they have left him food. After all the dashing and dancing and chanting and copulating, he would glide down almost vertically and soundlessly, his baleful shadow suddenly falling across the infant—the boy, the girl done to death in honor of Master Baal, Mistress Astarte, Master Satan, or one of the other presences—his beak and claws gouging into warm blood and flesh.

This morning, however, he smells a difference. Even the light of Shemesh is different. Too fresh. Too clean. No message of blood on the wind. No chanting, no screaming, no smell of writhing bodies. Shibtai is wary, therefore. Besides, he has heard a great shout from the ground. Then silence. All this is dangerous, unusual. And something else warns his old predator's instinct: the light. Too much of it! The peculiar and painful light.

As Shibtai shifts his weight and lets the wind wheel him away steeply to the left in the direction of the sea, he catches a glimpse of the dancer's upraised face. It is not twisted in the agony Shibtai has always noticed on the faces of worshippers. For this is David. The all-powerful king. The man whom his people look on as "the angel of Adonai." Not leading a sacrificial dance, as Shibtai first thought. Not celebrating with death. Not drunk with wine or victory, as one might think. Not reverting to some primitive ritual. No, this is David, merely stating as explicitly, as vividly as he can, before God and man, who he is. This is the entry of God's presence onto this hoary hill that nothing will ever again expel.

Yet David had started off this day merely as a very worried man. Armed and equipped as he was on any day of battle, he was a king who wanted to assure the centrality of his city by installing his people's only religious shrine there. He was, besides, concerned with the effect on his people of the act of theater he had organized.

About three hours before the procession began, while the night darkness still moved restlessly around the houses and the city walls, David and his retinue had ridden at a gallop for the farmhouse of Obededom, a mile and a half from Zion. From Obededom's farmhouse to the beginning of the slope up to the North Gate, the Ark was carried on a newly built four-wheeled oxcart pushed by the priests. At the slope's edge it was unloaded, slung on staves, and set on the shoulders of David's four special warriors, brawny men bulging with muscles, bristling with threat, each with the face of an angry Titan: Yashobeam, Adino, Eleazar, Shammah. Each of these could cut off the head of a bull with one sword stroke. Nobody had ever seen them smile. The cart was then burned on the spot.

Each man in the procession tied thick woolen cloth around his feet. The king's order: the Ark must enter in peace, with no sound of marching feet. Soldiers, officials, priests, and bearers had strict instructions from the king: once the head of the procession started up the slope to the North Gate, they were to use the royal pace: one step forward with the right foot, the left foot then placed beside the right, then one step with the left foot, then the right foot placed beside the left, and thus ponderously, solemnly, to enter the city until the Ark reached David's residence.

No sooner had the Ark been transferred to the shoulders of the four bearers than David dismounted, walked in front of the Ark, and stood utterly motionless. Every eye had caught the gleam of the stones on the Ephod, the sacred stole that hung around his neck. His left hand was on his sword, his right hand stretched straight up above his head, face set in hard lines, eyes watchful. He let his eyes travel slowly over all. The Ark and its four fierce-looking bearers. Behind the Ark, his captains: Joab, Ittai, Beneyahu, followed by the twenty-five hundred Cretans, David's special corps. Then the various divisions of his army.

David nodded to the trumpeter. The trumpet blared out one loud high monotone note. The get-ready signal! Then the counting started: one . . . two . . . three . . . four . . . The people waiting in the city heard that counting from more than thirty thousand throats as a deep, soft rustle, like surf breaking.

At thirty, the trumpet note sounded again. His right hand still held up at full length. David watched everything as the bearers took the first step forward. A rustle of movement stirred the whole long body of men, starting at the head and running down the slope, around the corner of the valley, and so to the rear guard. No sudden lurch. No initial shock. More like a huge vine tendril being pulled gently forward. In unison with the bearers, David took one step backward cautiously. He held his breath as the bearers lock-stepped once, stepped forward again, lock-stepped the second time. As the bearers moved forward slowly, David backed up step by step.

But he kept glancing at the faces of the bearers, at the rings of the Ark, at the Ark's swaying motion. Then up to the sky and the surrounding horizons. Then back to the bearers' feet. From inside the walls of the city came the rhythmic beat of timbrels and the old, old triumphal song of Miriam: "Adonai is my strength . . . my God . . . my salvation . . . my fathers' God. . . . I will build a house for his dwelling. . . ."

But after five or six paces the tension eased. David's darting glances ceased once the first few yards had passed without incident. One sharp look over the heads of the bearers told him that the whole long procession was now in motion, swaying from side to side with each slow step. The singing voices came nearer and nearer, the words clearer, the music louder and in

some way sweeter: "Adonai has triumphed! Gloriously!...
Sing! Children of Israel! Sing! Sing to our God!..." All fear
left David. They were on their way! They would make it this
time! The Ark was coming home! The God of Israel was with
him. Somewhere in his spirit a hidden transom swung silently
open and the first flecks of glory lit up his mind.

It was at this point that the sudden transformation of David
took place. As David backed in under the arch of the North
Gate, his face plunged from the sun's brilliance into the
shadow, as if a cloak of darkness had descended. Within these
few seconds David sensed unmistakably that same awesome-
ness he had known only once before: the day twenty-three years
ago when he had felled Goliath, just before he had walked out
between the armies of Saul and the Philistines to face the giant.
That day, while Goliath had run amok in idiocy and clumsiness,
David had felt power but no fear. It was a lifting, an exultation
of all he felt himself to be. He had merely said in a teenager's
loud, clear voice, "I come in the name of Adonai. I am going
to cut off your head and feed your flesh to animals." He had
done so. Today the feeling was the same. He knew, as sure
as he breathed, that an immense and irresistible power was
briefly sharing his soul and body.

After seven interminably slow paces, David appeared again,
backing into the sunlit street. The Ark was entering the street
also. Now Miriam's song struck David's ears in full volume.
The twelve trumpets filled the air with the long, stately notes
of David's royal acclaim. Directly inside the gate, the full
impact of David's staging took the procession by storm. Ranged
there on one side were the elders of the Twelve Tribes smiling
proudly, their tribal dresses and emblems a rainbow of color.

On the other side stood David's chief courtiers and officials
of the kingdom. His two prophets: Nathan, short, bald, white-
bearded, with an almost palpable air of peace; Gad, the black-
haired younger prophet, of medium height, wearing the perpetual smile of the visionary. The two chief priests: Zadok, a
thin rake of a man, expressionless of face because nearly always
alone in the preservation of the Law; and the globular Abiathar,
bon vivant and unwilling hero, witness to history but too stupid
to comprehend it.

A little apart from these stood the chief officials of the
realm: Adoram the Treasurer, a pygmy with obsidian eyes,
nicknamed the Mosquito—he touched you, they said, only to
extract blood; Yehosaphat the Secretary, bony, tall, marked by
a cringing politeness, who had the brain of an Arabian abacus

and knew where every arrowhead and oat grain in the kingdom was located; and Serayah the Scribe, a tidy figure with small round shoulders and mincing feet.

Side by side with these three stood David's chief councilors: Ira, the tallest, with an old soldier's scarred and rigid body, David's expert on the desert tribes; Uri the Hittite, a model soldier and loyal officer; and, finally, the remarkable Ahitofel, the wealthy Gilonite demon with the face of an archangel.

Marching behind the Ark in the procession was Joab, David's field commander and oldest comrade-in-arms. As he caught sight of the king within the city, his eyes grew round in wonder. That passage through the darkness of the gate's shadow was like a plunge through some invisible fire.

David seemed suddenly taller, elongated. He towered above the bearers and the Ark. His eyes were opened wide and riveted on the Ark somewhere between those two golden cherubim with bowed heads and outstretched wings. Both his hands were upraised. Beneath his helmet his hair was lifting in the wind. His chest was heaving as his breath came in long, deep draughts as he backed up the street. The sunlight seemed to be a reflection of an inner light, transfiguring David from head to toe. Joab had known David for more than twenty years. This David he had never known.

By now David was almost oblivious to all around him. He still moved backward in lock step with the others. But trumpets, timbrels, singing, colors, smells, distances, and the soft dull thud of padded footfalls had receded to the half-awake periphery of his consciousness.

He had the same feeling in his stomach as on that other day, the same thrill running in his nerves. It was the same fierce sensing, but this time accompanied by seeing. In between those two angels he finally saw what he later described as "the shadow of Adonai's glory." And beneath the cool shade of the gateway arch, the supple warmth of God's own love welled up in his heart. The crest of ecstasy.

Joab still matched his pace with David's every regular step backward. But he was beginning to feel in himself the anticipatory buoyance he saw in David. David was beginning to recognize what was happening. His body, the Ark, the bearers, Joab, his men, the city, the waiting people, the sky—his entire world was being washed in translucent waters. And he knew. Finally, he knew! Adonai's approval. At last! At last! After all the waiting. Finally!

What happened next took place just within the split second

of one backward step. Joab saw it all, detail by detail. As David lifted his right foot to step back, his left knee was bent, his body inclining forward gently. His right arm swept down across his chest, pointing over his left shoulder. His left arm was flung back level with the shoulder. Both palms faced skyward, the fingers splayed as for grasping unseen holds. His head bowed, his eyes on that unseen presence over the Ark. As if David had been about to fall flat on his face in adoration.

But no! David's right foot never completed that backward pace. His face did not bow down earthward. Joab had just enough time to hear David's staccato half-whisper: "So great! . . . God of my Fathers! . . . So one! . . . You! . . . O God of Israel!..." He saw the king's mouth opening wide in an access of passion. His front knee plunged into a deeper bend, then straightened out with whiplash speed. His right arm swung back from his chest, forward and upward, the convex chest thrusting to the heavens, the concave back straightening his body into a soaring rigidity, elongating the neck, jerking the head up so that his chin jutted out.

And neither Joab nor anybody in the entire city failed to hear the great shout of David as he leaped into the air, his hands reaching and thrashing for the sky, his head flung back, his eyes flashing.

So quick was that leap that it all took place within the span of one pace. And David's shout was neither battle cry nor scream of protest. It was the voicing of the pride, the pleasure, the exultation already gripping the marchers and the onlookers. From the watching crowds came a spontaneous murmur of surprise. "Aaaaaaaaaaaaaah!" And at the end of the murmur came the utter silence of expectancy. By the moment the bearers had completed the lock step, David was back on the ground and Shibtai had wheeled away.

In that waiting stillness David shed helmet, sword belt, body armor, shoulder plates, leg greaves, boots, undergarments, in one gliding movement, leaving only that sacred stole, the Ephod, around his neck. Now everybody hung on his slightest movement, but nobody knew what was going to happen. Just for one transfiguring instant he was motionless and naked. Then he was a flashing arabesque of action, his bare body ablaze with the filament of his dance. It was his face and his shout that sent the bird of ill omen streaking for the emptiness of the Great Sea.

Now every gesture of David's, every motion, is an invitation for the procession to advance, and to go on advancing. The Ark keeps moving forward on that regular uninterrupted lock step. The bearers, Joab, and the marchers nearest Joab feel David's every movement as the guiding strings, the power in their feet and the thrust in their will. And all David does, all he is at the moment, is a pictorial psalm of worship. The Law forbids nakedness. But the Spirit of Adonai can call prophet or king or—to use a favorite expression of David's—even "the least one who pisses against the city wall" to be with his maker as his maker made him. Invitation, pleasure, worship run like purple strands through the dancing pattern David creates in the city streets.

From the people there is no sound, not even that low hum of excited voices that comes from a crowd witnessing some unforgettable scene. All is stilled. All have been drawn into the effort of this one man soaring and leaping and weaving, ever aiming at the ultimate moment, the explosion from everything when he is taken and lifted aloft, he and all his watchers.

All the lightness that had poured out of him becomes strength and verve and a playful, tumbling cascade of gestures. He clears the street in three bounds, as if his sinews were made of steel. He is the lion he killed when he was fourteen. He is the victor of two hundred battles.

David's dancing carries him back renewingly, joyously, through all the miseries of banishment to his earliest hours and the springtime of his faith and hope, to the day when Samuel anointed him king but he had not understood when Samuel said that this would be ratified in "the fullness of time."

The Lord has undone all the painful knots. David is free. He is home. King. Anointed. Confirmed.

Up on the balcony his family waits. His wives: Mikhal, Abigail, Ahinoam, Maaka, Haggith, Abital, Eglah. His six sons: Amnon, Khileav, Absalom, Adoniyahu, Shefatyahu, Ithream. His brothers: Eliab, Abinadab, Shammai, Nethaneel, Radai, Amasa, Ozem. Even his concubines are there looking down at him with the others and sharing the moment.

The crest of joy sent into his soul by Adonai is carrying him into the company of the holy ones of Israel. He is, momentarily,

each one of them: Abraham gazing trustfully and wonderingly
at the night stars as Adonai's voice tells him of his innumerable
seed that will fill the whole earth. Jacob at midnight wrestling
with the angel at the foot of the heavenly ladder. Moses kneeling before the burning bush to hear the two awesome syllables
of God's very own name. Joshua commanding the sun to halt
in the skies. Elijah ascending to God in a fiery chariot. Blind
Samson shouting out to his God and pulling down the temple of
Dagon in Ashkelon on the heads of his Philistine captors. Samuel
walking in the dead of night and answering the call of God: "Here
I am, Lord. Send me!"

It is David's high moment. Right with God. Right with man.

David is now a being of beauty. His lips are moving in half-
heard syllables. And those watching him now hear the beating
rhythm of names familiar to them all: "Abraham!...
Jacob!...Moses!...Joshua!..." Spontaneously they join
in, their voices coordinating faultlessly with his, their hands clapping on the beat.

"...Elijah!...Samson!...Saul!..." He is no longer mere
striver, the watchers no longer mere watchers. Both work together, live as one, even as they chant and clap hands together.
They share in David's moment, are weightless with his weight-
lessness, experiencing beyond sight and hearing and touch the
visitation of the Holy One of Israel.

Long after David's death they were still telling different stories of how David's dance ended that day. Some spoke of a smiling angel who appeared and touched David's forehead, stilling
him and them, not abruptly but gently. Others recalled how
David fell prostrate in front of the Ark and lay there lifeless for
some minutes until the prophet Nathan called out his name. And
mothers told their children how the covering of the Ark opened
and a snow-white cloud descended from the sky over it, while
a deep voice was heard to say: "This is my beloved people. I will
dwell with them here forever."

BOOK I

DAVID
THE
BELOVED

The
Birth of David

⊠⊠⊠ Two weeks before Passover, tongues were wagging in the marketplace of Bethlehem—quietly at first, of course, because only those closest to Jesse's family knew the facts. And besides, Jesse's family was not to be trifled with. But there was no hiding it after Jesse hired two Hebrew midwives named Hushim and Shua to serve his wife, Korith, during her pregnancy.

Jesse's family was one of the oldest and best known in Bethlehem. And although the most famous member of the family had previously been Rahab the whore, who had let the Israelites into Jericho, Jesse's family was esteemed. It had always lived in the same house, possessed the same land holdings, tilled the same fields, pastured sheep and cattle on the same land. His sons would do the same. His oldest, Eliab, would have the house one day in his name. The other sons would work with him. Even given an atmosphere alive with disease and violence, at least one of the sons would live to pass on the family land to the next generation.

Jesse's house was one of the more elaborate ones in the town. Three solid walls of cedar wood were built against the side of a hill. They enclosed one very large room with a wide fireplace and stone chimney on one side. The sloping roof that topped the walls was slated with marl and provided with catchments for rain water that drained off into a large cistern at the lower end of the sloping yard. Beneath the roof of the house there was a shallow loft or attic where weapons and other family possessions were stored. The space enclosed by those three walls served as general living room for the whole family. They all ate there and the youngest normally slept there. Large closets lined the walls. One square table occupied the center. The hill itself anchored the two side walls and served as the fourth wall. Into the hill, at the back of the living room, a large second room had been cut. It was Jesse's bedroom. And there Korith lay.

Surrounding the three-wall structure on the outside was a yard that sloped with the hill down to a five-foot-high stone wall, its only gate giving access to the main street of Bethlehem. To the left, some distance down the street, lay the marketplace, a simple square paved with cobblestones, bounded by houses, with the public well at its center. To the right lay the principal houses of the important Bethlehemites. Years ago Jesse had built a large barn in his sloping yard to house his camels and donkeys and to store grain. The chickens took refuge there at night along with his older sons. And his slaves could sleep there in the bad weather; otherwise they spent the night in the fields with the flocks.

Jesse's house, like most of the others, faced eastward. In that direction the ground traced a gentle incline for about a quarter of a mile. Then it dropped sharply for some miles to the Dead Sea 1,300 feet below sea level. On clear days Jesse could see from Bethlehem to the purple-clad mountains of Moab that lay east beyond the Dead Sea. North of Bethlehem and a little to the west lay Jebus, which David would first call Zion and later Jerusalem.

Jesse had not married until he reached the age of forty-two. Before that he had been too busy working his land, fighting campaigns, and bringing up seven sisters after his own father was killed by marauders. No one could mistake the figure of this man whom everybody in the village called familiarly and respectfully *abba*—"our father." Everybody felt some quality of authority that was unmistakably a part of him. Yet he was not a tall man. His torso from shoulder to hip was almost square. He had a barrel chest and a thick neck. His hands were square too, equally used to the grip of a scythe or a sword, and they had crushed the brawny windpipe of more than one Philistine. His legs were solid, powerful, and he had the large head that marked his ancestry. His hair, which had been white by his twenty-seventh year, was long, abundant, and unruly.

Like those of the men around him who spent all their days outdoors, his face was lined and tanned. But in the eyes and the sensitive set of his lips was an expression that elicited love from his friends and inspired confidence in the weak. He was not a man of many words or of high thoughts, but rather a doer of deeds. For him, truth and reality were carved in tangible things.

Jesse's marriage to Korith had been arranged. It was always so in his society. Her family's standing, her dowry, and her personal beauty made her suitable in this match. But for all of that, Jesse loved Korith before he married her. She came from Hebron, a region famous for its grapes and for the comeliness of its women.

Jesse's child, it was muttered darkly, had still not been born and Korith was close to her tenth month. Cain, Onan, Jezebel and other villains in Hebrew history were all ten-month babies. If the birth did not come soon, the Hebrew midwives said, the child would be the spawn of Satan. "Wasn't Pharaoh who pursued our fathers into the Red Sea an eleventh-month baby?" Hushim remarked artlessly to a friend.

Rumors arose like plagues around Jesse. Perhaps, some said, the child was not his. "Robust Jesse may be, but still he is over sixty!" Also, Korith had been taken prisoner by a band of marauding Philistines less than a year before. She had been rescued, and had told Jesse that neither she nor her servants had been mistreated. Some weeks later, when Korith shyly told Jesse that she was carrying their eighth child, he had taken it as a sign of God's blessing and of their continuing love. Now he did not know what to think. Was this his child? Would Korith tell him if it weren't? She had borne him seven brawny sons and nothing like this had ever happened. Fainting spells and vomiting sickness plagued her now. The midwives put her to bed. Sharp pains kept her sleepless during the nights and the long days. Still the child did not come, and Passover was approaching.

Jesse was beside himself with worry until a suggestion by his cousin and neighbor, Joshua, gave him hope. He, Joshua, would ride next day to Jebus to ask his old friend and comrade, Uri, a Hittite, for the loan of Uri's skilled Egyptian midwife. Although former enemies, the Hebrews and the Hittites had made common cause against the dread Philistines, and Joshua and Uri had fought side by side. According to Hittite custom, Uri was sixteen when he married his wife, Hattishla, who by coincidence was about to give birth to her third child.

Although still only nineteen, Uri had become an officer on genuine merit. He was a soldier's soldier. Of medium height, he was built like a bear—husky, muscular, dark-skinned, with brown hair, brown eyes, and a thick beard that did not hide his strong features. His was a presence of strength.

"Hattishla's fine," he told Joshua. "So take Hatich"—the Egyptian midwife—"by all means. Her assistant, Heptah, goes with her. They're a pair."

Although Hatich was in service to Uri and Hattishla, she was very much her own person. Midwifery was a very honored profession among the Egyptians. She had entered the training in her teens and graduated with excellent results from the Royal Surgeons' Studio Workshop at Thebes. She had taken the oath to Ptah "to labor for the life of every man and woman and child" she treated, "and never to take life." Five years later, ritually, she was admitted to the exclusive Guild of the Pharaoh's Surgeons and Midwives, licensed to practice anywhere in the Kingdom of Upper and Lower Egypt and anywhere else in the Pharaoh's foreign domains. At the time of Joshua's visit it was her fourteenth year of service. She loved it and could have gone anywhere she wanted. She was with Uri and Hattishla—and for the time being with Jesse and Korith—because she chose to be.

Jesse and three of his sons ate their meal of boiled rabbit in silence. The Hebrew midwives had given Korith some light broth and she was resting.

Suddenly there was bedlam outside.

"Jesse, son of Obed, peace!" Joshua rounded into the gate. Right behind him clattered a whole party: Uri on his camel accompanied by five armed retainers and his big Anatolian hunting mastiffs with their long noses, short hair, and blood-shot eyes. Uri and his men rode in a formation that surrounded two veiled figures, Hatich and Heptah, riding sidesaddle on donkeys, their feet resting on *astrabas*, little wooden planks suspended from one side.

Jesse's heart jumped. Joshua's mission had been successful!

Yet in the week that followed, Jesse began to feel more like a lodger than the master of his own home. His household fell into a routine organized by Hatich around the care of Korith. Jesse was allowed to see Korith mornings and evenings. His sons stayed away from the house altogether. The servants from Joshua's house were called on to clean and prepare food, always under the close supervision of Hatich or Heptah, and always quietly. It was arranged for the Hebrew midwives to come when they might be wanted.

Hatich spoke to Jesse rarely, and generally only when he asked for her judgment about his wife's condition. Her answers were neither negative nor optimistic. "The night was passed peacefully," she might say. Or: "No sign of the end yet."

Finally, the hot desert sirocco had come, increasing everyone's discomfort, and still there seemed no progress. Blotting the sweat from his forehead with the sleeve of his robe, Jesse asked Hatich meekly, "Lady Hatich, Passover is only three days away. I must make arrangements. Korith—er, Mistress Korith—do you think it is possible that she will come to her time before the vigil of Passover? Before tomorrow evening?"

The pain in Jesse's eyes and the anguish of his voice reached Hatich. Her own voice became more gentle, but not less firm: "Master Jesse, son of Obed! Come with me!" As he hesitated, she added in a hushed voice, "Outside, sir! Please! Now! This conversation is not for the ears of my mistress! Outside!" The hot wind of the sirocco hit them both across the face when they stepped out the door into the yard.

"Everything I do for your wife is frustrated. The child turns in the womb, as though to start coming out; but it does not come. Then it turns again and appears to be in a wrong position. I work to correct that. I cure an infection in your wife, and another infection brings a fever. I tell you! Believe me! I am fighting, not against nature, but against some power not of this world.

"I can say no more," Hatich said. "I have broken the rules of my guild even saying what I have said. But your child needs protection. Go! Ask one of your own priests or prophets. You need *raham*."

"Raham," Jesse whispered to himself, racked; it was the Hebrew word for compassion. Then, "Why, of course, Raham!"

Jesse raced like a madman down the slope of the yard to the gate, up the street, across the marketplace, and up the little hill to where the village scholar, Raham the compassionate, lived.

Raham was a tiny man with short arms and legs, an oval face, and black eyes too large for the rest of him. He was completely bald, so that his outrageously bushy eyebrows gave him the appearance of a baby ostrich, and he had long ago lost most of his teeth.

People only guessed at Raham's age. He was in fact eighty-seven when Jesse's David was born. He always rose at cock-crow, went to bed with the hens, and was known to everyone in the village, for everyone came to him at some time for advice.

Yet he had never married, kept few possessions, had only squatter's rights to the shanty and garden where he lived alone with his bitch, Kalbi. The only resident scholar in Bethlehem, he was an untiring observer of human nature. He was an expert in the Law of Moses, knew the Story of the Hebrews, had traveled to Jebus and Shiloh and Bethel, had seen the Great

Sea, now called the Mediterranean, and the Great Desert, and—
rumor had it—had lived in the royal city of Thebes in the land
of the Nile.

No betrothals, no marriages, no births, no circumcisions,
no land sales, nothing of any import took place in Bethlehem
without Raham's blessing.

"Peace and grace between us, brother!" Raham said, looking
up blandly at Jesse. "Rest yourself a moment. Here, sit down
here." Jesse settled down, still out of breath and sweating in
the heat of the sirocco. He then blurted out his story, ending
with Hatich's observation. Raham nodded. "Come with me!"
He jumped up like a rabbit and, followed by an obedient Jesse,
trotted over to the gate of his garden. He pointed out across
the valley to the sparse copse of oaks at the foot of the hills.
"Look at them! Look well at them! What do you see, brother?"

Jesse narrowed his eyes. First he saw only movement among
the trees. Then he saw a herd of about twenty deer. Something
had driven them down from their grazing spots on the mountain
slopes.

"Did you ever see them so near, brother? And at nightfall?
And not grazing? Did you ever see that, brother?"

True, Jesse had not. The deer were standing, pawing the
ground, waving their heads, moving hither and thither in disquiet. "Yes," observed Raham, "something big's about to happen. This is a sign. So you go and see Shalama." Shalama was
a holy woman who lived in the mountains to the north, near
Nazareth. She was not a witch, for King Saul had forbidden
consultation with soothsayers and witches, and Jesse was a
man loyal to the Law and to his king.

"You must remember one thing," Raham added, "Shalama
cannot do anything for you. Or for your wife. Or for your
child. Of and by herself, that is to say. But she can be an
occasion. And that is *not* against the Law! You must go first
to Nazareth. Go before sunrise tomorrow. Seek out Malaki.
He is the blind beggar-fool of the town. He will show you the
way. Now that's all I have to tell you, except for one iron rule:
do exactly what Shalama tells you. Doubtless she will know
who you are and will be expecting you."

On his way home Jesse was startled again to see a horde
of rats and mice running crazed with fear across his path and
disappearing in the woods. He shook his head in wonder.

"Ozem," said Jesse to his youngest son as soon as he got
back home, "you must stay awake tonight. I must be up one
hour before sunrise. There must be no mistake or delay. Get

the camel packs ready for two days' ride. Ask Radai and Abinadab to prepare my arms."

Then he entered Korith's room. Hatich motioned to Heptah and they both withdrew. Korith lay quietly, her body turned slightly to one side, her hands lying on the coverlet, her eyes closed in sleep. She was breathing easily. Jesse tiptoed over and sat down on the chair close to the bed, facing her. Only then did he notice her right hand closed tightly around a carnelian necklace. Suddenly he felt miserable with some forgotten pain. He had never had it before, this sudden emptiness. And he had not seen that necklace for many years. He had bought it for Korith as a wedding gift. When they were alone on their first night, he had placed it around her neck. And Korith's joy at his gesture had been so genuine, so enthusiastic that he had almost knelt and worshiped her.

He reached out now and placed one callused hand over hers that held the necklace. Korith stirred and half opened her eyes dreamily.

"Jesse . . ." Her quiet voice trailed away.

"I will be gone for a day or two, my love." She nodded. "Raham says I should go. It's for the child—and for you. . . ." He stumbled over the words.

"I know. I know," Korith said almost in a whisper. There was a great peace in her voice. "I know it will be all right. All will be well. Don't fear, Jesse."

Jesse's eyes took in her face, her eyes, her body outlined beneath the bedclothes. For an instant he saw her again as she had been when he first set eyes on her, long-legged, narrow-waisted, high-breasted, flashing like an angel of Adonai through the cornfields of her father's farm in Hebron.

He stood up and bent to touch her lips with his, hands resting on her shoulders.

"Go, my beloved husband," she murmured. "Go now. And do Adonai's will. When you return, I will have my greatest gift for you."

Jesse's ride northward on his camel, Bara, led him up through gently inclining slopes and rolling hills that made the climb toward Jebus seem less steep than it was. He stayed away from the main caravan route as much as possible.

Within an hour Saul's fortresslike palace came within view, high on a hill from which a watch could be set east and west. Fire signals from peaks and mountaintops north and south could be sent and received. It dominated and controlled the great caravan route heading to and from Philistia. To attack the heights of Gibea successfully would be very dangerous and difficult, for, while the ground on which the fortress was built was flat, the surrounding hillsides fell away steeply on three sides.

From that height, looking down toward the Judean hills that had always been the defense and refuge of the Hebrews, the fortress-palace of Saul stood as the symbol of the Hebrew presence in this land where Hebrews were a weak minority.

Not that Saul's stronghold was a grand structure. In fact it was more fortress than palace. Compared with the Great Palace of Gaza or indeed, with that of any of the Philistine dukes, it was a poor thing. And there was no comparison at all with the buildings and palaces of Pharaonic Egypt.

The stronghold was rectangular in shape, protected by high walls of hammer-dressed stone fifteen feet thick. The walls, with their buttressing and their four high corner towers and the single set of tall heavy wood doors, enclosed an area of about 175 by 115 feet. Roughly in the center of the fortress compound stood King Saul's private two-story cedar-wood house, where the king, his family, his military leaders and his closest advisers lived.

The modesty of Saul's stronghold and the cramped quarters of his own "palace" were a reflection of the harsh reality: the "king" of the Hebrews was not in any sense the equal in external glory, pomp, wealth, and power of the kings that ruled in such places as Assyria and Phenicia. Yet Saul had made a huge difference to the Hebrews, starting a long counteroffensive against the dreaded Philistines. He was a fierce fighter and always entered battle courageously at the head of his own men. He had gained their confidence and their respect. Even their love. He had an easy grasp of the logistics of war and a sense of his own destiny. And he had been chosen for his role by Adonai and anointed by the great prophet, Samuel. But for all of that he was still more a tribal chieftain with an army than a king.

Jesse's approach up the slope to the heavy gate of Gibea had been seen. The wide doors opened and he entered the fortress compound.

Saul was only twenty-five at this time, slightly over average height, strong as a lion and just as lithe.

He wore the long, loose gown of the Hebrews, gathered in at his waist with a leather belt. He was barefoot, and his long hair was tied at the back of his neck. His dark, luminous eyes missed nothing as he moved his gaze everywhere. But most often he would seek the eyes of the prophet Samuel.

Saul turned his eyes now to the soldier carrying Jesse's request.

"Yes! What news?"

"A Bethlehemite. Jesse, son of Obed of the Tribe of Judah, seeks a safe-pass north."

"Yes." Saul spoke first to Samuel. "The man we saw approaching. I have been watching him down there." Then, to the soldier, "Where is he going? This is the eve of Passover. What is so urgent?"

"A case of compassion." The soldier was as brief as possible. "He says his wife is with child and both are in grave danger. He has been sent by the scholar in Bethlehem called Raham to Malaki at Nazareth, and he is to find the holy woman Shalama. He asks to look upon the face of my Lord King, and to be on his way as fast as possible with the King's pass."

"Raham is good. One of us," Samuel responded. A small man with very big hands, Samuel was twice Saul's age. His face shone with the light of holiness mixed with the shadow of sorrow, for there was no evil he had not witnessed. No man of his time had knowledge—and foreknowledge—equal to that of Samuel.

Samuel's was the advice and the blessing Saul valued and needed most in his heart. And Samuel, more than any man, had come to know not only the strength of Saul but the strange weakness that cut across Saul's personality like a jagged tear in a fortress wall.

"My Lord King," Samuel went on, "send this Bethlehemite on his way in peace, and add your blessing to the blessing of Adonai."

A shadow of doubt and anxiety fluttered around Saul's face for a moment. It was a look that Samuel had come to know well. He went on hurriedly, "There is no danger from this man, my Lord King. I know you are troubled in your mind by the strangeness of the wind and the unnatural behavior of the beasts and birds reported by our scouts. But they are not signs for you, Lord King."

"Let him go north, then," Saul finally replied to Samuel. "But I shall not see him." He turned to the soldier. "Tell this Jesse, son of Obed, that he may go in peace. Tell the captain to give him a safe-pass and to indicate to him the safest routes north and back again to Bethlehem."

"And tell the son of Obed," Samuel added to Saul's instructions, "to mind the words of Raham, and to listen well to all he hears from Malaki and Shalama. Tell him to take the time to pray at Kiryath-Yearim, before he makes his way to Nazareth. It will not delay him beyond his time."

Within the hour Jesse was on his way to Kiryath-Yearim.

He left Bara outside the forbidding high stone wall and walked through the gate with a growing apprehension at being so close to the awesome presence and the power that drew the face of all his days and all the history he knew. Here at Kiryath-Yearim the Ark of the Covenant had been placed when it was returned to the Hebrews by the Philistines, who had captured it in battle at Ebenezer twenty years before.

"You have come to pray at the Ark, my brother." A quiet, slightly sad voice startled Jesse. It was Eleazar, son of Abinadab, the appointed priest of the Ark.

Jesse stood speechless, fearful of approaching any closer to the sacred presence of Adonai. He had heard the stories of men who had approached this Ark and fallen dead in their tracks. And look at this man, this Eleazar! he thought. He had been a young man when he was selected as priest of the Ark. He could not be more than forty-five even now. Yet he stood in the doorway like an old man, palsied and shaking, leaning on a cane. His face was lined and hollow-cheeked. "I do not know how to pray." Jesse found his voice at last. "The prophet Samuel instructed me to come."

"Come, then. We will pray together. . . . No further than here, brother," Eleazar said to Jesse when they were a few paces from the Ark. His words were not rough nor even peremptory. Just a statement of fact. "This is the Holy of Holies of Israel." They stood there before the huge stone, the gold of the Ark glinting in silent reply to their presence there. Then Eleazar prayed aloud.

"O God of Abraham, of Isaac, of Jacob, look with favor on this son of your house, and grant his request so that his family be blessed with peace and health and serve your holy will this day and all the days of their lives." Silence again.

The next time Eleazar spoke, he spoke not to Adonai but to Jesse: "The Lord God of the House of Israel has chosen you and your family today. Have no fear. Not even in your trials. All fear comes to the chosen ones from the Adversary, the enemy of Adonai.

"For twenty years now, the Ark of the Lord has stood on that great stone, in this desolate place." Eleazar's eyes surveyed the arid land on which they stood together. "The end of my vigil is not yet, my brother. But in your hands, not mine, will lie the life of the Covenant. Do not fear, Jesse. Go in peace and strength."

Even though the morning was wearing on, and he still had a long trip to Nazareth, Jesse wanted to make a brief stop at Bethel, which lay directly on his way north from Kiryath-Yearim. It was sacred to all Hebrews as the place where Jacob had dreamed his historic dream and seen the Angels of Adonai ascending and descending on the ladder from heaven to earth. There heaven and the presence of Adonai had touched the land of men.

Yet Jesse knew that the holy places there, although still held by Hebrews, were now given over to the worship of Baal by the sacred prostitutes of Astarte, so in the end he decided not to stop. Instead he headed swiftly north for about ten miles through undulating terrain. Then he turned slightly eastward through a series of ravines, until he came within sight of the great caravan road.

Southward the road led past the Dead Sea and on to Egypt. Northward it led to Bethshan, held by Canaanite enemies of the Hebrews, and crossed the great caravan routes that led from Mesopotamia in the east to the Great Sea in the west. Jesse was preoccupied with thoughts of Korith, and before he realized it Bara's steady, rolling gait had brought him within a few hundred yards of the lower gate of Bethshan. There was a sharp buzzing sound and a loud clacking of wheels as the central gate of the wall at the base of Bethshan opened and a one-horse war chariot came racing out toward him.

Jesse reined Bara to a stop, a perfect target in the middle of the trail.

With movements as smooth and quick as long professional practice could make them, the bowman reined in his horse, drew an arrow, aimed and took his first warning shot. The arrow slammed into the trail in front of Bara. She arched her head in surprise. Jesse held her steady. He did not know which way to turn or move. Before the shaft of the first arrow had stopped quivering, a second hit within inches of Jesse, to his left. The bowman drew a third arrow and placed it ready, but did not shoot.

Jesse had been warned. If he came any closer to Bethshan, if he did not depart immediately, the third arrow would surely be aimed at him. He wheeled Bara around to his left and up

the slope of the hill, sending pebbles and stones scurrying
down, kicking Bara repeatedly until he was well east of Bethshan, where he turned north again toward the Valley of Yezreel.
Too close, he thought. I mustn't let my mind wander like that.

If ever there was a place where a troubled man could soothe
his soul, or a tired man could pause to take a bite of food in
peace, it was in the Valley of Yezreel of Jesse's time. As Jesse
came over the last rise in the mountains of Gilboa, he beheld
an extraordinary corridor of fertile land stretching like a narrow
ribbon of variegated colors. It wound before his eyes to the
west between sometimes gentle, sometimes steep rises in the
ground. The floor of the valley was carpeted in flowers and
green grazing grass. Anemones and chrysanthemums, cycla-
men and wild roses grew along the hills, their heads nodding
in the wind. Here and there at the top of a hill there was a
small Hebrew village overlooking small patches of green farm-
steads on the valley floor. Smallish flocks of grazing sheep
dotted the valley. Mulberry bushes, fig trees, vines, olives
danced with their shadows and bowed to the surrounding hills.
He could see Mount Thabor to the north, high, broad, majestic,
the perfect place for conversation between Abraham and
Adonai.

What struck every visitor to the Valley of Yezreel was, first
of all, the light. Over this luxuriant valley spread an effulgence
of sunlight that played magic with the imagination even as it
played with the flowers and green grass. The Hebrews had
named the valley "the pavement of Adonai's glory" the very
first time they had come here and been captivated by the translucence of its air. Before they came, the inhabitants called it
Sick-Heart Valley because for generations people who were
sick at heart had come here seeking restoration from their gods.

Wasn't this Valley of Yezreel the image of that Promised
Land that Moses had been promised by Adonai for all his
people? A land flowing with milk and honey? What had happened to all that—the promise, the land, the milk, the honey?
Had the people of Adonai been so unfaithful to him with Baal
and Astarte that he had deserted them? Adonai seemed to have
his own plans.

It was nearly four in the afternoon when Jesse caught his
first sight of Nazareth nestling high above his head on an
outcropping of a hill.

The town of Nazareth and its surroundings had been settled
for more than a thousand years; but the ancestors of the present

settlers had come only about two hundred years before. About thirty families of the Tribe of Zebulun had chosen this spot, and had won it by their swords from the Canaanites and Hittites who had settled the land long before them. Some twenty-five or thirty of the conquered families had chosen to stay and live as neighbors or as slaves of the Hebrew victors.

The tangible result of this union of people was noticeable in both the physique and the social mores of the Nazarenes. Of all the people in Galilee, the Nazarenes were by far the most attractive and the happiest, with a quick, purposeful intelligence. They lived their daily lives in an unflurried manner, and their town exuded peace and calm.

Nazareth had a special residence for a rather large group of scholars who studied and taught the Law of Moses. At one edge of the town there was a well-known lookout point, a flat table or rock jutting out from the land and ending in a sheer drop of some hundreds of feet. There Nazarenes and visitors alike came to talk and eat; and from its height of 1,300 feet they could look out upon the heaving body of the Great Sea to the west, spy upon Yezreel Valley in the east, look at Tyre and Syria in the north and Judah in the south.

As he passed under the arch of the southern gate, Jesse could already hear the calls of street hawkers, the whistling of drovers, and the sounds of shepherd's pipes playing the lilting dances of the Galileans. On the eve of Passover the marketplace was filled with townspeople together with visitors from the valley below, all come for the feasting and dancing and celebrations that would take place the next day.

The marketplace was not really very big. "Nothing is large in Nazareth except the hearts of the people," they liked to say. Jesse tethered Bara at the hostelry and asked the innkeeper where he could find Malaki. "Ha!" the man laughed. "You cannot miss him. Look in the marketplace. You'll know him when you see him!"

Jesse entered the crowds moving among the permanent stalls and little temporary booths that farmers had set up to sell their produce. He passed benches where people rested, slept, chatted. But he saw no beggar anywhere. He saw bearded old men in the pleated garments of elders, craggy-faced fishermen in white robes and little red head kerchiefs, towering farmers wearing leather coats and high boots, and the hard, leather-faced mule and camel drovers sweating and cursing their way through the milling square. He could see the more elegantly clothed townspeople in their wide Syrian hats, green and blue brocaded cloaks, and high-heeled wooden sandals copied from the Tyrians. But nowhere did he see a single beggar.

He bought some fried fish, finally, and some wine. He would eat something. As he raised his head to take a drink of wine, his eyes traveled over the heads of the crowds, and suddenly Jesse caught a glimpse of someone or something seated in a niche of a house wall on the opposite side of the marketplace. He almost spilled his wine. For this, surely, was Malaki. No one could ever be prepared for the first shock of seeing the beggar-fool of Nazareth.

Leaving his wine and fish half-eaten, Jesse pushed his way to within two feet of Malaki, his eyes staring in disbelief. Malaki was perched on a little box with a leather top. The box had been set into a niche of the wall.

His arms were short stumps, covered by red and purple skin that disappeared into the short sleeves of a linen gown. His legs were slightly longer, but they too were stumps, covered only partly by the gown and wrapped with strips of white cloth. The stumps of the arms stuck out straight and stiff from a torso no bigger than that of a ten-year-old boy, and in profile the figure appeared to be pointing or reaching out in endless supplication.

The small boy under the gown seemed to have only a thin layer of flesh hanging on shoulders and rib cage. It was bent to the right at a painful angle, as if some powerful hand had twisted it so and then frozen its very bones askew. The neck too was twisted, and its skin laced with furrows. The head was enormous, almost as wide as the shoulders, a small mat of thick hair covering its nearly flat crown. It, too, was cruelly twisted back to one side at an ugly angle.

The forehead consisted of two large bumps set above straight bushy brows. There were no eyes, only concave sockets the color of black cinders. Nor was there any nose, just two irregular holes above the mouth. Between the holes ran crisscross scars where the flesh had been knitted or somehow forced together. Irregular scars stretched along his cheeks. His chin had three notches in it, each as black as the eyeless sockets.

Only one feature of Malaki was intact: the mouth. And it was beautiful. If, on seeing him, you could somehow have blocked out the desolation and distortion on the rest of Malaki's face, and only contemplated those lips, your first thoughts would have been of the kiss that mouth would give, the smile it could radiate, the fine words it would surely mold.

Malaki had been born to the beggar's place, as he had been

born to his shrunken, stumped, and marred condition. His sy-
philitic parents had abandoned him at the edge of town very
soon after he was born. His armless and legless body was
already deformed and his eyes and nose already lost to disease
when a passing caravan of Nazarenes, homeward bound for the
Passover feast, had found him there and brought him to the
elders of Nazareth. The elders and the scholars had been unanimous. The child had come on the eve of Passover. Adonai
had sent him as the Stranger they were supposed to entertain
at the meal on that holy day. For all they knew, he might even
be the Messenger: the forerunner of the Messiah. The child
must be allowed to live, they said. And he must be cared for.

By some miracle of Adonai, the child had survived. Perhaps
he was truly the Messenger. So the elders named him Malaki,
because an old tradition said: "And Adonai promised: I will
send *malaki*, my messenger." They had decided that day, with
the firmness that only committed men can show, that Malaki
would be the town ward. And so he became the care of all the
citizens of Nazareth, lodged for one month at a time in one
home, then in another for the following month, then in another,
and so on the whole year round. And so Malaki had lived for
twenty years before Jesse arrived on the scene. The people had
taught him to speak. They sewed clothes for him. They fed
him. They constructed a small four-wheeled cart for trans-
porting him, and a little leather-covered box on which he could
sit in the fresh air and talk to the neighbors.

For some ulterior reason Adonai had visited this already
misshapen creature of his, invading his soul and his mind with
the light of divinity. That visitation had transformed the world
inside of Malaki; and that light had spilled over into his physique, so that even with his terrible scars, his sightless face,
his awful body, there was, after the first moment of shock,
nothing loathsome about him; but rather a radiance that could
not be ignored. Malaki was the most beloved and, because
venerated, the loneliest person in all of Nazareth.

"Malaki, peace!" Jesse said in a half-whisper, when he had
collected his wits.

"Tell me who you are and what you seek." Malaki's voice
was friendly. It was deeper than any voice Jesse had ever heard,
smooth and rich as it came from the beautiful mouth.

"I am Jesse, son of Obed, from Bethlehem in Judah. Raham,
the scholar of Bethlehem sent me. I must see Shalama. Raham
says you can direct me to her."

"Leave Nazareth by the eastern gate," said the blind seer.

"You must seek the trail into a sloping valley through which Mount Thabor can first be clearly seen. They call this valley Petahyahu, the Door of Adonai. But long before you reach Thabor, look for the Angel's Breasts. Nearby will be Shalama's Veil. There you will find the woman you seek. And remember, the fate of the Covenant goes with you."

Following Malaki's instructions, Jesse quickly came to Petahyahu. He tethered Bara at the entrance to the wadi, took some water from his pack, and set off as quickly as he could on foot. At the top of a shallow rise he stopped to survey the terrain. Looming in the near distance directly before him, standing as if to guard Thabor, was a mountain with two sharply rising peaks.

Down, down his eyes moved, straining, missing nothing, moving over crags and ravines until he saw the sunlight glint on the water that splashed and danced its way through gullies and down the mountain below the Angel's Breasts. Forty feet it fell, sparkling against the wooded shadows of stock-still evergreens. Shalama's Veil! It could be nothing else!

On a ledge far above the tamarisk bushes and the willows through which the stone trail wound its way upward to where she stood, Shalama watched Jesse begin his climb. It would take him some while to reach the ledge.

She turned away from the valley and walked to the hut at the back of the clearing. She ducked into the entrance, went through a short tunnel that led to a cave, and kindled a large fire in the pit at the center of the rock floor. That done, she went out to prepare some food for her visitor.

No one in Israel knew anything about Shalama's origin beyond the fact that, before living at Petahyahu, she had lived in Egypt, where she had been trained in the use of medicinal herbs. Later she had been a slave to Hebrew farmers who lived near Nain in the lower part of Galilee. Her blue eyes and the traces of blond hair that she still had marked her as a foreigner from the northern lands across the Great Sea. Apparently, while still a slave she had been converted to Judaism. Her Hebrew masters had set her free at the request of the prophet Nathan, who gave her a camel and some provisions, and told her she could go wherever she willed.

Totally at a loss as to what to do or where to go, Shalama threw the reins over the neck of the camel Nathan had given her, looked up at the sky, and began to shout: "If I have found favor in your eyes, Adonai, and if I have come all this way and all these years to find your will in this hard and cruel land, then help me now." Whether frightened by the protest of his desperate rider, or at the urging of Adonai's Angel, the beast charged forward out of Nain and didn't stop until it reached the mouth of Petahyahu, where it stopped dead.

It was early spring, and Petahyahu was fresh in its beauty and bountiful in its fruits. Its peace and isolation were balm to Shalama's spirit. After a careful search, she found a wide ledge with a well-hidden path, from which she could see anyone who came into Petahyahu. There was even a cave at the back of the clearing. Here she settled down to live.

One day she found three wounded Hebrew guerrillas lying among the bushes, bleeding and unconscious. With the skill she had learned in Egypt she tended their wounds for some weeks and brought them back to health. In gratitude they built her a simple hut.

As the months passed she tended others—shepherds wounded by wild animals, lone travelers near her valley. In time, word spread among the people of the blue-eyed Hebrew woman living in Thabor's shadow; how she had saved the life of this villager or that townsman, of the mysterious voices they had heard coming from the cave when she went there to pray. She became known not only as a physician but as a seer, a favorite of Adonai, one who had healing powers for the soul as well as for the body.

With the courage of desperation, Jesse climbed the last few yards of the steep path to the ledge where Shalama lived and looked about him. The sun's rays were still strong enough to cast a golden light on everything. In the shadows near a hut was the tall figure of a woman. A long, hooded mantle made of many patches of different-colored cloth was drawn around her. As Jesse approached she lowered her veil, and he looked into a pair of deep blue, heavy-lidded eyes resting on pouches of wrinkled skin. Jesse would never forget that face.

"Shalama . . ." It was a whisper, a question, a plea.

"I am Shalama. Who has sent you here?" The woman's voice was deep and musical.

"The scholar Raham, of Bethlehem. Malaki of Nazareth told me the way. I am Jesse, son of Obed. I seek your help, Mistress Shalama."

"I will help you, Jesse, son of Obed. Tell me your trouble."

"Mistress Shalama!" Jesse's anguish exploded into words.

"My child—it's late in coming—there's something peculiar about it all—I feel it in my bones and my flesh—"

Shalama's nod interrupted his breathless talk. He read her gaze: she understood. Every elderly Hebrew who had a child coming simultaneously hoped it would have a special destiny in the Covenant and feared it might be a spawn of Satan.

"—and this, my eighth, is so late, so, so late, Mistress Shalama—I am so old." He paused a moment, at a loss. Then, his features contorted in agonized pleading: "I must find out, Mistress! Please help us!"

"Be it on account of your child or something else"—she glanced down the valley—"something peculiar is afoot. Shibtai is too restive." She looked back at him. "Your Raham must have pointed out the signs. Look about you, Master Jesse."

The sirocco wind had died down. The air was eerie and still. But all around them there was movement. Animal movement. Flights of starlings and sparrows wove across the sky like black silk scarves; by now they should have been in their nests. Animals scurried about. They too should have been asleep in their burrows and lairs.

"Signs! Signs, Jesse! But only signs!"

There was genuine fright on Jesse's face. These things no man could fight with a sword. All of nature was awry.

"If you would have your answers," Shalama continued, "then follow me. You will hear the truth. But it will not be I who brings it to you. Raham said rightly. I shall be only the occasion of it, the way for you to find it. It is time. You must choose."

"I will have the truth, Shalama," he said.

"Good! Come quickly, then. Now!"

She led Jesse through the door into her hut, and across into the cave at its back. A large charcoal fire burned in a brazier, which was set over a huge crack at the center of the uneven rock floor. Over the fire stood a tripod from which hung a heavy blackened pot.

The cavern was round and appeared to be about fifty feet high, and more than that from wall to wall. The sloping walls and dome were white limestone flecked with silvery granules that shimmered in the glow of the fire. In the ceiling three very narrow fissures led to the surface and gave some ventilation. But in the stillness of that night, no air stirred in the cavern; and the smoke from the fire floated like a blue-green veil, waist high above the floor of the cave.

"I will sit here," Shalama told Jesse. There was a low, flat stone by the fire. "You will sit on that stone opposite me."

Suddenly Jesse was attacked by fear. I will never leave this awful place! The thought screamed at him in the silence. He half rose from his seat to be sure he was still alive, so oppressive was the atmosphere of fear pressing in on him.

He looked across the fire at Shalama's cowled head. He could not tell how much time passed before Shalama raised her head and her low, musical voice echoed in the cave as she recited a psalm:

> "Adonai is he who never ceased to begin.
> Before a man was begotten
> And when all men die, he is still eternal beginning.
> And in between he makes man's little hopes
> To blossom into passing glories,
> And then to molder down into dust.
> And women may weep.
> And men may pray and hate and fight and love.
> But when the silver cord is broken,
> Adonai sees all go down to the pit,
> And all shall rest in Sheol."

The sound—any human sound—was welcome to Jesse's ears. She rose, scattered something into the blackened pot— he guessed it was incense—and stirred the flames beneath it. Then she returned to her place, and the cave was silent again. The smoke gathered toward the ceiling and lingered there around the tiny openings that led out into the open.

The first movement was slight. Was it Shalama? Yes, of course. She had raised her head. She was looking—where? Jesse turned his head and looked up. But as far as he could see, only shadows danced around the ceiling.

Shadows? He looked more closely. There were forms. Not rock forms. Human. And faces. He struggled to recognize them but it was no use. He had entered the threshold of eternity from whence those shadows and all the past and future come, where time is but a finger that, if cut off, will wither and die.

Out of the silence a sound grew. Words formed. "Holy! Holy! Holy!...Lord God of Armies..." The sound faded again. The rest of the words escaped unheard. Even as the sound grew and then faded, so, too, the silvery shadows. The forms. The faces. But before they disappeared, yes! He knew them. He had never seen them. But he knew them.

In the new silence, Jesse felt desolate, abandoned. His nerves started to give way. He felt more alone than ever in his life. The presence that had surrounded him and grown within his being when those shadows were before him seemed now only an emptiness.

After how long he could not tell Jesse heard the voice of Shalama. A soft chant in her low, crooning voice. "Adonai. His body. Adonai. His body. Adonai. His body..." Over and over. He watched the darkness around him. He watched the fire. "Adonai. His body..." the voice chanted. Then, a subtle change. The sound expanded. It did not grow louder. It expanded. And Jesse realized they were again no longer alone.

There! There they came! "Adonai. His body. Adonai..." A new murmuring chorus, but with words repeating Shalama's chant. Men and women. The meaning escaped Jesse although the words he heard clearly.

Old nomads were there, glittering shadows of men who once had come and gone. Shades of stocky, broad-shouldered men with thick, short legs and huge hands and shaggy beards. These were the ancient men who, in their own days on this earth, had each prayed for a man child, a warrior, a "wise husband-man," a "father of many children." They did not pause, nor speak to Jesse. They chanted. "Adonai. His body. Adonai. His body..."

Shalama pronounced their names as they came and went. "Shem. Arphaxad. Shelah. Eber..." Ancient ancestors all! "Peleg... Reu... Serug... Mahor... Terah... Abraham ... Isaac... Jacob... Joseph..."

As they passed a form—what Jesse perceived as a shadow child, his shadow child—beyond the fire, beyond Shalama, each one seemed to impart a blessing, to link everything in that cave with a long destiny. And then they all stood to one side. They seemed to fill the inner recesses of the cavern, shimmering like the walls but distinct from them, their faces speaking of life that comes to its endtime, then passes through the interface of mortality and eternity, but, departing, never leaves life. Jesse understood in those faces what he could never understand with his mind alone, and what he would never be able to explain and almost never speak of in later years.

All was silence. But still Jesse listened. And then he saw Obed. Near. He was very near. Between Jesse and the child shadow, Obed's body was still wrapped in the shrouds of his burial. His head cloth had fallen away, and Jesse read on his father's face the silent suffering of one still waiting for liberation.

Obed looked at Jesse and raised his left hand to his mouth, one finger before his lips in a gesture of silence. With his right hand he motioned to the shadow crowd. All the figures moved forward at his bidding.

As Jesse watched them they seemed to rise above the floor, above the child shadow, above the rocks and stones and fire and the head of Shalama.

Jesse jumped to his feet, his hands reaching vainly for Obed above his head. As if to touch his father, rip the shrouds that bound him, free him, bring him back!

"The child!" he cried. "Father! The child! Korith! Father!"

For an instant there was only the sound of his sobbing. Only the fire crackling. Only his own shadow to be seen. Then Jesse heard the growling of thunder.

Ranging to the west of Jesse's home in Bethlehem, beyond the mountains that guarded Judah, lay the land of my lords the warrior dukes of Philistia.

At the time of David's birth, the Philistines—proceeding from Luqqawatna in what is now western Turkey—had been established in the land named after them for about a hundred and seventy years. Those had been a hundred and seventy years of swashbuckling conquests, murderous raids, and hard-fought battles against the Hebrews. The Philistines were supremely skilled in two things: architecture and the art of war. And, in addition, they had one other trait: absolute contempt for all that was not Philistine. If any petrifying danger hung over the daily lives of the Hebrews before and during the early part of David's time, it was those tall men with iron weapons flooding the land with war and beset with the dream of an empire they were to found in the name of their god, Dagon.

Philistia was a commonwealth, a chain of cities and garrisons dotting the coastal plains and the near hill country of Samaria and Judah. This chain was held solid by five major cities.

Inland, nearest to Saul's early stronghold of Gibea, and just north of the strategic Valley of Sorek, lay the city of Ekron, serving as a lookout on the eastern hills where the Hebrew natives lived. A few miles south, across the Valley of Elah, lay Gath, a garrisoned stockade of the Philistine First Army and a center for a race of giant people the Philistines had enrolled as their mercenaries. Westward from Gath and Ekron, across the plains of Philistia and ranged from north to south on the Mediterranean, lay the three coastal cities. Ashdod, protected on its western flanks by dunes, and famous for the flame-red oranges that all Philistia loved, was a city drawn with the pencil of rage. There was never peace or beauty or harmony in Ashdod. Storytellers pictured Ashdod as the mouth of hell and the gathering place for all the evil spirits who ascended from there to roam among men and women.

To its south was Ashkelon, ugly and smelling like a whale.

Farthest south lay Gaza the Magnificent, commanding the entrance to the great route leading southward to Egypt. Once upon a time the proud Egyptians had named that route "The Way of Ra." The Philistines renamed it the "Flight of the Swan." The Hebrews called it simply "the northern road."

Gaza was the apple of Dagon's eye, and Dagon was the supreme god who, according to the Philistines, had created the earth, founded the Philistine race, and protected its people. Gaza—palace, fortress, city, and monument to Dagon—had been planned and built as the center of Philistine life. It far outshone all other cities in this part of the world. Nothing west or east of the Salt Sea compared with it. Only Egypt had anything to rival its magnificence.

Gaza stood on a wide, rocky bluff overlooking the coast to its west, and the vast plains of the Shefela rolling eastward to the Judean hills. To the south lay the desert. Gaza, as the saying went, "begins where the desert ends."

Gaza itself was really a city within a fortress. Its planners had laid it out with a canny eye to sieges that could be expected in this prize territory. Surrounding everything were huge casemated walls, octagonal in plan, fifteen feet thick and forty feet high. Inside, three hundred paces from the first wall, was another, fifty feet high and also octagonal in its plan. Three hundred paces was a tough bow shot, an impossible spear shot, and a great enough distance to make any enemy laying siege to Gaza think twice before attempting to rush at the inner wall, even if he should be strong or clever enough to take the outer one.

Clinging to the inner face of one of the eight arms of the interior wall was the Great Palace, which by right of office belonged perpetually to the five dukes of Philistia.

In one wing of this palace was the temple of Dagon, a huge monolith rising well above the rest of the structure, dominating the skyline of the inner city, and capped by a lookout tower with windows facing in all directions. The temple itself was

bare except for the huge marble altar of Dagon and a staircase
that ran around the wall winding its way up to the lookout
tower. The altar of Dagon was adorned with flowers, and a
colossal statue of the god stood behind the altar, facing east.

In the wing close to the temple were the living quarters for
Dagon's priests as well as the army chief of staff, court officials, and guests. A third wing housed the Banquet Hall, the
Great Hall, and the Council Room. The five additional wings
formed ample living quarters for each of the five dukes.

Shekelath, the young Duke of Gaza, was always in residence, save when he was away on campaign. The other four
dukes might come at any time for council meetings or for
pleasure.

The ground beneath the palace was honeycombed with cellars and storerooms and water cisterns. The Treasury of the
Commonwealth was there. And a very complicated system of
tunnels and shafts connected this underground palace area with
almost every sector, street, and house in Gaza. The underground labyrinth had been designed for movements of men and
supplies in time of enemy siege. In a time to come, David
would see it another way.

Some small distance from the north gate leading out of
Gaza, Shekelath's father had built a water tower. A covered
mall ran from the water tower to the outer wall; and a narrow
passageway ran underground from the outer wall to the palace.

A little way north of the water tower was the race track
where Philistine warriors raced their chariots and horses. The
track could easily accommodate five chariots careening abreast,
but the architects had left just enough room for the head and
body of a sixth horse, not for the sixth set of chariot wheels
with their sharp rotating blades attached to the axle. Many a
warrior had found glory here, and many had met death, tricked
into trying to edge a sixth chariot through. All races were in
honor of Dagon. The victor was crowned with a garland of
silver leaves and greeted with the invocation: "You, like Dagon,
your father, have walked, flown, and swum through the air!"

The race track in its turn ringed Gaza's cemetery, filled with
graves marked by red tombstones in the form of a tree peculiar
to the Philistines.

At the center of the cemetery lay Dagon's Hoop, a grassy
field that rose gently to a green knoll the height of a two-story
house. There the priests of Dagon had built a gleaming white
marble altar and on it they had placed a great bronze statue of
Dagon. High above everything, dominating altar, statue, knoll,

and all else, and clearly visible from the watchtower over Dagon's temple in the palace of Gaza, stood the Great Terebinth, the celebrated tree that, as prevailing belief had it, Dagon had planted when the world was created. The Terebinth was called "Dagon's Body." It was worshiped as the visible sign of Dagon's life and power, as the source of virility in men and fertility in women, as the sanctifier of marriages, and as the father of all good and living things on the earth.

The Great Terebinth stood exactly at the center of the knoll. It took three husky warriors, their faces and bodies pressed against its rough bark, their hands barely touching, to ring it around. It rose seventy feet higher than the knoll it stood upon. The outmost reaches of its branches fully covered the slope in every direction and overshadowed the marble altar. In its full foliage the sky could not be seen through its branches.

When there was a high wind, the priests of Dagon had secret ways of reading the little spaces that opened and shut among the Terebinth's leaves according to directions from Hagon, the god's messenger.

At certain times of the year a priest would use a ritual knife to split the bark of the tree. Then he collected the milky brown emulsion that trickled out, and flung it on the sacred fire of Dagon. The emulsion made the fire shoot high with flames of extraordinary colors and varying forms. The priests would read prophecies, receive instructions, solve problems, explain dreams, predict the near future, by interpreting the behavior and color of those flames.

The Great Terebinth had spread its roots throughout the hill like a dense mass of gnarled arteries reaching deep into the ground. The knoll became an extension of the Terebinth's being, Dagon himself holding the earth's womb with sinuous grip.

As Jesse headed north from Bethlehem mounted on Bara, all five dukes lay asleep in the early morning hours at Gaza. Of these the youngest was Shekelath. In his twenty-one years he had proved himself to be a soldier's soldier, a diplomat's diplomat. For all his youth, he carried himself in every way like a man born to high station and to the command of the great forces entrusted to him.

Shekelath could map the strategy of a campaign, administer a large city, maneuver a fleet of warships, negotiate a treaty, drink anyone off his horse, and love a woman. He was in every way fit to be the powerful Duke of Gaza the Magnificent.

Shekelath rose that day with the sun. He greeted this day

as one of expectation and celebration. It was the Day of World Making, a major feast day in honor of Dagon. And it was a special day of happiness for Shekelath: his wife, Solka, and his three sons would return home from their winter-long visit to Solka's father, Makron, Saran of Luqqawatna in the "Land Across the Water," far to the north and west. Even as Shekelath rose from bed, Solka's ship would be well on its way toward the port of Gaza, accompanied by a flotilla of warships and supply boats.

But now Shekelath turned his attention to the affairs of the moment. He had much to do before he would greet his wife and hold her again that night. In just two hours from this sunrise there would be a council meeting of the five dukes. They must all prepare for the coming annual tax assessment council, and after that for the war council which would plan a renewed offensive against the Hebrews. Then at midday Shekelath would begin the solemn ceremonies inaugurating the feast day. At four in the afternoon the great banquet would begin and usher in carousals that would last till the following midday. For Dagon had created the earth in just that time: from midday to midday. Finally, by sundown today, Shekelath would leave the Banquet Hall of his palace and start the short ride from the city to the port, where he would embark on a swift courier ship to meet the flotilla that carried his beloved Solka and his boisterous young sons back to their home in Philistia.

At the stables early that morning Shekelath inspected his prize Arabian stallions.

"Ligam!" he called to the head stableman. "What has happened to the stallions?"

Normally Shekelath could make these animals do whatever he liked. But this morning they shied away when he approached. He caught one, then another, and then a third. They all shivered and neighed softly. Ligam shook his head. He had noticed too.

"Lord Shekelath..."

"Yes, Ligam?"

"Yesterday, my lord, just after sundown, but before the dark had settled in, I was bringing a pair of stallions back from the racecourse..."

"Yes, and?"

"Well, my lord, as we passed close by the garden, there I saw a large black beetle in amongst the flowers..."

"Fool!" Shekelath shouted. "Old wives' tales! You've better

things to do than smell flowers and watch beetles! See to the horses!"

But the color had drained from Shekelath's face. Every Philistine knew: a beetle seen among the flowers at the moment of sundown was a sign of death close at hand.

Shekelath was not the only one of the five dukes of Philistia who looked forward with special anticipation to the Duchess Solka's arrival escorted by the great flotilla of her father's ships. Achish, Duke of Ashdod, could think of nothing else. For on one of the ships a new and very revered statue of Dagon was being transported to Philistia.

Although only twenty-one, just a few months older than Shekelath, Achish was the most unfortunate of the dukes. This morning, as Shekelath was returning from the stables to prepare for the council meeting, Achish entered the temple of Dagon and stood alone before the altar.

Dalman, Duke of Gath, the prankster among the five, would have laughed to see Achish lost in thought in this solitary place. "Achish thinks too much," Dalman often said. "Someday he will think himself to death!" And then he would laugh till the tears came running down his cheeks. For a warrior nation like the Philistines, the thought of death by thinking was the funniest thought of all.

Achish's face should have reflected achievement and confidence, satisfaction, even nobility. Instead, it was etched with the tragedy and pain of a man who from the first year of life had been maimed. And Philistines had an abhorrence for physical handicaps.

Except for his withered right arm and peg leg, he was well built and well proportioned. But his face perpetually wore a hurt and tragic expression: Why, if Dagon was all powerful, had he not protected him from Adonai or at least cured him of his paralysis?

As he kept his quiet vigil in Dagon's temple, Achish lived again the events, as his father had related them, that had made him half a man. The day had begun in triumph in late September about twenty years before. Unparalleled triumph! Shekelath's father had been Duke of Gaza at the time, and he, Achish, had been the infant son of Kaluhag, Duke of Ashdod, who had fought against the Hebrews at a place called Ebenezer and led his men in frenzied attack. He had been merciless, skilled in strategy, boxing the Hebrews in between two solid phalanxes of iron shields bristling with Philistine lances. The Hebrews had fallen back in rivers of their own blood and tried to regroup. They brought into battle with them the most sacred thing they possessed as a people—the Ark of the Covenant.

And Kaluhag had captured the Ark itself! He brought it in exultantly and installed it in the temple of Dagon at Ashdod. It was his greatest day indeed! And his most bitter. When the victory carousals were finally over, Kaluhag took his infant son Achish and made his way to the temple to examine his prize. As he raised the heavy slab of gold on top, its weight began to slip through his hands. Perhaps it was the drinking. Perhaps the fatigue. But he could not hold it. It crashed from his hands and slammed onto the instep of his son's right foot as it fell to the floor. The baby cried out in pain but recovered rather quickly. Kaluhag thought no more of it, and, pursuing his interest in this Hebrew relic, found himself staring at four objects within the Ark. There were two long flat stones on which someone had scratched some short lines of Hebrew script. There was a wooden rod about three feet long. And there was a bronze figure of a serpent. Kaluhag lifted each object out, examined it, and put it back in the Ark; then he replaced the cover and left the temple.

Next day, his little Achish was crying with pain. His right arm and right leg both appeared numb, and he screeched in agony if either was touched. The doctors Kaluhag called in were not able to help the child. As the weeks passed, Achish's arm and leg became useless. Paralyzed. Within six months they had begun to wither like dead branches in winter. And the once beautiful, lively child grew up misshapen physically, although he compensated for this with a penetrating intelligence. In adolescence his infirmity caused him to shun women, even though his handsomeness and sharp wit attracted them. He found himself instead drawn to the companionship of young men.

The morning after Kaluhag's examination of the Ark, the news had been brought to him that the statue of Dagon had been found on the floor of the temple, lying on its face in front of the Ark. Even in his discomfort the duke had been dumbfounded. He had left everything in perfect order, he knew. The priests had not entered. No guard or casual passerby would go into that sacred place without permission.

The priests replaced Dagon's statue on the altar, made special sacrifices, and prayed for hours to the offended god. But the next morning they again found the statue fallen face down, and this time broken in a curious way. The head had apparently broken off, and it had rolled into a corner. The torso of the statue had split into four roughly accurate quarters resembling the condition of the prisoners whom the Philistines were accustomed to quartering in battle and as punishment for revolt. The legs and arms were in a thousand pieces, almost pulverized, as if someone had taken an iron hammer to them. The sight of the sacred statue in this dreadful condition had sent shivers through every man, woman, and child in Ashdod.

The news of what had happened in the Ashdod temple raced through the city. And with it a terrible fear arose. Had not the powerful Egyptian Pharaoh mocked this god, then been forced to free this people, and then been swallowed up by the thundering waters of the Red Sea when he pursued the Hebrews? What manner of god had they tangled with in Adonai?

But still they had kept the Ark at the Ashdod temple, even when strange happenings had begun to frighten them all. First, the men of Ashdod began to find that they could hardly walk: their rectums were blocked with painful, bleeding hemorrhoids. There was much joking of the kind one would expect; the great warriors of Philistia brought low with piles! But when within a few days every man in Ashdod had the same problem, the joking stopped.

Then the city was overrun by hordes of field mice. They were everywhere, in houses and barns and stables and storerooms. No matter what sacrifices and prayers the people of Ashdod offered to Dagon, the terrible and undignified afflictions continued. As if that were not enough for any city to bear, the menstruation period of every woman in Ashdod suddenly began. Finally, between the helpless agony of male and female, the whole city of Ashdod had come to a halt.

But it was only when the best warriors of Ashdod began falling like ninepins with a malodorous sleeping sickness from which they never woke that Duke Kaluhag realized it was the end. This Hebrew relic, this Ark of Adonai, had beaten him. He called for a meeting of the council and sent a crippled delegation, walking for all the world like castrated goats, to Gaza to find a solution.

With permission of the Pentarchy, the Ark had been transferred to Gath, the city that had bred a race of giants and where the men were the fiercest of all Philistines. But the same things happened there: the hemorrhoids, the hemorrhaging, the plagues and the death.

Emulsion was bled from the Great Terebinth, "Dagon's Body," and flung upon the fires; and there the answer was divined. The Ark had to be returned to Hebrew territory. Further, guilt offerings must be made to the Hebrews for the offense to the divinity of Adonai. About these offerings the priests and seers had been very specific: the offerings had to portray the punishment from Adonai, and they had to be of gold. There must be five replicas of hemorrhoid tumors made of gold, one for each of the five great cities of Philistia. There must be one golden mouse for each of those five cities, and for every other city, every town, every hamlet and farm throughout Philistia. These golden hemorrhoids and mice were all to be placed in a coffer of metal and transported with the Ark back to the land of the Hebrews.

It was done exactly that way, and in Philistia the plagues stopped as suddenly as they had begun. But Kaluhag's own trials had not ended. He was in disgrace. His little Achish was stricken. So desperate did Kaluhag become, and so impotent was the rage whose crest he rode, that he had tried to kill himself, but even that had failed, and it deepened his ostracism since it was against the Philistine code. He quickly became an embittered recluse, rarely going to Gaza. Little Achish, despite his permanent handicap, succeeded his father as duke when Kaluhag died, friendless and querulous. Achish was barely sixteen but already renowned for his learning and intelligence.

On this morning, as the great feast of Dagon was about to begin, Achish stood for a long time before the altar in the temple room. "Why could you not protect me?" he murmured aloud to Dagon in the pain of his heart, as he stood in the silence of that place. "Why have you not made me whole? If I could look upon the Ark and pray to Adonai, would I be able to walk like a man?" He waved the stump of his right leg, to which an ash-wood peg had been fitted. "Would I be made whole?" Would Dagon's new statue reverse his tragedy?

At four in the afternoon the most honored guests began arriving at the Banquet Hall in the Great Palace of Gaza.

Duke Ivordan of Ashkelon, some fifteen miles up the coast, was the first duke to enter.

As he and his companions arrived, the slaves removed their blue cloaks, their swords, and their footwear. These Nubians, mostly captured in childhood or early youth, had been trained in one thing: body service. And they did their work with gusto, always smiling.

When they had washed the face, hands, and feet of each guest in perfumed water, they combed his hair and helped him put on the Philistine carousal cloak. This was a short cloak that fitted over the shoulders and torso, covered the arms only to the elbows, and carried the embroidered emblem of Dagon on the back. The men wore it over their ordinary body clothes. The women wore it next to the skin. Every guest brought his own sandals. Once a guest was washed, dressed, coiffed, and sandaled, he was led by one of the slave masters to his place.

At the center of the huge mosaic floor of the hall a spacious circle had been set apart by a ring of couches. That central circle was divided by still more couches and low tables into five equal sections, each to be presided over by one of the five dukes of Philistia. At the very center of the circle was a statue of Dagon and a podium from which toasts would be offered and speeches made.

Except for a row of narrow windows set high up in the walls, the great Banquet Hall was sealed off from the outside by its massive walls. Long tapestries in blue, brown, and gold depicting scenes from Dagon's mysteries covered the white plaster. For light, five huge bronze oil bowls were hung by long, burnished chains from the ceiling, giving a flickering glow to the colors of the mosaic floor. Around the walls, pitch torches blazed in bronze brackets.

After Ivordan came Meluhhag, Duke of Ekron, once the handsomest warrior in all Philistia. He nodded to Duke Shekelath, then quickly turned away.

Hard behind Meluhhag and Shekelath came Dalman of Gath, preceded by his resounding laugh. But for all his 280 pounds, immense height, and fifty-five years, Dalman moved with an amazing nimbleness and delicacy.

Once the dukes had entered, the hall filled quickly and slave boys began pouring wine. The musicians, seated on a raised platform along one wall, began to play. The Philistines were famous for their fast-moving dances and their skill with the lyre, the flute, and pipes.

"By Dagon!" the Duke of Gaza shouted now, standing at the podium. "The first toast! By Dagon himself, and by the Great Terebinth of his strength, I vow that Dagon's rule shall extend over all! From the Green Velvet of the Fatherland in the north, down to the Golden Velvet of Philistia in the south!"

It was the customary oath that began the revelries, and it reflected the Philistine dream of empire. Great shouts and cheers answered this toast, and the banquet was under way. Wine goblets and flagons were kept full by the slave boys. Young slave girls bearing trays piled with food joined the crowd. They moved quickly through the narrow spaces between

tables and couches, as enticing to the eyes of the guests as the
food and wine were to their palates.

At a banquet as important as this, on the special feast day
of Dagon, on the day of Duchess Solka's return, on the day
the new statue of Dagon would come to renovate their national
shrine, Shekelath had spared no expense. The Philistines' mode
of banqueting was delightful in any case, but this occasion
outshone them all. Thirty courses were served—each complete
with meat and fish, vegetables, condiments, sweetmeats—accompanied by eleven different wines.

Even as the last course was served, the slaves began all over
again. And now the duke broke out the favorite drink of the
Philistines, great casks of rich black beer. And so it would go
through the night, feasting, drinking, toasting, dancing, shouting, playing music, laughing, joking. Shekelath's major-domo
supervised it all with a master hand, and all was very seemly,
as Philistines frowned upon lewdness in public.

As the feasting went on, Shekelath excused himself and set
out to meet the flotilla of his lady, Solka. Shekelath and his
aide-de-camp, Gonlan, approached the slips leading down to
the quayside. Then Shekelath stopped and looked up, surprised.
Gonlan stopped by his side.

"What is it, my lord?"

"Those sea gulls."

"The sea gulls, my lord?"

"Yes, why are they still up there so late at night? And they
are not even feeding. They should long ago have been in their
nests. And look at the sky. It looks like metal. Blue metal."

"A storm coming, probably, my lord. We'd best get under
way if we are to meet the flotilla by midnight."

Over the past forty-eight hours all that Samaria and Judah
and Philistia had felt were the random growlings of a chained
dragon, little murmurs of threat from its great throat, the occasional nasty flick of its tail, the scratchings of its claws—
which had sent starlings and sparrows and locusts flying in
fright, and animals scurrying in panic from their accustomed
places.

But now the dragon itself was unleashed. The whip of its
huge tail cracked the face of all lands and sent destruction
careening in one long, deafening roar over all the land and
people.

It came from the north at the instant of David's birth, spew-
ing rocks and boulders, splitting valleys, heaving through

mountains, sending up enormous tidal waves in the Great Sea, hurling streams and rivers from their courses, splaying flash fires across spring wheatfields, blowing buildings into rubble, toppling tons of earth upon fleeing men, women, and children.

In Jebus, cobbled streets split and a babel of cries from the dying and injured came from the sudden rubble of its houses. The house of Uri the Hittite swayed and its walls cracked. Its floors heaved and bucked. Furniture and pots and wall hangings were sent flying through the air. The torrential rain that came on heavy growls of thunder sent tons of water streaking down the sides of Jebus' hills into the valleys below. And those rains were like the tears of Uri's grief. The birth had been unexpectedly difficult. His new son had been spared, but his lovely wife, Hattishla, was dead.

At Gibea, the thunder erupted from the bowels of all the hills and ravines around the fortress of King Saul. The king was hurled from his bed, crying out in terror, his cries drowned in the sounds of the earth crashing against itself, and in all the shouts and cries around him. He ran from his room, quickly sent Ahinoam his wife, her children, his concubine, Rizpah, and her children scurrying from their beds. He shouted to everyone to get out, get out into the open air! The last to leave, he nearly plummeted down the stairs, thrown from side to side. The roof crashed to the floor behind him, and then the stairs collapsed. All at once there was a huge, resounding crack, more deafening than all the other noise, as the great fortress wall by the guard house heaved. Fifteen feet of solid masonry was split apart from top to bottom, and rocks and mortar tumbled out like entrails released from a belly.

Up in Galilee the valley rumbled. Villages on hilltops rocked on their foundations. In Nazareth houses vomited forth people through swaying doorways into the streets. Malaki lay on his little couch in the house that sheltered him that night. He listened calmly to the rumbling in the Yezreel Valley below, then rolled off his couch and put his ear to the ground. Then he shouted in his deep voice that no one could mistake: "Have no fear, Nazarenes! Listen to me! Stay where you are! This is not for us! Nazareth will be spared! Pass the word quickly and go back to your houses and to bed. Adonai will watch over us all!" And so they did.

No such reassuring voice came to the ears of Duke Shekelath of Gaza. A rough hand shook him out of a heavy sleep as he lay on his cot below decks.

He was awake in a flash. "What is it? Have you sighted Solka's flotilla?"

Up on deck, one glance was enough for the experienced Shekelath. The sea had changed. Its surface was black, ugly, seething with small sharp waves biting at the sides of his ship. Long underswells thumped beneath the waterline; and the helmsman was struggling with the rudder, endeavoring to hold the ship on course. In the clear sky the red evening star, Sirius, was gleaming like blood. And Shekelath could see Solka's flotilla about halfway between his ship and the horizon to his north, bringing his wife and three young sons home to him.

"What's the wind like, watchman?" the duke shouted to the crow's nest.

"Changing, my lord. Veering around toward the southeast."

"Southeast? You idiot! It can't be!" His voice was swallowed in the sudden violent luffing of the topsails.

"It's changing, my lord! It's changing right around."

"I cannot hold her, my Lord Duke," the helmsman shouted above the wind. "I cannot hold her. She's turning. If we keep on this course, she will capsize!"

"Come about, you fool. Come about! Quickly!" Shekelath leaped and threw all his might with the helmsman's at the broad shaft of the two rudders. The ship listed steeply as the prow came sharply around. Billows of water poured in over the side. Then she straightened with a frightening shudder, rocking violently from side to side, plowing and rearing fore and aft, as the fresh wind gathered speed each second. It whistled and rushed through the sails, bellying out every inch of the ship's canvas, lashing at the masts and bridge, bending and thrashing everyone on deck.

Shekelath looked back at Solka's flotilla. It was closing on them, so near now that he could make out the figures of people on the decks. Suddenly the duke's strong features melted into fear and misery as he caught sight of a high, fast-moving wall behind the flotilla. Shekelath could not believe his eyes. What was hurtling toward the ships from the shores of Solka's land of Luqqawatna, where the earthquake had originated, was the farewell gesture of the underworld dragon: the tsunami.

Tsunami waves could reach fifty or a hundred feet in height. They could race across oceans at 120 miles an hour. They would follow one upon another at a distance of perhaps a hundred miles between crest and crest.

Shekelath would never be able to tell anyone afterward with what helpless horror he saw the advancing wall of water seize

Solka's ship, lift it high, spin it around crazily, turn it upside
down, and suck it into the great black breast. His great shout
of despair and impotent rage was lost in the roar of water and
the high scream of the wind.

Then the wave was coming at the stern of his own ship.
Sea, spray, and spindrift blinded him. He was hurled violently
against the corner of the helm, the wind knocked out of him.
He grabbed at the deck railing and waited for the shock.

Shekelath had heard tales as great as Homer's of sailors
caught in giant storms, of ships buried in walls of water and
of what the Phenician poets called the "mercy window" that
sometimes appeared to spare one or another ship or hero.

Through one such "mercy window" Shekelath's ship escaped, dumped between towering cliffs of water that closed
together once they passed. Sails ripped. Wooden planks
creaked and snapped. Men were thrown around like straw as
the ship plunged into the vortex of the swirling aftercurrent.

As the first wave thundered on, rapidly outdistancing the
flagship, Shekelath could see high on its crest the overturned
hulk of some ship. He could not make out which one. All the
others had disappeared completely. Then that one, too, disappeared, borne like a matchstick out of sight, racing with the
wave toward the shores of Philistia.

Shekelath's ship would not find a second "mercy window"
easily when the next wave hit. And he knew now there would
be a second, and a third, and a fourth. Maybe more. He and
his crew took stock of the damage. Two sails had been torn
to shreds; they quickly hacked them loose and threw them into
the sea. The main sail had held. The bridge had been totally
shattered but the rudders were intact. Seven men had been lost.

As far as Shekelath could judge by the stars, they were
being pulled by the wave's aftercurrent back toward the coast
where Gaza Port lay. Right in the path of the oncoming waves!
He shouted to the helmsmen to veer right. He would tack
directly westward in the hope that they could outrun the westward stretch of the next tsunami. It was their only chance.

In the Great Hall of the palace in Gaza, the huge chandeliers
swayed above the gales of happy, raucous laughter and shouts
of the carousals. The floor trembled slightly under the dancing
feet of the revelers. The giant Dalman of Gath loomed up on
the podium, swaying from side to side, the flagon of beer held
high in his hand. "Earth's Power!" he cried in the first of the

great toasts. Answering shouts rose up from all around him: "Dagon's Power!"

Enthusiasm was at fever pitch. Everyone was cheering, spilling wine, and shouting in unison, "Dagon's Power! Dagon's Power! Dagon's Power!"

At this very moment on this night of nights, the incredible happened. The great cheer was prolonged by the roar of massive masonry tearing apart. An ugly crack appeared in the palace.

The mosaic floor split, grinned jaggedly, wider, tossing up the little colored squares of stones and glass like spittle. In a second the crack reached the walls on two sides, zigzagged up their length, cut across the graceful domed ceiling and sent a rain of stone and debris downward. Burning oil splashed from the chandeliers over revelers frozen in disbelief, until flames caught clothes and human torches shrieked for help.

All at once the crowd became a mass of human panic. The floor split wider, opening from one wall to the other. The dragon's roar swallowed all the screams of the terrified Philistines.

"The earth is listing! Philistines!" It was Ivordan screaming in his old man's voice. "The earth is listing! Look to your lives! Oh, Philistines! Look to Philistia!"

Over the heaving, cracking floor hundreds scrambled, bodies bursting, eyes bulging in fear, arms pushing and flailing, mouths open, throats coughing and choking in the dust, everyone trying to save himself. They trampled over shattered masonry, broken tables, overturned couches, smashed crockery, other bodies. They clambered, fell, dragged themselves over blocks of masonry, clawing and fighting their way to the outside.

Then all of Gaza heaved and trembled and seemed to tumble before their eyes, while great torches of flame shot up like jerking tongues from the fallen buildings.

One, two, three, four shocks came and went. They seemed to suck the air out of buildings all around, squeezing walls and roofs together and trampling them underfoot.

And then there was an uncanny silence as the pyramid of bodies and debris sank out of sight. A moment later the surface of each of the five radial avenues tilted, tumbling paving stones toward the center of what had once been the bath house—a magic and deserted garden of destruction that had been, a few minutes before, the hub of the busy capital.

Those people who had not been killed and who were not so stunned or panicked that they could not move made either for the dock side or for the Great Terebinth, guided by the light of the fires that had sprung up everywhere and were feeding upon the ruins.

By far the greatest furnaces were the city stables. There were sixty stables in Gaza, all placed strategically every few hundred feet or so in a ring between the inner and outer city walls. Each stable was built in tiers of three levels, two below ground and one above. Each tier of each stable held forty horses. The fires started in the hay and oats. The wood of the stalls quickly caught. And the wooden structures didn't last a minute, once sparks struck them. Soon the city was dominated by the fierce sound of the flames, the horrible neighing of the horses and the thumping and crashing of hooves. Over all hung the smell of roasting flesh.

When the worst seemed over, hundreds of survivors made their way through the main gate and down Palm Tree Road to the open spaces near the shore. There they huddled, stunned. And for a few moments some peace and some sweet release from the terrible trembling, the smell, the fire, and the din consoled them.

When those at Gaza Port and on the beaches heard the first roar of the tsunami, the wave was traveling at 140 miles an hour, and it was already too late for them. The wave entered the V-shaped bay of the port, and its huge shaking mass of water was fatally compressed by the narrowing sides of the bay as it crashed toward the quays and warehouses, rising ninety feet above the low-tide strand, engulfing the horrified inhabitants, boiling into the harbor, over docks and sea wall, carrying the wreckage of ships and human bodies. Then the water receded noisily out to sea, sucked by the magnet of the second wave already on its way. But no one at the harbor survived to see the second.

Achish's one thought when the earthquake hit had been to get to the Great Terebinth. He had been the first to scream out "To the Terebinth! To Dagon's Body!" In the wild onrush of the Banquet Hall, he was pushed and pulled by the crowd, thrown to the floor, trampled on, dragged along. He fought to his feet, pulling himself up on his crutch. He did not even know how he found his way out. What he saw around him and what he heard seemed so unreal that he stood for an instant in shock and disbelief. His one thought became: I must get to the Terebinth! I'll be saved at the Terebinth! I must get to the Terebinth!

On Achish went, stumbling, hobbling; through the race

track and the cemetery crowded with refugees from the devastation, as they gathered in little bunches among the graves of the already dead. As he drew near to the knoll where the Terebinth had stood, he slowed down, the smell of burnt flesh, clothes, and wood repelling to his nostrils. He raised his eyes, frozen, in fear of what he now expected to see.

All the ground before him was charred and blackened. The huge girth of the Great Terebinth of Dagon had been slivered from top to bottom. The split sides of the enormous tree had crashed down upon their own heavy branches, dragging huge clods of earth up with their roots, so that the grassy rounded top of the knoll no longer existed. One half of the tree had fallen headlong upon the statue of Dagon and across the altar of the god. The statue was crushed. The lovely white marble was shattered. The sacred fire was out, its ashes scattered among the strewn bodies.

In the open gashes of the earth where the Terebinth had stood, skulls and bones stuck out everywhere. It was like the refuse heap of a charnel house. All these years, Achish suddenly realized, Dagon's terrifying body had stood upon a mass grave that existed long before the Philistines had arrived. The Terebinth had been nourished on dead bodies. All this time it had been a tree of death.

Achish climbed to the top of the hill. He sat down wearily. "Who is this Adonai, after all? Who is this faceless god of the Hebrews? Is it he who has done this thing to us? Is it he who has killed Dagon?"

Shekelath made land safely, and hours later he found Achish sitting disconsolately on the skeletal ruins of the grassy knoll.

"It's all gone. Gone!" Achish kept repeating, looking on the devastation of Gaza the Magnificent. "This is no whim. No accident. If we had behind us the strength of the god who created this havoc, we could build an empire that would last five thousand years."

"Achish! I swear it!" Shekelath was shaking with anger and grief. "If the faceless god of the Hebrews has done this to us, we will have the skins of his people for our drums! I swear it!"

At the sound of thunder above the cave, Jesse raised his head. Shalama, he saw, was not looking up toward the sound but down at the floor.

"Jesse . . ." she began, but the thunder rose, invading the rock of the cavern. Suddenly a jagged cleavage opened from the cave entrance through the fire pit and over the opposite

wall. Red embers flew in every direction. The tripod and pot
tumbled down into the yawning crack. Flames and sparks and
smoke belched up from the crevasse that had been the fire pit.

Jesse, a prisoner of sound and shock, heard Shalama's voice
as from a great distance. "Pray! Pray that you do not die the
death or go down to the pit with them!"

Jesse thought she must be babbling in her fear. But a second
later, his head still near the jagged opening, he saw a garbled,
gangling rabble of bodies pouring out of the crack in the earth,
together with the smoke and flames. The mouth on each undulating face was cut like a gash. Each one screamed a name,
a sin, a curse. "Er!" "Onan!" "Hate!" "Death!" "Korah!"
"Sihon!" "Lick the Golden Calf!" "Garrote the Priest!" "Defile
the Ark!" "Curse the unmentionable All High!" Their curses
filled the cavern in an unbearable crescendo of filth and rage.

Jesse covered his ears with his hands and tried to roll his
body away from the jagged hole that vomited this desecration.
But the floor still heaved under him, and he moved like a
drunken man.

He shut his eyes as tight as he could, but the heat of belching
flame made him look in desperation at Shalama. What he saw
transfixed him. Shalama was standing upright, her face lifted
to the ceiling, her arms stretched out wide, the palms turned
upward. She seemed to tower over him and the black and red
jumble of bodies between herself and Jesse. Her hair seemed
like burnished gold. Her face shone with a clean and sunny
comeliness, her blue eyes were on fire with depths of seeing.

"Shalama! Shalama!" Jesse's voice was a croak.

"Adonai! Adonai!" Her voice rang out strong, clear over
the bedlam. "Adonai! This boy child will be the womb of
Adonai's body! Adonai's...His body...He will be the womb
of Adonai's body!"

Jesse would always remember each word she said. Yet it
was a contradictory phrase that left him totally confused.
Adonai's body? A man a womb? Another shock of the earthquake threw Jesse and Shalama to the floor. He was the first
to recover. They were alone in the shaking cavern. The fire
embers were almost out. He rushed over and found Shalama
crouching where she had been thrown by the last heavy jolt of
the quake. He pulled her up and dragged her after him through
the hut that creaked and groaned in the last heavings of the
earthquake, and at last they were out on the ledge, in the clean
dark air of the night.

Jesse tumbled to the ground and lay there, reveling in the

sight of ordinary trees and listening to the sound of falling water, grateful to be back in a world he could understand. Shalama slumped down beside him. When they had recovered, they talked sporadically in whispers.

"Mistress Shalama," Jesse stammered, "my child is a boy—how can he be a womb? What does it all mean? What am I to do?"

"I don't know, Master Jesse," she said sighing deeply. She was exhausted. "We know Adonai has neither flesh nor bones nor body. All I know is what I said—what they said."

"But is the child a blessing?"

She stared at him, a little angry. "He will be the womb of Adonai's body, Master Jesse—of course he's a blessing."

"But what am I to do?"

She heard the misery and puzzlement in his voice. "Take care of him. Special care of him." Her tone was compassionate. "That's all you need to do. Adonai will do the rest. Adonai takes care of his own. . . ."

"Great God! Great God! . . ." It was all Jesse could muster as a response.

When daylight began to appear over the eastern horizon and touch the sky with fingers of light, Jesse roused himself. All the questions he had had yesterday lay in his soul now like silent prayers. All the answers, like destiny and time itself, resided in the hand of Adonai. He said farewell to Shalama.

"Will I ever see your face again?"

"No, Jesse, son of Obed. No. But I will never forget your face. Never."

The late night air at Bethlehem was still. The wind had died down. The only sounds came from the village dogs. They were not barking, merely whimpering in fear at the unearthly silence and the whistling vibrations they could feel coming through the ground into their bodies. All the village slept beneath a blanket of darkness. The only light was in Jesse's house. Hatich had already gathered all the lamps not needed in the large room onto two tables near Korith's bed. Tallow candles and earthen oil lamps cast bright yellow pools over Korith, etching the pain on her face in light and shadow. There was alarm in her eyes. Her fingers clawed at the coverlet.

"Hatich! Hatich!"

"Here, Korith. Here I am. Be strong now. The child is coming!"

Heptah came quickly to Hatich's side. She put a great pot

of steaming water on the table and moved to the head of the
bed. With a towel cooled in water and balsam, she wiped
Korith's face and hair and soothed her temples.

Hatich spoke to Korith, telling her where to move, what to
do, how to breathe. Korith groaned in agony.

"Now, Korith! Bear down! Harder!"

Suddenly Hatich looked up at Heptah. She spoke quickly
and softly in Egyptian. "Get a midwife to wipe Korith's face
and another to help her move and shift. You come here. We
have trouble. The child is turned. The feet are coming first.
It is a breech. We must get this child out quickly and keep the
cord from winding around its neck."

Heptah, as cool and as quick as Hatich, who had trained
her, gestured the two midwives over to the bedside and by her
movements put them to their tasks. Then she moved to Hatich's
side.

"The ankle. The left is clear but the right is caught. We
must get it clear."

"Korith"—she spoke in Hebrew again—"one moment now,
one more moment of effort and we are through. I am going to
count to five. Then on six, I want you to bear down hard, bear
down and push with all your strength." Then to Heptah, "Place
your hands here and press. I will take the other side, when I
have inserted the instrument." Deftly, in perfect unison, they
went through the motions they had performed so many times
before.

"Korith, I am beginning to count. We are ready now. One,
two, three, four, five, and six!"

Korith gathered in her breath. Now she bore down on the
child with all the strength left in her muscles. She realized what
had happened. The child was caught. It was not moving.

"Again, Korith, please, daughter. Please. The same thing.
On my count of six. Come on now!" Then to the others, "Hold
her shoulders up. Support her."

The count started again, once Heptah and Hatich were ready.
"Again, Korith! Hard! Harder!"

Korith pushed down, her strength failing, the pain increasing. The pain became more than she could bear. She started
to scream. She screamed and screamed. And all at once it
seemed that all the earth was screaming with her. Lamps flew
from the tables. Water jars fell and crashed on the ground. The
whole house rocked back and forth crazily. Tables fell, spilling
towels and lamps and ointments. One midwife was thrown
backward, reeling. The other crashed against the bed, then fell

to the floor. Outside in the living room, Jesse's sons, who had gathered there with some neighbors, lay on the floor, frightened out of their wits.

Hatich's hand slipped from the child's foot as the force of the tremendous earthquake flung her away from Korith and slammed her across the room. Heptah was thrown against the wall near Korith. Hatich was momentarily stunned and dizzy, but she was the first to regain her senses. She tried to get up, but the floor heaved. "Ra, lord of life, have mercy," she prayed.

Korith could not tell whether she was alive or if this was what death was like. Her fear for her child was greater than everything else—including her pain and the general confusion. It rapidly brought her to the edge of unconsciousness, but she did not faint. She felt unarmed. Defenseless. Alone. She seemed to herself to be all blockage. She could feel the child low in her, struggling to be free. "Jesse!... Ah Adonai!... Hatich, help me! Help me!"

She felt Hatich's hands again. Hatich had regained her footing and braced herself between bed and wall and had the baby in hand now. One foot. The other. Her hand slid through the blood and mucous and grasped the baby's buttocks. Despite the rumbling and crashing and screaming, Hatich kept herself firmly wedged against the wall. She knew nothing except that the child had to be saved. Her concentration was a miracle, a gift. Her hands were strong, sure. They were guided by a power greater than herself.

One last long scream from Korith pierced through the confusion and din of the last great shock from the earthquake. And the child was in Hatich's hands.

"Heptah! Heptah! Quick, woman! Quick!" Heptah scrambled as best she could toward Hatich. "The knife, Heptah. Any knife. Quickly! Cut the cord!"

She hit the baby's buttocks. Again. Harder. Again. A cry. Again. At last, not a single cry but a sustained howl of protest from the baby's throat. The cry of life.

The floor beneath Hatich's feet still trembled but it was settling down. Somewhere in the room a jar fell and shattered. A metal urn rolled back and forth, and then stopped. The echoes from the earth subsided like receding thunder. The cord was cut and knotted. The baby was safe, but Korith was not.

Jesse had driven Bara long and hard, stopping only once, at midday. By late afternoon he rounded the stone fence in front of his house and turned into the familiar sloping yard. He slapped the camel toward the barn and headed directly for the house.

The first thing he saw was his new son. Hatich had heard Bara's clattering approach. The Egyptian stood waiting for Jesse in the middle of the large living room, holding the child wrapped in swaddling clothes.

"He is a fair, fine child, sir!" was her greeting.

Jesse did not see the glistening of her dark eyes. He saw only his child. He took the small bundle from her gingerly, as strong men often do, afraid he might damage such a small, soft being. He examined the little face, the fair skin, the lashes making tiny shadows on round cheeks as the baby slept in the cradle of his arms. He touched the forehead with one finger in a gentle caress.

Jesse looked at Hatich. He had fathered seven sons before this one, but the joy he felt in his heart was new. He smiled at Hatich. Then he handed the baby to her again.

"My wife, Mistress Hatich?"

"In the inner room, Master Jesse."

He started for the door of Korith's room, but Hatich stepped in his path.

"Master Jesse..."

"Is she all right?" His heart began to pound. "Is she all right, Mistress Hatich?"

Hatich did not answer. But Jesse knew. Korith was gone. "I knew." He tried to speak, but it was only a hoarse whisper. "I knew."

Jesse walked slowly past Hatich into the inner room. He sat down at the head of the bed, where he had sat two evenings before. He could hardly see through his tears. He bent over and kissed Korith on the forehead. Her face was peaceful, but her flesh had never felt like that before. He touched her closed eyes and her mouth lightly with his lips. As he raised his brimming eyes, a glint of color caught his attention. He reached, and felt the necklace she held in her hands.

"Master Jesse?" Hatich interrupted his thoughts. "It is not normally my place, nor, indeed, my desire. But now, as it is, there is no one else. Mistress Korith asked me to tell you. It is difficult for me to say; it is very personal. Master Jesse, your wife had heard the gossip. She asked me to be certain that you knew this child is yours. She swore on her love for you and your sons. I had hoped I would not have to be the one to tell you."

"Yes," Jesse answered. "I know the child is mine. And Korith's. And all our ancestors."

"She asked one more thing, Master Jesse. The child's name. She asked that you name him Elhanan—'God has given grace'—because surely it was by the grace of Adonai that you have this child today."

"Elhanan? There is no one by that name in our family."

"She said she knew that. But this child is different. The earth shook at his coming. And in her last few words Mistress Korith spoke of his importance. She said, *'Huwa davidum amihu'*—'He will be the leader of his people.'"

"Do you speak the Hebron dialect, Mistress Hatich?"

"No, Master Jesse. But Mistress Korith instructed me carefully. Those were her exact words."

During the day, a messenger had come from Uri telling Hatich of Hattishla's death and summoning Hatich and Heptah. Hatich had already made arrangements for nursing care for the baby.

"Mistress Hatich, you have told me things here that I will hold in my heart. Without you my son might have died too. Let me share one thing with you in return: I met the holy woman Shalama as Raham told me. We talked in the long hours after the earthquake. I did not know my son had already been born and my wife lay dying. Perhaps she did, I wouldn't be surprised. She told me that if Adonai wants a person to live, he gives that person love. Adonai gave Korith love. Mine and his own and the love of our sons. He gave your Mistress Hattishla the love of Uri, and I believe—I do not mean to be presumptuous—I believe your faithful love, as well.

"I think, Mistress Hatich, that they still live. Both of them. How that can be I don't know. But I pray it will comfort your heart."

"How does Adonai shake the earth like a bag of little stones?" Saul puzzled to Samuel as they watched the workmen repairing the damage done by the earthquake to his Gibea fortress.

"Did my Lord the King see Adonai making the earth and the stars and pouring the waters into the oceans and lakes and rivers?" Samuel queried sharply, lifting one eyebrow in reproof. Saul stared at the prophet as he went on. "No man, my Lord King! No man saw Adonai at work. He arranged all the rocks, all the earth, all the waters, all the sand, all the stars, as his slaves. Time itself was his slave. Then when he wants to, he has only to flex his fingers and all these things start shaking, as you say, like a bag of little stones—"

"But why, Samuel? Why do that to us, to his servants?"

"He does that to everyone—servants, enemies, the good and the bad. That's what Adonai—"

"But why does he?"

Fear now replaced puzzlement in Saul as he listened to Samuel's response. "An earthquake is the signature of Adonai," Samuel went on. "It is as if Adonai thundered out loud to all the world: 'On this day, a great event has taken place—a great battle has been fought, a great man has died, a favorite of mine has been born'—whatever Adonai wishes."

"But what about me, Adonai's anointed king? Have I ceased to be his favorite?"

Samuel looked away quickly. "We know only after the event, we humans. We have to wait." Then he looked around at Saul, his face clearing. He smiled. "Now I must go home, my Lord King."

Saul stood watching the retreating figure of the prophet on his mule wending his way down the hill slopes. "A battle—a great man dead—a favorite born . . ." The words kept bothering him for weeks afterward. Then he forgot about them altogether.

Jesse was not bothered that in the eight months since his new son was born no one had said a word to him, even out of politeness, about any resemblance of the boy to himself or to Korith. He was not even bothered by the gossip of the old crone Maaka, whose spinster daughter Shua was the baby's nurse.

"Hmm! He's big for his age," Maaka would comment when Shua brought the child to the well as she came to chat with her mother and the other women. "Growing like a desert cactus. All arms and legs. Not at all like his father!" And, peering at the infant's blue eyes and blond hair: "Extraordinary coloring! How unlike Jesse!" Or again: "Strange name, Elhanan! Well, Korith told the truth! *Huwa davidum*. He's a leader, all right. Maybe not of his people, but certainly of poor Jesse's house. The baby runs the master there, all right."

The only thing that troubled Jesse was his special responsibility to care for his son. True, he was healthy and robust for his sixty-three years, but he was still one of the oldest men in Bethlehem, and you couldn't cheat death forever in this hard land. His other sons had their own work to do. It was clear that David—even Jesse had begun to call him David—needed someone to care for him until he was a man, that is, until he was fourteen or so. Yet in this household of men, "the leader" lacked a mother.

A simple thing, Jesse thought at first. Why, even old Shem the miller still had five unmarried daughters. But Jesse wanted no more children. And the ambition of every young woman was to have many children because any child might be chosen by Adonai to be the promised deliverer of the Hebrews, the Messiah. But an older woman or a widow might not live to see David into manhood.

Another problem for old Raham, Jesse decided. And he was right. Raham knew of one woman who might be suitable.

"A distant kinswoman of yours, in fact." His black eyes glistened at Jesse from under his ostrich brows. "You remember Pelatyahu, who settled with all his family in Hebron some twenty years ago? Not long after you married Korith and took her from Hebron to Bethlehem."

"Yes, Raham, I remember."

"Well, all of Pelatyahu's daughters have married but one. Shoshanna. She is exactly right, especially because she is different. But that is not the problem, Jesse. The problem, as you know, is that you will have to have permission of the Council of Elders to marry a woman from outside Bethlehem, and the elders will not want any of your wealth to go to Hebron."

In Raham's mind the marriage was obviously settled. It was just a matter of details, and he was already running through the meeting of the Council of Elders in his mind. "Old Shem obviously would like you to take one of those spinster daughters of his. But I can handle Shem," he began.

"Just a minute!" Jesse interrupted. "This Shoshanna. In what way is she different?"

Raham grinned the satisfaction of a man who has solved everybody's problem with a simple stroke of genius. "Why"— he turned his toothless smile in his round old face on Jesse— "she is perfect for you. She has vowed an oath to Adonai to live and die a virgin!"

"How did you get yourself into a situation like that?" Joshua demanded as they rode to Hebron. "She's probably ugly and covered with hair, while most of the Hebron women are reputed to be great beauties. Just like you to get the gnarled old olive tree in a grove of orange saplings."

"Have your fun now," Jesse replied. "You'll soon be eating your words. What's wrong with a vow of virginity? It's an honored custom among our people—for those who want to serve Adonai in a special way. Ask Raham what Moses, our father, thought of a vow of virginity."

"Moreover," Joshua went on as if he hadn't heard, "she's probably been done out of whatever fortune she may have had, while you pay a pretty price!" And Joshua tugged at the gift-laden camel.

They arrived in Hebron with Jesse trying to remember just what his late kinsman Pelatyahu had looked like and trying to reckon how bad his daughter could be.

Joshua went to see Mahalyahu, son of Koth, a kinsman of Shoshanna's mother who had taken Shoshanna and her two small brothers into his house. Mahalyahu was well known as a tight-fisted but prosperous trader in perfumes. Indeed, all was in readiness, Mahalyahu agreed, and the wedding could take place immediately—provided, of course, that Jesse had held up his end of the bargain. Mahalyahu's eyes glowed as the slaves displayed Jesse's betrothal gifts, the bales of silk, the elephant horns, the silver talents, the iron dagger, the perfume. All very valuable and very tradeable.

"I think, Joshua, son of Ner," Mahalyahu said, without further formality and with a distinct warming in his voice, "we have an agreement."

It was late afternoon when Joshua went with Jesse from their hostelry to the place of the wedding—a house often hired out for such festivities—where Jesse, dressed in a long, full coat of pale blue, awaited his bride. The sound of a single pipe playing a marriage tune announced her coming. Then Jesse could hear little bronze bells rung by the bride's attendants. And then the bride came in, preceded by the young scholar Hokhni, with thin beard and harelip, with whom Raham had arranged the marriage. Three young women, friends of Shoshanna's, came with her, ringing the festive bells.

Shoshanna's dress was very simple. How different from Jesse's memories of Korith when she had entered into her marriage with him! Shoshanna's face and head were completely hidden behind a veil that reached past her shoulders; her hands were encased in the ritual white silk gloves.

"May Adonai, the God of Abraham and of Isaac and of Jacob, bless our brother Jesse, son of Obed," Hokhni began, his lip working overtime, "and bless his marriage to our daughter Shoshanna. May Adonai grant Jesse and his house prosperity and length of days. May Adonai bring Jesse and his house into the kingdom of his glory."

Joshua and all the bride's company answered with the ceremonial "Amen."

The scholar handed a ring to Jesse. Jesse took Shoshanna's right hand. He placed the ring on her index finger. Then he repeated the ritual words after the scholar. "I, Jesse, son of Obed, of Bethlehem in Judah, do this day take thee, Shoshanna, daughter of Pelatyahu, as my wife, within the Covenant of Adonai, and for the blessing Adonai gave to Abraham, our father, and his seed forever."

It was done. Jesse turned toward his new bride as Mahalyahu came forward in accordance with custom and removed Shoshanna's veil.

Whatever Jesse had expected, it was not this! He was not sure if this was a child or a woman. But she was as beautiful as Joshua's jokes had been ugly. Her face was young, vivacious, sensitive. Her skin white and unblemished. Her eyes were a deep hazel, and her look was open and steady as she returned Jesse's gaze. Her mouth was delicately shaped, a lovely mouth, open in a little smile as she watched Jesse staring at her. He saw that her hair, like her simple dress, was not adorned with pearls or wedding ornaments but was beautiful even so, raven black, encircled with a wreath of braided white silk that held it in place.

But the most striking thing of all for Jesse was that Shoshanna's extraordinary beauty shone, not with sensuality, but with some interior luminosity, filling him with awe as he remembered her vow to Adonai.

Clearly Shoshanna was not flustered by Jesse's stare or by his obvious surprise. When she spoke, her voice was as steady as her look, and her words were direct, but in no way harsh. "Our scholar, Hokhni"—she turned her head and threw a dazzling little smile in the direction of that young man—"has told me of your household. And of your infant son. You call him David, I am told. I know that my consent for this marriage is not required by the Law. But because of my own special vow to Adonai, Hokhni has shown me the kindness my own father would have shown if he were still alive. But you should know, Jesse, son of Obed, that I have made another vow—this time to you. I will be a good mother to your David. I will care for your house, all your sons, and all who come there. And you will have my honor and my love. This I vow."

Jesse waited a moment. His voice sounded rough to his own ears when he finally answered Shoshanna. But his meaning was as kind and as honest as Shoshanna's. "I am old enough to be your father, Shoshanna. I have a son who might be your brother. I pledge to you here as my wife what I pledged through Raham of Bethlehem before I saw you: You will find respect and honor in my house. You will be loved. And my David will be as your own son."

For just a second or two the silence itself seemed filled with blessing. Then the piper began to play, and Jesse began the first dance of the celebration with Shoshanna. The guests sang and clapped in rhythm, Mahalyahu's voice booming out above the rest as he drank to the marriage agreement. The bridesmaids rang the little bronze bells. The young scholar joined in with all the rest. And Joshua, bless him, blushed.

When David was still very little, Shoshanna would sometimes interrupt her busy day and take him with her down to the little vegetable garden near the fruit trees that David's grandfather Obed had planted. She took her knitting or some sewing and sat by the yew tree out of the strong sun. She would sing little songs to him, and David would roll, then crawl and toddle about, looking for baby mischief.

When time permitted, Jesse would look for them there in the afternoon, and he and Shoshanna would talk awhile quietly. Between Jesse and herself there grew a feeling of completeness in one another that did not need to rely on physical satisfaction. In such quiet settings Shoshanna and David heard stories of Korith, of the earthquake, of Hatich, and of David's birth.

There were other times when Shoshanna and Ozem would take David to the corner of the village down beside the Galligalli, the small but steady stream of mountain water, where there was a kind of village common. Apart from the well and the marketplace, where everyone had to go at one time or another, the Rabbit's Head was the most popular public place in Bethlehem. Years before, a deep inlet of the Galligalli had been enlarged to form a pond in the shape of a rabbit's head. Ozem and the older boys loved to swim in its cool waters, seeing who could hold his breath longest or swim the farthest. Elderly Bethlehemites, including Raham, would sun themselves on the benches by the Rabbit's Head, or stroll along the Galligalli, gossiping and watching the children.

As David grew, so did his lively curiosity. Boys did not start at Raham's school until they entered their seventh year; and until then their lives were very free. David's head with its reddish-gold hair became a familiar sight bobbing about in the marketplace, down at the Rabbit's Head, in the yards and gardens of neighbors' houses. *David hazahavi,* David the Golden One, he was called by all and sundry. *"David hazahavi!* Your mother will be looking for you!" *"David hazahavi!* Where are you off to now?"

David wandered farther and farther, making friends with other children, discovering wonderful places—the Witch's Road, a narrow shady pathway overhung with sticky spiders' webs woven from hedge to hedge; the watchtower, where the guard called out the hours and rang the bells that signaled the arrival and departure of caravans; the threshing floor and the grinding stones at the mill; and finally the sycamore trees up at Raham's, where hundreds of crows nested.

Raham used to say that crows lived for hundred of years, and that they talked to each other, and knew when someone was dying. He could listen to the crows, he said, and know when someone was approaching the house, even whether he was alone or not, and if he was walking or riding. "Listen," he would say to the children who visited him frequently in the late afternoon, "they're calling home the stragglers." And David and the others would cock their heads listening to the changing pitch of the cawing crows.

"Now," Raham would tell them all, as he had told their fathers when they were four and five years old, "if Adonai has made even the crows to help each other as one tribe, then surely he intended as much for the Hebrews of this land. Eh? What d'you think, Shammai? What d'you say, David *hazahavi?*" They always nodded solemnly at Raham, as their fathers had done before them, and then scurried home to eat and tell their families what "Raham said."

By the time David was five and already a head taller than other boys of his age, he used to trot alongside his older brother Ozem when he went out snaring rabbits, fishing, or gathering berries and wild fruit. The life of the house turned around the changing seasons and their respective holy days. Raham organized religious ceremonies that were adapted to the activities of the Bethlehemites—sowing, reaping, lambing, shearing, and so on.

The very first activity of this kind that David shared with his family was the time of the threshing. He stood on one of the threshing floors beside his brother Eliab. And while Eliab wielded the heavy leather scoops and whips to lift and scatter and winnow the wheat, David walked in among them, picking up the wheat and chaff, tossing them in the air to be caught by the winds blowing in from the mountains of Moab. He always remembered those scenes of the threshing because it was one of the few times that the work was done to the rhythm of music. And his first memories of keeping time with his feet and hands dated from those days.

One day, in David's sixth year, he lay chattering with his companions in Miller's Meadow, each child chewing blades of the long sweet meadow grass. At a certain moment David thought he heard a strange sound. "Raham's crows!" Yoldi, Joshua's son, said, and they giggled at the thought of talking crows.

"Wait!" David hushed his friends. He listened. It sounded like a very distant babble of sounds at first; then he could hear a rhythm coming from the caravan route beyond the sandy ridge.

The faint sound was suddenly buried in the raucous clang of the watchtower warning bell. Every child knew that, when that warning sounded, he was to run home if he could make it, or to the nearest house if he was too far away. The boys scattered; Yoldi and one or two others made for Raham's; Holdi and Malkan, old Zaza's sons, ran to the miller's house nearby. All were gone in an instant—except David. He fell prone and lay still in the tall grass, his eyes fixed on the road, waiting. The distant babbling sound came steadily closer. The rhythm became clearer.

Finally he caught sight of them. A rabble of figures straggling out from the curve of the hills, their forms wavy in the distant heat and haze, as they headed up the high road toward Bethlehem. It was a group of men, young and old. Some wore the loose robes of the Hebrews, gathered at the waist with a belt. Others wore only a loincloth, or a waist-skirt that fell from hip to ankle. All were barefoot and none wore any head covering. Two or three carried drums and beat out the mesmerizing thumping rhythm that David had first heard. A few played on pipes or small flutes. All of them were turning and twisting in a way David had never seen in the dances he knew.

As the little band bobbed and danced its way closer, close enough now so that he could even see the faces, David's fright gave way to a kind of attraction. All those rapt faces seemed to give off a radiance he had never seen. His own head, golden in the sunlight, began to bob. His feet and hands began to beat in unison with the thumping drums. Without thinking, without knowing, he slipped off his loose, knee-length robe; and, dressed now only in the tight cloth drawn between his thighs and about his waist, he moved forward, dancing, weaving, toward the band of men and boys who drew closer to him along the road. Closer. Closer...

"David! David!" He did not seem to hear the sharp cry of Shoshanna behind him. She came running across Miller's Meadow, skirts and arms flying, Raham trotting as fast as he could after her. She leaped at David, grabbed him by the shoulders, and twirled him around so that his back was to the careening medley of music, of bobbing bare bodies and writhing limbs. His eyes looked right through Shoshanna. She slapped him smartly on the cheeks; she covered his ears with her hands. "Raham! What is happening to him? David! David, I say, look at me! David!"

She pulled David to the ground and clasped him tightly with both arms. She could feel his whole body hot as with fever, sweating, vibrating from head to toe. Raham watched the company of dancing figures pass slowly by along the road; and he watched David relax slowly and finally fall asleep in Shoshanna's arms as the sounds died away.

"A company of prophets, daughter." Raham's breath was still a little short from his exertions in trotting through the meadow after Shoshanna. But his voice was calm. "When Yoldi told me David had stayed behind, I sent for you because I knew he would follow them. If you hadn't come immediately, you might have lost your son."

These companies of prophets had recently begun to wander the land. Everyone had heard that even King Saul had joined a band briefly, overcome as he was by the power of that rhythm.

"Not all is bad, I think, though," Raham went on, "Adonai has let loose a new spirit. I have seen it change ordinary men before my very eyes. They become ecstatic, as David was becoming. They praise Adonai and recount his greatness. They accuse Israel of its transgressions and prophesy its great destiny among nations.

"It is infectious. I have seen whole groups of men and boys taken by this call of prophecy. They leave their homes and families. No entreaty can make them stay. If they are brought back by force, many leave again. There are no boundaries for them in this divided land, and they talk always of the unifying will of Adonai. Certainly nothing else unites us now."

In the years of David's boyhood, the hope of the Hebrews had come to rest on two pillars: first, their faithfulness to Adonai, and their Covenant with him; second, the faithfulness of their king to the word of Adonai. The Hebrews had never had a king before Saul of Kish.

Yet any Hebrew of David's boyhood days would have found it hard to say whether it was Saul or Samuel who was more feared and respected. Saul's rule, even over the Hebrews, reached only as far as his sword—and that depended on three things: the will of Adonai; the guidance of Samuel, Adonai's prophet; and the obedience of Saul to both. It was the last of these three things that would come to trouble Samuel's soul, as David grew up in the sun of Bethlehem.

Samuel's power extended as far as the spirit of Adonai. But Hebrews everywhere were corrupted, it seemed, worshiping false gods in Adonai's holy places and being continuously infected by the heathenism of the peoples with whom they lived and traded. The Temple of Shiloh where Samuel had drawn close to Adonai and tended the very Ark of the Covenant; where Eli, the father of Samuel's heart, had been High Priest— even Shiloh had been destroyed in its own festering misery. And the shrine of Bethel echoed now with the wantonness of Baal and Astarte, proclaimed by Hebrews in their service. This weakness in the most ancient of pillars on which the hope of the Hebrews rested had troubled Samuel all his life. It would trouble him until he died.

It was often told how, when Samuel was only two and barely weaned from the breast of his mother, Hanna, she and her husband, Elkana, brought him from their home to the Temple of Adonai at Shiloh to present him to the High Priest, old Eli, of the House of Aaron.

"Adonai lent me this child in my old age," she told him. "Now I give him back to Adonai."

As he grew, everything about Samuel bore out Eli's first expectations that the child was special in the eyes of Adonai. So Eli entrusted Samuel with the care of the sacred Ephod. The Ephod was a square gold plaque attached to a piece of leather. It was protected by a flap of leather and provided with one long strap attached to the upper corners, so that it would be carried hanging around the neck, resting on the chest. It had been fashioned by ancient craftsmen according to the instructions of Moses. Inset in the gold were various precious stones and minerals. From Moses, too, instructions on how to use the Ephod to consult Adonai had been handed down from generation to generation.

It was through the Ephod that Adonai often made his will known. It had been so since the days of Moses, more than four hundred years before Samuel's time. The Ephod had been passed from father to son, from high priest to high priest, in the House of Aaron. But in the days of Eli it had been a very long time since the word of Adonai had been known through the Ephod.

Eventually it was the young Samuel, not old Eli, who heard the call from Adonai one night. The announcement that the Angel made to him was terrible: there would be a punishment against Eli and his house forever because of offenses committed by Eli's sons and because Eli had not restrained them. No amount of sacrifice and prayers could save them from this devastation.

After the Angel was silent, Samuel wept for Eli, whom he loved; and the message of Adonai weighed on his heart as a message of doom.

For Eli's sons, however, it was all the same. Days passed, months and years, and the word of this Samuel seemed hollow. The sacrifices came in as always, and the purses of Hofni and Phinkhas continued to fatten.

And then my Lord Duke Kaluhag attacked from the west with a great force of Philistines, and pushed all the way up to Ebenezer, with the result we have already seen.

Phinkhas and Hofni, who bore the Ark into battle, were captured with it. They were splayed and quartered, their eyes plucked from their heads, their bodies fed to wild beasts. Only one Hebrew defender reached Shiloh before marauding Philistines from Kaluhag's army raged into the city. Eli did not live to see the final judgment of Adonai on him. When he heard that the Philistines had captured the Ark, he collapsed, and in his fall broke his neck, dying instantly.

Samuel was able to escape only with the Ephod and the sacred Book of the Law before the Philistines looted and burned the temple. Even after the Ark was returned to the Levites, Samuel's message to the House of Israel was hard and unrelenting. Every year for twenty years, in all the Hebrew towns he visited, Samuel spoke the unchanging word of Adonai: "Like the sons of Eli who were slain before the Ark, you have deserted Adonai. Why do you say then that he has deserted you?" Slowly, slowly, the people began to take his words to heart, and it was at Rama, some twenty-three years after Shiloh had been destroyed, that the word of Adonai came to Samuel and told him that there would be a new beginning of friendship and love between the Hebrews and their God.

Samuel called for all the men of sixteen and over from every

Hebrew town, city, and hamlet to gather before him at nearby Mizpah. He said to them: "You have fought for twenty years since Ebenezer, but your strength has been like the strength of rabbits that run before every threat. I tell you, the Philistines, the most feared of all your enemies, will come against you with their weapons of iron and their chariots. But they will find now that the rabbits have become lions!"

And just as Samuel had said, before the Hebrews left Mizpah for their homes, the Philistine spies had reported on the huge gathering of Hebrews there. The Philistine dukes mistook it for a gathering army, and they immediately marched out against Mizpah with the intent of making it a second Ebenezer.

But before the Philistines could even range themselves up in proper order for their attack, the Hebrews, led by Samuel, poured on top of them from every side, thundering fearful cries to Adonai. The Philistines tried to fall back and regroup, but the Hebrews gave them no chance. The slaughter was immense, and the shame of Shiloh was wiped out.

But the Philistine threat never abated, and this deeply troubled the councils of elders in the major towns of the Hebrews. They came to Samuel: "Samuel, you must ask Adonai to give us a king who will be as strong as Shekelath and as wise as Achish," the elders pleaded, "but under your tutelage, of course."

Samuel went into seclusion at Rama. Was there a Hebrew free from corruption who was strong enough in his soul to serve Adonai and not himself? Adonai's choice fell on young Saul of the Tribe of Benjamin. Saul was the son of Kish, the wealthy landowner and animal trader who lived in the region of Gibea not far to the south of Rama. Saul came the few miles to Rama one day, searching for some breeding asses that had strayed in search of forage. This was the man Adonai had chosen as the first king of the Hebrews. Samuel knew by the word of Adonai. And so he anointed Saul king, and he knew that the *akeda*—the test of the new servant—would come, as it had for Samuel; as it would again for Samuel; as it came for every servant of Adonai. And he knew that then it would be a question not of the will of Adonai but of the answering will of Saul.

At the age of twenty-three, Saul of Kish was a man of dazzling gifts. He was striking and imposing, tall, dark-haired, quick-eyed. He had worked beside his father's men with the herds and flocks. He had tilled the land. And the rippling brawn of his tanned body showed it all. He had traveled north to Tyre and south to Egypt on his father's business and he knew the languages of both countries.

He could defend himself with sword, knife, and spear and had learned well the lessons that living on the land taught. But he had learned them better than most. He could measure a mile to within an inch with his eye. He was every bit as clever at trade as his father, yet he loved music and was a lusty dancer. He knew and loved the Law of Moses and lived by it as well as he could. And when he led the Hebrews to a brilliant victory over the Ammonites, his claim to kingship was settled. Yet there were not many who wanted to run afoul of his terrible temper.

When Saul was seventeen, Kish arranged his marriage to Ahinoam. They named their first son Jonathan. Saul was prouder of him than of his other sons, Ishui and Melkishua and Ishbaal, who came in quick succession. And Jonathan loved his father; but it was not necessarily any easier to be the favorite of Saul than to be the favorite of Adonai.

Some men said that Saul was as fierce as the great Joshua. Others told stories about him that rivaled those of Samson. But he won through fear more than love. And this was Saul's weakness as ruler over the Hebrews.

In Gibea, Saul refurbished a fortress that had been built by the Canaanites before they were driven north by the Philistines. A small permanent army together with a number of devoted officers began to gather around.

As he grew older, Jonathan learned all the skills that would make him a preeminent fighter in the land, worthy to be its next king. At the side of his father's chief lieutenant, Abner, he became as good as any man with the bow. He learned to fashion, weigh, and arm his own arrows. He could calculate wind and distance in the wink of an eye, and he never missed a target.

A figure almost as familiar as Jonathan in the fortress was Samuel. Every year before he returned to Rama at the end of his circuit through all the Hebrew enclaves, Samuel spent time with Saul at the fortress. He was ready at a moment's notice to come to Saul from wherever he might be on his travels. Samuel had loved Eli as a father. Now he came to love Saul as a son.

It was known everywhere in the land that the king would move only with Samuel's blessing and approval. Samuel's word was of greater weight than an army of thirty thousand men in counting the chances for victory or defeat. Saul easily observed the few inviolable rules Samuel laid down: no compromise with the enemy; absolute obedience to the exact instructions they received from Adonai; the need for Samuel to offer a sacrifice to Adonai before they went into battle; and, most important in Samuel's eyes, the absolute need for ritual purification of the king and his officers before entering battle. As long as Saul observed these simple rules, all would be well.

Yet the time came when Samuel thought it right to enlighten Saul about Adonai's grand design for his land and his people. It was autumn. They were walking in the compound of the fortress at Gibea early one morning, and Samuel decided to plunge right in with a history lesson, a lesson that, ultimately, David was to learn better than Saul—and what's more, to provide an answer.

"My Lord King, Adonai speaks not only to prophets through the sacred Ephod. He speaks in events! Events of moments, events of centuries, events of millennia. If that were not true, would we still scramble in our own blood for this land so many centuries after Moses, our father, led us out of Egypt? Time is nothing, my Lord King, except the tool of Adonai's will, of his plan, of his eternity."

Saul put one hand to his forehead and sat down on some planks near the wall. "My head spins at such talk." He rubbed his forehead. "Time may be nothing to you, but you walk nearer to Adonai than I."

Samuel's eyes reflected some frustration. If Saul would lead his people, he must begin to see beyond a series of little battles. Samuel did not know the details himself of what had to come. But he knew by the word of Adonai that this was a time of preparation.

"My Lord King, it's all very simple, really. Remember the game of seesaw we used to play as boys? If a boy heavier than you sat on the other end, he could lift you off the ground, control your position. But if you were heavier than he, you could lift and control him. And one boy standing on the middle of the seesaw could control the two ends, tilting them up and down as he liked."

"Yes, I do. But—"

"Listen, O King. Here, give me one of those planks. Put it on top of that stone. Now!"

He pointed to one end. "That's the south, the Bag of Sand called Sinai. You stand there. I'll stand here on the other end— it's the north, the Wheel of Galilee turning around the high ridge of Merom. Here's the Ladder of Tyre. And up there, the Twin Rivers of Tigris and Euphrates. Down south near you coils the Golden Serpent of Egypt. Up here by me is the three-headed Lion, Babylonians, Assyrians, Akkadians. Over here to the northeast is the Aramean Mule with its shattering hooves of forced trade and perpetual treachery. Over to the northwest you have the Hurrian Jackal and the Hittite Bear.

"Now, tilt the seesaw up and down! Once upon a time, the Golden Serpent of the south slithered up, occupied the center— and controlled the entire north and south. At another time, the three-headed Lion, the Hittite Bear, the Aramean Mule, the Hurrian Jackal, each one of them controlled it. And then the Sea Peoples over there on the Shefela and the coast of the Great Sea. Dagon! A new people! And a new idea! Not tribe against tribe! Not some Phenician whore-goddess. But Dagon against Adonai!

"Now at this time nobody controls the center or ends of the seesaw. The only ones who threaten to control it are the Philistines with their Dagon. You must attack and destroy them along with their god. The Hebrews must control and flourish from Dan to Beersheva, from the Jordan to the Great Sea. There can be no treaties between Dagon and Adonai, my Lord King! This is not a battle like all the others we have fought. This is Dagon and Adonai!"

For a time Saul stood still and silent with lowered eyes. Then abruptly he turned and strode across the compound. There he took a knife and a large fish, a carp, from the hands of a woman who was just about to clean it. Then he strode back to where Samuel awaited him on the farther side of the compound. He stripped away the flesh of the fish, then slammed the skeleton down on the center of a plank, the head still intact, its dead eyes staring up. The ribs of the fish played out in both directions, from the spine.

He turned to Samuel, and the question in his voice surged over his respect for the prophet, like flood water over a river bank. "You look and see the seesaw land of Adonai. I look and see a weak fish! Don't we all know how things really are? Look here! The spine of this fish: *that* is the land in which we live, a mountainous land. We live on hilltops and try to hold our tillage in the narrow valleys of the spine. Not even hold— cling to it, rather, like mountain goats! The head of the fish at the top of this spine of our mountains does not even reach the Wheel of Galilee. And its eyes stare north, beyond that Wheel of Galilee where you say the Bear and the Lion and the

Jackal and the Mule are of no account. But look with the eyes of the poor fish, and you will see the Arameans are still there and they still hate us.

"And here, at the tail of the fish, here in the south are the Amalekites. And here, at the belly, on the east, here all along the ribs of the fish are hordes of Moabites and Edomites; and the Ammonites have not gone forever. Daily all of them make inroads against the Hebrews. And the Jebusites are in our very midst controlling one of the most important cities and trading routes in all the land. And up there, where the open mouth of the fish takes no breath of life, there Bethshan is held by the Amorites, who control another major caravan route. And you tell me we have but one enemy! Look again!

"And even if there were only the Philistines, what have we to throw against their iron weapons and their phalanxes of chariots? I will show you what we have. In the north, cut off from the head of the fish, in the Wheel of Galilee, five tribes. Tribes? Remnants, better! If you gathered them all, even if you could unite them all and that is most unlikely, the men of Assher, Naphthali, Zebulun, Dan, and Issachar together couldn't stop a pack of blind mules.

"And over there in the east, can Gad and Reuben defend themselves? They are a pack of squealing mice before the Ammonite cat."

Samuel's face showed shock and anger, but Saul went on inexorably. "So here we are, the rest of us, clinging to the mountains and the wadis. The Tribe of Simeon here"—Saul moved the point of the knife to the center of the fish—"has been decimated. The Levites have no land, and anyway priests don't fight. That leaves four out of thirteen tribes of Hebrews. Judah here . . ." The knife moved to the ribs of the fish where Bethlehem would be. Then north: "Benjamin here; Manasseh and Ephraim here. Four strong tribes.

"But there is strength and strength. We control no iron and have no skilled smiths. We have no standing army, no chariots. Mountain goats! That's what we are, perched on the spine of the land, running hither and thither butting our horns to protect our peaks. But unable to stop anyone—anyone!—from moving upon us from the north or crawling up from the south to beset us! We are hard pressed to keep them from crawling up between our very ribs on either side." Saul threw the knife to the ground. "How many enemies can we fight?"

"In the sacred name of Adonai, we can fight them all." Samuel bent to retrieve the knife. "But we must know why."

"Why then, if not to be left alone on our farms and in our little toehold territories? Tell me, Samuel, is that not why?"

Samuel laid the knife across the ribs of the fish at the center of the seesaw. "Because Adonai wants something else. He wants to create, to fashion a sign for all the earth to see."

"A sign?"

"Yes, a sign! A sign of himself. Of his presence. Of his spirit. Something that men and women shall see forever until the end of all time. You, O King, were anointed for that purpose. If not you, Adonai will choose another and a more obedient man." Samuel turned away and left Saul brooding over the seesaw plank.

The first great event in the life of every Hebrew boy was his circumcision. The cutting off of the foreskin of the penis was a physical sign that each boy was a member of the Covenant of Abraham. But that occurred when he was only eight days old, so no boy had any memory of it. He had to wait thirteen years for the next major event: his confirmation as a member of the Covenant, when he became truly a "son of the Law" and an accepted "man of Israel."

Fortunately, in between those two events most boys could look forward to an event almost as important as circumcision and confirmation: their entrance into school at the age of seven. After the spring harvest in the year that David was seven, Jesse and Shoshanna made him a birthday gift of a clay tablet and a stylus made of flint to write with. They escorted him solemnly and importantly down the street from the house, past the marketplace, past Miller's Meadow and up to Raham's little garden, where Raham taught classes three mornings a week. In bad weather the pupils clustered in his barn.

All each boy needed for class was his tablet and a sliver of wood or a nail not longer than his index finger. The children sat in a semicircle on the ground around Raham. He sat cross-legged on the ground with a large platter of sand on his lap. Using a sliver of wood or his finger, he traced in the sand illustrations of what he was teaching. He also used wooden blocks, leaves, fruit, and little figurines to illustrate his lessons. The pupils used their slivers of wood or nails to trace on their tablets of clay.

The regular course of study lasted six years, with instruction on the history of the Covenant of Abraham with Adonai, the prescriptions of the Law that Adonai gave to Moses, and the meaning of many things in life.

The six-year course was cyclical. If you joined the class in the middle of one six-year cycle, you simply completed the latter half of the course during the first three years of your schooling; and then during the second three years you covered the first half of the course.

It all worked out very well, chiefly because the children were absolutely fascinated both by Raham's face and by his teaching methods. For instance, when he started teaching the letter *Alef* for *aretz*—the earth—he brought a little plate and a soft earthenware bowl and a bucket of water to class.

"Now this plate," he would say, "is the earth, *ha-aretz,* as Adonai made it, flat, rather round, with sharp edges and chasms all around it. And this bowl is the firmament of the skies, *ha-sham-mayim*. When Adonai had made the earth, then"—placing the bowl face down on the plate—"he placed the skies over the earth.

"You see!" he said, pouring some water over the bowl and plate, "none of the waters of the skies can reach the earth, unless!"—he would pause dramatically—"Adonai punctured holes in the firmament of the skies." He drove a thick needle several times through the bowl, then poured more water. It went through the bowl onto the plate. "And that is what Adonai did in the days of Noah when the Flood came." Then would follow an account of the Flood. Raham was thus always interconnecting his lessons. When he reached the letter *Nun,* the first letter of Noah, he would repeat the whole story. In this way there was a constant review.

As luck would have it, Raham was just starting a new six-year cycle when David began his instruction. In fact *Alef* was the letter of the day, and the word was *Adonai*. David quickly caught on to what he should do; watching the drawings of Raham and the others, he was soon tracing *Alef*s on his clay tablet and repeating with the class, *"Alef* is for Adonai."

Of course Raham had complete knowledge of the Law of Moses. This was called the Law because its most important part was a series of laws and prescriptions for the moral behavior of the Hebrews. But the Book of the Law also contained an account of how Adonai created the world; how he created man and woman; how the first man and woman, Adam and Eve, offended Adonai and were expelled from the Garden of Eden; and all the subsequent history of Adam's descendants down to David's century—a period of some four or five thousand years.

When David was a boy, the principal copy of the Book of

the Law was kept in the house of Samuel the Prophet at Rama. The senior scholars of the House of Israel came periodically to Rama to read the Law and to make copies. An old and diligent scholar, Raham had probably completed his copy over a period of twenty or thirty years. By this time the Hebrews had learned from the Phenicians to write in a cursive, spidery script quite unlike the script of Samuel's original.

Instead of writing on papyrus reeds as the Egyptians did (because the Nile River had a superabundance of those reeds growing on its banks) or on clay tablets as the Sumerians and Assyrians did (Mesopotamia was plentiful in mud flats), the Hebrews used parchment: the dried and treated skins of goats. Raham, however, had in his personal library hundreds of inscribed clay tablets as well as Egyptian papyri in languages which he had been trained to read. But he carefully kept them away from his Hebrews. There was always the danger that the religion of the Sumerians would influence an untrained mind. He used the tablets only for consultation about the history of medicine or practical matters like damming rivers, the calving of cows, and medicinal herbs.

Raham's copy of the Book of the Law was never opened for anyone else. It was in the form of a scroll, a long series of strips of parchment sewn together and rolled up when not in use. He kept his book in a special closet inside his little house and read it continually. From it he drew the materials for the lessons he gave his pupils.

David entered the last six-year teaching cycle Raham ever gave. The first day he admitted David to his class, Raham knew that he would see the boy through the full course, that somebody very important to Adonai was passing through his hands. But something equally deep inside him told him that would be the end of his teaching forever.

One day in early autumn when David was nearly ten, Raham began his lesson with the letter *Kaf*.

"*Kaf*," said Raham, his eyes darting around the young faces. "*Kaf* as in *kokav*, the star."

Then Raham drew a simple triangle on his sand platter. All the pupils drew a triangle on their clay tablets.

"Now attention, children!" Raham drew another triangle upside down on top of the first triangle. There was a gasp of appreciation from the boys, and each with his little stylus carefully drew the second triangle, and the six-pointed star appeared as if by magic on their tablets.

"Master Raham, please, why are there six points to this star?" David asked.

Raham's eyes glinted. He smoothed out the sand in his platter, reached for his stylus, and drew a large circle.

"What is that?"

"The earth that Adonai made with the power of his word!" came the well-schooled answer.

Quickly Raham drew a small rectangle within the circle and looked up questioningly.

"The land!" came the answer.

Then, as he sketched in to the left and right and the top and bottom of the rectangle, he stopped after each new element and gave his class that questioning look. The responses came in a regular swelling chorus.

"The Great Sea!" "The kingdoms of the Pharaoh!" "The land of Ashshur!" "The Great Desert!" And so on.

Then, within the land, he sketched the regions of each tribe of Hebrews.

"Reuben!" "Simeon!" "Dan!" "Naphthali!" "Gad!" "Assher!" "Issachar!" "Zebulun!" "Ephraim!" "Manasseh!" "Benjamin!" "Judah!"

Finally Raham's stylus fell directly on one spot in the land, and all the young voices shouted.

"Bethlehemmmmmmmmm!"—prolonging the last syllable and at the end breaking into cheers and laughter.

"Now," Raham went on, serious again. Darting his hand up to the far right-hand corner of the circle, he sketched in the Tigris and the Euphrates. "The land of the Rivers of the Star.

"David, son of Jesse, you asked why six points. Listen carefully.

"When Adonai decided to draw our earth and our skies from *tiamat*, chaos, what were his words?"

"Yehi ha-or!" came the chorus. "Let there be light!"

"Exactly! Light! Light from the star! Adonai caused a huge star to explode at six points on its body—to explode far and wide in a brilliant flame and fire of light! A six-pointed star!"

"What is the name of that star?" David was on his feet in excitement.

"Its name is *Mazal,* the brightly shining spot." Raham studied the faces around him.

"Why do we say *mazal tov* when we wish a person the best of things?" There was no answer. "We mean, surely," Raham answered himself, "may the light of Adonai's blessing, the light of his star, shine on that person.

"Now that star was Adonai's living word. For Adonai speaks through things. And his words are the roaring winds of the firmament, the newborn baby, the sword, the harvest. What other people has a god like ours?"

"There is no god but Adonai!" The class broke into another of its well-memorized refrains. "And Israel is his chosen one!"

Raham had taught his class the names of the chief constellations. The Hebrews guided themselves by the stars, and they recognized the change of seasons and the times of the year by the shifting pattern of the constellations. Raham smoothed out his sand platter and drew the circle of the skies. He started at the lower right and went around making little marks. At each mark the class repeated the name of the constellation at that location.

"The Yoke Star of the Sky!" "The Goat-Fish!" "The Bull of Heaven!" . . . "The All-Reaper and All-Crusher!" "The Swallow! . . ."

Finally Raham's stylus was down in the lower left-hand portion of the circle. He drew the six-pointed star there and looked up, his eyes querying the class. Then his stylus again filled in the squiggly lines of the Tigris and Euphrates enclosing the six-pointed star. He looked up again.

"There Adonai placed the *hadre teman,* the mystery of the southern sky. Then Adonai created Adam and Eve, our first father and mother, the parents of all the living, and he walked with them in the Garden of Eden, he and his angel.

"One of the things Adonai taught them was the meaning of the six gleaming points of the star. Each point stood for a great man, a leader whom he, Adonai, would anoint, his *mashiach,* his messiah, to lead his chosen people. Who was the first *mashiach?*"

"Abraham, our father!" David answered immediately.

"The second?"

"Isaac, our father!" Seven of the fourteen pupils had understood now.

"And the third?"

"Jacob, our father!" Now the entire class was answering in unison.

"The fourth?"

"Moses, our father!"

"The fifth?" Silence. One boy rose—Misha, son of Zaza.

"Samuel, our prophet and judge!" Raham shook his head. Ishkfar, son of Moker the merchant, suggested Saul, the king of Israel. Raham said nothing, only shook his head again. He gazed around at them all.

"We do not know. Yet." His voice was very quiet and deep. "Only Adonai can tell us. But the House of Israel awaits those two anointed messengers of Adonai."

"What will they do, Master Raham?" David asked.

"They will fight against Adonai's enemies. They will establish the Kingdom of Adonai, free it from its enemies, give blessings to our people and prepare all men for the reign of Adonai."

"What will that be like, Master Raham?" Young Evedyahu's eyes were shining with interest.

"In those days," Raham explained, "the mountains of Israel will run down with must wine. The hillsides will be clothed with white sheep. The meadows will be golden with grain. The sun by day will give warmth but never burn. By night the moon and stars will watch over us while we sleep.

"There will be no war. Men will beat their swords into plowshares, their spears into wheels for oxcarts, their arrow tips into fishhooks, their shields into plates and cups.

"For no man will fight with his brother. Nor will they fear the wild beast. The lion will lie down to sleep beside the lamb. The bear and the wolf will walk together. All will share the peace of Adonai.

"In the land, there will be complete justice and peace and law. *Mishpat* and *shalom* and *sedaqa!* Overall and everywhere!" Raham's voice had by now assumed an almost chanting note. "And the whole earth and the skies will be full of the glory of our Lord, Adonai, our God, God of all."

Raham rested for a moment in the silence that followed his words. David's eyes were fixed on the scholar's face, but he was lost in thought.

Up on his cramped roof terrace surrounded by a little parapet, Raham settled down, had a light meal, and read the day's portion of the Torah. As night fell, he lit a lantern, then took out his cedar box of clay tablets and went through them slowly, looking for one in particular. He found it finally. Holding it near the lantern, he scrutinized the wedgelike cuneiform signs. "*Zal-duk-ki . . . mul-nun-ki . . . ni-duk-di . . . nin-gish-zi-da . . . mul-nun-ki . . . mul-ud-ka-duh-a. . . .*"

The old scholar mulled for some time over that, speaking to himself and reverting to his Hebrew. "The Land of the Good Tree . . . bright shining spot . . . the star of special brightness . . . holy place . . . cat-faced, gape-jawed demon bird . . . with the serpent staff. . . ."

Long after he had put away his clay tablets, he lay on his pallet facing the stars, his eyes turned to the southern sky. He kept repeating *mul-nun-ki,* and gazing at the spot above his head where that brilliant star should have been.

Philistia

▨▨▨ At the time of the great earthquake, Philistia had been for about a hundred and seventy years the spearhead of Dagon's ambition, the southernmost mark of Dagon's expanding empire. But the earthquake that had ushered David into the land had so devastated Gaza and other Philistine towns that the central Philistine government sent word to all its lands that there would be a Council of Dagon. All commanders from every part of the empire would gather in Luqqawatna on the middle day of the last autumn month. There, under the supreme authority of Kalkodon, the High Priest of Dagon, it would be decided whether Philistia could and should be rebuilt to sufficient strength to remain Dagon's spearhead; or whether that honor—and that power—should now fall elsewhere. If the decision was in favor of Philistia, it would still have to be decided whether that command should remain in the hands of Duke Shekelath. Dagon's will in everything would be final, and that will would be conveyed through the priesthood. Thus all real power was in the hands of the priests.

The last council had been held after a disastrous defeat of the Philistines in a premature thrust into Egypt. The commander who led the attack against Ramses III had never returned from that council. His name, his family, every trace of his existence had been wiped out by order of Dagon. Control of Philistia had then been given over to Shekelath's great-grandfather. It could be removed from the family only by the high priest, Kalkodon.

Shekelath did not intend to suffer such a fate. He intended to fling back into the face of Adonai the death and destruction he was sure had come from the hated Hebrew god. So from the time the messenger from Luqqawatna announced the council until the time for departure, Shekelath set himself and Philistia a great task of rebuilding. Every man, woman, and child was urgently pressed into the work. It could not be completed before the council; it could barely be begun. But the damage had been so great as to provoke doubt in the council about Philistia's ability to recover. Shekelath was determined to put that doubt to rest.

And by the time the proud Killer Swan on the prow of his command ship nosed out to sea from the Port of Gaza, Shekelath had restored at least adequate defenses to most of Philistia. He left Duke Meluhhag in temporary command. Duke Achish commanded the second ship of the small flotilla, and if everything went as Shekelath intended, Achish would help in the requisitioning and supervision of the huge supplies they would bring back from Luqqawatna.

Of the five other commanders of Dagon's empire who were also preparing for the council, Makron was the closest to the center of Philistine power. Makron, Solka's father, was commander-duke of Luqqawatna itself; and he was as angry in his grief over Solka's death in the tsunami waves as Shekelath was. In addition, Makron had two younger daughters not yet married and no sons. So the loss of his grandsons along with his daughter might mean that the powerful leadership of Luqqawatna would pass away from his family.

Two of these five commanders, Ziekhale of Rhenan and Vogazil of Danuvan, traveled from the north, from the lands of the Rhine and the Danube. Their territories had been the northern gates of Dagon's power. Though reduced in size, the Philistine commands there were strong enough to protect Dagon's flanks and had great strategic value. Two other commander-dukes came from the southern bulwarks of Europe: Markalav of Sikaler from the toe of what is now Italy, and Arkavid from Makatan, just east of Luqqawatna. Their territories had been the earliest conquests of Dagon in the lands of the warm sun. Markalav was quite content with the earthquake that had necessitated the council because it might provide him with the opportunity to make his own move to the south. Arkavid's ambition was directed at Makron's command in Luqqawatna.

Shekelath knew what he had to face from the other commanders, but neither he nor any of the other five had ever met the six Strong Ones. They were from lands still unconquered by Dagon, but where Dagon's prophecy of empire was to be fulfilled. There was Amen-Ra-Hotep of Egypt; Gabala of Arabia; Sesebokassta of Africa; Mohenjo of India; Chuyanto of China and the Isles; and Ana-Ka-Ilu of Assyria.

Taken together, these were the twelve men on whom Dagon's prophecy depended. They were the tools of Dagon's will.

When he arrived at Luqqawatna after a four-day voyage of fair winds and good seas, Shekelath's first surprise was to find that the principal government buildings and the central palace had survived the earthquake intact, although the rest of Luqqawatna was in ruins.

The second surprise was more personal. No sooner had he settled into quarters in the central palace than a priest came to inform him that, although the council would not begin until the next day, he must come that night to participate in the mysteries of Dagon.

"The Representative will speak to you," the priest said.

The Representative? Shekelath had never heard of such a person or title. Did the cleric mean the high priest, Kalkodon? The cleric put up his hand for silence. "All in good time, my Lord Duke. And remember, at the mysteries you will obey all instructions. You will not be harmed. Never afterward are you to speak about the mysteries to anyone. Not even to the others who will be there. Any violators will die the death.

"When the mysteries are completed, you will participate in the council. Never afterward are you to speak about the council or what is said there, except to another commander."

Shekelath dressed quickly and followed the cleric to another wing of the central palace, through a set of heavily guarded double doors into a semidark vestibule. Quickly the other commanders and the six Strong Ones also arrived. All were stripped, examined, bathed, dried, perfumed, and then clothed in a black, sleeveless robe. The robes were so long that even the tallest of them had to lift the folds in front so as not to trip over them. Then each of them was blindfolded and led into the chapel, where they were guided to highbacked stone chairs.

In time, a sound began. Or, rather, Shekelath became aware of a sound, though he could not exactly remember its beginning. It was a tapping. Very regular. Like a light hammer striking a piece of metal ever so lightly. Tick-tick-tick-tick-tick-tick. He was almost sure it had been going on for some time. He heard the sounds of padded feet then, and caught the faint smell of incense. Tick-tick-tick-tick-tick . . .

When he least expected it, soft, unobtrusive fingers undid his blindfold. His eyes tried to focus in a darkness broken only by a single, faint luminescence. Fascinated, Shekelath watched as it seemed to grow stronger, then fainter; to come closer, then to move farther away. Tick-tick-tick-tick . . . It seemed to be approaching. From ever so far away. Ever so slowly, like a star, from an infinite distance.

Finally, he could see that the light was reflecting off something like a huge dark cube whose sides appeared insubstantial.

The cube came closer as if on wheels, smoothly and in total silence; as though it was from the void of the most distant space, pushing the frigid air of night before it. Shekelath shivered with a sudden chill. Tick-tick-tick-tick-tick . . .

At last it was before him, a giant cube the size of a room, completely draped in black cloth—velvet, perhaps. The black cloth shone softly in the light of four square lanterns. The whole assemblage, the four lanterns and the cube, rested on a large platform that moved silently into the chapel and came to rest beneath the flat black ceiling that was so high it barely caught the light of the lanterns.

Above and behind the platform Shekelath now saw a round hole in the far chapel wall, and through it filtered a pale white light. How could there be a wall so close behind the platform when the cube had come from so huge a distance? Shekelath's reason was as confused as his senses.

The figure of a man appeared from behind the giant cube. He walked around the cube to the empty space at the very front of the platform. His steps were in perfect rhythm with the metallic tapping that had, all this while, been the only sound Shekelath had heard. Tick-tick-tick-tick-tick . . .

He was completely bald. His forehead was high, narrow, wrinkleless. He was neither tall nor short, neither fat nor thin, neither white nor black. He could have been thirty years old. He could have been ninety. He stood stiffly upright, looking with his narrow, colorless eyes down at the twelve men, riveting each one of them with a look none could return.

"I am Kalkodon, High Priest of Lord Dagon." This was the man who was the key to Shekelath's fate. He could barely see the priest's lips move, but his whole being focused on Kalkodon's words, which came as clear and chiseled as marble.

"All must know what Dagon means. All must know what Dagon intends. Listen to the Representative. Then worship the will of Dagon."

Kalkodon became a shadowy outline of a figure in the fading light. The black hood draping the cube began to change. It became transparent, or it was drawn aside—Shekelath could not tell which—and a strange figure was partly revealed.

The only part of the Representative he could see with any clarity was the face and head. But he felt he was looking at a face that could not be: an impossibility. The forehead appeared to be a series of flat little panels of skin, like circles cut from parchment and attached piece by piece to each other. The nose was like a convex triangle, each nostril flaring at its base.

The chin was horseshoe-shaped. The teeth were rectangular and very straight. The lips were full. And all, forehead to chin, was the same off-white color. Except for the eyes. The eyes of the Representative were two perfect rounds of blue that seemed so close Shekelath thought he could reach out and touch them.

The stare of those blue eyes was steadier than a hawk's and seemed for a moment exultant as a hero's look but then changed to an expression of unconquerable sadness and regret. The blue of the eyes was so piercing that Shekelath felt all secrets and all knowledge were surely held there, but then it seemed there was only painful surprise and astonishment. Shekelath could make no sense of the contradictions he saw. Yet it was impossible to return that stare without accepting the Representative as more real than everything he contradicted, and when the Representative spoke, the sound of his voice was a confirmation of his face.

"I am the Representative. Of the Lord Dagon. My soul is his soul. My mind, his mind. My words, his words. My enemies, his enemies. My friends, his friends. My fate, his fate. My fate, your fate.

"You are all nothings. Will be nothings. Only Dagon becomes. Dagon has plans mortals cannot understand. He is everything because he becomes everything. Air. Smoke. Fire. Water. Earth. Fish. Bird. Worm. Beast. Man. Angel. God. He is the sperm and the egg, the womb and the baby. Dagon is in the strong hand that kills, the tongue that lies, the legs that run into battle. All is for Dagon. Dagon becomes all. The rising of the sun, the movement of the stars, the washing of the waters, the seasons of the land. Dagon is all. Know what you must do, what enemies must be destroyed. Dagon becomes all!"

Immediately, suddenly, all was an explosion of light. Shekelath's whole body seemed seared with heat, and he was blinded. Struggling with panic, he could hear the voice of the Representative rising in passion:

"Baal is not. Kemosh is not. Asshur is not. Ra is not. Wotin is not. Zeus is not. Adonai is not. Only Dagon is. Only Dagon becomes."

Instantaneously, it seemed, the light shrank to the size of a ball and there was a great explosion—it seemed far away, but the floor under Shekelath's chair shook. A billowing mushroom of smoke and fire spewed from the light, a black-tinged fireball blazing with purple, red, white, pink.

Now that shifting, shapeless, smoke-filled mass itself was becoming, ceasing, becoming. Smoke became earth. Earth became stone. Stone became tree. Tree became beast. Beast became swan. Swan became fish. Fish became man. Man became angel. Angel became fireball, spinning, blazing, dazzling.

Under the pressure of this relentless vision, Shekelath knew the deepest meaning of the Killer Swan and the Sacred Terebinth. His sole desire was to see Dagon become all, to be lost in Dagon, merged, melted, nullified. At any price.

All the anger Shekelath had felt for the loss of his wife and sons, for the devastation of Gaza the Magnificent exploded. He was weeping, shouting. Without being aware of it, Shekelath, inflamed with his anger, burning with vengeance, fell from his chair face down to the floor of the chapel sobbing tears of rage. "Adonai and the Hebrews will cease. I will become. They will cease. . . ." All around him the other commanders and the Strong Ones were similarly raging, "They will cease. I will become. . . ."

After a while, Shekelath heard only his own sobbing and the sobbing of those around him. He felt unobtrusive hands on his shoulders. He looked up. A priest stood beside him, expressionless, his hands outstretched. Around him the same thing was happening to the others. Shekelath reached out and was pulled gently and firmly to his feet. Kalkodon stood in front of the black-hooded cube on the platform. He looked at each man in turn.

"The sun is rising," Kalkodon said. "The council begins."

The council chamber into which the six commanders and six Strong Ones were led was an ordinary circular room topped by a flat ceiling. Entering there after the mysteries was a relief, like coming home from a fearful journey. They were given a meal of fruit and water with some pungent herb in it.

Then Kalkodon entered and took his place on a thronelike chair on top of a small dais. Twelve chairs had been arranged to the left and right of his throne in two half-circles. The six commanders were directed to the arc of chairs on his left, the Strong Ones to his right.

At last Shekelath was able to see the face and figure of Kalkodon in clear light. The high priest had neither eyebrows nor eyelashes, so that his pupils seemed to have the unblinking fixity of an Egyptian cat carved in lapis lazuli. And there was something peculiar about the way he carried his head. Not defiant, not challenging, yet strangely unfriendly and aloof.

Kalkodon spoke first to the commanders. "You all know that the power of every commander is only the power of Dagon. But you do not know much if anything about Dagon's servants, the Strong Ones," and he indicated the men on his right. "Dagon has Strong Ones in every age, in every land. They prepare every land for the becoming of Dagon.

"What concerns us today, however, is the one enemy that holds out most stubbornly against the will of Dagon, the Hebrews to the east of Philistia with their Adonai."

"There is danger very close to this commandership," Makron began. "The earthquake was Adonai's doing. There is no danger here in Luqqawatna that does not come from the lands and the god of the Hebrews."

Markalav was next. He leaned his compact little body forward and turned his small head toward the high priest. "I say abandon Philistia. It will take too long to rebuild it. Adonai is unknown in Sikaler. Except for Philistia, we are the southernmost command of Dagon. We too are in the lands of the sun. We are strong and ready. We can thrust straight into Africa and Egypt, and bypass this Adonai and his miserable Hebrews!" Markalav had brought into the open the very issue to be decided: the role of Philistia as the forward command.

"My Lord Duke," Kalkodon replied, "the damage done here and in Philistia was from the hand of Adonai. And we know that Adonai never does anything without a reason. We must discover that reason. Is Adonai merely defending, or is he reaching out from the Hebrew land to oppose Dagon? Let us find that out first."

If Markalav was disappointed, he was also intelligent enough not to contradict the silken reasoning of the high priest. Arkavid of Makatan squinted with his one good eye at Makron, whose post he coveted. "No doubt about it. Our fight is in Philistia. We must destroy the Hebrews. But this time"—he looked at Shekelath—"we must be sure of our strategy."

Kalkodon turned briefly to Shekelath. "My Lord Duke, we will not hear from you just yet." He gave no apology or reason. He simply turned his gaze immediately to where the Strong Ones sat. "We must know also if Adonai has shown his face in the lands where the Strong Ones serve Dagon."

Sesebokassta of Africa was called. An expansive smile spread over his face as he spoke, and it was all the more impressive because of the sharp contrast between his perfect white teeth and his pitch-black skin. "My brothers," he said in a resonant voice, "there is no power on earth so dominant in my Africa as Dagon's law. Neither Adonai nor his Covenant is known in Africa." And he threw back his head and laughed.

Amen-Ra-Hotep of Egypt had more concrete knowledge and advice, born of experience. "There was, some time ago," he said, "a danger that Adonai and his Covenant would prevail at Thebes and Memphis. But Egypt is weak now. There exists that confusion in which Dagon's will can prevail." Gabala, the Strong One of Arabia, added that such was the case in Arabia as well.

"But"—Amen-Ra-Hotep was back with a word of warning—"we know that Adonai deceives; he always reappears just when you think he has been destroyed. Yes, the Hebrews must be obliterated. Wipe out all memory of his worship, and you will surely destroy Adonai. But don't deceive yourselves that armies alone can do it."

Ana-Ka-Ilu of Assyria proposed that the task of eliminating the Hebrews be given to his people. But Kalkodon thought not: "You Assyrians had your chance. All you accomplished was to give the Hebrews a way of thinking and speaking about Adonai."

After Mohenjo of India and Chuyanto of China had told of the strength of Dagon throughout Asia, Kalkodon turned at last to Shekelath: "Before I hear you, Shekelath, I will speak:

"Adonai deceives. That is true, and when he has chosen a new leader or has momentous plans, he thunders or sends lightning bolts or shakes the earth. But there is not a commander here who is not better prepared than Saul of Kish. Still, Philistia has been badly weakened, and you are very young, Lord Shekelath. Now, tell me what you have to say of Philistia and of your commandership."

Shekelath was almost surprised by his own readiness to respond. He had been fearful when Kalkodon would not let him speak in his turn. But now he saw the wisdom of the way Kalkodon had run the meeting. All the facts, all the opinions, all the ammunition were in Shekelath's hands. He understood that his fate depended on how he used those weapons.

"We know that Adonai has caused the misery of the Philistines," Shekelath began, conceding the obvious ground. "And, yes, Philistia was badly crippled by the earthquake.

"But I say this: Dagon's great opportunity for continued triumph lies at this moment only in Philistia, the closest point to the enemy that must be defeated—if not now, then later. Adonai will be beaten.

"I say this: If we wait, if we shift the forward lines of Lord Dagon's prophecy to Markalav's command and thrust across the Great Sea to Africa and Egypt, we will only be repeating the mistake of the commander who struck at Ramses III at the mouth of the Nile. And we will only give the Hebrews time to grow strong before we face them. For face them we must. Without the corridor of land where the people of Adonai defy us, there is no holding the land to the north of it or to the south of it. If we move our commands forward without securing all the lands east of Philistia as we go, we shall fail. Philistia must be the strong forward dominion of Dagon.

"As to myself, I say this: I am young, yes. Younger, I would guess, than any commander here. But what other man here knows Philistia and the Hebrews as I do, I who have fought them and who learned from my father and my grandfather who commanded and fought there before me?

"Philistia was devastated by the earthquake, yes. But the eye of Dagon looks even now to revenge. I have already restored adequate defenses, and the arm of Dagon is growing strong again, to reach out and crush Adonai and his leader, Saul.

"If we do not do this, the non-Hebrew nations who live among the Hebrews and those who surround their borders will defect from their alliances with us. And we will see the iron deposits that we now control from Eilath across the Bag of Sand fall into Hebrew hands.

"I say this: I, Shekelath, must return to Philistia at the head of a great flotilla of ships filled with weapons of iron, with money and goods. So that every Philistine will hear and see that the strength of Dagon flows into Philistia.

"I say this: We must devise a plan for learning the mind and strategy of Adonai. And even as we rebuild, the forward command of Philistia and the central command of Luqqawatna must be bound again by the ties of blood. I propose to take to wife the sister of Solka, Pamaventa—Duke Makron's second daughter."

Duke Makron looked up in some surprise. How very clever of this young duke! He would have Makron as his supporter again in Luqqawatna, and Makron would depend again on Shekelath for a grandson and heir. So much for Arkavid's ambition!

"My Lord Duke!"

Shekelath turned to Mohenjo of India.

"If Adonai deceives, why should we suppose the earthquake was a sign of his exultancy in this miserable flea, Saul of Kish? Perhaps Saul is not the chosen one. Kill him, surely, but there may be another."

"Commander!" It was Makron. "Send spies among the Hebrews. Send clever Philistines. Bribe people of other nations who trade with the Hebrews. And—most valuable of all—corrupt the Hebrews themselves. Form a network of spies in the heartland of the enemy. Is there not one priest, one elder, one wise man to whom they listen?"

"Yes. Samuel of Rama. It is said Saul himself makes no move without Samuel. And we have learned from our spies that he travels the land and consults with other elders . . ."

"Good!" Makron pushed further. "And are there not seers among the Hebrews? And would they not know if something extraordinary has happened among them? If Saul is not the chosen one of Adonai, would their seers not know who is?"

"We shall seek them out," Shekelath agreed.

"And in Philistia itself, is there no one who knows something of the moves of Adonai? Captured slaves, perhaps, whose loyalty can be shaken?"

"The Hebrew captives have always been very stubborn," Shekelath replied. "Even the worst torture brings only bits of information. There are only the few surviving giants of Gath. They were in Philistia when we conquered the land. It is said these giants have some mysterious connection with the Covenant of Adonai, but we have not been able to find out more than that."

"You would be wise," Makron urged, "to find a way."

"Commanders and Strong Ones!" It was Kalkodon. He spoke always in the same even tones, but as his look pierced to the core, so his words could halt any conversation. "The decision of Dagon is that Philistia will be rebuilt. Shekelath will be its commander. The renewed union in blood between the family of Shekelath and the family of Makron is approved. We suggest that ten years should see the fulfillment of this plan.

"All we have said here will be accomplished. Adonai will cease! The Hebrews will cease! Dagon becomes!" Kalkodon clapped his hands and the council was closed.

The Dukes of Philistia were back in Gaza by the end of November. Pamaventa settled in immediately in the makeshift quarters set up for the duke, and Shekelath's first public act was to call a council of war for the middle day of December. The news was welcome to the Philistines. Discipline had become lax, trade sluggish, and the border garrisons spent their time repelling attacks. Philistines were not used to being on the defensive. Valuable allies among the local chieftains and kinglets were, as Shekelath had predicted, already defecting from their alliances with Philistia. All that would stop now.

Before the council began, Shekelath, in consultation with Achish, Meluhhag, and high Gaza officials, had chosen new dukes for Ashkelon and Ashdod. Achish, it was decided, would be shifted to Gath. On the morning when the council opened, the officers and officials, forty in all, assembled fully clothed in battle gear, as Shekelath, Achish, and Meluhhag mounted the platform. Then Shekelath announced the new dukes.

"Philistines! Hear! For Ashdod: look on my Lord Duke Balkarith! For Ashkelon: my Lord Duke Kolarak!"

Balkarith was not popular, but he was a leader, and he received the traditional accolade: "A Philistine! A Philistine! A Philistine!"

Now thirty-six, Kolarak had long been master of the slave galleys and the slave market at Ashkelon. Kolarak was infinitely resourceful and forever undaunted.

"Now, Philistines! Order, please, for our council!" Shekelath waved his sword above his head. It was the official signal, and according to custom the forty officers sat down on the ground in semicircular rows. When all were settled, Shekelath began.

"I announce to you a great joy! The conclave at Luqqawatna has authorized a great campaign—to destroy every trace of every Hebrew, blade and haft, bow and arrow, from the Great Sea in the west to the Jordan in the east, from Aram in the north to Egypt in the south, and thus wipe out every foothold of Adonai." A shudder ran through the officers at the mention of Adonai.

Shekelath went on. "I have a great score to settle with Adonai myself." His voice grated with hatred. "But fear not! Lord Dagon has instructed us how to proceed."

Shekelath then related the major decisions reached at Luqqawatna—the rebuilding of the cities and fortresses, the subversion of the Hebrews and the securing of an absolute monopoly on the iron supply. Five years were allowed to prepare for the campaign, five to execute it. Achish explained the subversion strategy, and Shekelath took up the question of the iron deposits at Eilath, the Viper's Tongue.

"That's Amalekite territory," Meluhhag interjected. "Didn't old Ivordan once talk with their king—Agag, wasn't it?"

"I was in that delegation, sir." It was a middle-aged officer, formerly of the Sinai Patrol.

"What was Ivordan doing talking with Agag?"

"A matter of young slave girls, sir." There were some hoots of raucous laughter at this. "But one thing is sure: between him and the Hebrews, there is no love lost."

"Your name?"

"Lapmar, my Lord Duke."

Shekelath looked the man over. "Could you find Agag again? Would he receive you?"

"With sufficient time and money, we can do anything with Agag."

"Duke Balkarith, your first assignment. Equip this officer for a trip to confer with Agag and establish a relationship of friendship with Amalek. Further, we need agreements with the authorities in all important cities to respect our monopoly.

"The other dukes and I agree"—Shekelath glanced sunnily at Balkarith and Kolarak—"that we must now have a single authority in charge of security and intelligence. We think that Duke Achish is best fitted.

"You and I shall talk of this later, Achish," he added in a quiet aside to that duke. Then to the assembly again, "And last, for now, we will begin to encircle the Hebrews by establishing close relationships with their enemies north, south, east, and west, for the gathering of intelligence. We do not engage in direct pitched battle—unless vitally necessary—until we are ready.

"We meet again in a month's time to review the final plans." The general meeting was adjourned, and the five dukes continued their discussion in Shekelath's quarters.

Shekelath began, "Militarily, we could exploit the giants of Gath. I'm told they are splendid and efficient warriors in addition to their connection with this Adonai. You must gain their confidence and so learn what you can about him. They could provide us with secret information from the councils of the Hebrews."

"You are prepared, then, to accept whatever I learn?" Achish asked dryly.

"Of course! Why should you think otherwise?"

"Because we are dealing with a mysterious mind, a mysterious power. I'll leave for Gath tomorrow."

Shekelath's eyes narrowed as he looked at Achish's retreating figure. He noticed the sneer of suspicion on Balkarith's lips and nodded silently in Achish's direction. Achish would himself be the object of some surveillance.

Later that evening, when Shekelath told Pamaventa the details of the day, he asked her, "What do you think of Achish?"

"My father always said: 'If you meet a Philistine who has any trace of tenderness—apart from his wife and children and close friends—don't trust him.' It's not Philistine to have tenderness. My husband, Achish has tenderness."

Achish was elated at his assignment to Gath. Gath lay at the southern corner of a long curving valley known as Refaim. And as Achish's convoy approached Gath he and his men were reminded again of the city's strategic position. Protected on all four sides by cliffs, Gath was almost impregnable. Like Jebus, it had a spring that perpetually supplied it with fresh water. It stood some fifteen miles inland from the Port of Ashkelon, at the hub of the valleys splaying out to the northeast, east, and southeast. Those long valleys stood like invitations to attack the Hebrews. Gath was the most crucial Philistine command.

By the time David was ten, Achish had done his job well, even though Kalkodon's schedule for the suppression of the Hebrews had not been fulfilled. Within two years of his arrival and installation as ruler of Gath, Achish had rebuilt all the city's defenses and most of its inner buildings, making it stronger than it had been before. He sent constant attacks against the Hebrews into the highlands of Judah and Ephraim and Manasseh. He gave Saul no rest.

Yet even with the huge tasks of rebuilding and harassment, Achish gave constant attention to learning the mind of Adonai. He tortured every Hebrew prisoner for information. He made Gath a haven for political refugees from Judah so as to learn from them and to use them as spies in their own land. Because of Achish, corrupt Hebrews like Anani of Bethlehem, an old enemy of Jesse's, had been joined in a network of informers.

Achish learned what he could about Samuel—when and how he spent his time in his yearly circuits, his relationship with Saul, the scholars he cultivated and taught and valued most. He learned of the seers, of Malaki in Nazareth, of Shalama in Petahyahu, of Avoiz in Carmel, of Miriam in Engedi.

He heard of the strange wandering companies of prophets and of the Valley of Naioth where they congregated. Achish became an expert on the Hebrews and their peculiarities.

All the while he was fighting and spying and laying clever plans, Achish did not ignore the neighboring nations. It was his spies who years before had first learned of the iron deposits at Eilath. It was he who suggested the building of a secret underground iron trail to Gaza. It was he who proposed the alliance with Jebus, as well as the setting up of Philistine ironworks there to arm the weaker Philistine outposts east of the Jordan and down its west bank.

The only thing Achish had not been able to do—despite enormous effort—was to learn the secret of the strange race of giants. He had begun by searching throughout Gath for anyone who knew the giants, had access to them, or had any knowledge of the strange relationship they were said to have with Adonai. Nothing. A total blank.

Eventually he found a Hebrew slave called Sava who said that she had lived with the giants. They came, she said, from an earlier and even larger race, the Nefil-im, or tumblers, men who were fifteen feet high and very quick and agile, with six fingers on each hand and six toes on each foot. This race had come out of Moab, originating in some distant place long ago when the Nile was still an ocean. Before dying out, the Nefil-im had impregnated ordinary women and sired the giants, who were only ten feet high and not as nimble as the earlier, larger race. Only a few of this generation had more than five fingers or toes.

"Could I learn their language?" Achish wondered.

"No," Sava answered. "They won't teach you. Neither will I."

"Well, what law do they live by? What sort of people are they?"

"They have always lived in caves. They are divided into two distinct classes. The curers, or Refa-im, and the warriors, the Anak-im. Anak-im means 'the men of the necklace.' Each man wears a necklace made of some shining metal. He cannot move without that necklace. If he takes it off, he—er—he—he disappears—he dies. And they do not fight unless attacked."

The only giants left had come to the area of Gath years before. The pacific Refa-im had died out, leaving behind them only the name of the valley where the Anak-im survived. A giant called Arba was their leader at this time. They had no women, but took them as they needed them. There were now about forty of them left.

"Whom do they worship?" Achish asked.

"He has no name they may pronounce or hear. They call him the Nameless One, and they await the fulfillment of his Rainbow Promise."

Achish was satisfied. He had found out what he wanted. He guessed that the giants were secret worshipers of Adonai. The Hebrews whose torture he had supervised over the years used to rant and rave in their excess of pain about two things, the Pharaoh and the Flood; and they usually mentioned the Rainbow in the sky as a sign of Adonai's promise. Although vague, evidence of a connection was emerging.

Early next morning Achish sent for Sava to guide him to the giants' enclave in the valley of Refa-im. Only one aide, who drove the chariot, accompanied them. Several miles up the valley they came to a flat floor of rock where rough-hewn walls extending from either side blocked their way. The walls were about forty feet high and so placed that they did not meet but overlapped, leaving a zigzag passage between them and through to the far side. Sava raised her hand to stop the chariot.

The three visitors walked to the corner of the first wall and Sava called out. An answering call came from inside, and without any hesitation Sava entered, the two men following her. They passed between the high overlap and rounded the second corner.

Achish caught his breath at what he saw. The slopes of the hills on both sides were completely bare of all trees and vegetation. Cut into those slopes, about six feet off the ground, were tall openings. Wider at the top, the long sides slanted down to thresholds narrower than their lintels. Farther on, about half a mile up the valley, Achish could see another pair of overlapping walls. Between these matching doors lived the giants, although he could see no sign of life. About midway through the space Sava stopped, called again, and waited.

The first giant appeared at the opening opposite where Sava stood. He was indeed about ten feet tall. To Achish's feverish eye the giant's head seemed almost as wide as his shoulders. The giant stood framed in the opening—five toes, Achish counted, on each foot. He wore a loose tunic and tight-fitting leather britches with an apron covering his genitals, and around his neck glittered the necklace of which Sava had spoken. Achish marveled at the smallness of the face and features compared with the rest of the giant's physique. Each thigh was as wide as a normal man's shoulders, and each finger was as thick as a normal man's wrist. But the nose and mouth were no larger than the largest Achish had seen among the Philistines. The eyes appeared within that giant frame like black-eyed peas. Only the ears were proportionately as big as the head. The hair was closely cropped and jet-black.

The giant's face was flat, emotionless. He looked steadily at Sava, raised one huge hand like a frying pan, opened his mouth, and spoke a strange language. It was, as one of Achish's captains had said, a series of clicks, buzzes, hums, and coughs. Sava answered in kind. Then she turned to Achish. The giant, who was named Anak, agreed to speak with Achish whenever Achish wished, in Philistine. "He says that his god, the Nameless One, wishes you well."

Achish wondered what Anak meant by that.

Back in his residence that evening, Achish dictated a long report to Shekelath and the council. In his opinion, he wrote, the plans of Dagon were as sure-winged as the Sacred Swan's flight. He, Achish, would be able to work with the giants; he had found and talked with them. Perhaps they could even be used as military forces. They must press ahead with the preparation of their war machine.

As he was finishing his report, Achish suddenly trembled with astonishment. Could it be possible? He thought he felt some tingling in his withered arm and leg for the first time since his childhood. Could that be a sign from Dagon? That would be truly extraordinary, for in all history Dagon had never cured before. Achish knew this for certain.

Little by little Achish learned that there were only eleven giant families in this valley. Anak and his brother Muzza were Arba's descendants. Anak had three sons: Sheshai, Ahiman, and Talmai. Muzza, his brother, had five sons: Ashibenov, Sar, Mushlan, Gamlasaf, and Goliath. As time went on, Anak's sons would come out to meet Achish. Then his brother and his sons.

After some months one or two other giants put in an appearance. And so it went, Achish slowly establishing himself with the giants as someone with whom they could speak. But for all of Achish's perseverance, the thing he most wanted to know—the nature of the connection between the giants and the Hebrew god—eluded him.

Achish asked Anak's permission to bring some soldiers into the narrow entrance to the giants' home for mock battles. Anak agreed, and Achish learned in that way that the giants were no use at all in a swift, running fight—they were, in fact, clumsy. But they struck absolute terror in the hearts of Achish's men when they first saw the giants; and in hand-to-hand combat one giant was worth ten of his men.

Achish proposed a great contest to select a champion of the younger giants, who would be honored among the Philistines. He would be provided with special armor, and with a sword Achish himself would present. Achish had seen the fear in his own men when they confronted the giants, even in their mock encounters. In his mind's eye he could already see the paralyzing fear and the demoralizing consternation in the ranks of the Hebrews challenged by one of these fearsome creatures.

Anak agreed, provided the contest be one of strength alone, that no weapons be used, and that no giant kill another. The contest was held in the zigzag passageway. It took three days, from sunup until the dark fell. The strength of the young giants seemed never-ending. The whole valley was filled with their terrible roaring as they wrestled and fought before the eyes of the unbelieving Achish. When boulders were in their way, they threw them aside like toys. When bushes or trees were a hindrance, they uprooted them. If only they weren't so ponderous!

Finally, at the end of the third day of the contest, Achish had his companion—Muzza's youngest son, Goliath. It took Achish's ironsmiths five weeks to forge armor for Goliath. When it was finished, eight of Achish's strongest men struggled to load it onto a cart and bring it to the mouth of the zigzag passage. Achish himself carried the special sword he had had made for Goliath. From handle to tip it was five feet in length. The blade of solid, well-tempered iron had a single edge, honed and sharpened so that it could split a human hair.

On Anak's instructions—he would not explain them—the blade was pierced along its center with six holes. The handle was protected with a haft of burnished gold that shielded the hand. On that gold haft, again at Anak's mysterious insistence, strange glyphs were engraved in a curious pattern.

Goliath was delighted with his prizes. He strutted cumbersomely for his brothers, dressed in his new armor, raising his new sword, laughing and bellowing in mock fearsomeness for his cheering comrades. Watching them, Achish was very pleased. In some way this meant that he would have a part of Adonai's strength on his own side, even though he had never penetrated the mysteries of the giants' origins and beliefs.

*　*　*

In the Hebrew towns and enclaves throughout the land, caravans brought news of Philistine activity everywhere. Philistines had been seen riding with the Amalekite nomads, who grew fat on trade in the deserts to the south of the Hebrews. Philistines were in Jebus and had formed an allegiance with the Jebusites. They were seen in Moab across the Jordan; and even the calm of Nazareth gave way to apprehension, as allies of the Philistines came to trade for leather and other supplies. Increasingly, small bands of highwaymen disrupted the fragile links between town and town. Isolated farms were raided and crops were burned. And, more and more, the tiny trickle of iron the Hebrews had managed to obtain by barter dried up. The Philistine grip on the iron supply was tightening.

The counterblows by Saul and his Hebrews were sporadic. Saul did not yet have at his command a well-trained corps of men, and the Philistines had adopted a military policy of surprise raids, "spear thrusts" they called them. They struck here and there, unpredictably, always with small forces that disappeared before Saul could counterattack.

In Bethlehem, Jesse and the other men of the town felt the change. They did what they could. Elder Zaza, the chief of muster, redoubled the guard. Citizens traveled in groups of three to five and took slaves for extra protection whenever they left the gates.

Fighting fever gripped the Hebrews. Even Ozem, on the days he was not in Raham's school or tending to his chores, hunted game with his friends and practiced with weapons. Every rabbit or deer or bird they killed was, in their imaginations, a Philistine soldier. But for the most part, especially in Bethlehem, which was of little strategic importance and possessed no wealth to speak of, there was comparative peace during David's early years.

The Anointing

In Jesse's house it was "Raham-said" time. Jesse and Shoshanna and David sat alone at the big table. Between every bite of his dinner David was telling and retelling the story of creation, adding his own embellishments, pointing over and over again to the clay tablet with the Star, which Shoshanna had had Shalamar, the potter, bake hard for him. It was David's prize.

"And Raham said that when the star exploded at the six points, the light from each point was brighter than the sun, and that the star went on shining from its heart. . . ."

Jesse turned his head toward the door and held his hand up for quiet. He had heard something. Before he could move, the door burst open and Eliab, Jesse's oldest son, strode inside. The surprise of the three was total, for Eliab was supposed to be at Gibea serving in the army of Saul.

"Father!" The urgency in that single word was clear. Jesse rose quickly and followed Eliab outside. In a moment he was back with Eliab and three other men, all fully armed.

"It is safe here," Jesse said, closing the door behind them. "Shoshanna, is there some food for Eliab and our guests?" The tallest of the three strangers came forward first. David could not take his eyes off the great bow strapped to the stranger's back, and he, for his part, felt David's insistent and very curious gaze.

"And who is this young man?" the bowman wanted to know.

"I am David, son of Jesse, sir," came the reply.

"Peace, David! I am Jonathan, son of Saul."

Shoshanna nearly dropped the dishes she was serving. But her surprise quickly changed to apprehension. Visitors or messengers from Gibea usually brought bad news. If the king's own son had come, what on earth could be going on? She looked over at Jonathan as he stood over David, smiling. Jonathan was just twenty-two and in his prime. From his father he had inherited his length of leg and arm. From his mother,

Ahinoam, he had received the delicacy of his movements. He was quite slim. His eyes were set wide apart in a long, narrow face. The cheek bones were high and rounded. When he smiled, two dimples appeared in his cheeks.

Jonathan was beyond dispute the finest bowman in the land and was commander of the king's corps of archers. Vastly different from ordinary foot soldiers, the archers constituted an elite fellowship of individualists; they knew their bows better than their wives.

Jonathan was an impressive commander, even though there was no persuading him to wear the beard that Hebrew men usually sported. He insisted on remaining clean shaven and was a very handsome man. He had married Yovav, daughter of Eleaba, and fathered one son, Meribaal, and one daughter, Yofipana. But they did not make him happy. Jonathan was really happy only when he was with his men. With men he blossomed.

"Jonathan?" David finally managed to say. "Son of the king? From Gibea? Champion bowman of the Hebrews?"

Jonathan laughed. "Yes, David. And this is Amos," he said, glancing toward one of his companions, "a captain in the king's archers. And this is Aholiab, a trusted captain of the king. We have come to ask your father's advice and take advantage of his hospitality." Why, his father must be the most important man in the whole of Judah, David thought.

As the men ate, Jonathan briefly outlined his mission and the deep secrecy that must surround it. In fact, he could say no more about it than that they needed someone trustworthy to guide them through the southern deserts. Eliab had told them that his kinsman, Joshua, was an ideal candidate. Would Jesse talk with Joshua about being their guide?

"We will not force him or order him. The mission is dangerous, extremely dangerous," Jonathan concluded.

Jesse thought for a moment, then turned to his ten-year-old. "David, it is better that Eliab not run the risk of being seen. Go quickly and ask Joshua to come at once. Take the back way to his farm. Speak to no one else." David was gone in an instant, and within what seemed a very short time he was back, not only with Joshua, but also with Ozem, who was just coming home as David and Joshua entered the gate.

"Did you meet anybody along the way?" Jesse asked David.

"Old Anani's servant was leaning over the wall when I ran past. But he didn't seem to notice me." Nevertheless, this information troubled Jesse because he had once had a row over a slave with Anani, an oil merchant, and didn't trust him. Something was the matter there...

Jesse quickly told Joshua what was wanted.

Joshua had only one question. "Does Samuel the Prophet know of this mission?"

Jonathan replied: "He does, and we have his blessing."

"Then I will guide you," said Joshua simply. "You will have to tell me your plan. I will not go into this thing blindly. And I will take one man from my own house, Abu Maher. He is my chief steward, a Bedouin. He will be very useful to us."

"Very well," replied Jonathan. "We know that the Philistines are hiring workers in great numbers. Their recruiters have been visiting all the Hebrew villages and hamlets south of Beersheva. They're speaking peacefully of high wages, good food, and a big bonus for everyone who contracts for a year's work in Philistia. Building and construction is what they say the work is. Everyone who wishes to go is told to sign up at their principal headquarters in Ziklag."

"But that is not very far from here." Ozem was puzzled. "Why go south into the desert and then north again to Ziklag?"

"For one reason. Philistines are only hiring men from the southern deserts. They will hire anyone from there—Hebrew or Edomite or African; but they will take no one from the land itself. That is already very strange. But on top of that, hundreds are taken; no one has been rejected. Yet no one has yet come back from the Philistine work camps.

"At the same time there are reports of increased supplies of iron in Jebus and in some of the Philistine garrisons east of the Jordan. Yet there have been no reports of iron coming overland from the north, from Luqqawatna. Maybe they are sending it by ship to Ashkelon, risky as that would be. We don't know. But we have to find out. If the two mysteries are connected, all the better. If not, we will attack one problem at a time.

"So, first, we will travel into the southern desert and, dressed as Hebrew laborers, make our way north to Ziklag to get ourselves hired by the Philistines, to find out as much as we can of what surprises they are preparing for us."

Joshua took up one of David's clay tablets, scratched a rough map of the Bag of Sand, and outlined their route. "We will have to travel down into the Aravah at the edge of the Bag of Sand. It is not possible to cut straight across the desert and survive. When we reach Shiroth, we will turn west to Arba, and then up the west side of the Aravah, through the Ascent of the Scorpions and then west again to Kfar Sarta. From there you will be able to go to Ziklag and look for all the world like anyone else coming up from the southern desert. We should be able to leave you at Kfar Sarta within two weeks of your departure from here." Joshua laid the tablet down.

"Eliab will return to Gibea tonight. My party will be Amos, Aholiab, and myself."

"And me!" spoken out Ozem, who was looking not at Jonathan but at Jesse. Jesse's heart cringed within him. Dear Ozem! With his eyes and mouth so much like Korith's! Ozem was always willing, always brave. "Father! Let me go, if Jonathan will have me. If four can go, the odds are that much greater of one coming back."

Joshua swallowed hard. He looked at Jesse. "Ozem is right, Jesse. A good man will increase . . ."

"I am good, too, Father!" Everyone's head turned toward David. Shoshanna felt as though every ounce of breath had been knocked out of her lungs. Surely not David! she cried out inwardly. He's only a child! "I am good, Father!" David insisted. "You know I am. I am even better than Ozem with the slingshot. I am as tall as the older boys and every bit as strong. I can help, too!"

Jonathan was moved by David's wanting to go, especially since it seemed more than mere boyish bravado, but Ozem said: "Little scholar, if we both go, who will take care of Mother? And who will Father be able to count on to help protect the house?"

"Your brother is right." Jesse put an end to it. "We need you here, David. We can't have all the men away."

In the dark of that night, with Joshua leading the way, Jonathan's party made its way out of Bethlehem, avoiding the main streets. Yet they were barely out of the village when Jonathan whispered to Joshua.

"We're being followed, Joshua."

"I know. There can't be more than two of them to judge by the sound. When we reach the next curve, keep your mounts going at a steady walk. When I slip off mine, you take the reins and keep him going on with you all. I will give our friends a little surprise."

At the curve, suddenly, with hardly a sound, Joshua was off his camel and invisible in the shadows at the roadside. The rest of them had gone only about twenty paces when a sudden quick clash of swords split the silence. Someone swore and there was a loud groan. In one move, Jonathan drew his own sword and dismounted and ran around the curve. He found Joshua standing over the body of a young man whose gaping side was pouring blood.

"The other one's gone down there. He's wounded. Quick!" The trail ended at the path to Anani's house. At their approach the guard dogs set up a din. Joshua ran his hand over the top of the postern gate. He found what he was looking for: "Blood," he said. "Our man went over the gate."

"Why didn't the watchdogs bark then?" Jonathan asked.

"Exactly! My question, too. Because they knew him. Anani, the oil merchant! One of his slaves probably. That greasy bastard would sell his mother. He must have seen you come with Eliab."

"Is this Anani a Hebrew?"

"Sort of. But he won't be anything for long after I get back." Joshua sent Abu Maher to tell Jesse what had happened. "And be quick. We'll wait for you here." To Jonathan he added: "We'd better get as far away as we can before daybreak. I don't like the way this business has begun."

Six weeks came and went. Still neither Joshua nor Abu Maher had returned. Ozem's leaving with Jonathan's party under such a cloud of danger had a deep effect on Jesse, who was now over seventy. In a way it was like losing Korith all over again. To cope with his anxiety he worked harder. Shoshanna and David understood how he felt and comforted him in every way they could.

About a week after the last heavy rains, in the middle of March, Jesse was coming home at dusk from his pastures in Beraka. As he entered the yard he heard a whisper.

"Jesse! It's me! Joshua!"

Jesse ran back to the gate as Joshua stood up and emerged from the deep shadows by the barn. As he caught his first glimpse of Joshua, Jesse stopped short. He could barely recognize his cousin. His head was bandaged beneath his helmet. His face was drawn, his beard unkempt and dirty. His clothes were caked with dirt and dried sweat; the whole left side of his tunic was stained dark and torn. Then Jesse saw the worst. "My God!" he gasped. Joshua's left arm was gone. There was only a stump wrapped in a dirty blood-stained cloth.

"Jesse, it's all right. But be quiet. I want no one to know I'm back until I settle a bit of unfinished business."

"Ozem?"

"I don't know. We were betrayed. Ambushed. He and Jonathan and Aholiab got away. More than that I don't know."

"He could be alive, then?"

"Yes. I'll be in the barn."

"I'll be there in a minute with food and wine."

By the light of a single lamp Jesse waited while Joshua ate like a starved animal.

"Abu Maher told you what happened the night we left?" Joshua asked.

"Yes. Zaza set a watch on Anani and on his household. You were right. He has a steady contact with the Philistines. Messengers have been followed all the way to Gath. He is a miserable dog, but I didn't think even Anani would betray us."

Joshua took a long draught from Jesse's wine flask and told his story.

The party had gotten safely to Kfar Sarta. But Anani obviously had betrayed them and, despite great precaution, they had been ambushed by a company of Philistines. Abu Maher had been killed instantly with a javelin through the throat, Amos mortally wounded, and Joshua had lost his arm.

Jonathan had slain the entire company of nine attackers with nine arrows. Then he, Ozem, and Aholiab went on, after treating Joshua's wound and seeing him on his way back to Bethlehem.

"The traitor must be killed immediately—before he knows I'm back. Tonight," Joshua said.

"Agreed," replied Jesse. "I'll go for Zaza and the guards."

They tiptoed out of the barn and down the sloping yard. At the end of the village they stopped at Zaza's house, woke him up, and explained their mission. In a minute he had joined them. He was armed and carried a bag of pitch, with some wood and kindling.

A select party of avengers was recruited, five in all. Once within hailing distance of Anani's house, two young men were sent in to dispatch the watchdogs and Anani's slaves. That was done silently, and then they all made their way up to Anani's door. Inside, sleeping, were the oil merchant, his wife, two sons, two concubines, and three servants.

"Anani is mine," Joshua whispered, his eyes glinting in the darkness. "I don't care who gets the others."

Jesse gave a low whistle, and the avengers poured into the main room and the two bedrooms of Anani's house. It was all over in less than a minute. A few groans, a woman's half-scream, the dull sound of metal on bone.

When he got home. Jesse stood in his sloping yard, watching. Presently tongues of flames were visible licking the pine trees that ringed Anani's house. The horn from the watchtower sounded out with one loud, clear signal followed by one short note, to tell Bethlehemites that all was well.

The next day a general assembly of the village was called an hour after sunrise. Raham read out the condemnation of Anani and forbade anyone to tell any outsider what had happened or why. Then Anani's goods in the warehouse and his animals in the public stables were sold at auction and the proceeds put in the village treasury. After this, a pit was dug and the charred remains of the house, of Anani's belongings, and of the bodies were placed in it. The townspeople filled up the pit, flattened the ground, leveled the stone wall that had run around the house. According to Hebrew Law: "When the evil is removed from your house, there shall not remain one stone or one blade of grass to show where the evil one once had his habitation." At spring plowing they would sow the land with meadow grass. It would henceforth be known as *Hakel-herem,* the Field of the Ban.

After the Philistine ambush, Jonathan, Ozem, and Aholiab headed roughly north, moving as fast as they could in the dark. By the afternoon of the next day they had come down from high ground to the road leading to Ziklag, where they fell in with a group of a dozen or so Hebrews who had heard about the Philistine offer of high wages and were coming to sign up.

Ziklag was a small garrison some miles inland and to the south of Gaza. The guards at the gate politely asked the would-be laborers to surrender their arms. They would get them back. It was just a precaution.

As the gate slammed behind them, however, all pretense was dropped. The small band of now unarmed Hebrews was quickly roughed back against the wall by armed Philistines, swords in hand. Their ankles and wrists were bound with chains on the spot; and they were prodded at sword point to a compound on the northern edge of the town. Jonathan was appalled by what he saw there. "That's Philistine wages for you!" He spat at the feet of the guard and was kicked with the rest into an already bursting compound. There must have been five hundred men in the confined space—runaway slaves from Egypt, Hebrew laborers, a motley collection of Edomites, Bedouins, Jebusites, Hittites, Amalekites, black men from Nubia and elsewhere, all in chains, cursing their stupidity for trusting the Philistines.

In the early morning light of the next day, guards burst into the compound without warning, kicking sleeping men, dragging some to their feet, beating those who were slow, killing outright anyone who resisted, herding the rest into rows four deep. The chains on their wrists were tightened. Jonathan thought Ozem was behind him somewhere in the same row. He lost track of Aholiab. They were all given some goat's milk and coarse oaten bread where they stood. After that, they were marched out of Ziklag and along the road to Gaza under heavy guard. The pace was fast, and there was no rest.

Jonathan, Ozem, and Aholiab had no trouble keeping up, but all stragglers were dragged from the column, killed, and left for carrion. The column marched west to the coastal road and then north toward Gaza. For many it was their first sight of the white-capped waves of the Great Sea, their first smell of brine in the wind. But for Jonathan the big surprise was Gaza itself. He had heard reports of Philistine rebuilding, but he was amazed and dismayed by what he now saw in the stronghold of the mortal enemies of his people. It was an appalling measure of Philistine strength.

The temple of Dagon, rising like the rounded head of a giant fist, dominated the city, and the ducal palace gleamed white in all its foursquare pride in the morning sun. By the time the fortress walls came into view, the prisoners were already caught in the buzz of activity that always surrounded Gaza the Magnificent. They were herded roughly to the side of the road to make room for chariots, oxcarts, and companies of soldiers. They saw exercise fields full of military recruits, chariots ranged in silent ranks, and long wagon trains of supplies headed for the city.

They began to hear the sounds of Gaza itself—the distant ring of hammers and chisels, the tramping feet, the sounds of many voices and many animals. All these sounds made up that steady hum that the Philistines called "the song of Gaza." Philistine bards had celebrated this "song" up and down Philistia as their army marched and conquered.

Jonathan took it all in. He craned his head to catch a glimpse of Ozem or Aholiab, but he couldn't find them. By midafternoon, the column of prisoners had been locked into a stockade within a few hundred yards of Gaza's great outer wall. For all of them, it was a fearful place to be.

Inside the stockade, each prisoner was chained to a stake

driven into the ground. They were left there, exhausted from the quick march, to bake in the afternoon sun. Toward sunset a column of Philistine soldiers entered carrying whips the like of which Jonathan had never seen before—long, flat strips of hard leather attached to a short handle. They set upon the prisoners, methodically whipping each one till he lay moaning and bruised, but alive. Only rarely did they draw blood. Some time later they were given goat's milk and coarse oaten bread again. Then they were left, to survive or not, in the chill of oncoming night. The process was repeated day after day until the guards were satisfied that those who survived were docile enough to put into the work force.

Finally, the overseers seemed content. Late one day the prisoners were all fed and differing signs were daubed on their chests with red paint. They were released from their stakes. Their feet still in chains, they were marched to the gates of the stockade in single file. As each man went through the gates, he was pushed by guards into one of five groups, depending on the sign daubed on his chest. Jonathan and Aholiab were reunited in the largest group, and they saw Ozem marched off in another.

Jonathan's group was taken to a makeshift stockade not far to the south of Gaza, at the edge of the dunes behind the beach. Each prisoner was given a shovel and a pickax and then taken a short distance inland where a gang of about a hundred were digging a huge trench. It was twice as deep as the height of a man and wider than two oxcarts. Cords marking where it would go disappeared into the distance. Whatever the trench was for, it was clear why a large labor force was needed to dig it.

The prisoners worked in four shifts of four hours each, always in chains, and with only a quarter of an hour's rest between shifts. The guards still did not speak to them, and always beat those caught speaking to one another. The laborers lived on raw vegetables, water, goat's milk, and the coarse oaten bread. They were bivouacked each night where the day's work ended.

Jonathan and Aholiab, both young and both hardened by discipline, survived well compared to most of the others, but their days of misery soon passed into months. It was a rare day when only one prisoner collapsed. Whoever did was pulled from the trench by the guards and buried, dead or alive, in the earth and sand thrown up by those still strong enough to work.

Each week, fresh additions to the labor force were brought in, so there was no letup in the forward progress of the huge trench.

The trench they were digging was to run parallel to the seashore until it reached the end of Philistia's fertile land. There the lines marking its course curved directly into the southern desert. One thing that puzzled Jonathan and Aholiab was the purpose of the trench. What the devil was it for? In the desert heat, progress was slow and the toll great. Aholiab began to weaken. Jonathan tried to work beside him and carry some of his load without the guards noticing, but soon it was apparent that Aholiab couldn't last much longer.

Then one day, in the last glow of daylight, almost a year after their capture, the prisoners had been bivouacked for the night and some Phenician peddlers had arrived with fresh fish to sell to the guards. Aholiab suddenly tugged on Jonathan's arm. "Jonathan, listen! Isn't that someone calling your name?"

Ozem had had better luck in almost every way than Jonathan and Aholiab. His group had been hustled along the coast to the main Philistine port city of Ashkelon and there set to work loading Philistine ships exporting timber and foodstuffs, and unloading supplies brought in from abroad. The prisoners were used literally like pack animals, and sometimes Ozem pretended to himself that he was an animal. It helped him to summon the animal strength he needed to survive the bone-crushing labor. Like the men at the trench, those who dropped from exhaustion were instantly killed. But at least the laboring prisoners had some shelter at night—even if only a miserable, rat-infested warehouse—and fish tails and heads to eat every now and then.

Ozem was as strong as he had boasted back in Jesse's house, and he was as brave and willing as Jesse had always known. Bone-breaking as his work was, he survived. He had no mysteries to solve like the purpose of the trench that confounded Jonathan and Aholiab. He quickly learned that the Philistines were bringing in only very small amounts of iron by ship. And if, as Jonathan had said, it was not coming in by overland caravan from the north, it was not coming from their homeland in Luqqawatna. The Philistines had another source. Once Ozem had learned this, he began watching for a chance to escape. The Phenician fishing boats that came and went with relative freedom obviously offered the best opportunity.

One of these was just hoisting sail nearby as Ozem and six others were carrying a heavy load of timber in the dim light one morning. A deliberate trip-up of the man in front of him sent the whole gang and its load sprawling across the dock and into the water.

Ozem took a deep breath and dived as deeply as he could, heading for the side of the Phenician boat. It took another feverish minute for him to claw his way under the hull at the prow to the side away from the dock, where he clung to a hanging net until the ship had cleared the harbor.

The Phenician relationship with the Philistines was based on mutually useful trade; but it certainly was not an alliance of friendship or admiration. The Phenicians who heard Ozem's shouts and pulled him up thought it was all a great joke on the "ugly Philistines."

Ozem did not make the best sailor the Phenicians had ever seen; but he tried, and he was a willing hawker of fish. With a mixture of Phenician and Hebrew that made the fishermen laugh, Ozem went ashore and sold their catch with the rest of the crew, and generally got a good price. And at every landing he kept a sharp eye out for forced-labor gangs, but it was many days before he saw the gangs in Gaza roofing over the great ditch with stone and covering it with earth to conceal it from view.

Ozem moved among the guards, as close as he could to the trench with his big pannier of fresh fish, hawking in a mixture of Phenician and Hebrew, smiling at the Philistines who tried to haggle with him and then paid his price because it was easier than trying to understand him. "My fish for a Jonathan," Ozem hawked in a loud voice, smiling. "My fish for an Aholiab." He made his way slowly, looking to see if any head turned among the prisoners. He was shaken to the core by what he saw—the huge open trench, deeper and wider than many a river, the dazed, filthy, helpless and hopeless corps of laborers. My God, he thought, Jonathan and Aholiab must be carrion by now if they are here. Still he persisted: "My fish for an Aholiab! My fish for a Jonathan!"

"I must be going crazy, Jonathan!" Aholiab whispered through cracked lips. "But I heard your name, I'm sure."

"Quiet, brother! You did. Stay here and be very quiet."

Jonathan began to edge slowly to the outer limits of the prison compound. Then he heard again, though still far off, the cry, "My fish for an Aholiab! My fish for a Jonathan!" The Bethlehem accent was unmistakable. It had to be Ozem. Jonathan thought quickly, then took a terrible risk.

He made himself stumble deliberately in his chains and fall heavily, letting out a curse over his hurt in as loud a voice as he could muster. "Ozem!" he shouted in his mock rage. "God damn you, Ozem. You shall pay for this, Ozem, you bastard!" The accident seemed only to amuse the nearby guards, who didn't understand Hebrew anyway.

Jonathan could only hope that his message had gotten through. But even if it had, how was Ozem going to get them out? The guards were many and vigilant. Aholiab seemed no longer to care, but even the glimmer of possible rescue infused new life into Jonathan. He encouraged Aholiab, and together during the night they slowly moved themselves to the outer edge of the compound.

Aholiab whispered to Jonathan. "If the Phenician ship is gone in the morning, let's get the Philistines to kill us. I can't take any more of this." Any prisoner could provoke his own death quite simply: he had only to spit in the face of one of the guards. Jonathan agreed to the plan.

As they lay in the dark, Jonathan could hear the same sounds he had heard every night for eight months, the endless sea breeze and the cries and groans of the sleeping prisoners. He was just beginning to fall asleep when he heard a subdued cry— "Gish! Gish! Gish!" Only a Bethlehemite would pronounce his family name like that, making the initial K sound into a G.

"Aholiab, listen! Ozem!" Jonathan answered softly. "Ozem! Ozem! Ozem!" Jonathan's message had gotten through! It was so dark that Jonathan did not even see Ozem until he was less than a yard away, wriggling toward them on the ground. Once he knew that he had found his comrades, Ozem unwound two lengths of cloth from around his waist and motioned to Jonathan and Aholiab to wrap their ankle chains so that they wouldn't rattle. When that was done, they started the agonizingly slow, wriggling crawl after Ozem, passing between the sleeping prisoners. Inch by inch they edged across the sand toward the dunes, then past the dunes and onto the beach.

There were some Philistines bivouacked a few yards down that beach; but their fire had gone out, and they appeared to be asleep. Still, the three inched forward on their bellies, silent as serpents until they reached the water's edge. They crept out into the water till their feet no longer struck bottom. A choking sound from Aholiab brought Jonathan to his side. The chains were weighing Aholiab down. And Aholiab was too weak to go any faster or, indeed, any further. He was at the end of his strength. "Let me die here, Jonathan," he sobbed in between deep breaths. "Let me die here in peace." Jonathan said nothing, but he held Aholiab's head above water.

Ozem in the meantime had swum away from them out into the darkness and returned some minutes later pushing a small raft. Jonathan helped Ozem heave Aholiab aboard it, and with his last strength he swam, chains and all, helping Ozem push the raft out to the ship. No sooner had they reached the ship's side than nets were lowered quietly and they were hauled aboard by several pairs of strong hands. All Jonathan remembered after that was collapsing onto the deck.

He slept for twelve hours straight, awaking only long enough to take some food and liquor, then slept again until noon the following day. The chains had been removed from his legs and he had been carried below decks without even being aware of it. But when he tried to stand, his legs gave way and his head spun. A young Phenician boy looked in on him and in a minute returned with bread, wine, and fish.

When Ozem and the captain of the ship came down a few minutes later, Jonathan asked after Aholiab, and the news was bad. They had buried him at sea that morning. Jonathan's tears were bitter. "You know," he said when he could finally speak, "toward the end he took more beatings than I did. He kept going on sheer courage. Now he is with Adonai." Neither he nor Ozem was able to mention Aholiab's name again for a long time.

In the day and a half that it took them to reach Dor, Jonathan and Ozem compared notes about what they had learned. "It can mean only one thing," said Jonathan, and he smiled for the first time in eleven long months. "We have discovered the Iron Trail of the Philistines. They are getting their iron from the south, and they are building an underground trail to transport it in safety."

Saul was in the upper room of his cedar house when he heard the shouting. He thought first that Philistines were actually attacking Gibea, the noise was so great, and he bounded down the stairs and out the door into the sunlight, brandishing a sword and shield. The excitement and the rushing around was indescribable. The walls were lined with his men waving their weapons and shouting. They had recognized Jonathan from afar as he and Ozem approached the gate, riding together on a single mule. The king ran with the others to meet them. The archers reached the mule first and hoisted Jonathan up the

slope on their shoulders. A flood of joyous tears overwhelmed
Saul. Wading through the soldiers, he reached forward and
pulled Jonathan down, clasping him to himself.

"My son, my son," he muttered brokenly through sobs and
laughter. "My own son!" Everyone gathered around, touching
Jonathan, crying, laughing, cheering. It was a sign to them all
of Adonai's blessing.

Eventually Jonathan was able to speak. "Father, I never
thought I would see you again, or Mother or Melkishua or
Ishbaal or Abinadab. I never thought. . . ." He wiped his eyes
and laughed. Then: "Where is he? Ozem of Bethlehem?" Nobody knew what he meant. "Ozem!" he shouted again in some
panic. Then he caught sight of Ozem still on the mule on the
edge of the crowd. "That man, Father," he said pointing to
Ozem, "without that man I would not be back today alive and
well."

"Bring him here to us!" Saul rapped out the order. "Now
let us all go inside. Abner, post the guards and send a fast
camel for Samuel. Tell him he is needed immediately. Let the
rest of us now rejoice and celebrate. My son has come back
from the land of the heathen alive and well. Adonai be praised!
Hallelu Ya! Hallelu Ya!" The shout arose again in unison:
"Hallelu Ya! Hallelu Ya!" That most ancient Hebrew cry of
triumph echoed over the hills and filled the valleys.

Samuel arrived about an hour and a half after Jonathan's
arrival, and immediately sacrificed a kid in thanksgiving for
his safe return. Then they all sat down to a sumptuous feast.
For the first time in years, Samuel could detect real joy in Saul;
the king looked young again. And when Saul's official musician, the aging Geshem, took his pipes and intoned the "Saul
Song," Samuel smothered the little fires of apprehension that
began to flare within his soul.

Geshem's arrangement was simple and suited to the rhythmic singing that helps soldiers to march, but it seemed too self-
aggrandizing to Samuel. It was simply a list of Saul's ancestors,
beginning with "Benjamin!" uttered in a slow, low-voiced
monotone. The guests imitated both the speed and the tone
of his voice. "Benjamin!" Then "Bela!" This time a trifle
faster and in a slightly higher tone. Up the chant went,
Geshem announcing, the guests repeating, through all
the names of Saul's ancestors, in an ever growing anti-
phony.   "Naaman! . . . Shararaim! . . . Abitub! . . . Beria! . . .
Michael! . . . Shimhi! . . . Elam! . . . Athalia! . . . Jercham! . . .
Kish! . . . Ner! . . . Kish! . . . " By the time they had reached the

second ancestor named Kish, the pace had reached a breakneck speed and the voices were straining to reach the topmost note, as Geshem hurled out the last glorious name: "Saul!" And all the voices shouted after him: "Saul!"

In the prolonged cheering that followed, Samuel bowed his head and murmured a fervent prayer to Adonai: "Lord, please, in your goodness, help the king, your anointed! Give him wisdom and holiness and victory over all our enemies. But, above all, wisdom!" The banquet went on far into the night. Early next morning, Jonathan and Ozem revealed to Saul, Samuel, and the high officers all they had learned in Philistia. "No doubt of it," Saul exclaimed, "the trench is their iron trail."

"And," Samuel added, "there is also no doubt the Amalekites are helping them. They are the only tribe strong enough to control the trade."

"That wolf Agag again," Saul snarled angrily. The Amalekites, fierce fighting nomads of the southern deserts, had been enemies of the Hebrews since the time of Moses. The dear price they could exact from the Philistines, if the Amalekites discovered iron in the region under their control, would make an alliance between Amalekites and Philistines very likely.

When the meeting broke up, Ozem went straight to the king and asked to be allowed to go home to see his family. Saul gave him permission and offered him an armed escort, but Ozem declined. The sun was standing in the south and Ozem still had five or six hours of light—and he needed but two on a fast camel to get home to Bethlehem. Saul and Jonathan, the officers, Saul's family, and crowds of soldiers led him out to the gates of Gibea. The king had provided Ozem with camel, food, and weapons, and his parting words were: "Peace and blessings be on you and your house forever. Henceforth, Bethlehem will come before any other village in the land!"

Jonathan went alone to see Ozem out of the gate. They embraced as brothers. There were no words for the comradeship they would feel for each other all their days, even if they never met again. Jonathan hastily took out David's clay tablet on which Joshua had drawn his map.

"Give it back to the boy, Ozem. Tell him I love him."

"I will, Jonathan, I will." Then Ozem turned his camel toward the southern trail.

"Ozem! Ozem!" Shoshanna cried as she flew down the slope of the yard toward the gate. She had seen the homecomer first, seated silently on his camel by the gate, paralyzed with joy, tears flowing down his cheeks. Within minutes the whole of Bethlehem knew it, and the entire town gathered in Jesse's yard.

The musicians started playing joyous music, and everyone began to sing and dance. Ozem stood in the center of the swaying, chanting crowd, Jesse and Shoshanna by his side. Someone cried out above the singing, "David! David! Dance, David! David *hazahavi!*"

Ozem watched with wonder as the swaying crowd of his kinsmen stopped and the circle widened to admit the tall, slim figure of David. He was at least two inches taller than when Ozem had left a year before. His luxuriant blond hair fell down around his shoulders. He had shed the long, loose house robe and wore only the short belted tunic. He had cast aside his sandals. All hands clapped in time to the music and the weaving mime which David performed, telling the story of Bethlehem, of his family without Ozem—the winter of their sorrow, and then the sudden burst of spring at his return.

Like all the spontaneous creations of David *hazahavi*, the dance built up to an ever faster climax—Jesse and Shoshanna and Ozem were joined together, moving and crying and laughing all at the same time, and the air was split by one long burst of clapping.

It was some time before Ozem could have a word alone with David, who hung shyly aside. "Little scholar!" Ozem said amid the laughter of all. "Not so little any longer! And I see you have taken good care of our family during my absence." He laughed with sheer pleasure at his brother. "I have a present for you." He handed David his little clay tablet. "That," he confided, pointing to the tablet, "has been all through Philistia and elsewhere. Jonathan, the king's son, who says he loves you, sends it back to you with his thanks." David flung his arms around Ozem and held him tightly.

The rejoicing went on for hours, and Raham led the whole village in a thanksgiving to Adonai: "His mercy is above all his works," Reham intoned.

"*Hallelu Ya!*" everyone responded.

"He has humbled the mighty and exalted the meek in his house."

"*Hallelu Ya!*"

David had learned the harp from Raham, and he loved to play and sing the songs he composed about life in Bethlehem. One that Ozem had him repeat again and again celebrated the little droplets of dew—David called them the *kokave el,* the stars of God, that glistened in the spiders' webs and thick hazel bushes in the Witch's Road.

But there were many, many other songs, playful, loving, descriptive of all the things that he and Ozem loved about Bethlehem. The tramp of soldiers' feet when the company of the king's spearmen passed through the village. Bees humming in the sunny afternoons above their heads while the boys lay flat on their backs in Miller's Meadow. The hand of Adonai drying the rivers with his sun, and whitening the bearded barley in the cornfields.

David, accompanying himself on the harp, sang the songs in the evening as Shoshanna knitted and Jesse and Ozem listened. In a little over a year David would leave Raham's school. He would be confirmed in the Covenant, a man in Hebrew eyes. But the change that now began in David was much deeper than the one marked by an external ceremony.

At that age, David had not yet emerged from the realms of fantasy, half-childlike, half-demonic. Not yet a man but no longer a boy, he was passing through that in-between age in which the snakes of dreamy belief and painful longing lay entwined. He was on the brink of invention, of creativity, but not there quite yet. Thus he could use words like "love," "perfect," "pure," "happiness," yet he did not know what these words meant. All they conveyed to him was some inner ache. Still, he performed outside Bethlehem in neighboring villages. During the high holy days and on Shabbath festivals he was always chosen as cantor and musician.

Young Hebrew males left boyhood behind quickly, and old age began at thirty. Only a few lived past fifty, and a tiny minority went beyond. Adulthood, therefore, began at puberty, and puberty itself came early. But David's arrival at manhood was more poignant and painful than it was for the majority.

Only Shoshanna appraised his inner turmoil. She found that he did not want to be kissed on the face by her or by his father. And when he was about ten, she found out he no longer wanted to be naked in front of her.

One summer afternoon, when David had been swimming with his companions, he took a short cut home through a pine grove, and he heard the wind soughing in the trees above his head. At that moment, in that solitude, surrounded by the cool, green darkness of the grove, listening to the voice of the wind,

David had an impression of some invisible voice calling him from an immense ocean of peace and happiness. Yet it also made him sad.

He invoked Adonai's Angel and, of course, felt protected. But deep inside he began to realize that there was more to him than the love of Adonai. It frightened him to think that one day he might be defiant to the Lord of Israel.

Another time he started composing a song about the cries of birds at evening time. But the emotion became too much for him. He dropped his harp and ran back to Shoshanna at home. She put her arms around him and held him.

Finally, he put together a hymn of praise that delighted everybody without exacting too great a toll of pain from his spirit. That hymn became known as "David's Psalm of Bethlehem," and he repeated it on request by anyone. It had something from each portion of his life. His "Psalm of Bethlehem" told what everybody experienced in their daily life. Yet when he tried to sing about imaginary people and places, he felt dissatisfied and unhappy. Thus he learned he could not toy with a gift so delicate.

The only area in which David did not develop as fast as his contemporaries concerned love between men and women. From about the age of eight, when the normal boy and girl of his time became acquainted with the "facts of life," some veil seemed to have descended over David's perceptions. Shoshanna and Jesse both tried at various times to enlighten him, but he showed no interest.

When Raham, under prodding from Shoshanna and Jesse, discreetly inquired of David's fellow pupils and companions, he found that they all had an unspoken agreement among themselves: for some reason or other David had no curiosity about human love, so that when he was present they never recounted what they had furtively seen happening in their own homes, nor did they allow him to share in experimentation among themselves.

Jesse, however, was more concerned with something else. "What bothers me, wife, is his growing strength and his skill with weapons."

"But, husband," Shoshanna retorted, "in this land those skills are a blessing!"

"Exactly, my Shoshanna. Exactly! But this boy must not be called into the king's army. I have been warned to protect him, perhaps even from the king himself."

* * *

The news from Gibea indicated a widening rift between Saul and Samuel—Saul's behavior and treatment of those nearest him had become erratic and heartless. Something was very wrong. Jesse had no means of knowing how far King Saul had deteriorated in spirit and outlook. But the signs that Jesse read were disturbing enough, and the Michmash campaign was one of the clearest. Although it ended in a brilliant victory for the Hebrews over the Philistines at Michmash, in the center of the region of Benjamin, it revealed a number of distressing things about Saul. First, when Samuel failed to appear, the king took upon himself the function of priest and sacrificed a heifer. Samuel denounced Saul publicly for this irreverence, warning him that he was in grave danger of losing Adonai's protection.

Even more disquieting was Saul's behavior toward his own son, especially since it was Jonathan's stunning surprise attack upon the Philistines that finally precipitated their total rout. Saul had ordered that no man should eat or drink until full vengeance had been exacted from the enemy. Jonathan never got the order, and he stopped to eat from a hive of honey he had come upon in a wild oak tree.

A company of Hebrews saw Jonathan eating and told him of Saul's prohibition. Nettled, Jonathan responded: "If my father had been more diligent in battle and had seen that his men ate well, many more Philistines would have been killed!" Although Jonathan meant no disloyalty, his words had fearful consequences.

When Saul found out, he flew into a towering rage. "You are going to die right here and now," he said to Jonathan, his face black with anger, his hand raising his javelin. But all the officers ringed Jonathan with their weapons in a unified gesture of support.

"O King," Joab, son of Zeruiah, said menacingly, "do you mean to say that Jonathan, who gave us this great victory, is going to die? As Adonai lives! This will not be!" And they stood there glaring at Saul the king.

Saul was beaten and knew it. The anger fled from his face as he turned ashen with fear. He called for his mule, mounted it, and rode back to Gibea.

The battle was over but the damage was done. Word was out among his men that all the love in Saul was being transformed by some evil spirit. Jonathan had seen his father's eyes filled with black, unreasoning anger. Samuel heard and knew that this was an indication of worse to come. Had Adonai indeed abandoned Saul to evil?

In solitude, Samuel at Rama prayed for guidance. He visited the ruins of Shiloh, but owls and bats fled screeching from the blackened hulk of the ruined temple, and he chased a family of foxes from the room that had served the Holy of Holies. Outside, he wandered disconsolately, in utter silence, around the oak groves. The trees were bare, the ground thick with fallen leaves. He had the sensation of being followed, of something unpleasant reaching out to touch him and just missing. He trembled at the slightest sound, a frightened bird taking wing, the scurrying of a rabbit in the undergrowth, a twig cracking beneath his foot.

Sometimes—was he imagining things?—he thought he heard the faint scraping of some heavy animal's tail as it dragged itself through the undergrowth behind him. But when he listened intently, he could hear nothing except the sighing of the wind and his own uneasy breathing. With a heavy spirit he returned to Rama.

It dawned on him one evening that the noxious presence he felt was something that opposed and excluded Adonai. A storm had raged all day and passed at evening, leaving the sun choked behind sullen gray clouds tinged with the redness of freshly spilled blood.

Samuel went indoors and knelt before the Ephod. He drew back the leather flap and contemplated the mysterious emblems depicted by those precious stones. His body was aged beyond his years, emaciated from fasting, traveling, and deep worry. He had lost most of his hair and allowed his beard to grow untrimmed. He had a permanent tremble in his hands, and all his joints were attacked by arthritis. He prayed: "O Adonai, God of Israel, where is the evil I have admitted into my life? What is this shadow that is now always with me?"

Through his tears, at last he saw the Ephod lighting up, the red and the white and the blue-green of the stones at last luminous with meaning, and a voice thundered: "This is the shadow of my adversary. The shadow of evil. Of the enemy who once fought for Heaven with me. That shadow is now carried by his servant."

"Who carries it, Lord?" he asked breathlessly. "Who carries it? Whose is that shadow?"

"You will know when you will know. Do not despair." The stones went dark again and the voice was still.

As he lay down to sleep that night, he thought about the shadow. It had haunted him for years now, flitting from rock to rock, staining the golden sand in the desert, floating beneath the ripples of the Jordan. Just before he fell asleep, he suddenly realized that the shadow had appeared with Saul.

The news of Saul's deterioration had a devastating effect among the ordinary people as well. It was carried by soldiers returning to their homes after Michmash. Inevitably, Jesse's sons brought all the details, and Jesse became more and more concerned for David. It was bad enough that his other sons were so often called to serve this king. But if David fell into his hands, only Adonai knew what would happen to him. And David's prowess with weapons had become outstanding. It was Shoshanna who finally persuaded Jesse to discuss the matter with Raham.

"Make him your shepherd," Raham counseled. "When the year is up and school is finished, send him out with Omri at Beraka. They can't take him as a shepherd unless there's a general conscription."

Jesse liked the plan and so did David, although he did not learn the real reason. He liked being with Omri, and Beraka, with its wide-open spaces, had always attracted him.

So life went on uneventfully, until one afternoon the Egyptian nurse Heptah came from Jebus escorted by some of Uri's men. Hatich, she said, was dying, and it was her deepest wish to see David before she died. Would he come with Jesse?

"Tell her, Mistress Heptah, that we will come gladly," Jesse answered. "Is there more?"

"Yes. I have a message for you and Master Joshua from Master Uri. If you come—when you come—he asks that you travel with a caravan—fifty men or so, all trusted, and with pack animals. Come as traders before the spring fair at Jebus is ended. The city is at its most crowded and busy during that time. You will not be noticed. He says no more except the word 'iron.'"

"I see. I see. But the fair has already begun, hasn't it?"

"During the first week it is a carnival, celebrating Astarte. The trading fair goes on for a second week. Beyond that I know nothing. Master Uri expects me back before nightfall, and I am anxious to return to care for Mistress Hatich. I shall tell her that you and David will follow. What answer shall I bring to Master Uri?"

"Tell Master Uri to expect our caravan." Although it was a question the elders would have to decide, Jesse knew what their answer had to be. The villagers couldn't defend themselves with their weapons of bronze, flint, and stone, and copper-tipped arrows crumpled when they hit the hide-and-wood shields of the Edomites. More than that, without iron farming was difficult. Wooden plows and shovels broke in the hard ground. If there was a chance that with Uri's help Bethlehem could get iron, the elders would jump at it. They did. The dispute at the Council of Elders meeting was not about the iron but about Jebus and Uri's motives.

The whole countryside knew of the Jebusite trade fairs held at the spring and fall equinoxes. In the matter of fairs and trade in general, the Jebusites were apt above all other people. They were a mongrel breed, a mixture of a dozen different peoples from Asia, Africa, and the many nations who had lived in that land. In skin color they ranged from pitch black to stark white. Their behavior varied equally.

The Jebusites had conquered the city many years before, but by now, the fight had largely gone out of them. They were governed by a group of greedy old men who had lied and robbed their way to the top and ruled shrewdly. They taxed everything, but they knew how much the goose could be plucked without squawking. They made friends with neighboring cities and chieftains, and above all they traded. Their city dominated the main caravan routes.

They protected the virtually impregnable city with mercenaries—Hittites, Egyptian deserters, Edomites, Nubians, and a general riffraff of expatriates—ex-robbers, ex-pirates, escaped felons, runaway husbands, sons, and slaves. Gold was the glue that held this force together.

Merchants, peddlers, caravan masters, slave dealers, craftsmen, personal representatives of some three dozen kings, and every sort of religious fanatic were always to be found within Jebus's walls. Even the Philistines found the city useful. At fair time, even more people crowded in. They came to trade, to discuss, to learn, to worship, to amuse themselves, and to spy. They came, above all, to participate in the wild, erotic celebrations that greeted the equinox of fertility in the spring and said a lusty farewell to the sweaty pleasures of summer in the fall.

"First of all," Zaza began at the Council of Elders, "can we really trust this uncircumcised Hittite, Uri? Who speaks for him?"

"I do." Jesse's tone was calm. "I know him. I trust him. And I know why he proposes this. His days are numbered in Jebus, if we Hebrews cease to be a threat to his masters.

Without iron, we will be overrun—you all know that. They'll keep him as long as our tribes in Judah threaten their caravans."

"All right! So we need iron," Raham broke in. "But at the time of the spring fair? No Hebrew must even witness, let alone participate in those vile rites. Why, even the name those heathens have given to the city—Jebus—means the whoring belly of that infernal goddess they adore. I tell you, my brothers, at those celebrations of the Jebusites, no girl remains a virgin, no man or boy is merely a male—in fact, no animal is safe! Filth and desecration, brothers! Desecration and filth!"

When Jesse told Joshua what Raham had said, Joshua wanted to leave as quickly as possible so as not to miss anything. But Jesse explained that the elders had agreed to send the caravan only on the strict condition that it arrive in Jebus after the carnival, stay no longer than their business required, and then come home with every last man.

"Three days at most! With or without the iron!" This was the iron rule, as Raham put it.

David was very excited as he rode his mule between Joshua and Jesse at the head of the caravan. Except for his visits to the Beraka pastures, David had never been out of Bethlehem. He had heard stories, of course, but he had never dreamed of such a sweep of land as he saw before him in the clear air of that spring morning. David knew nothing of Raham's fears. He did know that everyone who had been to Jebus talked of its beauty and grandeur.

"Wait until you see it!" Joshua said to him as they rode. "It's the biggest city you'll ever see. It's beautiful. And the people are special." A look from Jesse stopped Joshua before he got to the bare-breasted women dancing in gossamer skirts.

"Look!" Jesse pointed ahead. They had at that moment topped a hill, and a fairly level plain sloped gently before them to the horizon. "Do you see that cluster of hills in the distance?" David nodded. "Now, look just above those hills. Do you see those two bright spots?"

"I see them." David's face was intent. "The spot on the right is rounder."

"Well, now, that taller one on the left, that's where we're headed."

"And the round one on the right?"

"That's Mount Moriah, where Abraham offered Isaac as a sacrifice to Adonai."

How many times David had marked those places on his clay

tablets and repeated their names and histories in Raham's class! But how different to catch even a first distant glimpse of them. It was as if a new door were opening in his life, and he could hardly wait to step through it.

As they drew closer to the eastern side of the city, he could make out the figures of men with tall spears and plumes in their helmets walking to and fro on the walls that had become tanned and yellowed with the passage of time. Joshua pointed out a structure of seasoned oak wood that seemed to hang on the outer face of the eastern wall: the Millo barracks.

"A long time ago, Phenician engineers cut a tunnel to let the waters of Siloam flow from outside the eastern wall through the rock of Zion, right under its streets. Then they cut a well from the city street down to the tunnel. No one laying siege to Jebus can get to the water for themselves; and no one can cut it off from the city. It is as great a defense as a whole army fitted with weapons of iron!"

Then Joshua pointed to a spot at the southern wall. "Right about there, that's where the well drops inside the city to meet the tunnel from Siloam. And that's where Uri has his house. He is in charge of the security of Siloam and that whole sector of the city as well."

As David was taking it all in, the caravan continued its way along the western path, then turned north again, skirting the hills they had seen from so great a distance, until they were well north of Jebus, past Mount Moriah.

Finally, by midafternoon, they approached the city itself. It looked like a walled ellipse, forever guarded by its cliffs rising from valleys on three sides. Even the northern approach was difficult, rising from the Ophel Valley south of Mount Moriah, up a steep ramp that was completely dominated by the fortifications of the north wall. As Joshua signaled for the caravan to draw to a halt some distance from the gates of heavy oak, crisscrossed with stout bars of bronze, David watched uneasily the fortifications that jutted out over the gate. Six tall window slits were clearly visible, and the sun glinted on the arrows aimed at them from each one of those windows.

As the caravan waited, the gates swung open. An officer mounted on a mule came through the gate and rode slowly toward them, holding a sword high over his head. He had only to drop that arm and the arrows aimed from above would kill every man, every animal, in their caravan. It happened often. Joshua left the caravan and rode up to meet the officer. "I am

Joshua of Bethlehem. I bring a caravan to the fair to trade and buy. Our patron is Uri, servant of the governors of Jebus. We ask permission to enter with our trade goods and then to stable our animals here at Ophel. We will stay with Master Uri."

The officer's only reply was to turn his mule toward the gate and then wave the caravan in. At the gate the caravan was counted—ten pack camels, six oxcarts—and the name of each man recorded. The carts and animals carrying the trade goods were inspected and then stabled. They would be inspected again on their way out. Joshua paid the entrance tax of five silver talents for the caravan, and each man was given a little inscribed clay shard as his pass within the city. He would return it when he left the walls.

From the bright sun outside the gate they entered a short, dark, zigzag passageway covered over by a stone ceiling pierced with several round holes about the size of a man's head. After a few seconds they emerged again into the light of day and into the sudden noise and hubbub of the main street of Jebus.

David caught his breath. The colors, the smells, the buildings, the shops, and the crowds of people were overwhelming. Stretching before him was a long, wide, cobbled street that ran the whole length of the city, from north to south. Every inch of that street seemed lined with three- and four-story houses. The upper stories were gaily decorated with bunting, flags, tapestries, streamers of all kinds. On the balconies people were drinking, shouting, and waving down to the crowds in the street.

The first story of each house was a shop. David had never thought there was such plenty in the whole world! Store fronts were piled high with every kind of goods. There were pyramids of melons, oranges, apples, bananas, white and red grapes, lemons, cucumbers, mangoes, pomegranates, plums, and varieties of fruits and vegetables unknown in Bethlehem. There were huge round baskets of raisins, figs, chestnuts, walnuts, red berries, blackberries, bread loaves, and extraordinary platters of cooked food—chicken legs, steaks, fish pies, quail, lamb, mutton. At open braziers cooks were stirring copper caldrons of steaming soup.

The men of the caravan tried to stay together as Joshua led them through the crowd of people wearing every conceivable dress: the red-and-blue-bordered white robes of the Bedouins; tall Galileans in leather jerkins and boots; quick-witted Phenicians wearing fine, close-fitting linen shirts, their women in flowing byssus robes with exposed breasts. And everywhere there were the haughty Philistines in body armor and helmets, their short iron swords at their sides.

And the women! David was used to the Hebrew costumes of Bethlehem, where women wore veils even at the village well. Here he saw bare-faced women walking in the streets or standing in open balconies. They wore low-cut dresses, their breasts showing, the sides of their skirts split to display their legs! All during fair time the women were supposed to display their charms as an expression of their love and devotion for the goddess Astarte, to help men celebrate her mysteries of love.

No one had warned David about the images of Astarte. You could not travel ten yards in Jebus without running into one. Plaques hung at every corner and above every lintel. These displayed the figure of the goddess naked, with distended belly and large breasts, her hands grasping either lily stalks or serpents, for Astarte was the patroness of love and fertility.

For Hebrews, the most awful abominations were committed in Astarte's name.

By the time Joshua finally got through to the southern end of Jebus, where Uri's house stood, David was no longer at the front of the column but at the rear, staring in amazement at everything. One of Uri's slaves went off to the barracks to find his master.

Uri's house, like all houses of men of wealth and influence, was built in three stories around a more or less circular courtyard, with family quarters on the side farthest from the street and quarters for slaves, servants and guards on the other. Uri had gotten Jesse's message, and all was in readiness to receive the caravan. Slaves showed Jesse, David, Joshua, and some of the others to quarters in the family dwelling. The rest were given rooms in the servants' wing. By the time Uri appeared, most of the men had washed and refreshed themselves after the dusty journey. They were already gathering in the courtyard, where Egyptian slave girls, naked except for light woolen stoles around their shoulders and wooden sandals on their feet, served them a meal of fresh fruits, cheeses, and wine.

As Uri came into the yard, he was greeted by a burst of loud laughter. David, it seemed, was as much a curiosity to the Egyptian girls as they were to him. They had never seen a young man so tall, golden-haired, and blue-eyed. In their country only the gods were reckoned to have such colorings. They surrounded him and tried to touch his hair, while David ran from one to another in a bewildered attempt to break out of their circle.

Joshua spotted his old friend and rose from his place, still laughing and wiping tears from his face. "Come here, old friend! Bow and salute! Your lovely little slave girls think our David is a young god! They said the one who served him first would marry a handsome husband at the next blue moon! That lass over there, Lassatha, won the race!" Lassatha was a long-haired Egyptian girl with pale, ivory-colored skin and long, elliptical dark eyes. "And to crown it all, they asked why David wore clothes! They wanted to see his golden pubic hair! Really, Uri, it's all too much for us poor Hebrews! His golden pubic hair indeed!"

David rose from his place too, laughing with the rest, but red-faced and embarrassed. Uri looked at this boy whose mother had died, as his own wife had, in childbirth. "As the king lives!" Uri swore in mock protest. "This golden god has already taken my favorite concubine."

David, blushing and choking with embarrassment, said hastily: "Oh, no, Master Uri! Never!"

Uri looked at him in mock solemnity from beneath his eyebrows. "As the king lives," he swore, "you will have to kill me or have me killed before you take my woman away from me!"

Everyone, including David, laughed at that, and they set to eating their food.

When David awakened well before dawn the next day, neither Hatich nor iron was on his mind. He was ready for more adventures in Jebus. When he entered the courtyard a few others from the caravan were already there. Jesse, Joshua, and Uri were huddled together. Lassatha, the young Egyptian girl who had been so taken with David, offered him fruit, bread, and cheese with white wine. Returning her smile, he joined his father's group and took quick refuge in the conversation.

"The situation is a lot different than it was the last time you were here, Joshua," Uri said. There was no trace of last evening's humor in his voice.

"You mean the Philistines?" Jesse asked. "They're everywhere."

"Yes. They have always found Jebus useful for trading. But now they've made an alliance with the governors. They've set up an iron forge and warehouse. They bring ore in—from where we don't know." Jesse and Joshua exchanged glances. "It goes into their warehouse, then they forge it, and it leaves with a convoy for their garrisons up north. They pay a heavy tax to the governors, and in return the governors give them free access. It's a nice deal for both.

"But"—Uri looked at Jesse and his trusted friend Joshua— "I see a way to stick these Philistine pigs. My men and I can safely sneak a good quantity of iron out of the forge and the warehouse. It's easy during the fair, when there's so much confusion and half the guards are drunk. We can hide the iron briefly in my cellars. It's risky, but I can do it. The trouble is getting it out of the city. The guards at the gate can be bought, all right, but they can't be trusted. They'd take your money, and then get a bonus for turning us in. And there's no way at all to get past them."

Jesse suggested lowering the iron in batches over the south wall.

"It won't work," Uri replied. "It would take too long, and one clang would have every soldier in Jebus on our trail.

"The fair goes on for two more days. We have until then to find an answer. After that, the crowds thin out too much, and there'll be no excuse for your caravan to be here." Uri looked at Jesse and Joshua. "Let's take a walk. I have one idea I want to talk over with you."

The rest of the men went out on their errands. David happily joined one of the several parties. But first Uri cautioned everyone. "One single word about any of this and we're all dead men! Believe me! The crowds are swarming with the governors' spies."

"And you, David," Jesse added as sternly as he could manage, "stay with your group. Keep your mind on business and your eyes where they belong!"

"Yes, sir." David took in Joshua's wink and Lassatha's smile as he ran to catch up with the others.

Their task was to locate about twenty sets of the wheel-made pottery imported from the north. It was decorated with sharp carination points covered with a thick coat of red or cream slip. This type of ware, highly prized for the Shabbath seder, was found in the Aramean stores.

Second, they had to buy about forty vases, bowls, and jugs of various sizes for ordinary use. These wares had a highly burnished black surface decorated with chalk-filled geometric designs. David, in addition, had been instructed by his father to buy one of those delicately shaped piriform perfume vases with a button base. It was to be Jesse's present to Shoshanna.

While David and his group were making their purchases, two other groups of five were out foraging for other necessities. One group bought a series of wooden utensils—bowls, spoons, ladles, cups, buckets. The other was concerned with obtaining some outsize copper cooking pots, supplies of clay tablets and papyrus and copper styluses for Raham and for the Council of Elders, and one large bichrome vase with painted ornamentation in friezes as a gift for Raham from the village.

Of all the people they met during that day, David liked the Phenicians the best—laughing, independent people with ready smiles—and they marveled at his golden hair and blue eyes.

While the craftsmen finished Raham's gift vase, decorating the friezes with six-pointed stars, the Phenician shopkeeper invited David and his companions under the awning at the back of the shop, where David talked with his two children, a boy called Elkesef, a little older than he, and a girl, Safith, somewhat younger. While the men chatted the young people soon became friendly. Safith showed David some golden statues of Astarte that Elkesef had stolen from a drunken Jebusite soldier who had killed a Phenician peddler to get them. Elkesef's father planned to smuggle them out with other goods before the fair was over.

David's interest suddenly magnified, but he gave no sign. Turning one little statue in his hand, he asked idly, "How?" Elkesef realized he had made a mistake. This young Hebrew could now betray them to the guards. He liked David, but could he trust him?

His sister laughed. "Don't be silly, Elkesef. Everyone who can does it, and the Hebrews don't love this place any better than we do. Who wants to give the Jebusites all his money in taxes?"

So Elkesef said to David. "Swear by your god you'll tell no one."

David swore by Adonai.

"Through the shaft of Siloam," Elkesef confided. "It's not easy. You have to swim the stream, and it's all under water. I almost didn't make it last year. But no one guards the pool at the other end. You bury whatever it is at a marked place in the desert, and pick it up when you leave. The hard part is getting back into the city. Last year I just swam back up the stream and climbed up the well rope. That's risky because guards come by the well a lot. Hittites they are."

"I wouldn't like to try it," David said modestly, and yawned. "But don't worry, Elkesef, your secret is safe with me." Soon David and his party sauntered off with their purchases and went back to Uri's house.

David waited anxiously until he was alone with Jesse and Joshua and Uri. "I know how we can get the iron out." He had to struggle to keep his voice even. "Siloam! The shaft of Siloam! That's the way, Master Uri!"

Jesse looked at David as though he couldn't believe his ears, and then in astonishment at Uri.

Uri smiled. "David, what kind of security commander would I be if I didn't know that people try to swim the shaft from time to time? The trouble is, although few try, even fewer make it. We find about two bodies a month in Gikhon. So it's no secret, but as your father and Joshua and I have just been saying"—he smiled again—"it is one solution. But you have to be an exceptional swimmer to have a Hebrew's chance. But then you people are Hebrews, aren't you?" he added, laughing.

"I *am* an exceptional swimmer," David broke in. Jesse frowned him down and Uri continued.

"We know so little about the shaft, how it curves, how wide it is. We know that some people have gotten through, but very, very few."

"Well, I could," declared David. "I know I could. I'm almost exactly the same size as the man I met who did it. Both ways! And I'm the best swimmer in Bethlehem."

Uri's eyebrows went up a little. Maybe he'd better step up security a bit. But not just yet. Joshua stood up with a sigh. "Even if David could make it, there's no way to get the iron through."

"Yes, there is." Uri leaned forward and looked intently at Jesse. "Look, my friend. I know how you feel. If it were my son, I'd feel the same. But if he can do it, we can do it. We can get the iron tonight. Small weapons, already forged, and some pig iron, maybe small ingots.

"I have a few sets of Philistine armor. No, don't ask how I got them." Uri patted his sword. "I just got them. Dressed like Philistines, about five of you should be able to get a cart out the gates and in again. And no questions asked. Remember, their alliance gives the Philistines free access to the city.

"You take the cart down to Kidron, as near as you can get to the pool of Siloam. There are no guards down below, as David knows. Just keep close by the cliffs, David," Uri went on, "and be as quiet as you can. I'll have trusted men at my end of the walls over the Millo. That's the easy part.

"Now, as to David and the shaft—if Jesse agrees. David will take no iron through; only a rope. That will be heavy enough, but the water should be some help. The rope will be double, a big circle. We'll fasten it at the middle around David's waist and pay it out behind him all the way through the shaft. He can signal us with pulls if he gets into trouble. At the Millo end, Joshua, you and Jesse dressed as Philistines will set up a sturdy stake and drop the rope around it. Then you signal us—so many tugs. We'll tie our ends on the beam over the well mouth. All we have to do then is tie the iron goods to the rope at intervals and pull them on through the shaft. Then we work fast to get the iron hidden in the desert."

"And how does David get back?" Joshua asked in growing anxiety.

"Father, let me try." David knelt by his father's side, his eyes pleading. "You're the one who said how desperately we need the iron. I know I can do it. Please let me."

Jesse bit his lip. How could he measure iron against David's life? He groaned. He took his son's head in his hands. He looked at Uri, at Joshua. If anyone can do it, he thought, David can. That is true. But dear God in heaven, how could I ever forgive myself? He turned again to Uri. "Well, how *does* David get back?"

"Back through the shaft. It's easier than going out. He'd be swimming with the current on the way back. And he'd have the rope to pull himself along. We could try to get him back in the cart, but remember this: even though the Philistines have free access, they're still subject to gate inspection. You might need to explain the extra person on the way back."

For a moment Jesse remained lost in thought and prayer. Then his features relaxed. He had reached a decision. He regarded his companions calmly and said:

"All right. He can go."

Before helping to smuggle out the Philistine iron, David had a personal mission to accomplish—to meet and comfort the dying Mistress Hatich, without whose skilled knowledge he would never have been born.

Uri and Heptah showed him and Jesse the way. In the semidarkness of Hatich's room, David could see at first only the silhouettes of five Egyptian women sitting near the simple window overlooking the courtyard. One plucked a lyre and all softly sang of the death trip across the sky on the wheel of Eternity.

Then in the dimness he made out in the corner nearest the chorus a slim statuette of a woman standing on a pedestal and holding in her right hand the ankh, ancient Egyptian symbol of life. The figure's features were composed, its eyes tranquil. A brazier of incense smoldered soundlessly beside the pedestal.

The whole effect on David was sobering and, in its strangeness, frightening. He felt Jesse's hand on his shoulder. Together they moved across the room to where Hatich lay, covered with a long blue robe, a veil hiding the ravages of sickness on her once handsome face.

"Master Jesse?"

"Yes. I have brought David to see you, Mistress Hatich."

"David." A pause. Then: "Yes. I have heard you are called David. Please come near." Hatich turned to appraise his tall, lithe figure, his blond head, his deep blue eyes.

David knelt, leaning on her couch. He smelled the heavy perfume of roses and sandalwood that did not quite mask the smell of corrupting flesh.

"David." Her voice was tender, yet resonant, of a timbre utterly new to him.

"David," Hatich continued, "you were born on a special night. Never have I felt myself in the focus of such power as that night. It took over my hands and directed them." She shifted her body painfully.

"Soon, David, I will be a part of the past. But I learned something from your Adonai that night. There was death and life that night you were born. There was old and new. Past and future. You are a link, David, and I was fortunate to be there. Now, no tears, David."

David had not realized that he was crying.

Even in her frailty, the authority that had always been so much a part of Hatich was still there. "There will be no tears here, *David hazahavi!* What matters is the task in front of you. And you must give it all your strength. The light of your Adonai shines on you, dear David."

Hatich turned her head toward Uri. "Master Uri, one favor."

"Tell me, Hatich."

"I do not want my bones returned to Egypt."

"But you have always said . . ."

"I know, but things are different now. Or I see something different in things. Here is where my bones must remain. Outside the walls in some quiet tomb. Outside until David returns to stay in this city. Then—only then, mind you—my bones can be brought back here."

"Until David? . . ." Jesse repeated, confused and baffled.

"Yes, Master Jesse. David will be back. Of that I'm certain."

"What you wish shall be done," said Uri.

Hatich was silent, her veiled face turned slightly toward David for a last look. A slight movement of her hand was her farewell and blessing.

If only the events of this visit could have been arranged differently, Jesse thought as they left the sickroom. Uri was a fighter; he had seen death hundreds of times. And every man Jesse's age, warrior or not, had seen it often enough. But David had not. Oh, animals, yes. He had hunted; he had seen sheep killed by wolves or lions or men. And, of course, he had known people in Bethlehem who had died, or never returned from battle. But until now he never had to stare death in the face.

Uri had a suggestion. "Don't let the lad brood over this," he told Jesse. "The thing to do now is busy him with life."

"David!" Uri called. "Come with us. Lassatha! Lassatha! Where are you, girl! Lassatha!" Uri strode across the courtyard bellowing orders. Without looking back, he knew Jesse and David were behind him. Lassatha appeared, too. Uri gave her some quick instructions in Egyptian and off she hurried. Uri threw open the doors to his own quarters.

"Come in, Jesse. You too, David, and strip off your clothes."

David looked at his father.

"Come, come!" Uri pretended impatience. "You're not a baby. Strip! You've got a big job ahead of you. Lassatha will get you ready."

David kicked off his sandals. He undid his belt slowly and took off his knee-length robe. Lassatha came back into the room with two other slaves, carrying an assortment of towels, blankets, trays of oil vases, and a large metal box. Lassatha laid the things she was carrying near a low couch and spread a blanket. Then she turned to David. Before he could even blush she had undone his waist cloth and led him bewildered and stark naked to the couch.

The two slaves, giggling at David's embarrassment, took steaming hot towels from the metal box and gave them to Lassatha. David howled as she slapped one on his chest, then another across his middle. Uri laughed until he wept. "David," he said, "by the time Lassatha finishes with you, you'll be ready to swim the Great Sea itself." He pulled Jesse after him out the door.

"Don't worry, Jesse, the lad will be fine. Lassatha will rub him down and give him some good hot soup that'll put him to sleep. Then they'll cover him with thick oil. Lots of it. He'll need it in that cold water. But he doesn't need you to fret over him! We've got to get you dressed as a Philistine, anyway. So let's move along."

By the time Uri came back for David, half an hour before midnight, the iron had been stolen and Jesse and his crew had started for the gate. Uri's trusted men gathered at the top of the well. David was wrapped in a blanket and glistening with oil. It hadn't taken him long to get used to a beautiful naked young woman rubbing his body with oil and massaging it into every muscle. He was talking and laughing with Lassatha as Uri and Joshua came in.

"Ready, David?"

"Ready." There was no hesitation.

"Let's go, then."

Lassatha removed the blanket and David stood naked in front of her. She took a cut and measured piece of leather, slipped it between his thighs, and drew the two ends up, covering his sides, stomach, buttocks, and gathering his genitals in tightly. With needle and thong thread she sewed the sides, so that finally David stood there clad in tight-fitting leather briefs. Leather sandals were bound tightly on his feet, and he was ready. Lassatha surveyed him, then uttered a few words in Egyptian that David couldn't understand. Uri laughed and threw a soldier's blanket-cloak over David, covering him from shoulder to toe. As he left the room Lassatha stared after him, her index finger placed horizontally over her heart. Uri noticed and laughed again.

"That means she wants to make love with him when he gets back," Uri whispered to Joshua. "What she called him in Egyptian was 'my midnight fish.' Clever girl, no?" Both men laughed.

When the strict curfew of the fair had started and all of Jebus was asleep, they left Uri's house and crossed the street to the House of the Fountain, which consisted of a tiled roof resting on four pillars without walls and lit by torches. Off to one side of the well, covered with tarpaulins, some of the iron was already stacked into bundles, guarded by Uri's men, ready to go as soon as David made it through the shaft.

"Have you changed your mind, David?" Joshua asked.

As an answer, David threw off his blanket. While they tied the rope around his middle, over the top of the leather strapping, Uri went over with him for the third and last time as much as he knew about the underground tunnel.

"The water starts about forty-five or fifty feet down. Once you hit the surface, it's about twenty-five feet more to the bottom. Up here, it's about thirty-five or forty feet horizontally to the eastern wall. As you know, it could be longer down there, if the shaft curves.

"If you have any trouble at all, just give two sharp long jerks on this rope, hear me? We'll pull you back and that will be that. No nonsense! Understood?"

"Yes, sir."

"Your father and the others should already be at the pool. They'll hold one lantern close to the water. It can't be seen from up here. When you see that light, you'll know you're just about there. Once you're through, the rest is up to us."

David tested the heavy rope fixed around his waist. It was secure and not too tight. "It feels heavy, but I think I need more weight. Let me take a couple of ingots. I want to get to the bottom of the shaft as quickly as I can. Then I can drop them."

Joshua and Uri helped David over the lip of the well and he braced his feet against the smooth stone. Four Hittites held the rope taut. "On the way down, whistle once if you want us to stop," Joshua said. "Twice if you want to come back."

"We'll keep the rope taut till you reach the water. Then whistle three times and we'll let out the slack and you're on your way."

"Once to stop, twice to come back up, three times to go," David repeated.

"And two sharp pulls to come back once you're under."

David nodded that he was ready. Uri gave the signal. The men started to lower him very slowly. The only sounds were the rubbing of the rope against the edge of the well and the breathing of the men. No one spoke. Uri held his arm straight out, indicating with a continuous motion the speed at which they were to lower the boy.

By the time David was ten feet down, he could no longer see even the lanterns up above and could hear only his feet brushing against the stone and the scraping of the rope.

The first shock of the cold water was over quickly. "Just like the Rabbit's Head," he told himself. When he was in the water up to his shoulders, he whistled once. The rope tightened, and he stayed where he was for a few seconds. He knew they were passing it over the winch pole that stood over the top of the shaft in order to use the pulleys from then on. He dunked his head, came up again, took a series of deep breaths, then gave three short whistles. The rope was already going slack. He filled his lungs as full as he could, dived head first, and kicked straight down.

He had his eyes open, but down here it was pitch black so he closed them. His arms hit the side once or twice. With the iron to weigh him down, he was at the bottom sooner than he expected and cracked one wrist against the solid stone floor.

He kept the iron as weight while he felt around for the horizontal shaft opening. Ah! There it was! He dropped the ingots and felt for the dimensions of the opening. Twice his size! was his quick calculation. He could feel the very gentle current coming in against him. He was colder now for sure than at the Rabbit's Head. Yet within seconds after his dive he was into the shaft, kicking his legs, feeling his way with his hands for any curves or narrow places. He couldn't get any real sense of how much distance he was covering, but he began to hear a gently low, faint roaring in his ears and began to feel the pain of holding his breath.

The rope started to drag a bit and rasp his skin. Were they giving him enough slack? His ears were now pounding with the sound of his own pulse, and his lungs were bursting. He fought back his instinct to breathe in and kicked harder, groping along the wall. Where were those lights? Adonai! Where were those lights?

In spite of himself, three quarters of the way through that shaft he was taking in small amounts of water and his energy was going. The pain in his chest was so great that in a moment he would have to open his mouth. He could see nothing. The little grains of hope started to wither. He could not make it. Air! Where was the air! He thought he heard a voice. No! It wasn't a voice. Finally, it was light! He could really see light! And what looked like two columns. And then he could remember no more.

Strong hands took hold of him. The "columns," as David learned later, were Jesse's metal-sheathed legs as he stood in the center of the pool holding his lantern near the face of the water and watching that slender sliver of flesh slithering, jerking spasmodically, pushing laboriously, plugging away toward him.

Jesse feared the boy's head would crash against the top of

the shaft, but up he came, water cascading from his head and face. His mouth opened wide, gasping, sucking. His eyes stared. His body was taut and rigid. As Jesse held him up, other hands undid the rope. Blood trickled from the weal the rope had cut around his waist.

"David! David! You've made it, boy! You've done it! David!" David's rasping cough as he gulped air made his whole body heave and his perceptions returned. "David!" Jesse cried again. "You've made it!"

Jesse picked him up and waded with his son in his arms to the side of the pool. Two of the young Hebrews took the rope and dropped it over the stake they had planted deep and strongly at the side of the pool. They gave the rope three very hefty sharp pulls. They helped Jesse spread out some blankets for David and rubbed him with warm oil to get the cold out of him. Gradually his heaving breath subdued. Jesse poured some Phenician barley whiskey into his mouth, and David began to feel his legs and arms again. He started to shiver violently.

"Father! I don't think I can go back through the shaft. I don't think I can do it!"

Jesse stroked David's wet hair back. "Don't worry. You've done enough for now. Lie back there and sleep. You're safe."

In the hours that followed, the iron came through on the rope in a steady stream, and David slept without stirring. The five men worked like pack animals. Two of them cut the packets free of the rope as they arrived and stacked them at the side of the pool. Jesse and the other two lugged packet after packet out to the cart. Each time the cart was full, they hauled the load off to bury in the desert.

David felt someone shaking him. He opened his eyes, and then sat up with a start. He was surrounded by Philistine soldiers! It took him a second or two to realize who they were.

"David, it will be light soon. The iron is safe, waiting for us in the desert. You've done it, son!"

"It's time to go back, then, Father?" David knew that he could risk everyone's life if he tried to get through the gates of the city by hiding in the cart, and the sleep had renewed his strength. "I'll go back through the shaft."

They all waded forward to the mouth of the shaft. David looped one strand of the rope securely around each hand. He knew better now than to trust his grip in that icy water. When he was ready, he gave a nod.

"Adonai protect you, son!"

"I'll see you at Uri's, Father!" The farewell was like a knife cutting through each of the five men looking at David's face in the semidarkness. Jesse and the others then all grasped the double rope in front of David's hands. On Jesse's count they gave two sharp, hard pulls and saw the slack come up. David dived forward, kicked once, and was gone.

One of the men said quietly to no one in particular, "That is a brave young fellow."

"Yes!" The remark galvanized Jesse. "Now let's get out of here fast!"

Joshua was leaning over the well a little, holding the rope, when the signal came. "That's it," he cried. "Pull!"

Uri jumped to the front of the line of men pulling for dear life. Hands moved over hands. Arms hit each other. Bodies bumped against bodies. They pulled like a machine, the wet rope coiling in a growing mound behind them. David down in the shaft had the advantage of experience this time. The cold got to him very quickly, but he had the current with him, and the rope pulled him faster than he could swim. His main worry was to keep from being scraped against the sides of the shaft.

He freed one hand from the rope and used it and his legs to keep himself away from the hard stone as much as possible. When he felt the current lessen, he knew he was in the wider part of the shaft. He grabbed the rope again so that he was holding it with both hands; and he kicked as hard as he could. The pain in his lungs began again. But he must be nearly there, he must be nearly . . .

Suddenly he was jerked roughly upward. His body slammed against the stone above him. In spite of the shock, he still managed to hold some air in his lungs. He hadn't realized the speed at which he was being pulled back; he'd have to guard against hitting the top of the shaft where the rope pulled upward into the well itself.

Joshua felt the sudden tightening of the rope that had been slipping so easily through his hands. "Hold it, hold it. He must be at the mouth of the shaft below there. Give a little slack!" Joshua pulled and guided the rope to get David clear. "Easy! Easy! Now pull. Not too hard! Easy!"

When David's head broke through the water's surface in the well, it was just in time. He gasped for air, but the rope was too tight around him and he couldn't get enough. In trying to draw in breath, he only succeeded in expelling his last remnants of air. Then he was just dangling at the end of the rope, his head above water, unable to breathe, panic and helplessness closing in around him again. Dear God! What now!

The sharp-eyed Uri realized the problem in a flash. "Pull like hell!" he cried. "Everyone pull! Pull!" David's body shot up the well. Joshua and Uri lifted him out, and even before they laid him on the ground Uri had cut the rope that had tightened around his waist at the base of the rib cage. They let him lie still until he had drawn some deep breaths. Then Uri picked him up as if he were a sack of feathers and ran across the street, through the courtyard and into his own quarters, Joshua hard on his heels.

Lassatha and three other slaves had a large fire burning in the brazier in Uri's room. Hot soup and warmed wine were waiting. Uri put David down on the couch, then turned to Lassatha. "He's done it but he's exhausted. Do everything for him that needs doing. Everything! He's a hero!"

Lassatha went into swift action, tenderly bathing David with hot towels and applying soothing balm to the ugly weal at his waist and to his other cuts and scrapes. When David had been warmly swaddled in a cocoon of blankets, they gave him soup and wine. Finally he looked at the two men standing silently by like worried owls and smiled.

"Well, it worked!" he said. "The iron is safe."

Joshua gave a whoop of triumph. "Now there's a job well done! If Jesse and the others get back through the gate all right..."

The wish was answered immediately as the door burst open and Jesse rushed in dripping wet, his eyes searching for one thing only. He stopped suddenly when he saw David, then he hid his face in his hands and shook with sobs of relief.

Uri turned to practical things. "Let the lad be for an hour. The rest is easy, but we can't waste valuable time. You and your men take off that armor and get your caravan ready."

As the rest of the household—guests, servants, and slaves—set about completing the night's work, David fell asleep again. Only Lassatha remained with him. She lay down beside him on the couch and put her arms around him, one hand caressing his forehead and temples, the other gently cradling his shoulders. She lay there listening to his breathing and to the rain falling outside.

Uri told Joshua and Jesse how he planned to dispose of the Philistines who had contributed their armor to the project. He would load their bodies and their armor into sacks and mix them up with the usual loads of garbage and debris that were carted out of the barracks each day. Dumping the garbage was a commonplace in Jebus, and he could count on his position to get the whole convoy through the gates with minimum inspection. Once outside, they'd go as usual to the Valley of Hinnom, southeast of Jebus, to dump their garbage.

The stink that arose from Hinnom was notorious, and the surface of the valley was covered with nests of mosquitoes, horseflies, and various beetles who bred on the refuse, dead bodies, and the Jebus sewage. Anything dumped in the cesspool there sank irretrievably into the black waters.

The city authorities had bonfires lit from time to time to consume the garbage and putrefying bodies. The result was that the name Hinnom became synonymous with a place that looked and smelled of fire, flies, filth, and death. And over it, up in the sky, hovered Shibtai the vulture. It was his favorite station. The name, *ge hinnom*, passed into popular speech among Hebrews as the name of hell, of Gehenna, where the Lord of the Flies, Satan, the adversary of Adonai, dwelt in fire, filth, and living death.

"May all their Philistine brothers end up in the same stinking tomb," said Joshua lifting his glass of wine.

Life in Jebus was full of sharp contrasts. As Uri laid out his grisly plan, David woke lazily from his brief sleep. Warm in his blankets, he listened for a minute or two to the rain hammering on the roof. Slowly he became aware of the arm lightly encircling him, the body beside him. He opened his eyes and saw Lassatha's face beside his own, her eyes resting lovingly on him. Instinctively he smiled. Around Lassatha's lips a gentle expression played, half-smile, half-statement. He stirred slightly, feeling her warmth.

He removed her arm and hands, and she got up noiselessly from the couch, her eyes still looking into his. She picked up her stole and draped it around her shoulders, standing there for a moment, her arms by her sides, palms outward, the lamplight flickering over her otherwise naked, glowing body. David could not take his eyes off her. He realized he was now walking on what for him had been untrodden ground. And he was quietly asserting his right to be there. Her nakedness now seemed to him normal.

"It is nearly time for you to go, David," she said in accented Hebrew. But he knew there was something else between them that had to be played out. She was standing in front of him, her legs somewhat apart, her right hand stretched out to him.

He sat up, obeying some inner voice that softly dictated the ritual to him. It was as if he had always seen her beckon him in this fashion, as if he had always known her as part of his life. He swung his feet onto the floor, easing his body off the couch, and stood up.

She came forward and stripped him, removing the blankets from around his shoulders and body as well as the linen bandages they had placed around the red weal that marked his waist. When he was completely naked, she lifted her face to his. His lips moved wordlessly, and she read the question in his eyes.

"Lie down on the couch. It won't take long." He did as he was asked, and she started talking gently, softly in Egyptian, all the while her hands slowly caressing his body. She started with his hair and his head and face. And as he gazed at her and listened to her words, he realized there was a rhythm, a metric beat to her words, and that her hands were in unison with that beat. She seemed wholly abstracted from him, wholly absorbed in the ceremony, as if his body held a meaning for her that only her words and actions evoked.

Lassatha touched his eyes, his lips. His nose. His ears. His cheeks. His shoulders. His breasts. His belly. His hips. His genitals. His groin. His thighs. His knees, calves, ankles, feet, and toes. Her hands lingered nowhere but touched everywhere.

"Give me your hands, David." He lifted them and placed them gently in hers. She turned them over palms downward, placing one on top of the other. "Stretch your arms out at full length. He did. She took a small sip of wine from the vial and placed both his hands on top of his pubic hair and genitals. She bent down, her hands leaning lightly on his hips, and kissed the back of the topmost hand, letting some of the wine in her mouth flow over his hand and onto his body. Then she placed her lips on his. He felt her tongue parting his lips—they were quite yielding—and the little rush of warm wine over his teeth and gums.

She had straightened up by the time the wine was tingling on his tongue and in his throat. She lifted his hands from his body. "Sit up now and let me sit with you. It is almost over." He did so, and his body curved in order to look at her as she sat beside him, still holding his hands.

Outside, all were ready to depart and only David was missing. Uri and Joshua and Jesse waited about five minutes, then they made their way toward the inner rooms where David had been carried. At the door, they stopped. Uri held up his hand for silence. From inside, they could hear the sound of Lassatha's voice. They moved aside the curtain and looked in. David sat naked on the bed, Lassatha beside him. Jesse had never seen that look of joy and happiness on his son's face before. He glanced at Uri. The Hittite put his finger to his lips to quieten any tendency on Jesse's part to intervene. They withdrew noiselessly and went back to the courtyard.

"Uri, what the devil is going on?"

"That, my dear Jesse, is an Egyptian ritual. The Egyptians say that only a woman can release a boy into manhood—no! My foolish Jesse!" Jesse had become rigid. "No, no! Not that! That comes later! You don't understand the Egyptians. They know more about the human spirit than your scholars do. Believe me!"

Inside, Lassatha was just finishing and was speaking in Hebrew:

"... nakedness is not shameful. Lewdness is. Nakedness is for birth and for love and for death. You submitted to my control of your body now. So you ceased, in spirit and in will, to be independent. And this ceremony is a symbol of what the man, the real man does. He submits to a woman. She encases him, possesses him—if he submits without fear. You may enter many women. You may have much sweetness, but never love until you submit."

The spring following David's famous swim to Siloam brought him into his fourteenth year, to his passage into manhood and full participation in the life of the Covenant. It was also the spring that saw old Raham come within reach of his one hundredth year, a wholly stupefying age for that period.

It was a happy crowd gathered in the dappled sunlight under the trees in Raham's garden one morning. Everyone knew that in a few days more Bethlehem would have its best spring harvest in years, thanks to the farm implements that had been made from some of the iron brought from Jebus the year before. Jesse had decided to combine David's confirmation with the annual feast of his family. Everyone in the village had been invited.

Of the four boys to be confirmed, David was the youngest to be received as a man among men, a Hebrew among Hebrews.

When Raham spoke, there was no pain in his voice, only the joy of the day and the triumph of his vision. "Let our praise be full and let our hearts be echoes of the great *Hallelu Ya!* of the saints," he began. "For this day the Covenant is renewed once more. Not in flesh merely, as in the rite of circumcision of an unthinking child, but in the spirit and soul of a willing man who freely confirms his belonging in the Covenant and is freely accepted by Adonai through the other members. On this day, in accordance with the holy word given to our father, Moses, by Adonai, four young men are assembled in the presence of Adonai to be consecreated to his will and to his service.

"It was our father, Moses, who wrote down all the words of Adonai and who first related them to Adonai's people. And they all answered Moses with one heart and one voice: 'We will do the holy will of Adonai!'" Raham here raised for all to see his own precious copy of the Torah.

"These four young men are going to swear that they will defend the land, the Ark, and the Law. That they will see in every person and every thing the truth of Adonai. The Law tells us to open our eyes and see the glory of Adonai through the things of this world, but not to confound those things with that hidden glory. To all that! You, Eliel, son of Abdon! And you, Arad, son of Malcham! And you, Jether, son of Haniel! And you, David, son of Jesse! To all that you are about to swear."

Raham stood, then, and called each youth in turn to his side to swear loyalty to the Covenant, to the Law, and to the will of Adonai. It was a terrible oath, and although it was only five short words in Hebrew, those words remained with each one of them for the rest of his life.

David's turn came. As the three boys before him had done, he laid his right hand on the copy of the Law that Raham held out to him.

"What do you seek to do now, my son?" Raham intoned ritually.

"As Adonai lives, I swear on this Holy Law," David pronounced the oath unfalteringly. But when he started to remove his hand from the Scroll, something stirred in Raham's heart. For an instant the old man straightened up in his seat. His eyes were alight. He looked up at the young boy now over five feet eight inches tall, taller than most fully grown Hebrews. The sun shining from the east lit up the blond curls, so that David's head was encircled with a filigree halo of burnished gold. His clean-scrubbed skin, ruddy and fair, looked like new ivory in its youthful smoothness. The blue eyes looked directly at Raham's, frankly and trustingly, and now with a quiet question.

"Master Raham?" David had some idea that he had made a mistake. But David had not made a mistake. For a few moments Raham was transported far from that place. He was somewhere else in spirit. In long, wide paved streets crowded with Hebrews gaily dressed. In a great city graced with ample houses, crowned with tall towers, set among the mountains, in view of all the nations. And David had become immensely tall, immeasurably stronger and intensely beautiful, with the height of Adonai's heavens, the strength of Adonai's right hand, and the beauty of Adonai's Angel. Raham knew instinctively it was an end vision, the sort of "second sight" Adonai granted to his faithful ones just before they were called away to the eternal sleep.

"It's all right, child. Go in peace. I'm all right. Your mother, father, and brothers are waiting."

A few days later Jesse met Raham at the Rabbit's Head. The scholar spoke urgently. "There are things I must attend to now, Jesse, without delay. Right now, today. Please come to see me before sunset. Bring David with you. For sure?"

"For sure, Raham. For sure!"

Back in his own garden, Raham let his eyes wander over the hedge of bushes, beyond to Miller's Meadow, over to the copse of sycamores and oaks where the crows nested, and over to the falling slope of the terrain toward the Great Salt Sea set against the purple and blue mountains of Moab. He glanced up at the sky, noting the position of the sun. Unsurprised, he acknowledged the distant presence of old Shibtai high above him.

His gaze came back to his small garden where he had taught and the barn in which classes had been held on rainy days. He would not end this day sitting by the wall of his house as he had often done to watch the lengthening shadows.

The heaviness in his chest grew oppressive as he went upstairs, laboriously climbing each step up to the sleeping terrace on his roof. His breath came in short, inadequate gasps. As he lay down on the pallet, he did not put his copy of the Law back in its place but kept it with him. He stayed there for the rest of the day. Sometimes he slept a little. Whenever he awoke, he said the prayers he had taught so many others, prayers against the traps of the Evil One. Prayers for light. For peace. For refreshment. For joy. For an end to exile. For an endless day.

By the end of the afternoon the air had become chilly. He heard the evening wind beginning to sing in the trees and wrapped his blanket around him. But he continued to feel cold. As the shadows spread and the disk of the sun sank, he turned his head and watched all the colors of daylight turn gray and then black. He dozed again, but within minutes was awakened by a voice calling at the garden gate.

"Raham! Master Raham! Are you here?" Raham struggled over to the low parapet.

"Come, Jesse! Come up the stairs. Come, David! I have been waiting for you."

When Jesse saw Raham lying on the pallet, he knew for certain what he had only suspected before.

"Now, good friend, sit down beside me. And you, David, come sit beside me too. But first you must fetch my harp. You remember where it is? I keep it where I always kept it when I was your teacher."

"I remember, Master Raham." David's voice was quiet. He knew he would sing for the last time to this beloved old man.

"Jesse." Raham did not wait for David to return. "I must tell you, I am tired. Very tired. I am looking forward to a long, long sleep and to waking up to the sight of the glory on the face of Adonai. But there are certain things I want to be sure will be taken care of when I am gone."

"You know we will do whatever you ask, Raham."

Raham was quiet for a little while, listening to the sounds of day ending. There was no hurry. He watched David come back, holding the harp as Raham had taught him to do when he was so little he was barely able to span its seven strings.

"Jesse, you will take my copy of the Law here and my library of scrolls and papyri and tablets. Keep them all for my successor. Tomorrow you must send word to Samuel at Rama. He will appoint my successor. As to my burial, I want to be buried in the Field of the Scholars near the Ark at Kiryath-Yearim."

"That shall be done."

"Watch over David. I know you have always done that. But things will change now. Watch over him with great care. But when his time comes, don't hold him back. He will not be a shepherd all his life."

Jesse prayed he would know what to do when he was without Raham to consult.

"You will know." Jesse was startled that Raham seemed to read his thoughts. "Stubborn as you sometimes are, Jesse, you will know; and you will obey in the end.

"Now, my David"—Raham turned his head in the dusk— "you are a man."

"Yes, Master Raham. But I don't feel like a man just now. I don't want you to leave us!"

"Ah, David, let me tell you something. One day many years from now, when your blond hair is gray and your eyes have seen much more, and your heart has loved and pained, and your deeds for Adonai are done, you will know that there are those who have always watched over you, and that I have been and will be among them.

"Now the time is coming for you to leave me, my friend. But first, play a little for me, one last time. What will you play?"

"*Kokave El*. The Stars of God, Master Raham."

"*Kokave El*," Raham repeated, his eyes opening wide as he succumbed to his own thoughts about the stars of Adonai. "Good. But without tears, all right? Remember what I have told you. You are a man now. And I am just going home to rest."

The sound of David's harp was pure; not masses of notes this time as on many other occasions, but a melody of simple chords. His voice was clear. No tears, as Raham said. David sang of the Bethlehem he and Raham knew, of the Bethlehem he had known through Raham's words, of its sights and sounds, of the alphabet and other lessons Raham taught, of the peace at evening time, of the haze over the wheatfields. Each of his verses ended with the appearance of the stars of God, the *kokave el*, at the fall of night over the village.

The melody drew to its close before Raham realized it was over. David's music had put the dying man into a drifting meadow of dreams and recollections. He turned his head and looked at David. The boy was watching him expectantly. Raham struggled to a sitting position.

"I had something to say to you, my son. Something quite simple." He moved his head, taking a last look at the landscape he loved. The evening air gave an azure tint to trees, hills, slopes, fields. They could hear the lowing of the last cows being driven in from pasture. Over in the sycamores the crows had begun to congregate and caw, sending out the first signals that all were to come home for nightfall.

"A good evening for a parting," Raham said pleasantly. "Now, David, shortly in your life you'll find large gates opening. At present you're knocking at the door of Adonai's universe, the door of his divine mysteries. It's going to open. And you're going to find out about fate. You must release yourself and your desires from Bethlehem, your family, your

tribe of Judah. You must blend all you are with the greater
message of destiny." David, his hands holding Raham's shoulders, could feel the old man trembling with his efforts.

Raham continued, "Remember never to hesitate to say you
were wrong. Always be able to say you've erred, you've
sinned, you need forgiveness. Always. It is not so much sin
but obduracy in sin that angers Adonai."

The crows, at that moment, set up a very loud cawing.
Raham blinked over in the direction of the sycamores. "Our
friends are right. It's time for bed and sleep. Now lay me down,
son. Gently, for I ache in all my bones." Then he waved both
Jesse and David away. "Go now. Both of you. You, Jesse,
come back tomorrow morning early and take care of everything."

When they were gone, Raham settled down for the remainder of his struggle. As the last light was disappearing he felt
the weight on his chest lifting. But his feet and legs had gone
terribly cold. As the night darkness gathered around him, he
began to recite the old prayers he had recited at hundreds of
deathbeds during his years in Bethlehem.

It was then that he began to hear a low, murmuring sound,
as if many people were approaching the side of the bed talking
in low voices. He had the distinct feeling that they were his
friends, talking about him, coming for him. All the while his
breathing got more and more difficult, and his vision began to
fade away. That cold numbness now advanced up his belly and
invaded his lower chest.

The sounds of those voices kept on increasing in volume
and grew closer. And he began to weep because he thought,
When they arrive, I shall not be able to see them or recognize
their faces. Then there was a violent wave of pain—it seemed
to him it started in the tips of his fingers and toes and rushed
through his entire body, foaming through his arteries, bones,
muscles, organs, up to the top of his head. He heard himself
crying out, heard the death rattle in his own throat, and the
expulsion of the last little pockets of air that had remained in
his lungs. And he felt all this as if he were completely separate
from his body yet still in some way tied to it.

At that moment he saw them all and knew them all. Their
names came back to him. Hanna and Eli, and Abner, and
Ifibosheth, and Malki, and Tamyahu, and all the others, maybe
a thousand of them whom he had helped to die over the years.
All of them loving, ushering him onward to a new destination.
"Come home, Raham! Come home, old friend! Come and see

what we all have prepared for you in the Great House of Adonai's Blessed Ones."

Raham answered, but he couldn't hear his own words. He reached out to the loving voices, smiled at the smiling faces. Just a moment more. And one vision before he left his body completely. It was the face of Samuel, he thought, but shining in a wisdom more than Samuel's. And then it was the face of David, but smiling in a beauty greater than David's. As he moved away, he knew he saw not those beloved faces but the source of what he loved in them, the source of their very gifts, of Samuel's wisdom, of David's beauty. He knew that all his life he had been the servant of what he now began to see. His tears had been for it. His desires had been for it, just as his sins and his weaknesses and his infidelities had been against it. His labors, his travels, his hungers, his loneliness, all had been for it. All the good he had ever done, all the love he had ever given and felt, all of it now shone upon him from the very face of good, from the very eyes of God. His last thought was a prayer: "Adonai, our God, you are One."

The streets and cultivated lands of Bethlehem were draped over a highland spur of Judah like a patchwork gown whose skirts trailed over the pastureland of Beraka, the "Blessing," some seven miles to the south toward Hebron.

In this often dry and always unpredictable land of Judah, to own sheep meant the difference between starvation and plenty. Sheep gave milk for cheese and yogurt and a kind of liquid butter. They provided wool for cloth and skins for warm cloaks and jackets and britches and gloves against the cold winds that came in from the desert cutting across the hills like a knife. They gave tallow and meat. Their horns could be made into weapons, containers, or pipes. Their ground-up bones served as mortar, their hooves as a source of glue, their tails, genitals, eyes and ears as delicacies. Even the droppings of the sheep could be dried and used for fuel.

For as long as anyone could remember, Beraka had always been in the care of Jesse's family. Its lush, rolling land, roughly a mile wide and twice as long, sloped down to the deserts on the south and east. It was fenced off from the rough, thickly forested hills and gullies rising to its west. Its northern side was protected by rocky cliffs whose caves had for centuries given protection from sudden rainstorms to shepherds and sheep alike. The thick grass of Beraka was fed by those rains, by the morning mists, and by the waters running off from the higher ground to the west and north. Beraka had an especially nutritious mixture of herbs and grass plants which produced sheep and lamb meat renowned for its delicacy.

The Beraka pastures were broad and rich enough so that all the flocks of Bethlehem could forage there. Yet it was small enough so that a shepherd with nine or ten good men and a few well-trained sheep dogs could protect it.

Since the time when Jesse and Raham had decided that David would replace Omri when he retired, Omri had walked nearly every inch of Beraka with David and taught him all he knew, how to keep the pasture evenly grazed, the signs that meant wild animals were near, the great grottolike caves where sheep could be sheltered from weather or wild animals. They hunted together for rabbit, deer, wild goat, quail, and partridge. They watched ewes drop their lambs, tended to sheep sores, worked the dogs, mended fences, and penned the flocks below the cliffs at night. There was nothing that could be taught that Omri had not shown David. The rest David would have to learn by himself.

It was a brilliant morning, cleared by the late rains that had fattened the harvest, when David rode out with Jesse to take up his post. Jesse had given David his own favorite camel to be his mount at Beraka. But the parting from Shoshanna had been hard, even though Ozem had reminded her that David would be home for all the feast days.

"Well, at least you're not marching off to Gibea," Shoshanna had said.

David took very little with him. A few clothes, his sling and slingshot pouch, some precious iron throwing knives, Raham's harp, some warm clothes.

"You'll be all right here, son," Jesse said as he turned to leave. He wanted to say that he'd miss David, but words like that did not come easily to Jesse.

David was a born shepherd. All his skills suited the life at Beraka. He quickly earned the respect of the men who worked the flocks. They were all Hebrews and all Bethlehemites.

If there was any doubt that David could lead them, it did not last long. He was up before any of them every day, inspecting the fences, noting the wild animal tracks, testing the flow of springs, examining the flocks. The men found that none of them could best him in the use of sling or throwing knife, and that he could ride harder and longer than any of them.

By nightfall every evening the sheep had been penned. Then

David and his men built a charcoal fire and cooked their evening meal. Sometimes they chatted. Sometimes David played his harp and sang. At shearing and lambing time, just about all of Bethlehem came to Beraka and lived in black-brown goatskin tents. There was dancing and feasting among the shearers, and it was always an occasion for flirting. In good weather they all slept in the open. In winter they sheltered in the caves and grottoes.

In less than a year Shoshanna could see already the change that Beraka was working in David, and it made her both happy and sad. Although just under fifteen, he was already six feet tall. His dark blond hair was bleached by the sun, his fair skin bronzed.

Shoshanna also saw something else—the self-reliance that David had developed. Each time he came home she looked for the boy, and each time she saw him more a man. And the years passed quickly.

Jesse commented less than the others on David because he saw his son often. He rode down to Beraka with Ozem or Shammai every week or two to take David some of Shoshanna's griddle bread and other supplies.

"There's been talk of a hard dry season to the south," he remarked to David on one of his visits about three years after Raham's death.

"Has there been enough rain in Bethlehem?" David asked. He knew, as everyone did, that Hebron or Beersheva or any town could bake in the sun while a village barely two miles away might be drowning.

"Adonai has been good to us."

When Jesse left that day, David went off alone to the place he had come to love above all others at Beraka. It was a low rise not far from an overhanging cliff some distance to the east of the sheep pens. There were two large wild oaks there and a cluster of maples, acacia, and cypress. If ever the shepherds needed David and could not find him, they learned to look for him there. They began to call the place David's Rest; and so it was called ever after.

As much as the flocks or the rolling pastures, those trees spoke to David of all the things Raham had taught him. Of life in death, of Adonai's constancy, of hope and renewal and purpose in the majestic passage of the seasons.

One occasion for passion and maturing occurred just about three years after David came to Beraka, when he was almost seventeen and fully six feet tall. All the pens were full of lambs.

It was four days before the Day of Atonement, which David planned to spend in Bethlehem. Toward evening he passed by the southwestern corner of the pastures and chatted with Joram and Merari, who were stationed there for that night. He guessed from their breath that they'd had a barley whiskey or two. He wandered slowly up toward the fences that ran along the edge of the western slopes, and there he noticed fresh tracks. It looked like three sets—a jackal for sure, almost certainly a bear, probably a lion. He returned to Joram and Merari to warn them and hurried back to his grotto for food, extra shot, and knives. By the time the sun was setting, he was back at the shelter with Joram and Merari.

"You each take your regular watch. No drinking. I'll be outside," he promised. He passed through the fences, following the animal tracks and climbing into the rocky terrain. He examined his surroundings until he found a small cave up on the slope, overlooking the tracks but giving a view down to the pens.

Night came on suddenly and he lay down, his head cushioned on the palms of his hands, looking at the stars. He woke to the early morning light, his nose warning him of what he would find. Only Gora the jackal had that smell, rancid and dirty, reeking of death. He rose and surveyed the surrounding undergrowth, eventually spotting the black-brown form lying between two clumps of bushes. Gora was waiting patiently for her morning meal, which would be whatever the predators left her. He settled down to wait, too. It took about an hour.

The birds suddenly stopped singing. There was a quick scurrying in the undergrowth and the squeal of a weasel, then the telltale grunting and clumping farther up the track. David's mouth tightened. Only Dov the bear had that arrogance; most other animals crept along as silently as possible. David was not mistaken. It was a young male, about five foot tall, David calculated, about two years old and between three and four hundred pounds in weight.

David glanced over to Gora's covert. The wily jackal had not budged. She lay there, her belly flattened to the ground, her muzzle between her front paws, her yellow eyes fixed greedily on Dov, who would provide her breakfast.

David made up his mind. He laid aside his slingshot and selected a heavy throwing knife. At this age, perhaps Dov could be frightened off because of his inexperience. But Gora's behavior was puzzling. She still had not budged. Normally by now she would be slinking along parallel to Dov. Dov never

attacked Gora. Gora never interfered with Dov. She only
wanted what Dov left. Nevertheless, David felt it was time to
act.

When Dov was close enough, he stood and hurled the knife.
Chunk! It hit Dov in the side between the ribs and haunches.
In a rising scream of pain, Dov reared to his full height, then
rolled over roaring, pouring blood. But he had fallen on the
haft, which only drove the blade in deeper. He got up screaming
and growling and pawing at his side. Crawling on all fours,
he lurched into the underbrush. As David watched, he heard
another sound that chilled his heart—the unmistakable bleating
of sheep in danger. Then the barking of the dogs and the shouts
of the shepherds.

Gora lifted her heavy-bellied form and bared her teeth. The
kill was near. Bounding up the slope came Ari the lion, his
head lifted, a lamb between his jaws. About fifty yards behind
him came the dogs. The shepherds were not yet in sight. Obviously, the dogs had surprised Ari as he crept in on the flock.
But he had snatched a lamb and was making for the high
ground.

David forgot Gora and Dov. The thing that transfixed and
enraged him was the sight of that inert white form caught in
Ari's jaws and its weak bleating. David's nostrils flared, his
eyes narrowed. In an instant he was transformed. He did not
know it then, but the lust to kill was on him in full force, and
now he was its instrument.

Joram and Merari got there just as David was about to
spring. From their vantage point, David crouched above them
on the ledge, seemed to have doubled in size. He held a knife
in his right hand; his legs were apart and slightly bent at the
knees, his body flexed.

The shouts of the shepherds died on their lips as they saw
his face. It was still David's face, of course, but completely
changed. There was no longer any beauty there, only hate.
They froze at the scream of rage that came from his throat as
he leaped heavily across Ari's back, the left arm hooking
around the lion's neck, locking its windpipe, his two long legs
clamping like a vise around Ari's withers, his right hand drawing the knife across Ari's throat in deep, furious slashes.
David's belly and chest were lying on Ari's back, the side of
his head resting on the back of Ari's neck and head. Ari opened
his mouth to breathe, to expel the blood from his throat, to
punish this sudden lethal nuisance.

The lamb dropped to the ground, but the lion's momentum

carried him and David on another few yards. David was still screaming, but now he had driven the knife in under the left forepaw, piercing Ari's heart. Joram and Merari watched as man and lion rolled over and over and then lay still.

For a moment the shepherds thought David had been hurt, too, for he continued to cling to the lion's body. But he was merely tasting the death of Ari, feeling the warm, inanimate bulk, listening to the last drop of air fleeing from the lungs. Then, with a quick movement, he slipped out from under the dead lion, his face still white with anger, the dagger cocked in his hand, seeking the lamb. But he whirled as the raging, wounded form of Dov came crashing through the bushes, its front paws raised to smite.

In what seemed one motion, David dropped the dagger, pulled a knife and threw it. Chunk! It stuck quivering beneath Dov's left shoulder blade. Another followed it instantaneously. Chunk! It hit just below the solar plexus. David sidestepped the lurching body and the murderous sweep of those paws. His third knife split the small of Dov's back. Dov went down, roaring and screaming. He raised himself on his front paws, his face and body matted with dust and blood. That dreadful hand of David's drew another knife. He drew back and flung it with all his force, haft-deep into the animal's throat. Dov fell back, thrashed once, and died. There was a rustle in the bushes behind David. He turned, saw, and threw in one long, smooth deliberate movement. Gora yelped and groaned. She came out staggering, the knife deep in her eye. She fell and rolled down the slope on top of Dov.

"Here, Merari! Joram! Here! Come here!" It was David's voice, harsh and commanding. "Help this little one." Already David had scooped up the lamb and was running down to the shepherds. When they took the lamb from him, they could not bear to look into David's eyes, but they marveled at how tenderly he handled the helpless little bundle of wool. His knees were bleeding from the struggle with Ari, and either the lion or the bear had slashed through the leather on his left arm. Otherwise he was unhurt, although covered with blood. "This little one," he continued, "may have had a rib or two broken, or the legs. Take care of him. I'm going to skin these carcasses. The other jackals will be here with the vultures very soon.

"Didn't you see the lion?" he asked Merari and Joram. They started to stammer.

"Were you drinking?" Their eyes betrayed the answer.

David's fist crashed into Merari's face, knocking him back-

ward over the rocks and bushes. The back of his hand caught
Joram in the temple, and he reeled off like a top to fall across
Merari.

"Get up! Both of you."

They struggled to their feet. "If this ever happens again, I
will kill you both with my bare hands. Now get back to work."

As his anger subsided, fear suddenly came upon David.
Fear of the killer lust that had consumed him, of the strange
exultant pleasure he had felt when the animals died beneath his
hand.

On his first evening back at home for Atonement, the feeling
suddenly came to him again, although in a fresh way. As he
stood in the assembly of the men of the village, David found
himself measuring his shoulders and height against those of the
men around him. Without thinking he was comparing their
strength with his own, and as he did so, traces of the blood
lust flickered.

Later, at a village celebration, he found himself evaluating
the women in a way he never had before. It wasn't any particular physical attribute—slimness of waist, fullness of breast,
glossiness of hair, nimbleness, age, beauty—it was rather
something framed within their physiques, and only now as
obvious to him as their eyes or feet.

Whenever this happened—it was never deliberate—he felt
that same disturbing power which the encounter with the animals had awakened, and it frightened him.

At no time during his stay did he become so conscious of
the change in himself as when he danced alone or sang and
played the harp to entertain his fellow villagers. They noted
the difference with satisfaction, but David found it disturbing.
Before he had danced with the grace and abandon of a young
boy, now it was with a passion and verve that mesmerized his
audience but abstracted him. It was the same when he played
the harp and sang. "We're now listening to a man," the villagers
said, but David felt the passion and the rage—he did not even
know for what—coming through his voice and his fingers.

Shoshanna's reaction capped his fear. She became shy with
him, almost embarrassed. And by some tacit agreement they
never once held each other as they used to, and they simply
abandoned the frank conversations they used to have.

In all of this David betrayed no exterior sign of his uncertainty. He affected not to see the admiring looks of the mar-
riageable maidens or the appraising glances of their parents.

He simply refused to acknowledge that he himself was spontaneously assessing women. He clung to the family ikon of him as the beautiful and protected Benjamin, even though in practical matters he now stood in no need of any protection. But deep down his fear lurked, and his questions echoed painfully: Must a man, to be a man, have passions so vivid and so dangerous?

On the last day of David's stay, Joshua came over with surprising news: there was an expanded market for Bethlehem lambs in Jebus. Joshua and Uri had confirmed four buyers for all the live lambs Jesse could spare for delivery within a month. It was the first time since his Siloam exploit that David might be able to visit the city.

"Have them all sorted and washed and ready to go," Joshua said to David. "Put plenty of straw with them in the carts to cushion the bumps. I'll come over to Beraka at the full moon and we'll take them up together."

Three weeks later, when Joshua and his usual retinue of slaves, servants, and bodyguards arrived, David was ready. He even had packed his harp. They set out immediately and reached Jebus late that same afternoon. After delivering their lambs and collecting payment, they went straight to Uri's house for the night.

It was almost four years later since David and Uri had seen each other. David was now a little bit taller than Uri, and Uri was astonished by David's size, strength, and grace.

"Nothing could make me happier than seeing you now a man!" he cried. "By God! You could be a king!"

David smiled shyly in response, and from that day on Uri treated him as he would any other man. For Uri, the boy David was gone.

Uri announced that he had taken a wife, a Hittite woman— "not a famous beauty, but she's a good mother for my children and a good wife for me," he said with his usual precision.

His memory sparked, and before he knew what he was saying, David asked: "Lassatha? What's happened to her?" Uri and Joshua broke into delighted laughter, and David, after spluttering a little, joined in.

Lassatha, Uri explained, was still with his household and was now in charge of all the servants and the marketing. "I don't know if you want to see her," he added, "but Lassatha certainly wants to see you. Dinner is in two hours; how about a wash and a rest?" Uri took them to their rooms.

When he entered his room, David knew she was there, and when she came to greet him he was shocked. He was now looking down on her, whereas four years ago she had been a bit taller than he.

"Master David!" she said with a smile. "Welcome! Your bath is ready." During the four years Lassatha had blossomed. Her breasts were now full, her hair long, lustrous and aromatic. She led him into the bath, which was square in the Hittite fashion and sunk to floor level and made entirely of marble. And the Hittites had acquired the Egyptian habit of perfuming the water and the soap.

Lassatha stripped David and fingered barely healed wounds on his left arm and knees that were a result of his encounter with the lion and the bear. "You must tell me later how you got these, my lord," she said. "Now sit in the bath, and I will scrub you clean." He stepped in and sat down, and for the next ten minutes she thoroughly scrubbed and rinsed his entire body.

Between his sensations four years ago and now, David could detect only one small difference. Then, he had been vividly conscious of the pleasure of being bathed. Now, he was conscious of her hands in another way. Lassatha wrapped him in an enormous towel while she changed the bath water, and he told her briefly how he had gotten his scars.

"If it happened like that, my lord, then you have tasted blood. And that marks a new thing in a man."

"Is that what a man is for you, Lassatha, someone who has wanted to kill?"

"It's one way to become a man, my lord." She sprinkled some perfume powder in the fresh bath water and beckoned him. Lassatha trembled slightly as he stepped away from the towel, naked. She rinsed him clean, dried him thoroughly, perfumed his skin, then provided him with the long house robe that was customary among the Hittites.

"Those Hittites have some good ideas!" David remarked good-humoredly when she had finished. Lassatha laughed.

"The best is yet to come, my lord," she teased. "Follow me!"

She took him to his bedroom and installed him on the couch. She propped him up with cushions and served him the heated wine so coveted as an aperitif.

"Lassatha," David said, "for four long years I have wanted to ask you a question."

"Yes, my lord."

"Suppose you had not 'awakened' me in the manner of your

people four years ago—is it possible that I would not be as troubled now as I am?"

"No, dear David." The use of his familiar name gave him a strange sensation. She seemed to have a power over him that he had not guessed. "One way or another, every man wakes. And you would have awakened, too. Tell me, while you were slaughtering that lion and bear, what was your uppermost thought?"

"My lamb," he said truthfully.

"That is not usual. And I believe that you were saved from waking up to be a killer by the fact that a woman—I myself— consecrated your manhood and opened it to love." As she said this he felt that, unbidden, his whole self, body and soul, was opening to her and that some strange force was welling up in him. All, somehow or other, at the bidding of Lassatha. His muscles tensed.

She saw his fright and stood up. "But why must we 'wake up'? And what do you mean by 'love'?" he asked almost sadly.

"If you were observant of your famous Law, you would say: 'Because that's the way Adonai made us.' That's why and that's the answer. And that's why the Lady Hatich, who saved your life, I believe, asked me to awaken you. Do you think she would have done evil to you?"

"No."

"Then what do you want?" Lassatha was becoming exasperated by his refusal to understand. "To breed babies by an ever fattening, ever aging wife, while you loaf off, like Joshua and Uri, for a turn with a half-raddled whore? To lie with men or dally with beautiful boys?" Her tone was almost contemptuous. "Or perhaps you'd prefer to lie naked and alone in the sun as the young Jebusites do on the roofs of their fathers' houses, your eyelids dazzled, soaking up the sun's warmth as though it were some distant lover? Perhaps you would content yourself with that monster Shemesh in his sky, and you fool yourself that the sun's rays are merely warm hands, and sweet sleep overcomes you, until old Shemesh drives you into momentary rigidity while you sleep and forces every drop of semen from you, and you turn on your side to dream safe dreams? Is that what you want?"

David stared at her, astonished by her vehemence and imagery. This was a woman, and he was awed.

"Now it is my turn to ask forgiveness, my lord." There was genuine affection in her eyes, and David saw it.

He was deeply puzzled. "Can we talk again later, after dinner?"

"Yes, my lord. Now rest."

Uri led his two guests out onto the high balcony of his house, which looked south over the walls of the city and down over the desert. They sat there sipping after-dinner wine and discussing Saul, Philistines, and the Hebrew clans in the central highlands. All three felt that soon a major clash would develop. Finally Joshua stood up and stretched himself.

"Uri, my friend! You promised to take me to see those Cypriot dancers."

David waited until he heard the clatter of the bolts in the doors below and Joshua's belly laugh fading down the street, then got up, intending to fetch his harp. Lassatha stood in the doorway.

"My lord desires company now?"

"Yes! Yes! Come and sit down." She came over smiling; calmly she lay beside him. David, very much at ease, leaned on one elbow, looking out over her at the valley and the desert beyond.

"When you see—when a man sees—a young girl with that peculiar pining look on her face, how should he deal with it?"

"More or less like a girl or woman who sees the same stupid, cowlike gaze on the face of a boy or a man." Her tone was as tart as the answer. David laughed. He saw the amused smile on her face. He ran a finger over her cheek in mock reproof. Her eyes remained closed.

"As long as you can laugh, we Egyptians say, you can be saved. About the pining: it is not love. Avoid the piners, David. They only love themselves. And they are a bore." He laughed again. She placed her hand lightly in his. Her darkened profile was silhouetted in the moonlight.

"This 'awakening' business. Does that mean learning to love?"

"Yes. Chiefly. But much else besides."

"What else?"

"Just as in shedding blood, much else." They were silent for a while. Somewhere up the street, people were dancing to music. David could hear the soft beat of drums and the ting-tong-tang of a lyre.

"Is this peacefulness part of love?"

"Yes. But there's much more to it." He felt he understood, at least in part. Since they had lain there holding hands, he had experienced an increasing sensation of sweetness and freedom, an incalculable and pleasurable lightness, as though he had been cushioned in such soft material that he could feel nothing on his skin—except the touch of Lassatha's hand.

Because he had no emotion corresponding to the feeling from her hand, he was suddenly frightened. Her eyes were open and shining with some searing absorption in him, some penetration of his inner being. He jerked his hand away and sat up.

"Does Adonai forbid love, David?"

"Not between man and wife."

"But men and women become lovers, don't they?"

"Yes, but it is forbidden."

"I am not talking about fornicating with a whore. I am talking about making love."

"I know. I know. It is forbidden."

"Well then, my Hebrew, you Hebrews have a far greater problem than we. For we worship Astarte, who will bless the fulfillment of our desires as lovers and will lead us down the mystic corridor of love. She will not—some say she cannot—protect us from the ills that flow from that fulfillment. There is always and ultimately our Lord Baal." She shuddered. "He stands towering at the end of that corridor lovers have entered. They must pass by his throne. He makes the final decision."

"For the Hebrews, there is only one God. Adonai. Your Astarte and your Baal and all the others—Kemosh, Asshur, Ra, all of them, are false gods. They don't exist. And Adonai has told us that to love other than your wife or husband is fornication or adultery."

"Do you really believe that?"

"Yes."

"But how does Adonai help at those awful moments?"

"What awful moments?"

"Like now, David."

He answered feebly. "What's particular about now?"

Lassatha groaned. "David, it's what you're doing now, sitting on a balcony viewing life from on high. You can't descend into the street and mingle with the rest of us. You don't want to descend. You insist on being safe. Well, you can't have it always and not pay a penalty." She began to sob quietly.

"Lassatha," he said. His lips were dry. He drank some wine.

"It's rare, you know. For mortals." She ignored him. "But it does happen. Someone remains loveless for decades, living for half a lifetime or more without ever feeling the warmth, seeing the light of precious love.

"In their ever growing desperation, these luckless people get to know everything about love except love itself. They mimic its words, act out its glory—like an artist freezing in winter cold who paints the picture of a fire, thinking that he can warm himself at its side. Finally, the goddess takes pity. Once! Just once! Without warning or notice, she smiles on these abandoned creatures.

"Believe me, David!" Her even voice vibrated with passionate resonance. "There can be no forgiveness in heaven or on this earth for someone who shrinks from that touch. He will pay his debt in a bitterness beyond telling." Lassatha fell silent, her eyes closed tightly but her lips moving soundlessly. David could see the gleam of tears on her lashes.

"Lassatha, what are you saying?"

"I am praying, David," she said simply through her tears. "Praying that you will not pay that terrible penalty. Perhaps"— she gave him a wan smile—"your Adonai has a special alchemy for mending human hearts. Perhaps."

"But," David protested, "what penalty? What will I have done wrong?"

"After all your locked-in safety. After being with so many who love you and offer you love that you never return, someday, somewhere, you will meet a woman. She will mean everything to you. In a flash you'll know that you waited for her all those years. But when once you have her, it will be too late. Not too late for love. You *will* love her. That's the pity of it. But too late, I mean, for love's celebration. You'll be merely love's custodian. You will not create the happiness of that one woman because you will not have cared about the happiness of so many before her.

"I love you too much to wish that misery upon you. My lovely David!"

He shivered at that phrase. He knew she was waiting, but he said nothing.

"Say to me, David, at least that it is because your god Adonai forbids us to be lovers. Say at least this!"

But he could not because that was not the reason. He could not admit to himself that he knew what she desired and what he too desired and that only fear of losing himself kept him from her. "I don't know what you mean, Lassatha," he began.

"God help you, David, my lovely David." Her voice broke. "May your god help you. For I cannot."

* * *

One day David stayed so long at David's Rest that he decided to sleep there that night. It must have been after two in the morning when Falash, the best of his dogs, woke him with her deep, insistent growling. David quickly saw what had roused her supicions. A band of some twenty or so men, all on camels, was coming up a gully on the desert side, but not very distant from where David lay.

Trouble for sure. No armed groups traveled here at night without nefarious intent. And there were too many in this group for it to be a simple poaching expedition. David listened. The other dogs were quiet. He sent Falash back to the pens, tested his sling, counted his knives. He swiftly edged down toward the gully. As the camels drew cautiously closer, he could see that the riders were not Hebrews. They looked like Amalekites.

Trouble indeed! The Amalekites had always hated the Hebrews, even though they too were descended from Abraham through Isaac's son, Esau, who had been tricked out of his rightful inheritance by Isaac's other son, Jacob, ancestor of the Twelve Tribes of Israel. The enmity of the Amalekites was a constant reminder of Esau's undying resentment. Moses had had to fight the Amalekites on his way out of Egypt.

The Amalekites were warrior nomads of the southern desert and a formidable enemy. They swept in from the horizon in a welter of arrows and javelins, killing, burning, raping, looting, and disappearing just as rapidly back into the silent Negev or the plateaus of Sinai. As a people, they had abominable customs and mores. The word of an Amalekite was synonymous with betrayal. "The Amalekite trick" was a common expression for poisoning. Every pact was sealed in blood. Every wrong was settled in blood. Every celebration was crowned with human sacrifice.

Normally the Amalekites kept to the desert, and woe to the caravan that crossed the Negev or the Sinai without the weapons to protect itself or a costly pass from the Amalekites. But when rain water failed and drought hit the oases, the Amalekites would come north to raid the nearest fertile land—Judah. If this was an Amalekite scouting party checking to see if any of Saul's army was near, it was as certain as sunrise that the Amalekites would soon be swarming over the land like locusts.

David was well hidden in the brush when the camels drew level with his hiding place. He waited until they had all passed, then slid out until he had a clear view of the last rider. There was a swishing sound as his sling gathered speed, a whistle as the shot sped through the night air, and suddenly the pained shrieks of the camel as the shot pierced its rump, sending it into a sudden gallop that stampeded the entire cavalcade. No sooner had David's shot hit the camel than he sent a knife sailing in a sure, quick arc between the shoulder blades of the rider on that last camel. The man flung his hands up, screamed, and fell to the ground as his camel and the other riders disappeared into the night.

David gave Ahitai the Amalekite's clothing and sent him speeding north to Bethlehem. "Give this bundle to my father. Tell him exactly what happened. There was a party of about twenty scouts. They've made it this far north; so they know we have no soldiers between here and Beersheva. It won't be long before they'll be back for the kill."

When news of the Bethlehem incident reached Samuel, it seemed to him that this was how Adonai would pay the treacherous Agag and his tribe for their wickedness. The drought could be Adonai's instrument to drive the Amalekites north into the trap which Samuel could spring.

Samuel placed the shimmering Ephod around his neck and knelt for hours in earnest contemplation. And when he rose he had learned from Adonai what had to be done.

By the time the gates of Gibea closed behind Samuel, the high heat of the day had passed. The prophet went directly to the cedar house and sat with Saul, Jonathan, and Abner in the room where they often held council.

Samuel said, "The Lord who sent me to anoint you king speaks this day to you. Listen well, Saul. The Lord Adonai says: 'I will punish Amalek. Their nation shall be destroyed. They have opposed my people, and they have not repented. Now go, Saul, and smite Amalek and utterly destroy all that they have and are; kill both man and woman, infant and suckling, ox and sheep, camel and ass.' And it will be a test for you, anointed of the Lord and beloved of this old, weary prophet."

Saul sat silent and solemn. When he spoke, his thoughts were practical. "What you say is well and good, Samuel. Our people have fought the Amalekites for four hundred years. Now they have made their greedy alliance with the Philistines, fattening themselves with gold and Shekelath with iron. Certainly I want to destroy them, but how am I to do it? How am I to obey the Lord?"

"We know the drought has driven Agag close to Beersheva.

He knows by now that we have no armed camp anywhere from Bethlehem to Beersheva.

"Soon he will be ready to attack and plunder Beersheva. Adonai has put the whole Amalek nation in reach of your sword. We will plan well, we will move swiftly, with surprise as our ally, and we will fight on terrain that will make twelve thousand Hebrews more deadly than two hundred thousand Amalekites."

Saul understood. Before dawn he had dispatched fast-riding messengers to every part of Judah with the now familiar call to battle: "The king commands every man who can fight to bring arms and food and assemble this day at Telaim. So commands Saul. So commands Samuel."

In the first gray light of morning, after a nightlong discussion of strategy, Samuel repeated in Saul's ears the exact command of Adonai. "Destroy the Amalekites."

The long shadows of early morning seemed to cast dark fingers into Samuel's thoughts as he made his solitary way back to Rama. He pondered on Saul's actions, remembering all the times he had begun in obedience only to waver in fear or arrogance.

All those times Adonai had forgiven him, but this time there would be no forgiveness. This holy war against Agag was to be Saul's *akeda,* the fearful final test that Adonai gave his most important servants before he finally confirmed them in his service.

Some measure of *akeda* was demanded of all Hebrews. In faith and trust and obedience they had to turn from all other gods as enemies of their very jealous and unseen God.

But it always seemed there was a special *akeda* for the great ones of Israel: "He who receives more is asked for more." Early or late, that moment came, as it had for Moses, for Joshua, son of Nun, for Gideon, for Abraham, for Samuel himself.

And now that moment had come for Saul. Saul had only to slay the enemy whom he hated, and destroy all that his enemy possessed. Surely he would be worthy. But, Samuel thought, what if he were not?

Never had the Hebrews responded to a battle call with such alacrity as to Saul's summons to fight Agag. Everyone knew that bad times in the desert meant Amalekite raids in the land.

Abner led the standing army of three thousand men down from Gibea. Jonathan led his five hundred archers. By the time

Saul arrived, ten thousand Judeans waited at Telaim, together with men from Benjamin and Ephraim and Manasseh. Abner had already sent scouts into the desert. "The whole Amalekite nation has assembled. And the Kenites, too." Abner sketched a rough map in the dirt for Saul. Telaim was about three miles north of the desert valley where the Amalekites were encamped. "Their spearhead force is here, a little to the eastern side of the cliffs. Their main force is close by, right about here. Agag's tents lie between the two, here. The remainder of the Amalekites are to the rear. There must be at least twenty-five thousand of them."

"How many fighting men?" Saul asked.

"Probably twelve thousand, or a little under."

"And the Kenites, where are they?"

"Toward the rear, behind Agag's army, near the Amalekites, here."

The Kenites, Semites also, lived in the lands roamed by the nomad Amalekites. They were a peaceful, mostly sedentary people who supplied the Amalekites with arms, musical instruments, and dairy products.

"After dark, Abner, when the Amalekite fires are dying," Saul instructed him, "send scouts back to the valley with a message for the Kenite leaders. Adonai's word is clear. It is the Amalekites we are out to destroy. The Kenites are not our enemies, although they are forced to serve Amalek. Adonai remembers how they helped his people as they fled from the Pharaoh out of Egypt. Therefore, tell them to flee tonight."

When darkness fell on Telaim, Saul's battalions began their preparations.

It was an hour or more before sunrise when the Amalekite women, rising to build their cooking fires, saw that the Kenites had gone.

When the word was brought to Agag, he gave a terrible roar. Known popularly as "Bloody Belly," Agag, like all Amalekites, was short, broad-shouldered and brown-skinned, with the tightly cropped hair of a desert fighter. What distinguished Agag was his girth and weight. Agag's broad frame was one irregular mountain of overlapping fatty flesh. His two breasts puffed up to his chin and cascaded over a bulging middle and a still more protuberant belly. He could not hang his arms by his sides or join them in front of him.

The body sloped in from the undulating hips to the tips of the feet, each thigh and calf as round and puffed as a camel's behind. The grossness of his body was further emphasized by the frightening bulk of his genitals. Testicles and organ hung in front of his thighs wrapped in a vivid red cloth. He had gargantuan sexual appetites, ate voraciously of red meat and drank gallons of desert wine several times a day. Although he had to be lifted on and off his camel, in close infighting he had never been bested. He had the brute strength of a mountain bear in his arms.

Agag, in addition, was a very powerful man because of the ferocity of his tribe and the almost fanatical following he had among them. Alliance with him was sought even by some Pharaohs.

"Disappeared!" Agag roared again. "Those stinking dogs of Kenites! I smell treachery. Wake the camp! I want all my chieftains here immediately!"

Agag had barely begun the council of his chieftains when the first scouts were back. Their reports were reassuring. There were Hebrews assembled at Telaim, but they had built no earthworks. They were still asleep, and even the guards were asleep at their stations. There were not more than three thousand of them, and they were not even formed into battalions. Agag's triumph already gleamed from his pig eyes. He moved his huge bulk with surprising speed, leading the way out of his tent. "This valley will be their cemetery. To the camels! We'll eat the entrails of the Hebrew dogs tonight!"

The roar of Agag's angry threats was drowned in a sudden bedlam from the camel pens. Burning arrows like shooting stars were arching through the air, falling on the piles of straw where the camels were kept. Flames suddenly licked their flanks and heads. Shrieking animals stampeded in every direction, knocking down tents, trampling the shouting men who scattered everywhere trying to escape flying hooves and hurtling bodies. More burning arrows were streaming in from every direction. Every tent seemed aflame. It was Saul's first surprise for Agag.

Then a greater bedlam arose. Thousands of Hebrews poured down the two sides of the valley on top of Agag's disordered army, shouting, running, killing: Saul's second surprise. Agag's position between the spearhead force and the main army gave him some slight protection. He was hastily lifted onto his camel, surrounded by about half a hundred warriors on camels, and together they raced for the open ground at the south end of the valley.

But when Agag was within two hundred yards of the narrow mouth of the valley, companies of Hebrew archers commanded by Jonathan suddenly sprang from holes they had dug in the sand. Saul's third surprise! A rain of arrows blackened the sky. The thunder of camel hooves gave way to the bellowing of wounded animals, the shouts of men thrown to the ground, and the groans of the dying. Agag's camel was shot from under him. He was thrown to the ground unconscious, rolling over and over until arrested by a boulder. Saul's order had been concise: "Agag is to be brought to me alive. Kill all the others. Save as many camels as you can."

When Agag recovered consciousness and rolled over on his back, endeavoring to stand up, the tip of a spear pricked his stomach.

"Lie still, Amalekite fox! Or else you die." The young Hebrew gazed down at Agag longing to kill him. But Agag did not budge.

Meanwhile, the rout had started. Saul's surprise tactics had carried the day. The main body of Amalekites had been caught in the tents away from their camels and their arms. They were cut down systematically by the Hebrews, who literally hacked their way through the camp, killing everybody they met, men, women, and children. No cattle were touched—on Saul's orders. All the gold and silver was left intact.

The Hebrews quickly pursued those who fled. From Havila at the end of the valley down to Shur on the borders of Egypt, the slaughter of the Amalekites continued all day.

It was nightfall before the first of the Hebrew army returned. There was still much to do. The countryside was full of armed, fleeing Amalekites who had to be caught and killed. And there still remained the Amalekite belongings to be piled up and burned.

Joab wanted to talk this over with Saul. The soldiers were spent, hungry, battle-worn. They had achieved one of the greatest Hebrew victories since the time of the great Joshua. Surely Adonai would grant them, the warriors, a reward—the best sheep and oxen. Surely Saul would agree.

Actually, Saul was among the last to return to the camp, blood-stained, tired, but exultant. He made straight for the oily mound of flesh trussed and gagged and waiting. Agag lay helpless on his side in the dust and watched Saul stride toward him, hand on the haft of his sword. Saul unceremoniously rolled Agag over onto his back with his foot. He looked down at his enemy sweating with fear and noted with satisfaction that the whites of his eyes were bloodshot and stark. Saul drew his sword and with a flick of its tip he split Agag's nostril and one whole side of his nose. Agag spluttered and coughed, choking on his own blood. The gag in his mouth reddened.

"What shall we do with this Amalekite pig?" In Saul's voice rang the hatred of the Hebrews, who were gathered around in a great circle, twenty men deep on all sides. "What say you, Jonathan? Abner? Joab? Shall we pull him apart with his own camels, as he has done to our kinsmen?"

Shouts of bloodthirsty approval came from all around Saul. "Or is that too pleasant a death for this smelly animal?" More shouts for blood. Saul's sword hovered. "Shall we begin by scooping out his eyes?"

"O King! A word!" It was Joab, son of Zeruiah, stepping out of the crowd. "My King. We can use this Amalekite fox. His blood will bring nothing. But if we let him live, his allies in Arabia and the Negev may ransom him handsomely. Remember the reports of his hidden treasury!"

Agag's eyes shifted to Joab. Here was the voice of greed and cunning that he knew so well. A chance for him?

"Joab! We have fought a holy war. Agag is to die. No remnant must survive, but above all, not Agag. Adonai himself spoke to Samuel and commanded this!" Saul did not really oppose Joab. He was playing for time, seeking a justification for what he wanted to do. There were murmurs from the men.

"Then let us deal as the Amalekites deal!" Joab persisted. "Let us hold him for ransom. And when we have what we want, let's kill him then! What does it matter when he dies? Die he will. Let us take the richest of the booty that lies in that valley, and the fattest of the cows and sheep, and divide them among us all."

Saul was engulfed now by the approving shouts of his men. Abner stood quietly at the edge of the circle. As was his wont, he said nothing. Jonathan came forward, his own sword drawn. "Father, if Samuel has told you this is a holy war, then kill this fat stoat now and slay the animals. I will do it if you will not."

Saul was alarmed. He grasped Jonathan's arm and would not let him raise his sword. "There is truth in what Joab has said. Samuel said we are to slay the Amalekites. But can it matter if we disembowel this dirty bull today or tomorrow, at dawn or at dusk? All that matters is that he die! Listen to your own men shouting for their prize. Can it matter if they slaughter the animals here or in their own homes?"

"Father! Listen to me, please!"

"It is decided, Jonathan. I will hear no more from you!"

* * *

"Samuel! Samuel!"

The voice that roused the old prophet from his sleep in the dark night at Rama was one he knew well. The same voice had pronounced the terrible punishment of Eli at Shiloh years before.

"Speak, Lord. Your servant is here."

"Saul, whom you love and who is my chosen and anointed king, has disobeyed my commands. He has listened to the voice of greed and vainglory. He shall not be the leader of my people any longer. And his house shall not rule over the land."

"Adonai!" Samuel started to weep. "Perhaps it was my failure! God of heaven and earth! Perhaps I did not make him understand your will. Have mercy, Adonai, on your chosen one."

"He shall not be leader of my people." The voice of Adonai was insistent, definitive.

No words will ever tell the misery and pain of the weary old man in his weakness of body and mind, still devoted to the errant Saul and still gripped by his love for him, struggling helplessly with the iron decision of Adonai.

For this was Samuel's *akeda* also, his own test. Adonai's hand had passed over Saul and was pointing to a time beyond Samuel's time, to a time that Samuel would not see but to which he had to be true. He prayed for Saul, even though he knew that Saul was finished, and he wept for Saul as he had wept for Eli. God's forgiveness had run out.

In the cold light of morning, Samuel finally rose from his knees before the altar. This day, with all the brightness and renewal of its dawn, was going to be the saddest of his life.

The news of Telaim had spread with the sun. Saul strung Agag on a tree trunk tied between two asses and placed him at the head of the best of the sheep and lambs and cattle saved from the slaughter. Directly behind them came the carts filled with booty and drawn by the oxen of Amalek. With his commanders and his troops, with Agag as his trophy, Saul paraded through the land from Telaim toward his own territory. In every village people spat vile curses on Agag and covered his body with buckets of waste, cheering Saul and his warriors.

At Carmel of Judah, Saul stopped and raised a monument to his great victory. Then he led his procession onward through all the towns and villages to the sacred place of Gilgal, where he had been anointed king. There he offered thanks to Adonai in sight of all the people, and there was rejoicing and dancing.

When Saul's pride and triumph were at their very peak, the prophet arrived. He had stayed apart, watching, unnoticed, as he sat on his mule on the hillside overlooking the jubilation of Saul and his Hebrews. Saul had built a new altar on the hill and a priest had offered a sacrifice.

So absorbed was Saul that it was some time before he even noticed that silent figure on the hillside. A few dancers stopped. Some singers fell silent. Then quickly, silence fell on all.

Then Saul shouted, "Samuel! Prophet of Adonai! Come! See! I have performed the commands of the Lord. The Amalekites are no more!" Samuel gave no sign of answering.

Saul left the high place, shouldering his way brusquely through the crowds and up the hill where Samuel waited, and renewed his plea. "Come! Offer sacrifice for us and bless your people and their king!" He took the reins of the mule to lead it.

"Shall I bless you, O King?" The sound of Samuel's voice, filled with pain yet cold as ice, stopped Saul where he stood and paralyzed his fingers.

"Samuel, man of God! The Amalekites are no more! I have done the will of Adonai." Saul's voice was low, urgent.

"What then do I hear with my ears? Is that the bleating of sheep I hear? And the lowing of oxen still standing with their traces fastened to carts full of booty?"

"The people, Samuel! The people have brought these things, Samuel! They spared only the best of the booty, the pick of the flocks. The rest we have destroyed utterly. What we spared is here for our sacrifice." Saul was almost whispering in anxiety.

When the prophet finally answered, his voice terrified Saul.

"Puny. Such was your victory, Saul. You do not exult in your victory for Adonai. You exult for yourself—in your pride and stubbornness. For you have failed. You have failed to do the one thing Adonai commanded you to do! Like Esau, father of the detestable Amalekites, you have sold your inheritance!" A physical blow could not have stunned Saul as Samuel's words did at that moment.

"But, Samuel, my father, I *have* performed the commandment of Adonai. And I have offered sacrifice to him in this place! I have..."

"Enough." Samuel held up his hand for silence. "How little you are in your own eyes, Saul! Are you not the head of the House of Israel? Why then did you not obey the voice of

Adonai? Adonai himself has rejected you as king over the House of Israel. I cannot return with you to the high place."

Samuel turned the head of his mule in order to leave. But Saul leaped like a tiger after him, taking hold of Samuel's robe. In his frenzy he tore off a piece of the garment. It came away in his hand, dangling there like a remnant of Adonai's blessing. Samuel paused, looking over his shoulder, his face an ikon of sorrow and pain.

"Just so, Saul." His voice sounded infinitely sad and remote. "Just so, my King, has Adonai torn your kingship and your kingdom from you, in order to hand it over to another, a better, man."

Saul was now beside himself. "Samuel, I beg you! Worship with me this day before the people! I beg you! Please! Help me, at least in this! Help me!" Without a word the prophet looked down, his gaze flickering over the altar, the assembled soldiers and people, and Agag still slung between the two asses. Finally he turned his mule back. He headed slowly down the slope and over to the high place. Saul followed behind. Murmurs of relief arose from the waiting crowd. Samuel would sacrifice for them to Adonai. When Samuel had finished his prayers and blessing of the people, he turned gravely and stared at Saul.

"I have one more thing to do before I go. Bring Agag to me."

Several of Saul's men went from the high place over to the two asses between which Agag was hung. They cut the ropes. He fell heavily, thudding to the ground. They pulled him to his feet, turned him toward the high place.

Breathing heavily and swaying along, Agag arrived at the top of the high place. He stared at Saul unblinking, then at Jonathan and Joab and Abner and the rest of the tall, armed warriors around the king. But then his eyes fell on the bent and hoary figure of the prophet. He could not bear to stare in the old man's burning eyes. Something was wrong. He threw a look at Saul; the king's eyes were red and fearful. A movement caught his eye. The prophet was reaching for the sword in the scabbard at Saul's side. Hypnotized, Agag watched the sword drawn and raised on high. Agag, mouth agape, eyes bulging, the mountain of his flesh instinctively leaning back, stared at the blade.

"Son of Satan!" The prophet's curse struck him first. "You are worthy only to sit forever in the cesspools of Gehenna! As you have made our women childless in the land, so shall your mother be childless among women. So says Adonai!" Agag's mouth started to form some syllables. He could promise more, give them more than they had ever dreamed.

But all he saw then was the sword flashing in the sunshine, and all he felt was the agony of the cut. Agag's right arm lay dismembered on the ground. The Amalekite shrieked. His blood spurted on Saul and Samuel and down his side. A gasp went up from the crowd.

Samuel lifted the royal sword again. Agag staggered back, trying to get out of its terrible way. But the sword fell again, slicing Agag's left arm. Blood mixed with curses came from Agag. A low moan from the army filled the high place. The Amalekite's eyes were fixed on Samuel in utter fear. He staggered back a few more paces, stumbling, vainly trying to get out of the way of that sword. But it flashed again and came down again on Agag's right thigh, slicing away a huge hunk of flesh, then down on his left thigh, then down on his left and right calves, then the tendons of his legs. He crashed forward, a mountain of flesh scrambling and thrashing in the dust and blood, trying to roll over and away from the sword. Again and again it tore at his flesh—his back, his buttocks, his legs, his feet. Still, life persisted in the Amalekite. He kept rolling, screaming, cursing. His breasts were hacked away. His side was opened up. His groin was split so that the two femurs appeared white and pink. By now Agag seemed to be nothing more than a mass of groaning blood and cursing strips of flesh and fat.

With every slash and cut of his sword in Samuel's hands, Saul crouched closer to the ground in horror. The ceaseless onslaught of blows, the blood, the screams, pierced Saul's soul like a judgment on himself. The agony of Agag's body was the agony of Saul's spirit. Still the sword flashed and cut. Samuel was bathed in blood. His face glistened red and ran salty with his own tears.

Agag's brute strength was his death torture. For he was still alive. Only pain and hatred burned in those blind eyes. He felt the blade slip into his belly and open his chest, drawing out entrails and organs. He felt his lungs pierced and immediately tasted the blood gorging his throat. His still-beating heart was sliced from its moorings. At last he lay still.

Samuel, however, had not yet finished. With a few quick cuts, he opened up the Amalekite's chest, plunged the sword through the heart, and lifted it out. He held it up dripping before Saul's eyes. Tears streamed down Samuel's face. He cried out for the last time to Saul. "Never once did you raise this royal sword, as Adonai commanded you, to pierce this heart that beat in purest evil! Never once, O King! Are you a coward who shrinks from death? Are you so craven that you think that to let evil live will bring you riches on earth or in heaven? Or that to ransom evil can be made holy with the burning flesh of heifers and sheep?

"If you had once, so much as once, raised your own arm to slay Agag, pehaps the Angel of Adonai would have stayed your hand, as he stayed the hand of Abraham. But you did not! And it was your own hand, resting on your own sword, that sealed the fate of the king of Amalek, and the fate as well of the king of the Hebrews!"

Then Samuel flung the heart of Agag in the dust. He raised the sword with both hands above his head. With a great shout of grief and pain that echoed throughout Gilgal as in a great and empty cavern, he brought the sword down with all the force in his body and split the head of Agag from crown to chin, cracking bone and slivering brain.

Samuel did not look again at Saul. For an instant he stood there, his hands holding the sword as it lay buried in Agag's skull, his eyes staring dully at the Amalekite's ruin. His fingers loosened nervelessly from the sword haft. Now the prophet was completely subdued again. Tears blurred his path as he turned away wearily from the king, the silent thousands, and the slaughtered Agag. He went away slowly and alone, climbed on his mule and left.

A week after his return from Gilgal, Samuel set out on the northern leg of his circuit. Out of fear of reprisal that Saul might attempt during his absence, Samuel packed in his saddlebags the two most precious objects he possessed: the Ephod and the scroll of the Law. He would be accompanied by his two faithful servants and his five Elamite slaves.

For five weeks Samuel circuited through Shechem and Salisa, Dothan and Gilboa, Ibleam and Shunem. He rested for two days at Gilboa, then set out northward through the passes for the southwestern corner of the mountains ringing the Valley of Yezreel at the south. He crossed the Moreh Hill and headed west to Nain, there to see Nathan, Nain's resident scholar.

By the time Samuel had reached Nathan's house, he was preceded by a joyous crowd spreading out in the path of Samuel's party their rugs, cloaks, palm branches, and anything they could lay their hands on. Everyone in the land wanted to be able to point to a carpet or a cloak and tell his grandchildren: Over that carpet—or on that cloak—once walked the mule of the prophet Samuel with the prophet on his back. Or: On that rug fell the dung from the prophet's mule.

Nathan the Scholar was waiting outside his house. He helped Samuel off his mule, kissed his hands, embraced him, and led him inside. A score or so of the men took up positions around the scholar's house. As long as Samuel was there he would be guarded with their lives.

Tired from his journey, Samuel lay down and rested. While he slept Nathan sat outside in his garden to look at the Valley of Yezreel beneath the rays of the declining sun. And for the first time since he had come here almost sixteen years before, he felt that the sun was setting on his sojourn in Nain.

After he had rested, Samuel questioned him about his life here.

"In Nain, everything is secure and fine, Samuel. But two things are worrying me. First, the Philistine marauding parties."

"And second?"

"Witchcraft. Many of our people are beginning to lose belief in the strength of Adonai and their hope in the king he appointed by your hand. So they have been consulting witches. They buy images of Baal from the Syrians and Phenicians and Arameans. They offer sacrifices, and on the high places they perform strange rites. I have forbidden our townspeople to go to Endor."

"Why? It used to be a peaceable little place."

"Now everyone who remains there is under the spell of the witch—a famous one. From Petahyahu—you remember when the pilgrims used to go to Petahyahu to see the holy woman Shalama?"

"Of course. Of course I remember." Samuel scratched his beard in astonishment. "She? This does not happen in the House of Israel to someone who belongs to Adonai—" Samuel broke off, his eyes wandering.

"We know some details about what happened," replied Nathan. "Apparently the Philistines learned about her, and they visited her several times. We have eyewitness reports."

"But how or why would she renounce her belief in Adonai?"

"Renounce her belief? I never said that, Samuel."

"It's the same thing!"

"Very well. But we don't know why or how. We may never know. All we know is that she's gone from us."

Samuel shivered. "I'm afraid we are entering a long night,

Nathan. God help us all!" He turned around slowly, looking meditatively at Nathan before speaking again.

"Nathan," he said finally, "it is the will of Adonai that you come south with me." Nathan was not surprised but his face fell. "I know, Nathan. I understand you do not wish to leave your home. But down there is where the real struggle is going to take place. And this is the call of Adonai.

"The terrible fact, Nathan, is this: Adonai has rejected Saul for his disobedience. The will of Adonai is that you come south with me to become the scholar of Bethlehem. When I get home to Rama, Adonai will tell us whom he has chosen and I will anoint him king. Now"—his tone relaxed and he smiled at Nathan—"let's go and tell your Council of Elders. We have much to arrange, for we leave at sunrise."

It took Samuel and Nathan four full days to get down to Bethlehem. They decided to avoid the central highland route— that would take them straight through the heart of country constantly patrolled by King Saul's men. They could not risk the lowland trail that ran down past Philistia—there they could not avoid the forward pickets of the Philistines. So they traveled eastward as far as the Jordan and then down the west bank of the river almost as far as Gilboa. Saul country lay ahead. So they forded the Jordan at night and went down the east bank to within a half mile of the Salt Sea. At the village of Bethar they crossed back into the land and made toward Jericho. They camped one moonless night in the orange groves on the outskirts of Jericho.

Before he went to sleep that night, Samuel knelt down in his tent to pray to Adonai. Nathan, who was sleeping outside on the ground, could hear the old man crying and sobbing to himself as he prayed. His prayers were all for Saul.

At first Nathan lay there listening, his mind full of dark forebodings. Then he must have slept because suddenly he became aware of the silence and he saw near the ground, all around the lower edges of Samuel's tent, a gently wafting luminescence, as if the tent were a hooded dome full of an unearthly light. One look was enough for the learned Nathan. He pulled his cloak over his head. "Adonai," he prayed desperately, "let me not look on you or your glory. Let me not die."

He was still lying there an hour later when Samuel stirred him with his stick.

"Nathan." Samuel's voice was deep and confident. "Get up. We have to be out of here within the hour."

As they rode along, Samuel uttered only three sentences. "You will find a heifer wandering in the road near Bethfage—be sure and rope it in." A pause. Then: "The word of Adonai came to me, Nathan. There will be danger, but we will have our king, and Adonai will finally have the land to himself and his people."

The last leg of the trip south to Bethlehem was uneventful. Outside Bethfage, Nathan roped in the wandering heifer. From there on, past Netofa and Rachel's tomb, right up to Bethlehem, they journeyed without incident.

The watchmen in the tower, Dedan and Ever, were distracted by their running argument about who was right, Saul or Samuel, when the dogs started barking and the two guards saw far off the living embodiment of their dispute approaching. Samuel, glancing at Nathan, cackled at the frenzied tolling of the tocsin. He was by now well accustomed to the galvanizing effect of his appearance.

Hardly a soul was up in Bethlehem. Maaka was just preparing to toddle out to her post by the well. But within minutes all the elders were arriving, half-clothed and unwashed, talking quietly among themselves.

When the travelers arrived, a peculiar hush fell on everybody in the presence of Samuel's unmistakable grandeur and force.

"Peace, my brothers!" Samuel greeted them.

"Peace upon you, O father of the people! Peace!"

"May we enter your village in peace?"

"Prophet of Adonai, we are poor miserable dogs in the sight of Adonai and clods of dry earth in the eyes of our king, Saul. Are we to have our lives forfeit because you come among us? Or do you bring the peace of our God and our king with you?"

Samuel's face was an unreadable mask. Saul had warned all the Hebrews under his rule: If Samuel comes to your village, remember that I am king and he is my subject too. The Bethlehemites did not wish to be caught in any cross fire between the king's arrows and the prophet's anathemas. Samuel, however, was prepared. He waved his hand airily toward the heifer.

"Brothers, the Lord told me last night to come and sacrifice a heifer to him here in Bethlehem and to sanctify you all, because today Bethlehem receives its new scholar, Nathan of Nain, whom I have fetched all the way from the north." Nothing could have been more plausible.

Zaza answered for them all. "Peace upon you, O Prophet of Adonai. You are welcome, you and Nathan of Nain and your followers." Jesse, who stood with the other elders, had a foreboding, however, that Samuel's appearance somehow had something to do with David. And he was afraid.

Samuel refused all refreshment, protesting that he was about to perform a religious ceremony. They all accompanied him to the high place of public sacrifice. The heifer was muzzled and tied down on her side on the altar.

"May Adonai, God of Abraham and of Isaac and of Jacob, God of all our fathers, bless you and, in the sight of the blood we are about to shed, forgive you your sins and make you holy in his sight for eternal dwellings."

The knife in Samuel's upraised hand flashed for an instant in the morning light, then plunged into the animal's jugular vein. The blood spurted over the altar's edge, down its side wall, and into little rivulets along the ground as the heifer struggled and died. One by one the Bethlehemites filed up to Samuel. Old Zaza was first.

"I am Zaza, son of Samla, O Prophet."

"May Adonai bless and sanctify you, Zaza, son of Samla." And looking steadily into Zaza's eyes, Samuel dabbed a little speck of blood on Zaza's forehead between the eyes. So it went for each individual Bethlehemite, adults and babies, young people and children.

Nothing out of the ordinary happened until Shoshanna had been sanctified and Jesse's turn came. Then it was as if a fire had suddenly kindled behind Samuel's eyes. And Adonai spoke to his spirit: "This is Jesse, son of Obed. One of his sons will be my king. Sanctify them all, and I will tell you which son is he who is to be anointed and who will come into power in the land." A new confidence surged through Samuel as all the distress and uncertainty of the previous months melted away.

"May Adonai bless you and sanctify you, Jesse, son of Obed. Where are your sons?"

"Coming behind me, O Prophet."

"It is good, Jesse. It is good." Then privately to Jesse he said: "Now stand here and present them to me, for Adonai has chosen one of them for great things."

Eliab, Jesse's firstborn, came up, towering in the full strength of his youth.

But Adonai again spoke silently to Samuel: "Samuel, my servant, this is not he. His heart is trammeled with pettinesses." Samuel blessed Eliab.

And so it went through all the sons of Jesse who were

present: Abinadab, Shammai, Nethaneel, Radai, Amasa, and Ozem came forward. Adonai refused them all.

"Are these your sons, Jesse? All your sons?"

"Yes, O Prophet!" For they were.

"Make them, each one singly, pass by me once more."

Once more it was done, and once more Adonai said no.

"Are these seven all your sons, Jesse?"

At last, Jesse was caught. "There's one more, our youngest—our Benjamin. He's out with the sheep in Beraka."

Samuel's command rattled like a drum roll. "Send for him. Now! I will wait here until he arrives."

He continued with the blessing of the other people while Jesse sent Eliab on his fastest camel to Beraka. "Go like the wind! Fetch David. The prophet is angry!"

When Eliab returned with David two hours later, Samuel had long finished the blessing and only Jesse and his family were left at the place of sacrifice.

As he waited, Samuel's anger had cooled. He could understand why a man would want to protect his son. He talked amiably with Jesse, and slowly the story of David's birth came out. Samuel's understanding grew. He now knew the ways of Adonai better than ever before.

Jesse concluded, "He has always belonged to Adonai from the moment of his birth, and I have always been charged to protect him."

"Of course, Jesse," was Samuel's soft reply. "Fear not." Then to Nathan: "The fall of Shalama was greater than you had thought."

Nathan's face clouded. "Greater indeed, Samuel, and sadder."

It was high noon on a sunny day with very little wind. All of Bethlehem was hushed and would remain so until the prophet had shaken the dust of the village from his sandals. Eliab galloped up the hill with David just behind him; he slithered from his camel without waiting for it to kneel and ran forward.

"He is here, O Prophet."

David calmly reined in his camel. It had been raining in Beraka, but here the sun was shining. He saw his brothers, Jesse, Shoshanna, a stranger with an extraordinary face, and, alongside him, the fierce-looking ancient whose hand Eliab was now kissing.

David dismounted, took off his shepherd's cap, and walked toward the group gathered by the altar, his eyes fixed on Samuel's face. It was Nathan's first sight of David, and he seemed to the young scholar to be some representative of another, golden race whom Adonai had favored with a special grace and comeliness. All, even Samuel, felt the gentling effect of David's presence. And Samuel heard the voice of Adonai: "This is he."

Samuel turned to Jesse and all his family and said to them with great deliberation: "In the name of Adonai, you members of the family of Jesse, and by the Covenant! If any one of you ever speaks before the time of Adonai's desire about what I am about to do here, I will bring your bloodless carcass to the Vale of Hinnom and there throw it in with the cadavers and excrement of the Jebusites. And your soul will die in eternal torment.

"Now turn away and cover your heads and stop your ears, all except you, Jesse, and you, Shoshanna."

When they had done as he commanded, Samuel waved Jesse nearer.

"Stand by your son and put your right hand on his shoulder." As he did this, Jesse's fingers felt the necklace beneath David's jerkin—Korith's necklace!—and some new confidence sprang up in his heart. Samuel went on: "You begot him, Jesse. You protected him. You risked your life to save him whom Adonai confided to your care. Now give him back to Adonai, son of Obed! Give him back in the name of his mother who died that he might live. For from this day forward he belongs to the Chosen Ones of Adonai. Give him back so that your bones may be gathered in peace with your fathers', and your spirit may return to Adonai who created it."

Silence. David could feel the trembling in his father's hand. Jesse's eyes were on Samuel's face, his mind just opening on the vista Samuel's words implied. He struggled to speak. "My son . . ." he started to mumble. But the tears blinded his eyes, and he could taste their salt on his tongue. He could only bow his head in assent. And suddenly a great feeling of buoyancy possessed him. All the anxiety that the years had laid upon his spirit vanished.

"Truly"—Jesse could hear the triumph in Samuel's voice— "you are here, Lord, with your servants."

While Jesse was being made whole in those moments of grace, that same all-loving hand of Adonai was opening a new dimension within David. He lost all sense of Jesse's hand, of Samuel's voice, of the smell of the heifer's blood, of the hard stone beneath his knees.

For a long time afterward he never knew which came first,

the ecstasy in his body or the exaltation of his spirit. In reality the first was the wash, the wake, of the second. But he knew the exaltation when the ecstasy seized him. A clear, unimpeded thrill running at blood-speed through every nerve. He became one fierce sensing unity of body and spirit that was bigger than he was, a spacious room expanding. And in it were swallowed up, like so many wisps of dust, all the smallnesses that harassed him: Eliab's jealousy, his loneliness at Beraka, the priggishness of his sensuality, the hardship of his days. It was Adonai saying: "I will plant my tent beside yours." And David cried out in a whisper: "Adonai! Your servant! Adonai! Come!"

It was the moment. Samuel took out his special horn of oil, uncorked it, held it with both hands over David's head and lifted his eyes to heaven. He tilted the horn and the thick oil dripped down in transparent golden globules, gathering at first, then slipping slowly down over David's face and temples and onto Jesse's hand. Jesse looked at Shoshanna, then at Samuel, and his eyes locked on the old man's face. For the exultation in Samuel's eyes changed to questioning, to apprehension, to amazement and, finally, acquiescence. A hidden conversation and vision were reflected there. At last Samuel lowered his gaze to look at David. It was over.

"Stand up, David! Stand up, son of Jesse! Embrace your father and your mother and your brothers. Henceforth you belong to Adonai."

BOOK II

DAVID
THE
WARRIOR

BOOK II

DAVID
THE
WARRIOR

The
Giant Slayer

▨▨▨ At the moment Samuel was pouring the oil over David's head in Bethlehem, two related events took place at distant places.

In his Gibea fortress, King Saul suddenly leaped from his chair, grabbed a spear from its hooks, and tried to slay his eldest son, Jonathan.

And in Gath, the giant Goliath awoke in his cave and sat up, his eyes gleaming. Then he went out and shouted for one of the Philistine guards. "Get Duke Achish!"

These two widely separate events were related to David simply because every move of the military protagonists in the fight between Hebrew and Philistine reflected one fundamental reality: the military clash was the visible theater in which the invisible struggle between Adonai and his eternal adversary was conducted by its human participants.

Since the tragedy of his disobedience at Telaim, Saul had been subject to increasingly uncontrollable attacks of rage. They came upon him suddenly and were always directed at someone he loved—at Samuel, at his wife, Ahinoam, and now at Jonathan.

The king and his son had been discussing an expected Philistine offensive up north by the Valley of Yezreel. Jonathan, like everyone else, had heard of Samuel's recent visit to Yezreel. He suggested that they call in the prophet and ask his views. His suggestion was a torch to dry straw.

Jonathan was saved by his quick reflexes; he ducked his head and the spear stuck quivering in the wall behind him. Joab, Abner, and the other officers jumped Saul and held him. He screamed and ranted all the way up to his bedroom, where they tied him down to his bed. Soon all of Israel knew: "The king has an evil spirit since the prophet left him."

In Gaza, Shekelath wrote in his diary: "Dagon is winning our battles in Saul's head before we cut it off." But before

177

Saul's madness was known in Gaza, the giant's message reached Duke Achish.

He was at home in his living room sipping wine with a young friend when the messenger from Goliath arrived. Without hesitation he placed his half-finished glass on the table and went directly to Refa-im. Goliath was waiting for him.

"Friend," he said, "it is the time to plan the first spear thrust at the heart of the Hebrews. As you will learn soon, Dagon is afflicting the mind of Saul. Soon Dagon's spirit will bend his judgment and put him in our hands."

Achish hurried back to his headquarters and ordered a chariot for a trip to Gaza at sunrise. Throughout the night he met with his staff to draw up the plan of attack. Goliath had suggested the Valley of Elah, which ran in a curve from west to east between the two towns of Azekah and Shoko. Its western end led into the Shefela and pointed straight to Ashdod on the coast. Its eastern end pointed straight at Jebus. Whoever held Elah had direct access from the coast to Jebus and the central highlands. Saul knew the strategic value—and danger—of Elah. He lacked the power of chariots. Only one-fifth of his men were equipped with iron weapons. He therefore could not risk a battle on the open plains of the Shefela. So he preferred to maneuver in the narrow spaces of the valley and the mountains around it. He had wisely constructed fortified camps at the northeastern end of Elah, and there he kept the main contingent of his forward army, about eleven thousand infantrymen. No army could pass through Elah as long as Saul occupied the northern rim of the valley.

The plans of Achish were cunning. In mid-January, after the Philistine holy days, a company of one hundred and fifty chariots would be positioned at the western opening of Elah, ready to attack when the signal came. Three battalions of Philistine infantrymen totaling twelve thousand men would take up a position on the southern rim, opposite the Hebrew camp. Goliath would go out each day on the valley floor and challenge the Hebrews to settle the battle by a single combat of champions. Whether they accepted or not did not matter. While Goliath was thus striking terror into their hearts, four flying columns of Philistine archers would make their way behind the Hebrew camp via the Valley of Sorek, north of Elah. If all went well, Goliath would kill successive Hebrew champions, thus depriving Saul of his best fighting men. And, at a given moment, the simultaneous attack by the Sorek columns would drive the Hebrews off the slopes of Elah into the valley, where the chariots and the main Philistine contingent would close and crush them.

Over all the Philistine deliberations and decisions floated their persuasion that Dagon was fighting their battle for them: the battle for the soul of Saul.

The day of the anointing, David went straight back to Beraka alone. The bad weather had continued there all day, as though Beraka mourned while Bethlehem rejoiced. A rainstorm swept over as David reached the ledge outside his grotto and looked down at the countryside. The mountains of Moab were hidden in clouds, and a thin, misty drizzle fell over the hills. He could hear the bleating of the sheep and the barking of the dogs. Soon they would all be coming in for the night. All was exactly as he had left it that morning, yet all was changed and changing.

There was no doubt that these would be his last days at Beraka, which he had come to love. His enjoyment of the place was now edged with sadness.

He climbed to the top of the ridge to watch the sunset. The sun, red and round, was about to sink. Above it the sky was still black with rain clouds. Below it lay the dark of the earth. In between, the sun peered as through a slit, shedding an unearthly glow that for a brief moment washed with glory the rock and the wooded hills. And David saw his life as a small blaze between the mysterious darkness of the past from which he had emerged and the mysterious darkness of the future which would swallow him.

From then until the end of winter he gradually withdrew from his work. He went to Bethlehem every two weeks to spend the night there, returning to Beraka next day.

Several times when he returned from Beraka he found Nathan talking with his father and mother. Obviously a friendship had grown. And although David never really got to know Nathan in this time, he noticed with some dismay that the scholar always deferentially stood up when he came in.

Toward midwinter Saul's recruiters appeared to conscript more young men for a huge spring offensive. Jesse's three eldest—Eliab, Abinadab, and Shammai—were marched off. David, as shepherd, was exempted—"unless we are all invaded."

The intimacy between David and his family grew deeper and sweeter during that period. And for those few weeks David savored the loving affection of both Jesse and Shoshanna and the deep contentment of their company.

In mid-February the company in which Eliab, Abinadab, and Shammai were enrolled was posted to the camp at the Valley of Elah. The Philistines, delayed by heavy winter rains, were setting up their camp on the opposite side of the valley. Jesse forbade David to go to Elah. When Shoshanna had food packages for his brothers, David took them to Gibea, and from there they were carried by the king's commissariat to Elah. Then one day a servant arrived in Beraka carrying ten griddle loaves and an ephah of parched corn. "Your father says: 'Go to Elah and deliver these by tomorrow mid-morning to your brothers.'"

When David questioned him, all the messenger could say was that the prophet Samuel had visited Jesse and then he, the messenger, had been dispatched. Then David knew: the instructions he had just received were his summons out of Beraka.

As he ate his last meal with the shepherds that night around the fire, he felt a sharp poignancy and had to turn away when his eyes suddenly burned with tears. "O Adonai!" he prayed silently to himself. "Why is it that I must walk alone?"

David left Beraka an hour after midnight. He embraced his ten shepherds warmly, giving each some small gift from his belongings—Zichri got his rabbit snares, Joram his bronze drinking cup, Merari his double-lined wool blanket. He made a special bundle of the things he wished to keep—his harp among them—and told his men to hold it for his father.

"Will you not be coming back as usual, David, tomorrow night?" Merari inquired.

"From this day forth Adonai alone knows the time, the place, and the manner of my going out and my coming in. Blessed be the name of Adonai."

"Blessed be his name," each one said as he received David's farewell embrace.

David's path took him up in a northwesterly direction to the village of Bether, then straight westward following the trail between Beth Shemesh and Sanoa. He passed Sanoa at daybreak and two hours later was within sight of Timna. It took him another two hours to climb the first steep slopes of the north side of Elah Valley, where Saul's camp lay. The rear guard pickets directed him to the topmost ridge, where his brothers were quartered.

His brothers weren't in their tent. "They're on watch up there," a soldier said, cocking his thumb at the very top of the ridge.

"What's that thunder?" David asked. "There aren't any clouds."

The soldiers looked at him curiously. "Just look over the ridge and you'll see," another soldier responded. David climbed up the last few yards and looked. The Valley of Elah fell away beneath his view. Immediately beneath him were the forward tents of the Hebrews, irregular gray, black, and brown goatskin rectangles. He could make out the king's tent in the center: it was circular, a shield attached to the top of its center pole. Beyond the row of tents, looking down on the valley floor, were ten lines of Hebrew infantrymen, shields, swords, and spears at the ready.

Across from the Hebrew camp on the southern ridge stood the round blood-red tents of the Philistines, each one flying a pennant. In front and behind these tents the ridge was literally flashing and blinding with armor-plated warriors. David's heart shivered at the sight of that gleaming iron. And because he could see no Philistine face distinctly, his first impression of the Philistine war machine was of a dragon, its scales glittering in the sunlight, its red spine pulsating with poison.

As he took in this scene, the thunder again split his ears. It came from the floor of the valley. A giant of a man was walking there slowly and ponderously, a long sword in his left hand, a spear strapped across his back. In his wildest dreams David had never imagined anything like this man. It was Goliath.

At that distance he seemed about twice David's own height, which was frightening enough. But he was obviously built proportionately large. Each arm was as thick as his own waist, David calculated, each leg was a mighty oak. From head to foot he was clad in polished iron armor. The only part of his body that was bare was the strip of his face that included his eyes and a small patch of his forehead. Behind him walked a Philistine carrying nothing but a huge shield that looked to David as big as the door to Jesse's barn at Bethlehem and as resistant as granite.

As the giant walked, his left hand raised the sword and brandished it above his head. David listened spellbound while the giant roared out as he paraded up and down: "Am I a dog, Hebrews, that you send out those fleas to prick my skin before I kill them?"—pointing to the corpses at his feet. He stopped roaring and walked another length of his beat before starting again: "Am I a dog, Hebrews? And are you fleas that you still cling to your king? Is he not the rump of an old mule where you nest? Am I not going to kill you all?" Now and again some Hebrew archer would fire an arrow at Goliath. The arrow only brought out that contemptuous thunderous laugh. "Must you throw old women's needles at me, Hebrew fleas? I am a Philistine. Come down and fight!"

David saw his brothers then, and ran down to where they stood watching. Eliab was angry as soon as he saw David.

"What are you doing here, little brother? You had food to deliver? Very well! You've done it! Now get out of here before you get hurt."

"How, Eliab?" David asked, facing his brother. "Nobody's fighting. That Philistine dog is insulting you all, the soldiers of the living God, and you just hide up here. How shall I get hurt?"

"Son." It was an old soldier who spoke up. "Whoever kills that monster will be great in the land."

"No matter the reward!" David was already shaking with anger. "The Philistine insults us, insults the king, insults Adonai. He must be killed." His voice was getting louder as he stood there towering over most of the soldiers in the pride and glory of his youth.

If nothing else, David was certainly a distraction for the encampment. The word spread through the lines and down to the tent of Saul. "A young shepherd, It's a young shepherd who says the giant must be attacked and killed." Some laughed. Others shrugged.

Inside his tent, Saul was sunk in despair. His scouts had just arrived with the horrible details of how the Philistines had massacred his men in Sorek and were now marching unimpeded to his rear, threatening his supply lines and escape route. Other scouts had discovered the Philistine chariotry at the western end of Elah. Saul saw the strategy in a flash—an iron vise ready to close and throttle him. Then came the hubbub. "Find out what's happening," he told an aide.

The aide was back in a few moments. "A young man says he will kill the giant."

"Kill the giant? Who is he?"

"I don't know, O King."

"Bring him to me."

There was silence when David entered Saul's tent. Two officers stood at the entrance; the king's armor hung on the central pole; and Jonathan, standing beside the tables, was contemplating Saul as he leaned with both elbows on the table, studying a diagram of the battlefield. He did not recognize in

David the little brother of Ozem. David recognized Jonathan but said nothing.

Saul looked up from under his eyebrows and eyed this shepherd, who now spoke directly: "I will go as your champion and kill this offensive and grotesque Philistine."

Saul looked on David's youth and his shepherd's clothing and the stave in his right hand and smiled.

"Son, go home. This Philistine is a grown, experienced warrior. Go home, son, to your family and your sheep."

David did not budge. "I have fought a lion and a bear and killed them with my hands. I have fought the Philistine and Amalekite and Edomite, all of them, like the animals attacking my flocks. Adonai gave me a victory over them all. Now he will give me victory over this Philistine."

Saul grunted and stood up to take a second look. It did not take him long to find what he sought in David's eyes.

"Why not, shepherd lad? Why not?" He snapped out orders. "Get my armor down and put it on this lad. Hurry!" At the least there would be another challenger to raise the spirits of his Hebrews.

David was quickly dressed in the king's armor and stood in it, both hands holding the haft of the sword, the point directed at the ground. But something wasn't right. David lifted an armored leg and took one long stride, stopped, then drew a deep breath.

"Help me out of this, my brothers. Unless you are accustomed to it, you cannot fight in it. You can only die in it!"

From down in the valley came Goliath's bray again: "Is there no man among you to fight me?"

"How then, shepherd, are you going to fight?" Saul wanted to know. David looked at the king. Everyone present was struck by his eyes. The blue was very, very blue. The whites were very, very white.

"As I fight best, O King. As I fight best. At present I am best if I am lightest." David's voice was not loud nor did it sound passionate. But Saul recognized the coldness correctly as the coldness of a man determined to kill.

He said one word, simply. "Go."

Jonathan was thunderstruck. He looked from his father to David, from David to his father, and back and forth again, like an enthralled spectator at some village tugging match. He could not understand what strange emotions they shared. Something was wrong, somebody was making a mistake. Was his father mad? David must be stopped. Saul, who knew his son, sensed his reaction. He put his hand on Jonathan's arm.

"Don't," he said quietly. "Don't. Let him be. He knows exactly what he is doing."

David's hand twitched as he walked slowly through the entrance of the tent. He glanced right and left at the Hebrew soldiers, then over at the Philistines. He bent down at the mountain stream which ran past Saul's tent, cupped his right hand and scooped up a mouthful of water. He stood up, licking his lips, took a few paces forward, and stopped. All his immense concentration now focused on the giant. He took in every movement.

Saul, Jonathan, and the two officers came to the tent entrance and stood just outside it to watch. A violent cascade of jeers, shouts, and curses arose from the Philistines at the sight of the Hebrew king. The Hebrew soldiers around Saul's tent stood up when the king appeared and removed their helmets. One or two started the traditional greeting: *"Yechi ha-melek!* Long live the King! *Yechi ha-melek!"* But Saul held up his hand for silence, then pointed to David. The word passed along the lines. Everybody fell silent. Only the taunting bellow of the giant echoed around them.

"Shall a flea kill a Philistine? Huh?"

Men glanced at each other, at the king, at Goliath, and then back at that lone, still figure. Saul said to Abner: "Abner, what is that boy's name? I forgot to ask him his name."

"As your soul lives, O King, I do not know who he is," Abner replied.

The Philistines were surprised into stopping their jeers. What on earth was this? A champion he was most certainly not. No sword. No shield. No helmet. And those knee britches and tunic! A priest with his magical rod? A shepherd with his stave? But this was war!

Jonathan felt the cold tingle of sweat on his scalp. His father contemplated the scene with eyes hooded, upper front teeth clamped over the lower lip, breath coming in long, slow respirations.

David was aware of none of this—so intensely was his attention fixed on the giant. He watched Goliath march up once, march back once. It was enough. He glanced up briefly at the sun. Almost due south, it shone into the face of the giant as he marched back.

David took two long sideward steps to the stream, knelt briefly, scanned the edge of the water, and picked up a smooth

stone here and there, dropping each one into the shepherd's
purse he carried on his belt. Five smooth stones in all. He
straightened up and stood absolutely still, a polychrome statue.
The giant was just reaching one end of his march. As he turned
into the sun David threw his arms straight above his head and
let out a scream pulsing with blood lust and hate that echoed
from ridge to ridge and up and down the Valley of Elah. It
stopped the giant in his tracks and sent the hands of thousands
of armed warriors on both ridges reaching for their swords.

David flew down the slope from crag to crag, bounding
across ditches, sure-footed, light, breathtakingly fast. His shepherd's cap was torn from his head and his golden hair streamed
behind him. A murmur arose from the Hebrews. He was down
on the valley floor before those thousands of hands had released
their sword hafts. The giant, squinting into the sun, suddenly
saw a streak of gold and brown and heard the shout.

"Philistine! Come and die!"

Goliath put up his hand to shield his eyes from the sun, took
one look at David, put back his head and roared with laughter.
His shield bearer struggled around the giant, offering him his
shield, but Goliath put out a large hand and knocked him down,
shield and all. He bared his teeth.

"What is this they now send out to fight me? Not even a
Hebrew flea of a soldier, but a Hebrew flea of a boy! What
am I?" he asked, looking to both sides of the valley, baying
at the top of his lungs. "What am I? Huh? Am I not a Philistine?"

An answering roar arose from the fighting men of Philistia
up on the ridge: "Goliath! Goliath! Goliath!" It was a resounding chant beaten out to the accompaniment of sword hafts on
iron shields. "Goliath! Goliath! Goliath!" David did not stir.
On their ridge, the Hebrews watched in stark fear. Only Saul
did not change. He stood still, teeth clamped over the lower
lip.

The giant held up his sword for silence and roared at David:
"You miserable flea! Come! I will feed you to my sword in
the name of almighty Dagon. Come!"

David's voice rang out clearly, his mouth firing each word
sharply into the face of the giant. "You have insulted me. You
have insulted my king, the anointed of Adonai. You have
insulted the army of that living God, Adonai. And you have
insulted Adonai the terrible." A short pause. Suddenly a change
came over him: like the change he had felt that day when he
confronted Ari the lion. In a psalm he would compose in his

old age, he would sing: "Yea, Adonai, my flesh and my bones and my soul were yours when I faced my enemies." It was that force, not his own, that drove him, controlled him, and directed him.

"Now, Philistine dog, I am going to kill you." He spoke very calmly. "I will cut off your head while you are still alive. I will drain your body of its blood. I will take off your armor. I will carve up your carcass. I will place it on this very ridge above you. And the vultures will come in the evening and perch on the bits of you, and peck at your vitals. The jackal will come and start eating you. The lioness and the wolf will feed their young off you. And all the world will know that no one, no one, I say, insults Adonai."

While these words were ringing out, Goliath's mouth drew back at the corners. He lifted his sword in both hands and shoved it back in its scabbard. He looked at David. For a moment their eyes locked. David started running forward, his hands moving expertly. He quickly took his sling from his belt and loaded it with a stone. He swung the sling around and around, his right arm and hand tracing in the air a figure like the funnel of a tornado and developing an enormous force as the swing accelerated. David's eyes were fixed on the naked patch of forehead between the giant's eyes. He had performed this feat hundreds of times since the age of five. Now everything he had ever learned went into the distilled fury of that swing.

Nobody watching saw the precise moment when he loosed the stone. All they saw was his outstretched hand, the dangling end of the sling, and the sudden awful recoil of the giant's head. They heard the strangled scream of pain as Goliath fell flat on his back, stunned, blood pouring out over the visor of his helmet and around his neck.

David, who had stopped in his tracks once the stone left his sling, now raced to Goliath's side. With both hands he took hold of the huge helmet, put one foot to the giant's shoulder and dragged the helmet off his head. He pulled the sword from its scabbard, lifted it with both hands and brought it down with a single triumphant shout across the Adam's apple of the giant. Then there was blood everywhere. On David. On the ground. On the sword. Once more it fell, this time cutting through the neck, severing the tendons, breaking the bones. He dropped the sword, seized Goliath's lolling head by its crinkly hair and held it high in his hand, the blood streaming down his arm and over his body.

A great roar sprang from the Hebrews. Saul, galvanized,

was giving orders as he ran, and the Hebrews were moving like mercury down the slope, across the valley floor and up the Philistine slope, a mighty embodiment of the wrath of Adonai. David dropped the giant's head, seized the huge sword, and charged with the first ranks at the Philistines.

The fall of Goliath shattered the Philistines' courage. Their weaponry was still far superior, but the manner of Goliath's death and the youth who killed him rendered them baffled and helpless.

At the moment David rushed forward swirling that deadly sling, all the Philistines would have sworn by Dagon that they saw the famous "blue fire" that David was later said to emit from his eyes and hair whenever the fury of battle came upon him. And in Philistine lore, "blue fire" was the special weapon used only by the gods. That small round stone was another fatal element. Nothing dismayed the Philistines more than invisible death. They did not flinch from all manner of bloodletting with sword and spear and whip and dagger. But the sight of a huge giant, faced with a youth half his size, suddenly falling on his back and then being carved up—this was too much. They fled in terror.

The rout was complete and the toll was terrible. The Hebrews cut the Philistines down mercilessly, pursuing them down the slopes through the thickets and all the way over to the borders of the Shefela and into Philistia as far as the gates of Ekron and Gath and Shaaraim. The capture of spoils in iron weapons was enormous, and the defeat was so sudden that no signals could be sent either to the chariot corps waiting at the western mouth of Elah Valley or to the Sorek columns stealing in behind the Hebrew camp. Saul grasped the situation immediately.

He took four prisoners and tied them naked to four posts facing each other. He took a dagger and gouged out the first prisoner's eyes, then he drove the knife into the solar plexus and ripped the man down to the crotch. He stood in front of the remaining three: "The signal. The signal for the chariots: what is it?" None of the three spoke. Then there were two. He repeated the question. Neither spoke. He moved toward one of them.

"Three arrows—three flaming arrows," the terrified Philistine shouted. "Don't!" Saul did anyway. To both of them.

Saul was on his mettle that day. "Shepherd boy!" he said to David. "You are a general now. Take three thousand men and lie in wait for those Philistines coming up from Sorek.

Tear the faces off them. Jonathan, you and your archers station yourselves midway in the valley on both sides, well camouflaged. Stay hidden until you get the word." He dispatched another seven thousand men under the command of Joab, son of Zeruiah, around the south ridge of Elah with instructions to reach the mouth and block it. The remainder of his army he placed back at the original Hebrew camp site.

An hour and a half after Goliath's death, three flaming arrows soared into the sky. The chariot commander gave the command. Within ten minutes the Hebrews could hear the cracking of whips, the war screams of the charioteers, the thunder of hooves, and the rattling of chariot wheels. The chariot corps burst into Elah in a hurly-burly of metal and hurtling horseflesh, coming in for the kill. When they had passed the halfway mark, the trap was sprung. A hail of arrows eclipsed the sun. Then a second hail. A third. A fourth. The air was full of agonizing shouts and crashing metal as horses, men, and chariots toppled over, collided, and struggled, and died. Some of the chariots at the head of the charge escaped the deadly arrows and thought to reach the Philistine camp at the upper end of the valley. But only the Hebrews were waiting for them there. Others turned around and managed to flee westward to the mouth of Elah. But Joab was waiting there. None got through to the Shefela and home to Philistia.

Almost simultaneously the Sorek columns walked into David's ambush. Caught on the north slopes of Elah between David's men and the Hebrew camp, they were cut to pieces methodically in the melee that followed. Some stragglers escaped back into the Sorek woods and ravines and made their way at night back to Gath. The bulk perished.

By four o'clock that afternoon it was all over. Saul returned to his tent on Elah's ridge and received the reports from his officers. Thousands of iron weapons and pieces of armor— enough to outfit whole battalions. More than a hundred chariots intact, about sixty chariot horses, the Philistine camp supplies of food, arrows, tents, and equipment, hundreds of slaves, but no prisoners.

In the evening, as the sun was setting, most of Saul's men were back at the camp site celebrating. Fires had been lit and food was being cooked. Soldiers sat around drinking and eating and singing. The musicians from Gibea entertained. On the outskirts of the camp, the Philistine corpses fed huge bonfires, but at Saul's order the head and corpse of Goliath were left lying where the giant had fallen, for only he who slew a champion in single duel had the right to burn the body. But the king ordered the armor of Goliath brought and laid outside his tent.

"Where is that shepherd?" Saul kept asking. "If he is dead, we must find his body and bury it with honor. Who has seen the shepherd? He belongs to us and to my house. Alive or dead, bring him to me."

At sundown a great commotion resounded through the camp. As the shouting and cheering continued, Saul and Jonathan rushed from the tent and looked down into the valley where the main body of the troops was camped.

Soldiers were waving their weapons as they ran wildly toward the eastern end of Elah. Finally the watchers on high could see David returning at the head of the force Saul had dispatched to Sorek. The soldiers engulfed the shepherd and those nearest to him. Then he reappeared borne along on the shoulders of the men. He brandished a sword and smiled as he looked over that sea of naked weapons and heard the joyous chanting: "David! David! David! David!" Cries and chants filled the air as he was carried to where Goliath's corpse lay. David then looked up and saw the king standing outside his tent.

He slipped off the shoulders of the men, picked up the head of Goliath by the hair, and turned toward Saul. Suddenly all was silent.

In the darkening light Saul watched the young man approaching. His face was serious now. He was covered with caked blood and dust. He had been wounded in both arms and on the forehead. Sword and spear were clasped in his right hand. In the fingers of his left hand swung the head of Goliath, its mouth gaping vapidly.

Saul watched him as he climbed. "Who is this extraordinary boy?" Jonathan heard his father mutter. "Is he someone I must watch?" Then David was there.

"I am David, son of Jesse of Bethlehem, and the king's servant. I give you, O King, the head of your enemy in the name of Adonai." All that was good in Saul, all that was noble, all that had retained hope for peace, for victory, for Adonai's blessing and favor, welled up in him. He stretched out both hands and shouted at the top of his voice.

"Welcome, David! Champion of the Hebrews!"

Then came the chaos of delirium. Saul was beside himself with genuine joy: his army was victorious; his hero was home.

After some minutes Saul held up his hand for silence. "Bring up the corpse of the giant!" They carried it up in a tarpaulin and laid it in front of David. Saul sent for his sword and handed it to him. "You promised to cut him into pieces, shepherd. Do so! And we will feed him to the animals." In the light of the campfires and surrounded by the king and his Hebrews, David hacked the massive arms and legs off, carved the huge torso into four portions, and laid them with the head on the highest spot on the ridge, where vultures and wild animals would soon feed upon them.

While his men returned to their bivouacs, Saul led David into his tent. David reported on the Sorek battle and then asked permission to return to his flocks.

Saul stood up, his face a mask of stone: "From this day on, David, son of Jesse, you are part of my house and army. As I live and as Adonai, God of Hebrews, lives, you will never leave me!"

"The king's good servant," David said, bowing low in obedience as was the custom. "If the king wills, his servant will go and see his brothers."

"Go! Speak to them and send one of them to tell the good news to Bethlehem. Then eat, rest, and tomorrow we return to Gibea together!"

When David emerged from Saul's tent, it was the occasion for another scene. Saul heard the chant starting again: "David! David! David!" For after the hardship and oppression of six weeks at the mercy of Goliath's taunting they were victors because of this man alone! Abner, the only one who remained with Saul, noticed the disquiet creeping into the king's manner.

Jonathan led David to his own tent, where they washed off their battle stains and bound up their wounds. Jonathan gave David a fresh tunic and an ankle-length house robe. Eliab, Abinadab, and Shammai came. Joab with his brothers, Abishai and Asahel, arrived shortly after. Zeruiah, Joab's mother, was a sister of Korith, David's mother. Suddenly Jonathan realized who David was. They ate, drank, and sang together. When brothers and cousins left, David sat with Jonathan in front of the campfire.

"Do you remember," Jonathan said, "what I wished for you when Ozem and I went looking for the Iron Trail?"

"Yes. That I be a lion in the land." David smiled into Jonathan's eyes.

"Well, you are now," Jonathan said with deep feeling. "You are now, David—our lion."

After that they said very little for a while, now and again exchanging stray thoughts, being perfectly content to savor those moments of quiet. They were both aware of a new and surprisingly strong bond between them that they only now sensed, and neither of them wished to appraise it with words just yet.

Finally Jonathan spoke: "I heard that Samuel visited Bethlehem and blessed you all."

"Yes. And he anointed me—I don't know for what, except that it has changed my whole life." The words came out of him before he realized he had violated old Samuel's command.

"God in heaven! Did he? My father must never find out. He would have you killed." They looked at each other, the confidence deepening their new relationship. In silence they sought wisdom in the fire until the guards called out the midnight hour.

"I don't think I have felt so close to another human being as I feel to you this night," David said very simply. Jonathan nodded. "Some months ago," David continued, "a young woman whom I know now I loved told me that I was selfish— that I couldn't celebrate love because I couldn't give myself, that I was obsessed with safety. I wish I could see her now."

"Have you ever loved a woman?"

"No. Not yet." He let a few moments pass by before adding: "I've always felt that means the start of a long, long journey. Up to now it's a journey I haven't felt ready to begin. Perhaps Lassatha—that was her name—perhaps she was right, that I can't love."

"Have you ever been with a woman?"

Again David shook his head.

Again they consulted the fire, now mostly dying embers. Jonathan finally stirred. "I am sure you will see her again. And you will discover the sweetness of the love a woman can give." There was another pause, and Jonathan continued: "There's something I would like to say to you. Now, I think, is the moment, if ever, to say it. I would not like you in any way to misunderstand, God knows!" Jonathan stumbled on. "But can you understand if I tell you that I love you?"

David picked up a stone, threw it into the embers, and meditated briefly on the resulting sparks. Neither of them felt any urgency to speak. "Yes," David said at last, "I can understand it very well. I love you too. Don't misunderstand. I am young but I have seen men who love each other and whose kisses are as warm as the kisses of men and women, who sleep together, who enter each other's bodies, and whose hearts are as bound up with each other as the hearts of man and wife. All

that I know. And"—a slight frown wrinkled his forehead—
"I know what the Law says about that love, what old Samuel
would say, and King Saul."

He squared his shoulders wearily and looked at Jonathan.
"But I know the love I have for you is not that kind, but
something else. Something very strong, very sweet. I seem to
love you more than a brother or a father. And yet I don't
know—it's quite a different love." He flung up his hands.
"I don't understand it, Jonathan. But"—a smile lit up his mouth
and eyes—"I want to keep it, to make sure it grows."

Jonathan looked at him and joined in his smile. They turned
away, David's arm falling around Jonathan's shoulders, Jonathan's arm around David's waist. They smothered the embers
with sand and walked slowly back to the tent.

Inside, Jonathan loosened his heavy silver-embossed belt.
He took off his long outer robe of Tyrian purple, folded it
carefully, and laid it on the tent rug; placing the belt on top
of it, he removed his sandals and placed them beside the robe.
He took out his embroidered shirts and kerchiefs and stockings
from his baggage and laid them on the robe. Finally he took
down his beloved bow and quiver, which he had made himself,
adding them to the pile of his possessions. Standing there in
his tunic and bare feet, he said smilingly, "David, I have little
in this world. But what I most dearly possess I give you as a
seal to the bond of friendship and love that I now swear to keep
between us. For it is apparent to me that you are the anointed
of Adonai. And my soul belongs to you."

They embraced each other, and David kissed Jonathan on
the forehead and hands. "Jonathan, my friend," he said, looking
into Jonathan's eyes, "I swear to this bond as to a pact between
us. Let nothing separate us. I will never dishonor you, nor you
me, I know. And I will honor your family all the days of my
life." For one short instant Jonathan, his head bowed, was still,
holding David's hands in his. He did not dare lift his eyes to
look into David's. Some imperious demand was stirring in him.
He hung in doubt.

David felt the tightness of Jonathan's fingers around his
hands. "Peace, now, my brother," he said softly. "Peace! There
are many more days and nights to come." His words broke the
tension.

Jonathan loosened his grip and looked up at David. He
smiled through his tears. "You are wiser than I, David," he
said quietly with a certain wryness.

"Not wiser, Jonathan. Just that whatever you and I do must

be done with the blessing of Adonai. For if we have love for each other, it must be from him. And while I have today become and do intend to remain the king's good servant, I belong first of all to Adonai."

"I will always love you, David. More than you love me, I dare say. Perhaps that is what your lady meant." He stopped. David was crying, his shoulders heaving. "What have I said, David? What is it?" He found the tear stains on David's face almost unbearable.

David slowly regained control and answered: "I am now walking a narrow path, a razor's edge between two precipices, and I must go on, unless I refuse my destiny. In accepting it, I know I am hastening the day when love will come." He was seized again with a fit of sobbing.

Jonathan became brisk. "Come, now! Come! There is your blanket. Lie down and go to sleep." Sleep was certainly the answer then for David, or part of it. But when he woke at first light, he saw that Jonathan had not gone to bed at all.

In Gaza, the defeat at Elah had a predictable effect. Duke Shekelath sent a fast boat to Luqqawatna asking for advice. The answer was categorical. For the moment, there should be no more frontal attacks on the Hebrew heartland. Almost a hundred and fifty chariots, charioteers, and chariot fighters had been lost in the battle. Five to seven years would be required to replace these threefold and to develop the necessary infantry for a final, overwhelming assault. Luqqawatna therefore counseled a return to the strategy of "spear thrusts" rather than "hammer blows," of raids rather than frontal attacks.

The commander most affected by the directive was Achish. He had just returned from an inspection when he heard his name called out. "Duke Achish! My Lord Duke! Duke Achish!" The young captain ran through the long corridor of the palace at Gath. Achish heard the shouts and knew the voice. His servants continued to remove his body armor as he turned to face the breathless young officer who burst through the door.

"My Lord Duke! Duke Shekelath has been to Refa-im!"

"To Refa-im? Shekelath? Why was I not told? When did this happen? What did he want there?"

"My lord, I only just learned the news. He is already back in Gaza. He took one of his own regiments. They found the caves, my lord. They searched every lair and stronghold, hundreds of them. Every giant they found was asleep. Not a normal sleep. They didn't stir. Not one of them."

"And?" Achish closed his eyes. He almost knew the rest without being told.

"Duke Shekelath knew about the strange necklaces of the giants, my lord."

Of course he did. Achish himself had told Shekelath every detail he had learned of the giants.

"He gave orders that the necklaces were to be torn from every giant found, and every giant was to suffer the fate of Goliath."

"How many were killed?"

"All of them, my lord. After it was over, the caves were filled with dry bush and the entrances were piled high as well. The whole enclosure was set ablaze. It's still burning."

When his captain had finished and left, Achish dismissed his servants and let the silence of the room fall around him like a cloak. He dressed himself slowly, lost in thought. Later, the slow, even tapping of his peg leg echoed through the darkened marble corridors. He stood at the battlements looking out over the Shefela that stretched away to the southeast, as seventeen years before he had looked out from Dagon's hill at the destruction of Gaza. He watched the fiery halo in the darkness far off above the zigzag pass.

How your god puzzles me, Anak, he thought. Will I never understand this Adonai?

The next blow came when Shekelath and the council called Achish to account for his intelligence gathering. It was Achish against the council, and Achish won, of course. None of them, singly or together, was a match for his ability, intelligence, wit, and delivery. Lean and intense, he limped into the council chamber and hammered home his point:

"This is Dagon's war against Adonai. Every piece of information I have garnered points to one conclusion. We are being drawn into a trap, a snare. We all want to get rid of Saul. But suppose that itself is a trap? Will any of you, my Lord Dukes—will any of you take that risk without making sure? Now I will say it once more and I will say it again. Somewhere up there in that foul nest of Hebrews there is someone, some man, some woman, some baby, carefully hidden from us by the cunning of Adonai. We have to find him or her and kill him or her. For what happens here in Philistia is what happens to the entire Philistine dream."

"Did they ever catch that miserable shepherd?" Meluhhag asked without much interest, to fill the silence that followed.

"We don't even know his name," Shekelath snorted, "and

he doesn't matter. He's nothing. By now he's back guzzling goat's milk, hair and all. Achish is right. There's a snare here. Even Luqqawatna is cautious. From now on it's spear thrusts, no hammer blows until the moment is ripe."

As Achish limped to his chariot, Shekelath's comments ran through his mind in an endless loop: "We don't even know his name... and he doesn't matter." But suppose, Achish mused, he did matter? Suppose he wasn't just a "miserable shepherd" at all? Suppose he was the key man, Adonai's emissary? At the least, Achish would find out his name, his family, and his home town.

For the next five years the Philistines executed Luqqawatna's strategy with great fidelity and considerable success. They became exceptionally adept at the hit-and-run spear thrust. Life and property in the land were never secure.

It was Achish, not Shekelath, who was right about David. Literally overnight, David the obscure shepherd boy of Bethlehem became, at seventeen, David the champion of Israel. Within days of his amazing victory over Goliath and the rout of the Philistines, David's story had entered the history of his race.

The magnitude of his triumph and the way in which it was won combined with David's youthful freshness, beauty, and strength to make him instantaneously mythic among his people, while corroding Saul's very soul with a blind hatred and jealousy that the king seemed powerless to resist or even control.

Emotionally David was still an adolescent when he was suddenly taken up and made an official member of the king's own household. For the better part of two years he was a commander in Saul's army, had his own quarters at Gibea, and at Saul's table was assigned a place next to Jonathan. He participated in all war councils and led the Hebrews into battle. He was fully established but often puzzled and anxious.

The primary cause of David's anxiety was the erratic character of Saul himself. One day, all Saul's greatness and nobility would shine out in everything he did; the next, he would be angry and withdrawn. He would leave the fortress by himself and be away for days. Occasionally at night David and others in the compound would be awakened by doleful groaning from Saul's bedroom. Yet Saul often called for David to play his harp after the evening meal, and he would take great pleasure in the music. To David he was unreadable, unpredictable, and exceedingly dangerous.

Another thing that puzzled David was the increasing trust

Saul placed in his steward, a strange man called Kelebai. Kelebai managed Saul's personal property and affairs as well as the finances of Gibea. He had only come to prominence since Samuel left the king, but very quickly he seemed to become Saul's alter ego, and his malign influence increased almost daily. Even the placid Ahinoam seemed ill at ease when Kelebai was around.

A third thing, too, distressed David. During his first winter at Gibea he often talked with Saul about taking the initiative against the Philistines. Saul valued David, and he listened but seemed oddly indecisive. And when spring came, it was the Philistines who had planned well. They jabbed into the Hebrew clans everywhere. A chariot sweep into Shekhem desecrated the shrine; a night raid into Beersheva left hundreds of cattle and sheep slaughtered, houses burned; other raids destroyed two of Saul's forward garrisons east of Gath near Refa-im.

Only then did Saul throw off his indolence and begin a frenzy of activity himself. In the ensuing weeks David campaigned everywhere: northward into Galilee and as far west as the Ladder of Tyre; east beyond Nazareth as far as the Jordan. He led attacks into Ammon, Gilead, Edom, and Moab. He defended Hebrew villages all through the central highlands in the heart of Judah. Yet by midsummer it seemed that the Philistine attacks would never end. Like a swarm of wasps, the enemy stung the Hebrews everywhere and proved almost impossible to destroy.

Saul had been back at the fortress but a week toward the end of summer when his spies reported a planned Philistine move against his garrisons guarding the eastern reaches of Sorek Valley. He rode out with David and intercepted the Philistines, took prisoners and tortured them. They learned of two planned thrusts, one again near Refa-im and one at Hebron in the south. Saul laid his plans. He would take most of the men to defend Refa-im. David would ride south with five hundred men and conscript villagers along the way to defend Hebron.

By the time he reached Hebron, David led five thousand men and carried out a classic ambush. For the Philistines it was a minor if bloody defeat. David rode at once from Hebron to strengthen Saul's defense at Refa-im, and there again his help was decisive. In those two campaigns alone the Hebrews counted ten thousand of their enemy who would never fight again. At last, some wasps had been swatted.

Cheers and celebrations greeted king and champion everywhere as they rode back to Gibea. David listened to the shouts of the men and the music of timbrels in the streets of the towns they passed, and the simple songs of victory the women sang— "Saul has slain his thousands! *Yechi ha-melek!* David has slain his ten thousands! *Yechi ha-melek!*" But everyone noticed that once back at Gibea, Saul left David without a word and made straight for his house.

At dusk the gates opened twice, for Jonathan and for Joab, each with more victories to lay at Saul's feet. When he would see neither of them, they joined the impromptu celebrations and feasting. Well after midnight Saul still watched from the window. When he saw Jonathan and David together, his anger flew out of control! "He conquers the hearts of my people, even my son! What is left for him to take from me but my kingdom?"

Saul waited for David at the top of the stairs. The scream that then came from the upper stories of the house froze the blood in the hearts of every soldier in the compound. David raced for the stairs, sword in hand, Jonathan only a step behind. Another scream, and then a sight that stopped David stock-still. Saul himself was on the landing above David. He had the face of a man possessed—teeth bared, eyes flashing, face white. The veins and muscles in his neck bulged with his fury. His hands flashed forward and his spear flew for David's heart.

David's twisting leap saved him. The spear buried itself to the haft in the wall. Before David could recover, the king was down the stairs four at a time, past David, screaming again. With all his might he pulled the spear from the wall, and as he turned to try again, he was pinioned from behind by the captain of the guard, who had burst into the passageway. It took the captain and a dozen men to hold Saul down. David fled.

"He could have killed you, Father!" Jonathan screamed at Saul. "His sword was drawn. Your spear was thrown. You could not have saved yourself. He is your loyal servant, Father! He has sworn it to me as well as to you! Are you mad that you attack him?"

But as always now, it was not his son or his stricken and terrified wife whom Saul listened to, but Kelebai. The wily steward had raced from his bed at Saul's first scream and had watched the whole scene from the top of the stairs. It was he who succeeded in calming Saul. In the semidarkness of his room, Saul watched, the whites of his eyes gleaming, as Kelebai poured a cup of wine and soothing herbs to help the king sleep.

"The King is right." Kelebai's voice was quiet, reassuring. He handed the cup to Saul. "But the method is wrong. The King fears David, and so do I. The people make too much of his victories. But for that very reason the King cannot kill him so crudely. The people say the Lord is with him. So we must arrange it that the Lord will slay him before he seizes power."

"You have a plan, Kelebai?"

"I knew my King would know my thoughts," the steward smiled. "It occurred to me that if the King would promise his eldest daughter, Merab, as David's wife..."

"Kelebai, you are mad! To give him Merab would be to give him the kingdom!"

"Hear me out, my King. I said *promise* him Merab, not give her to him. The King can offer Merab as token of his sincerity. But of course a mere shepherd of no account will have to perform great deeds to earn so great a prize. The King can be expected in such circumstances to send David everywhere, into the worst campaigns, the most dangerous battles. The idea, as the King says, is to see him dead, not crowned. But let the Philistines do it for us. And while he is away fighting, Merab can be safely married off to another. She cannot be expected to wait for a dead man!"

After Kelebai had left him, Saul lay in the unearthly quiet that gripped the fortress. Kelebai is right, he thought: I do fear David. And the people are right: the Lord is with him. And Samuel is right: the Lord has departed from me. But still I am king, the anointed king. And even Samuel cannot change that. Saul chased these thoughts for hours, as a cat will chase its tail, with equal results.

Ahinoam was as constant and loving a wife to Saul now as she always had been. Even when Saul was so cruelly beset by these evil spells that seemed to come without warning, Ahinoam hoped that each one would be the last. The morning after his attack on David, Saul came to her bedchamber and begged her help in persuading David that he sincerely repented, that he valued David, that he proposed to pledge Merab to David as the dearest token of his word that he could give.

Ahinoam found David in the sanctuary of Joab's protection. She told David all that Saul had said to her: he would make David a commander of thousands, a rank held only by the king's own son, Jonathan, by his kinsman, Abner, and by Joab. And, more than that, Saul would make him his own son-in-law. Merab, Saul's daughter, would be his wife, Ahinoam explained. Now David had seen Merab many times. Like everyone else, he found her comely; but her chief advantage was that she was the king's daughter.

"Does that seem to you a little thing, David, to become the king's son-in-law and to marry the woman you love? Return to his services, fight for the Lord."

David kissed Ahinoam's hands. "So be it," he said in genuine delight at the prospect of marriage with Merab. Still, some of the innocence of his own heart had been slain within him. He was wary. He agreed to stay, but he no longer fully trusted Saul.

Saul was ecstatic at the news Ahinoam brought him. From then on, before he would send Abner or Jonathan or Joab, he sent David to defend the land. And everywhere David piled success upon success. Spoils from his battles against the Philistines poured into Gibea. David's fame increased over all the House of Israel.

Kelebai was forced to reassure the king: "Keep David away from Gibea. Keep him fighting. It will only be a matter of time before the enemy will do our work for us." When Merab was given to Adriel the Meholathite in marriage, Ahinoam tried to intervene for David, who was near Hebron again, fighting. Saul would not listen to her:

"These are not women's matters!" he told her roughly.

The dry season extended well into the winter of David's second year at Gibea, and the king did not lack for Philistine offensives to keep his young commander in constant peril. But David's life seemed charmed, and there finally came the day when Saul stood with the steward, Kelebai, at the window of the upper room and watched David coming at the head of columns of weary men drenched by the rain, up the mountain trail toward the gate of the fortress. Saul's voice was full of despair. "How will I keep him from turning my people against me now when he learns that Merab has been married these many weeks to another man?"

"Easily, O King, if I know my man." Kelebai's resourcefulness at scheming was limitless. "There's always Mikhal. Your second daughter can be as useful a snare as your first. They will be promised to each other publicly, so there will be no room for doubt in David's mind. If he performs just another task or two and still comes back alive! Will the King leave the matter in my hands? I will have a full report before a week has passed." Saul agreed, and that evening Kelebai went to lay his proposal before David.

"Yes, Kelebai," David began, "I see the king's esteem for me. The first news I had on entering the gates was that Merab has already been married to another."

"You must understand, David, we had reports of your death. Merab loved you, and the king would not let her pine in her grief. When we knew the reports were false, it was too late. The king is quite upset about this. Quite. It would not surprise me to see you as the king's son-in-law yet. There is Mikhal, you know; the king knows she loves you, too—every bit as much as Merab—and it pleases him."

But this time David's smile didn't reach his eyes.

"If you will leave the matter in my hands, David, I can promise that there will be a different outcome this time."

"Tell the king, Kelebai, that as Adonai lives, I am the loyal servant of his anointed king, and I will wait to hear from him." Although David in fact did not love Mikhal, nor she him, it meant acceptance for him and a chance for Mikhal to leave a father whom she hated.

The matter was quickly arranged. Saul himself made the formal announcement of betrothal, declaring that he desired no marriage gift except a hundred Philistine foreskins.

During the winter months of his betrothal, David lived apart from the king in his own house outside the compound, but he was expected to join Saul's family at the evening meals during the feasts of the new moon and for high holy days. He found the king quiet but generally even-tempered. Ahinoam, however, seemed pale and could not easily meet David's eyes, although he often tried to reassure her with his own.

"I will force your father's hand this time, Jonathan," David told Jonathan as they walked alone one day. "If he fulfills his part of the test this time, and Mikhal is given to me, then that will be the Lord's sign that I am to remain here. If he betrays his word again, then . . ."

"He will not, David. I know this time he will not. He cannot."

Even before the winter rains had stopped, David led his command from Gibea. To give Kelebai his due, the steward was hardly surprised when David returned not three days later, without so much as a scratch on him, and called Kelebai to his house. He flung a leather pouch on the table between them. He spoke evenly, decisively. Not yet twenty, David was learning how to make his power felt.

"Here, Kelebai, are two hundred Philistine foreskins. Give them in full number to the king. Now I warn you! By his own word I have doubly fulfilled the test he set me, and I will be his son-in-law!" And he was.

There had been grander wedding feasts in the land. Kelebai, as steward, made all the arrangements for this one, and he saw no reason for suffering the indignity of having to prepare a lavish celebration for David. And after the simple ceremony, David and his new wife took up residence in a small house assigned them within the Gibea compound. Mikhal, at that age, was attractive in a flinty way. Small, wide-hipped, black-eyed, sharp of tongue, she was determined to make this marriage a happy one. She had, after all, been married to the most desirable man in her father's army. David, however, found himself indifferent to her charms. Yet he dissembled well, for he felt her loyalty. In the ever tense atmosphere of Saul's court, he had few allies; and Mikhal, he realized, could be an invaluable source of information about Saul's intentions. If things had turned out differently, Mikhal might have become the mother and ancestor of a whole dynasty of kings in Israel. The hardness of her character might have been softened. But future events were shortly to deprive her of her beloved David. And when she was returned to him many years later, she had turned into a woman full of bitterness and hate.

Barely three weeks after their wedding, Saul's wife, Ahinoam, took Mikhal aside:

"Don't ask me how I have learned this, my daughter. I have reason to be very watchful. But if David stays even this night in Gibea, by tomorrow he will be killed."

"Lord God! Mother! Are you sure?"

"It will be a risk for you, child, but you must help David flee."

As soon as she could get David alone, Mikhal told him of her father's treachery. "You should kill him, David! He has become hateful!"

"No, Mikhal, I can't. He is the anointed of the Lord, and I cannot raise a hand against him. But neither will I stay to be killed by him. You must help me get away."

David had barely time to outline a plan with Mikhal when they heard heavy footsteps approaching the door.

"Delay them, Mikhal. I will let myself out through a back window."

As he lowered himself silently to the ground at the back of the house, David could hear Mikhal's voice at the door. "You can't see him now. He doesn't feel well and has gone to bed. Tell my father to send for him tomorrow."

Mikhal knew her father and his rages well enough to know she hadn't more than a few minutes before his men would be back. She did exactly as David had told her. It was Kelebai who came the second time, with a dozen men.

"Your father will not wait until tomorrow. If David is sick, as you say, my men will carry him to the king in his bed. You are to come also." And Kelebai waved his men to the bedroom.

When the messengers laid the cot at Saul's feet, the king caught the bed coverings with the tip of his sword and threw them aside. There, where he had thought to find David ready to be slain, lay a large image of Dagon, a trophy of one of David's victories.

"Find him, Kelebai." Saul's voice was as cold as death itself. "Find David or you are as dead as he will be. I swear it as an oath!"

This time, David realized he could not return. He knew only one place to go: to Samuel at Rama.

"You can't stay here," the aged prophet said when he had heard David's story. "He'll come here at once. You will have to go into hiding. I will show you the way." By the middle of the morning they were miles north, at Naioth, a tiny valley where the wandering companies of prophets assembled and prayed.

The next day Saul's men arrived back in Gibea as Saul sat alone brooding.

"David and Samuel are at Naioth, O King!"

"Kill them and bring me back their heads and hands." Saul leaped up, his face twitching. "Go get them, you dogs! Kill them!"

The appointed assassins arrived at Naioth and soon found David and Samuel standing quite calmly in the middle of a group of ecstatic men. Saul's messengers plunged in among the babbling prophets, leaving two of their number outside the valley to cut off any attempted escape. But before they could take Samuel and David, the spirit of prophecy took hold of Saul's men, and they tore off their clothes, fell to the ground, and started to babble. The two who had remained outside dashed off in terror to tell Saul. The king sent a second group, and then a third to Naioth, but whoever dared to enter among the companies of prophets was immediately seized by the spirit and enchained in that immobilizing ecstasy.

In desperation, Saul, followed by his bodyguards, hurried

up to the small valley, took one furious look at the wriggling, raving prophets, drew his sword, and plunged into the crowd. But he had just stepped over the first prone body when the spirit took hold of him as well. He dropped his sword, ripped off his armor and his body clothing, and fell gurgling to the ground. His alarmed bodyguards drew their swords and made a bold attempt to reach the king, but they also immediately succumbed. Samuel's crinkled face spread into a slow smile as he and David watched. He said to David, "I think we can go now. We have a small margin of safety." They went swiftly to Ramathaim-Zofim, where they went into hiding.

Some time later, Saul, his bodyguards, and the messenger-assassins he had sent woke up to find themselves lying alone and naked in a sea of mud. The prophets were all gone and the winter rains fell heavily. Hungry, cold, angry, mystified, they made their way back to Gibea under gray-black skies, lashed by driving rain and cold winds. Nobody said a word to Saul. His face was white, his eyes unfocused. He lay down on his bed and remained staring at the ceiling.

It was fully ten days before the king reappeared. His eyes were round and lit by some frightening gleam; the expression around his mouth was vacuous. He seemed to have a complete lapse of memory about recent events. He frequently spoke of David as dead. Once or twice he asked Jonathan where David was. Then he would start weeping while he looked at David's empty place at the table.

It all became too much for Jonathan, who concluded that the issue had to be resolved one way or the other. He made elaborate inquiries—and when he got the information he needed, he sent a secret message to Ramathaim-Zofim to ask David to return. David's answer came back swiftly: "I will meet you, dear friend, at the south end of the king's threshing floor the night before the next full moon."

Two nights before the full moon, David slipped down to Gibea in the dead of night. He climbed into one of the tall cypress trees that stood at the north end of Saul's threshing floor and remained there all night and through the next day until evening. He had to make sure that the meeting was not a trap.

About ten o'clock he heard footsteps along the gully leading from the fortress ramp to the threshing floor. Jonathan emerged onto the moonlit floor and stood there, calling out David's name softly. David did not budge. He could take no chances. He kept his eyes on Jonathan and on all the approaches for two hours more. By midnight, he was sure that Jonathan was alone. He whistled as he often had done during night raids. Soon Jonathan was in among the cypress trees, answering David with a corresponding whistle. They were beside each other immediately, embracing without speaking. David scanned the sky.

"In a few moments, Jonathan, the moon will be hidden by those clouds. Let's make a run for it through the gullies behind the cypresses." They waited, and in the darkness scurried across the open space into the Ezel Valley. Then they sat down side by side, their backs against the rock wall.

"David," Jonathan began, "you must come back to Gibea. It's the only hope for my father and the kingdom. The Philistines are increasing their attacks. You must return. You can help him get well."

"He wants to kill me!"

"He doesn't really. It's because he is ill."

"Jonathan, Jonathan! Your father knows we love each other. You're the last one he'd tell." David clasped Jonathan's hand. "Believe me, Jonathan, at this very moment I am at death's door, and I cannot defend myself. I am not allowed to touch the anointed of Adonai even though he wants to kill me."

Jonathan started to cry. "It cannot be. Even if my father is in the hold of an evil spirit, that doesn't release him from the Covenant."

"My beloved friend," David replied, "I am tired and baffled, and Adonai has not shown me what to do. If truly your father wants me dead, *and* you know this but cannot bring yourself to tell me, then please, Jonathan, kill me now." And he handed Jonathan his bare sword. "At least love will be with me at my death."

Jonathan dropped the sword and buried his face in his hands, sobbing. Finally, he managed to speak: "David, let us swear a new pact. I swear to you that you and your family will be most precious to me, and that I will defend you with my life."

David hesitated an instant, then: "I swear, Jonathan, by the Covenant that here and hereafter you and your family will be sacred to me, to be guarded with my life."

They made their plans. Jonathan was to find out as soon as he could if his father really wanted David dead. They arranged a secret signal. David would remain hidden at the end of the Ezel Valley beside a well-known monument called the Ezel Stone. When Jonathan had ascertained the truth, he would come down to the valley to practice archery as usual and tell

David what he had learned. If he was followed and the news was bad, he would simply shoot an arrow to strike the stone, and David would know that he had to flee.

But Jonathan's experience at table next evening was frightening and humiliating. Out of the blue Saul without moving a muscle put the question to no one in particular. The king gazed at the ceiling and asked in a steady monotone, "And where is David?"

Abner and Joab looked at their plates. Mikhal shot a warning glance at Jonathan. Kelebai, standing behind the king's chair, smiled. "Jonathan must know surely," he said.

"David has gone to Bethlehem, Father. His family offers a special sacrifice at this time of the year. He asked me to tell you, Father." Jonathan was not ready for the storm that followed.

"You," Saul said, suddenly switching his gaze down from the ceiling to glare at Jonathan with burning eyes, "you filthy sodomite, you faggot whelp of a whoring mother! Don't think you fool us! I know you have slept with that smelly stallion!"

"Father! Father!" Jonathan cried, half rising.

"And where were you the other night? Kelebai couldn't find you in your bed! Out polluting yourself with him, he soiling you with his sweat and filth! Abomination in Israel." Saul's voice rose and his mouth filled with spittle. "Don't you know that as long as he's alive you will not be king after I die? Don't you know that? Or has he promised you his bed as king, too?" Saul had risen with the force of his abuse. He now sank back in his chair, a satisfied look on his face as he saw the stricken look on Jonathan's.

"Now there is only one thing you can do." He took out his sword, tested its edge with his thumb, and laid it down on the table beside him. He lifted his head, grinning from ear to ear. "Go and fetch the filthy sodomite. Bring him here—tell him the king loves him and wants to embrace him." Saul threw a wild look up at Kelebai. "Tell him anything you like, but bring him here."

Jonathan could not move or speak. Saul screamed violently. "Go! Get out of here! Find him! Bring him back!"

"Why should he die, Father?" Jonathan asked plaintively. "What evil has he done?"

Saul never took his eyes off Jonathan. His eyes and voice changed radically. Blood suffused his face. "I'll fix you properly this time, my dirty little pig!" Before anyone could guess what he was going to do, Saul seized his spear from the wall and hurled it at his son, but haste and rage affected his aim and the spear went wide.

Jonathan stood up. Watching his father all the while, he walked to the wall rack and picked up his bow, strapped his quiver over his shoulder, fingered his arrows until he found a favorite one, took it out, and strung it on his bow. There was dead silence in the dining room. Saul licked his lips and looked at Jonathan. Kelebai cowered behind Saul. Abner's fist was on his sword, but Joab clamped a rough hand over it and shook his head at Abner. No one dared move. They knew Jonathan's accuracy. He was cold, taut-faced. He stood utterly still, his eyes filling with tears. Kelebai knew that if he moved he was a dead man.

But Jonathan had eyes only for his father. He stared down the length of that arrow at his father's right eye. He could plant that arrow right in the center of the pupil. Then he remembered David's pathetic words: "I cannot touch the anointed one of Adonai..." His anger subsided. He removed the arrow from his bow, weighed it in his hand for a moment, then turned on his heel and walked out of the dining room with his long, loping stride.

"Jonathan," Saul croaked hoarsely, and when his son did not turn back, Saul collapsed crying over the table. Mikhal rushed from the room. Kelebai stayed with Saul. Joab stood up and blocked Abner's way.

"If either of you makes one move in the next twenty-four hours, I will cut out your entrails," Joab said to Abner and Kelebai.

Joab left the king's house and went in search of Jonathan. "Make sure David gets away," Joab whispered. "I'll see that you are not followed."

Joab kept his word. The next morning Jonathan got up early and went down to Ezel Valley. He was not followed. He called and David came out of his hiding place. Jonathan told him of the king's madness, and David was too overcome to speak. At last he knelt down and kissed the dust on the valley floor three times, his tears flowing freely, his body shaking with emotion. Jonathan heard him murmuring, "Blessed be the name of Adonai...blessed be the will of Adonai...."

For an instant Jonathan looked at David through his tears, then he whispered, "Go! Go!" It was the last time Jonathan was ever to look into David's eyes.

The Outlaw

No sooner was David out of Jonathan's sight than he broke into a desperate run, in case Jonathan had been followed. He had no food, no weapons except a small throwing knife, no roof to shelter under. Where could he go that Saul's dreadful anger would not reach?

He ran for about three miles northwest of Gibea and stopped on the bank of a stream flowing swiftly westward. He paused for a moment to consider a place where he might flee. Nov, perhaps, at least temporarily. He entered the stream, wading upstream eastward for about two miles before a downpour of rain blanketed the land. At least he need not fear being tracked. He proceeded quietly for another half a mile and climbed cautiously up a hill to reconnoiter. Far to the left the land rose to a little plateau, and there it was, the high place of Nov, the stone tower and the chapel encircled by a high stone wall.

Because it was near Gibea, Saul consecrated all his war trophies there—the sword and armor of Goliath, Ammonite shields, Philistine chariot wheels, Edomite helmets, Egyptian saddles, all hung there. The current high priest was Ahimelek, who had one wife and five sons. Nov itself was a town of eighty-five priestly families, and people said the air was peaceful in Nov night and day. To David's eyes now it looked like a haven. But there was a difficulty: to appear on foot, alone, without arms or companions, would surely arouse Ahimelek's suspicions, since Saul's animosity to David was already well known.

Suddenly David heard the sound of hooves and whirled. Joab and his two brothers, Abishai and Asahel, were less than fifty yards away, leading their camels toward him by the halter. David, cursing, drew his knife, determined to fight, but Joab held up his hand.

"No, we come in peace, David. Jonathan told us everything. We don't want to stay in Gibea, where we will surely be killed. Saul knows that we are your kinsmen and that you and I are close friends as well. As for Abishai and Asahel, well, they go where I go. We want to join you. See! We have brought you a camel." David said nothing, still wary. Then at a sign from Joab they unbuckled their sword belts and flung them to the ground. Spears, daggers, shields, and helmets followed. Unarmed, they walked forward.

David held out his hands in sheer relief, and the three men rushed forward and fell to the ground. "David, you are our leader," Joab said. "We will follow you. We swear it on the Covenant!"

David saw that, together, the four of them had hope—small but real—and his spirits rose. Laughing, he embraced them. "Well, my warriors! Swear to me then, as I to you, that my enemies will be your enemies and my friends will be your friends. Swear to me on the Covenant!" Again Joab spoke for all three:

"We swear it, David. We swear it on the Covenant. And as the sign of Abraham's oath, we place our hands beneath your thigh!" Each man in turn then placed his right hand beneath David's scrotum and said, "I swear in the name of Adonai!"

David looked at his cousin. Plain Joab certainly was, but he had the panther's instinct to kill. Joab would be the man to guard David's back. No man alive was better suited to that task.

As for Abishai and Asahel, they were Joab's creatures, both strapping young men with the same black hair as Joab. Asahel, the younger and slighter, had a certain pleasing quality about his mouth. Abishai, renowned executioner of prisoners, had cold, dead eyes.

"Rearm yourselves," David said, "and we'll go to visit Ahimelek." As they rode on to Nov, David asked Joab how he had known where to find him.

"I asked myself: Where would David go—without food, without arms, without a mount? Either to Rama or to Nov. But not Rama—"

"Why not?"

"Because you love Samuel. You wouldn't want to endanger him. So I came straight to Nov!"

"If you can think like that, so can the king."

"I doubt it. I doubt that the king knows yet what your circumstances are. But we must be quick about things because he soon will."

Ahimelek, alerted by the watchman, was waiting for them behind the barred gate. David the champion, but only with his cousins? No soldiers? No weapons? Saul's messenger came every week to find out who had passed. It did not pay to act unthinkingly.

"Peace, David! Why are you come with such a small company?"

"Greetings, Ahimelek, my brother!" David's voice was confident, authoritative. "I am on the king's most urgent business, and I need food and weapons."

Ahimelek was a frail, hunched man of about seventy, perpetually racked by arthritis. He revered David but knew of the growing breach with Saul. He also knew the reputation of Joab and his brothers. If Saul had sent these three as David's helpers, theirs was a blood mission. No need for questions. He made a sign to the slave to open the gate. The three brothers deposited their arms with the gatekeeper—no weapons were allowed in the high place—and the four rode in and dismounted. David kissed the hem of Ahimelek's robe. The priest said: "Food I have not, except the sacred loaves for tomorrow's holy feast. Have these men been with women in the past three days?" David shook his head. "Very well, I can see no difficulty." He led the way into the common room where worshipers prayed and indicated a large pannier filled with the dark brown oaten loaves. "Take what you need," he said, and they filled their saddlebags. "But I have no weapons here.. The Law forbids it. We do have, of course, the sword you took from the giant."

"That will do. Where is it?"

"Wrapped up in cloth and put behind the Ephod. You must lift it down yourself. Only you and the king are allowed to handle it."

As they walked back toward the gate, David noticed a young Edomite named Doeg, Saul's chief shepherd, standing there. David and Joab continued walking nonchalantly toward the camels. David tied the sword to his saddle and nodded to Joab.

"As the king lives, Doeg! The king has sworn to kill anyone who reveals our whereabouts." Joab's delivery was even, but every word resonated with menace.

"I have seen nothing, nothing at all. So help me Adonai!" Doeg swore. The group retrieved its weapons and mounted.

"Ahimelek, my brother!" David saluted the old man. "May Adonai bless you and bring you great peace. I will not forget your help."

Ahimelek peered up at David. "Whatever you do, may Adonai be with you." The party rode out the gate with deliberate calm, and not until they had crossed the stony plain and were hidden in the gullies did they start galloping.

"Where are we going?" cried Joab.

"Just follow me," David shouted, whipping his camel to a frenzy.

Back at the high place, Ahimelek returned to his house and called his youngest son, Abiathar: "Son, there is going to be trouble, and we must be ready. Take our Ephod and our copy of the Law and wrap them carefully in a canvas. Have a camel ready, but keep it in the stall. Tie the canvas bag to the saddle. Don't let Doeg or anyone else see what you do."

"What is it, Father?"

"I don't even know myself, but we are both going on a long journey, and the House of Israel will be filled with sadness and blood."

After ten minutes of swift galloping, Joab shouted to David, "There are the towers of Jebus!"

"We must get beyond Saul's pickets," David shouted back. "It's our only chance."

David intended as soon as possible to head for Adullam, where he had found a hiding place while he was herding sheep at Beraka. But first he had to make sure that Jesse and Shoshanna were gotten safely out of Bethlehem, because Saul's anger would surely fall on them. There was really only one available solution. "We must go to Gath," David told the others. "It's open to all refugees from Saul, and it's the only way I can get word to my family and make sure they are protected. Has any of you got any money?"

"Some Tyrian silver talents," Abishai answered.

"Good!"

Within another hour's ride they met the first Philistine guards. Declaring themselves refugees from Saul's kingdom, they were given passes and allowed to continue into the crowded streets of Gath, where they mingled with a vast throng of many races.

Duke Achish had initiated this policy of hospitality in the hope that with a widely spread net he would catch some valuable fish. None of the refugees left Gath without being interrogated. The Philistine authorities here, wholly unlike those in the other great cities of Dagon, regulated affairs with a lenient but firm hand, discreetly watching over all that happened. This was entirely due to Achish himself.

The officer in charge of political refugees interviewed David's group: "Hebrews, you are welcome here as long as you are willing to fight Saul. But at all times the innkeeper must know where you are. And keep your passes with you."

"By God, we are enemies of King Saul," Joab swore. And no one could have doubted the sincerity of that declaration.

The Philistine smiled. "Let that hate last, Hebrew, let it last! You're safe here and welcome at the compound of Duke Achish this evening for a warm meal and entertainment."

The compound was in the center of the city, and a large crowd had gathered. Achish sat on a low balcony giving onto the walled courtyard where the refugees sat around a circular platform. Cooked meat, vegetables, bread, and wine were served, and a naked Philistine dancing girl pranced onto the platform to the sound of flutes and pipes. Soon the crowd accompanied her with handclaps and shouts, and now and again a man would leap up to join her in the dance.

David felt the tension of the past day beginning to ease. He began to feel the pull of the music and the attraction of the girl. Imprudently, he leaped to the platform to take a turn with her.

Joab swore, but too late. Already David had thrown aside his robe and was twisting, stamping, bending, and matching the girl's wild configurations with even wilder ones of his own. Delighted by David's beauty and prodded by the challenge of his dancing, the girl accelerated her tempo, and the music matched it. The handclapping got louder, more rapid. The shouting and whistling faltered and halted as everyone became enthralled with the sensuous geometry of the dance. Achish on his balcony fastened his eye on the Hebrew. "Know him?" Achish asked his guest, who was the political officer.

"Yes, my Lord Duke. He is called Elhanan. Out of Bethlehem of Judah, a refugee from Saul's army."

Achish was silent.

The last wild throes of the dance brought the whole crowd to its feet stamping and clapping, and as they finished the cheers burst like a dam. The girl hurried off the platform and disappeared as David went back to his companions.

"Who *is* this Elhanan?" Achish asked.

"Either a madman or a genius, my Lord Duke," his aide answered.

"But what a body! What legs! What arms! Bring him to me!" As the officer left on his mission, another from Achish's intelligence unit entered the balcony, spoke briefly to the duke, pointed in David's direction and quickly withdrew.

David had barely sunk to the ground beside Joab and only

begun to see his foolishness when the Philistine aide stood over him. "My Lord Achish wants to greet you. Come with me." The other Hebrews froze. David stood up and started to greet the officer. Then, as though suddenly galvanized, he began to quiver. He stopped his ears. He stuck out his tongue, laughing and spitting on the ground. He fell to the ground to lick the dust with his tongue and rolled over, grunting and grinning. He stood, bent down from the waist and broke wind, then started to laugh shrilly and to jump spastically, landing on his buttocks with a resounding thump. "Oh! Ah! Oh! Ah!" he moaned. "My arse is broken. My arse is broken." It was a convincing performance, although not clinically correct. The Philistine drew back in disgust and fear at what he took to be an epileptic seizure. The whole assembly crowded around to watch.

Joab, quick to understand, whispered to the officer: "My brother has the curse of the snake pit, sir. All our family are epileptics. He's harmless, but when he dances, the evil takes him." The aide spat in David's direction. Philistines believed that an epileptic was possessed by Dagon's devil, which made husbands impotent, women barren, children die, animals vomit. If you shed the blood of an epileptic, the devil was multiplied in as many drops of blood as were shed. The Philistines always drove epileptics out of their towns and left them in the wilderness to die.

"Stay here!" the Philistine snarled, his fear rising. "But keep him quiet." He hurried back to Achish with this news only to find the duke pacing the balcony and gleefully rubbing his hands. "My Lord Duke," the officer began, "that man, the dancer..."

"I know, I know. It is David, their champion. I've just been told. Dagon be praised!" The political officer had no idea what Achish was talking about.

Before he could ask, the commotion in the yard had grown so great that the guards at the gate had noticed it and were shouldering through the crowd toward David, swords drawn. Achish grabbed his aide by the arm:

"Quick! Tell the guards they must not touch that man unless I say so. Hurry!" Achish's brain was feverish with possibilities. If this was indeed the slayer of Goliath, then he was Adonai's champion. And if Adonai's champion would fight on the Philistine side, well, what more need be said?

Achish's officer returned with the sergeant of the guard, and as the three men walked over to where David was performing, Achish explained that no harm was to come to the madman. As Achish stood over David, he was disgusted by the spittle and dirt and smell. David had already urinated and defecated, and still thrashed around drooling, eyes rolling.

"Now tell me," Achish said to his two companions but keeping his eyes on David, "would you really believe that this quaking fool could be the champion who slew Goliath?" The aide and the officer laughed. But, ah! Achish saw the merest flicker, the merest gleam of thought in those presumably mad eyes.

"If this disgusting Hebrew goes on like this, I'll have to throw him out!"

Another flicker. Achish waited.

David rolled over again and sat in front of Achish, then climbed to his feet and swayed drunkenly. For an instant his eyes met Achish's, and in that fleeting look he got Achish's message. He fell back on his side, scrounged in the dirt, picked up a little pebble, crawled and slid across the dirt until he reached the gate to the compound, dragged himself up on the gatepost, and stood swaying and grinning.

He started to scratch a six-pointed star into the wood of the gate. "Oh, don't kill him," ordered Achish in mock exasperation, "just kick him out—and his pals with him!" The officer needed no further encouragement. David felt the nailed boot hit him in the coccyx. He hurtled through the doorway and rolled into the street, followed by Joab and his brothers, who had been hurled bodily after him.

"You have half an hour to be out of Gath," the political officer shouted after them. "Or else!"

The whole assemblage hooted with laughter.

Achish walked back to his balcony and drank some red wine. He called for his chief of operations, Maraghal: "Find out what is happening in Gibea, what Saul is doing. And, by the way, find out if four of Saul's officers are missing."

Out in the street, the four picked themselves up and made for the hostelry. Joab paid their bill and they made their way to the eastern gate of the city. As they came up to the gate, David still pretending to be mad, the other three praying and moaning, the guards turned the points of their spears and swords away, fearing that the madman might throw himself on the naked weapons and thus shed his pestilential blood on Philistine ground.

They kept up the performance until they were out of sight of Gath, heading southeast.

"Now where do we go?" Joab wanted to know.

"Just follow me," David said shortly. He reined his camel around due south. As they followed him across rocky gullies and through wild groves, David spoke only once: "When you see six fingers of rock sticking up into the air, tell me."

By noon of the day that David fled, Saul knew that Joab, Abishai, and Asahel had also gone. He stormed down to the camp of the archers and had Jonathan seized and tortured by driving wood slivers under his fingernails, until he was satisfied that Jonathan knew nothing of David's whereabouts. In a rage, Saul called for his camel and the tracking dogs.

The weather was foul. Rain flailed the earth. Saul cursed. No tracks would have lasted five minutes. He drew his sword and wildly struck at the ground in frustration as the rain streamed down his face and body.

Suddenly he swiveled and shouted at Abner. "Rama! Rama!" he exclaimed. "They're with him! On your camel, man! Armor bearer! Hurry up! We'll have their gizzards yet." In minutes the three men were thundering through the rain up the sloping trail toward Rama.

To his surprise, the first person Saul saw at the top of the narrow passage leading up between the rocks to Samuel's property was Samuel himself, sitting on a rock in the rain. Saul brought his camel to a scraping halt in the mud. The prophet did not move. The other two men rode up.

"O Prophet," Saul said harshly, "we are looking for David, and the three sons of Zeruiah."

"They are not here, O King," Samuel answered without lifting his eyes. His clothing was sodden. Saul glared at Samuel while Abner and the armor bearer waited in fear. No one could read the expression on Samuel's craggy face. Saul made a decision.

"O Prophet! A blessing on us, and we are on our way."

"May Adonai bless the King, and may Adonai's will be completely fulfilled in my lord," Samuel said in a low, deep voice. He stood up and bowed, lifting his eyes to look at Saul for the first time. Abner wasn't sure whether Samuel was crying or if it was merely the rain. They turned their camels around and trotted off a way. There Saul halted.

"He wouldn't dare return to Bethlehem." Saul was thinking out loud. "He'd know it would be the first place I'd go. Philistia would be suicide. It must be Bethel or Shiloh, or else the Jordan. Let's try Bethel."

Saul's arrival at Bethel struck Abner as bizarre. For years the high place had been in the hands of Hebrews who had become pagan priests of Baal. The temple housed the sacred prostitutes of Astarte. Yet King Saul rode in boldly, as though he hadn't a thimbleful of fear about ritual impurity or contamination. More disturbing still for Abner was the familiar way in which Asarhadad, the priest of Baal, greeted Saul. Abner and the armor bearer sat on their mounts in the rain while Saul walked away with Asarhadad into a one-story building. Soon the sound of laughter reached them and they watched as servants led three of the sacred prostitutes over to the house. Two hours passed. A servant came to Abner. "The king suggests that his faithful officers bed down for the night. There are accommodations, food, and amusement for you."

Abner stiffened. "We will camp in the valley and return for my lord at sunrise." All through the night Abner counted the hours, his soul perplexed with a growing apprehension.

While Abner waited and Saul dallied, David led his little company on through the night, aided by the moon that followed the rain. All four watched for the rock fingers.

It was Joab who suddenly reined in, pointing: "Away to the east, over there. Huh?" Sure enough, rising up from the mountainous terrain, they could see the "six fingers."

"That's it! That's it!" David said. "We're safe, my brothers. Let's go."

One side of the valley rose perpendicularly in the rock; the other was covered with woods. All was silent. They picked their way among the rocks and boulders on the valley floor and gradually began to hear the sound of running water. Soon they came to a shallow stream flowing out from the wooded side of the valley and disappearing again through a crevice in the rock face opposite. Above their heads the rock face shot up, ending in the six huge columns.

"This will be difficult," David said. "Better lead the camels. Watch carefully what I do. Joab, you come last." He led the camel down to the hole where the stream disappeared into the rock face. He stepped into the stream, pulling his camel, then disappeared into the hole. Abishai and Asahel followed, then Joab. He saw the rock roof slanting down in front of him until it left only a foot-high fissure ahead through which the water foamed and hissed. "Where are you, David?" he shouted.

"Here! To your left!"

"I see only rock."

"Yes. Go straight ahead toward the place where the stream enters the rock. Then bear left."

Joab waded forward. Cautiously he picked his way over and found that the slit was an invisible entrance to a steeply sloping cave where David and his brothers were stretching their weary arms and legs.

"We still go on foot," David said. "After a few yards it's going to be dangerous, so watch the camels."

Following David, they passed through a rather level cave for another twenty yards and then emerged into the moonlight. Their path now ran eastward around a sheer face of rock that faced north. The path was just wide enough for a camel. To their left and separated from them by a chasm of about twenty feet, a similar rock wall rose. On their right, their shoulders brushed against red sandstone that went straight up about a hundred and fifty feet to the "six fingers." The chasm to their left seemed to Joab to fall perhaps eighty or a hundred feet to the stream bed below.

As they continued, the path narrowed and the stream vanished. Scores of owls, eagles, hawks, and bats poured on the intruders a cacophony of hoots and screeches.

"It won't be long now," David kept saying. "We'll soon be out of this."

And suddenly they were. The north rock wall swung away, and the pathway widened out. Again they heard the babbling of water and the night sky unrolled overhead. David led them over to one side of the expanse of rock, where the water swirled in a pool. In the darkness they could make out trees and bushes.

"This is it," David said. "We're safe here."

"And tomorrow?"

"Tomorrow, Joab, before dawn, ride to Bethlehem. Tell my father, my mother, all my brothers, all their families and friends to pack up as quickly as possible. Then lead them here."

David explained that they were in Adullam in the heart of Hareth Forest. Once while shepherding at Beraka he had wounded a mountain goat and followed it here.

"By Adonai," Joab breathed, taking it all in with a sweeping glance, "you are either the destined one or the luckiest man alive!"

At the earliest light Abner and the armor bearer were back at Bethel's high place, where they found Saul already mounted and in high spirits. It was a bright, cold day with a sharp wind.

"All is well," said Saul. "Nobody passed through here yesterday. Asarhadad is paid to know these things. Our prey is still near Gibea." He swung his camel's head around and swept off, followed by his two officers. By nine in the morning they were close to the fortress, and Saul reined in. "Let's wait under those trees," he said. Saul sat down, his back to a tree, his sword, helmet, and shield by his side, his spear stuck in the ground. All of Israel knew this waiting posture of Saul. It always boded trouble for his enemies. "Signal to the fortress that we are here," he told the armor bearer. "Then patience, my friends! We will have news."

At the shrine of Nov, four miles south, at about the same time, Ahimelek the High Priest called his youngest son. "Abiathar, it's time to go. Take the camel. Go by the east trail until you can see the Salt Sea, then turn south and head for Bethlehem. Go immediately to Jesse, son of Obed. Tell him to flee with his family and his friends. Stay with them. David will find you. Tell him that Doeg the Edomite betrayed him."

Toward ten o'clock, Saul and his companions heard the sound of hooves. A man on a mule galloped up the Gibea ramp and into the fortress. A minute later he emerged and galloped over to Saul. It was Doeg, his face flushed with excitement.

"O King! I have come from Nov"—he drew in his breath—"David with Joab and his brothers came there yesterday. Ahimelek received them as honored guests, fed them the sacred bread, and gave David the sword of Goliath. Then they went away."

Saul was black with anger, screaming as he ran for his camel: "That filthy, treacherous son of a whore. I knew it! The priests are all in league with that son of Satan!"

The others had trouble catching up with Saul as he sped toward Gibea. Saul jumped off his camel inside the gate and shouted to his troops: "Bring me Ahimelek and all his sons, every priest and every son of every priest in every family at Nov. Bring them now! Here!"

An hour later Ahimelek and the eighty-four other priests entered the Gibea compound under guard. Every one of them wore the white linen Ephod tunic. They said nothing but stood quietly in front of Saul, who sat on his judge's chair outside his house, his head lowered, looking out from under his eyebrows.

"Ahimelek, son of Ahituv, you supplied food and weapons to my enemy, David. You plotted against me and my kingdom!" Ahimelek opened his mouth to speak, but Saul clicked his fingers and looked at his personal guards. "Kill them! All of them!"—pointing at the eighty-five priests. A wave of fear and consternation swept over the guards. No one moved. No Hebrew would lift a sword against a priest. Saul glared around at the guards, his eyes burning with anger. He turned to Doeg, who was with him. "Kill them, you, Doeg! All of them! Right now!"

Without further ado, Doeg drew his sword, advanced quickly and drove it into Ahimelek's belly, twisted it and drew it out entwined in entrails. The other priests started to pray out loud as Ahimelek fell forward groaning. One by one, in the broad light of day, Doeg killed all eighty-five priests of Nov. When the last had died, he wiped his sword on the dead man's tunic.

All this time Saul had not moved. He had watched each one die, grunting at every sword thrust by Doeg, his two fists closing and opening. Now he sprang to life as if renewed in spirit. Within minutes he had assembled his elite corps of spearmen.

They rode to Nov, entered the town, slew all the women, children and cattle, and set fire to every building. It was midday when Saul and his men returned. The king was by now exhausted. He stumbled up the stairs and fell on his bed in a deep slumber. Later, Jonathan arrived. He had been up north with his archers. He crept into the house and found his mother, Ahinoam. "Stay out of sight, Jonathan," she said. "Go to Beth-horon. I will send for you when I think it best."

That evening, an hour before sundown, David was sitting with Abishai and Asahel in the Adullam redoubt when Joab appeared. Behind him David could see the grizzled head of Jesse, who was leading a mule on which Shoshanna sat. Then came Joshua and his family and all David's brothers, their wives, children, servants, and slaves. They led pack camels and asses with the belongings they had hastily gathered. In the rear was young Abiathar, clutching to his chest the Ephod and the Law.

Rapidly, each family was assigned living quarters in the caves that honeycombed the rock walls of the hideout. Their available supplies of food, drink, and arms were checked. The animals were allocated to one part of the redoubt, and each adult was assigned daily duties. Guards were posted at the hole in the valley itself.

Within a few days Joab brought back word of Saul's massacre at Nov. David sat down with Abiathar: "I am responsible for the destruction of your entire house. I can't reverse that, but I will avenge it. Stay with me, Abiathar. You will be safe here. Someday I will cut out Doeg's heart."

"That I fully believe, Lord David. But now my father instructed me to hand this Ephod over to you." He held out the leather bag containing the Ephod. "He said to tell you: Do not fear. You are now the anointed of Adonai."

"I don't know how to use it." David shivered, full of apprehension.

"I am to show you." Abiathar smiled gently. "Here!" He undid the buckles. David held his breath. Abiathar drew the Ephod out and laid it flat on the rock between them. David saw a piece of leather about fourteen inches square. At the center was a gold plaque set with fourteen different-colored stones, each one with a letter etched on it. A semicircle of five transparent stones curved around the lower portion of the leather.

"There are three rows of four stones each," Abiathar pointed out. "One single stone, a blood-red carbuncle, above the rows; and another single stone, an amber, beneath the rows.

"There's one stone for each of the Twelve Tribes. *Ahlamah*, the amethyst, for Manasseh. *Tarsis*, the yellow serpentine, for Dan. *Soham*, the dark-green malachite, for Naphthali. And so on. See! The first letter of each tribe's name is on its own stone. The *kadkod*, the carbuncle, is for Gad. The amber is for Benjamin! I'll teach you all the names in a moment. The semicircle of five at the bottom contains the Name—you can read it. No one, save Moses, pronounced it ever."

David read to himself the letters etched on those five stones: A - O - U - E - I.

"Now, Lord David, give me your right hand. Spread your fingers. Palm up, please. Listen carefully. The thumb is for life, for love, for race. This, the forefinger, is for Adonai. This, the middle one, is for the fool's finger: it is for Satan. This third is the leech finger: for wisdom and heart. The little one is the ear finger, for secret messages from Adonai's spirit. The center of your hand where the haft of your sword rests in battle is for war. The heel of the palm is for death: by its force you drive the javelin through the heart of the enemy. The upper bank of the palm is for victory.

"Next, the finger letters. Each finger has three or four letters assigned to it. Here, then, is how you use the Ephod. The thumb here, the little finger here. There! Now, rest the center and heel of the palm down—so!"

For a full hour the others looked over with great curiosity at Abiathar and David, as the one gesticulated and talked and the other nodded, repeated, and gestured.

"Remember," Abiathar's last words of instruction ran, "when you have positioned your fingers and hands, and you've repeated the rhymes and spelled out the letters, then, according to my father, you'll spend one dreadful moment hanging on the precipice of silence and utterly dependent on Adonai's response. Do not fear! You are Adonai's anointed!"

For the second time in three years, news raced around the land. Every Shabbath assembly stirred with consternation: "The king wants to kill David." "David has gone into hiding in Philistia ... in Zoba ... in Egypt ... in Phenicia ... in Nubia. ..." "They say he's dead" ... "Samuel has vanished" ... "Whoever aids David will die the death" ... "Saul had every priest at Nov killed" ... "Doeg the Edomite is now champion." ... Around and around the rumors swirled.

Within the House of Israel, a great foreboding grew and spread. Men asked each other: "What is to become of us now that we are fighting among ourselves?"

Achish was summoned to a court-martial by the council in Gaza, accused of having let a man who was probably David escape.

Achish insisted, however, "I did not let this enemy of Dagon escape. On the contrary, if it was he, I made sure that he will come back to me willingly as the champion of Dagon and the enemy of Saul and Adonai."

And Achish stumped off, once more victor over his enemies. He had taken a long shot, to be sure, but he was certain it would pay off. His last gibe as he left the chamber: "Today, each one of you can sit in his garden plucking oranges in peace. Shortly, I tell you, we will pluck this ripe fruit off the tree— in peace."

Lassatha heard the news of David's flight from some caravan drovers and rushed off to tell Uri. He wasn't surprised. "David is a very special man. There hasn't been anybody like him in my lifetime, and he has a special destiny. This is just the beginning of things for David. Be patient. You love him, I know. Wait! We'll hear from him soon."

* * *

When the news reached Nazareth, the elders asked Malaki's advice:

"Two things are sure, my brethren," replied Malaki. "We cannot touch the king—he's the anointed. But also, as far as we know, David has done nothing wrong. Let us wait until Adonai speaks as only Adonai can. Through events. In the meantime, let us go about our business and trust in Adonai."

For the moment the object of their concern, David, had evaporated like mist in the sun. Down in the redoubt of Adullam, during the remainder of the winter and all the following spring, he kept his little band under tight control. Comings and goings were strictly regulated and were always by night. David and Joab traveled to Beraka to talk with David's trusted shepherds, who supplied them with food and news. The news was always bad. Saul raged continually and killed anyone who spoke or acted in even the slightest way favorable to David.

In Adullam, although food never lacked, it was always scarce, and David began to see a certain deterioration in Jesse, who was too old to be uprooted from a comfortable home and hidden in a cave like a hunted animal.

As summer faded, things started to crystallize in David's mind. Joab and Asahel returned from Beraka with surprising news. They had found a group of some forty-five men from all over Judah and Benjamin and Manasseh—with even one or two from the coast. All of them had come to find out where David was hiding and to join him.

"What did you tell them, Joab?"

"Now don't get angry, David," Joab answered. "They can't be spies. Some you know—soldiers who served under you. Some owe you heavy debts. Some, no doubt, are fugitives. All want to serve you."

For what? David asked himself. He was not in revolt against Saul and didn't want to be. He needed no army. Any day now Saul would relent—he always had before—and he, David, would be back in his rightful place. He explained this to Joab, but the wily Joab persisted: Why not accept the forty-five refugees? Wasn't he always afraid for the lives of the old people of their band? Well, here was a ready-made bodyguard. Besides, how long was he going to hide like a badger? Couldn't he see the hand of Adonai in all this too? Why think that Adonai only sent failure and suffering?

In the end, David said yes, partly for the reasons Joab supplied but chiefly because it had become increasingly apparent to him that his hope of reconciliation with Saul was in vain. So he went to meet Joab's men.

He was shocked. Eleven were thirty or more, but the rest were all between thirteen and seventeen. "They are children!" he exclaimed to Joab. Each had a mule or an ass. Some had weapons. All were hungry and miserable. "The younger ones are bound to be straightforward, but let's have a talk with the others," David said. Each was questioned at sword point for an hour or more, and each was genuine, as far as David and Joab could judge. They had just one ambition: "To fight in my Lord David's army and to enter his kingdom!"

The addition of those forty-five created new problems for David. There was room in the redoubt, literally a hundred caves or more. But food and weapons were already in short supply, and mounts were needed for most of the new arrivals, since the mules and asses they had brought down with them were mostly poor beasts that soon had to be killed and eaten. When Joab rode in a few weeks later with twenty-two more recruits, David and Joab made the only decision possible: they had to plunder some caravans.

After a few days' watching and waiting by the southern trail that skirted Philistia, David's scouts came back with news of a large Syrian caravan encamped five and a half miles from Adullam.

It was just past two in the morning, in a blinding downpour, when David's raiders struck. First, the men watching the animals were silently liquidated. Then the perimeter guards were picked off one by one. Finally, with about a dozen men assigned to each tent, a silent general attack was made under Joab's command. David and his forces encircled the camp to cut off all the stragglers. David's orders were explicit: no one, male or female, adult or child, was to be spared. No one was. Joab made sure of that. The fact that the caravaneers were Syrian made the ugly job easier for David. His first raid was a total success because the surprise was total.

The weapons, mounts, and clothes captured insured that everyone would be warm in winter and that the fighting force would be equipped. They still went to Beraka for meat. But in successive raids they supplied themselves amply with food, utensils and furniture.

Even though David never interrupted a caravan at the same place, the word gradually trickled out that he was operating somewhere south of Judah. As more and more of Saul's recruits deserted to David, his general whereabouts became known.

Saul could not, however, venture south of Jebus all that winter because the Philistines had started to push deep into Ephraim and Manasseh. But he vented his rage on any family that had a member who couldn't be accounted for. "They have sinned against the anointed of Adonai, their king. And they consort with that filthy onanist, David. They will all die," he swore to Abner and Jonathan. Saul posted a reward of twenty gold Tyrian talents for anyone leading him to the "refuge of sinners," as he described David's secret hiding place. Saul was confident that sooner or later David would be betrayed into his hands.

It was winter and its hardships that decided David to move the older members of his group. After more than a year, he found it increasingly unpleasant to see Shoshanna in an armed camp full of roughly dressed, unwashed men, bleating camels, and champing horses. Dirt, blood of battle, primitive conditions, were slowly wearing down both Shoshanna and Jesse as well as Joshua's aging parents. Eliab had little children, and his wife was pregnant. Moreover, the presence of a few young women in an almost all-male camp created an unbearable tension. They had to move, David told himself, and winter was the time to do it.

David sent Joab to Jebus with a message for Uri: "My father is old. My mother is frail. If we come to the city, can you find them a safe and comfortable place?"

He would do so, Uri responded. He also wanted to see David about a matter of great importance and had arranged their admission to the city as his guests.

A week later, leaving Abishai and Asahel in charge of Adullam with absolute authority and strict orders not to budge until they heard from him, David set out at the head of a small caravan for Jebus. They traveled mainly at night, approaching the city from the northwest. In the intervening week the loyal Uri had arranged everything.

"Your parents, Joshua's parents, and Eliab's wife will go to Mizpeh, city of Moab," Uri explained to David on the afternoon of their arrival. They sat in Uri's living room, Goliath's sword, which was never far from David's side, lying on the table between them. "Abikemosh"—King of Moab—"is my personal friend. He is married to a Hittite, and he owes me several favors. Besides," he added with a new gleam in his eyes, "Abikemosh cannot but welcome the slayer of the giant! The giants originally came from Moab, you know, and Kemosh, their god, was himself one of them." David detected some new sentiment in Uri, and he had a thousand agonizing questions. How could he pay Abikemosh? How could he be sure of his parents' safety? How long could they stay in Moab? His puzzlement showed on his face.

"I will explain. First, it's easy to reach Moab. You go to the landing stage halfway down the west bank of the Salt Sea, take the flat-bottomed boats there, and sail to the Eagle's Beak, a huge promontory sticking out into the sea. Once there, the rest is easy. I've arranged guides and boatmen."

"Wait, wait, my good friend," David said, laughing. "Who says we're all going to Moab?"

"You will, when I have finished explaining." The Hittite went on calmly and firmly. "Now you'll find Moab strange. They're not Hebrews. They have habits and customs you Hebrews cannot abide—brothers marry sisters, aunts marry nephews. They offer sacrifice to Kemosh—and you only worship Adonai. I know all that. But look, they believe what they believe. You believe what you believe. Leave them alone and they'll leave you alone. You'll have to meet Abikemosh in person. Don't be surprised at what you see."

"What's that?"

"Never mind, for the moment. Abikemosh is a very private person, rarely seen in public. He governs from his palace. You'll find all that out in good time. Besides, you'll learn a great deal. Did you ever hear of the Mirrors of Moab?"

"The what?"

"The Mirrors of Moab. For instance, in order to tell Abikemosh you're coming, all I need do is send a messenger to the shore opposite the Eagle's Beak. Within five minutes, Abikemosh in Mizpeh knows who's coming with how many men, camels, and horses."

"How?"

"Mirrors. And a special system of signals. They use polished bronze shields to flash signals from peak to peak. Do you know, Abikemosh can send a message from Mizpeh to Zoba and get an answer back within half an hour."

"Can I deliver the old people over there and be back here all in one day?"

"Yes, but I think you should think along other lines." Uri stared hard at David and repeated: "*Along other lines.* I mean, David, the king's 'high matter.'"

"Go on."

"First, David, what is it that you intend to do? With your life, that is?"

"Uri, all I know is that I was anointed by the prophet Samuel and that I then became the king's champion. This seems to be the will of Adonai. And that's what I want."

Uri stood up and looked out over the city through a window.

"How do you know Samuel anointed you to be Saul's champion?"

"Because he did—"

"Did he say so?"

"No, but—"

"You assume he anointed you for that?"

"Well, yes..." David broke off, a wider interpretation just dawning on him.

"There are two kinds of rulers, David," Uri went on reflectively, still looking out the window as if scanning the empires and kingdoms and nations that lay around the land. "The first kind is the kind you see everywhere. The second is rarer. A Pharaoh is of the first kind. The office of ruler makes him what he is, is all he finally becomes. Like a general who obeys all the rules of strategic battle: infantrymen in the center, cavalry on the wings, supplies in the background, archers on raised ground on both sides. Heaven speaks to such a man through his people. A Pharaoh. An Assyrian emperor. A Hittite king. An Ammonite chieftain. A Bedouin sheikh. Fate. Heaven. He is the high priest, the prophet for his people, the repository of power, a clay which is molded by that power. And that's all right.

"But the second kind is like rare metal. He makes the office. He creates, he generates the power. Heaven talks only to him, not to the people. He is heaven, in one sense, for the people. The power comes to him, and thence to his people—"

"Where is all this leading to, Uri?"

"To this, my friend." Uri came over and sat down again, facing David. "Saul is neither one nor the other. Now. Whatever he was before. He has not got the marks of such a high destiny. Look at me! I am a Hittite. I have no use for your Adonai, Abikemosh's Kemosh, the pharaonic Ra, the Phenician Baal, the Syrian Hadad, or whatever. It's all rubbish. But of late, I've had second thoughts.

"David, there's a unity in your life. The things that happened at your birth, your looks, your strength, your slaying of Goliath, and now your going to Moab, the original home of the giants. You have power with that sword of Goliath and prestige with the Philistines"—he gestured toward the sword lying on the table between them. "Saul's anger against you, Samuel's anointing of you, your escape, the gathering in of Hebrews to you—all that, my friend, betrays to me some guiding hand and some pattern which is extraordinary. I am almost ready myself to believe in your Adonai. The most extraordinary part of it is that events seem made to fit you, you are not called upon to fit in with events.

"But not if your aim is to be a one-time champion of a bug-ridden ass breeder like Saul, or a hunted bandit because this king—king!—is jealous of you. Be sensible! If your Adonai exists, have more respect for his intelligence."

David laughed helplessly at the innocent irreverence of the Hittite. "But, Uri, what can I be?"

"What were you *anointed* to be? What would you be? And don't say Saul's champion. That's over! Do you hear? Over!"

"Well, what am I to do then?"

"Give your Adonai a chance."

"How?"

"Stay in Moab for a year or two."

"In Moab? Doing what?"

"First of all, Abikemosh lives off the trade routes. He needs an efficient military agent, someone to enforce his treaties with Edom, Ammon, Gilead, Bashan, and even Zoba in the far north, not to speak of the tribes in the Great Eastern Desert. And if there's one place Saul will not seek you, it's in Moab. It's also the perfect hiding place for your old people. And you can—"

"Why should Abikemosh favor me?" David broke in. "Oh, his debt to you, I suppose. But how long can that hold? I don't know, Uri...I don't know..."

"Then you don't know. Then go to Masada. It's impregnable. It's not far from Moab. I'll show it to you. An army of giants in armor couldn't take it. Only eagles live there. At least stay out of Saul's reach for a year or two. He'll have enough to do to hold what he has without following you around the Salt Sea into Moab. The Philistines are already keeping him busy up north. At Masada you'll be safe."

"Very well, Uri," David said. "Very well. Moab it is. And Masada. Perhaps after a year or so Saul will forgive—"

"Forgive what?" Uri shouted. "In the name of Saul's camel dung, forgive what? What have you done?"

"Uri, he's the anointed of Adonai. I cannot harm him. I cannot fight him like an ordinary enemy. I must avenge him if anyone damages him. Only Adonai can decide the issue between King Saul and me."

No sooner had David left Uri and started down the corridor when Lassatha was there in front of him. She said nothing, only laid a finger on his lips and took him by the hand past the door of the room assigned to him by Uri, and over to her own door.

"Now we will sleep—this time together, you and I."

Finally it was Astarte's turn, and the goddess did not disappoint.

Later, as they lay side by side savoring the sweet indolence of satiety and delight in each other, they talked the way lovers talk.

"Did you really love Merab?" Lassatha asked, not out of any jealousy but simply to know more about this man she loved.

"Will I ever know?" David answered, puzzled. "I never touched her. We were never alone. We never talked about ourselves."

"And Mikhal? You married her."

"Yes . . . in a way. I know now that Saul proposed my marriage with her as a tool to plot my death—that plot cost the Philistines two hundred lives. Yes, technically Mikhal and I were married, and in fact she saved my life. She is attractive, but she didn't attract me. I did what I was supposed to do, no more."

"Why was that?"

"I don't know. I couldn't bear the sight of her naked body. Each time I lay with her—when it was over, I was disgusted with myself."

Lassatha moved over to place her wine glass on the table. "So there's only been Mikhal?"

"Only."

She was back on the couch. "You spoke about Mikhal's nakedness. What about mine?"

"That I don't understand either. It seems completely natural with you. Forgive me"—he appealed to her with his voice and eyes—"I don't think, at least I don't know, if I love you. Yet your being naked or my being naked with you doesn't bother me in the slightest. It must have something to do with love. You told me once that nakedness is for birth and love and death."

"Yes. Haven't you noticed that you don't see the nakedness of a baby. You see a fresh new expression of life beginning. And a dead body. More than their nakedness, you see their death—the pathos, the indignity, the immobility, the death.

"In love, you don't see the nakedness of your lover as nakedness. You see it as all-lovable and all-accessible. Without love, a living naked body is out of place. Dirt is nothing but matter out of place."

"Yes, that is so. Being with Mikhal always made me feel dirty. Yet I must have her back even if I never touch her again. It is a point of honor."

The deep silence of the dead of night hung over the house. Far off, the pluck of a lyre could be heard, and a woman's laugh.

Lassatha broke the serenity: "David, I love you. You know that. But let's be quite clear. I am only, I can only be, a door for you."

"Door to what? To where?"

They looked at each other. David found it extraordinarily restful just to be there and to return her gaze. She was entering him in some mysterious way, becoming more accustomed to his near presence, as he was to hers.

"I was never so much 'with' anybody as I am now," he confessed, emphasizing the "with," while a slow smile lit up his eyes and mouth. Lassatha said nothing. But her mouth opened ever so slightly, permissively. Gradually a new current of feeling ran between them, independent of what either said or did, but more interior to them both than sound or movement.

"David, what do you now want out of life?"

"What I've always wanted. *Ha-kol!* All! The all of life!" He lapsed into momentary silence. "From as early as I can remember, people like old Raham, my teacher—may his memory be blessed!—and Jesse, my father, even Shoshanna, my stepmother, led me to think about life outside Bethlehem, outside Judah, to expect achievement. They taught me to look on the land as a mirror of Adonai's universe, but I never realized it until Samuel anointed me. At that moment, all my desire seemed to shoot up the narrow flue of Bethlehem and plaster itself all over the sky. And now I long for this sense of totality."

David lay silent and Lassatha drew close to him, touching, guiding, caressing. It was Astarte's turn again. David saw the deepening color of Lassatha's eyes and the sensitive flare of her nostrils. He marveled that making love with a woman could be so graceful, so quiet, so gradual. Lassatha never hurried. She waited for him to assimilate each stage while he became more and more hers.

"I cannot give you your totality, David, as you call it. But I am your door to it."

Then, Lassatha was all around him, engulfing him, drawing him inexorably upward with some strength superior to his own, through the forms and figures and bodies and faces and desires of hundreds of unknown women. It was as if all women, through Lassatha, laid their claims on him for themselves, but also for him and for all lovers. And Lassatha was suddenly all women, a simple profound womb of desire, a single irresistible passage for his seed, a single pair of heavy, fruitful breasts to shelter him.

He heard himself cry out in surprise and wonder as he had never cried before, in tones he had never used but which he recognized as deeply his, fearing that his very fulfillment would undo him, drawing him into a pool of pleasure from which he might never emerge.

As they put out in the flat skiffs to cross the Salt Sea to the Eagle's Beak, the morning sun shone down like flaming copper on the turquoise blue of the lake, burnishing the white crystals that speckled its surface. Across the sea the early sun sparkled the mountain peaks and slowly ate into the deep blue mists in the valleys.

From the moment they landed it was quite apparent to David how different Moab was from any place he had ever known.

Moab was a high and rocky plain, perhaps two thousand feet above sea level. It had great stretches of good grazing land, plentiful water, and abundant fruit groves. Its chief advantage was its function as the funnel through which all caravan routes passed. As David's party climbed from the shore to the plateau, David caught sight of a dazzling pinpoint of light on the heights. The Mirrors of Moab were already talking about them.

Soon they were in the country of soft, flame-colored sandstone, traveling along a wide, well-used track bounded by smooth sloping cliffs hung with pink oleander and dotted with wild flowers. All around them the rims of the cliffs ended in fantastic headlands and grotesque peaks, natural sculptings of strange heroes, dragon's ears, and gargantuan faceless beaks. More surprising still was the abundance of sacred stone circles and crude altars that dotted their path, set up thousands of years before by some long-dead people.

The road suddenly turned southward, and after a long climb up into what appeared to be an increasingly deserted country of rocks, they saw an eagle with a serpent entwined around its body carved out of natural rock. Mizpeh, Abikemosh's capital, must be near. A turn in the track brought them onto a wide plateau carpeted with short mountain grass. It was flat at the center, its sides sloping up to sandstone cliff walls that climbed up hundreds of feet to level rims, on which they could see rows of buildings and, again, those flashing pinpoints of light announcing their arrival. Ahead they could see the black basalt walls of Mizpeh, city of Moab.

A small detachment of spearmen on mules came out to meet them. David halted his convoy and together with Joab and Abishai rode ahead to meet them.

As they came within hailing distance, David dismounted and walked forward alone, holding the sword of Goliath high over his head with both hands. It had an immediate effect. The detachment halted. The riders got down and prostrated themselves on the ground. Their officer knelt, removed his helmet, and cried out.

"Who are you and what is your mission?"

"This is David, warrior of Adonai and conqueror of the giant," Joab yelled. "Master Uri of Jebus has sent us."

"Come in peace. King Abikemosh awaits you."

Preceded by the riders, they rode the last mile to the gates of Mizpeh. Once inside, they found themselves in streets thronged with people. They were led immediately to the king's palace, where the officer led David, carrying the sword, to meet Abikemosh. He was gone one whole hour but returned smiling and confident. What had passed between him and Abikemosh remained a secret for many years.

"We're home, brothers and sisters! We're home! Be easy in your hearts!" David cried out in a loud voice. Jesse and Shoshanna together with their servants and slaves were led into the building. The escort remained outside. After half an hour Joshua's parents and the others were taken inside. Eventually David came out again, this time accompanied by slaves carrying jars of date-palm wine and trays loaded with figs, melons, apples, oranges, pomegranates. When all had refreshed themselves, they mounted again and headed off across the plateau to Masada, the mirrors flashing again from the surrounding cliffs.

"What happened back there with Abikemosh?" Joab asked.

"Joab, I have taken an oath. I will tell you when I am free to tell you. But there is no way you can guess what I have seen today. No way at all!"

*   *   *

During the year and a half that David spent at Masada, he and his men traveled the entire west shore of the Salt Sea. David's rules of procedure were simple and unvarying: Get to know the terrain—the wells, oases, caves, defiles, valleys, the hunting grounds of animals, the routes of caravans, the Bedouin tracks. Most important, know the avenues of escape. Again and again David said, "Never stay overnight in a house without a back door."

In those sandy wastes, spring and autumn were pleasant and livable while summer was hot. As the weather allowed, David sailed to Moab once a week to visit Jesse and Shoshanna. The Moabites had long since devised a way of living in the summer heat that David envied. They had hewed entire dwellings out of the sandstone. These, together with a complicated system of rainwater catchments feeding into underground cisterns, assured them of both adequate water and natural refrigeration.

David's agreement with Abikemosh made him protector of the caravans, which were required to pay customs and excise taxes and served as Mizpeh's main source of revenue. Two major caravan routes crossed Moab. One ran from the Persian Gulf, then called the Arab Sea, to the ports of Tyre and Sidon in Phenicia. The other began by the Tigris and Euphrates in Babylonia and ended in Egypt. Some miles north of Mizpeh, the two routes crossed. Moab guaranteed the safety of all caravans within Moabite territory. Moabite treaties with Ammon to the north and Edom to the south extended that protection to their region. All three kingdoms benefited from the taxes levied. But Abikemosh and the Moabites were responsible for enforcing treaty stipulations.

David perpetually marveled at the ceaseless activity in the marketplaces and around the government buildings: the convoys of pack camels and mules and carts; the teams of clerks taking stock of the merchandise and reckoning taxes; the motley assembly of drovers and military escorts; and the warehouses, built of wood or carved into the naked rock, where the goods were stored.

Among the Moabites, David and his men were regarded as supremely efficient mercenaries but as semibarbaric and of a lesser cultural standard and breeding. "But," as David remarked again and again to Joab, "if the Moabites, inspired by Kemosh—a lump of stone—can achieve this glory, shouldn't the House of Israel, which is backed by the hand of the universal God, Adonai, be able to achieve much more?"

But circumstances did not allow David much time for

dreams of glory. He was still a hunted man, living by his sword and his wits. The thought of the avenging Saul was with him night and day.

His function as protector gave him access to and a knowledge of the lands north and south of Moab east of the Jordan as far as Zoba, later to be called Syria. There David learned the dangers of tangling with this feisty race of merchant-soldiers. "Zoba," he was to say later, "is the thorn that Adonai has stuck in the backside of the House of Israel."

David finally chose a place called Engedi, quite near the Salt Sea, as his favorite residence. It had a constantly flowing stream of sweet spring water, a medicinal moss grew there the whole year round, and there were hundreds of caves for shelter and defense.

One Shabbath eve as David returned from Zoba, he camped for the night on the bank of the River Yarmuk. Abishai came to him and announced a visitor. It was Gad the Prophet, a tall, middle-aged man, his red hair already sparse, eyes flashing with intelligence, with a special message for "David the Golden." After the Shabbath meal was over, Gad spoke in his language of image and metaphor.

"Oh, my brother David! Nothing here is for you. Neither the bulls of Bashan nor its golden grain. Nor the perfumed orchards of Gilead. Nor the black basins of Moab. The milk of Judah and the honey of Benjamin are yours. And the glory of the House of Israel would be your dwelling. Return to Judah. For this is the word of Adonai to you."

"But will I again be the king's champion?"

"Adonai will show you! You will defend the glory of the House of Israel."

"But," David asked in puzzlement, "the House of Israel is only Judah and Benjamin and Ephraim and Manasseh and Reuben and—" He stopped. Gad had jumped up and was off into the darkness toward the river. David could hear him splashing around there talking to himself. He was back in a rush with a cloakful of wet stones.

"Feel the weight of them," he said breathlessly, shoving the cloakful at David. "Now!" He opened the cloak and let the stones tumble at David's feet. "Look at them! Look!" He kicked one aside. He spat on another. He crushed a third into the ground with his heel. "Now they are nothing. Just strong little stones!"

David looked up slowly at the flaming eyes of the prophet. It was a moment of awe for him. "Meaning, O Prophet?"

"Meaning the House of Israel, and the tribes of that house, David the Golden One!" He dropped to his knees and gazed meditatively at the stones. "Ever since Moses and Joshua led the tribes of Jacob into this land Adonai promised to Abraham, our father, those tribes have been just like these stones, kicked, spat upon, crushed, isolated, falling over each other." He paused and looked at the young man. David's head was lowered. He was looking at Gad from beneath his eyebrows, David's characteristic pose when in deep thought.

Gad read his thoughts. "Yes! Surely! They have their Covenant. Oh, yes! And their language. And their dances. And their marriage festivals. Oh, yes! All that—except! No peace. No security. Each one waiting to be kicked or crushed." The prophet picked up stone after stone, giving each one the name of a Hebrew tribe: "Judah...Gad...Reuben...Ephraim..." and dropping the stone into his cloak. "And Assher! The twelfth!" He stood up and looked down at David. "Feel them! Feel their weight now. Here! Take it!"

David took the cloakful of stones, weighing it slowly in his hand. Gad smiled at him. "We have stones. But no house. Go back to your Judah and build that House of Israel. Now!"

"But the king—Saul—"

"Yes," Gad said ecstatically. "Yes! You'll be the hunted, Saul the hunter. At the beginning, that is. And then? Adonai has his plans. Just go back to your land." Gad turned to go, then stopped, a dark silhouette. He spoke without facing David, and his voice was no longer vibrant. "David, son of Jesse! Unborn generations depend on what you do. Be careful. What you do decides the life and the death of whole nations."

When Gad was gone into the night, David stayed a long time thinking.

At Adullam, the most immediate problem was Saul's harassment. His messengers were everywhere in the land, cursing David and his sympathizers. In spite of his position, however, Saul's information about David in the first five years was extremely skimpy. No one at Gibea knew even whether David was alive or dead. But Saul's wild persecutions sent a new flood of refugees fleeing to Adullam. Within three months of David's return there, more than a hundred had arrived, and the numbers swelled daily.

The majority were Hebrews from the Twelve Tribes, but

mixed in were also Syrians, Hittites, Egyptians, Moabites, Ammonites, Phenicians, Cretans, Sicilians, Philistines, Greeks, Nubians, Berbers, and a sprinkling of strange Nordic men with blond hair and blue eyes, speaking no known language, who fought like lions.

Out of this bedlam of nations and languages, it was the Cretans who found special favor with David. Called Kerethites by the Hebrews, they were slender men of smaller than average height and splendidly proportioned bodies which they exercised continually. They were dark-haired, with black, almond-shaped eyes. They had tight-fitting helmets that encased the head completely, wore mail armor, and introduced David to the shell phalanx, locking their square shields in a way that presented to the enemy an eight-foot arched wall of armor that looked like an open umbrella lying on the ground. David quickly understood their value as a separate corps and would not allow them to be absorbed in the general mass of his men. Instead, he organized them as a permanent bodyguard for himself.

One of the most difficult problems now was to find accommodation for the hundreds of recruits who needed food and arms. The difficulty was solved piecemeal. First David set up another center at Masada, then a third garrison at Engedi. Before his whole status changed with the death of Saul, David would have almost a dozen of these "oases of strength," as he called them, throughout the land.

Even in the course of that first year, Saul's control over the land began to break down. Heavy drought had led to a noticeable increase in hunger and general poverty. Highland tracks and even regular roads became infested with bandits. Increasingly David's men found themselves hired as protectors. The caravans found it necessary not only to add more guards but to employ someone to police the routes. Farmers, cattlemen, and shepherds also required protection, and David was the only one who could provide it.

The contract was simple. He would guarantee with his life the safe conduct of people and goods along a given sector between two determined points. The agreed payment in cash or kind was automatic and on the spot, at the destination. Failure to pay promptly was punished then and there by the death of all in the caravan and the confiscation of all goods and animals.

Only once, in fact, did David have to demonstrate that he meant what he said. The Ziphites contracted for protection as far as Beersheva, then refused payment. That evening one hundred and twenty human heads, all of prominent Ziphites, were flung over the walls of Ziph. One Ziphite was released to explain why.

David assembled a team of organizers. Joab was field commander; Abishai ran the commissariat; Asahel managed the domestic and war animals; Adoram of Gilead kept the accounts. Yehosaphat the Judahite was David's accountant; his scribe was Serayah the Benjaminite; Abiathar, son of Ahimelek, the murdered priest of Nov, had charge of Ephod and Scroll; Ira from Naphthali dispensed medicines and cared for the sick. These men stayed with David all their lives and served as a framework for his later administration as king.

David's most important early client was that great and powerful city kingdom of Tyre. He and a column of men were riding north parallel to the coastal caravan route when they heard the clash of weapons and the shouts of battle. Scouts informed him that a Phenician caravan had been ambushed by Geshurites, a seminomadic tribe that lived in a barren stretch of land between Judah and the Shefela. The Phenicians were doomed.

David had no use for the Geshurites. With characteristic decisiveness, he ordered an immediate attack. His force of eight hundred Kerethites was all that was needed to surround the caravan, corner the Geshurites, and kill them to a man. Paltibaal, the commander of the caravan, never forgot who saved him from certain death. Nor had he ever seen such a smooth liquidating machine. David conducted the caravan to the borders of Tyrian territory. A few months later he accepted a contract for protection from the king and the council of Tyre.

Now and again Saul heard of David's activity, but Saul was continually assured by the seers he consulted and by his inner counsels that David was either dead or in exile. It did not matter to Saul. He had no visible rival, and the Philistines seemed to have chosen this time for a lull while refurbishing their military apparatus.

David's idea of what was really happening to himself and the land was incomplete—at least in the beginning—but Saul's was fatally erroneous. The only observers who understood with any accuracy what was going on were the Philistines. This was the period of Duke Achish's greatest influence. Unlike Saul, who relied on biased reports and his own fantasies, Achish had a double advantage. He received accurate reports about both Saul and David, and to his own satisfaction he had identified

David as important to Dagon's supreme enemy: Adonai. This was the shepherd from Bethlehem, the surprise champion of the land, now turned into a powerful warlord and, as far as Achish could assess, at daggers drawn with Saul.

"Wait," Achish again counseled Shekelath and his fellow commanders. "Let the Hebrew strength disintegrate. Every month Saul's supporters diminish and his control over the territory weakens. David is emerging more and more clearly as the countervailing force. Saul will soon be ripe for the harvest."

The reports that reached Achish about David's movements and achievements whetted his desire to see David quit the outlaw life and come over voluntarily to the Philistine side. At the beginning of David's seventh spring at Adullam, Achish was informed that David was back in central and southern Judah, near Beersheva.

"It's time we two met again," Achish stated to his aide as they rode with his bodyguard toward Beersheva. "At least I want to see what he has become." Some distance from the town they branched off into the hills, where the bodyguards would remain. Then Achish and his aide removed their Philistine armor and clothes, changed into the customary tunics and loose robes of the Hebrews, and mounted two mules to ride into Beersheva.

It was the day of the monthly fair, and every street was full. Achish and his companion made for a tavern owned by an agent of Achish's and climbed to the second-story balcony to sip beer and look over the crowd while awaiting David's arrival.

They feared he might pass undetected, but David, though a regular visitor to Beersheva, still stood out in a crowd. Suddenly, not only Achish but everyone in the huge marketplace knew that the almost legendary, giant-killing warlord, David of Bethlehem, was there, announced by a momentary lull in the uproar of the marketplace.

Achish craned forward and saw striding into the market square a man in his late twenties who towered over everyone around him. He was followed by three armed Hebrews. He wore knee boots furnished with throwing knives attached to the outside of each boot. Tight-fitting leather knee britches, the sort used by riding men, clothed his legs from knee to waist. His low-necked tunic was sleeveless, and the skin on his arms, chest, and face was bronzed. A light blue cloak of dyed sheep's wool, its loops around his neck, hung down his left side.

He carried a sword belt with a wildly oversized sword and scabbard, but it hung loosely over his left shoulder beneath the cloak. His long golden hair hung almost to his shoulders, and he had a short, trimmed beard.

So this is David, son of Jesse? Achish thought, noting the way the intensely blue eyes moved ceaselessly from side to side as David advanced. His eyes swept over the crowd and the buildings of the square and, before Achish and his companion could move, over the balcony where they sat, gleaming for the moment as they met Achish's own, then passing on.

"Shall we accost him, my Lord Duke?" the aide asked Achish.

The duke shook his head. He had seen what he wanted to. "I don't think so. This is not our territory. If that man walks casually through the marketplace, you may be sure that the square is full of his men. No," he said, standing up, "no, my friend. I want to sleep in my own bed tonight."

In the autumn of David's seventh year at Adullam there was a disastrous crop failure in Philistia, and the Philistine commander at Ziklag attacked the grain center of Keilah in Judah, setting off a new series of events that would lead Saul and David into even more radical opposition.

The Keilahites were the subject of much ribaldry and often bitter sarcasm. They were a collection of self-made, self-important merchants: hardheaded, pretentious, and mercenary. And their harvests were luxuriant. "Oily as a Keilahite," was the common description of anybody hard to pin down.

Keilah was an obvious target for the grain-hungry Philistines, who attacked its city walls. The Keilahites sent messengers scurrying for help from David.

It was a new venture for David. Since he left Saul's army he had never attacked the Philistines, and he knew nothing about fortified cities. He summoned Abiathar, the priest, and told him to bring the Ephod. When consulted through the Ephod, Adonai answered quite clearly.

"Go down. Attack the Philistines. Deliver Keilah."

Joab and his officers immediately objected, saying that they were all hunted people who were wanted alive or dead by the king. What now possessed David to want to go and fight the Philistines? David once more consulted the Ephod, but the answer was categorical: "Destroy the Philistines."

When David approached the Philistine encampment, his scouts reported on the weakness of their position. Certain that they wouldn't be attacked, they had set up no real defenses. In the dead of night, David's men crept in and stampeded the animals, which ran right over the sleeping Philistines, through their hastily constructed earthworks facing Keilah, and on toward the walls of the city itself. The Kerethite phalanxes then advanced immediately into the center of the surprised Philistines, crushing all opposition.

After a victory meal, David threw his mighty sword and stuck it into the ground. It was the traditional sign that a parley should begin. The Keilah burghers drew their cloaks tighter around their fat shoulders and looked at each other complacently. But when they heard David's price, their faces fell and they quickly excused themselves for a private discussion. Later that evening, one of his men on watch reported to David that Keilahite messengers had surreptitiously left the city heading north. David did nothing hastily: he consulted the Ephod. "Have they sent for Saul and will Saul come? And will the Keilahites betray me?"

The answers were unequivocally yes and yes, and David leaped into action.

"Gird on your weapons, lads. Kerethites! Come with me!" He marched them to the Keilahite treasury, broke down the double doors, and seized every one of the three thousand gold and silver Tyrian talents in the vault. He and his men then left Keilah in their dust. The Keilahites had to send a second—and different—message to Saul.

When Duke Achish heard it all, he laughed, shaking his head in disbelief. "Strange! Strange! What next, Lord Dagon?" How could David have shut himself in with a pack of weasels like that? he wondered. Achish sent a sharply worded admonition to the commander of Ziklag to make sure that his back and flanks were covered before he undertook any more raids. He then called for Benimaat, commander of his most experienced field spies.

These were all Bedouins of the Arbati tribe, small, brown-skinned men who traveled faster on their feet over rough terrain than any mount. Expert in tracking, with uncannily keen smell and sight, the Arbati never fought with weapons. Their only service was scouting and spying. One of Achish's singular achievements had been to establish the Arbati as a special signal corps. One man would be stationed secretly every quarter to half mile within a given area. A hundred men thus could form a signal line up to fifty miles long. Achish called the Arbati "my long eyes."

"Set up a signal line from here to Keilah," he told Benimaat. "I want daily reports if there's activity."

* * *

When Saul got the second message from the Keilahites, he cursed them roundly, but decided to search for David anyway. It was a fool's errand. There was no way he could trap David or find his hiding place. From his concealment David could see Saul and his men fruitlessly searching the valleys with Jonathan and Abner and all the other captains he used to know.

Had he wished, David could have toyed with Saul endlessly, but on the eighth day a messenger came from Mizpeh: "Jesse keeps asking for you, but calls you Elhanan most of the time." It was David's original name, although he had been familiarly called David for as long as anyone could remember. Three months before, Jesse had had a stroke and hadn't recognized anyone for some days. The Moabite doctors called it the "first blow of darkness." David had to get back to Mizpeh. First, however, he had an aching desire to speak with Jonathan.

David sent out his best man to flood the area with false and confusing tracks. Saul plunged deeper and deeper into impassable woods, winter streams, and rocky gullies farther and farther away from David's hiding place. Then one evening as Jonathan and his men were returning to camp from a hunt, with Jonathan in the rear, three light arrows lodged almost noiselessly into the earth behind him. David! He was near and would meet him that night where the arrows fell. Jonathan slipped away when the camp was asleep. It was a moonless night, and all around he could hear only the rustling of dry leaves in the wind and of night animals in the thickets.

"Jonathan!" It was a faint whisper from behind him. "Do not move, my friend. Stay still." Jonathan's eyes welled and his throat choked. David said, "Before morning, I will be moving. My father is dying and I must get to him. I just wanted you to know that I will keep my oath never to harm the king or any member of your house."

"David..." Jonathan whispered. "My father will never be able to track you. I recognize the false trails and I have been directing the men—"

"Will the evil spirit never leave the king?"

"My beloved friend...my friend..." Jonathan's whisper grated in his throat. "My father knows he has lost the hearts of the people. And he knows that you'll be king one day. So does all of Israel. Adonai will take him soon, and I had hoped to be beside you when you came to power."

"You shall, Jonathan! You shall."

"No, David. I used to think that. But now I see that I am

destined to go with my father. Perhaps it's better. My blood may spare you suffering..." His voice ceased as he contemplated the enormity of the future, and for a few moments the only sound Jonathan could hear was the thunder of his own heart.

"David! David! Don't go yet!"

"I'm still here, Jonathan. I want you to know that I love you. May Adonai protect you."

The invisible hand of panic tightened around Jonathan's chest. "Please, let me touch your face, just once." He waited, almost persuaded he heard or saw David coming. But it was only his desire fathering the illusion. There was no sound. He buried his face in his hands and cried silently in the darkness.

Next morning Saul rose in a fury. He had apparently decided that David was nowhere near. "Send out messengers. If anyone has seen the dog, let him tell us. We're going back to Gibea."

But he was barely back in his fortress when two messengers arrived from Ziph and offered to lead Saul to David. Their scouts were on his trail, they said. They hadn't forgotten the hundred and twenty heads that David had lopped off.

"Where?" Saul shouted, dancing in a raging delight. "Where is he?"

In the neighborhood of Hakila, they said, just south of Yeshimon.

Saul's face lit up with gratitude: "As Adonai lives! You will be rewarded, my brothers from Ziph. If I take that mangy dog, I will make your city free of taxes for one year. Now listen. That dirty fox knows that you have come to me. He has eyes and ears everywhere. So we can be sure he has either left Hakila or is about to. Follow him if you can, and if he stops somewhere for a day or more, come and tell me. I'll be near Ziph tomorrow morning."

Saul was right. David's "eyes and ears" had noted the Ziphite messengers, and by the time Saul was on the move again David had left Hakila for the wasteland of Maon. But the Ziphite scouts tracked him there, too. David dared not move any farther eastward with Saul blocking the way. Yet he knew that Jesse might die before he reached his side. He thought, then acted quickly, sending five horsemen south in full sight of anyone watching, deep into the sandstone desolation of Maon where it stretches down to the Sinai.

The Ziphite scouts duly reported back to Saul and the king came thundering after them while David hid his forces in what was almost a replica of Adullam, but even more inaccessible.

There was only one way in or out, a narrow, barely six-foot-high fissure. The local tribes called the place Sela Hammaveth, the Sojourn of Death. For if you took refuge there, you could easily keep everybody out, but you might not get out yourself.

But Saul's informers had noted that move too, and within a day, Saul had recovered himself and positioned his troops outside Sela Hammaveth. The situation was frozen in a deathly stalemate. David easily blocked any attempt by Saul to enter, but Saul ringed the red sandstone bluff with five thousand men and sent back to Gibea for supplies and additional detachments. He had only to wait. Time was on his side.

David had been forced into this corner because his eight hundred or so men were no match in open combat with Saul, who could easily summon ten times that number. Moreover, he was sworn not to touch Saul, and he must not betray to Saul his parents' hiding place in Moab. The combination of events had trapped him.

The Arbati reported to Achish: "The Hebrew king has his enemy bottled up in Sela Hammaveth. He is settling in for a long siege. There is no escape for David."

Yet if David was to serve Dagon's ends, he must be saved from Saul. Achish sprang into action. His chariot corps rattled up the coastal road and into the Shefela in the direction of Gibea, and a regiment of spearmen with a battalion of archers marched directly up the Refa-im Valley, curved west of Jebus, and halted within four miles of Saul's fortress. Hasty messengers told the king of the Philistine threat, and within the hour Saul and his army were flying back with the speed of terror. David and his men then emerged and streaked northward to Engedi.

When Saul reached Gibea, the Philistines were already retreating back down into the Shefela. Saul chased them fruitlessly and returned to Gibea, where he sat in a daze muttering about "treacherous dogs" and "black hands of death."

Jonathan and Abner and Ahinoam tried to calm him, but he flew into blind rages. Then a new group of Ziphite scouts came with information that David had been seen heading toward Engedi. This time Saul was meticulously careful. He chose an elite corps of three thousand camel riders, and left the bulk of his army to defend Gibea. He set out at night, stayed hidden during the day, crossed to the west shore of the Salt Sea, and crept stealthily down toward Engedi. "That vile piece of dung slithers around at night like a rock lizard," he railed to Abner. "We'll do the same."

David, Joab, and five others had ridden north from Engedi to buy mutton from the shepherds of Malakhoth. They decided to stay the night in one of the caves near the pens, and leave in the morning. With his usual eye for detail, David tethered his camels among the camels of the shepherds, and then carefully chose a cave about six feet off the ground, which narrowed inside down to a small crevasse at the back and then opened again into a large chamber. They all wriggled through the crevasse and lay down in the chamber to sleep.

The sound of loud voices roused them from slumber. As their hands went for their weapons, they heard raucous laughter from outside, and then someone climbing up and walking into the outer cave. David and the others froze as they recognized that voice.

"When I, the king, cover my feet," Saul shouted, "even the Angels of Adonai don't see me." To "cover the feet" meant to defecate, for the squatting posture brought the Hebrews' robes over their feet.

Looking out through the crevasse, David could see by the dim light of Saul's lantern the broad back of the squatting monarch, the hem of his robe lying within arm's reach. One spear thrust and it would be over. David knew that more than half the men waiting outside for Saul hated the king, and that the rest would be indifferent to his fate. Who but Adonai could have delivered his mortal enemy into his hands? And when David drew his knife, his little company was sure that he would strike and kill. A smile of triumph appeared on Joab's face.

David wriggled out silently to where the back hem of Saul's robe had fallen on the lip of the crevasse and very, very quietly cut off a square of it while the king was relieving himself. He then drew back, his finger to his lips, as Joab's smile turned to numb amazement.

Saul finished and left the cave, jumped to the ground, and walked over to his camel. David and the others were out through the crevasse in a flash and lay flattened inside the mouth of the cave, watching the waving lanterns of Saul's party some thirty-five yards away. Another fifty yards or so off, they could make out the black forms of Saul's main force waiting.

As Abner helped the king mount, he noticed the damage to Saul's robe and jokingly remarked, "O King, you left a portion of your robe in the cave!"

"What? That's strange!" the king muttered, fingering the damaged place, which had clearly been cut. "Here, hold the reins. I'm going to find out what happened."

At that moment, to Joab's consternation, David rose and jumped from the cave mouth to the ground below.

"My Lord! My King!" It was the first time Saul had heard David's voice in more than nine years. It brought him up short, filling him with some strange, sweet calm. He was no longer chasing some monster of his imagination. He was instead face to face with the man, and listening to the voice that had sung so sweetly to him many years before in the heyday of his reign.

"Is that David?" Saul found himself asking plaintively, as one would inquire after a long-lost friend. He peered through the darkness to see a tall, dark figure bow his forehead down to the earth three times.

"Accept my homage, O King! Anointed one of Adonai! It is I, David." Saul was speechless. He did not even grope for his sword.

"I know," David went on, "that evil tongues say I am your enemy. But, my Lord King, look at this!" David stooped, picked up a stone, wrapped the patch of Saul's robe around it, and threw it toward Saul's feet. "If I had really wanted to kill my king, I could have done so. Adonai delivered my king into my hands to kill or to spare, and I spared him." Saul picked up the stone and held the cloth wonderingly, his mouth open. He stared at that dark, still figure, his heart breaking inside him.

"O King, hear me! The only judge of you and of me is Adonai. I swear I will never harm Adonai's anointed. I pray only that Adonai save me from the King's sword. For in comparison with my Lord King, I am what Goliath called me, a dirty dog and a filthy flea." Then a deep silence fell. Only the snorting and fidgeting of the camels broke the stillness.

When Saul found his voice, it was weary and aching. "God knows! God knows! I have surely wanted to kill you with my bare hands. But unjustly, for you are innocent. And you could easily have killed me just now." The truth of his situation flooded Saul's soul.

"My beloved David! Look at me! Evil has me in its grip, and Adonai has rejected me. You who will rule over Israel"—sobs choked his voice—"swear to me that you will have compassion for my family when you come into your kingdom!"

"I swear it. On the Ark of the Covenant, I swear it, O my Lord King!"

"Then let there be respect between us, for I can already smell my death. Farewell, David." And Saul turned wearily, stumbling in the dark to where Abner and his companions waited. David stood there until the sound of hooves died away and, in the distance, the lanterns of Saul's main force moved slowly northward toward Gibea.

Back at Engedi, David's men had brought in a Hebrew who had been held in bondage at Gath. He said, "My Lord Duke Achish freed me and told me to tell David of Bethlehem: 'When David was trapped in Sela Hammaveth, Dagon sent his troops against Gibea. Salvation lies with Achish and the god Dagon.'"

Even when they drove splinters deep under his nails, the man's message was the same. Joab finished him off anyway with a spear thrust through the chest. The rule was never to spare anyone who had worked with the Philistines. Exceptions were very rare. But the message distracted and dismayed David. Why had he gone on fighting all those bitter, lonely, hard years only to be saved by Dagon? Was Adonai really in control of good and evil? Or was Dagon stronger? And was David finally to become a servant of Dagon? In his solitary agony of spirit, David wept.

In Mizpeh, Jesse had had another stroke. It was the "final blow of darkness," the doctors told Shoshanna. But where was David? Please bring David, Shoshanna prayed. And David was now free to come.

But five days after that last stroke, the end seemed near— and still no David. Jesse was laboring for breath, inhaling noisily and exhaling slowly. Shoshanna knelt by the bedside and held one limp hand. She hid her face in the coverlet and cried.

Then she heard the clatter of feet and the jangle of arms and David, fully armed, burst into the room, his face white, his helmet under his arm. He ran forward, dropping his helmet, and, falling to his knees by the bed, reached out for his father. He felt the old man's whole body vibrating in his arms and Jesse's eyes found David's. David stayed with him, holding him, until Jesse fell into a peaceful sleep from which he never awoke.

"We will bury him here until it is safe to take his bones back to Bethlehem," David told Shoshanna. "But I want you to come with us. I have talked with King Saul. We've a peace of sorts. For now."

And in the following months David led a less hunted existence, although he continued to maintain his garrisons and scouting expeditions. Every month, in fact, saw fresh increments of men—some now with their families—rallying to his side.

The next autumn, David took a contract to protect a vast sheep shearing about to begin near Carmel of Judah for Nabal of Maon, an exceedingly wealthy landowner who had enjoyed King Saul's protection until Saul's power failed. Nabal himself never went near his land or flocks. He left that to his stewards and servants and slaves. He was arrogant and irreligious. He had married a very beautiful woman, Abigail of Bethhoron, but they had no children. The rumor was that Nabal was impotent.

Nabal maintained a magnificent three-story house in Maon, where he counted his money and lavishly entertained his rich cronies. He was extremely jealous, and any man who looked twice at Abigail might find his fields burned, his cattle slaughtered, or his daughter raped. Nobody crossed old Nabal with impunity. Yet Abigail had managed to have several lovers, because she was intelligent and discreet.

She was always splendidly dressed in the silks, furs, and precious stones which Nabal provided, so that when she appeared with him, Nabal felt proud of her as a unique possession. Besides, he used to dally childishly with several of her beautiful handmaidens. And they, carefully instructed by their mistress and sure that their chastity was perfectly safe, so treated him that he constantly lived in the hope that soon, very soon, they would renew his potency.

At this time David was about thirty and Abigail in her middle twenties. She had always been beautiful in an extraordinary way. The raven-black hair was common among Hebrews, but not the extremely white and delicate skin. And her eyes were of so light a green that at times they seemed transparent. There was not another such pair of eyes in the land. Her hands were renowned for their grace and expressiveness.

It had been a lean year in Judah, and robbery and looting were on the increase. The two weeks' shearing time for Nabal's three thousand sheep and thousand goats proved a strenuous test for David's men. Moreover, there were five different shearing centers that had to be guarded twenty-four hours a day. So well did they perform, however, that not a single bale of wool was lost, although nineteen men had died in raids and half a dozen had been injured by wild animals trying to get at the sheep.

David sent a contingent of ten young riders to pick up the

agreed fees from Nabal at Maon. Nabal, alerted to their presence by a slave, glared drunkenly out an upper window, a jug of wine in his hand. He had been celebrating the successful completion of shearing.

"Who the devil does this David think he is, demanding that kind of price? He's just a camp slave running away from King Saul." And he banged the window shut and returned to the party.

But the young men persevered. Their spokesman shouted at the closed windows: "Our master provided protection for your sheep and shearers, and we were promised the payment we have come to collect, Master Nabal. Master Nabal! Please give us an answer for my Lord David!"

Nabal flung open the window again: "If you think I'm going to give my money and my fine-milled grain to that dirty bandit, you are mad. My Lord David indeed! Now be off with you before I have you spread on my land as dung."

David's young men repeated Nabal's insulting words. David's reaction was predictable and immediate: "Buckle on your swords. On your camels, Kerethites! We'll teach this filthy goat a lesson he ought to have learned years ago. Two hundred of you stay here. The rest follow me." David rode out at the head of six hundred angry men, Joab riding beside him.

The news of her husband's foolishness put into motion a plan that had been in Abigail's mind for some time. She rushed around giving orders, and by midafternoon of the day following Nabal's discourtesy her preparations were complete. She had a team of pack donkeys fitted with panniers and loaded with two hundred fresh loaves, forty stoneware jugs of fine Carmel wine, ten whole cooked sheep, a hundred clusters of raisins, two hundred fig cakes, and several jars of wild honey. Then she decked herself in her finest silks and jewelry and rode out with five of her most attractive handmaidens, all wearing low-cut blouses, skirts split from waist to ankle, and gossamer veils.

She rode with her retinue down the curving road as David was coming up it with his men. The hill at the curve blocked their views of one another.

David was still breathing curses and vengeance: "I will make glue from that gelding's bones. Why should the blood of my men be shed?" He would fall silent for a while, then suddenly erupt again: "I shall reduce him to dog meat bit by bit, his whole gross, whimpering carcass. I'll burn his house to ashes."

The avenging party of six hundred, with David and Joab in the lead, swept around the curve of the hill, their blue-eyed leader still fuming, and the next thing David beheld was perhaps the most beautiful woman he had ever seen lifting her veil to display a perfectly made-up smiling face with hypnotic pale green eyes.

Six hundred men stopped as though paralyzed, with a great bleating of camels and cursing. David sat stupefied by the vision that now approached him.

Abigail, still smiling, bowed to the ground, then rose and kissed the tip of David's scabbard. After a quick glance at his face to reassure herself, she pressed home her advantage.

Her voice was low, infinitely soothing, musical. "My Lord David, son of Jesse, protector of the weak and the lowly, I, Abigail, am married to a man called Nabal. He is a fool, my lord, a fool through and through, as are all those who seek to harm you.

"But let my Lord David accept my gifts and be not a fool to shed blood over the words of a fool."

David was enchanted. A low smile broke over his features. "Truly, you, Abigail, come from Adonai! If you hadn't come to meet me, I swear, not one man or woman or child would be alive this evening in Maon."

He alighted from his camel, led Abigail back to her white donkey, lifted her up and placed her upon it, then sent her home under escort and returned to his stronghold. When Abigail arrived back at Nabal's house, she knew exactly what she was going to do and what its effect would be. Nabal was still celebrating. Tranquilly Abigail dined and slept. When she had risen and bathed and dressed in her usual leisurely fashion, she made her way with great dignity over to her husband's quarters. Nabal was slumped on a couch in a drunken stupor. There was vomit and filth everywhere. She had one of her handmaidens pour a jar of cold water over Nabal, who sat up swaying and blinking.

"Do you know, husband, who came to kill you and everybody in Maon last night?" she asked sweetly. Nabal's eyes opened wider. She bent forward and hissed into his face. "David, son of Jesse, wearing the sword of Goliath the giant. With six hundred armed and angry men to cut you into dog meat. He left because I asked him to, but may return—" She broke off. Nabal gave a low, choking sound, swayed backward, then forward once, then fell heavily backward onto the floor, his head rebounding off the slate.

"Pick him up and put him on the couch," she told the slaves.

"And get the doctors." But it was already too late, as she had hoped it would be.

A month after Nabal was dead and buried, David heard the news, and the wily Joab commented, "Maybe you could comfort his widow? Isn't it about time you took a wife? You need children, and the comfort of a woman to come home to."

Intrigued, David sent his kinsman Joshua to sound out Abigail. He went loaded with gifts and accompanied by camel-riding spearmen. Within two weeks Abigail was at Hakila. Shoshanna and David's brothers welcomed her into their house, and Abiathar performed the ceremony. According to custom, David would not touch her for three months, until her mourning period was over.

The respite from Saul's bitter enmity was not destined to last very long. Within a year of Saul and David's encounter at the Sojourn of Death, the old spirit of murderous hate was once more rampant in the king. The final act in the tragedy of Saul, first king of the Hebrews, began to play itself out in his blood.

Among those whose fates were intimately bound up with the destiny of that flawed hero, no one of them—Samuel, Jonathan, Achish, David, Uri, Joab, Abner—communicated fully with the others, so each had only a partial view. Yet all felt themselves witnesses to an event that would literally change the world. Until he died in defeat and disgrace, Saul of Gibea was the caldron of change.

Samuel the Prophet was heir to the ancient tradition of Abraham and Moses, by which the Hebrews' worship of Adonai and their fidelity to his Covenant was the cement that held them together. Therefore, when Samuel, against his deep instincts, anointed Saul as king, he never thought of him as a monarch like those in the nations surrounding the Hebrews. There the king or strong man was identified with Baal, Kemosh, Ra, Hadad—whatever the god was called—and this was utterly abhorrent to Israel's ancient tradition: Israel had one God, the true God, the only God. The Hebrew king was still a man and a servant to Adonai.

For Samuel, then, Saul's downfall began when he started to wield power autonomously. And there can be no doubt that Samuel regarded David as Saul's successor.

In his declining days, Samuel stayed close to his beloved Rama, seeking what news he could of a king who no longer consulted him. He could see that Saul was steadily faltering before David's continually expanding power and prestige. All that kept Saul in place was his army, plus David's refusal to attack him and Samuel's unwillingness to move against the man he himself had anointed.

For Samuel the cardinal sign of deterioration was Saul's gradual dependence on the occult, on warlock and witch, astrologer and magician. To Samuel, every one of their "darkling revelations" was the malicious work of "the angel of false light," the nameless adversary of Adonai: Satan, antique source of Dagon and Baal. And in abandoning himself to them, Samuel believed, Saul placed himself in the power of the ancient liar who, at the dawn of human life, deceived the first man and woman and brought death into the world.

At Hakila, David enjoyed his first taste of a loving marriage with Abigail. She would never be the love of his life, but she was the perfect wife. She gave him no children at first, but was always at his disposal. She never questioned him about the women who had preceded her, nor those who would come after. She did not demur when David took another wife, Ahinoam of Yezreel. She lived in perfect harmony with Shoshanna, and she was quite content with her status as first woman of David the Golden.

David had married his Ahinoam to cement an alliance with the single most powerful family in Galilee.

"Ahinoam by name and Ahinoam by nature," was a current joking phrase uttered by David's companions—her name meant "my brother is delight." And indeed, Ahinoam had a very handsome brother, whereas she herself was a plain, homespun little woman, broad-hipped, big-breasted, and short-legged, with massive nose and mouth, powerful arms, and what was called in Israel "fallen buttocks." But, besides a quick sense of humor, she brought a big dowry to David and she liked nothing better than to serve this man whom she adored, housecleaning, sewing clothes, polishing arms, and bearing children. For David's other women she felt absolutely no jealousy. "One of us may be lucky," was her comment to Abigail. "We may bear a king, or even the Messiah!"

The evening he brought Ahinoam home, life had never seemed so good to David. He moved now with relative impunity north or south of Gibea. He was respected. His strongholds were flourishing, the year's income was substantially higher than ever before. When sunset was almost over, he went up onto the roof of his house, took his seven-stringed harp, and played to himself. It was a habit he had developed during the early hunted days at Adullam. For months on end, in those hard times, the only pleasant thing his family and companions knew was the sound of that harp after sunset, and occasionally the voice of David singing.

David's music was, for him and his band, their sacrament of communing with Adonai, in whom finally all their hopes reposed. David the Golden was just as frequently referred to as David the Holy in those hard days.

This evening David stayed on the roof longer than usual, playing, pausing, and playing once more, into the early hours of the morning. Then, to his surprise, he noticed Abigail. He had thought himself alone. It was a moonless night lit only by the stars. Abigail was wearing her nightdress, her hair loose about her shoulders.

"Abigail?" It was half-question, half-exclamation.

Wordlessly she came over to him and slid quietly to a sitting position between his knees, her shoulders between his thighs, her head resting on his belly. She felt his hands on her temples. They remained like that, silent, calm, for some minutes, looking into the night. David knew she had a question, and he had come to love the way she delicately set the stage before raising the curtain.

"Only by coming up here when you are playing at night," she said dreamily, "can I realize why the roof is your favorite place."

"Yes," he said slowly and leisurely, "it is very peaceful."

"Will peace continue for us, Lord David?" Not her real question, David told himself, but an approach.

"Adonai knows, Abigail! Adonai knows! What he wills will be."

"What chance, then, have we all, my lord?" she whispered. "If we are going to be forever like this, can we speak of happiness?"

"Adonai always makes his own choices, once men have taken theirs, my dear wife. And thus there are sudden turns in our lives, little unexpected twists of mercy, perhaps. In spite of Saul's betrayal and my weakness, I hope Saul—or at least Jonathan—will find mercy. Or so I must hope, Abigail."

After this she lay silent for a while, then she began again. "Ahinoam should have strong children, whenever she starts conceiving." There was a gentle humor in her voice, and a questioning uplift at the end of the statement.

"When she is given children—yes! They should be strong

and healthy." He glanced down at her, waiting. She could not see, but she sensed that he was smiling again.

"My lord smiles."

"And my Abigail."

She turned gently around on her knees, put her hands on his hips and laid the side of her head in his lap, her eyes lightly closed. He stroked the long hair back from her face. "I don't need to smile, Lord David. To be with you gives my soul a life that no mere smile could characterize."

"Abigail," David said, "you should know—I don't want any children yet. I made a vow to have neither wife nor children until I regain what is rightfully mine. Right now I need wives, it seems, but children are another matter."

"My lord, up to this point I have been more a friend than a wife. And I know that for you friendship is holy, but..."

"But?"

"Of late, my lord"—her voice choked a little—"of late, I have begun to ache—I mean inside me, some part of me has started to pain—oh, I don't know any longer what I'm saying—what I want."

He bent down and picked her up in his arms and carried her down the stairs to his bedroom.

"But you really have not asked me what you wanted to ask, so I think you should know now what I value in you, in your love."

"You didn't say 'our love,' David," she said. "Don't take that amiss. I understand—I think I understand—but please, you must then try to understand that little ache in me."

"Don't you think I have an ache too, my Abigail?"

"But if that pain and ache in both of us is not removed, what good has our—does my—love do you, David?"

"Abigail, woman, I knew immediately that you would do one thing for me: you would be more than a friend, you would be a lamp of light, a haven of repose and warmth and trust."

She opened her eyes wide, looking at him. "You want no more than that?"

"Abigail, my wife, Adonai has not given me to know more. To imagine more, yes! To hope for more, yes! But to have more, to be capable of achieving more, no. Not yet, anyway."

"And when did you know that I could be that one thing at least for you?"

"I knew it on the day you first came to greet me at—" He was interrupted by a sudden rude hammering at the door.

"David! David! Wake up!" It was Joab.

"Samuel is dead," he shouted. "He died yesterday at Rama. He was buried this morning, and Saul is moving against us again."

Because of the remoteness of Hakila, David was late in hearing of Samuel's death. The prophet apparently had died alone, as befitted a man who had spent his life in solitary strength. Jonathan, who visited him frequently, had gone as usual to Rama and heard the mournful howling of Samuel's watchdogs, which lay outside the closed door that led into the windowless little back room that no one except Samuel ever entered. Samuel was nowhere to be seen. Jonathan stumbled back in terror. He sensed doom and ran for his camel.

Within half an hour he was back with Saul, Abner, and a handful of officers. Saul stood, sword drawn, in front of the door into that back room. The dogs bared their fangs, snarling. "Kill them, Abner," Saul ordered, his eyes glittering with hate. Abner drew his bow and sank an arrow into each dog. Saul stepped over their bodies and cautiously pushed the door open with his sword point. But he did not dare enter. He turned away as if blinded, murmuring, "Jonathan! Jonathan!"

Jonathan jumped forward. All was still and cold in the semidarkness within. The body of the prophet, clothed in a long, wide-sleeved robe, sat on his judgment seat, the head leaning back against the wall, the eyes wide open, lifeless. Samuel had put on the sacred Ephod; and the light breaking in from the living room made its red, blue, white, and green stones wink and gleam. The Scroll of the Law lay on the prophet's lap, partly unrolled, the bulk of it standing in the crook of his left arm and shoulder. The right hand had closed around the other rolled end. Samuel had installed himself in this way to wait for Adonai to call his spirit back to the world of eternal life.

Saul sent messengers to Gibea and the countryside announcing the death of Samuel and the burial at sunrise on the morrow. Scholars and priests from nearby towns prepared the body and went through Samuel's effects. The cedar chest with Ephod and Torah they took to Kiryath-Yearim and placed in the safekeeping of the Levites who guarded the Ark of the Covenant.

By the time the burial was over, Saul seemed to be in magnificent spirits, barking orders as he made plans to call up a few thousand recruits and undertake a vigorous campaign. He also dispatched half a dozen riders to Judah. Jonathan was excluded from the war council, but he learned from Abner and the others that Saul was planning all-out war to the death against David.

Late that night, two of the riders returned with three perfumed citizens of Ziph who were chewing on Egyptian mint candies.

"We know, O King, precisely where David hides this time," they told Saul. "It is on the mountain of Hakila that stands before Yeshimon. If the king wishes, we will guide him there."

"You and your town will be blessed forever by me and my house," Saul answered warmly. Leaving a strong detachment to guard Gibea, Saul set out at the head of three thousand picked troops.

By an hour after sunrise on that same day, David had sent his mother, Shoshanna, his two wives, and their servants and slaves, under armed escort with Joshua in command, westward to Adullam, the only stronghold David was completely sure of. Fast riders had gone to alert all his other oases of strength. He himself led his faithful eight hundred Kerethites out of the Hakila stronghold and up to the top of the mountain to hide in the wooded thickets. From there he could keep a watch on all approaches.

Watching from his covert, David saw Saul's army approach and then move slowly up the slopes, swords drawn and spears pointed. One detachment of five hundred men started to march around the mountain, stationing pickets of five fighters every twenty or thirty yards. Saul's tactic was obvious. Then a company of fifty soldiers rushed through the gorge into the stronghold. Faintly, from far below, those on the mountaintop could hear the cries of that company as they ran back out: "The birds have flown! The birds have flown!" Saul settled down for the night. The last thing in the world Saul expected was that David would be hiding above him.

David had dug a trench across the mouth of the gorge in front of Hakila to channel the winter streams, but it was dry now and offered shelter from the wind. Saul, with his commander, Abner, made his personal camp there. David noted carefully where Saul stretched his blanket and placed his provisions of bread, meat, and water by his side. Characteristically, he had stuck his spear into the ground beside his shield and helmet and sword. Abner and his men lay about ten yards from Saul, guarding all access to their king.

A plan started forming itself in David's mind as he watched all this. When night fell, he asked for a volunteer. Abishai stepped forward. "Take only a knife, follow me, and do exactly as I do," David instructed him, and they disappeared into the darkness.

After what seemed hours of slow and careful descent, David and Abishai found themselves on the crag which formed one side of the gorge entry. Beneath them lay Saul in a dead sleep.

"David," Abishai whispered, "let me go and drive that spear through him. One thrust, and it's all over for him!"

"No, Abishai. You know what I have said about that. I will lower you down, so you can steal his spear and that water skin without waking him."

A few seconds later, the point of Saul's spear came up to David with the water skin attached to it. David took both, hauled Abishai up, and they moved back to the high ground about thirty feet above Saul and his guards and perhaps twenty-five yards distant.

"Abner!" David shouted out in the night, as Abishai froze in fright. "Abner, commander of King Saul's armies! Are you listening? Abner! Abner!"

Abner shook himself like a dog in fright and sat up shouting: "Who is calling me? Son of a pig!"

"Abner," David answered, "a man just crept up to kill the king. And what were you doing? Sleeping, Abner! Sleeping, my friend! Oh, we know you're brave and valiant. But why do you not guard my lord the king?"

"What do you mean, you fool? Who are you?" Abner was on his feet now, looking wild-eyed at Saul.

"Well, Abner, where is the king's spear? Eh, great Abner? And where is the king's water skin? Where are they?" And Abner saw that the objects were gone. "Where are they, Abner?" David's voice taunted out of the darkness.

Saul, waked by the shouts, did not even look at Abner. He had recognized David's voice and its sound melted him.

"Is that my son David? Is that my beloved David?"

"It is David, my lord! My King!" Saul began to weep. "But, my King," David went on, "if Adonai has told you to pursue me, that is one thing. If my enemies have done so, then my curse upon them. For my enemies are the King's real enemies." David's voice was cracking. "They only want to drive me from the land of Adonai to serve alien gods, my Lord King! That is a terrible crime!"

If one went to live in a foreign land, one of course had to worship the god of that land, at least nominally. But David had not yet concluded that Adonai was the God of all the earth and of all the cosmos forever. Abishai saw David wipe the tears from his eyes. "My King," he went on, "why should you, the anointed of Adonai, shed my blood? I am nothing—a bug in a bush, an ant in the desert—and you are the slayer of lions—" David could not go on.

"David, my son, I have sinned," Saul called back. "I am a fool, a simple fool, and a blasphemer besides. I listened to those fat Ziphites with their greed and treachery. You could easily have killed me just now, and you did not. I now reject the death I had planned for you."

"Never, never, my King, will I touch Adonai's anointed one. But please, value my life as I have valued yours. I will leave your spear and your water skin here. I am going now. You can send an officer to fetch them."

Saul looked up in David's direction. "David! David!" he cried. "Go in peace, David!" Then to himself, "Beautiful David, go in peace."

After some shifting and grumbling the camp again fell silent. Suddenly there was a stentorian shout from the recumbent Saul: "Kick those Ziphite pigs out of the camp. If they're here at sunrise, I myself shall feed them to the foxes."

"David, what are you looking at?" asked Joab next morning as they watched the horizon swallow the last of Saul's army.

"Death, Joab. Death. Saul rides with death. God help him and all with him, and all in the House of Israel."

Then he turned abruptly to Joab: "And you are riding to Ziph. Spare no male under thirty. Destroy all the animals—all of them. And all the spring wheat, burn it. And all their furniture, too. We have had enough from Ziph. But listen to me! Touch no woman, no female child, and no elderly man. And try to find those three sons of pigs who betrayed us. Make sure they die slowly."

And that's how it was done.

It was late summer. Soon the huge prewinter caravans would roll and it would be harvest and shearing time throughout the land: David's busiest season was approaching. Sitting in Adullam around a fire, his officers were full of enthusiasm about their prospects.

"The new recruits are coming every day," Eliab remarked, "and the night riders are riding again." This was a reference to the communications system among David's various fortresses: dromedary camel riders rode from stronghold to stronghold each night, thus keeping his whole organization informed.

David shrugged and stood up. He walked around the fire and over to the eastern lip of the Adullam plateau—they were about a stone's throw away. There he planted his feet and his eyes swept the surrounding mountaintops and valleys.

The conversation around the fire lagged and halted as the group waited for its leader, until finally the crackle and hiss of burning pitch was the only sound to be heard.

At last David returned. "It's not as sure as you think," he began. "But if we are going to have real peace, we will know before winter. However, we must now act and arrange our affairs as if still preparing for war. We will refurbish Hakila—you, Joshua, will be in command of it. My family will stay here in Adullam." He then reviewed the commands of the other oases of strength and the disposition of forces at each.

"All of you prepare for trouble. And *stay prepared!* I will see you all at least once over the next three or four months. Those months are critical for us. It means peace or war. Life or death. Believe me. I do not believe the king will keep his word. There is an evil spirit that consumes him."

Up in Gibea, Saul was preoccupied with the work on his lands. Like his father, Kish, he was an expert ass breeder, and he exported the animals to Phenicia, to Syria, to Egypt, and even to lands beyond the Great Sea. Neither he nor his agents penetrated very often into southern Judah, so that contact was minimal between the king and the communities where David's influence was strong. Israel was effectively divided between Judah and the north. But both north and south were prospering.

Saul's personal condition continued to give his intimates cause for worry. To all others he seemed a prosperous leader in full stride. He appointed judges, enforced the law—and he was still one of the strongest warriors in the House of Israel. But although he was accessible to the ordinary people, he seemed to have dropped all ideas of any central authority for the various tribes and clans, and his monarchy steadily shrank. In consequence the king's officers also saw their dreams of power and wealth gradually disappearing. But Saul seemed at ease, if distracted.

"I sometimes think your father is a totally different person, or that he is wearing a skin-deep disguise," Saul's wife, Ahinoam, told Jonathan. "What does he do on those mysterious trips? You don't know. Abner doesn't know. I certainly don't know. If only it were another woman! But it isn't. I know that. He always seems as brittle as pottery. Adonai forbid that anything should shatter him." But even that unquiet peace was soon shattered. Late that September, Abner and two other officers found Saul naked and trembling inside one of the large wicker baskets used for the winter storage of dried figs. They had to use main force to drag him from the basket and tie him down, screaming, to his bed, where he lay with eyes closed.

The fit vanished as quickly and mysteriously as it came, however. Saul shook himself, opened his eyes, and laughed heartily. Ahinoam broke into tears and left the room. His sons crowding around him kissed Saul and served him some food, which he ate voraciously. From that day on, however, Saul was gripped by a new anxiety. It seemed to him that he needed special counseling.

He would ask even casual visitors if they knew of any effective seers. In this way he was put in touch with a certain Barissa of Tyre by Imibaal, a Tyrian trade agent. In the first week of October, therefore, Saul, accompanied by Imibaal, set out with a drove of prize asses to market in Tyre.

Once that business was over, Imibaal took Saul to the house of Barissa. Like all important Tyrian residences, it was built on the west shore of the harbor, overlooking the eternally moving waters of the Great Sea. Barissa was a dusky Phenician born in northern Africa and, while yet a child, brought back to the Ladder of Tyre. Her father, a Phenician, had been assistant high priest at the shrine of Melkart. Her mother, an African, had been a temple prostitute there. From them Barissa had learned the trade of astrologer and witch. Now in her early thirties, unmarried, she was small-boned and lissom, but taller even than Saul, with pitch-black eyes and sharply chiseled features.

Saul had never seen anyone like her. Each of her features was in proportion, but the whole was elongated forward, her forehead sloping flatly, her nose prolonging the slope of her forehead, her mouth and chin sloping still further. Her head, according to an African custom, had been bound when she was quite young, so that when she developed physically it was in this distorted fashion. She had the short, black, crinkly hair of her mother's race and conversed easily in four or five languages including Hebrew.

She was always cool and self-possessed. And the moment she laid eyes on Saul, she knew that he was somebody she could profoundly influence. She received him as a guest in her house, fed him a quiet meal alone during which she let him pour out all his fears and jealousies about David. He spoke about the anger he felt whenever he came across that symbol of David's person and David's power: the six-pointed star.

"But, surely, Master Saul, you must know that the evening star, the star of Helel, is seven-pointed," she commented to him. She said little else. Afterward, when night had fallen, she took him to a little chapel overlooking the Great Sea. An altar stood to one side; it had a single silver seven-pointed star carved into it. On the other side was a long couch covered with a leopard skin. She sat beside Saul and, playing a lyre, sang to him a well-known Phenician song to Helel ben Shahar, Helel, Son of the Dawn.

The music, the words, the scented wine, the good food, the soft hand of Barissa, all this added up to a paradisiac experience for the rough Hebrew highlander, who felt so much in need of understanding.

After the singing was over they stayed awhile, listening to the lapping of the waves against the sea wall, watching the crescent moon, and dreaming dreams. Saul laid his hand on Barissa's shoulder. She spoke quite simply: "My Lord Saul! If I be with you tonight willingly, you must consent to become my Helel ben Shahar! I was consecrated to him at my rites of maidenhood. And if love has been born between us two, and that love is to heal your wounds, then you are to speak to me with the mouth of Helel. And our love will be supreme."

Saul made no answer, but in his eyes she read his consent. She lifted his right arm straight above his shoulder and bent forward, sinking the teeth at the left corner of her mouth into the fleshy part of his underarm. A suppressed scream of pain came from Saul's clenched mouth. But it was all over in a flash.

"See! My Lord Saul!" she whispered quite calmly, a little trace of blood on her lips. "Helel is now with us." And she sang in a low voice:

> *"A great sacrifice of nighttime,*
> *Molchomor!*
> *Breath for breath!*
> *Life for life!*
> *Oh, Son of the Dawn!*
> *Helel, my Beloved!"*

In the morning before he left, she told him: "You have Helel's mark, my Lord Saul. It will protect you." She drew aside the left corner of her mouth to display the upper and

lower canines. Their surfaces had been filed into a certain
shape. "In a few days' time you will find the seven-pointed
star incised in your flesh where no enemy can find it," she
added. "And ever afterward that star will bring you victory.
When Helel's bird, the owl, hoots at the crescent moon, you
will remember!"

Two days later a sudden dust storm thundered up the ramp
into the fortress at Gibea. It was Saul. He leaped off his camel
and shouted for Abner and his officers. Jonathan was absent.
From an upper-story window Ahinoam watched her husband
gesticulating with flashing eyes down in the compound as officers and aides ran hither and thither. At one moment she
heard Saul talking, then breaking into a wild cry, flinging both
arms into the air—"Victory is mine! Victory is mine! David
is finished!"

In Adullam, David was just setting out for Hebron on a
minor piece of business. Shoshanna and Abigail and Ahinoam
went with him. "I have not been home to Hebron since I left
over twenty-five years ago," Shoshanna had reminded him. It
was an appeal David could not resist, and he decided to make
it an outing for all his women.

All went smoothly until midafternoon, when at the main
road to Hebron they realigned the convoy. From the oxcart
carrying Shoshanna and David's two wives came laughter and
cries of excitement. David smiled, throwing a characteristic
sweeping glance up at the sky. Suddenly he stopped short.
"What in the devil's name!" Joab followed his gaze. High in
the sky a flock of vultures was winging southeast, directly
toward Hakila.

"God protect us!" cried David. "Turn the carts back to
Adullam! Now! Everybody!" Within two hours they were back
in the redoubt. David left for Hakila with Joab and his Kerethites right after sunset. They were fully armed and fearful
of what they might find.

About three hours before David's convoy turned back to
Adullam, Joshua in Hakila placed his grandson and namesake,
called familiarly Yashua, or Yashya, on the saddle in front of
him, and rode out on his camel with six guards, more or less
following the trails to the gorge. The guards obligingly flung
their spears to amuse Yashua, who was five. They engaged in
mock races, which Joshua's camel always won. For the real
gallop in those races, Joshua swung Yashua around onto his

back. The boy clamped his hands around Joshua's neck and his feet around Joshua's waist, clinging like a limpet and squealing in delight. Finally it was time to go home.

The light of the sun was already reddening and the first gusts of the evening wind were blowing, but the air was still warm. Joshua could see two thin spirals of blue smoke ahead, from the chimneys of Hakila's two cooking fires. Supper would be ready when they arrived. Tomorrow would be even better. David was due for a three-day stay. An involuntary shiver shook Joshua's body as they faced up the last slope. Little Yashua laughed. "Grandfather has the itch! Grandfather has the itch!" he teased. An old children's story told how the angels of Adonai invisibly tickled the bodies of good Hebrews with the feathers on their wingtips.

Joshua and the guards laughed too, and then Joshua noticed a third spiral of thick black smoke from the stronghold. "There must be a fire," he cried, pointing. "Let's get back fast." They set off at full gallop—right into the well-sprung trap.

The six guards and their camels went down in screams and shouts, riddled with spears. Just as he reined his camel in an effort to turn and flee, Joshua felt Yashua's grip loosen. The child crumpled to the sand, a spear in his back. Then a hail of spears hit Joshua from all sides. The last thing he heard was the whoops and cheers of his killers.

Saul's new tactics had paid off admirably. Hakila was the one stronghold whose exact location he knew, and he knew he could get into it by going over the mountain. Abner, who led the raid, had enlisted some of the surviving Ziphites. It had taken three days and three nights to work their way over the mountain in utter secrecy. When they attacked from the back, it was with total surprise, and everyone had perished. Afterward, Abner hid his men in the nearby gullies. There was still one more act to the drama: David's night rider should appear after midnight. He would lead them to another stronghold.

Sure enough, about three o'clock in the morning the night rider appeared, took one look at the smoking ruins, and headed at a gallop northwest toward Adullam. Once the sound of hooves had safely died away, Abner sent two experienced trackers after him. "Stay far enough back so that he can never see or hear you," he cautioned.

David and his Kerethites reached their destination some five miles from Hakila at about the same time the night rider was fleeing to the stronghold. They had settled down to wait for dawn to proceed when they heard his camel's hooves approaching. "Whoever that is, we'd better stop him," said David. Joab and a detail waited on either side of the trail. David waited behind them. Within a few moments, the panic-stricken rider was surrounded by an armed ring and blinking in the light of the pitch torch that Joab had lit and thrust toward him.

He expected to die then and there, then he recognized the torch-holder as his eyes accustomed themselves to the light.

"Joab! Joab! It is I, Imla, rider for David. Hakila is in ruins! Everybody's dead! Even the dogs!"

"Then where are you going?"

"To Adullam! To warn David!"

"You ass," cried Joab, snuffing the torch. "To lead the wolves there?"

"Hold, there!" David came up. "Tell me quickly all that happened."

"Adonai be merciful to my comrades!" he exclaimed when the rider had finished. "The king surely has someone on your trail. We must find them before they find us."

He took Joab and a band of Kerethites and rode for a couple of miles parallel to the trail, to a wooded area. Here David ordered everyone to take cover. He sent Joab with ten Kerethites another mile forward to lie in ambush. The rest waited. It was nine o'clock in the morning when Joab and his men returned, swinging the heads of the two trackers.

As he waited, David had been thinking. The tactic of tracking his night riders could eventually lead Saul to his other strongholds, even to Adullam. The riders had to be stopped. David sent messengers immediately to all of the strongholds with that order. Expect to be attacked, he warned. Stay inside. Don't show yourselves.

He and his company then rode farther westward, covering their tracks and doubling back in order to arrive at Adullam from the hills in the northwest. When they arrived late that afternoon the news was already bad. Five of the eight strongholds had sent out riders to Adullam before David's messengers arrived. The next day David's scouts returned with worse news. Maon and Sela Hammaveth had been taken and their garrisons liquidated. Masada was surrounded. Saul had installed his own garrisons in Hebron, Bethlehem, Carmel, Keilah, and Beersheva. His scouting parties were out day and night. One curiosity: a red seven-pointed star had been daubed on rocks near the entrances to the raided strongholds.

To Joab's surprise, David's decision in the face of Saul's

latest scourge came out effortlessly, as though it had been arrived at long before—and it had.

"We're going into exile, Joab. We leave at sunset. Those who wish to may stay behind or go where they like."

"Where to, David?"

"To Gath."

"To Gath? To Gath? To Duke Achish?" Joab was stupefied.

"Yes, Gath. Yes, to Duke Achish. If Saul insists that we serve other gods, then we will. We have to survive."

Joab did not hesitate. "We'll be ready," he said.

The
Servant of Dagon

⊠⊠⊠ Never in the whole varied chronicle of Dagon in Philistia had such a great council been called. Great councils were very rare. They involved every member of the ruling classes. Such a meeting was called a "Heave of Dagon," and a whole theology underlay it. As the priests of Dagon explained—for only they could initiate a "heave"—at very critical moments the supreme god "heaved" himself into a more elevated and resplendent condition, for Dagon was in the eternal process of becoming. "Dagon becomes!" was therefore the Philistine greeting of everyday life.

When Achish came privately to Duke Shekelath to tell him of the triumph of his policy, of David's arrival in Gath as a refugee, Shekelath nearly swooned with relief and delight. At last, vengeance was near at hand! Vengeance for which he had been storing up hate for thirty years, since both he and Achish were young men. He went dutifully to his monitors, the priests, and they called the heave.

Their words were exalted. "From the darkness of chaos, Dagon heaves in strength and light. Forever. Through water primeval. Through unbreathed airs. Through masterless winds. Through the inobedient earth. Through the oarless seas. Philistines! Assemble for the Heave of Dagon to a greater glory!"

By an hour after sunrise one day later, the Philistines had assembled in the great audience hall of Gaza. After the earthquake Shekelath had rebuilt and redecorated it more lavishly than ever before. It was filled this day with great names, beautiful women, handsome children, venerable elders, all in a magnificent panoply of robes and coronets. The five dukes sat on their thrones clustered around the high priest, Manaath, and looked out over the might, the wealth, the nobility, and the hopes of Philistia.

After Shekelath had incensed the altar of Dagon, he motioned to Achish, who limped to the podium. This was his supreme moment.

263

"Philistines!" he began. "In the name of Dagon, I am authorized to declare this a Heave of Lord Dagon. Some days ago Dagon called across the lowlands. He sang across the highlands. And out of the darkness beyond, a golden-haired giant came riding. He has moved over the hills like an avalanche. He has flown over the plains like the magic winds of Osterman. He has run ahead of all the wise men of Babel and of Israel and of Tyre and of Thebes and of Ammon and of Zoba. The sunrise was the fire he heated himself by. He came enameled with adversity, stained by brutality, hardened in hate. He brought with him the greatest gifts, the wind-rise of rebellion in the land and the water flow of refugees from the land." Achish paused again for effect. Men and women looked at each other. Who had come, did the duke say?

"The one who comes," Achish went on loudly, "is the herald of our success. He is the greatest gift of Dagon, the proof of Dagon's power. While our enemy Saul of Gibea languishes in his mountain pigsty, battered by evil spirits, abandoned by his soldiers, cursed by his priests—this slayer of giants, this mortal enemy of our mortal enemy, this warrior"—Achish stopped again, waited a moment before continuing—"this David, son of Jesse of Bethlehem, fighting arm of Bashan, of Ammon, of Edom, of Judah, of Galilee, of Zoba, this David, the golden-haired one, is now one of us!"

The effect of the announcement was overwhelming. The other dukes on their thrones were round-eyed in amazement. A flush of exultant excitement appeared in the whole assembly, as if an invisible hand had brushed sudden color there. Almost a thousand throats uttered the name of their god in hushed reverence, starting with a long rising and falling tone. "Daaaaaaa-gooooooooo-nnnnnnnnn!" and ending with that humming nasal twang characteristic of the Philistine language.

Achish, the perfect master of ceremonies, let the reaction run itself out. Then, with a mocking stare at his old adversary Duke Balkarith, who sat impassively on his throne, he went on with his more usual staccato delivery.

"A question of strategy, Philistines! There were those who counseled quick action. Hotheads! There were those who wanted perpetual war. Meddlers! There were those who thought all day. Dullards! And there were those who read the signs and saw that it was best to wait. Those relied on Dagon. Believers! True believers!

"Now he has come to us, this favorite of Adonai. And the anger of Adonai has been turned away from us. No longer need we fear the deadly hemorrhoid for our warriors, nor the crippling flow for our women, nor disease for our children, nor the white teeth of mice and rats for our wheat, nor the brown rot in the eyes of our watchmen! Adonai, who sent all those plagues, has now sent his champion to serve us. With the sword of Goliath on his belt, he is ours! Ours! Ours! Philistines! Ours!"

It was too powerful a draught. All control and convention broke down. The whole assembly rose, chanting: "Philistines! Philistines! Ours! Ours! Ours!" Even the four other dukes joined the chanting. Men embraced each other. Women and children clapped and cheered. The servants and slaves at the door took up the chant. Those outside in the five courtyards of the palace started chanting and clapping. The watchmen on the walls of the palace, the people standing on the streets, even those sitting at the windows of their houses heard it and joined it. A great wave from Gaza the Magnificent flowed out into the fields around.

The "roar of Philistia" was heard for miles. The drovers of passing caravans on the coastal road listened in wonder, and soldiers on picket duty in the hills gazed at each other in astonishment.

While the assembly was filing out, Shekelath summoned the dukes and high priest Manaath into a strategy session. Achish began with the details. Now he spoke in normal fashion—succinct, clear, unadorned, from time to time consulting his notes.

"He came in the evening with a company of two thousand. With him: his two wives, Abigail and Ahinoam, their slaves and servants and baggage; his seven brothers, four of them married, with children and servants; his aides, who are his cousins, Joab, Asahel, and Abishai; one priest, Abiathar of Nov. All in all, fifty-seven, including children.

"His military escort was a company of eight hundred armed Kerethites on camels, and another six hundred infantry—mainly Hebrews but also many Ammonites, Egyptians, Moabites, and others. He also has three companies of Galilean archers and some seventy cavalry. Just under two thousand men.

"He is willing to become a vassal of Philistia and to fight for Dagon's cause. He has asked for political asylum.

"We have three alternatives. We can kill him and all with him. Judging by their condition, this would cost the lives of about three to five thousand of our men. These men are awesome fighters. Our losses would be heavy. Or we can let him go freely and depart from us. He is talking, half-talking I should say, about going north to Zoba or even further. We would then be allowing a new power to settle up there; given two or three years, this David would undoubtedly build a kingdom of his own.

"Or we can, finally, accept him as one of our own. This will take time. He must be tested. We must be sure. But one thing we must remember: he is the champion of Adonai. And now I will say to you all, as I have been saying always, that with Adonai's champion on our side, we have Adonai on our side—"

"If you are in any way suggesting that Lord Dagon is not supreme, my Lord Achish"—Balkarith was on his feet—"then this is blasphemy—"

High priest Manaath lifted his right hand. "Achish has the floor," Manaath said with his thick sibilance, "and so far all he has said coheres with the mind of Dagon and Luqqawatna." Balkarith sank back on his throne.

"I just have one thing more, my Lord Dukes! There is one additional circumstance of David that argues the wisdom of selecting the third choice. This is the condition of soul of this Hebrew—"

"Yes, yes! Tell us! What is it!"

"In my judgment, he is in total revolt not only against Saul but also against the very foundations of Saul's kingship: the approval of Adonai. He blames his reliance on Adonai for the hardships and humiliation of his present state.

"For instance!" Achish held up two fingers. "Twice, my Lord Dukes, twice he had Saul at his mercy in the last few years, and each time he spared him in the name of his god, Adonai!

"But now! Let me quote his own, his very own words to me as taken down by my scribe: 'My Lord Achish, I request political asylum and military protection. I further request to be admitted to the ranks of Philistia. My god has rejected me. My king has hunted me. Neither the Covenant of my race nor my belief in that Covenant has served to protect me and mine. All I have lived by has failed me. I am now at the mercy of the Pentarchy. With the sword of Goliath I am here. At your disposal.'" Achish stopped to enjoy the low hum of excited conversation.

Shekelath stood up. "In your opinion, my Lord Duke, is this David reliable? Can we believe him?"

"Yes, on both counts."

"Then, let's get to specifics, Achish. What do you suggest?"

"The following. It is now the middle of winter, I need—he, David, needs—time. He must stay in Gath. I must be near him—say for some months. That brings us to, say, the end of next summer. During that time I suggest we deploy our forces so that by the end of next autumn we are in a strategically favorable position to winter safely and, at the beginning of the spring, to deliver the final hammer blow to Saul and his cabbage-patch kingdom.

"By next autumn, if all goes well, I propose to transfer some minor but important command, say Ziklag, into David's hands. Later, at a more apposite moment, I propose to present David to this honorable council. Philistines! I have spoken."

Shekelath stood up beside his throne and looked over at Manaath. The high priest nodded benignly. The duke went to the podium. "The assembly wishes to thank Duke Achish for this long and arduous pursuit of a policy which I, for one, doubted could be successful. But it has been. And now, Philistines, now we shall meld Adonai into Dagon. We shall enslave his people and consecrate his Ark to Dagon. We shall substitute the empire of Dagon for the Covenant of the Foreskin!"

A roar of laughter rose from his audience, easing Shekelath's tension. "We hereby grant full approval to Duke Achish's proposals. Members of the general staff will examine Achish's strategic proposals for the last hammer blows against Saul. Philistines! I have spoken!"

The Heave of Dagon was over.

As the dukes and their accompanying officers were leaving, Shekelath chatted with Achish, and Balkarith strolled over. Achish sensed the danger in this still-young bull of a man and was ready for Balkarith's assault. "Watch out, Achish!" Shekelath whispered out of the side of his mouth. "The ox is coming to gore you." Balkarith had been nicknamed the ox by his troops because of both his size and his strong, rank odor.

"Well, I suppose, my Lord Duke," he sneered at Achish's back, "having this fair-haired man in your house will help your insomnia." The sly and contemptuous reference to Achish's homosexuality was infuriating. Shekelath froze, seeing the sudden flash of rage in Achish's face. But the limping duke had his answer ready.

"It will be interesting, my Lord Shekelath," Achish said in

a loud voice, keeping his back to Balkarith, "when you meet
David of Bethlehem. They say he fells an ox with one kick of
his right foot. A far more humane way of killing a sheep or
an ox, don't you think, my Lord Duke, than approaching them
from the back and penetrating their stomachs with the penis."
It was a direct reference to Balkarith's favorite pastime of
bestiality. Then Achish took Shekelath by the arm. "Shekelath,
there's an odor in here. Shall we get some fresh air?"

"If David is brought here," Balkarith shouted after them in
fury, "I won't come." Wit was not Balkarith's strong point.

"Neither will the shit lifters of Gaza," Achish fired back
from the doorway.

David and Abigail sat with Joab and Eliab and Abiathar in
Achish's quarters in Gaza. The atmosphere was sober. They
had heard that mighty roar of Philistia. Now from the windows
they watched the Philistines streaming out of the hall. The
crowd was exultant but peaceful. David and his two thousand
would be staying in Philistia.

David stood up. He seemed paralyzed, like a man trying
to walk with his feet in a trap. He struggled for breath and
began to sob, burying his face in his hands. Abigail touched
his arm and gently led him back to his seat. No one said a
word.

Eventually David spoke. "What I now have," he said, "is
sorrow without tears. I have no juice. I have no god. I'm
finished. We can survive, but I am finished. This is death for
me. But I will play it out to the end."

The immediate effect on Saul of David's disappearance was
predictable. He had no way of knowing that David had gone
into exile. For all he knew, his enemy was still lurking in the
wastes of southern Judah or on the mountain fastnesses in the
Wheel of Galilee. David was not, Saul ascertained through his
informers and spies, in either Jebus or the Ladder of Tyre. He
probably was not over in one of the east bank nations, certainly
not in Gilead—Saul had good allies there—nor in Bashan,
Ammon, Moab, or Edom.

He might possibly be in Egypt. The Egyptians needed slaves
and mercenaries. But if David was there, he was really gone.
Hebrew refugees rarely returned from Egypt. To get there involved an arduous journey through the death-dealing Bag of
Sand and through fiercely murderous tribes.

Philistia was a possibility, but if David had gone there, then he was finished as a rival. The Philistines would give David two choices: death or subservience. The Philistines meant business, and David's name would stink forever in the nostrils of Israel if he became a vassal of Gaza. If he were killed by the Philistines, then someone else had done Adonai's work!

To get Jonathan out of the way, Saul sent him to guard the eastern territories. Saul then scoured Judah and Galilee for David, but David was nowhere to be found. Saul captured and gutted eight of David's strongholds, but never found Adullam in Judah or Merom in Galilee. David, he concluded, could not be in Judah.

On the morning before he left Bethlehem, his base headquarters, he spoke with two Bethlehemites, Nathan the Scholar and Maaka the crone.

During his whole stay at Bethlehem he had met Nathan face to face only once before. That was at the general assembly of all Bethlehemites on the day of his arrival, when he had denounced David and his supporters to the elders and the people. Afterward each elder passed by Saul's chair to do obeisance by bowing to the ground while touching forehead, mouth, and heart as a sign of allegiance in thought, word, and feeling.

When Nathan's turn came, Saul was troubled. Nathan did not avert his eyes like the others, but looked steadily into Saul's. And Saul found that he could not stare back, which made him angry as well as afraid. Saul called Nathan in again.

At this time Nathan was in his mid-fifties. There was nothing impressive in his physical appearance. He was of average height, dark-skinned and bearded. He dressed simply and spoke quietly: "an average man."

But some detail, some trait, something about him resonated. Nathan could read the geography of a man's spirit with his penetrating gaze.

Again Saul could neither return the scholar's stare nor speak to him. He tried to stand up. He could not. Abner and Doeg the Edomite, standing by Saul's chair, noticed his difficulty. They watched over Saul like jealous hawks, for their lives depended on his safety. They drew their swords and, clanging their scabbards threateningly, advanced in front of Saul's chair and looked coldly at Nathan.

The scholar did not move. He said simply, "Under the shadow of the Hebron gate, I see the sword stuck under the fifth rib of Abner. On the roofs of silence in Beersheva, I see the sword of Goliath asleep in the neck of Doeg." The swords fell from the hands of both men and they reeled away, moaning and writhing to the ground. The elders of Bethlehem standing around Saul drew back in fear. Abner had his hands clamped over his ribs. Doeg's head was shaking back and forth. Nathan looked at the king. "If the King wills it, I shall go."

Saul could only stare. He knew he wasn't being asked for permission. Nathan was already about ten paces away, when the king found his voice and shouted: "Be gone in the morning, Nathan. Be gone out of here forever. Forever!" The scholar turned on his heel and transfixed Saul with a look. Then he went on his way. He would be gone that evening.

The crone Maaka was now of very great age. If anyone heard news, it was Maaka. And if anyone knew the best astrologers and witches, Maaka did. Saul therefore questioned her closely. She knew nothing about David's hiding places, but she had one interesting detail about his birth—Jesse's visit to Shalama at Petahyahu. Maaka had learned of it from her daughter, Shua, who had assisted Hatich during Korith's confinement.

"Apparently, O King, Shalama could call up the shades from Sheol and have them speak to the living! Now I hear that she has moved to Endor, and they say she's a witch."

"Give the old woman food and drink and some money," Saul told Abner. "When we go north to Galilee, we must visit Endor."

A week or so after the Heave of Dagon, Achish inquired about the Hebrews. David and his family were well, the servants reported. The Hebrew leader did a lot of walking outside by himself. The Hebrews kept to themselves, were extremely deferential, and modified their ways to fit the Philistine manner of life. They refused to eat certain foods, however, and would not drink milk with meat.

He sent an officer to David's quarters to tell the Hebrew that he, Achish, would come to see him that evening. Then he turned to the day's business.

The two met in the dining hall assigned to the Hebrews. Wine and cakes were served to them as they talked. Achish found David calm, subdued, but charming and grateful. With the mutual respect that was growing between them, they chatted civilly about his family and the weather. He has news for me, David thought. He is feeling his way and has no plans, Achish told himself. They were both right.

"I often reflect in wintertime," Achish said, glancing out the window at the leafless trees and the flowerless beds, "that we humans should retreat as nature retreats." He contemplated the sky. "Days are narrowed down to a mere slip of light between two darknesses. The heavens weigh down on us with clouds. All living things go under. Winter is a cruel god!" He looked over at the Hebrew.

David smiled. "Yes, Achish, but even a rough character like winter melts before that gentle maiden, spring. In spite of all his teeth, she will come in her time, leading her lamb children and flower children, putting winter's cold kingdom to rout."

"Yes," Achish said, smiling with pleasure. "Well, enough of this poetry." David waved a hand in mock dismissal of all poetry. "We had a very successful Heave of Dagon, as I told you briefly. And there will be more about it later between us. First, as to Saul, he cannot find you or where you've gone. He thinks you're still in the land. He has taken and destroyed eight of your former strongholds. And at present his base camp is in Bethlehem. Yes, Bethlehem." Achish saw the look in David's eyes. "And he is rampaging like a mad bull around Judah and its environs with his army and two commanders, Abner and Doeg—"

"Doeg!" David's voice grated.

"Ah! An old score to settle there, eh? Well, you'll settle it, David. In good time. But, my friend, Saul is really mad now. He is killing scholars and holy men, desecrating shrines, consulting seers, violating your Shabbath rules—he's rebelled totally against your sacred Law. It's only a matter of time until he goes over the edge completely. Nothing can save him now."

"But what's the difference between what Saul has done and what I've done? We have both rebelled against Adonai."

"Yes, you both came to the edge of the same precipice. When that awful moment comes, some demon or some angel holds up before a man the polished mirror of his life. There was a difference between you and Saul at that moment. Saul looked into his own eyes in the polished mirror. His eyes were already glazed with madness. And he said to himself: 'You are beaten. You've been dead for a long time. Why wait any longer? Leap! And forever you shall inherit the glory of the brimstone kingdom where you will reign surely forever.'"

"And?"

"And Saul will leap. Be assured. But you, you stopped at the edge. Without madness. You said: 'I am broken but I shall survive.' And you could see the devil clinging to your back grinning over your shoulder. You saw how you had been dead.

Now you want to shake that devil. To live again. With your music. Why can't you play?"

"Achish, Gath is exile for me, a life I cannot accept as permanent. And I am no longer pure. Only a pure hand can plant a sacramental flower."

"I thought you were a bird that could sing on any bough." Achish flung his arms out in a wide gesture. "I can give you the bough of Philistia, all Philistia, and soon all of this sunbathed land. Soon music will burst from your throat and fingers. Dazzling lyrics! All men will listen to you."

"No, Achish. My harp will be silent here in Philistia." He looked over the roofs of Gath. "I need God's whole world for my poems. I feel hemmed in here by these roofs and gables and walls and cornices. They are too full of unhappy echoes."

"I am sorry," said Achish. "I hope that feeling will pass. Talking about revolt and rebellion, however, brings me to my next subject." Achish stood up as he said this, and stumped up and down as he spoke. "At the Heave of Dagon, it was unanimously decided to offer you the honorable position of vassal to Philistia." He stopped and waited for a reaction from the Hebrew.

"Yes?"

"Yes. The hard facts, then, as the moneychangers say." Achish's voice became a monotone, and as precise as a military report. He was now the Philistine duke, emissary of the Pentarchy.

"You will consent to serve and swear allegiance to the Pentarchy as a free vassal—you came of your own accord. You will be assigned living quarters. You and your people will benefit from our Philistine way of life. Your soldiers and riders will remain under your direct command. You may also recruit Philistines freely. When we destroy the kingdom of Saul, you will consent to be our vassal among your own people of Judah and Benjamin as part of greater Philistia. You will be respected.

"You and your family will be quartered here in my palace until late spring. Your men-at-arms will be given barracks and exercise grounds, and the daily pay of Philistine soldiers and officers. All of you will have freedom of movement within the military code; that is, a superior officer must always know the whereabouts of each man under him."

"What determines the length of my stay here in your palace?"

"A direct question requiring a direct answer." Achish took a long draught of wine. "Until I am satisfied that you no longer fight against Lord Dagon." His eyes were like frozen stones now as he looked at David. "Until I am satisfied that you do, indeed, serve Dagon." He stopped.

David stood up and folded his arms across his chest. "Until, that is to say, Duke Achish, I become a Philistine. Isn't that the price?"

"Yes." The answer was abrupt, cold. This was the crux. Without realizing it, both men held their breath: everything between them would stand or fall on David's answer. The Hebrew stared unblinking at the Philistine. Then he sighed and spread out his palms before dropping his arms to his side. Achish breathed in relief. At least the answer was not no. He would return to the question by another route, perhaps on another day.

"David," he said, pouring him wine, "tell me about Adonai. Where is he?" The question provided an easy transition. David started to answer spontaneously.

"Raham taught me that—" He broke off and looked away, some fleeting expression passed over his face whose meaning evaded even the sharp-eyed Philistine. He began again, wistfully: "I used to believe him to be everywhere, Achish, and always with me, at my sitting down and my standing up, in my very deepest thought, on every path I walked. Behind me, in front of me, around me." David was almost chanting. "And that I couldn't hide from him, whether in profound darkness or on the mountain peak. That he knew my every thew and sinew, every bone and limb and nerve, every thought and fancy and memory, all of me, always, even in my mother's womb."

"And now?"

"I don't know." A terrible look of anguished loss crossed his face. His voice rose. "I don't know. For if he is all-knowing, all-seeing, everywhere, at all times, why am I hunted, exiled, disgraced in the House of Israel?"

Achish was pleased. "David, no one knows the mind of Adonai, or of Dagon, for that matter. We are mortals, after all." He smiled deprecatingly. "But that is what Adonai in all his strength has done. Put you in the arms of Dagon."

David did not reply and Achish rose from his chair. "Enough for tonight. Rest now, David. We have much to do together.

"In the next few weeks I will give you a tour of Philistia. We will prepare for the Spring Festival Games in which you will be urged to compete." He looked David up and down searchingly. "And, by the way, I almost forgot! A small point, but important in its way! You know, perhaps, that all Philistine athletes perform naked at the games?"

"That's all right, Achish."

"Very well. But the sign of your Covenant—your circumcision—would only provoke derision. Philistines are proud of their foreskins. Besides, as long as you're without one, they won't see you as genuinely Philistine. But"—he looked speculatively at David's crotch—"I think we have a solution for that." Achish walked to the door. "We have plenty of time."

Upstairs in the living room of his own quarters, Joab was incredulous. "Proud of their foreskins? Did you tell him how we once cut off two hundred just to win you a wife?" They hugged each other, laughing.

"Perhaps he'll lend you his!" Joab shot at him as he fled laughing out the door.

"Was Achish serious, David?" Abigail asked.

"Completely so. The sign of the Covenant is important. But far more serious is my belief in Adonai *and* my becoming a vassal of Philistia."

"Do you believe in Adonai?"

He ducked the question with a question: "What does Adonai mean to me now?"

"Well, whatever you do, my Lord David, I will love you."

"Why do women think that love is the solution to all problems?"

"Isn't it?" Abigail asked with a slow smile.

David's life at Gath gradually assumed a regular and peaceful course. Achish's word was his bond. "David's Hebrews," as everyone called them, could move freely between the barracks in the Field of Thaya and David's headquarters in Achish's palace. Occasionally high Philistine officers came to watch David's men on maneuvers and to spot check David on code enforcement: "I see you list as spearman a certain Aminadab, son of Yoram of Carmel in Judah. Where is he at this moment?" The queries were always satisfied.

Achish visited David and his family regularly. "And how is our candidate today?" Achish would say this teasingly, and David took it in that spirit, but he knew there was serious intent behind it. Gradually, also, Shoshanna, Abigail, and Ahinoam organized the household. With their own slaves and servants they did all the cooking, washing, and marketing. The Hebrews were highly visible in the normal population of Gath, but Achish had made it abundantly clear that they were not to be harassed. And they were not.

David and his intimates were provided with teaching slaves who instructed them in the Philistine language, which was wholly different from Hebrew or any Semitic tongue. Within a couple of months they had mastered all the Philistine they needed, although David and Joab were the only ones who became proficient.

Toward the end of winter Achish took David on a tour of Philistine territories ending in Ashkelon, the fortress city and port governed by Kolarak. There David spent three weeks lodged in the duke's palace on a promontory jutting out into the Great Sea. Achish, together with Shekelath and Kolarak, departed across the Great Sea on a secret mission: "We will talk when I get back," he told David, not divulging his destination. "Meantime, you have thinking to do," Achish reminded him. True. Soon it would be time for the Spring Festival Games. Well before that David would have to choose sides, and as he saw it he really had no choice.

It was the first time David had ever seen the Great Sea. He marveled at the rising and falling tide and the salty taste of the water and its briny smell. He found its buoyancy for swimming peculiar but satisfying—if a big frigid so early in the year. He was enthralled and mystified by the ceaseless sound of the sea. It seemed that some great power was flexing itself in the restless surf, soothing, keening, threatening, exulting.

Throughout the doldrums of the sirocco and the rasp of the hurricane, he kept listening, as years ago he had listened to the wind in the pine grove in Bethlehem. Would the wind or the sea have an answer for the ache in his soul?

The morning Achish was expected back, David went out early to walk on the beach. The sea outside the surf line, barely flurried by the landward winds, looked like the light-colored marl floors he had once seen in Gilead farmhouses. But long, stately waves rolled up to the shelf of the beach, breaking in a ruffled white line toward the headland on which the duke's palace stood. He heard shouts from the jetty and saw the harbor guards lighting the signal fires. Far out but clear against the horizon he could see the topsails of the duke's lead ship. He strode over to the jetty and inquired how long before the flotilla made port. About an hour, he was told.

He sat in the shelter of the dunes and pondered the mysterious strength of the sea that made him lonely for Bethlehem. He yearned for something—some power—that might be his inner food no matter where he was, sitting in Gath or riding the deserts.

In those moments he did not want any human being near him; this solitude was deliciously painful, as an honorable death might be. Except, he thought, that I would like to be able to thank someone for the gift of this feeling and this beauty. And I would want someone to know that I was dying and, later, dead. The shouts of the dockers shattered his reverie as the lead ship drew up to the quay wall.

Achish was in marvelous humor, smiling, rested, full of benignity: "David," he said, his face lit up in laughter, "I've been given authority to give you all your heart desires. Just take that little step we discussed. Then, my friend, then it's all for you!" He flung his arms wide in his customary expansive gesture. They walked arm in arm back to the waiting chariot, and were soon rattling down the coastal road and in through the rising country to Gath, "the cap of Philistia," as Achish described it to David. They agreed to have dinner together that evening.

Achish's rose garden was the apple of his eye. He led David that evening down the meandering pickaback surface bordered with roses to a rectangular marble-lined pool shaded by tall palms. The floor of the pool was lined with green slabs, so that the water always had a green translucence. Achish called it the Palm Pool. He bathed there, sometimes slept there under an awning, and held private conversations under the palms.

"We must plan carefully, David," he began. "There is no fiercer hell than failure in a great enterprise.

"Now," he said comfortably, "as you have no doubt surmised, I have been across the Great Sea to confer with the ultimate authority for all Philistines. It rests there in Luqqawatna in an enormous and enigmatic building. And please don't reveal that I have even spoken to you of it. The priests would not approve."

"But just what *is* over there?" David asked.

Achish shook his head. "Don't, David."

"But without Luqqawatna, without that power?"

"All would wither, David. All! Overnight. But that's enough. No more questions. Please!" There was a pause while Achish collected himself. "Now listen, my Hebrew. We have to present you to the Philistines. We have only six weeks before the games, and we have two things to take care of: your training, physical and mental; and the matter of your circumcision. As for the training, it had better be thorough. The single combat in the games is to the death.

"Still, training is training. So let's get on with it. But the circumcision—"

"Achish," David interrupted, "there is nothing one can do about that. I'm circumcised. That's it."

"No, friend, it's not," Achish said roundly. "We've had this problem before, with Egyptians and Arameans. The Egyptian surgeons are of good service in this matter. They have a tremendous science at Thebes. I have already sent to Gaza for the chief surgeon to the army, Maat-men."

"But what can Maat-men do? Is he a magician?"

"Not a magician. A surgeon. Maat-men has been trained in attaching artificial foreskins. I've seen the finished article— well-treated leather and sweet Arabic gum. Of course you can't fiddle with it. But it looks all right, and it's no more annoying than the gummed wigs of court ladies. It can be worn permanently, once you get used to it.

"Now if you are to participate in any of the games—the spear throwing, the slingshot, the knife throwing, the horse race—and you must do so to signify your allegiance to Philistia—you cannot do so as a circumcised man. The foreskin has a tremendous religious and social significance for Philistines. Have you ever noticed the hood over the head of Lord Dagon's statues? And the statue itself?"

"I have; I thought it was a symbolic crown or miter."

"Haven't you noticed? It's attached to the forehead just above the eyebrows and then around the temples, and it is in loose folds. Do you know the word for foreskin in the Philistine language?"

"*Selmat.*"

"That originally meant hood! And the whole glory of Philistines comes from the uncovering of Dagon's power to become more and more and more and more." The Philistine's eyes were aglow.

"All right! All right, Achish. So be it. It's only a detail."

"A detail, David? I wonder!" The Philistine looked at David with great concentration. "You know, unlike you Hebrews, we Philistines are not supposed to have much religion. But we have cultivated one great quality: *lapathalna,* the quality of evoking deep spiritual enjoyment from the commonplace. *Lapathalna* doesn't seek to impress, leaves all becoming to Dagon. And so *lapathalna* impels a man to leave things as they are—things like the foreskin.

"True, the Hittites and the Egyptians and who knows what other nations remove the foreskin because it gathers its own type of sedimentation and dirt. Doubtless—you may be angry at this suggestion—some wise lawgiver of the Hebrews had the same idea, but gave it a religious significance in order to place an irresistible obligation on you to observe his law.

"Philistines, following *lapathalna,* prefer to retain the foreskin as a sign of masculinity as well as a symbol of their unity in Dagon."

"So that's your *lapathalna.*" David leaned back, grinning, his hands joined behind his head.

Dinner was then announced, and after dinner Achish had a surprise for David. "An important meeting, David, for you and for me. You may bring him in now," he told the officer-in-waiting.

A lone figure escorted by four guards entered the dining room. And David found himself looking into the eyes of the single most powerful religious figure in the House of Israel since the death of Samuel: Nathan.

"Peace, my Lord David." Nathan's words brought David to his feet, his heart beating wildly.

"I did not know . . ." David faltered, still speaking Philistine. He took an awkward, half-hesitant step toward Nathan, then stopped, his face paling beneath the bronze sunburn. Achish sat composedly. Only his eyes had changed. They were hard, glittering, watchful. This was one of the finest pieces of theater he had ever organized. What better way to test David than to confront him with Nathan, whose religious importance the shrewd Achish had recognized long before most Hebrews had ever heard of him?

If he was aware of Achish's intention, however, Nathan gave no sign. His eyes and David's were locked.

David started to return Nathan's greeting in Hebrew, then said in Philistine: "Achish, please, with your permission . . . ?"

"Of course, my Lord David," Achish replied graciously in Hebrew. "Everyone here speaks Hebrew."

"Nathan, my brother, peace be upon you!"

"And again, peace upon you, my Lord David. I arrived in Gath yesterday. The duke has been most kind."

When Nathan had been seated, he told of Saul. Expelled from Bethlehem by the king, Nathan had gone north to Nain and then across the Yezreel Valley to Nazareth to see Malaki. The blind seer of Nazareth had welcomed Nathan openly, unafraid of the king's wrath. Not two weeks after Nathan's arrival,

Saul had swept up to Galilee in his feverish search for David and his sympathizers.

Saul's method was brusque and thorough. He would first meet with his supporters at whatever place he was and get from them a list of Davidites. Then, if they had not already fled, Saul had the Davidites beheaded in public along with all their blood relatives, wives, servants, and slaves. Their lands, houses, and all chattels were confiscated and distributed among the king's supporters. The Saulites therefore had reason to fight the king's battles. Saul's treatment of the family of Ahinoam, David's third wife, was especially cruel. All the males were castrated and blinded. All females were sold into slavery. All children under ten were slaughtered. Nathan recounted all this in an uninflected factual manner that won the admiration of Achish.

Then Saul came to Nazareth and everything changed. He was met outside the gates by the elders and scholars, who stood clustered around Malaki as he sat on his little four-wheeled cart. Malaki and Malaki alone would speak for the town, Tay-Amim, the chief elder, told the king. Saul had never before come up against such a strange coagulated power and resistance in the whole of Israel. He looked upon the ranks of sullen faces, and deep instinct impelled him to caution. "The king," he bellowed harshly, "will talk alone with your spokesman."

Only the king and his personal bodyguard were invited to enter the town. Once Saul and Abner and the twenty swordsmen were inside, the citizens closed ranks. For one tense moment, Saul looked at Malaki, at Abner, at the crowds, and back at Malaki, then ordered the others to remain outside.

At Malaki's house, Saul found a further irritation. Standing in the front garden was Nathan.

"O King!" Malaki's voice reverberated. "The scholar Nathan is my guest. My honor is involved. And yours, O King, as his fellow guest!" Nathan stayed. They sat Saul down, washed his hands and feet, and gave him cooled wine.

"O King," Malaki said, before Saul had time to take a second sip of wine, "last night the owls of Endor all flew over and clustered on the walls of Nazareth." Saul's wine cup shattered on the flagstones, and the red wine pooled in the fragments at his feet. A choking sound came from his throat at this reference to Barissa's promise. He peered into Malaki's brown, sightless sockets as if trying to see his thoughts.

"O King," Malaki went on imperturbably, "last evening the evening star shone for one hour and then went out. The watchmen reported it to me. It reappeared only at dawn, shining and luminous." Saul was now on his feet, the vein pulsing in his forehead.

"O King," the seer went on, "the owl and the Son of the Dawn have cruelly deceived my Lord the King. For Adonai made all the stars, and all the birds of the air, and the beasts of the field, and all the fish in the Great Sea. But the adversary, Satan, uses all things to destroy those whom Adonai loves. Yet," Malaki finished in a low, tender voice, "there is salvation and peace for my Lord the King. But Adonai does require satisfaction for our offenses."

The ambivalence and the tragedy of Saul were never more clearly seen than at that poignant moment. He burst into uncontrollable weeping, falling on the ground, his body wracked by sobs, his hands reaching out and gripping the stumps of Malaki's legs.

"Can anything save me, Seer of Adonai? I have betrayed the Covenant. I persecuted Samuel and all the holy ones of Israel. I have driven my beloved David into exile. I have killed and tortured and starved thousands. I am damned. Satan holds me. I fight against it, but it is no use. O Seer! Pray for me."

Malaki said nothing until Saul's torment had spent itself.

"Sacrifice there will be, O King!" he concluded. "A sacrifice pleasing to Adonai. Adonai will show my Lord the King, for he will not let his anointed perish. But . . ." Malaki's voice sank to a whisper and Saul had to place his ear close to Malaki's lips to hear.

When Saul stood up, his face looked like an empty water skin, drained and lifeless. He could look at no one and walked with evident pain. Nathan had to turn from the wretchedness in Saul's eyes. Saul dragged himself back to the gate, mounted his camel, and left Nazareth at a gallop, his retinue trailing behind him.

There was silence for a time as David and Achish digested Nathan's amazing account.

"And why have you come here, O reverend scholar?" Achish asked.

"Because this man, my Lord David, is the anointed of Adonai," Nathan answered simply. "Adonai has driven him out into the lands of Dagon. Adonai's will is that he be with the sons of Dagon. Therefore I, as scholar of the House of Israel and of Adonai, should be with my Lord David."

It was the same answer Nathan had given when he arrived

in Gath. Achish had merely wanted David to hear it from Nathan's own lips.

"What, Nathan, do you think Malaki told the king?" David wondered.

"How, where, and when he would die, my Lord David, and how he would be sacrificed to make satisfaction for his offenses, covered with the same disgrace he planned to pile on others."

All of a sudden David saw the future.

"Very good!" Achish stood up. "I think we have all heard enough. Now," he said briskly, "Nathan will live in the quarters of my Lord David and come and go as my Lord David does. David, tomorrow you and I have business to conclude."

Once he was alone with David, Nathan lapsed into the taciturn reverence he had always shown him. They sat together in the living room for a short time.

"I don't know what you know or think of the new way of life I am leading," David began.

But Nathan raised his hand and said mildly, "I think I know most of it, including the professional attentions of the Egyptian surgeons." There was not a trace of reproach in his voice.

But David repeated Achish's argument against circumcision anyway, adding: "If we accepted everything handed down from generation to generation, I would still be using flint instead of iron arrowheads."

"My Lord David," Nathan said dryly, in his habitual use of parable, "a young man went to an old man: 'Give me some money, my friend. I have to go abroad and see the world.' The old man reached into his pocket and handed the young man a purse full of experience but empty of money. 'Here! I have paid for what is in that purse with the coin of my life. My experience is all I have.' And so," Nathan concluded, "the Hebrews keep the riches earned by their ancestors." He bowed and got up to leave.

David gently laid a hand on his arm: "First, Nathan, could you tell me the real reason you have come?"

"My Lord, when a king has a beautiful bride whose safety is his only concern, the king always keeps his watchdog on guard outside her door, so that her beauty not be marred by ugly men. Good night, my lord."

Alone in his room, Nathan knelt and prayed: "Even though he wanders now in darkness, O God of Abraham, Isaac, and Jacob, let the day come when he sees your light again."

Adonai did use Nathan as a watchdog, but his gifts destined him to be much more, to be prophet to the man who would fashion a Hebrew nation. Like most prophets before their day comes, Nathan was unaware of his gift. Starting as a scholar, he was convinced that most scholars saw things as clearly, as prophetically, as he did. Only with time did he discover the rarity of his gift.

When David returned to his rooms, Abigail found him pensive but apparently happy. "All is well, my Lord David?" she asked demurely, when they lay side by side.

"Yes," he said slowly. "Yes, but..."

"But what, my Lord David?"

"But let me love you tonight!"

The prudent Abigail said nothing. But it was the first time she had ever had to feign desire for David—and fulfillment. Some vital quality had suddenly disappeared from him, to be replaced by something of the animal she had found in all the men who had slept with her in previous years. And that animal grew and flourished in the weeks ahead.

Those weeks before the Spring Festival were filled with a blizzard of events that penetrated and modified David's very soul. The genius master of it all was Achish. He had the champion of Adonai in his power. He had probed the man in long, intimate conversations, listening to what David was really saying when he spoke of his ambitions, his sufferings, his fears. This Hebrew was an extraordinary human being, Achish learned, with an extraordinary destiny. And the deepest wound that had been dealt him was exclusion, exile long before he chose exile.

Under Achish's direction, therefore, everything and every circumstance having to do with David was orchestrated so as to say, "Welcome! Be one of us!"

So David's personal household was allowed to remain intact. He came home at evening to Shoshanna, Abigail, Ahinoam, Abiathar, Nathan, and Ahimelek the Hittite. They spoke Hebrew among themselves, but it reminded him of disappointment, hardship, and hate.

On the contrary, the activities of every day outside that home meant freedom, honor, and hope for the future. Gradually, home and all it signified—what was Hebrew, what was of Adonai—began to assume the character of beloved relics and to lose their vitality.

There was, first of all, the tour of Philistia, especially of Gaza, and all its architectural, engineering, and military marvels. How could Saul stand up to that might?

Then the Egyptian surgeon arrived to attach David's foreskin. It was very carefully fitted, but as the gum dried, it hurt a bit for an hour or so. It could be removed with a solvent and reattached with more gum. David was shown how to do it. "Well, that's that," said Achish, beaming.

Day after day, in the cool of early morning and twilight, David trained hard for the games. Then there came the hot baths, the sumptuous meals, and the women—the Philistines had a wholly uninhibited view of sexual activity.

As they witnessed the change in David, his family and friends withdrew into themselves, realizing that their only hope of survival in faith was to remain separate and, if necessary, ultimately to die. Only Nathan was never perturbed or surprised. At first David snubbed him, but then he found himself putting problems to Nathan. The answers were always to the point. Could David worship Dagon? Nathan answered coolly the question that would have horrified any other Hebrew. Then, too, Nathan spent long hours walking up and down in the rose garden with Achish. David could not understand this.

The one person who remained close to David in this period was Shoshanna, whose health was now obviously declining. She never doubted, and often told the rest of his circle: "David will never betray his race and his Covenant. Be patient. He will come back to us."

The afternoon before the games, Duke Shekelath rode over from Gaza. He, Achish, and David dined alone. The two dukes told David what he had to do if, as they assumed, he survived the single combat and gained the championship.

"You have made a wise decision to join Philistia," Shekelath began. "You should have no trouble with the war council or the assembly that will be held tomorrow."

"In fact," Achish took up the commentary, "we are so confident that you'll be approved that we've already given you your own command—Ziklag."

"Most important," Shekelath concluded, "you will play a vital role in our final assault on Saul. We'll soon get to the specifics of that." The meeting was essentially a ratification of all that had been planned and discussed at length.

David went by himself into the rose garden afterward. An hour or two later, Achish joined him. He was in high spirits.

"Do you mind being alone, my Lord David?"

David shook his head, smiling.

"May I go with you?"

David nodded. They walked on in silence for some moments.

"Have you walked in the garden of love, David?"

"A few times." The blue eyes held Achish's stare. Achish ached to reach out and caress David's cheek, but dared not. "It was all I ever wanted," David went on. "In that garden, Achish, I have seen—you too, I'm sure—hundreds of lovers, men and women, all clothed in the radiance of their beloved's presence." He shivered. "But then in the shadows I once saw a young man crying his heart out alone. 'My love is a forbidden love,' he told me, 'and so it hurts to love.' You know, Lord Achish, it hurt me, but I could not bear to join him."

"I see." Achish was glad of the dusk that hid his flush. He changed the subject. "Where do you walk, David, when you walk alone?"

"Down the paths of remembrance, Achish. All that I have seen, done, felt. Sometimes I search for a particular sensual record—"

"For example?"

"Oh, the smell of griddle bread baking in my mother's oven on winter evenings, the first time I kissed and desired, the crowing of the cock just before dawn, the smell of camel sweat on my saddle. That sort of thing." They sat down on the edge of the Palm Pool.

"Sometimes what I am looking for can't be found. But I go on looking, looking."

He traced with his finger on the water.

"And what are you looking for now? Just now?"

"I was about seventeen. A girl, a girl who was really a woman..." Achish's face fell. David's expression softened. He placed a hand gently on Achish's wrist and the Philistine felt the chill of the cold water still on it.

"She said you always pay a penalty for not returning love," David continued. "But to take the step you desire me to take, I shall have to forsake the Covenant of Adonai." To the Philistine the shrug of David's shoulders was eloquent of his quandary. Achish sat upright. His eyes had lost their languor and regained their usual sharp look.

"But Adonai has protected you, David. He brought you here..."

"Did he, Achish? Or was it my own right hand? My own judgment? My own swift camel?" Achish heard the little grating note of anger in the other man's voice. He shivered and stood up slowly. It was dawning on him that a far greater crisis was upon him than the crisis of his own desire for David and David's reluctance to satisfy it.

"Let's sleep on the matter, my friend, eh?" They walked together back to the house. Achish clapped his hands and the slaves appeared immediately, nodding.

"Our beds are ready, Lord David," Achish said, and they parted. But Achish could not sleep. He got up and stood at the window, and again and again his eyes swept David's window, as the hours slipped away. Then suddenly he saw a single candle burning in David's room.

Hastily Achish draped a cloak over his shoulders and limped along the corridor to David's doorway. He pulled aside the hanging beads. David was lying on his back, naked. His body shone like polished oak in the candlelight. His eyes were fixed on Achish. The Philistine walked over near the couch. He noticed the sudden, almost imperceptible tensing of the muscles in David's thighs. The foreskin was gone.

"I saw the light."

"Yes, my lord. I put it there."

"Why?"

"Because something is unfinished between us." Achish sat down, hunched, on the chair beside the couch. He was listening more to the sound of David's voice and what it told than to what David actually was saying.

"I have a certain worm of fear gnawing at me, David," the Philistine replied. "You know I desire you. With love I approach you. But you make me afraid now."

"Why?"

"It is not love that impels you. You will give yourself, but you will not take. In the last ten or twelve years you have been a many-stringed harp. All your strings have been strummed again and again—pain, fear, guilt, joy, expectation, disappointment, anger, hate—all of them. And those strains have summoned some snake into you. It slithers into a man, enticing, hypnotizing, urging him to surrender to loneliness, to take refuge with it, safe from the strumming strings of his agony. The name of that snake, my friend, is despair! Once you yield to it, you cease to love your god, you cease to love yourself. You cease to love."

"But tell me, Achish"—David raised himself on one elbow, impatient—"What has my belief gotten me? Twice I could have killed that filthy ass breeder Saul. Twice!" David held up two fingers. "I could have destroyed him. Did I? Oh, no! Observant David! David the anointed! David the pious!" His voice was vibrant with contempt. "And then what? Adonai says: Run like a rabbit because my favorite donkey farmer does not like the smell of you. Run and run and run and run! Hide in Gath!

"And now, Achish, you talk to me of love! Look here! You can have pleasure in my body, and I in yours. I will draw every drop of seed out of you. You can sink your tongue in me. We can get drunk on top of each other. Isn't that the love you want?" In the rush of his words, David had not noticed Achish. The Philistine held his hands over his face, shaking quietly.

"Achish?" David asked, concerned. "Achish, what is it?"

"Your Adonai wins, David."

"Wins? Wins what?"

The Philistine flung up his hands in a gesture of helplessness. "I want you as lover, but you can't because of your Adonai. If you lose your faith in Adonai and are willing to give yourself to me, I cannot love you because without Adonai you are unlovable and unloving. Any way I look at it, I lose. He wins!"

He looked at David, shaking his head. "Truly, this Adonai has great power, David. If I knew such an Adonai I would serve him all the days of my life. Good night, David."

The Philistine Spring Festival was not primarily an athletic occasion. The Philistines had little cultural refinement but a very strong religious belief. Thus the activities in which the strong men of Philistia participated were acts of worship. The very term used to describe the games was *shakmet,* whose literal meaning was "strivings" or "efforts," and the "strivings" of the warriors were seen as foretastes of Dagon's coming successes.

The whole festival, therefore, had the wooden and elephantine ritual that one would expect from a vigorous yet literal-minded people. Each contest was governed by ponderous rules and lumbering protocol, but performed with brevity. They had little or no wit, and a heavy-lidded love.

Their culture was a mannered technology, polished muscle was their idea of handsome. What they called beautiful was essentially symmetry without harmony, and therefore sterile. Their only original possession was their asserted descent from the god Dagon, of whom they were the sole favorites.

And so, the games. Although the audience was huge, it was perfectly regulated. The stadium was a vast square with tiered seats south of the race track. At the end a single row of seven steps led up to a bare altar, where a statue of Dagon stood with a charcoal fire burning before it. Victors in the games would mount those steps, drop a pinch of incense on the charcoal, and turn around to be acclaimed by the crowd. The chariot races were held in the race track. All other contests took place in the Games Square, as it was called.

David had been entered by Achish in slingshot, spear throwing, and the all-important swordsmanship. The slingshot was no trouble for him. It required speed and accuracy. Seven pigeons were released simultaneously from one spot. The contestant had only that one chance to bring down all seven with a series of swift and straight shots. The record up to that day had been four hits. The other competitors, eleven in number, tried hard. Two of them brought down three pigeons. Five hit only one. Four knocked down three. But David's advantage was unfair: every person at the games knew that his terrible sling had felled the giant. And the speed of his shots in this contest was so great that, it was said, "the hand of Dagon killed all seven pigeons at the same time."

The spear throwing was a different exercise. The target was a living tumbler, one of that small, lithe race of men from the town of Urbillum in Mesopotamia who specialized in tumbling. The target, the best tumbler, stood on the end of a seesaw that rested on the ground. Two other tumblers, standing on a ladder above the raised end of the seesaw, jumped in tandem down on the raised end, thus propelling the target tumbler many feet into the air. As he shot up and down, he wriggled and twisted every possible way to avoid the spear thrown at him by the contestant. But he had to land on his feet. Otherwise he was disqualified, which is to say killed, and replaced by another tumbler.

The spear throw was very popular because the sacred drum players beat a low, steady tattoo until, at an unspecified moment, they boomed out one loud report. On that, the two propellant tumblers had to jump. As the target tumbler flew up, wriggling and twisting, and the contestant took aim, the trumpets blew a long, rising note and the crowds took up a correspondingly long, rising roar, ending at the apex of the tumbler's flight. Then both trumpets and roar diminished with the target's fall. The optimum and only time to hit the target tumbler was at the apex of his flight. Any other time was second best, except for the tumbler. If he landed unhurt, a pandemonium of boos broke out. If he was speared at the apex, the spectators went wild with joy. For Philistines, an alien was an animal, really not a human being, and his death bothered them no more than the death of a flea.

There were only four contestants besides David, and the only serious threat was Duke Balkarith. They all preceded him. The first two missed the tumbler. The third hit his tumbler before he hit the apex. Balkarith hit his tumbler right at the apex, as did David. It now was a contest between him and Balkarith.

There remained swordsmanship. Here it was David and seven others, one of whom was Balkarith. For the Philistines, the only victory in any hand-to-hand contest was to kill the opponent. It was literally an elimination tournament. In consenting to allow Balkarith to possibly fight David, the Pentarchy reflected a division. Of course some Philistines objected to David's presence at all, and it was decided that the only way to choose between two factions was to see to whom Dagon gave the victory. For in the end it was Dagon who wielded the sword, just as it was Dagon who brought down the pigeons and speared the tumblers.

David, with the sword of Goliath, had no trouble arriving at the finals, and Balkarith if anything had an even easier passage. Both David and he, according to custom, were naked. There was to be no sound during the action—no cheering, no shouts, no curses from either spectators or contestants. Just the clang of iron, the breathing and grunting of the fighters, and the shuffling of their feet. Only when the final and lethal blow was struck would an overwhelming roar of triumph break from the throats of those thousands of spectators.

A swordsman struck at his opponent until he broke his weapon or was too tired to lift it any more, and then the victor split him from his forehead to his crotch.

David had difficulty from the beginning: his sword was unusually heavy. Balkarith was at him from the start, weaving a regular shield of beating iron around himself against which David made little headway. It was the official silence of the contest that helped David. As the rain of blows continued, David began to hear the Philistine whisper, "Dagon," as he delivered each blow in an accelerating tempo. "Dagon!... Dagon!.... Dagon!... Dagon!... " In the avalanche of blows and grated whispers, David suddenly felt himself threatened, weakening, backing away, stumbling, barely holding on. Every mention of Dagon's name and every blow seemed laden with malignant strength. Some old instinct awakened in the Hebrew. As always, when he was physically outdone, David's mind sought some wile. With Balkarith a perfect fiend in voice and blow, out of David's very depths and without his willing it, there came a muffled cry: "Adonai!"

The effect on Balkarith was instantaneous, as if the name cast a spell over him and made him momentarily musclebound. An almost imperceptible gap appeared in his fierce rain of blows. His sword hung for that split microsecond in the air, and that was all David needed. The sword of Goliath became lightning in his hand. It swept down lethally in an arc of light and a crack of skull and muscle and bone and flesh. One second Balkarith was there, breathing, acting. The next second he was on the ground, neatly sliced in half like a melon. He did not even cry out. For the first time in the memory of Philistia, the scream of the crowd was late. But when it came, it was ear-splitting. Surely Dagon was with this golden-haired Hebrew giant!

With each of the seven steps David took up to the altar, a shout arose from the crowd: "David!" The cries mounted in volume until he stood on the platform facing the altar and Dagon's hooded statue and charcoal fire. As he climbed, he thought of Samuel and Saul and their horror of alien gods. He thought of Adonai and realized that only in Adonai's name had he been victor—saved from public death by Adonai! Now something he could not control or silence was speaking in him, forcing words to his lips that he had never consciously willed.

He stretched out and took the ritual pinch of incense between thumb and forefinger, and as it sent blue smoke billowing, he heard himself saying: "O Adonai! It means nothing. Please, Adonai! God of my fathers! It means nothing except my life. If I die, who will be your champion, O Adonai? It is nothing. Have mercy, Adonai!" He then turned to face the spectators, bathed in perspiration, spattered with the blood and brains of Balkarith, the sword resting on his shoulders, his foreskin duplicating the head on the statue that towered above him.

"Lord David, we wish you to tell the council what you think is the best way to attack Saul," Shekelath said to David at the council, which was held right after the games.

David, forewarned by Achish, had given much thought to this. He had his answer ready. "It will be impossible from the west."

"Why?" Shekelath, as commander, asked the questions.

"It is all uphill, very rough. Besides, the people there are completely loyal to Saul. There'll be nothing but continual resistance and harassment."

"Therefore?"

"From the north." David and Saul had discussed this strat-egy—for defensive purposes—many times. "You move your main force up the Shefela, past Mount Carmel, then into the Yezreel Valley, over along the south shores of Kinnereth, and up through the Shunem defile leading to the town of Aphek. While the main force is moving, place another contingent on the edge of the Shefela opposite Gibea. The king will not know which is the real strike force. He will be obliged to split his army. For he cannot afford to lose Gibea.

"Just before you launch your main attack southward from Shunem, you should send a large diversionary force south in plain view of Saul, this to make him think that the main thrust is coming from the Shefela through Sorek or Elah Valley. When he has begun to shift more of his army south, the general attack should come from Shunem-Aphek."

"Why is the Shunem-Aphek defile so desirable?"

"It is barely 330 feet wide for about a quarter of a mile, so it will be easily defended. The holders could be attacked from the flanks, of course, if Saul could command the northern passes on Sussita ridge and the gorge of Barbara. But you could occupy these before Saul knows of the danger."

"So the main attack would flow into Yezreel, up to Gilboa, and then on to Gibea?"

"Yes."

"Couldn't Saul attack the diversionary force, and cut it to pieces?"

"Yes."

"Under these circumstances, if you were Saul, and if you had failed to attack the diversionary contingent, where would you take a stand?"

"At Gilboa."

"Why?"

"It's most defensible—and the last defensible plateau before Gibea."

"What advantage do we have in letting him occupy and defend Gilboa?"

"The advantage of making him take a stand. He can run and fight forever around the hills and mountains of the land. The western slopes of Gilboa are easy terrain for your chariots. The fire from the chariots should prove decisive."

"What does the council think of this plan?" Shekelath asked.

There was apparently complete unanimity except on one point: who was to lead the diversion. Achish stood up: "You have the champion of the Hebrews. You have his plan, which to me at least seems excellent. Do you want him to lead the diversionary contingent, knowing that he runs the risk of being massacred by Saul? All right then! You have it: David will lead the diversionary contingent."

After that, unanimity was complete, and the council decided to penetrate the Shefela the following June and July. Shifting of the main detachments of chariots and infantry north to Shunem-Aphek would begin in September and October. They would settle in for the winter there, and in earliest spring, once the monsoon rains had ceased, the main attack would be launched as David had outlined. Meanwhile, David would go to Ziklag as commander.

The feasting and carousals ending the games went on till well past midnight. It was close to dawn when David and Achish got back to their quarters. Following behind them was an oxcart carrying David's trophies: three small chests of silver coins. In the other cart, besides some jars of liquor, were five Philistine slave girls, "one for each dukedom in the Pentarchy," whom David had picked out at the public baths. "I am just about to rape all five dukedoms, Achish," David gurgled drunkenly. Achish let him be. It was a side of the Hebrew he disliked intensely.

Achish, the experienced Philistine, was quite sober in spite of the eight-hour carousal. But David, who never drank or ate heavily, was drunk in a novel way. He could walk and talk without much difficulty and he did not get ill. But he became loud, aggressive, rude, and vulgar. The Philistine left David coldly, glancing up at the officer of the guard, indicating that he'd better keep an eye on the Hebrew.

David disappeared into his quarters with the five young women, and disported himself for some two or three hours until his desire and the liquor ran out. Abigail, Ahinoam, and Shoshanna, who had accompanied him to Gaza along with Nathan, sat waiting for David in the gloom of an unlighted room. They heard his wild laughter and the giggling of the women change into shouts of anger and whimpering screams. David had become furious at his own impotence and the empty liquor jars. He blamed the women and flung them out bodily.

There was a dead silence for a while. Then they heard David weaving down the corridor, ricocheting off the walls and muttering, "Abigail! . . . I need you!"

He stumbled into the room, but all he could see was three black figures huddled together, their veiled heads bent. He stared in puzzlement. "Abigail! Shoshanna! Ahinoam!...Speak up, for the love of God." But there was no answer.

He lurched out and down the corridor again until he found a door into the open, where he stood taking in lungfuls of the night air. He noticed Nathan kneeling on the balcony of what apparently was his room.

"Scholar!" David yelled. "Scholar! No time now for praying! Sleep or celebrate! But no praying! I, David, say so!"

Nathan stood up. "My Lord David, it is a terrible thing to fall into the hands of the living God. It is even more terrible to be the chosen one, the well-beloved son of an all-powerful father. Good night, my lord."

David sat down, leaned his back against the wall, and looked out into the darkness. He felt sober and sad all of a sudden. The silence of the house, the gloom of his women, Nathan's penetrating comment, all contributed to this effect. The day's events closed in on him. But nothing really bothered him—not even giving his readymade plan to the enemies of Saul—except—except that little pinch of incense.

The week following the games, Achish accompanied David to Ziklag. Achish was proud of Ziklag.

At this time it was home to about two thousand people, although it had the capacity for many more. The Philistines had settled there for economic reasons. Some miles due east there were long stretches of meadowland, and the first commander of Philistia had planned Ziklag as a meat center. Its inhabitants would raise cows, sheep, and goats for the Pentarchy. But harassment by the Hebrews and the desert nomads had not allowed this dream to come true. With the construction of the Iron Trail, Ziklag became a posting town for the army corps guarding the lower end of that valuable trail as well as a base for launching punitive raids against the nomads.

The city was built in the sand around some ever fresh streams. The stone and wood for its buildings had all been brought there to construct a square-shaped town on the one raised area in an otherwise flat countryside, so that it dominated the land for miles in any direction. The Philistines had surrounded it with several rings of defensive bunkers linked by a signal system.

Before he left to return to Gath, Achish gave David his last instructions: "Now, David, remember you are here as lord and master with power of life and death. You have a right to levy taxes, recruit for the army, to do what you think will help the Pentarchy.

"We both have enemies in Gaza—Balkarith was not the only one—and also throughout Philistia. But they are of little consequence. What will weigh with the council will be three things: control of the nomads, safe operation of the Iron Trail, and the combat-ready condition of the men under your command.

"One more thing." Achish took a deep breath. "It's about Adonai. We are entering the last phase of our long struggle against Saul. He is doomed, we all know that. And we are going to seal his end because Adonai has put you in our good Philistine hands." They stood alone together on the battlements looking westward over the sandy wastes. "One thing I have learned, David, is that your Adonai has power. And another thing is that he is very jealous. Dagon? Why, Dagon will drop you like an old toe rag. But Adonai? Why, if he chooses a beggar man of eighty, he will never let that miserable wretch go. And this troubles me. Because here you are! Here we are! You are our vassal. Yet I never fool myself. Adonai has a plan. And it may mean he's stronger than Dagon in the long run, that Adonai is indeed the highest divinity!" The Philistine turned and looked David in the eyes.

"If Adonai wins the last battle—and that is the one that counts—know this, David, that I belong to Adonai. I am too old to be taken in any longer by statues of wood and stone, but I don't know—yet."

"But I have turned my back on Adonai!" cried David.

"Have you, David?" Without another word the great Achish left David on the battlements. David stood awhile, watching the cloud of dust Achish's party kicked up as it departed.

"David, we've work to do." Joab's interjection shook him from his daydream.

"Yes, my friend. You're right." David was instantly alert. "First put up a poster in the square calling for recruits for a special corps. Then send our messengers quietly through Judah and Benjamin to say, 'David is recruiting. Come to Ziklag immediately!' Then send Ahimelek the Hittite and Abishai with gifts to the Bedouin leaders and say to them: 'David lives now in Ziklag, and desires brotherhood with you against his enemies.' This will be a beginning."

"But we are supposed to be fighting the Bedouins."

"We're supposed to but we will not. We'll be leaving here soon. And we will need those Bedouins to rely on."

The next week, David rode over to Gath to see Achish about his special corps: "I want permission to recruit from among the felons condemned to death."

"Why?"

"Because if you grant a man his life, you have made him your slave for life."

"And if the council argues that it will build a corps of malcontents?"

"Tell them politely they are mistaken. We are going to have a magnificent infantry."

Achish liked the idea. He obtained the necessary permission and, with David, searchingly screened twenty-four hundred candidates from all the prisons in the Pentarchy. David finally selected an elite of eleven hundred. The "Pelethites," as they were called in Hebrew, were all transferred to Ziklag, put on normal pay and rations, furnished with armor and weapons, and sent into intensive field training. David himself supervised the first days, and soon nourished in them a deep personal devotion to himself.

In the meantime, many of David's former comrades who had gone into hiding at the time of his flight now came forward. They had one trait in common: hate for Saul and devotion to David. These men formed the hard core of the army he now proceeded to form. Each member of it swore a special oath of allegiance and had David's six-pointed star inscribed on every shield, sword haft, and helmet.

By the end of June of that year, the main Philistine army was moving on schedule to the rim of Shefela to fulfill the first phase of the planned assault on Saul. No sooner did he know that the Philistines were actually on the move than David took his first major step. He had two objectives: to try out his new army corps and—unbeknown to the Philistines—to get rid of certain Philistine allies among the Canaanite tribes. Already David foresaw the day on which he would turn against his Philistine hosts. If he could now eliminate some of their allies, his struggles on that day would be all the more easy. The tribes he had in mind were Geshurites, Gezrites, and Amalekites, all southwest and southeast of Beersheva. The campaign against them carried David into late August. To keep the Philistines from discovering what he was doing, his methods had to be thorough, and the massacre of those tribes had to be so complete that no one survived to report back to the dukes. He sent out three forces, each one with orders to surround, then pin down the inhabitants of the main encampments of the three tribes.

Then he himself set about obliterating them by siege and assault. Every man, woman, child, slave, and servant—even foreigners accidentally resident with those tribes—was killed, and all booty was divided half for David, half for the soldiers.

He reported to the Pentarchy that he was punishing the Hebrews and Bedouins, and so thorough was his liquidation that no survivors ever reached Philistia to give him the lie.

"He will surely be my faithful servitor forever," Achish told the council. The Philistine command, deeply occupied with the logistics of their assault on Saul, pursued the question no further.

David held his own war council. Joab, Abishai, Asahel, Ahimelek, Nathan, Hellakath, commander of the Pelethites, and Makrion, who commanded the Kerethites, all sat with David. Serayah the Scribe took notes. All the religious figures, priests, scholars, and prophets, were excluded. "War is one thing," David explained, "scholarship and prophesying are different. If we need prayers, we'll ask for them."

The decision was a shock, even to Joab. No chieftain, no king, no Pharaoh would ever have treated his "holy men" so cavalierly. The officers looked at each other questioningly.

Seeing the expressions of surprise, David continued, "I am a Hebrew of the Hebrews, Hebrew to the thirty-second generation! I will live and die a Hebrew and I was anointed by the prophet Samuel. Don't let anybody think that a little bit of flesh hung or not hung on your penis makes you a Hebrew. It doesn't. It's Adonai." He inspected a hangnail on his finger, sucked the finger, rubbed it vigorously. "Yes, it's Adonai." He sat back and folded his arms. "I was unfaithful to him—out of fear, stupidity, whatever you like. But he did not forsake me. The proof?" He cocked an eyebrow at Joab and the others. "We're here now. We're intact. We are together. How I settle my account with Adonai is a matter between him and me.

"In the meantime I want all of you to concentrate on one thing: How can we fight in this campaign against Saul without forever being abominable to our fellow Hebrews? Joab, what do you think?"

"David, if we flee now, we'll be opposed by Saul as well as the Philistines. That would be crazy."

"So we go along. For how long?"

"For as long as we have no alternative. They will bury Saul. No doubt of it. If you play the game well, they'll send you back to the land of Judah. Then we'll see."

"And you others? Do you go along with this?" Every head

nodded. "Then it's decided. In three weeks, we move up the Shefela on schedule and join Shekelath at Shunem-Aphek."

At the door, as he left with Joab, Nathan joined them. "Scholar," David said conversationally, "tell me one thing. I have known only one scholar, really, old Raham. He was a holy man. Are you holy? I don't know yet. But you're something else, too. And I don't know what this is, either."

Nathan walked with David. "I see," he began in an equally conversational tone, "a very, very large room. It contains a wide bed. The room has twenty small windows, five in each wall. The bedposts are gilded. And in that bed is a very, very old person." David stopped, his mouth agape, his hand—as always when he was surprised—straying to his sword haft.

"I see a tall warrior enter that room. Two tall Nubians bar his way—they carry large silver fans in the left hand but each has a double-edged sword in the right hand. A musical voice calls out: 'Let me see the golden-haired slayer of the giant. Let me see him, I say!' The slaves stand aside, and the warrior approaches the bed.

"Wonder of wonders. The person has practically no face. It is eaten away by leprosy. But I see the fingers and the breasts. It is a very, very ancient woman. And do you know what she says to the tall warrior?" Nathan looked at David for the first time in the conversation.

"You devil!" David breathed, not in anger or exasperation but in stupefaction.

"She says—"

"Enough! Enough, Scholar—or whatever you are!" He stood there looking down at Nathan. His expression had softened. "There's always the trap, his trap, isn't there, Prophet?" he said in a quiet voice. "Achish was quite right, and you were right. Once Adonai makes up his mind, he always has his way. It is a blessing from Adonai that you are here, Nathan.

"We have another hope," said David, turning to Joab, who had witnessed the preceding exchange in total bewilderment.

"What's that?" demanded Joab.

"A prophet, my friend. A prophet. Adonai does not waste his prophets on a man he has rejected."

When Saul learned of the first massing of the Philistine chariots in the Shefela, it didn't surprise him. In fact it reassured him. "Those asses' sons keep making the same mistake year after year," he told Abner. He didn't sound a general alert, nor order a mobilization. Any chariot assault on Gibea from the Shefela could be easily repulsed.

Moreover, Saul was now reasonably sure that David had joined the Philistine cause. His intelligence was meager, but all of it suggested the same things: that David had become the lover and the serf of Duke Achish of Gath, and that Philistine sorcerers had restored his foreskin. He was therefore a *meshummad*, an apostate from the Covenant, and a *herem*, an abomination in the House of Israel. And Saul lost no time in informing every Hebrew of all this.

In September, however, new reports poured in: the Philistines were moving north. Saul went personally to confirm the news. From a lookout in the foothills he watched the iron-wheeled chariots rumble ominously northward. Within a week, Saul knew that their final destination was the Shunem-Aphek defile. He began to make sense of it all. He and David had often discussed the best way to invade the land. "Whoever holds the highlands," they had agreed. And: "The only way to unseat the one who straddles the spine of the fish is to strike from the north."

At this point Saul proclaimed a general alert and universal conscription for a holy war "against the uncircumcised heathens and against the apostate, David of Bethlehem." With Abner and Jonathan he spent ten days moving stealthily around the ridge of mountains that formed the southern side of Yezreel. They reconnoitered the terrain between Yezreel and Aphek. As soon as they knew the location of the Philistine forces northeast of Aphek, Saul's first plan was to battle them there by having Jonathan and his archers take the Sussita and Barbara heights. But the Philistines, following David's plan, had already taken them. Saul would have to fight farther south, and as David had foreseen, he finally chose the mountain called Gilboa. As long as Saul held his highlands and enjoyed numerical superiority on Gilboa, he could fight a winning battle against that army gathering behind the Aphek defile. Gilboa mountain, then, became the assembly point for the conscripts, as well as for Saul's allies and his regular army. Before the rainy season, Saul had set up his own permanent headquarters on top of Gilboa.

His situation was far from desperate. He could not be attacked on the western slopes of Gilboa under normal conditions; his anti-chariot corps, over ten thousand men, had dug in and was amply supplied, and for the time being, at least, the rains precluded any Philistine attack by chariotry. His main forces, twenty-five thousand infantry and five thousand camel riders, were placed along the northern ridges of Gilboa. The sixty-five hundred archers were posted at the east and west flanks of that main force, and the archers were extremely mobile. Every day saw more recruits coming in. With bravery and luck, his position would be impregnable.

Saul even considered attacking the Philistines. But because they held the high ground around Aphek, the only way to do it would be from the north, from Zoba. He sent emissaries proposing an alliance.

But David had been there before him. Zoba not only rejected alliance with Saul but proclaimed friendship with David, dating back to the time he had been military protector of the trade treaties involving Zoba with Moab. There was no help for Saul there. Zoba would be neutral. And David was at Aphek, ready to join battle against Saul.

"At least they are all here facing us," was Saul's comment. "Once we've beaten the Philistines and those apostates, we'll teach Zoba a lesson—and Moab as well."

The torrential rains reduced visibility and made scouting difficult, but Saul was puzzled and troubled by the report of twenty thousand men detached from Shekelath's army at Aphek and moving westward in Yezreel. And when the heavy rains stopped in the first week of March and were followed by days of brilliant sunshine, Saul's heart contracted with fear. The mud on the western slopes of Gilboa would dry fast. He could be caught between two Philistine forces and pulped like grapes in a press. He had no priest nor Ephod to consult, only the sinister Kelebai, whom he called in: "Go find Shalama, the witch of Endor. I must get advice."

David had arrived in Aphek with his force of twenty thousand at the beginning of January, leaving only a skeleton force at Ziklag. Since Ziklag was well within Philistine territory, it was deemed safe, especially after David's attacks on the desert tribes. He had gained much prestige with the dukes by pointing out the danger of a rear attack from Zoba, and then solving the problem by negotiating Zoba's neutrality with the help of Abikemosh of Moab.

"Splendid work, David," said Achish. "I know now that I could put my life in your hands."

"David," Joab asked him as they walked around in Aphek, "you have sworn never to harm the anointed of Adonai."

"Who says we're going to?" David answered primly. "We're going south. We won't be here for the battle."

"Suppose Saul wins, and then pursues you?"

"We run, Joab, and wait. So far Adonai has preserved me from having to fight Saul."

"Adonai, eh?" Joab looked at David quizzically.

"If not he, then what power?"

At the beginning of March, David led his troops westward along the northern slopes of Yezreel, then south to Arad in the Shefela. Together with the Philistine force of seventeen thousand already there, he was now poised on Saul's west flank. David's orders were to take Gibea when the Philistine push began across the Yezreel, and then to march north to take Saul's rear.

"In the name of goodness, will someone stop those two sluts fighting?"

Abigail, on the ground floor of David's house in Ziklag carding fresh wool with two slaves, could hear Shoshanna's shouts of exasperation coming all the way from the fourth floor across the courtyard. She glanced up demurely, one eyebrow raised quizzically, as she caught sight of Shoshanna's irate face in the frame of the window. Abigail herself was imperturbable.

"What are those two squabbling about?" Shoshanna shouted.

The shouting and fighting continued at the far end of the building, where David's concubines were housed. Shoflagai, the Philistine from Gaza, and Aleshine the Arabian had never got along together. And ever since David had left for the north four days ago, they had been at it. At the sound of footsteps Abigail gave her two slaves a silencing look and bent over her work. Ahinoam arrived breathless, her eyes bulging and filled with tears, her hands clasped on her chest. From dawn until dusk every day, Ahinoam followed the same schedule, working strenuously between the kitchens, the yard well, the washing room, and the bedrooms, her voice always raised in song. Any disruption of her schedule threw her into a panic.

"Mistress Abigail! Mistress Abigail! What's happening? They're killing each other! What shall we do, Mistress Abigail?" Everyone turned to Abigail when there was trouble, for she as the first wife of his exile held a very honored position in David's eyes.

"Nothing that will not settle itself, Ahinoam." Abigail's voice was calm, patient. She accorded a pleasant glance to Ahinoam in her long white apron and high bonnet. "Go back to your work. It'll be all right."

"But Mistress Abigail..."

"I'll send Mishlam." Abigail nodded to one of her slaves. "And I myself will visit Lady Shoshanna. Anyway—listen." The fighting had stopped. Ahinoam lost her frightened look and dropped her arms by her sides. But as she turned and walked away with her waddling gait, the noisy concubines started up again.

Mishlam, the elder eunuch, stood up and sauntered casually down the corridor. Abigail went on carding, while Ahinoam stood and watched him. Mishlam disappeared into the concubines' room. The screaming and curses stopped suddenly. Abigail heard some quick scuffling, the sound of some sharp slaps, two little screams. Then silence.

Mishlam returned as unruffled as before. He bowed his head to Ahinoam at the door of Abigail's room, handed a small parchment to Abigail, and took his place on the floor again. "If you could only speak, Mishlam!" Abigail smiled at him. The eunuch's eyes filled with satisfaction. "So"—unrolling the scroll—"this is why our young birds were scratching each other's eyes out." Ahinoam departed to her work. The two slaves went on carding the wool.

Some minutes later, when she entered Shoshanna's room, Abigail found David's mother calm once again. The two women even managed to laugh about the incident.

"They sounded like two Egyptian cats," Shoshanna said with a smile. Abigail chuckled.

Shoshanna suddenly became serious. "Disgraceful, though! Don't you think so, Abigail? My son should never have touched a daughter of the heathen. There are plenty of young Hebrew women here now in Ziklag." Shoflagai and Aleshine had been the two latest additions to David's harem of concubines.

"I warned him," Abigail said gently, "not to bed the new ones as frequently as he does. At least in the beginning. Otherwise they get ideas of their own importance."

David's habit was to sleep with a different concubine each night, and once a month with each of his two wives, Ahinoam and Abigail. Mishlam was in charge of the entire harem, wives and concubines. Of Mishlam it was said: "He is dumb, but you will always know what he means." And he had other advantages. He could, for instance, calculate a woman's fertility. Abigail was delighted to have him in charge—he was her slave and would inculcate respect for her as the number-one wife of David. David liked him because Mishlam would never allow either Abigail or Ahinoam to conceive. "Until I return to the land of Judah, I will not ask Adonai for a child from my wives,"

David had sworn. Children by his concubines were of little consequence for David and his family.

"Has he made either of those screaming women his favorite?" Shoshanna asked confidentially.

"No! Not at all! But Aleshine claims he did."

"Oh! The little monkey!" Shoshanna snorted at the thought. She looked sharply at Abigail.

"I know you're not jealous, Abigail, but Ahinoam? Doesn't she feel—at least sometimes—that . . ."

Abigail leaned back in her chair. "Oh, no. Not a bit of it. She loves him too much to be jealous. She wants only to work for him. She even bathes the concubines if Mishlam is too busy. No, no. Do not fear. Those other two, they hate her."

"What were they fighting about, anyway?"

Abigail held up the parchment scroll. "Would you believe it?" She burst into merry laughter. "A poem of David's. And a poem meant for neither of them!"

"A poem?" Shoshanna was incredulous. "You mean the one we heard him singing the night before he left?"

"Yes! He heard some Phenician players singing at the playhouse, and when he came home he composed a song of his own."

"A people without shame who sing songs of shame." Shoshanna's tone was severe as she took the scroll and unrolled it. "I have always said that concubines should not be taught how to read or write."

"All the same it was a lovely song," Abigail said softly. She knew how far she could go with Shoshanna. But she well remembered the sound of David's harp and voice: night had just fallen, and his words rose to her memory as Shoshanna read them to herself.

> *You came, Beloved, from the Plains of Tyre*
> *As a spring queen*
> *Garlanded with the purple lilacs of Yadai,*
> *With the lilies of the field from Kinnereth.*
> *Among the amber cedars of Lebanon,*
> *From Amana and across Shenir,*
> *Even to the summit of pure white Hermon,*
> *The comeliness of your eyes and the grace of your*
> *   limbs*
> *Outshone the sharpest sunlight.*

When I saw you in the orchards
Of the Tribes, love told me
To kiss your mouth,
To adore your breasts,
To taste the hanging pomegranate of your love,
To let love's liquid flow between your thighs.
But my heart shrank back,
Mindful of the dirt upon my hands,
Of the blood upon my sword,
Of the lies between my lips.
And my warriors growled:
"Who shall gentle you, fierce fighter,
That you caress her?
Who shall cleanse you, man of the road,
That you never soil her skin?"
And you whispered:
"I am black but beautiful, my Lord.
The gracious sun has smiled upon me
In the meadows of my fathers.
Can the golden fairness of my Lord
Mingle with my darkling mysteries?
Can the moon mate with the sun?"

But let me take you, Beloved,
To the mountain of Myrrh,
Beyond Shiloh and Labrum.
Upon the Hill of Frankincense
There we will have our couch.
There we will sleep deliciously . . .

Abigail's reveries were interrupted by Shoshanna. The older woman sighed deeply. "I think what started it all was that Shoflagai had been with David just before he sang that song. And afterward, if you will believe it, Aleshine stole up to his room unbidden!"

Shoshanna expelled a deep breath of disgust. The two women were quiet for some moments. David's mother, wives, and concubines watched his lovemaking like hawks. It was the central interest of their lives as a household.

"I wonder who he was thinking about when he composed that poem." Shoshanna thought out loud. She had heard stories about Lassatha, Uri's Egyptian house mistress.

"I don't think he has met her yet." Abigail looked into the distance. "No woman has really yet possessed David."

Shoshanna shuddered. "I do wish that Adonai would allow us to return to the land of Judah," she commented a little bitterly.

"We will, Mother," Abigail consoled her. "We will. Be sure of it." She went on, "At least David is alive. We are alive." She looked at Shoshanna and read the apprehension in her eyes. "And don't worry. He will not even be in the battle up north. He will return here shortly."

In mid-March, Achish and the other dukes came down to Arad and declared themselves quite satisfied with the readiness of the armies there. They were just about to return to Aphek when Shamkal, the Philistine ruler of Arad, stood up. Shamkal was a taciturn man.

"My Lord Dukes, the other governors and I do not want to fight side by side with the Hebrews."

"But," Achish objected, "you don't know what you are saying. They are the men of my Lord David, slayer of the giant, the mortal enemies of King Saul."

Shamkal rose again. "I repeat, my Lord Dukes," he said stolidly, "we Philistines will not fight by the side of these Hebrews."

"Why?" Achish thundered. "The man has proved his loyalty. What are you talking about?" He looked over at David, who sat with arms folded, chin sunk in his chest.

"We have no absolute guarantee he will not turn against us in the thick of the fight," Shamkal persisted.

"It will be a matter of vote, then," Shekelath broke in. "Those in favor of retaining my Lord David and his Hebrews for battle, please stand up." No one stood up. "Very well," Shekelath said. "The meeting is over."

Achish, trembling with disappointment and rage, went to David. "My friend, I don't know what to say." The two men embraced, both weeping. As David and Joab walked to their tents, Joab noted David's wary smile and said out of the side of his mouth: "I suppose that too is the work of Adonai?"

The morning before the battle, David and his forces moved out of Arad and headed back to Ziklag.

The Philistines at Aphek and Arad were ready to begin their great assault, for the rains were surely over and a vague haze of heat rose up from the meadowland and the woods as the translucent green of spring began to appear, first here and there, then everywhere.

The ground was hardening, the troops were ready, and

David's diversionary move had worked. Saul had been forced to split his forces and send many battalions down to Gibea. His concern was not the fortress itself but his own rear.

As the hour of battle neared, tension grew among Saul's men at Gilboa. Night and day across Yezreel a continuous stream of sound fell upon Hebrew ears. Sometimes it was the hour-long beating of drums. Sometimes it was the clashing of the silver cymbals Philistines used at their dances. Or it was the voice of trumpets, the rising and falling chants of the Philistine soldiers singing around their campfires. And sometimes it was the Great Shout of Philistia. Each Philistine, no matter where he was or what he was doing in the camp, would stop and on signal shout at his loudest: "Dagon! Dagon! Dagon!" full seventy times. They did this at irregular intervals, day and night. The undulating echoes pierced Hebrew ears like the threatening crackle of thunder.

But tension was greatest at dawn, when the Philistines had their sacrifice. A temporary altar had been set up behind the defile of Aphek. Beside the statue of Dagon lay his sacred golden mask, with the neck of a swan, the chin and mouth of a man, the nose of a lion, the eyes of a fish, the forehead of a bull. Around that forehead the folds of Dagon's hood. Each day, just before dawn, pitch torches lit up the place, and the army followed intently every movement of the high priest Manaath as he ascended the altar to sacrifice a pig. The Philistines, like the Hebrews, considered the pig unclean, and the death of the pig symbolized the death of all enemies of Philistia. All was deathly quiet until the knife flashed, which it did precisely when the first rays of the sun shone over the horizon.

If the priest then left the altar, there would be a rattle of drums but no attack. But if at that moment he began the Great Shout of Philistia, it meant attack. Combat. Death.

The Hebrews knew all this, and day after day they waited for that first glint of sun. If all they heard afterward was the drum roll, they fell back on their blankets and breathed with ease. Not today! Thanks be to Adonai!

The day before battle was actually joined, Saul and Kelebai, with the king's bodyguards, surreptitiously left Gilboa for Endor. Endor was a peculiar place, shunned by the nearby farmers and villagers as a haunt of fugitives. It was a deep, virtually sunless fissure in the mountain about an eighth of a mile in length, about sixty feet at its deepest, and not more than two hundred feet at its widest. The fissure, which ran from east to west, had cracked open during that terrible earthquake more than thirty years before in which the original village of Endor had perished. A few lean-to houses stood on the floor of the fissure, and their occupants lived year-round in perpetual twilight.

At sunset, Saul and Kelebai entered the fissure, leaving the guards and their weapons outside, as the witch had insisted.

Shalama had become hunched with age. It would have been impossible to recognize any physical resemblance in her to the impressive woman who had greeted Jesse. She wore a patch-work robe of every imaginable color, and her veil was so heavy that no trace of her face could be seen.

"You need no torch, strangers." Her voice was authoritative and not unpleasant except for a somewhat querulous tone. Kelebai stuck his torch in the earthen floor. She drew a hanging red blanket aside and motioned them to enter a back room where, in the dancing light of a candle, a red-embered charcoal fire brooded alongside a low stone table. Saul entered warily, in mortal dread.

"I am Shalama, the servant of Lilith and Maveth. What do you wish of me?" She removed a black cloth from the stone table, or altar. She sat on one side and motioned Saul and Kelebai to sit across from her.

Saul licked his lips and swallowed. "We wish," he squeaked, then cleared his throat and found his voice. "We wish to speak with the shade of Samuel the Prophet."

The witch's head jerked back as if someone had physically attacked her, and she started keening, her head in that same awkward position. It was a rattling noise like water rushing over pebbles, more as if she were scraping her throat than talking, and it went on until Saul's head ached.

Then, as abruptly as it had begun, the keening ceased and a profound silence descended. Gradually, over the stone table the ghostly head of a man began to appear. Then the features became recognizable.

"Samuel!" Saul croaked. "Samuel! My father!" Kelebai, stiff with fear, could only listen. Saul was on his knees.

"Why have you disturbed my sleep, O King?" The face had acquired a voice that had a quality in it of the dead prophet, but no mortal ever made that toneless sound.

"We face the Philistines nearby at Gilboa, my father. And they are also attacking Gibea. Should I attack them from here or go back and defend Gibea?" Saul was crying as he spoke.

"Neither the one nor the other. Tomorrow the Philistines will attack you on Gilboa. They will defeat your army, cut off your head, desecrate your body, and then destroy Gibea fortress. Your kingdom is at an end. Your seed will die out. You broke the law of Adonai. Nothing can save you."

"But, Samuel, my father!" Saul rose and went forward, but the shadow had vanished, like smoke in a strong wind, and Saul fell unconscious across the stone square.

The journey to Ziklag took David and his men seven hours. While they were still two or three miles away, they could detect smoke rising above the mound on which the city sat, and as they galloped the last distance, the smell of burning flesh reached them. There was no living person to welcome them, and all the houses had been burned to the ground.

It was the first time in David's fourteen years as a commander that he almost lost control of his men. All the wives and daughters, children, concubines, servants, and slaves had been left safe and secure in the very middle of Philistine country, where military convoys always passed. Besides, sufficient men had been left in the city to defend its walls and gates.

Now, as they pushed those broken gates aside in deathly silence, the only sign of life was a small colony of brown desert rats who fled squealing from a pile of spilled grain. There were no bodies, no blood. Nothing. Everywhere the camel dung of the invaders' mounts, and everywhere the pathetic traces of useless struggles—a girl's sandal, a woman's veil, a brooch torn off, a baby's cot crushed, a ribbon in the dirt. David looked at the rubble where his own stone house had stood when he left his wives and Shoshanna and wept. "May God damn them!" he shouted. "God damn them all! God damn the Philistines! God damn this war! God damn everything!"

Joab beside him heard the crying of the other men coming from what had been their street and house. Keeping his hand on his sword, he walked quickly and warily down this street, up that one, peering cautiously through windows and doors of the gutted stone houses that still stood, his mouth open, aghast at the instantaneous demoralization of his fiercely loyal men.

But the worse it became, the cooler and more calculating became Joab. Joab did not shock easily; it was a function of his killer instinct. So as the situation worsened toward anarchy or mutiny, Joab thought. Then Joab acted. Joab tore out his sword and slashed his left arm superficially, so that the blood splattered his blade and breastplate. It was the traditional way David and his riders in the old days had signified an instant oath to shed the blood of those who had offended them. Then

Joab started running and shouting, eyes bulging, voice raucous with rage: "To your weapons, Hebrews! To your weapons! Let's get the bastards who did this! To your weapons!"

It worked. The frustrated soldiers scrambled for their weapons and their mounts. David, who had summed up the situation exactly as Joab had, was already on his camel, waiting for his men as they came shouting his name. At David's signal, the trumpeter blew the two strong, high notes, one short, one long, for silence. Automatically the men took up the cry that had inspired them in past crises, their leader's name: "Daaaaaaveeeeeeeeed! . . . Daaaaaaveeeeeeeeed! . . . Daaaaaaa-veeeeeeeeed!" Then a great silence.

"Abiathar!" David shouted. "Bring the Ephod!" Everyone watched the winking gleam of the jewels as Abiathar slipped the sacred stole over David's shoulders.

"Adonai!" David shouted. "God of Our Fathers! I, David, your anointed, ask you in the name of the Covenant and in your sacred unmentionable name! Shall I pursue the ravagers of our city? Shall we overtake them? Adonai! One God! Answer your anointed one! For your name's sake!"

Men who stood there in front of David that day would later tell their children and grandchildren that in the silence that followed a blinding, dazzling light beamed out from the sacred stones over David's face and golden hair. They had to avert their eyes.

"We will overtake them. We will slay them. We will recover all that we have lost!" It was David's voice, bell-like, triumphant, like the Angel of Adonai himself speaking to Adonai's people. When they looked again, David had already handed the Ephod back to Abiathar and Joab was rapping out the orders: "Pelethites, surround the city! Hebrews, start clearing the houses! Archers! Kerethites! Two hundred of you, guard the northern road. The rest of you, follow David!"

Five hours of hard riding brought them at nightfall close to their quarry, the Amalekites. The raiders had camped in a small valley and were celebrating their success. "They're all drunk as pigs and raping our women around the next bend," the head scout reported back to David. He and his men swooped down on them immediately. The vengeance they took was terrible. Within half an hour the four hundred raiders had been killed to a man.

"Shoshanna? Where is Shoshanna?" David cried to Abigail.

"In that cart, David," Abigail replied gently, indicating an oxcart nearby and hiding her annoyance at his apparent lack of concern for her. "But steel yourself. You must understand. We all have been raped many, many times."

Everyone left alive in the valley was frozen by the scream of agony that split the night air. The camels tethered at the center of the camp cowered down, ears flattened, muzzles on the ground. Joab rushed from the other side of the camp, sword in hand, sure that David was in mortal danger. David lifted Shoshanna out of the cart, and the whole long night he cuddled her in his arms like a mother holding a child. She had been savagely treated and was hemorrhaging badly.

The next morning they all returned to Ziklag, where Nathan was waiting with news. "They will join battle at Gilboa today," the prophet told David.

It was sunup, absolutely still, the soldiers rooted like trees of iron sweeping rank on rank up from the altar into the hills around. High priest Manaath turned, holding the Mask of Dagon to his face. The sweat of excitement broke out all over Shekelath's body. Today would be the day. Revenge! Achish's eyes narrowed. He held his breath.

"Philistines!" the high priest screamed suddenly, his voice splitting the vault of silence. A short pause, then—"Dagon!" His voice sounded hollowly through the funnel mouth of the mask.

"Daaaaaa-gooooooooon!" The answering cry arose from the massed army. It spread like a wave to the nearest units, armed, massed, ready, on up to the walls of Aphek, down to the defile, ringing in the throats of the archers guarding the Sussita and Barbara ridges, and on to the forward pickets at the edge of Yezreel. The thunder of hooves and the clank of bladed wheels started simultaneously with the shouted commands. Saul's Hebrews over on the other side had heard the Great Shout of Dagon. They saw that bright flashing stream pouring toward them across the plain. At last the battle was upon them.

Saul's sons, Jonathan, Abinadab, and Melkishua, together with Abner, Kelebai, and Saul's commanders, were standing with the king at the moment of the Philistine shout. They all knew what to do. There was no panic. Only Jonathan turned for a few instants. Saul, in good form this morning, was about to take his spear and shield from the armor bearer when he caught sight of Jonathan and stopped abruptly. Father and son had not spoken together intimately for more than two years. It was time to close that rift.

In Jonathan's eyes Saul read only love, hope of being loved.

On Saul's face Jonathan could see the old look of combativeness and courage that had made him a hero. That look was altered now with age and deep regret. But it was still there. He looked again at the royal insignia his father wore: the bracelet on his right arm, the thin band of gold around his forehead. Saul, still embracing Jonathan with his eyes, pulled on his helmet. "My father is going to battle like a king," Jonathan thought, "as bravely as ever before. Surely his bravery comes from Adonai."

For one instant, Saul was tempted to order Jonathan out of battle and south to safety. But it was only a moment. Jonathan saw the flicker in his eyes and gave the battle cry of the Hebrews.

"Chai Adonai—Adonai lives!"

"Chai Adonai!" Saul repeated in a deep voice, adding the response of hope and confidence. *"Weanachnu chayyim*—And we are alive!"

Their guards standing by heard the king and his son and yelled the words of attack. *"Mowth yemoothun*—They shall surely die!" Then everyone ran to his post.

The battle unfolded as David had predicted. The Philistine chariots swept westward along Yezreel, then up across the western slopes of Gilboa, testing the firepower of the most forward of the Hebrew archers, who showered the careening chariots with arrows. The Philistine strategy was to erode the strength of the archers, clearing the way to the top of Gilboa and Saul's camp. The day was bright, the earth bursting with promise.

The main Philistine army of over twenty thousand men-at-arms, in four battalions flanked by two wings of seven thousand camel riders each, marched steadily across the plain toward the north slope of Gilboa. Saul and Abner, watching the approach, were mystified by one thing. In the center of each of the infantry battalions was a number of greatly oversized six-wheeled ox-carts, each pulled by a team of six mules. Nothing could be seen in the carts.

"Weapons?" Saul asked Abner.

"Who knows?" They would have to wait for the answer.

Over to the east, the Philistine corps of mounted archers circled around and around, well out of bowshot, apparently under orders to wait. Saul evaluated the threats and gave his orders. The main shock of the attack, he decided, would come on the north slope. He was certain that Jonathan and his men could keep the chariots at bay in the west, but he dispatched one of his two remaining regiments of archers as insurance for

Jonathan. The other one he detached and sent to the east to parry any attack by those mounted Philistine archers. He ordered his veterans to mass with him on the north slope, slingshotmen in front, then spearmen, then swordsmen and macemen, in that order. The heart of the battle would be fought by these men.

The Philistine chariots were already sweeping in and out in ever wider and higher curves on the west. Three quarters of the way across Yezreel, the main Philistine army halted. Then silence. In that silence Saul saw a new body of men on mules coming down at a gallop from the Aphek defile and heading toward the western slopes of Gilboa to reinforce the chariotry there. A messenger arrived from Jonathan to tell Saul that they were falling back to a second line of defense. After two hours of continual sweeping attacks by the chariots, they had suffered heavy losses. Saul now wondered if the main attack wasn't coming from the west after all. Abner thought so. Saul still thought the chariot attack was diversionary. There were the archers to the east to worry about, too. No, he couldn't help Jonathan. He instructed the messenger: "If Jonathan has to withdraw farther, come and tell me before they move."

In another hour the messenger was back: Jonathan had to withdraw. Saul refused permission. Instead, he sent over a thousand of his veteran javelin throwers with orders to hold that second line no matter what. The mule riders from Aphek were drawn up now behind the chariots in the west, but out of bowshot. The chariots kept up their murderous sweeps.

Suddenly, trumpet commands came from the immobile Philistine center. The ranks opened and the outsize oxcarts lumbered forward. The battalions closed ranks and started to trot forward behind the carts. The move seemed pointless and stupid. The moment the mules were within slingshot and javelin range, the Hebrew marksmen brought every mule down in its tracks, about a hundred yards from the Hebrew front line. The Hebrews then braced for the onset of the Philistine center, trotting forward at an easy pace about seventy-five yards behind the now-stalled oxcarts.

As the infantry reached the carts, it split into streams to go around them and the Hebrew slingshot and javelin throwers prepared for the order to fire. At that instant a canvas was thrown back from each oxcart and the helmeted heads and strung bows of Philistine archers appeared as if by magic. Simultaneously the divided wings of the Philistine center joined and launched into a fierce frontal attack under a sky thick with their comrades' arrows, which fell in a hail of death on the completely surprised Hebrews. The forward lines of sling-shotmen and javelin throwers were decimated. Saul took an arrow in the calf of his left leg. A second and third shower of arrows finished off the forward defense lines. Everybody else, including Saul, retreated back up the slope, leaving Kelebai and Saul's son Melkishua dead on the field. A messenger came with the news of Jonathan's death.

They were in the confusion of seeking fall-back positions when the Philistine center hit them like a battering ram. The two wings of camel lancers closed in on the sides. And then began the deadly melee of hand-to-hand combat. The remnants of Jonathan's archers had taken flight up the western slopes. They were now being slaughtered by the chariots and the force of men on mules that had been called in.

The desperate fighting went on for three quarters of an hour. Around Saul there gathered a hard core of his veterans deter-mined to effect the king's escape. But escape there was none. They were able only to hack a passage for Saul and Abner so that they could retreat to the top of Gilboa. Saul then ordered Abner to run for Gibea, to save Ahinoam, the king's wife, Ishbaal, his youngest son, and his favorite concubine, Rizpah, with her two sons by Saul. Abner went, but Saul never knew if he got through. Two more arrows found their mark in him. One went through his right wrist and lodged in his side. The other struck his right thigh. He now could not walk nor lift his sword. In the screaming confusion of battle shouts, the cries of the dying, the clash of weapons, and the merciless heat, Saul knew it was the end.

His veterans formed a human barricade around him. But everyone, including Saul, saw the chariots sweeping over from the west; all the defenders there had been killed. The cavalry that had been circling out of range in the east was now charging up toward the top of Gilboa. All escape routes were closed.

"You!" Saul screamed at the nearest of the soldiers. "You! Come here, man! Come here!" The soldier ran over. "Who are you?"

"Doshlag, Sire." He was an Amalekite Saul had freed after the battle of Telaim.

"Doshlag, do me an act of kindness now. Kill me! The Philistines must not catch me alive. Hurry! Kill me!" Doshlag hesitated. "Hold your sword—haft on the ground—at a slant." Doshlag bent down and held the sword there. "So! Hold it firm, man. When I am dead, take off my bracelet and the headband. Get them to David of Bethlehem. Swear it!"

"I swear it, O King, but—"

"Hold that sword steady, you fool!" Saul turned his chest toward the point of the sword, calculating for one brief instant, and then fell heavily, so that the sword entered between his ribs and went through his heart. He fell across the wrist and arm of Doshlag.

The Amalekite jumped back, then stooped and took the bracelet from Saul's arm. He slipped the helmet off the dead man's head and removed the gold headband. He tucked them in his tunic, then he rolled over and over beneath the legs of the men still fighting. In a short time he was able by careful maneuver to crawl under a heap of groaning, dying Hebrews. He heard shouts in the language of the Philistines and knew that the battle had passed over him.

A short time later he heard one great sustained shout:

"Sha-ul! Daaaaa-gooooooon! Sha-ul! Daaaaa-gooooooooon!" The Philistines had found Saul's body and were yelling the triumph of their god as they drove their spear points into the dead Hebrew king.

The defeat was total. As far as the Philistines could see, there were only a few survivors. They knew that Abner had escaped because his body had not been found. But the victors had paid an expensive price. Philistine losses had been twice as heavy as expected. A third of the charioteers had been killed and their chariots badly damaged. Losses of camels, mules, and horses were extensive. More than eleven thousand officers and men were dead. At least another twelve thousand were wounded.

The dukes decided to invest Gilboa with a garrison and then to retire to Aphek. The Hebrew camp, the dead bodies and useless equipment were torched. Before the incendiary squad reached the bodies where Doshlag lay, he was able to steal off westward and down to the Shefela. He had to get to David of Bethlehem.

On his return to Ziklag that day, David's first care was for Shoshanna. His carpenters and masons worked feverishly at repairing enough of his residence so that he could move her into at least a temporary shelter by nightfall. The doctors feared that she would not last long, however. They could not stop the hemorrhaging. Moreover, she couldn't eat, and was in constant pain from her ruptures. Most difficult of all for David, she wept continuously and insisted on hiding her shame behind a veil.

David sent a force to the Amalekite camp to haul in the vast booty the nomads had taken during a three weeks' spree in southern Judah. Not only had David and his men recovered all their family members and goods; they had acquired great stocks of cattle, sheep, cows, goats, and camels, along with silver, gold, and iron weapons. But this sudden acquisition of wealth brought on a fresh crisis.

By right and custom, David's portion of the booty was half, with the other half divided among his men. But many of the men objected to any portion being given to those who had stopped at Besor or those who hadn't been on the raid at all. David assembled the men and stood in front of them holding the sword of Goliath.

"Listen to me now! Men of David! For I, David, am speaking. And listen to no one else, neither yourselves nor the seer Nathan, nor the prophet Gad, nor the priest Abiathar, nor anyone else. They would be neither priest nor prophet nor seer if Adonai had not sent me, the anointed one, and given my right arm the strength to kill our enemies. For I, and I alone, am leader and do hear and execute the will of Adonai. And here is the will of Adonai for you. Listen to it very carefully! For whosoever violates it, I shall kill him myself with this sword.

"There has not been, there is not, and there shall never be any distinction in this matter of battle spoils between the old man who empties the chamber pots of our wives and the jauntiest warriors who go off to battle. Between the cook who prepares your food and the archer who kills an enemy because his arm has been strengthened by that food. No distinction! Ever!

"For we are one body. And every part of that body plays its part. You defecate with your arses and you urinate with your rods. Suppose you say: I don't need my dirty arse. I can do without this stinking rod!" There was a huge roar of earthy laughter at this. "Let me tell you, men, we need them! By God we need them! Every man receives according to his due. And this will be the law among us forever!"

The next day David had Nathan write letters to the elders of the main towns in Judah where he had been received and treated well—Bethal, Ramoth, Yattir, Aroer, Sifmoth, Eshtemoa, Rachal, Horma, Chorashon, Athach, Hebron, Beersheva, and to all the towns of the Yerahmeelites and Kenites. They all had backed David in the past. He would soon need their backing again. A special delegation led by the prophet Gad, who had joined David at Ziklag, went across to Moab, Bashan, Gilead, and Ammon.

Next morning, as David was sitting with Shoshanna, Joab burst in: "Saul is dead and his army destroyed. Jonathan too. The messenger to Hebron found a soldier there who escaped. The soldier says he has a message from Saul for you. He's here now."

David went quickly, his emotions in a turmoil. He found himself looking at a light-skinned young man with bright eyes and a volatile mouth. He still wore a blood-spattered breastplate, but the rest of his armor was gone.

"I am David. Your name?"

"Doshlag, Lord David. I have a message from the king. This will be a great joy and glory for my Lord David!" With a grandiose gesture Doshlag drew out a cloth package and handed it to David. David opened it gingerly, his eyes hardening as he picked up Saul's bracelet and headband.

"Hold him, Joab! Now, friend, where did you get these?"

"From King Saul's body, Lord David." There was an unearthly silence. Ahimelek, Nathan, Abiathar, Hushai the Arkite, Serayah the Scribe, and several officers crowded around.

"Who killed Saul?"

"I did, Lord David. He called me in the thick of battle. He was mortally wounded, with three arrows in him. Jonathan and Melkishua, and Abinadab, and Kelebai and his commanders were dead—all except Abner—"

"Trust Abner!" David interjected, glancing at Joab. "Continue!"

"Saul's armor bearer was dead. The Philistines were not ten yards from us—only the veterans stood between Saul and the Philistines at that moment. The king said to me: 'Kill me, so that I do not fall into the hands of the uncircumcised.' And I slew him as he begged me to do."

David's control broke. He dropped the bracelet and headband and turned away quickly, his eyes flooding with tears, his hands pulling and tearing his robe. Those around him also broke down. Doshlag stood in amazement.

"But, my Lord David, Saul is dead, and all those who persecuted my Lord David are gone to Sheol!"

David spun around, his voice rasping. "And were you not afraid to put out your hand and kill the man anointed by Adonai?" The words were heavy with a dead weight of threat.

Doshlag sensed the threat, and a wild fear swept over his face, leaving it bloodless. He opened his mouth to speak, but could say nothing. David looked over at a young officer. "Pull out your sword. Strike this dog once, just once! But make sure you kill him." Most of the men present had never seen the cold-blooded look in David's eyes before this moment. Nathan shivered and turned away.

The young officer stepped forward, pulled out his sword, raised his right arm and took aim carefully and coolly. With his left hand he raised the chin of Doshlag ever so slightly, so that when he struck the blade could pass through the neck and out the other side without hitting Doshlag's chin. One quick swish, and Doshlag's head rolled off his shoulders, cleanly cut. His body remained standing stiff and shaking for about three seconds, then it simply collapsed on top of itself like a pile of clothing.

"That was a good stroke. Hang this dog's body up for the vultures. Nail his head to a board, and send it to Saul's family. At least they will know we avenged Saul. Double the guards around Ziklag, Joab. And tomorrow I want a war council at dawn." He turned away, picked up the bracelet and headband from the ground, and went back inside the house.

Once he had closed the door, he fell to the floor, again crying bitterly. Nothing could relieve his pain or stop his tears at that moment. He would never see Jonathan alive again. Never had he realized how much he loved Jonathan.

A sudden, almost imperceptible sound distracted him. It was like a sigh or a rustle of silk. He lifted his head but could see no one.

"David, my son! My son, David! Why are you crying?" It was Shoshanna, leaning against the doorway behind him, her face white and strained. David carried her back to her bed. He knelt down and put his face on the coverlet and cried his heart out, telling her of the death of Jonathan and Saul.

"David," she said. "Do you remember that chest I took everywhere with me? It's there in the corner. Please bring it to me here."

She asked him to take out of it a long cloth package. "I kept this for you," she said, and he found himself holding Raham's seven-string harp. Neither of them said anything. He fingered the strings and examined the wood.

"Please play," Shoshanna said simply. She lay back on the pillows. "As you used to in Bethlehem."

He struck a chord and listened, wondering how he had done

without this sound for so long. He struck another chord, and
then another. He ran his fingers up a half-scale, played a chord,
then started to strum quietly, humming all the while, his eyes
lifted to the window glowing with moonlight. Gradually the
words of his lament for Jonathan and Saul came to him as he
played, and Shoshanna heard the voice of her beloved David
once more.

> *"From Israel all grace has fled.*
> *All beauty has been slain*
> *Upon the heights of the mountains. . . .*

> *"But on Gilboa let my curse rest forever!*
> *Never let the sweet dew fall on you!*
> *Never let the rain water your trees and flowers!"*

Joab and Abishai and Asahel, who slept, as was usual, in
the small compound of David's residence, woke up from their
sleep. They had not heard that harp or that singing voice for
years. In the night silence of Ziklag the liquid music rose and
fell. The keening tones of David reached across the street into
the tents there. The guards on the walls and down in the square
heard it. It penetrated into the tents of Kerethites and Pelethites.
Slowly men got up, hypnotized by this strange voice of beauty
and sorrow, drawn by the resonant Hebrew syllables. They
wandered sleepily toward David's house, gathering there in
silence, some standing, some sitting. Old veterans, young men,
lonely men, weary men, brash men. They listened as David's
sorrow sang out in the quiet night.

> *"Ah, Saul! Ah, Jonathan!*
> *You were lovely and graceful in your lives.*
> *And in your death*
> *You were not separated.*
> *You who were swifter than eagles!*
> *You who were stronger than mountain lions! . . .*

> *"Women of Israel, weep for Saul!*
> *He placed fine linen on your limbs.*
> *He clothed you in fine purple.*

> *"Adonai! The mighty are fallen in battle.*
> *Jonathan, my beloved darling. You fell fighting.*
> *My heart will never be at ease again,*
> *Never again, my brother!*

"For from your hands I accepted a love
   More wonderful than life
   Surpassing the love of the fairest of women.

"Adonai! How are the mighty fallen!
   Adonai! How are the weapons of battle broken!..."

He finished and started to tiptoe out. "Sleep well, my beloved David," Shoshanna whispered. "I won't die this evening."

David left the house and stopped, bewildered. The compound, the yard, the street on either side was a mass of silent men, all looking at him. It took him a few seconds to take in the silent sympathy of these rough men.

Joab and Ahimelek were at the door, their eyes glistening. They came forward and embraced him, not saying a word. Another officer came forward and touched his arm softly. Some kissed his hand, others embraced him quickly, others touched his shoulder, his arm, his face, his hands, his back. When they were all gone, he sat alone until dawn.

BOOK III

DAVID
THE
KING

The
Grapes of Hebron

▨▨▨ Neither David nor any of his people took part in the three-day victory celebration that the Philistine Pentarchy decreed after the defeat and death of Saul. Only Philistines who had fought in battle could share in the victory. So David was spared that torture, too.

On the morning of the tenth day after Gilboa, a messenger arrived from Achish summoning David to appear before the Council of the Pentarchy in Gaza one month from that day. The messenger also brought the official announcement of Saul's death.

In a private message Achish asked for a secret meeting with David and Nathan next morning in the valley of Shimshon. Shimshon was ideal for such a meeting, a deserted and reputedly haunted place, where the body of the old Hebrew hero Samson had been temporarily buried in dishonor by the Philistines a century before.

"Why do you think Achish asked for you?" David wondered.

"Adonai has his ways," Nathan answered mildly. "And, Lord David, you must send Abishai and Ahimelek to Bethshan."

"Must I? Why?"

"Because that's where the body of Adonai's anointed, Saul, is lying, and the bodies of his sons. They must be buried in accord with the law of Adonai. Send your men to the warriors of Jabesh-Gilead—Saul once delivered them from the Ammonites. Together they will manage to recover the bodies."

David looked at Nathan. "You started as a scholar. Sometimes I wish you had remained one."

"You started as a shepherd, my Lord David. I never wished you to have remained one."

David laughed. "Very well, private Prophet! Be ready to ride tomorrow at noon."

"If we start tomorrow at noon, my Lord David, we should be back by dusk?"

"Well—yes—er—I suppose so. Why?"

"It is Shabbath, Lord David."

So Abishai and Ahimelek were dispatched to Jabesh-Gilead, and David and Nathan went to Shimshon. Achish was waiting, alone. Both David and Nathan noted his lack of spirit, and David realized that Achish was struggling with forces within the Pentarchy of which he, David, knew nothing.

He explained that Shekelath had sailed from Luqqawatna and would be returning with instructions on how the Pentarchy should proceed with the complete subjugation of the land, now that Saul was gone. Many large pockets of fiercely independent and well-armed Hebrews still existed, and there was always Abner and the remaining son of Saul, young Ishbaal. Abner was already raising another army among the northern tribes to support Ishbaal's claim.

Achish thought David should know beforehand what Shekelath and the Pentarchy proposed to do. David would be offered the vassaldom of Judah with orders to subdue all the tribes and to liquidate Abner. But once David had accomplished this, he and every member of his family and every one of his personal followers and bodyguards—his Kerethites and Pelethites too—would be put to death during a public spectacle at Gaza. For this was the ancient prophecy of Dagon, Achish said, wryly quoting the words in Hebrew: "The search of a thousand years for the sun-drenched Empire of the Philistines will end when the Mighty One is slain in Dagon's capital."

Shekelath, still consumed with vengeance, would never be content until everybody directly connected with Adonai had been slain in his own blood. Why, Nathan asked mildly, did Achish appear to disagree with the Pentarchy's plan? Because, Achish answered trenchantly, the Philistines had achieved their victory over Saul only with the help of Adonai's champion. To rid themselves of that champion would be to alienate Adonai, and Achish feared Adonai's power and anger. Moreover, he loved David, but this he did not say.

It was Achish's convoluted belief that Dagon needed Adonai's connivance to attain his full divinity. Dagon would eventually become Adonai—as he would, of course, become everything. But until then it was madness to alienate and anger so powerful a divinity as Adonai. Achish did not speak of his thought that Adonai might be even more powerful than Dagon. Nathan greeted his explanation with a lift of his eyebrows.

Achish's advice to David, therefore, was not to accept the vassaldom but to take refuge again in the mountains and desert wastes he knew so well. David's name was already anathema to many northern tribes and clans. To become Philistia's vassal in Judah would only add to his list of enemies. Unless—and here Achish turned to Nathan—unless Adonai had a message. Had he?

David had never valued Nathan sufficiently until then. The seer asked Achish to walk a little way off with him. Nathan's back was turned, but David could see Achish's face. Achish seemed to be listening, and his expression changed from questioning to surprise and finally to reverence. Apparently Adonai *had* delivered a message, for when the Philistine and Nathan returned to David, Achish had lost all his anxiety and hesitation and had completely reversed his position. "Nathan and I advise you to accept the vassaldom, David," he said briefly, adding, "and once you're there, we'll be able to see more of each other, I hope." David did not ask why Achish had changed his mind.

As they rode back to Ziklag, David said nothing for a time. Then: "Well, if I accept the vassaldom, we will have Hebrews killing Hebrews again."

"What's wrong with killing?" Nathan asked. He did not look at David nor David at him.

David was cautious, fearing a trap, but finally offered: "I remember old Raham years ago reading the Law of Moses, and if I'm not mistaken, Moses said: 'Do not kill.' I even remember Raham's face as he told us that."

"You are mistaken, Lord David," Nathan offered.

A little way farther on, David said suddenly with a note of delight in his voice, "Ah, yes!" He then quoted the Law as he remembered it: *"Lo tiqtol.* That's what Moses wrote. Do not kill."

"Lo tirsach is what Moses wrote, my Lord David," Nathan answered. "Do not murder. And we know the difference between the two words."

"So," David commented sarcastically, "you teach us that we may kill, but we may not murder?"

"Adonai has given great wisdom to my Lord David," Nathan answered with a smile.

When they stopped to rest their animals by a stream, David lay on his back, his eyes closed. Nathan as usual remained standing.

"Nathan, tell me," David said seriously, "if we are to survive, we have to go to war. There will be killing—whatever word you use for it."

"Oh, the word matters, Lord David. The word—if you are

truthful—reflects your mind. And it's your mind that makes the difference."

"I'm not looking for an argument, Nathan," David responded. "I need light." He sat up and looked south toward Ziklag. "When Adonai made this world, did he foresee death and dying and killing?"

"Adonai foresaw everything. That doesn't mean he wanted a world of dying and death and killing. Cain was not fulfilling the will of Adonai."

"Yes, but Adonai foresaw it. So why did he create that sort of a world?"

"We don't know. Why should we be able to understand what the great and awesome Adonai does? But he must have preferred it to any other sort of world."

"Is that the only answer you have?"

"Yes. Except to add that for no believer is life the highest value."

"What's more valuable than life?"

"Your honor, for one thing. Your belief in Adonai, for another. Truth also. And the beauty of a graceful life."

"Are you saying that Adonai can ask you to sacrifice your life or to sacrifice the lives of other men and women?"

"Yes. Even if Adonai himself appeared in the form of man, the life of that man as a man could not be regarded as supreme."

"And where's the limit?"

"The voice of Adonai within you. If you want to, you will know when it's wrong to shed blood and when you may do so."

"And for that," David said laughingly, "we poor ordinary men need you, Scholar, eh?"

"It's one of our functions," Nathan answered seriously. "Yes, Lord David. Indeed it is."

When they got back to Ziklag, a secret delegation of elders from some towns and cities in Judah had arrived and waited to see David.

There were seven of them, and David knew them all. Each was a respected leader in his town—Hebron, Beersheva, Maon, Bethlehem, Socoh, Devir, and Lachish. They had a simple message: They wanted David as king of Judah.

"It's not so simple," he told them. "The Philistines can crush anyone now. We have no army, no supplies, no bases, no organization. Besides, of all the Twelve Tribes, only part of Judah—the small part you represent—will accept me. Remember, I am regarded as a traitor and an apostate to the

Covenant. On top of all that, there's the House of Saul. I hear that Abner is promoting Ishbaal."

"We know you never betrayed the Covenant, Lord David," their spokesman, the Hebronite, answered. "And we do not want Ishbaal. Under what conditions will you come back?"

"I will come back only as the vassal of Philistia," David answered. The Hebronite blanched, but David went on reassuringly. "But that's only for convenience. I need time to establish myself, build an army, tame the House of Saul, subjugate the other tribes—especially the northern ones. Then we can turn around and claim the freedom of Adonai for ourselves."

The Judahite delegation retired and conferred by themselves for some minutes. When they came back, they had a clear and unanimous decision. "We are ready to swear a secret oath of loyalty to you, Lord David. And we will fight your battles and support you as king, not only of Judah but of all the House of Israel."

David rose to the occasion as if he had planned very carefully beforehand what had to be done, which indeed he had. "Joab!" he called. "Bring in the others." David and the delegation waited while David's councilors and officials filed in: Ahimelek, Abishai, Asahel, Abiathar, Nathan, Hushai the Arkite, Serayah the Scribe, Adoram the Treasurer, Yehosaphat, Ira the tribal expert, David's brothers. They stood around the delegation. David sat down on a chair. Abiathar took out the Scroll of the Law. When he called each elder by name, the elder stepped forward, laid his hand under David's scrotum, and swore a double oath: of loyalty and secrecy. When the ceremony was completed, David embraced each elder.

"Within six weeks, I shall be with you," he told them.

The meeting in Gaza went smoothly. But there was one surprise for David. When he entered the council chamber, he found the five dukes seated around a sixth man, a large, absolutely bald individual with strange eyes. The look on Achish's face told David to be wary. Try as he could, David could not take his eyes off the face of the stranger. Shekelath introduced him to David as "my Lord Kalkodon," but the name meant nothing to David. While David conferred with the dukes, Kalkodon's eyes never withdrew from David and never blinked. He said not a word, but it was clear to the Hebrew that everything said and done was done with continual reference to Kalkodon.

"You, David of Bethlehem," Shekelath said imperiously, "are to be the servant of Lord Dagon and vassal of the Pentarchy in the land of Judah. You will take up your residence in Judah, from which you will wage war and subdue all the tribes in the south and north, securing the borders of the land against the nations on the east bank of the Jordan and south of the Bag of Sand. Those nations in the north you will leave alone for the moment. If they attack you, you may defend yourself, but on no account are you to attack them.

"Your vassaldom will stretch from Dan to Beersheva, and from Philistia to the Jordan. We will supply you with iron weapons. You will pay Philistia an annual tribute of ten thousand goats, fifteen thousand sheep, two thousand she asses, seven thousand camels, and two thousand oxen. There will also be a coin tribute of four thousand shekels in silver and four thousand shekels in gold. You will supply five thousand male and five thousand female slaves to the Pentarchy each year by the opening of spring. Once a year you will come to Gaza to present yourself. You cannot form any alliances with anyone without the permission of the Pentarchy. Have you any questions, Lord David?"

"May I take the Pelethites as well as the Kerethites with me?"

"Yes."

"May I have an allocation of five hundred chariots with Philistine instructors?"

"No. The chariotry is solely for Philistines."

"When do I go to Judah?"

"Immediately."

And that was the end of the discussion. Both Shekelath and David turned and looked at Kalkodon. It was only then that David realized that he could read nothing in Kalkodon's eyes, neither interest nor contempt, neither opposition nor friendliness. They regarded each other for perhaps five full seconds. Then Kalkodon looked at Shekelath and nodded. The presiding duke rose.

"All hail, David *saran-ta-Avrinon*—saran of Hebrews!" Shekelath said solemnly, using the Philistine expression.

"All hail!" the others chorused stiffly. The meeting was over.

Achish walked to the door with David, a look of deep misery in his eyes. What had happened to the mighty Achish? David asked himself. What terrible instructions had Shekelath brought back for Achish from the dread place Luqqawatna?

"*Saran-ta Avrinon...saranma...*" David repeated the Philistine words. "Achish, translate *saranma* into Hebrew."

"What the Arameans call *medina*—region, territory, province. It means a land inhabited and owned by one people, held together by one common set of laws, one principal army, one ruling authority. *Saranma*."

"Then we Hebrews would say *medinath yisrael*. What must that be like?" David said wonderingly. "We've never had that... *saran-ta Avrinon...saran-ta Avrinon...medinath Ivrim*... Samuel would have liked *medinath Ivrim*, but he never thought of a *medina*."

Achish sighed. "Farewell, my Hebrew," he said. "Your ignorance is your blessing. Walk carefully!" David, on his camel and smiling, looked down at the duke.

"It needn't turn out as bad as you expect or they plan, old friend.... Suppose, Achish, just suppose Adonai wants a *medinath yisrael?*"

Achish turned away with a dismissing gesture of his hand, as if to dismiss David's idea as pure fantasy. David spurred his camel and departed.

The city of Hebron was more than four hundred years old now. The first Hebrew tribes that fled from the Pharaoh had discovered the place almost by chance. In their desperation to get away from their pursuers, they had headed straight across the twenty-four thousand square miles of lifeless wastes in the Bag of Sand. Only a fraction of those who set out survived the killer sandstorms, the burning sun, the freezing nights, and the marauding nomads. The fertile land of Hebron seemed like paradise to those few who made it. They formed a new association for mutual protection, and they called their new-found paradise *hevron*—the "association," or "league." Without realizing it they were not far from a spot called Mamre, where Father Abraham had built an altar to Adonai. They learned only later that history had come full circle at Hebron.

It was a pleasant valley with gently sloping sides covered with meadowland. Water was plentiful, and tall shady palm trees. Large stretches of land were well timbered with cedar, sycamore, oak, and pine. A large rock platform jutted out at the northern end of the valley, accessible only on one side from the high ground, with a sheer drop of over forty feet on the other three sides. Although only half the size, Hebron shared this characteristic of inaccessibility with the city of Jebus. The early Hebronites settled on this rock plateau, sowed their crops in the meadows, grazed their flocks in the valley, and with the passage of time strongly fortified the one accessible side of the plateau.

Hebron flourished with the rise and fall of successive generations. The Hebronites terraced the south and southwest slopes of the valley and planted vines. With care, and the caress of the southern sun, the grapes of Hebron became famous throughout the land. From them the Hebronites pressed an array of delicious wines that were in great demand. The Hebronites also became famous for their women. A daughter of an Upper City burgher was bound to have three things: pure Hebrew blood, an ample dowry, and large black eyes as luminous as Indian onyx. Both of Jesse's wives, Korith and Shoshanna, were "daughters of the Upper City."

Only descendants of the original settlers had the birthright privilege of living in the Upper City. Those who came afterward were allowed to join the association and build their houses in the western and eastern ridges and down toward the end of the valley.

Hebron was governed by a Council of Elders that levied taxes, maintained the guard of well-paid mercenaries, regulated prices. As the Hebron council went, so went any city or town of importance in the area. Hebron's treasury was chiefly enriched from the dairy farming and the vineyards. But Hebron was also an important focal point for the main caravan routes, and tolls added to its revenues. At the time of David's return to the land, the most prominent member and influential councilor was a certain Gilohite known as Ahitofel. The name means "my brother is evil and foolish." The man started off as David's trusted minister, but subsequently betrayed his kind. And David never forgave him.

Ahitofel's distinction was that, although he was not really "Upper City," he had successfully married into it when he was barely seventeen. Sole heir of a very wealthy family of winemakers at Giloh in northern Judah, Ahitofel brought not only great riches to the Upper City, but also some ancient formulas for winemaking that further enhanced the Hebron vintages.

Besides this, Ahitofel was extremely intelligent and well educated—speaking Egyptian, Phenician, and Assyrian as well as his native Hebrew and Canaanite. Tall and thin, he had a narrow, sensitive face ending in a closely trimmed beard, languorous eyes, sparse hair. He was always washed and delicately perfumed, although he had little interest in sex of any kind. His wife had died young, after giving him one son, Ammiel.

Ahitofel never married again, but immersed himself in public affairs; by that time he had won his place as the deciding voice at the private sessions of the Hebron council.

He married Ammiel off to a rich heiress who slept with her husband only briefly and then retired into a deep melancholy from which she never emerged—but not before giving birth to a girl who was called Bathsheva. From the start, Ahitofel dominated the life of Bathsheva, as he completely overshadowed her father. Ammiel was a tragic figure, afraid of his father, capable only of fighting; he eventually became an officer in David's army.

Ahitofel was virtually monosyllabic, mainly because of his contempt for the slowness of others. His agile mind leaped where others labored. He signaled his conclusions in staccato phrases, veiled by the apparent indifference in his eyes. But in fact Ahitofel was always watching, calculating. He regarded any man of twenty-five and over as a jackass if he still believed in "that Adonai business," as he referred to the religious history and teaching of the Covenant.

The other council members could not resist his remarkable gifts, so they ignored his godlessness and contempt in order to benefit by his cunning and sagacity. Following Saul's destruction, it was Ahitofel who suggested negotiations with David—"a lout but a good soldier, who will eat the grapes of Hebron and be our lackey." It was Ahitofel who drew up the plans for the installation of David in Hebron and saw to it that it was done smoothly. He overrode and overruled objections about David's apostasy and Philistinism ("A distinct advantage!" was Ahitofel's retort) and the rumor about the "abomination" of his having taken a male Philistine lover—"A duke, no less!" one old elder wheezed. "To be sure, to be sure," Ahitofel replied.

The council approved Ahitofel's plans, and a few days later he walked Ahimelek and Joab up and down the terrace of his Upper City residence and told them how the installation of David should be achieved. Then, having fixed the date and all other details, he dismissed his visitors, closed his house, and retired to the peace of his country villa two miles down the valley. Ahitofel always left the melee the better to perceive its issue.

The first day after the first Shabbath in May, the night watches on the walls of the Upper City were under the command of Jarak, an Egyptian who had been in service at Hebron for

over twenty years. Nighttime officially ran from six at night
to six in the morning and was divided into four watches of
three hours apiece. The night officer had to supervise the
change of guards in person. He himself sat in the guardhouse,
a small wooden room behind the northern battlements. It was
a sultry night, some six weeks after Gilboa. Jarak was waiting
for the hourglass to tell him when the fourth and last watch
should take over.

A knock at the door brought him to his feet. Outside he
found Shechanya, president of the council, Ahuzam the treasurer, Malkiram the militia chief, and Ahitofel the all-powerful.

"Jarak, my good fellow, we are replacing you and the guards
of the fourth watch with a new contingent," Malkiram said
pleasantly but firmly. "The council has made an important
decision. We need your full cooperation!"

"At the council's command!" Jarak said shortly.

Ahitofel then gave the orders: "Tell the guards on watch to
go to the courtyard. Then send them to quarters. Then go to
your own. You and they are confined to barracks until further
notice."

"Very well, sir!"

As he stepped off to comply, Jarak noticed two tall, bulky
men on the battlements. They had short spears and square
shields decorated with blue six-pointed stars, they were clad
in chest and leg armor, and they were watching him. At their
feet, Jarak saw some object wrapped in sacking. Jarak knew
better than to ask questions. He called his trumpeter, ordered
the signal for assembly, and marched his men off to their
barracks.

When they were gone, Ahitofel stirred himself. "Gentle-
men," he said dispassionately, gathering his cloak around his
shoulders, "I'm sure you can manage the rest. Malkiram knows
how. I'll be at my villa."

"Joab, Abishai!" Malkiram called to the two armed men.
"Go ahead!"

Joab went to the edge of the battlements, drew back, and
threw his spear in the direction of a small copse about thirty
yards distant. He opened the sacking and took out a rope ladder,
looped its ends around the battlements, and dropped the other
end over the wall. Shechanya, Malkiram, and Ahuzam stood
aside and listened. All was quiet, and a full moon shone. After
a few minutes they heard what sounded like the hooting of an
owl. Joab leaned over the wall and gave an exact imitation.
Shortly afterward the helmeted head of a man appeared at the

edge of the battlements. He leaped in. He was as big as Joab and armed in the same way. He was followed in quick succession by two hundred others. None of them spoke. Every one of them seemed to know what to do. Within an hour, and two hours before the beginning of the first day watch at six, the battlements, watchtowers, and arsenals of Hebron's Upper City were manned by David's men. It had all been accomplished in complete silence and with a swift efficiency that amazed the elders.

These warriors were disciplined and used to night action. The elders were overawed by the muscular militancy of these rough men, by their strange armor, their large heads, long hair, and full, untrimmed beards. They smelled of camel sweat and convinced all who saw them: these were fighting men.

When this phase of the operation was over, Joab went to the battlements again and whistled three times. The elders again watched in fascination as another stream of armed men appeared over the wall and leaped in nimbly. They were all slightly built, narrow-waisted, and small-headed, with tight-fitting helmets that left only their eyes visible. The Kerethites. They squatted down behind the battlements with their bows and arrows, their backs against the wall. There were over two thousand of them, and it took them all a little over an hour to take up their prearranged positions around the entire length of the walls.

Some three quarters of an hour before the official start of the Hebron day, David's troops were in place. The three elders then went to the public hall. They sat down, took some food, and waited for dawn and the arrival of the other members of the council. Joab, Abishai, and Ahimelek remained on the battlements in charge of the soldiers.

Promptly at six o'clock the official city dawn call rang out, as the caller struck the town bell twenty-four times. Slowly the city came awake. The gates were opened and the day's work began. The first people about, food merchants, garbage collectors, slaves and servants going to fetch water, noticed the strange-looking guards at the gate and the still line of gray-clad soldiers strung like a garland of weaponry around the battlements. "Strangers are in town! Armed strangers! Remain in your homes!" Very soon the streets were deserted again, but at all the windows hundreds of eyes gazed out apprehensively. Then the full city council, with the exception of Ahitofel, came marching through the main streets calling the citizens to a public meeting. The Hebronites assembled in front of the public hall without delay, and Shechanya addressed them from the podium.

"Hebronites! You elected us to guard your interests. The council has decided that there is no way Hebron can survive unless we put ourselves under the protection of my Lord David, son of Jesse, the slayer of the giant." There was a certain amount of murmuring at this, but Shechanya went on anyway. "It's all very well to grumble, my brothers. But there is no longer a king in Israel. There is no longer a prophet in Israel. We are defenseless sheep. There are only the Philistines to the west, the nomads to the south, the Edomites to the southeast, the Moabites and Ammonites to the east, the Arameans to the north, and always the Egyptian serpent down south.

"We live by trade. We must have protection. You want your wives and children to live, your houses safe, your servants unharmed, your valuables protected.

"We can do this only under the protection of my Lord David. You decide."

Somebody handed Shechanya two cages, each with five pigeons in it. The citizens watched as Shechanya opened the cages and let out the ten pigeons. The birds rose up, fluttering and weaving irregularly as pigeons do before they find their homing direction. In dumbfounded silence, the citizens heard a sharp command rapped out in a language they didn't understand. There was a series of whizzing noises, and every one of the birds fell, an arrow through its neck. All the heads in the crowd swiveled around. They glanced up to the battlements. No one in that gray line had so much as risen to his feet. Two of them from a sitting position had whipped out their bows and arrows and brought the birds down in a matter of seconds.

"My brothers," Shechanya said almost apologetically, "you take my meaning!" There was no sound from the Hebronites. Shechanya braced himself for the next part of his announcement. "At eight o'clock—that is, in less than one hour, my Lord David will enter the city. After the oath of allegiance, we will install my Lord David in the Center House. Normally, you know, this is reserved for visitors, but under the circumstances it is better if my Lord David stays there until he builds his own residence. The council expects everyone to welcome my Lord David." That was the end of the town meeting, and everyone hurried home.

At about eight o'clock the nervous ears of the burghers picked up a distant sound. At first they thought it was the wind rising, but gradually, even though still distant, it could be distinguished as the wailing cry of shepherd's pipes. It was the voice of the wild, of a world they all had hoped would never interfere with their well-ordered town life. Down in his country villa Ahitofel sat on his marble terrace, sipping dry wine from a golden goblet. He wore an embroidered morning gown of Tyrian purple. His left hand toyed with a tiny glass vial filled with a bright red liquid. He took another delicate sip of wine and listened to the pipes, a speculative look in his eyes. "It's all foolishness," he said calmly to himself.

The pipes came closer to the wide-open north gate. The gray line of archers were all standing now, each bow loaded with an arrow, taut and ready to shoot. But the eyes of the apprehensive citizens strayed back to the gaping north gate and beyond it to the curving road that led up to it.

Around that corner came the first contingents of David's convoy, two small drummer men beating out the marching rhythm. Behind them, the soldiers, the famed Pelethites. No Hebronite had ever seen Philistine soldiers or any soldiers of this ilk. They marched six deep. Each one was not only tall and long-legged; he was broad in the shoulder, big-headed and big-footed. He wore armor on head, shoulders, chest, arms, thighs, and calves. A sheepskin cloak hung over the left shoulder, and a long spear was strapped across his back. A shield was strapped to his left arm. The first ranks entered the gate and peeled off, six to each side. They stood back to back, one man facing the houses, his fellow facing the street. Each pair was one sword's length from the next pair. Over the scene, the wild music of the pipes sounded continuously.

As they entered in sixes, the main and side streets became lined with those armed soldiers. No Hebronite in his home was in a position to count them all and know that eight thousand Pelethites had filed in. But that was only the beginning. Immediately on their heels came three thousand Hebrew spearmen, followed by contingents of fifteen hundred men each of slingshot and mace fighters. In the heart of the Upper City the detachments started to form around the public hall. Shechanya and the council remained sitting; nobody stirred to look out the windows. As the council listened to the steady, monotonous beat of the drums and the eerie piping, the excited citizens began crowding into the street to see the show.

The Hebrew infantry entered, followed by ten mule-riding detachments of thirty men each and a long three-deep file of camel riders. Behind them came important officials—Abishai, Asahel, Ahimelek, Ira, Serayah, Yehosaphat, Hushai the Arkite, and a score of others, some on camels, mules, asses, and small Arabian horses. Then came a long line of oxcarts pulled by four oxen apiece. One armed man sat beside the driver of each cart. As each of the twelve carts passed by, gasps of astonishment went up. The carts were filled with shining gold and silver coins, with carved ornaments and shining garments.

But this awe at all the glory was suddenly stilled by a sudden increase in the pipe music. They looked through the gate just in time to see the first line of pipers swinging around the curve in the road. All were young men, long-haired, heavily bearded, all clad in shepherd's clothes: tight-fitting leather tunics and britches, leather boots, and round caps, oak staves strapped across their backs, throwing knives protruding from the tops of their boots. David's shepherds. The full blast of that pipe music grew and grew as the shepherds swung through the gate. The regular beat of the drums suddenly grew louder and faster as a long, covered cart pulled by six oxen leisurely rounded the curve, followed by a second, a third, and a fourth. By the time the first one was entering the gate, the onlookers had caught glimpses of the veiled face of a woman, the robe of a slave. And all realized that David's family and servants sat in those covered oxcarts. Directly behind them were three men on mules. Nathan and Gad were there, and the third man was Abiathar, the keeper of the Ephod.

Ten yards behind these three riders came a group of twenty men on camels, headed by a crinkly-haired giant of a man, all brawn and muscle: Ramram, a Hittite, chief of David's personal bodyguard. Ten yards behind the twenty-man bodyguard and coming around the curve by himself on a tall camel there appeared a lone figure.

The camel's body was hung with a light blue covering that swept the ground on each side. The sunlight flashed on the reins its rider held in his left hand. The figure straddled the camel as a horseman sits on a horse, and his long legs draped down over the sides of his mount. He was fully erect, his head held high and steady. Every detail about him seemed to enhance his awesome effect.

First there was his long curling golden hair, confined by a circlet of slightly darker gold. Then there were the flashing blue eyes.

His clothing was simple: breastplate, leather britches, high boots, his shield and helmet hanging on the camel's neck. But what finally drew all eyes was the flashing, gleaming sword in his right hand. He held it straight up at arm's length. It was enormous. Quietly the word was whispered around: The sword of Goliath! There was a sudden intake of breath by every man there, an overriding rush of emotion welling in every heart and every eye.

One man shouted suddenly: "Long live David!" Forty took it up. Two hundred voices joined in. Hands were waving feverishly. Women and children began to cry and cheer. The wild outburst spread from house to house, street to street, until the whole of the Upper City resounded.

At the gate, Shechanya himself, in his embroidered robes, stepped forward, took the reins of David's camel in hand, and led him slowly up the street. Joab rode beside Shechanya, Ramram at David's side. Behind them came other elders. Outside the public hall, ringed around by his soldiers, David dismounted and stood until they brought out a ceremonial chair. Shechanya called an officer and whispered instructions to him: he was to fetch Ahitofel from his villa. Meanwhile David sat down, the sword of Goliath lying across his lap. Abiathar placed the sacred Ephod over his head and around his shoulders, then sat at his feet holding the Scroll of the Law open at the place where Moses teaches his followers to recite the prayer of belief in Adonai. Abiathar read out loud the first words: "Hear O Israel! Adonai, our God! Adonai is One!"

The council elders came forward one by one, all twenty-five of them, knelt in front of David, and placed one hand on Abiathar's Scroll, the other on the sword of Goliath. When David administered the oath of allegiance, the elder bent down and kissed David's instep. David then gave him his right hand to kiss. Then the elder rose, backed away until he reached the ring of soldiers, and turned to find his place. After the elders came all the important burghers, the chief landowners from the Hebron countryside, the heads of towns and villages in association with Hebron, and the chieftains of the southern Bedouin tribes allied with Hebron. Shechanya looked over his shoulder for Ahitofel but he did not appear. The ceremony took till midday.

Finally, when it was over, David stood up. Joab whispered in his ear.

"Shechanya," David called out sharply, "have they all come?" The president of the council jumped with fear.

"Yes, my Lord David . . . that is . . . er . . ."

"Who is missing?"

"Master Ahitofel, my Lord David. We sent a messenger—"

"Who did not leave the city, Master Shechanya. During my entry and installation we allowed no one to leave the city. Your messenger is for the moment my prisoner. He will come to no harm."

"Yes, my Lord David."

"Send an officer with Joab to fetch Master Ahitofel. We will wait." David sat down again, sword across his knees.

Within half an hour Ahitofel arrived, detached as ever. He was riding a pure white donkey. When he dismounted and walked toward where David sat, Shechanya whispered to him. The lanky councilor bent to listen. He knit his eyebrows in puzzlement and straightened up, sighing resignedly. But David acted first.

"Joab!" he shouted, nettled. "We have received all those who matter. Lift this man onto his donkey, take him to the gate, and tell him to go home and wait there until he has learned how to behave. He obscures my view of the sun."

A sudden twist took hold of those fine features. Ahitofel had been publicly humiliated for the first time. He would not forget it.

The rest of the day was spent installing David and his family in the Center House. There was a long and sumptuous banquet starting at four o'clock. Ahitofel arrived, composed and dressed in his finest clothes. He approached David and performed the rite of homage. "Events took me by surprise, my Lord David," he said. "Having negotiated your entrance to Hebron, I look forward to a long collaboration with you. You will find my services valuable, I believe."

"I am sure I will. You are most welcome, Master Ahitofel," was David's answer. "Teach me to trust you!" Ahitofel smiled smoothly and bowed. The matter was closed.

When the banquet was over that evening, Ahitofel led Joab and his two brothers, Asahel and Abishai, off for some more night drinking at his villa. David's house was quiet, emptied of guests. Before he went to his own room David had one more duty to perform: visit Shoshanna. He found her lying awake in bed, the oil lamp extinguished.

"Come and sit a moment, David. I've something to tell you." He squatted on the floor by the side of the bed, one hand cradling her head, the other holding her right hand. "When your father Jesse sought advice about you, just before you were born, he saw a holy woman up near Nazareth—"

"Shalama, Mother."

"Yes, Shalama. What you don't know is what Shalama

actually told your father—he would never tell you. He didn't understand what Shalama told him about you...

"I never told you before, son. I felt the time hadn't come. It's different tonight..."

"Mother," David said, the tension in him obvious to her, "what did Shalama say?"

"She said"—Shoshanna spoke slowly, enunciating each word carefully—"she said: 'Your son will be the womb of Adonai's body.' Don't ask, my son—" Shoshanna broke off, feeling his hands go limp. He stood up, perplexed. "Son! David! Wait!"

He heard the alarm in her voice but could not heed it. Adonai's body? Womb? He, David, a man? He remembered what the Philistines believed about Dagon and Dagon's body. The crassness of all that belief had always seemed ludicrous and blasphemous to him. Raham, Nathan, all the scholars taught that Adonai had neither face nor form. Then he heard his mother again.

"Son! My son! Don't go from me like this. Kiss me."

He took hold of himself with an effort. "Mother, sleep well, now. All will be well. I'm fine."

"For this you were born," she whispered to him as he bent to kiss her good night. "Adonai will let you know. Trust him! Please trust him, my David."

"I will, Mother. I will. Now sleep."

He went up alone to the roof and looked out over the city and the countryside. It was the hanging twilight moment that immediately follows sunset, just before the fall of total darkness. He wanted to catch the luminous pale color that bathed the earth at sundown, and, in that luminosity, to contemplate his life and hopes. Shalama's words to his father kept coursing through his mind as he looked out over the city. "Adonai's body." "The womb of his body." "Form his body." He could not put those words together to make any sense.

The city streets below him were almost empty, but there were lights in the windows. People were sitting and standing in doorways, still tingling from the events of this day. The watchmen were in their towers. The city gates were shut and barred. The walls were lined with David's men. He was master of Hebron. But...to be the womb of Adonai? That was something else entirely.

All around the city, as David lifted his eyes, the hills rose and fell, gold, yellow, pink in the reflected glow of the endless desert that rolled out from the foot of the hills in every direction.

The sides of rocky ledges and wadis were already graying in long shadows, but the slopes of the hills were flecked with brown and gold. Far off, directly north beyond the woods, in the immaculate clarity of the air, he could just discern the distant hills and mountain land surrounding Jebus. Someday, he mused, he would march up that rough land and enter Jebus, making it his own. Immediately above him was Mamre, the mountain where Adonai had talked with Abraham.

To the south and northwest the sloping sides of the Hebron valley swung gently upward through the vineyard terraces, and then through the carpets of white and pink cyclamens, scarlet anemones, poppies and tulips. Later, he resolved, when the blue lupin and the daisies and phlox covered that hill, he would build a residence there for himself and his mother and his family. Perhaps then Adonai would give him a son. . . . To the east David could see the dip of ground that led down to the Salt Sea. And, beyond that sea, he knew, was Mizpeh of Moab and the quiet cave where Jesse's bones waited. The glowering mountains of Moab were now hooded in darkness.

He shivered as the cool winds of evening began. It was said in David's Israel that "the wind blows where it will—you hear the sound of it, but you cannot tell where it comes from or where it is going." The mystery of that wind recalled him to the other great mysteries unfolding around him. Darkness was now complete, and a great full moon rode the horizon like a golden bowl. A sense of the divine, of some communicated greatness, came over him. Would Adonai accept him back? The question hung in his mind.

A soft rustle distracted him. He turned. Nathan and Abigail, favorite councilor and favorite wife, had silently joined him. They understood him. They loved him. Abigail had brought his harp, and David sang a song he would sing again and again in variant forms all his life.

> "Lord! You have probed me and known me . . .
> How can I escape from you?
> Where can I hide from you?
> If I climb up to the skies,
> You are there.
> If I penetrate the depths of the earth,
> You are there.
> If I make my bed in the center of the earth,
> You are there.

*"If I fly on the wings of the morning light
    Out to the edge of the Great Sea,
    Even there your right hand holds me!*

*"If I say: Surely, the darkness shall hide me!
    Then the very night will be light around me.
    Darkness and light are the same for you..."*

As David sang, Nathan rose, to leave husband and wife alone. He nodded to Abigail and started to go. David paused at the shuffle of sandals and looked around.

"Prophet! Do you think Adonai sees us now? Do you think he hears my song?"

Nathan retorted over his shoulder, "Do you think he who made your eyes to see cannot himself see? He who made your ears cannot himself hear?" And he continued on his way. The strains of the harp and of David's voice grew fainter as Nathan descended to the ground floor and out the main door. Now he could hear the music and the words clearly again. He drew in deep breaths of the fresh night air. Gad the Seer still sat there alone. Nathan looked over at him quizzically. "What say you, Gad, O Seer? This night of all nights!"

"In the Book of the Law"—Gad's voice was quiet and meditative—"the first word Moses wrote was 'In the beginning.' This night, Prophet, is the beginning of the beginning. If he comes to trust his fate in Adonai's hands, this night is the beginning of a great beginning."

Nathan squatted down beside the other man. The music continued above their heads. "Perhaps, but it is hard to believe," he replied. "After all, he fled Adonai's land. He adopted Philistine customs, spoke their language, slept with their whores, burned incense to their god, wore that filthy foreskin. He gave the Philistines the plan of battle to destroy Saul, Adonai's anointed. Now he's back here. Can Adonai forgive all that?"

"He didn't really apostasize, Prophet. He panicked. And he mistrusted. Just mistrusted Adonai."

"Yes, but Adonai is a jealous God—"

"Adonai is more than that, Nathan. You, a prophet in Israel, and you can't see that? No wonder our Hebrews are split in a thousand ways!" The reproach was gentle but firm. Nathan stared at the bright eyes of Gad.

"What's this 'more' you speak of, my brother!"

"For one thing, Adonai is not merely the jealous God of the Hebrews. He's the God of Philistia, too, and of the Great Sea, of the mountains, of Egypt, of Assyria, of Phenicia, of all the earth, of all generations. Jealous? Yes. But also caring. Loving. David doesn't realize this yet, but he will see it one day."

"You said 'For one thing,' Seer," Nathan remarked mordantly. "Is there a second thing?"

"There is, very wise but puzzled Prophet." Gad's voice was gently teasing. "There's more to the 'more' I spoke about. It's simply that Adonai needs something. He has talked for hundreds of years with prophets and seers and holy men and women. Through sacred oak trees, ephods, and other things. He has even shown himself to a few—Moses, Abraham, others. He has performed great miracles, wondrous events. All that, surely! But finally it's not enough. You remember the saying of Samuel—'Adonai's pleasure is to be with men and women. Adonai wants to make his dwelling with his creatures.' You remember?"

"Yes. But I always took it to mean his constant presence with the Ark of the Covenant."

"No matter, Prophet. No matter what you thought. This time, Adonai wishes more. He wants a body. He wants his footprints to be seen clearly in the sands of time. Finally, we men and women must see a body of his—"

"It's blasphemy!" Nathan's voice was hoarse.

"Careful, Prophet! Careful! I said: 'a body of his.' Listen to me!"

"And?"

"What David must do is form that body."

Nathan stood up. "I don't understand."

"Neither does David. He will be a great king, the king of kings. Adonai will not merely exalt him as a model for all other kings, but as the maker, the fashioner, the womb of Adonai's body among men."

"I don't understand, but blessed be Adonai, who makes the seer of Israel see what the prophet cannot," Nathan mumbled good-humoredly as he departed to bed.

In Ahitofel's villa, Joab and his two brothers watched and listened warily as they drank continuously, and the Gilohite, at his smoothest, filled and refilled their cups, talking volubly about David and the near future. All the while, Ahitofel secretly marveled at the unslakable thirst of these three desert fighters. They had nothing in common with Ahitofel. The Gilohite knew that much. He was fishing, however, for possible allies, probing for weaknesses. The Hebrews, he said, had always lived in separate enclaves, never grouped around a king in his royal city. To be sure, they had this Covenant with Adonai. But that apart, and apart from the common danger which always brought them together, they had never been gathered together and ruled by one man. Not under Samuel. Not under the hero Samson. Not under Moses. And certainly not under Saul. Nor had they ever inhabited a land they could really call their own. Moses said they were promised the land of Canaan. But they lived on little isolated patches of it—the worst patches, at that. Guests and sojourners, wherever they had lived, this is what Ahitofel called them.

And then there was Philistia. How long would the Philistines be patient with David and his Hebrew marauders? How could Hebrews stand up against Philistine armor? And then the northern tribes and the Saulites, they abhorred Judah and the Judahites. They didn't even worship the same god—or did his listeners think that the El of the northerners was the same as the Yah of the southerners? And so the Gilohite rambled on, without eliciting any response from the three brothers. The sons of Zeruiah liked Ahitofel's beer. They obviously did not like him. After an hour and a half, Joab stood up in the middle of Ahitofel's sentence.

"Master Ahitofel, for the beer, our thanks. As for David, fear not. He is now in his thirties. Most men start to die at this age. Not David. He's only beginning. I swear by Yah or by El or by the breasts of Astarte or the rump of your camel: My brothers and I, on the day David marches into Jebus, the day he wipes Philistia off the face of the earth, the day he is acclaimed by all Hebrews, the day Hebrews possess this land from Dan to Beersheva, from the Jordan to the Great Sea—on that day we intend to be present." He glared at Ahitofel, then at his brothers. "I hope you do too, Master Ahitofel." He belched contentedly. "Come, my brothers. Let us go."

No one who listened to David singing on that Hebron rooftop in that enraptured gloaming—not even the prophet Nathan nor the seer Gad—had any view of the near future, although Gad trusted in it. Yet as David played his dreamily ascending scales, caressing mid-register melodies and overlapping patterns of sonorous bass notes, Abigail and everyone else who heard him soaked up the peace of the moment and the joy of the music. They knew that they were with David the Golden, and that was enough for now. Indeed, that was delight itself. They knew now only that the dusk had deepened into night, with a slight chill descending.

For a few moments David scanned the city and its surroundings. Northwest of him lay Philistia. He rolled on the tongue of his mind the perpetually biting question: Would his gamble work? Tomorrow and on subsequent days, he would receive the submission of the principal cities in Judah. When that was done, he would be anointed king of Judah. Then the northern tribes had to be faced. And then the Philistines! And then— whatever Adonai willed. Abigail tugged gently at his sleeve. Together they left the roof and went down to bed.

But Shoshanna in her room had been listening also. And the last few lines of David's song rang in her memory:

> *You know me, God!*
> *Through and through*
> *From having watched my bones take shape,*
> *When I was being formed in secret,*
> *Knitted together in the darkness of the womb.*

In the darkness of the night, Shoshanna prayed. "Forgive him his anger, Adonai, his brutality in war, his distrust and his disbelief. He is your child. And aren't you, Adonai, his father—and more than his father? Did you save him from sudden death at his birth to drop him now like a soiled rag? Forgive my son. I beg you, Adonai! Forgive him."

Events forced David to take two more wives. He and the Hebron council negotiated with the cities and towns of Judah. Hebronite economic power plus David's military weight created a very impressive combination. But the pursuit of Hebrew unity dictated that the adhesion of the Judahites be voluntary. So the delegation of David's men, Nathan and Gad, and Hebron's elders, Shechanya and Ahitofel, made visit after visit all over Judah. In two key cities, Keilah and Beersheva, the price of unity was a political marriage. So David took to wife Maaka, daughter of Talmai, prince of Geshur and chief elder of Keilah; and Haggith, daughter of the chief elder of Beersheva. By August's end, therefore, he had four wives of his exile. And within a month, all four—Abigail, Ahinoam, Haggith, and Maaka—declared themselves pregnant by David. Under these circumstances, and with the blessing of the Hebron council, he dispossessed six Upper City families, expropriated their stone houses, refurbished them as his own residence, and installed his pregnant wives there. Shoshanna remained in the Center House with David, her room adjoining his own. And each of his wives vied with the others in her attentions to the dying woman, knowing that David valued her beyond all other persons.

At the beginning of October, David decided not to wait any longer for his official installation as king of Judah. In the middle of the month, the elders of all the Judahite cities gathered in Hebron. In the public square of the Upper City, Nathan anointed David with the sacred oil. Abiathar read out the Law of Moses in its entirety. Serayah the Scribe, read the chronicles of Israel from Samson to Saul, and Gad addressed the assembled people. David then called on Shechanya and the group of presiding elders from the forty-three cities and towns of Judah. Shechanya took the gold headband and bracelet of kingship, held them up in front of all the elders.

"In the name of you all, I place this headband and this bracelet on David, son of Jesse—David of Bethlehem—as the signs of your acceptance of his powerful right arm to defend you and your acceptance of his wisdom to rule you."

He placed them on David, stood back, and gave the traditional salutation: *"Yechi ha-melek David!"* The elders repeated the cry. "Long live King David!" And it was taken up by the people. *"Yechi ha-melek! Yechi ha-melek David!"*

Ahitofel, who stood with the other elders, had little to say. He had been extremely useful and wise in the negotiations, just as he had been in the earlier discussions that brought David to Hebron. But even he was surprised at the mode in which David chose to be crowned. He glanced at David's armored soldiery, noticed the look on David's face, and remarked to old Malkiram, "Our king obviously believes in the Covenant but intends to keep the prophet and the priest in their places." Malkiram only grunted. He did not like Ahitofel. And he liked the idea that politics and military matters were in the hands of politicians and soldiers.

Ahuzam, who stood by, was louder in his reactions: "If Saul had known how to act like David, his rotting corpse would not have been nailed to the walls of Bethshan."

But the coronation festivities swallowed all differences. Everyone, excluding the skeptical Ahitofel, was caught up in the excitement of the new era: They now had a real king! But as Ahitofel soberly reminded David in private: "The Philistines still regard you as their vassal, you know, and they do not interfere with your progress. But for gaining the loyalty of the northern tribes, your vassaldom will be *the* obstacle." David had to acknowledge the bitter truth of this comment.

"Then you, Ahitofel, must advise me in this delicate matter. I will know how to reward you. We both know you could lose as much as I if the Philistines turn on me or if I do not win the loyalty of the Hebrews. Walk this narrow bridge with me, and we can both survive and flourish. What do you say?" The offer took Ahitofel's fancy. He laughed easily, and kissed David's hand in homage. For the moment, David had won Ahitofel.

"One thing we're changing right now is my title, Ahitofel. For the Philistines I am a vassal governor, a *saran*. And my territory is *saranma-ta Avrinon*, the province of the Hebrews, for our long-nosed friends."

"What a barbaric language!"

"But you and I, Ahitofel, and everyone else will refer to me as *melek yehuda*, the king of Judah, and to my kingdom as *medinath yehuda*, the territory of Judah. Understood?"

"I understand, O King of the territory of Judah!"

Shortly after this day, Joab came with a piece of bad news: messengers David had sent to Jabesh-Gilead were back and the warriors had politely rejected David's suggestion that they become his subjects.

"Rightfully," they said to David through his messengers, "the throne of Saul belongs to Saul's son, Ishbaal."

"Sire," Ahitofel said when he heard Joab's account, "you should by rights attack and destroy both Ishbaal and Abner. Now!"

"That I cannot do, Ahitofel. I would violate my word not to cut off the seed of Saul from the House of Israel."

"Then, Sire, do the next best thing! Go north! Through Philistia. Manifest your power through some of the northern areas. Thrash some of the more rebellious tribes. Then withdraw south again. Perhaps Ishbaal and Abner will understand."

"I support that idea, David," Joab said quickly.

"Let's do it!" David decided. "Immediately."

Circumstances frustrated that decision, however. Shoshanna had a great crisis the day after David's coronation and hung between life and death for more than six weeks. By the time she was out of immediate danger, the rainy season had begun. David set the coming March as a new date for his "javelin diplomacy" in the north, but again he had to postpone leaving, this time because Ahinoam went into premature labor. It was well he waited because, at the end of the first week in March, she gave birth to a seven-month baby, a boy whom David named Amnon. David finally set out two weeks after Amnon's circumcision.

Before he left, Shoshanna begged him to detour to Moab on his way home and bring back Jesse's bones:

"Adonai will give me strength to wait for them, David. I am very tired and I would like to rest with my creator, but I cannot, I will not, until Jesse's bones are buried in Bethlehem, where I can rest beside him." David made a solemn promise to do as she asked.

Driving the yearly tribute of animals in front of him and accompanied by his Kerethites and Pelethites, David marched west into Philistia and up north to Gath. There he gave his yearly report to Achish. He found the Philistine friendly but cautiously reserved about David's becoming king of Judah.

"What is the next step, David?"

"What do you counsel, Achish?"

"First, what you are about to do—to awe the northern tribes with a show of strength. Then to seek out Abner and to make some arrangement with him. At Gaza, last week, we—the dukes—were warned by our instructions from Luqqawatna to proceed with extreme caution regarding the central highlands. Philistine memories are long. We do not forget what happened when we seized the sacred Ark. As you know, I have strong personal reasons to remember. The dukes are willing to wait. You still have time."

The interview lasted only an hour, and David went on his way through Philistia. He traversed the Plain of Sharon and, swinging east, entered Yezreel, camping at the entrance to the valley and setting out on particular forays. He expelled the families to whom Saul had given the houses and lands of his wife Ahinoam's family. He raided Dothan, Jezreel, and Horon, cities that had openly supported Saul and now stood with Abner and Ishbaal. In each place he destroyed the walls and killed every tenth male over twenty. He also took a sizable number of cattle and demanded a large payment of money for leaving each place. Then he set fire to their cornfields in farewell. By then it was the end of June. As yet he had no reliable information concerning the whereabouts of Abner and Ishbaal.

At the beginning of July he marched up to Nazareth. Here the wise elders and scholars received him with a gala welcome. They installed him in the official guest house, and all of them—including Malaki—turned out to acknowledge David as their future king.

"When Adonai anoints you king in the House of Israel, the

land will be blessed," Malaki told him. Although David was fascinated by Malaki, his principal purpose in coming to Nazareth had been to find the Witch of Endor. He had heard the story of Saul's having visited the witch the night before the battle of Gilboa, and how she had cast a spell over him, foredooming him to defeat. David wished to avenge Saul by killing the witch. Nathan, who spent long hours with Malaki, eventually found a man who could guide them.

"But," cautioned Nathan, "Malaki says you should not enter the house at Endor. Have Joab and some of his men bring the woman out, and do it in broad daylight." Fear of the occult was great among the Hebrews. "Before you do anything to her, listen to her, Malaki says. She was once the favorite of Adonai. She helped your father. Adonai does not easily repent of his choices, does he, O King?" And David smiled.

When he arrived with his retinue at Endor, David waited outside the eerie fissure while Joab and a company of Pelethites went in and returned shortly, carrying the inert figure of Shalama, whom they threw on the ground in front of David. He stood with the sword of Goliath in his hand, the tip toward the ground.

"Remove her veil, Joab," David ordered. Joab bent down and tore the cloth away, but her face was toward the ground. "Let me see your face, woman!" David said quietly. Shalama lifted her head and David found himself looking into a pair of heavy-lidded, faded blue eyes resting on pendules of wrinkled skin. The face was a serried arabesque of wrinkles that recorded some cup of unutterable bitterness that she had been forced to drink.

At last, Shalama thought, at last I see David!

"What is it you wish?" she asked him.

"The night before King Saul died, he came to you. What did you do to him?"

"He asked to speak with the shade of Samuel. I called up that prophet's shade, according to my art."

"Did he cast a spell on him?"

"No, my Lord David."

"What did Samuel tell the king?"

"I don't know. Samuel did not speak with the king. The shade of Samuel spoke with the king." David stopped, perplexed.

"My Lord David. Those we invoke are the powers of deceit—those who sleep with the Father of Lies. Samuel the Just sleeps in Adonai's care. What spoke as Samuel's shade—who knows? But the king asked me to tell you that he loved you, and to say to you these words: 'If you trust in Adonai, Adonai will trust in you.' That's all." She looked up at David fearlessly.

"One last question, woman. You—once you were called the holy woman of Petahyahu." He saw her eyes dilating with memories. "My father came to you. You helped him. Good help! Holy help! He said so all his life. What happened to you? Did you make an agreement with the spirits, with Eleb? Did you?" The question was a lethal one. Eleb was the chief of all the evil spirits whom warlocks, witches, magicians, sorcerers called up for nefarious purposes. A yes to that question and David would be obliged by the Law to kill her as she lay at his feet.

"No, Lord David. No, I didn't . . . Lord David, Adonai sends true prophets and false prophets, true seers and false seers. The true he sends to guide good men. The false he sends to misguide false men. I was sent to misguide false men. I did. Now, my Lord David, in your mercy, liberate me according to the Law, and send me back to Adonai, if he will have me."

There was a long silence. No matter how David turned the matter over in his mind, he kept running into blank walls. He could not see clearly. And he was afraid. "Tell me, woman, what you said to my father about me." He noticed the sudden delight in Shalama's eyes. "Tell me: What does it mean?"

Shalama closed her eyes and turned her head away. David and those near him could hear the half-whispered words: *"Amar Adonai . . . mashichi ca-ima yotzer gufleneshami . . . amar Adonai . . ."* She went on repeating the words. "Adonai said . . . my anointed one like a mother will form the body for my spirit . . ."

Joab—always ready for the quick dispatch—looked inquiringly at David. But his leader, abstracted, ignored him. He sheathed his sword and called over four of his men. Together they lifted Shalama and carried her to a camel litter.

"You are coming with us, Shalama. You will live in Nazareth and wait for Adonai. Joab! Put a torch to those houses."

As they rode westward to Nazareth, the smoke of Endor stained the sky. Figures of men and women ran out of the fissure, howling and falling on the ground, endeavoring to put out the flames that devoured them. David knew it was cruel, but a place of abomination had to be cleansed by fire.

On his return to Nazareth, the elders had news for David. Abner had fled with Ishbaal, Saul's son, to Mahanayyim, a fortified town in Jabesh-Gilead on the east bank of the Jordan. Ishbaal's name ("man of the Lord") had been changed to Ishbosheth ("man of shame") in keeping with the custom which dictated that men should reflect in their name any deep disgrace that had befallen their family. The death of Saul, his father, was such a disgrace. Abner, meanwhile, had sent messengers all over the north proclaiming Ishbosheth as king and successor to Saul.

"He knows you are here, my Lord David," the chief elder said. "They say he is raising an army to come and give you battle."

"I leave tonight for the south," David answered quietly. "Is there anything I can do for your people?"

"Yes, Lord David. Take Malaki with you. Saul blamed Malaki for having so few Nazarethites in his army at Gilboa. We fear for his safety. Perhaps if Malaki is gone Abner will leave us in peace."

"Men of Nazareth, you know I cannot fight Ishbosheth. And you know why. Take care of Shalama. She has very little time left."

"We will care for her, Lord David. And we will tell your story to all of Israel. Go in peace!"

David left with his army the next day, accompanied by Malaki. He descended the highlands as far as Giveon, then went east and down the west shore of the Salt Sea to the Eagle's Beak. There David crossed with ten companions to Mizpeh, saw Abikemosh, and retrieved Jesse's bones. A day later he was in Bethlehem, where he buried Jesse's remains beside those of his father, Obed. He was back in Hebron by the end of October.

By then he was the father of three more sons, already circumcised. Abigail, Maaka, and Haggith had given birth. Abigail's son was named Dodiel; Maaka's, Absalom; Haggith's, Adoniyahu. And those infants were bright lights in a sky that was otherwise dark for David: war with Abner and Ishbosheth impended and his mother was dying. About two weeks after his homecoming, word came from Nazareth that Shalama had died and been buried in her beloved Petahyahu.

Malaki settled into a new life in Hebron. His name meant "messenger" or "angel," and he soon showed himself to be both of these—and much more—to David. He identified everyone by voice and footstep. He relayed messages for everybody. He was consulted by Nathan and Gad and Abiathar. Malaki perceived David's moods merely by listening to his first greeting. Joab came to like him and extended to him a brusque protectiveness. "The little bastard," Joab called him, with that peculiar affection that otherwise loveless men sometimes display.

David had found that the blind seer carried a blessing with him. When he accompanied David, the mission generally was a success. So he became a sign of David's presence, and his name took on a heightened significance. He became "David's Malaki," and "the Doorman."

That winter, Shoshanna died in her sleep. When he was in Hebron, David visited her every night. On the last evening she said to him as he left: "Don't worry, David. You will have more protection soon." He thought she was referring to a northern tribe he was wooing and to the daughter of its chief elder. She was called Abital and was to be his next wife. But when Malaki sent his slave to wake him up at five o'clock in the morning, he knew something was wrong. He hurried to Shoshanna's room. Her body was still warm, but she was gone.

The next day he took her home to Bethlehem. The rain mixed with David's tears as they buried her beside Jesse. Malaki said: "Please, Lord David, weep no more. She is now in the bosom of Adonai. From there she will protect you."

David spent that winter training a new army of Judahite recruits, and at the beginning of March made his yearly visit to Philistia, carrying his vassal's tribute in slaves, animals, and money to Gath. He and Achish discussed the developing crisis. Ishbosheth, with Abner's influence and prestige, had been accepted as successor to Saul by the tribes of Ephraim, Issachar, Zebulun, Naphthali, Dan, Assher, and Manasseh. The Geshurites, the Ashurites, and the warriors of Jabesh-Gilead had also acknowledged Ishbosheth. This meant that David, as sovereign of Judah, could not venture much farther north than a line drawn from Gezer in the west to Jebus and Jericho in the east. This was bad enough. But what troubled the Pentarchy, and therefore Achish, was that the fearsome Ark of the Covenant was still at Kiryath-Yearim, just a few short miles from the ruined fortress of Gibea and within the strongly pro-Ishbosheth territory of Benjamin.

"We cannot lay a hand on that Ark," Achish told David. "And if Ishbosheth rebuilds Gibea, and lives near the Ark, the Pentarchy will not let us attack." He held up the stump of his leg to display his own dread of the Ark.

"Your strategy should be to wear down Ishbosheth's allies

by harassment. Cut off supplies. Prevent recruits from reaching Mahanayyim, so that he cannot strengthen his army. Assassinate chieftains who support him. Or corrupt them with gold. Fight minor battles. You say you've made a vow not to harm a hair of his head. Very well. But there are more ways than one to skin a goat! We must cripple him and Abner. Their territories should be made to fall like ripe oranges into our hands. Once that happens, we'll decide about the Ark—" He looked away for a moment. "Or perhaps Adonai will tell us what to do with it." He looked back, and his next question surprised David. "When am I going to see Nathan again?"

"Nathan?"

"Yes. Nathan. He's alive, isn't he?"

"Why, yes, but..."

"Let him come with you next time. I'd like to talk with him. And for the moment fear not. Gaza is holding. I'll warn you if there's a change."

"You once counseled me not to stay on as vassal, but to run. If it comes to that, where would I run to?" asked David.

"That was before I talked with Nathan, but I was thinking of Phenicia. You're still friends with Tyre and King Abibaal?"

"Yes, but the Pentarchy dominates Phenicia. I couldn't stay there."

"No. But their long ships could carry you across the Great Sea. There are many strange lands out there. Why not go and see Abibaal, anyway? He's old. His young son, Hiram, is of age now, and he's going to be king someday. You ought to get to know him. It's good policy."

"I have wanted to visit Tyre for some time. There is a Tyrian woman there called Barissa. I have learned, from Malaki and Nathan, that she inducted Saul into a dark compact that was one direct cause of his corruption and failure. She must die. Abibaal will root her out for me, if she is still alive."

"I thought," Achish said pointedly, "that Adonai said: 'Vengeance is mine!'"

"Achish!" David said heatedly. "Some things Adonai wills firmly—and inevitably they take place. Other things he seems merely willing to approve or permit. Achish, my friend, with all this talk of Adonai, one would think that you were a Hebrew!"

"Perhaps I am! Perhaps I am!" They both laughed at that, and David left for Hebron.

At a war council in mid-April that year, David proposed two moves: a blockade denying all supplies and reinforcements not only to Abner and Ishbosheth in Gilead but to all the Saulite tribes; and the military isolation of Kiryath-Yearim and the Ark.

To cut off the supplies was logistically simple. But the plan to isolate the Ark at Kiryath-Yearim was a hazardous undertaking. It grew out of a bold and totally unacceptable plan put forward by Joab. "Let's capture the Ark and the priests with it," Joab proposed. "Let's transport them all with the Ark down south here to Mamre. All of Israel will come running to you after that. The Ark is the only thing that stands between them and the Philistine pigs."

"I like the idea," David said slowly, "even though the priests and the prophets would be against it. The idea is fine. But on one point I will not budge. No one must touch the Ark with his hand. God knows, he might be killed instantly. We *all* might be killed instantly. The whole army! No!" He sat back, folded his arms, and was silent.

"How then do we capture it?" Ahimelek the Hittite asked plaintively. "Do you want us to stand around in a circle and say: 'Go away, wicked Abner! Avaunt there, Ishbosheth!'"

"Wait a moment! Call in the priest!" directed David. Abiathar was brought in. "Abiathar, tell us about Kiryath-Yearim."

"Ah, Kiryath-Yearim! Ah, yes!" Abiathar said ecstatically. "The Ark stands on a raised—"

"We know all that, Abiathar. I want to know what the rules of the tribes are for the Field of the Ark?"

"Ah, the rules of the tribes for the Field of the Ark. Ah, yes!" Abiathar took this theme up as ecstatically as ever. "Very strict! Very, very, very strict! Indeed strict, O King—"

"How strict?" David's eyes were hooded in leaden patience, but his voice was rasping.

"No one enters without permission of Abinadab. Once inside the enclave, you cannot—"

"How big is the enclave?"

"About the size of a large meadow. And once inside, you cannot be arrested, attacked, shot at, or otherwise assaulted."

"Those inside, what can they do?"

"Anything, except take the Ark. They can defend themselves, for instance—"

"Shoot arrows out, for example?"

"Yes."

"Priest! I thank you. You may go now."

Everyone in the council had seen the point of David's questions. They could isolate the Ark, so that none of the tribes would be able to visit it. They would be immune from attack.

Like every other decision of David's, the moment it was made, execution followed. The very next morning he rode up to Kiryath-Yearim with three thousand archers. But Abinadab, the chief priest, had a surprise for him.

"I was wondering how long it would take you to come here, Lord David. You are the only one who can protect the Ark now. Welcome, come in and take up your residence here."

From that day forward, until David became king of all Israel four years later, the Ark was ringed around with a guard of David's archers. By late June that year, the whole of Israel knew what had happened, and the word finally reached Abner and Ishbosheth: "David's men ring the Ark. No one can approach the enclave without risking his life."

The isolation of the Ark and the denial of supplies were two new pressures which saved David from attacking Ishbosheth and yet prevented Ishbosheth from strengthening himself. That August, when David's latest wife, Abital, gave him a son whom he called Shefatyahu, David began to feel for the first time that the tide was turning in his favor. If he could only keep the Philistine Pentarchy happy, he could foresee an end to his waiting.

But as things turned out, David himself had very little to do with the elimination of Ishbosheth, Abner, and the surviving Saulites. Only after his installation as king in Hebron did he learn the full facts about the remainder of Saul's family: that Abner had fled to Mahanayyim with what remained of Saul's treasure; that, all in all, about twenty-five hundred Saulites had gone with Abner, including Saul's wife, Ahinoam, his concubine, Rizpah, with her two sons by Saul, and Rizpah's two brothers. And David had to wait more years before he found out that Jonathan's son, Meribaal, who was lame in both feet, had fled with an old Saulite servant, Ziva, and taken refuge with Saul's old friend Machir. In keeping with the custom, Meribaal's name was changed to Mephibosheth. He and his wife and child, Mikha, remained in hiding for almost ten years.

Joab's advice to David had been that he track down Abner and Ishbosheth and kill them. David, by reason of his pact with Jonathan, refused to do that. But Ishbosheth and all with him were ill starred from the beginning. Over a period of seven years, David's prestige and power grew and spread. Ishbosheth skulked in Mahanayyim and never attracted the active allegiance of the northern tribes. And when Abner deserted him after a quarrel over Rizpah, whom Abner had married, his day was over. He and Abner finally attempted to placate David by restoring to him his first wife, Saul's daughter Mikhal. But it was misfortune for all three: Abner was assassinated by Joab with David's connivance; Ishbosheth was butchered in his bed by two of his own captains; and David took Mikhal into the obscurity of his harem. He wanted her there only because she was his.

Yet David could say honestly that during his Hebron period he had technically kept his promise to Saul and Jonathan. Personally, he never "cut off their seed." With the death of the last surviving son of Saul, the only genuine Saulite claimant to the throne of Israel, he believed control of all the land should fall easily into his hands, provided he could deal successfully with the Philistines. The danger from them, however, was of the greatest magnitude. As he entered his seventh year at Hebron, he was nominally king of that city, but really the vassal of Philistia and under ultimate sentence of death at Philistine hands.

The Horn of Power

In February of that seventh year, David's worry increased daily. In two weeks he had to make his annual visit to Gath, to pay his tribute, give an account of the past year, and outline his policy for the next one. The pentarchy would know by then about the death of Abner and Ishbosheth and its effect on David's power. It would be a time of maximum danger. Was he to wait? Was he to run? Was he to fight?

David had a deeper worry concerning Adonai. He thought over and over about the "body for his spirit" of which Shalama had spoken. What was it? And what did it mean to "form it"? Indeed, did these words have any meaning at all? Perhaps Shalama had been sent by Adonai as a false seer in order to deceive him?

He came to an abrupt decision one day after a talk with Malaki, his "angel" who sat perpetually at the door. David was entering his house when the blind seer called after him.

"Lord David! Lord David!" David stopped but didn't turn around. "Do what you must do. Adonai will do the rest."

"What must I do?" David was somewhat testy.

"Take all the parts of this land. Not merely Judah. Take them all. And bind them together into one compact body. Tie north and south together. Galilee is the head. The central highlands are the chest. The Shefela and Moab are the hips. Judah is the belly. Sinai and Edom are the legs. Phenicia and Ammon are the arms. Jebus is the navel. A man's body frame is compacted at the navel, not in the belly. The whole body is Israel. *Gufleneshami*, Adonai says. 'A body for my spirit.' So says Adonai."

David turned around and said wonderingly to the seer, *"Guf,* eh? A body? And my spirit? *Neshami?"*

"Do what you must do. Adonai will do the rest."

That evening David sent for Ahitofel. He wanted to be invited to spend a few days incognito at Ahitofel's country

354

villa. And would Ahitofel also arrange for two unnamed persons to join a large caravan going up to Jebus?

"Who else is going with us, my Lord David?"

"No one."

Ahitofel was both flattered and intrigued. Delighted at the prospect of secret moves in the game of power, he departed, and that very afternoon, Ahitofel's steward delivered an invitation for the following day to "my Lord David to spend as long as he wishes at the villa of Master Ahitofel, away from the cares of state."

The trip to Jebus was uneventful, and on the evening of their arrival David and Ahitofel dined with Uri.

"Do you want to visit Lassatha when we're finished?" Uri asked David.

"Not this time." David heartily wished otherwise, but it was imperative that they conclude their business and get back to Hebron as soon as possible.

Uri was actually relieved. "I cannot completely trust even my own servants and slaves," he told David. "Lassatha, of course, I would trust with my life, but Philistine informers are everywhere, and they distribute gold like cups of water. In fact I myself will soon have to leave before I come to some ill fortune."

"That is what we have come to discuss, Uri. Master Ahitofel is already aware of the issues." He went over his situation in detail, revealing also what Achish had told him about the fate the Philistines had in store for him. "So," he concluded, "if I wait, I'm a dead man. If I fight, I'm a dead man. But on our way here, Ahitofel and I had what we think is an excellent idea."

"The idea, Master Uri," Ahitofel said loftily, "is simple. Jebus is the most nearly impregnable of any city in the land. One could hold out here indefinitely. Besides, from it one could dominate all, I repeat *all*, the caravan routes. So if fight we must—and I'm not so sure we have to—my Lord David and I have concluded that he should take Jebus and make it his own city!"

"It will not be enough," Uri answered shortly. "Even if you could take it, which I doubt, in forty-eight hours the Philistines can surround this place with twenty corps of chariots. A wall of iron! Then they bring up their infantry. You would die in here hemmed in by an army of fifty thousand men. No, that wouldn't do at all!"

"Quite accurately said," the wily Ahitofel retorted. "And

so we concluded also. For your reasons, and for others of our own. Still, we believe we can take it, as we'll discuss in a moment. But there is another problem. Bethel, Hebron, Gilgal, Gibea, or Rama would seem good to Hebrews, but this city stinks in their nostrils. So we have a double problem. How render it inaccessible to a Philistine siege? How make it acceptable, even valuable, to the tribes?"

"It may seem nothing to you, Uri." David took up the argument. "But there is only one way to solve both those problems."

"What's that?"

"The Ark! The Ark of the Covenant. The Philistines will not attack the place where the Ark is. The tribes will gather around that same place!"

David sat back. "So we bring the Ark up to Jebus—"

"After you take Jebus!" Uri rejoined with spirit. "And that by no means sure."

"Yes, Master Uri," Ahitofel broke in. "But we have full confidence we can accomplish that with your help. I, of course, am no longer really moved by this Ark business." He sniffed. "But the people, the ordinary Hebrews, are. And, of course, the Philistines, being utterly primitive, are in fear of the Ark for their very foreskins!"

They ate dinner at that point. Uri served it himself—roasted lamb from Beraka in David's honor. When they had finished, Uri gave his views. To take the city of Jebus, he said, you would need to gain control of seven major points: the north gate, the government house, the battlements in their entirety, all five watchtowers, the Siloam pool and well, the Millo barracks, and the arsenal. He could guarantee the Siloam pool and well and the Millo barracks. But he and his men could not take the entire city. Even if you held all those major points, you would then have to go house by house and root out all Philistines, all Jebusites, and all other possible troublemakers. But how could you get the necessary troops into the city unnoticed to do this?

"Well," Ahitofel answered, enjoying himself, "we have thought about that too, and we think we have the solution— if, Master Uri, we have your help. We have the corps of Kerethites, all small men, all excellent swimmers. All magnificent at hand-to-hand combat. If my Lord David at the age of twelve was able to swim the shaft of Siloam, then I think the Kerethites can. They are all sons of fishermen in their native island in the Great Sea. They swim from the age of two."

"It's now late February," David came in, thinking out loud. "I'll need until September to train them. I'll probably send them to Bethlehem, to the Rabbit's Head, where I learned to swim underwater myself. In small groups so as not to attract attention. But it will take until September, not to speak of the other preparations."

"If your Kerethites can do it," Uri answered, "I can supply short swords and bows and arrows. But they'll have to bring their own armor."

"That's one reason why I need some months to train them," answered David.

"One more thing, my Lord David," Ahitofel broke in. "Suppose, just suppose the Philistines do the clever thing and attack you in Jebus before you get the Ark here, what then?"

David stared at Ahitofel. This one stumped him. He shook his head like a boxer who had just taken a hard blow. "I don't know. I don't exactly see..." He was silent. The two others watched him closely; they too were at a loss. Then David spoke again. "All I know is that this city is going to be my city, my eagle's nest, my Zion... Jebus will cease to be. It will be the city of David, Zion. And I suppose that, if we fail to get the Ark here in time, then it's all or nothing, my friends." His voice seemed listless to Ahitofel. But Uri could read it accurately. Twenty-five years before, standing above Siloam shaft, he had seen the same stillness on David's face, heard the same apparent listlessness in his voice. David was looking for his "signals" now.

"Yes," David said, expelling a sigh, "it's all or nothing," and his eyes sparkled as he contemplated the exquisite risk. "So I will strike first—right for the heart."

"Gaza, you mean?" The other two almost chorused the question, apprehension growing on their faces.

"No!" David lifted his eyebrows and gave a quick smile. "No. Not Gaza. Gaza is secondary. Luqqawatna!"

"Luqqawatna!" Ahitofel and Uri looked at each other in total astonishment.

"The same! A friend told me once that the Pentarchy and all its power would dry up like a fig in the sun if Luqqawatna ceased to exist."

"Yes, yes, yes," Ahitofel replied. "To be sure, to be sure. But Luqqawatna? Luqqawatna? Who knows where it is or what it's like? We know the name, that's all! Who is in Luqqawatna? What is the center of power in Luqqawatna? Why does the Pentarchy depend on Luqqawatna? What does Luqqawatna hold that is so terrible in power? How does one *get* there? How does one penetrate it? We know none of this."

"I don't know, my friends. Neither does my friend, I suspect. But we've got to find out if we want to survive." David spoke slowly and deliberately. "Sometime in August, Uri, I shall send Master Ahitofel to go over all the final plans. Are you with us? Good! We will have just one dark night for our work. And it must be fast! Uri, my friend, we cannot succeed without you. I will never forget this."

"David, my friend, I cannot survive here much longer. You offer me a way out."

Back in Hebron, they found delegations from some of the tribes already waiting for David. Within two weeks they were all there. Representatives from the Twelve Tribes, the elders of the principal cities, the chiefs of the various guilds, the elders of leading families. The speech they all made in their own words came down to a simple acknowledgment of facts: "You, David, are Hebrew of the Hebrews. Like us. You are bone of our bone, flesh of our flesh. You slew the giant. Under Saul, you led us always to victory over our enemies. And Samuel told us that the word of Adonai was this: 'David is anointed to be the general of all my armies.' Your name is *davidum*. Your destiny is *davidum*. You are our commander. Our leader! We will have you as our king!"

David listened to them all patiently. His answer was couched carefully and categorically. "If you want me as your king, go back to your tribes and your homes. Let this matter remain between you and me. But meet me on the first day after the high holy days in September, at Mamre. And then, if you are still of this mind, swear allegiance to me. If you accept me then, I will consent to be your king."

This response produced a marveling wondering in his audience. For he said it with obvious sincerity, and with a decisiveness and a self-confidence that promised strong leadership, yet with a mildness that augured well for his rule. The powers of the Hebrews talked among themselves: "If he thus patiently can wait, if he thus humbly can give us time to think and consult each other, if he thus sparingly approaches our offer and shows no lust for power, what manner of king will we have in him, do you think, my brothers?" "An angel of Adonai who will walk in the ways of justice and mercy," others answered. And some excitable ones rushed around shouting: "Oh, men of Israel, to your tents! We will be one people as

Adonai our God is one God!" Ahitofel stroked his chin and whispered to David: "Wisdom, my Lord David! What wisdom! All the ordinary people are hungry for you!"

At the end of March, David reached Gath for his annual visit. Besides his Kerethites, he had brought Nathan with him. He was surprised when Achish met him at the gate of the city. Achish tried to warn him by looks and David understood. He found the entire Pentarchy council waiting for him in the council chambers.

"Well, my Lord David," Duke Shekelath said when David finished his report, "you have certainly done everything you promised to do. The Pentarchy has been enriched by your yearly tribute. Abner and Ishbosheth are dead, although there is a poor lame grandson of Saul hiding out with his nurse in some Galilean village." David made a mental note: he had thought that all Jonathan's seed had perished.

"Now," Shekelath said, verbally closing one door and opening another, "how do we proceed from here?"

"With caution, my Lord Duke," David replied. He felt the silence. This was not the answer they had expected. A harsh look descended over the long noses, heavy eyes, and jutting chins.

"Caution? But haven't the tribes offered you the crown? Get it! Bring us their allegiance." Shekelath looked around, a great gleam in his eyes. The other dukes nodded.

"There's just one detail, my Lord Duke. There is the Ark."

"The Ark," Shekelath repeated, raising his eyebrows in displeasure. "What do you propose?"

"You all know, my Lord Dukes," David went on smoothly, "that I have maintained my troops around the Ark day and night for years.

"I propose to persuade the priests to transport the Ark to a very remote place in the land. I thought six months a reasonable time. There's a lot of diplomacy involved."

"To where, for instance?" several voices demanded at once.

"The top of Mount Thabor, for instance?"

"Not there. We have mapped that for a lookout fortress."

"Well, then, the middle of the Eastern Desert?"

"Excellent idea, my Lord David," Shekelath said sententiously. "Shall we say by year's end, then, this annoyance will be removed and isolated?"

"The end of the year will be fine," David said with an air of indifference.

"One thing more, my Lord David. The Pentarchy has two restrictions for you. First, on no account do you touch Jebus. Jebus is already ours by—er—proxy. Two, when there is a crowning ceremony of you as lord of all the land, the Pentarchy must be advised and there must be Philistines present—in disguise, surely. You will observe both of these regulations." David nodded assent.

Achish spoke up. "My Lord David and I are going to spend a week together in the country."

"Fine," Shekelath said. "Fine. Now, my Lord Dukes, we must return to Gaza. My Lord Achish! My Lord David! We bid you good day!"

When they were alone, Achish dropped his façade. "Why did you promise to settle events to their satisfaction by the end of the year?" he asked. "Are you mad? Don't you know that you've set the date of your own death?"

"Do not worry for the moment. I have a friend waiting outside—Nathan. You wished to have him as your guest. He's here. I will not go to the country with you. Nathan will. You remember we discussed a visit to Tyre? Well, I'm going to Phenicia. King Abibaal is expecting me!"

Achish's face cleared and he began to smile. David had chosen to flee before the Pentarchy seized him. At least he would not be tortured and sacrificed in front of those silly statues of Dagon. "When will you sail?" he asked David quietly.

David looked at him before answering, knowing that Achish was ignorant of his purpose. Should he tell him now? He decided against it.

"Oh, sometime in late September or the beginning of October." Then, jocularly, "Do you want to come along? They say the mussels at Massilia are delicious." That port of call would later be known as Marseilles. Achish smiled.

"To spend my old age with you, David!" he said softly as they went out to meet Nathan. "That would be quite a pleasure!"

David's delegation to Tyre had preceded him there by several days. Ahitofel had conducted all the official talks with Abibaal. Hushai the Arkite had searched out Barissa. By the time David arrived, all arrangements had been made.

"We've found the woman—Barissa. We know where she lives and every move she makes. We can take her any time we like," Hushai reported. "I've hired some men here. The thing will be done after our departure. She will know why she's being done to death, but she will never hear your name."

Old King Abibaal received David magnificently. Tyre was a unique city built on two large chains of rocks just off the coast. The city proper, situated on those rocks, was a fabulous place, with gaily painted villas and monuments, and only reached by boat. On the northern side was a natural harbor; and there David marveled at the lines of closely packed ships, some two hundred of them, at the wharves and jetties and loading ramps and out across the harbor from one side to another. The harbor swarmed with sailors from over two dozen nations. The people of Phenicia were children of the sea, and the sea was part of all they said and did. But they were much more than a nation of successful sailors.

They were uninhibited dancers and painters and poets. All these castes were organized into guilds flanked by the sculptors and metalsmiths. The king traditionally maintained one whole street for each guild. Their contemporaries said of the Phenicians that they excelled in four things: in being happy in love, laughing at fate, writing poems, and making money from water.

The Phenician smile and laugh were the outcome both of their discovery of romantic love and of commercial success. For some inexplicable reason these particular Semitic nomads took to the sea like porpoises, playfully yet intelligently. At the time of David's visit, Phenician caravels were nosing their way down the west coast of Africa and across the Indian Ocean. Others were touching on the Atlantic coasts of England and Ireland. And still more were exploring the land of the midnight sun in Scandinavia.

David was given a tour of the entire city, but what interested him most was the Phenician fleet. He boarded the heavy troopship, the speedy scout ship, the transports, the long sailing ships, the high-pooped ships the Phenicians used for northern seas. He asked all sorts of questions: how many men could fit in this or that ship, the speed of each type of ship, the condition of wind and tide in the autumn, the use of oars and sails, the relative distances of lands across the Great Sea. His questions were endless. Abibaal was very shrewd. He and his twenty-four-year-old son, Hiram, found David's questions intriguing. "Why did he want to know this?" they asked each other.

"My Lord David," Abibaal said at their final meal, "I have the impression you wish to take a sea voyage."

"O King, that is the final subject I wanted to discuss with you. But I want to do it within the framework of an alliance between us, an offensive and defensive alliance, a mutual treaty."

"Yes, yes, that is my wish, too. We will continue to discuss it. But this voyage of yours, is it long or short?"

"It would take your military transports three or four days, if wind and tide were favorable—and if I understood your answers."

"Come with us, David, to the map room," Abibaal said. Inside there, David put his left index finger on Tyre and his right index finger on the coast behind which lay Luqqawatna.

"The Land of the Philistines!" Hiram breathed in awe. "But, Father, we are forbidden to sail anywhere near there. We have no maps of the harbors or reefs or shoals." David turned and faced father and son.

"The fact is, O King, unless we do something, we will both be swallowed by Philistia—and within a year." Both men nodded. They knew this too. "I was informed about Luqqawatna and what it signifies for the Philistines by a very dear and loving friend of mine. He did not tell me much, but he did say enough for me to know that as long as Luqqawatna stands firm, the Philistines cannot be beaten. Destroy Luqqawatna's strength—whatever it is—and the Philistines are finished. I now propose," David went on, pointing to where Luqqawatna lay, "to make one quick raiding attack there. To cut Philistia off forever from its base. I must transport at least seven thousand men and their weapons. The only times suitable for such an attack by such a small group of men are the Philistine carousals, which are held at each season one week before the new moon. They are totally off guard at that time. Can you— will you—help me? If you don't, it is exile or death for me and all mine. It will be exile or death for all of you, too, sooner or later."

"You know, my Lord David," Abibaal said, sitting down by the map, his face grave and lined, "I love only this one." He looked at young Hiram. "And I have been worried about his future. I have not been remiss. I have built a palace for him across the sea in a safe place"—he jabbed at the map, resting one finger on the coast of northern Africa, where the city of Carthage would later stand—"called New City. Oh, it's only a trading post now, but it could become important." He smiled at Hiram with pride and pleasure. "I would like my son to live, you see, my Lord David!

"Now, you come with a plan which takes my breath away. And, frankly, if you were anybody else, I would reject it with

a laugh. But you"—he paused and looked into David's eyes—
"you are not anybody else."

Hiram broke in. "Between now and September's end,
Father, let me take a fast sculling ship and find a suitable
landing place on that coast. I'll chart the place."

"We intend to attain Luqqawatna via the river which flows
in from the west coast of Luqqawatna country, Hiram," David
said. "We don't know what men or arms we will find there,
but we do have maps of its physical features."

They walked back to the dining room. Abibaal was silent
for a long time. "Is it this or else?" he finally asked.

"Yes, O King. This or nothing!" David answered.

"I suppose," Abibaal said finally, "such times come once
or twice in a century. And a man's behavior is a measure of
the man in such circumstances. For these are the highest circumstances. They involve heaven and earth and the underworld. All the powers that rule us. Very well!" He suddenly
brightened up. "Very well, young men! It's decided! Now"—
raising his voice to his servant—"where are those girls, my
good fellow? And the wine? Is there no more wine left in my
palace? More wine, I say!" Hiram and other Phenicians broke
into their famous laugh, and the celebration went on.

Just after dawn on the first ordinary day following the high
holy days of September, David, accompanied by his chief advisers and surrounded by his Kerethites and Pelethites, arrived
at the shrine of Mamre, outside Hebron, the place where Father
Abraham had talked with Adonai. Every one of the Tribes of
Israel, all the major cities and towns, and each of the great
families and guilds had sent representatives. And all had one
intent: to crown David king of the land and leader of their
armies. No representatives of the Pentarchy were present.
David had not sent word to the dukes.

When they had crowned him, Ahitofel read David's coronation proclamation: "I will rid the land of the scourge of the
Philistines. I will establish an army, appoint local judges, reg-
ulate the caravan trade, feed the poor, liquidate robbers, and
install the worship of Adonai from Dan to Beersheva and from
Jordan to the Great Sea. Adonai, our God, Adonai is One!"

By midday, David had returned to Hebron. His Kerethites
and Pelethites departed immediately from Mamre, following
a circuitous route to join a force of twelve thousand infantry
who already lurked in the hills east of Jebus. By now, David
hoped, the machinery of his plans would be in full action at

Jebus. He had a quick meal and left Hebron about two o'clock in the afternoon, so as to reach the assembly place by nightfall.

At about the same time Hushai the Arkite, at the head of a three-hundred-man camel regiment, rode up boldly to the north gate of Jebus. His brazen request: "Open the gate of the city for King David!"

The Jebusites laughed loudly. "Go back," they yelled at him, "and tell that smelly bandit that he can come when the blind begin to see and the lame begin to walk!" Hushai, according to plan, led his troops back into the hills and set up camp in plain view of the watchtowers. When night fell, he lit large campfires. His position would always be visible to the Jebusites from their walls. Their attention would be concentrated on him. Meanwhile, down in the valleys surging around Jebus, Joab and a detachment of javelin throwers on mules patrolled the western passes making sure that no emissaries from Jebus could escape westward nor any messengers from the Philistines reach Jebus. David, with his Kerethites and a force of twelve thousand, lay in hiding east of the city. Dispatch carriers passed between Hushai, David, and Joab every two hours.

An hour or so after complete darkness fell, David led his first batch of two hundred Kerethites to the pool of Siloam beneath the Millo barracks at the foot of the eastern cliff of Jebus. One by one the little men plunged into the pool and swam away into the shaft. Inside the city, at the top of the shaft, Uri waited with his Hittites. When the head of the first Kerethite, Makrion, the commander, appeared, Uri threw down the saddle rope to him. The Kerethite slid it over his shoulders, sat in the loop, and was hauled up. Before they had him up on the ledge of the shaft, another Kerethite appeared, gasping and blowing water. The Hittites threw down several straight ropes knotted at intervals. Very soon the rounded wall of Siloam shaft was swarming with Kerethites climbing like monkeys. Each was led away immediately to the barracks to be provided with weapons. It took almost two hours and a half for all eight hundred to reach the top. But well before midnight the Kerethites were fed, armed and ready.

Uri and Makrion divided them into companies of sixty, each in charge of a Hittite captain who knew the walls. When all were ready, the first took the government house, overpowering the guards and killing everyone inside quickly and noiselessly. Jebus now had no president and no privy council. Next came the two south-wall watchtowers. Four Kerethites dressed in

Jebusite armor scaled the ladders at each tower. A few seconds' quick scuffling disposed of the unsuspecting guards. The arsenal was more difficult. Uri himself appeared there on the pretext that he wished to lodge a valuable assignment of iron spears. One Jebusite managed a scream before he died, but it was lost in the night.

The last objective was the north gate. Again Uri went first. He offered to help the officer in charge handle those Hebrews on the hills, and went with him to view the situation from the top of the tower. There Uri and his men took the officer and his six guards by surprise and killed them. Then they opened the tower to the waiting Kerethites. One by one the Kerethites entered and stormed the guardroom, slaughtering the remaining guards as they slept. This done, they flooded over the battlements of the city.

At a signal from Uri, the battle for Jebus was on. David with his twelve thousand and Hushai with his camel corps galloped up to the north gate, now wide open and unguarded, and poured into the streets of Jebus. A sudden rising roar of battle filled the night air. Jebusites sleeping in their houses woke to the screams of fighting men, the clash of weapons, and the thunder of hooves.

By the time the men in the houses rushed out with their weapons, it was no use. The main streets and the marketplaces were filled with David's men, and they outnumbered the Jebusites. The battlement guards were picked off by archers or killed by what seemed to be endless groups of little men wearing tight-fitting helmets and wielding strange short swords. It was only a matter of time before all the Jebusite soldiers were dispatched. Before daybreak the city was totally conquered, and a great tower of corpses rose in the cesspools of Hinnom.

"This city," David announced, "will henceforth be called Zion—the nest."

When the sun rose, David, who was directing cleanup procedures from the government house, stood up, put on his armor, and went outside. It was a bleak morning. High above he could see the still form of Shibtai, the vulture, watching the city. David knew the story. Every day the Jebusites threw Shibtai a body—some slave that had died naturally or been killed the night before. That practice would now come to an end. He mounted his camel and, followed by his Pelethites, galloped to Kiryath-Yearim to bring back the Ark of Adonai and install it in the city. After the success of the night attack and the taking of Jebus, he was jaunty, even arrogant. It was his own decision to fetch the Ark, and he did not even consult the sacred Ephod. Hadn't Adonai already delivered the city into his hands?

At Kiryath-Yearim he talked with the priests. Abinadab was dead. Zadok, a friend and admirer of David, was in his place. He would be delighted if the Ark were in safekeeping within the walls of David's city. The priests, all of them, would go along. The priests loaded the Ark on an oxcart and all set out. Within two hours they would be safe within the city with the Ark. They would be impregnable!

It may have been the curious half-light of dawn, the uneven track, or perhaps the hand of Adonai. Whatever the cause, somewhat over a mile from their destination, the four oxen pulling the precious load stumbled. They were crossing the track at the opening of a dried-up river bed. The oxen may have taken fright because at that moment Shibtai swooped down and swept away again in a malevolent rush of wings. The Ark started to slide off the cart. Uzzah, one of David's trusted officers, automatically steadied the Ark with his left hand. And Uzzah dropped dead on the spot.

David called a halt, wiped the cold sweat from his forehead, and reflected. Perhaps Adonai was displeased. Or angry. Or offended by some undetected impurity. Perhaps he had not yet accepted David as his anointed. It appeared, David concluded, that Adonai wanted him to remain in the valley of contention. And David did not want any more of his trusted officers to be punished for what might have been David's own offense. His plans would have to go ahead without the protection of the Ark.

Hushai the Arkite, who knew the area well, told of a very pious man near there, a farmer called Obededom. Better leave the Ark on his farm, Zadok counseled, until Adonai made his mind clear. Adonai would tell David when to bring the Ark up to the city. So they turned aside and deposited the Ark in Obededom's largest barn. David would have to wait a while longer. He rode back to Jebus, held council with his officers, put Uri in charge of the city, took some food, and within two hours was gone with his Kerethites and Pelethites to Phenicia. They stopped only to refresh their camels and mules and to collect some fresh water. By noon the following day they were riding into Tyre. Abibaal and Hiram were expecting them.

"Five nights from now, David," Abibaal said, "there will be no moon. And when you get to Luqqawatna it will be the height of the Philistine autumn carousal. It's either now or in three months' time."

"I do not have three months," David answered. "I will be under sentence of death in less than a week, when the Philistines find out I've taken Jebus. I can't get the Ark into the city. I must destroy their power now. It's our only chance."

Some time after midnight four days after their departure from Tyre, eleven Phenician transports arrived at a place about five miles from the mouth of the principal river on the west coast of Luqqawatna. Hiram, on his scouting trip, had discovered vast stretches of reeds in the delta marshland where they could hide the long, low-decked ships that had brought David's Kerethites and Pelethites.

In the covered cabin of David's ship sat twelve young men. This was Abibaal's gift to David: the team of Mesopotamian tumblers which Abibaal had purchased some years before for the amusement of his court. When David explained his plan for getting into Luqqawatna, Abibaal thought that the tumblers would fit in admirably. Actually, they were to become the key element to its success.

While the ships were still out of sight of the coast and its lookout stations, the Tyrian crews had struck sail and stepped down the masts, so that each ship could be rowed into the tall delta reeds to nestle there unnoticed. They lay in hiding all that first day. The following evening, after sundown, five more ships arrived loaded with archers.

Some eight miles up the river was Luqqawatna city itself. When darkness covered the river mouth and the land, the crews set up the masts and spread their sails. They sailed to the river mouth and started up the river, running in front of a strong breeze and aided by the strokes of muffled oars. Within three hours they came around a bend in the river and could see the lights of Luqqawatna. But in the moonless night they could not make out any details of its towers or buildings. A small party of men landed downstream from the landing stages, stole up on the few guards there, and quickly garroted them. The ships were then signaled in. As quickly as one emptied its human cargo, it drew away and another eased into its place. The empty transports then went down river to lurk around the bend. The sails and masts were again removed.

David and his men had fixed arrangements. If they had not returned one hour before sunrise, or if they were in danger of detection themselves, the ships were to put out to sea and wait one day near the coast. If no one appeared by then, they were to sail for home as fast as they could with wind and tide.

With his eight hundred Kerethites and eleven hundred Pelethites and the archers in safe hiding among the woods along the river bank, David readied his men for the attack. They had been over the plans dozens of times. There was one Pelethite, Harkath, who years before had been in Luqqawatna as a member of Duke Shekelath's bodyguard. With his help, David had mapped out the mode of attack. Harkath and those he consulted in Tyre spoke of the Great Temple, and in particular of the Globe Room in the Great Temple. If there was any central source of Philistine power in Luqqawatna, it must be in the Great Temple and, specifically, the Globe Room. Harkath knew this much: "In the Globe Room, they meet for all solemn occasions. The priests with the famous high priest." And with whatever else might be there.

David had been informed that, apart from its ordinary citizens, Luqqawatna normally housed approximately eight to ten thousand Philistine infantrymen, with another fifteen thousand in the large barracks just to the south. But David's objective was not to take the city, but to destroy the Great Temple and get away without being detected. The one advantage he had was that the temple stood behind the north wall. Had it been in the center of the city, it would have been a thousand times more difficult to reach. But even so, Harkath told him, the lowest row of windows in the temple wall was well over forty or fifty feet—Harkath was guessing—above ground level.

David, Joab, and the tumblers set out, wriggling along from bush to bush, from tree to tree, David in front, the tumblers immediately after him in single file, and Joab at the rear, paying out a black guide line as he went. They took almost an hour to cover eight hundred yards and reach a spot a stone's throw from the temple wall. Behind them were the archers, following Joab's guide line. After the archers came the Kerethites. The archers distributed themselves along the bushes and trees facing the wall. They were there to cover the retreat.

Now David could see the brooding bulk of the enormous round tower heaving up into the night sky. The row of windows was visible. David's heart sank. The height looked more like sixty feet. But it was too late now. He turned back, whispered to the leading tumbler, Banipal: "Keep your best man until last. He may have to jump a few feet!"

"That's me!" Banipal grinned at him in the darkness. "And if I fall, try to catch me, please!"

Then the operation began. In utter silence. The first three tumblers ran forward and took up positions. Then one by one, first at intervals of some ten seconds, then fifteen and twenty-five and increasing each time, the tumblers ran forward noise-lessly and climbed up on the shoulders of the preceding one. The intervals were long and excruciating for the last four tumblers. As Banipal's turn came, David tied a thin rope around his waist. Banipal ran and started to climb. David watched the wriggling blur climb the human ladder. He waited. Dimly he could make out Banipal's figure finally standing on the shoulders of the last man. Before David realized it, Banipal had jumped. The row of windows was actually some short distance from his hands, and without that jump, there was no way of reaching the window sill. David saw him dangling by his hands from the sill of the central window in the row. He saw him disappear. Banipal was inside! The other tumblers quickly undid their human pyramid, came back, and took cover. David turned and nudged Joab.

Joab ran forward to the wall, seized the dangling rope, gave it two short jerks, and tied a heavier rope to it. Then Banipal from above started to haul it up. Joab watched the heavier rope mount. When it was near its end, he tied a rope ladder to it, and sent it up. Then he ran back to David.

The rope ladder was in place. David began to climb. When those on the ground saw him disappear through the window, the Kerethites started to mount, one after the other.

David found himself on a wide, circular gallery that ran around the inside of the tower. It was almost an hour past midnight when all nineteen hundred Kerethites and Pelethites were within the gallery. David now had a little less than five hours to accomplish the mission.

While his men were still climbing in, David had explored the gallery. There was only one doorway. A staircase wound down and away into the darkness. When Joab, the last to arrive, was with him, David started down that stair with the sword of Goliath unsheathed. One by one the soldiers fell behind him. David had counted more than fifty steps before he reached a fork in his path: the steps ran down farther to the left; to the right, through an open doorway, he and Joab could see an altar, a statue of Dagon, a row of thrones facing two double rows of high-backed chairs. There was nobody there. A red light burned in front of the statue of Dagon. In the far wall they could see seven doors set close to each other. They listened. There was no sound. Even the wind was muffled within that tower. But from the city the faint echoes of singing voices and martial music wafted through the thick walls. David looked around at Joab, gesturing close to Joab's face, his index finger pointing to the stairs.

David was about to start down when he felt Joab tugging at his sleeve. He looked around. Joab held something in his hand. He peered at it, mystified. He put out his hand and touched it. The moment he felt the hard round heads of the stones, he knew what it was: the Ephod! Joab! Hardhearted, unbelieving Joab! He, not David, not Abiathar, had thought of the Ephod. Joab slipped the sacred stole over David's head and let it fall softly on David's shoulders. He reached out and touched Joab on the cheek. It was the first and last time in their long association these two men displayed any emotion toward each other. Then David started down the staircase into the yawning darkness.

Suddenly all of them, from David at the head of the descending file of men up to the last Pelethite at the end of the file, realized they were listening to a faint medley of sounds coming from deep within the tower, but no one could make out what they were. The sounds did not rise and fall. Rather they seemed to come nearer and then to distance themselves again, as if produced by projectiles that whizzed by. At their loudest—and that was still faint—the sounds produced a certain confusion in each man. They had barely adjusted to this anxiety when David and Joab passed the word that they had seen a ray of light ahead of them.

David was the first to reach the bottom and look around the corner of the staircase wall. Ahead of them was a wide, long room or hall, rectangular in shape, with a high ceiling, lit by a series of oil lamps on the side walls. At this moment they could hear a buzz of conversation from the other end of the hall. David turned and whispered instructions to Joab. The word passed. The main body of the Pelethites remained behind and the Kerethites went into action immediately.

As quietly and as quickly as they could, they entered the hall, lining up in twenty rows, each one ten men deep, forming themselves into the Kerethite shell phalanx. The shields locked into each other, forming a shell of metal five feet high to provide a roofing over the heads of David, Joab, and some forty Pelethites. As the first shell phalanx advanced down the hall, another two hundred Kerethites formed a second one, and another forty Pelethites took cover beneath it. The two phalanxes moved slowly down the long hall toward the far end, the Pelethites falling into formation behind the second phalanx. Peering through the slits between the shields, David saw heavy

wooden double doors ahead. As they approached them, Pelethites leaped out of formation and extinguished all but one of
the oil lamps, creating almost total darkness. A command from
David and one Pelethite rose from his cover and flung a javelin
that struck the doors resoundingly and fell to the floor.

They heard the sound of curt commands spoken in Philistine
on the other side of the doors, and then running feet. Someone
was unbarring the doors on the other side. David, with a sudden
thought, opened his chest armor and slid the Ephod beneath
it. If there was fighting he did not want the Ephod damaged.
At David's command the front of the phalanx opened wide.
The double doors opened. A stream of armed Philistines—
perhaps twenty in all—rushed out into the darkness and into
the waiting jaws of the phalanx, before they realized what was
happening to them. A fierce, quick hand-to-hand combat took
place, while the phalanx as a whole moved up to the double
doors. A shower of javelins from behind the phalanxes sped
in through the doorway and struck the Philistine soldiers rushing
forward. David shouted for the phalanxes to dissolve and, followed by the Kerethites, headed into the inner room.

It was obviously an anteroom, low-ceilinged, round, lit by
the usual lamps, and large enough to contain a guard of about
a hundred Philistines. Now the fighting began in earnest, David
and Joab in front, the Kerethites all around them, the Pelethites
picking off their targets with those light javelins. One by one
the Philistines were overcome by the superior numbers of
David's men and the fierceness of their attack. When the last
Philistine guard was cut down, a sudden silence fell on them
all. They looked around for David.

In front of them David and Joab could see red-and-black
brocade curtains hanging over a narrow doorway. Behind those
curtains, surely, lay their objective. David looked at Joab and
lifted his sword. Just as he was about to advance, the curtains
parted silently. A figure David recognized as Kalkodon the
high priest emerged and stood there looking at them. He was
as bland and expressionless as on that day seven years ago
when David had faced him at the council meeting in Gaza.
Kalkodon stared at David for a few moments before speaking.

"You, David of Bethlehem, you must know that to desecrate
this place means death." David's deepest instinct told him to
answer nothing. He advanced two paces and stood quietly. The
others pressed behind him. Kalkodon, still with the calm, blank
look, kept his eyes on David. He spoke again.

"Within these walls is a power no mortal can fight." Kal-

kodon's eyes never left David's. Now David, followed by Joab
and the others, walked steadily toward the high priest, swords
pointing menacingly. Joab turned around once and caught the
eye of the Pelethite commander. A second later, two javelins
hurtled over the heads of the advancing men and struck Kalkodon in the chest. On their impact, a look of intense pain and
shock cloaked those bland features. The high priest's hands
came up and touched the handles of the protruding javelins.
He looked at them unbelievingly. The look of pain gave way
to bewilderment. His mouth opened and blood poured out.
Kalkodon in his agony stretched up on the tips of his toes,
whirled around, and fell backward over the curtains, tearing
them down with the weight of his fall.

The advancing men walked on over his body. David and
Joab were the first to enter that last room. It was huge and
perfectly hemispherical, made of some black stone like basalt.
All around its enormous dome, circles and triangles of silver
glittered in the light of a great fire burning in its center, its
flames ascending and entering a round chimney hole in the
vaulted ceiling. Seated on a low stool by that fire, its back to
the Hebrews, was the figure of what appeared to be a wide-
shouldered, white-haired man. All around them in the Globe
Room were those faint sounds—hissing, whistling, moaning,
clicking, rushing, swishing—like the sound of thousands of
little bodies rushing through thousands of narrow passages.
David held up his hand to call a halt.

"If you look upon my face, you will not live, David of
Bethlehem. You have neither the authority nor the strength to
confront me. Your sins have given me power over you. Over
all of you." The voice was granular in timbre, deep in tone.
It filled, or rather occluded, all space, rasping out each syllable
with a thumping resonance painful to the ears. "If you retire
now with your men, you can have much glory from my hands."

Joab was the first to sense the effect of that voice upon
himself. In the sudden heaviness of his body and the lassitude
seeping into his mind, the old warrior saw danger to his fighting
prowess. And all his life Joab had relied only on that prowess.
He turned with a growing helplessness, looking at David, his
eyelids paining him, his eyes filled with desperate fear, his
throat contracting. One glance at David was sufficient: he was
obviously falling beneath the same terrible, invisible burden.
Joab swung his gaze with aching difficulty around the room
at the soldiers crowding in behind him. The same was happening to them. Strong men were twitching like palsied beings,

their legs buckling, the weapons falling out of their hands.
They heard that voice again.

"The Power! The Power! No mortal can resist it. The Power!
The Power!" The seated figure was slowly starting to swivel
around, all the while repeating those words.

Joab tried to speak to David. He couldn't. He dropped his
sword, stumbled over to David, tore at David's breastplate with
weakening fingers. David, even in the agony of resisting that
baleful influence, understood what Joab was trying to do. The
Ephod! The Ephod! How had he forgotten the Ephod? Together
they tore at David's breastplate.

The voice suddenly changed from its deep, thumping, der-
isive rasping to a rising scream. "Stop! You miserable creatures
born in a bed! Stop!" The scream rose higher and higher. "It's
no use! Stop!" But they had the Ephod out. It hung over David's
breastplate, its red stones shining and smiling at the flames of
the fire. Pandemonium broke loose. Every man in the Globe
Room felt some invisible release from the fearful pressure and
binding heaviness that had fallen upon him. And in his growing
relief, every man started shouting. The screaming words still
coming from the figure in the center soared away in a jumble
of clamorous voices. David advanced, swordless, the Ephod
gleaming on his chest.

"O Adonai!" he shouted. "O Adonai! O Adonai! Holy!
Holy! Holy!" It was all he could remember to say. It seemed
to come spontaneously, as if he had rehearsed it at a now
unremembered moment. The cry was taken up by Joab, by
those nearest to Joab, and then by all. "O Adonai! O Adonai!
Holy! Holy! Holy!"

As David advanced, the figure seated on the stool stood up,
whirling around, its back to the fire. David had one momentary
look into the eyes that seemed to have nothing human in them,
then the fire advanced, swallowing it up. As it disappeared into
the flames, David heard the last words of a scream that ended
in a threat: ". . . return, I, the immortal. . . ."

Then they saw the flames licking their way hungrily toward
them. David stopped and shouted in alarm, "Out of here! All
of you! Quickly!" Retrieving their weapons, they rushed out
of the Globe Room, followed by smoke and flames. David
passed down to the back, and from there he led a mad dash
through the double doors, up the long hall, into the winding
staircase, and up to the gallery. The smoke was with them
everywhere, the flames following behind. Their descent to the
ground from that row of windows was agonizing for all. The

fire was crackling in the deep interior of the temple tower, feeding on its wooden floors, staircases, and room frames. Wreathing smoke was everywhere. The heat was almost unbearable. By the time the last man descended the rope ladder, the flames were eating away at the window frames and shooting higher and higher through the upper stories, out through the roof toward the night sky.

From Luqqawatna a strange sound arose: a loud keening and crying. David left the archers, as he had planned, to cover their retreat to the river bank. But they never had to fire an arrow. No Philistine guards appeared. There were no pursuers. The temple tower was a huge conical mass of smoke and flames as they boarded the ships. But all the while from the city of Luqqawatna the only sound that came was that dreadful wail of sadness and mourning. The heart of Philistine power and the life of Luqqawatna was slowly being consumed. And its children were mourning the death of the ancient dream.

They landed at Tyre six days later. They had left a hundred and fifty dead Kerethites and seventy dead Pelethites in the flaming inferno of the temple. Another three hundred men were wounded. King Abibaal had news from the land: three days ago the Philistines had sent a large invading force to take Zion. The main bulk of the force was encamped in the Valley of Refa-im, obviously awaiting instructions from Gaza. David set out immediately, and by forced marches reached a place called Baalperazim. He fell upon the Philistines there and took them by surprise, massacring about four thousand of them and putting the remainder to flight. Joab and the others counseled him to proceed immediately to the safety of Zion. But David took out the Ephod and consulted Adonai.

"Shall we, this time, return to Zion? Or will the Philistines again come up against me?"

"Do not return to Zion now. The Philistines will indeed come up against you soon. They will aim at Zion. Do not attack them directly, but conceal yourself with your army in Bechaim wood. When you hear the rustle of the winds in the tops of the trees, attack them. You will be victorious."

In Bechaim wood with his troops, David waited. The main body of the Philistines was coming back into Refa-im, setting up camp there. Toward midnight he heard the wind rising and rushing through the trees. He passed the word. Their footfalls muffled by the ever rising wind, the Hebrews crept forward and fell on the camp.

The Philistines had not expected to be attacked from that direction, and there was a general stampede. The Philistines tried to escape into Philistia through the Valley of Elah, but David had posted a regiment of archers there in ambush. Most of the escaping Philistines were cut down. Some sixty or seventy survivors got back to Gaza.

In the morning David and his men marched north to Zion and were met with celebration. The king, David the Golden, was back safe and sound. He had successfully destroyed the center of Philistine power and also routed the local Philistine armies. David entered the government house, which he took as his residence, and was received by his wives and children.

The next day, talking with Joab and Ahitofel, he decided that it would be unwise to relax vigilance. The Ark was not yet in Zion. The Philistines could still field an army of over sixty thousand men. "Pray to Adonai," David said to his councilors, "that we have time to get ready." Week after week, month after month, reports filtered into Zion telling David of Philistine preparations. An air of crisis gradually took over in David's citadel. The only one who went about with his usual air of calm was Ahitofel. Some three months after the Luqqawatna expedition, Ahitofel was in the government house to transact some caravan business. As he was leaving, he sought out David and threw a remark at him that changed everything.

"By the way, my Lord David! I was out hunting yesterday. Up by that little farm—what's the name—er—Obededom. Yes! Obededom! And do you know, his wife gave him twins last month. His cows have calved without a single loss. And he has so much wool and lamb tails that he doesn't know what to do with his new-found wealth."

David was on his feet in a flash, quivering with excitement. "Repeat all that, Ahitofel! Repeat it all!"

Ahitofel did, adding: "I thought my Lord King would be interested."

"Why?"

"If this Adonai is responsible for what most people call blessings, and if Obededom has received all these blessings while the Ark affair is reposing in his main barn, then why does my Lord King not decide to bring such a source of blessings to his citadel here in Zion! Peace and goodbye, my Lord David!" And with that the lordly Ahitofel went on his way.

"Joab! Joab!" David shouted at the top of his voice. "Joab! Call a meeting of the council for this afternoon!"

* * *

The following day David successfully brought the Ark into his new Zion, saluting it with his unique dance of adoration, and feeling for the first time that the fearful and exacting Adonai had finally confirmed him as king over the land. The Ark was laid in a special shrine that he had built for it near his residence; and there sacrifices of animals and fruits were offered to Adonai. David gave a blessing to all the people. Nathan, Abiathar, and Zadok had wanted to give the blessing, but David waved them aside: "Am I not the chosen and the anointed of Adonai? None of you would be priest or prophet in this land if I were not king!"

The sun was sloping into the afternoon when David returned to his house flushed with happiness, leading a cluster of notables to the council room—Joab, Ira, Uri, Ahitofel, Barzillai, Hushai, and Ahimelek. As they came in the door Mikhal was waiting for them, arms akimbo, feet apart, jaw set, ready to attack. She had watched David dancing naked along the street. She was outraged, and totally oblivious of David's retinue.

"The people have had a great example, haven't they, the whoremasters in the marketplace and the dung lifters in the alleys. They'll be lying stark naked tonight around the streets smelling of cheap wine and copulating like rabbits. And why? Oh, my children of Israel, because our beloved king danced naked with his genitals flapping around the people's ears. Vile!" she spat out at him. "Your actions are vile!"

When David answered her, his voice was deep with anger. "What you do not realize, woman, is for *whom* I was dancing. For the Lord, I say, woman. Yes!" His voice rasped. "For Adonai who made me king of the land!

"You say I was vile. Well, I will be viler still, viler than you ever dreamed. I'll be baser and lower than you can imagine. In my own eyes. In your eyes. In the eyes of all the people. And in the eyes of those scullery hens and bedroom biddies you care so much about. I will sleep with every one of them. Every one! They will have my seed in them! You won't!"

His right hand touched the winking stones of the sacred Ephod he still wore, over the battle gear he had only just reassumed. "I swear it! As the Lord lives, I swear it! They will be honored. You will be dishonored! Forever!" David shouted. "What you said just now will rot in your soul until all of your inside is as bitter as sour wine. Are you satisfied now, daughter of Saul?"

David would never again touch Mikhal, nor even smile at her, never again address one word to her directly. The whole palace, the city, all of Israel would live her disgrace and banishment from day to day. The heart went out of her that evening, and it finally stopped two years later, dry and loveless. David would not even view her dead body.

In the council, David listened patiently while his next moves were debated. The air was full of cities and nations and tribes, logistics, strategy, weaponry, demographics. The politicians gnawed away at the bone of Hebrew disunity, citing the obstinate independence of the three hundred main walled cities and towns that dotted the land, and the total lack of a uniform trading policy.

David heard it all, then stood up. "There is no point," he said, "in going on with this detail, or I will be dead in the dust. If I even begin to think singly of the tribes and of the nations around us, I begin to lose heart, then I begin to lose interest. Merely to survive, we would have to spend the next twenty or thirty years fighting. Does anyone here want that? Don't we all wish to sit in peace beneath our own olive tree and drink the wine of tranquillity with our familes? And see our children grow to manhood?

"So let's look at the problem another way. Look at the face of this land and tell me where the life's blood of those cities, all of them, flows."

"Along the caravan routes," Ahitofel shot back promptly, "but—"

"Ah! Ah! Ahitofel!" David broke in. "Right! If we dominate the caravan routes, we dominate the cities. The most effective weapon for dominating the routes are chariots. Therefore, we need chariots. That's problem number one.

"Second question! There are now only two foreign powers that can possibly destroy us: Philistia and the Syrians who live in Zoba and Damascus. We cannot fight them both at once. Which do we turn to first? I think the Philistines are badly shocked. They will wait for months for instructions from Luqqawatna. They will wait a very long time. I can vouch for that myself—"

"Yes," Ahitofel interrupted, "you would know about the Philistines, my Lord David." His voice was sardonic, but he was smiling. Then, seeing the black look on David's face at the implied reference to David's status as Philistine vassal, he quickly went on: "I mean, you've the advantage of having lived among them. . . ."

"I know what you mean, Master Ahitofel," David said in

a deadly voice, glaring. "I always know what you mean." He went on: "I think, therefore, that further destruction will demoralize the Philistines even more, until one day soon they will be ready to fall before us.

"I therefore propose that we invade Philistia each year at the end of spring and again at the end of summer, that we burn every crop, cut down every tree, kill all the animals we don't want as booty, hack their vines, burn the farms. We scorch Philistine earth twice a year.

"Now Zoba and the Syrians are another kind of nettle altogether. We must pluck it, destroy all resistance, and hold it. Hadadezer, king of Zoba, has a thousand iron chariots, thanks to his Philistine friends. There is our chariotry!

"As to the Hebrew tribes, look at them! They are poor. This is a poor kingdom of poor people. Now they grow their own food and remain at the same level of poverty. But why shouldn't they sell their harvests and their wares? This is a bountiful land. Why shouldn't they be able to feed foreign markets? Why shouldn't Hebrews trade with Phenicians, with Assyrians, with Arabians, with Zoba, with Damascus, with Egypt? Why shouldn't they trade across the Great Sea where the Phenicians sail—to Africa, to Crete, to Sicily, to Massilia, to Tartessus?

"The second thrust of our policy, therefore, should be to create at least two trading triangles, one running between Zion and Phenicia and Tartessus. On triangles the Egyptians raised their pyramids. On trading triangles we will raise the poverty of our people to plenty. Do that, and there will be unity."

His councilors had listened in rapt silence. But now a shadow of worry had gathered on the faces of the military men. Joab voiced their fears. "David, all this sounds fine. But the Philistines are still strong. Zoba and the Syrians are still formidable. They are waiting for us to collapse. What shall we do before they come after us—probably next spring?"

"We don't wait for spring, my friend, we act now." David looked at Uri. "I am hereby putting Uri in charge of the defense of Zion. My brothers Eliab and Ozem will take charge of Judah, operating out of Hebron. In three days' time, rain or no rain, we're leaving. We will march through Philistia from north to south, then cross over Judah to Edom, then up through Moab, Ammon, Bashan, Gilead, and as far as Zoba. We will destroy Zoba once and for all."

"I suggest you hold up all other plans until you finish that trip and see how it goes," Ahitofel put in coldly, still smarting.

David looked at the Gilohite just as coldly. "If I do not

reenter Zion by the end of the summer with all our objectives achieved, Master Ahitofel"—he rasped out the Gilohite's name acidly and sharply—"then I suggest you go back to Giloh and hang yourself. For I will be dead, and all your hopes will have died with me. But I don't plan to be dead. In a few days Abibaal of Tyre will be sending his workmen to build a cedar palace for me. I have drawn up all the plans for them. My brothers, I intend to live in Zion and live there for my threescore years and ten." He rose and strode out of the council room.

"David," Abigail whispered to him as they lay side by side that night, "what happened today, to make you dance like that? Did you see the glory of Adonai above the Ark?"

"No, wife. No." His voice had a dull, almost sullen tone. She turned her head to look at him in the darkness. "Not his glory. Only the shadow of his glory." Abigail was filled with puzzlement at his mood. Had Mikhal's words hurt him so deeply?

But he guessed her thoughts and went on, a note of sharp resentment in his voice. "No, no! It's not what that bitter old bitch said! But"—he stopped a moment—"why should Adonai show me his glory? I'm merely a fighter." His bitterness made Abigail wince. "All Adonai wants from me is to kill, kill, kill, kill." He turned his back to her.

"My husband, what about the body of Adonai you mentioned to me before?" Immediately she was almost sorry she had brought up the subject.

He half-turned as if something struck him forcefully. "Yes! What about it?" His voice was raised querulously. "Don't you think I've done more than Abraham or Jacob or Moses or Joshua or Samuel? They all saw him and his glory. But not me. For me it is just killing." He turned away again.

Abigail lay awake for many hours, feeling the weight of David's disappointment.

The weather was misty and stormy when they started David's slow, guarded campaign through Philistia. It was an eerie experience for commanders and troops. He himself knew more or less what to expect. When he lived as a Philistine he had learned of "the fist of Dagon." When they were in a tight corner or uncertain what move to make, the entire Philistine population lived as if under siege, contracting to form "the fist of Dagon."

To enter Philistia in the safest way, David went north to Shechem, then branched west into Philistia as far as Jaffa on the coast. David rode with the Kerethite column on his right, the Pelethite on his left. The rest of his army followed the Pelethites. From the moment he crossed the Philistine border at Methegammah, he had the shepherd's pipers out in front playing the loud, threatening wail of the desert fighters. In the rear, the corps of drummers kept up the relentless boom! boom! boom! beat that David had invented.

Within Philistia he followed the coastal road south past Ashdod, Ekron, Ashkelon, and Gaza. After Gaza, he veered southeast to Gath and then into Judah. Throughout Philistia there was no fighting. No chariots. No camel patrols. No javelin pickets. Not even ships on the Great Sea. Philistia was a land of total silence, on guard, waiting. Even when David's axmen proceeded to cut down every fig tree and every olive tree, to hack every vine to bits, and to set fire to every isolated farmhouse, barn, and hay silo, no Philistine hand was raised in defense.

It was an eerie experience. At Ashdod David halted his columns within a quarter of a mile of the walls. The battlements were bristling with javelins, lances, flashing helmets, and arrows strung on bows. Outside and near the walls, chariot corps were harnessed and manned and standing ready. But beyond the pawing of a horse or the swaying neck of a camel, there was not a move. Not a sound. "They have even muzzled the war animals," Joab remarked. David held his troops there for about an hour, pipes wailing, drums beating, then, with a satisfied look, he gave the order to march on, scorching the earth as they went.

They found the same condition at every one of the five ducal city-fortresses, at every garrison town and fortress, and around all the army camps. David calculated there were about twenty-five thousand warriors massed outside Gaza, to say nothing of the garrison inside. Yet Gaza was pathetic in its walled silence, its hooded impotence.

David turned east toward Gath on the sixth day. Again the now customary deathly stillness, accented by the heavy rain and the mist that shrouded the walls and watchtowers. David, who had walked every one of Gath's streets and battlements, went over with his eyes what veteran campaigner Ira graphically described as "a bristling hedgehog." He was about to give marching orders when his eyes fell on the Tower of Silence on the east wall. On its top the Philistines had placed a four-sided iron grille. To that grille they used to tie criminals and traitors whom they wished to punish with a slow death by the beaks and claws of vultures. There was always a body spread-eagled on one side of that grille, and there was one now, which prompted David to ask himself aloud: "I wonder what they've done to Achish? They are sure to have blamed my defection on him, and their vengeance is terrible."

But it would be a long time before David would learn Achish's fate. Achish had been the first to know that David had violated Shekelath's command to have Philistines at his coronation. He immediately informed the council of dukes in Gaza, advising them to delay any response for a time. "David," he wrote, "is too wily. He must have a good reason to do what he has done. And nothing in his behavior since he came to us and since he became our vassal suggests even remotely that he is doing anything but advancing our interests." The answer of the council was ominous and immediate: a team of twenty officers clattered unannounced into Gath and marched into Achish's residence.

"My Lord Duke," the officer in charge told Achish, "I am Daglashan, servant of the Pentarchy Council. We have been sent by the council as your special assistants. You are to report to me, Daglashan. I will transmit all dispatches to Duke Shekelath on behalf of Gath."

Achish was now a virtual prisoner. And he guessed that Daglashan had orders to kill him at the slightest sign of betrayal. Daglashan had a bland baby face, large staring eyes, and a lugubrious manner. Men like Daglashan killed and tortured as blandly as they spoke.

Although Achish was still free and unharmed, his dominant emotion was confusion. When the news arrived that David had taken Jebus, Achish learned it the hard way. He was bathing in the Palm Pool with a young friend. Daglashan arrived on the double with the other officers. They yanked both men out of the pool, drove a killing sword thrust through the youth, knocked Achish unconscious and threw him in an oxcart. When he woke up an hour later, he was bound hand and foot and on his way to Gaza.

There he was first whipped unmercifully, the four other dukes delivering the first four blows. Afterward he was left to nurse his wounds all night. As a Philistine, he knew what was coming next. At dawn he was taken to the temple of Dagon and there tried in secret by the other four dukes. They satisfied themselves that he had known nothing of David's intentions. And all would have gone relatively well for Achish—he would have been allowed to retire into obscurity with only the stigma of failure attached to his name and his life—if Lalardan, now the Duke of Ashdod, had not thrown a stray and pointless question at him toward the end of the trial.

"Do you now recognize the error of trusting this Hebrew?"

"Yes, my Lord Duke." Achish should have left it at that. But even in his misery and degradation he could not suppress his contempt for Lalardan; and he could not resist the sight of the duke's huge, red, bulbous nose—the butt of many popular jokes. He added: "It's as plain as the nose on my Lord Duke's face."

The other dukes suppressed their smiles at this unexpected sally, but the Duke of Ashdod was nettled. "And I suppose you'll be more careful in the future about whom you take to bed with you, my Lord Duke Achish?"

Achish blanched with anger. "David and I never were lovers, my Lord Duke. He never loved me."

"Oh-ho!" Lalardan leered around at the others. "So our little golden-haired Hebrew pig wouldn't snuggle down with you? Ha-ha! Tell me, my Lord Duke, did you—er—love him? Did you want him—you know what I mean." He laughed at the others.

"Yes." Achish looked contemptuously at Lalardan.

"Oh-ho!" Lalardan said in a mock seriousness. "You didn't by any chance offer to cut off your foreskin just—er—to facilitate things sort of—er, you know? Be a good little smooth Hebrew for a night? A little secret sucker for Adonai—just for an hour or two? Eh?" The other three dukes looked on all this as a good joke. Shekelath was in fact getting to his feet and gathering up his documents, about to call an end to the proceedings.

Something snapped inside Achish. Lalardan's leering face suddenly became utterly abhorrent to him, and at the same time completely unimportant. He looked around at the three others. Shekelath, with an indulgent smile, was half out of his chair. Another had his mouth open ready to guffaw with laughter. A third was making a lewd gesture over to the fourth. Above their heads towered the new statue of Dagon, all thirty feet of it, long, rugged, with fin-shaped hands, webbed feet, and that peculiar face—half-swan, half-human—clad in the cold fixity of unfeeling stone. Achish saw it all now. He saw the dukes as perfectly suited to that Dagon. And the image of David's beauty and of Nathan's sensitivity came back to him as dear memories of a wholeness he had always desired but had not consciously sought. He knew now what he had always wanted.

"If being a little Hebrew, even a little sucker for Adonai, meant victory! I would, my Lord Duke, I would!"

Shekelath froze at the blasphemy, then sat down heavily on his chair. A cold silence gripped the dukes. They looked at each other. Shekelath's eyes glittered.

"You once told me, my Lord Duke, that if this Adonai could guarantee an empire of a thousand years with *his* power, you would worship him. Would you? Have you done so?"

In that split second before he answered Shekelath, Achish underwent the biggest change of his life, or rather that great change had already taken place and he was now becoming aware of it. He did not care any more about anything the council might do to him. It seemed to him that Shekelath and the three others had suddenly become pygmies, mechanical gesticulating toys whose arms and mouths and eyes and heads were jerked and controlled by invisible cords held in the palm of some hidden puppeteer.

"You don't know—" he began, and broke off; he could not find the words he needed. Great thoughts rose above the dukes' heads, above Dagon's statue, erasing every breath of human respect and fear from his mind. None of these people or what they represented mattered any more. What mattered was that he not lose the peace of this new-found courage and inner cleanliness. "... I have no part in your filth ..." he started off again, helpless to express what he really wanted so desperately to say.

Shekelath shouted at the top of his lungs, so great was his anger. "Declare your allegiance as a Philistine to Lord Dagon. Declare it now!"

Achish was momentarily stupefied by the words that he now heard himself deliberately crying out. He was speaking half in memory of what he had once heard Nathan say, half in memory of a song David had once sung in his presence. "Adonai is my guardian. Whom shall I fear?... Adonai is one in his heavens...." He stopped. For the dukes he was making no sense, only talking blasphemy.

True to form, his fellow Philistines said no more. They were, after all, Philistines. They knew the law. Shekelath called in the official executioner and gave him instructions. The man stood in front of Achish, placed his palms gently around Achish's temples, the tips of his thumbs softly resting in the inner corner of each eye on top of the tear ducts, the rest of the thumbs lying as quietly as butterflies over the eyeballs. On signal from Shekelath, the palms gripped Achish's temples like a vise, the tips of the thumbs drove in and around the eyeballs, separating them from their moorings and scooping them out. Achish screamed and fell to the floor unconscious. They had him taken out and thrown into a cell. He was destined to die in public after a couple of weeks. In the meantime his nails, his hair, his genitals would be removed one by one. Then his arms and remaining leg would be hewn off. Always the wounds were cauterized and the bleeding stopped. He had to live for the day of execution. The living trunk with the sightless sockets would be impaled on a stake, until he was quite dead and rotting. It was Philistine law and the will of Dagon for all blasphemers and traitors.

Achish's hours were now passed in continual agony. But he found himself continually repeating those words he had pronounced in front of the council. For long periods he slipped away into gracefully accepted unconsciousness. But they came to wake him up regularly. He must suffer. Some days later he was lying in his cell, having lost all his nails and hair, when he heard that strange sound, the Cry of Dagon! Huge, long, undulating wails Philistines set up when death was facing them. His torturers did not come for him the following day. In the evening of the next day, Shekelath arrived. Achish could only sense his fury and hatred.

"Luqqawatna is silent. Kalkodon is dead. The mysteries of Dagon have been violated. We don't know what's happening. Your Hebrew lover is responsible, we are sure. The law will be enforced."

Achish knew nothing of David's raid, but he knew what Shekelath meant. In their onward thrust to empire, the Philistines had been told that if ever the mysteries of Dagon were violated and his guidance suspended, only a lengthy sacrifice of the violator or someone closely connected with the violator could restore Dagon's favor. The sacrificial victim had to be held ready to die, but not killed until Dagon spoke to them again, either by lightning or through an oracle. It meant a long torture for Achish.

He was given some water and food, and his wounds were periodically cauterized. He lived on from dawn till dusk, then through the night, then from the next dawn to the next dusk, then through the week and subsequent weeks. It was a good omen. Dagon was keeping the victim alive for the grand moment of deliverance. But time passed and Philistine fortunes did not improve. They began to take better care of Achish. They might need him. He might one day be their passport to safety and—who could tell?—to victory.

Achish himself was left severely alone by the dukes. He found himself asking Adonai to let him hear David's voice once more before he died. He became aware of the "bunched fist" status of the Pentarchy. As the days stretched into months and the year rolled around from spring to spring, his agonies died down to a dull heavy pain. But gradually the darkness of his blind man's world started to fill with a new light.

It was gentle. It came unbidden. It fled when he tried in a worldly way to "look" at it or understand it. It returned at unguarded moments. He finally accepted it with the humility of mind which betokens total submission to the movements of the spirit and to whatever force was moving his spirit. For it was thus that Adonai burned out the roots of false pride in any man whom he loved, favored, and destined for final happiness. Gradually that light filled all the darkness of his days. He understood that this inner light came partly through the loss of the light of days. And he joined that fortunate company who find out that the light of Adonai's truth and the brightness of his love are too dazzling for living eyes. They blind at first and produce darkness, the darkness of soul through which everyone who ever turned to Adonai must walk before reaching his goal. Only later was it possible for Achish to begin to see with other eyes, flesh into spirit and earth into heaven. He entered a period of waiting and hoping.

Most of the next year David spent consolidating and extending and securing the borders of his kingdom. He spent three and a half months in Hebron, establishing in collaboration with the Judahite elders a system of Davidic enclaves on all the fallow lands, where he settled hundreds of his veterans. Before he left at the beginning of March, he gave his soldiers a general directive— David's famous order of the day to his soldiers.

"Once we enter any territory that is not linked to us in brotherhood or race or alliance, the watchword is: Punish! Kill! Kill as many warriors as we can. Burn every farm. Cut the hamstrings of every horse, every camel, every mule, and every donkey we don't need. Destroy every vine and fig tree and olive tree. Knock down the walls and towers of every town. Make slaves as we will. When we conquer, one half of all the booty goes to the kingdom. The other half is divided among you, the warriors, each according to his division and rank. The women are at your disposal. The old men and women must be left alive."

He took his main army directly south past Beersheva and raided two Amalekite and Geshurite camps. He was on his way toward Edom when, at Kadesh-Barnea, messengers arrived from Uri in Zion: "Abikemosh of Moab has been assassinated. Mikash, a northern Moabite, has seized power in Mizpeh. Be careful." David halted at Kadesh-Barnea for a day and held a council.

"We have to deal with Edom and Moab in one blow," David announced. "Mikash may well invade Judah if we delay."

"What happened?" Joab asked.

David's unguarded answer took Joab and the others by surprise: "She was killed in her bed," he answered simply.

"She? What do you mean 'she'?"

"Abikemosh was a woman, a woman of a very great age. Moreover, she was a leper. Always confined to bed. I will never forget the first day I was brought in to see her in the palace of Mizpeh. She was my friend, and the friend and protector of my parents. I will avenge her."

"So that's what Nathan was referring to in Ziklag that day," Joab said. "By God! How did he know?"

"It could not be otherwise. He is a prophet. I'm going to send Abishai south to Edom, and Ira north into Moab. You'll take only camel riders and bowmen. Your purpose, both of you, is to provoke a battle, then leave. You, Abishai, will draw the Edomites northward after you. You, Ira, draw the Moabites southward after you. I will proceed with the main body of troops and lodge myself on the Plain of Kikar."

Kikar was at the southern tip of the Salt Sea. It had a central valley opening at the northeast and the southwest, and at its center there were thick woods. David's aim was to draw his enemies into that trap. "If Edom and Moab take the bait, we should join battle by tomorrow afternoon."

The following morning the trap was set. His archers and slingshot men and javelin throwers lay concealed at the two openings into Kikar. He, with Kerethites and Pelethites, hid in the woods at the center of the plain. The rest of his infantry he placed outside Kikar at the north end.

By midafternoon David and his men heard the thunder of hooves. Within half an hour Abishai with his men streamed in from the south pursued by the Edomites, while Ira rode down from the northeast with Mikash and his camelmen in hot pursuit. The subsequent carnage was particularly gruesome because David's men interpreted his instructions literally. No prisoners were taken. No escape was possible. The killing went on far into the evening. Mikash was captured alive and brought to David, who sliced him in half with the sword of Goliath, then ordered the remains to be wrapped in sacking and tied to Mikash's camel.

Abishai was sent with eleven thousand troops to set up a string of Davidic fortresses from Kadesh-Barnea down through Edom right to the waters of the Red Sea at Ezion-Gezer. David and the remainder rode to Mizpeh and took the city easily. David assembled all the Moabite nobles, all the chief merchants, the elders of the ten Moabite towns, and the army officers on the plain in front of Abikemosh's palace. He had Joab drag the two halves of Mikash around in full view of everybody. Then he had them all stand shoulder to shoulder in ranks ten deep, to form a long human rectangle. He stretched a line diagonally from one corner to another. All those to the left of that line were killed then and there. All those to the right of that line were stripped naked and scourged with thong whips loaded with metal tips.

Those who survived were freed. David imposed on them a fine of three thousand gold Tyrian talents, one thousand camels, one thousand lambs, and four hundred horses. He appointed Malkikemosh, the son of Abikemosh, king of Moab, recovered the remains of Abikemosh and buried them with honor. "You will be my son and my vassal," he told Malki-kemosh. "Let there be peace and alliance between us, and let us trade together."

He stayed in Mizpeh for three weeks, setting up the trade alliance, then marched northeast into the friendly territory of Nahash, king of the Ammonites. Here at Rabbath-Ammon, Nahash's capital on the edge of the Great Desert, David stayed while he sent Joab north through Bashan and Gilead to reconnoiter around Damascus and Zoba. It was the latter half of April when Joab returned to report that the Syrians of Damascus apparently had heard of David's victory at Kikar. They were mobilizing chariotry and infantry.

"If we tackle them head-on," David decided, "they will call on their lackeys in Zoba. We must take Damascus from behind. That means we have to go around by Galilee. Get the men ready to march westward. Ira will go up to the boundary of Damascus, threaten them, harass them, and keep the Damascenes looking south."

David then took the main bulk of his troops across the Jordan directly westward from Rabbath-Ammon until he reached

Shechem. He streaked north into Galilee past Dan, passed into the mountains of Phenicia, climbed the Ladder of Tyre unnoticed by the Syrians in the cities of Berutha, Betah, and Hamath, and assembled for battle on the borders of Zoba. He allowed his troops a week's rest, took in supplies, and bided his time.

Early one morning in May, three hours before sunrise, he sent in the Kerethites, who silently found their way to the chariot barns and stables, overcame the guards, and took possession of Zoba's pride, the chariotry. Then a general assault was launched. David's army burst in on all the hamlets and townships and the main city of Zoba. The sleeping were destroyed. Hadadezer, the young and brash king of Zoba, was in bed with his favorite concubine. He woke up to hear the door of his bedroom hacked down and found himself looking at the tip of Goliath's sword in the hands of a huge warrior with golden hair and blue eyes. From the streets outside came the groans of dying men, the cries of fighters. Hadadezer was spared in an act of mercy that David would later regret.

He had thoroughly occupied Zoba, placing his divisions strategically, when twenty-five thousand Damascenes arrived and attacked. But the captured chariotry was decisive. Of the Syrians, almost eighteen thousand perished in three days of continual fighting. On the fourth day, Joab came to David in Zoba and told him the main Syrian body was in total flight and disarray.

"After them! Cut them down! They must not get back to Damascus!"

One corps of three hundred chariots was sent ahead of the fleeing Syrians to cut them off from Damascus and force them back into the arms of the pursuing Joab. Another three hundred chariots made for Damascus and thundered into the city before any resistance could be mustered. They were followed in force an hour later, and the fight was over.

Day after day David received delegations from the various Syrian cities, Helbon, Khur, Rivla, Zedad, Hazor, Qadesh, Shumatu, Ad, Qatna, all suing for peace, all offering themselves as vassals. The northern threat to the kingdom was eliminated.

David's trade routes to the Euphrates and beyond were in his grasp. It took David and his army over a month merely to load the booty. Hadadezer had furnished his own personal regiment of bodyguards with ceremonial shields and helmets of solid gold. Every goblet and plate and spoon used in his palace was of silver or gold. All the doors, beds, chairs, window frames, cupboards, tables, and staircases in Hadadezer's palace were of solid brass. And his treasury was packed full of Egyptian, Phenician, and Assyrian gold and silver. His armories and arsenals were furnished throughout with the invaluable iron weapons David needed so much.

When David returned in mid-June, he found Zion almost unrecognizable. Uri with an honor guard of Hittites met him at the head of his advance column a mile north of the city. Behind David there stretched a three-mile-long procession of pack camels, pack mules, oxcarts, and loaded donkeys. As they entered Araunah's threshing floor, David's eyes bulged at the sight of the long holding barns Uri had specially built there to house the tribute and taxes levied on Amalekites, Geshurites, Edomites, and Moabites.

"We can buy the world now, Uri!" David shouted as he realized what those barns held.

"Ah, wait, friend! It's only the beginning." The Hittite plunged ahead up the ramp, in by the North Gate, and through the main straight street leading to the south end of Zion.

Minutes before they arrived there, pressing their way through a frenzied populace that lined streets, windows, balconies, and rooftops, a look of wonderment crossed David's face. Towering over the bubble-shaped roofs of the houses and taller than all the long watchtowers of Zion, there appeared the red-brown pinnacles of his Cedar Palace that the Phenicians had been building in his absence. The plans had been his, but what they had created was beyond his wildest dreams or imaginings. And as he drew nearer, he could see his family waving from the topmost floor.

"You should really close your eyes until you turn the corner and enter the courtyard," Uri said, half-joking, half-serious.

"No man on earth will prevent me from enjoying every moment of this hour, my friend," David breathed in awe.

When they rounded the corner, David and his party saw the full bulk of his Cedar Palace. There was a long, thunderstruck silence, when everything was frozen in their amazement and in the tense expectation of those awaiting David's homecoming. For everyone, by concert, was waiting for David's reaction. David saw Nathan and the priests standing silently over by the Shrine of the Ark. On the other side, around the opening shaft of the precious Siloam, were Uri's faithful Hittites. And directly in front of David: his Cedar Palace.

He ran his eye up the shelving walls, past the crowded second-floor balcony, up story after story, from balcony to balcony, over cornice piece and crenelated windows, up past the sixth and seventh floors to the roof, until his eyes met the clear blue June sky. As his gaze ascended, some deep feeling long unnourished had been welling in him. It burst from him now, as he opened his mouth and let out one of those mighty yells for which he was famous—triumph, thanks, joy, defiance, fun, pride, satisfaction. It expressed them all and something else besides: the happiness of coming home. Then pandemonium broke loose. Everyone started cheering, shouting, dancing, laughing, clapping.

David slipped off his camel, and the others followed him up the steps and into the Great Lobby. They gazed at David's war trophies on the walls, the rugs of lion and bear and deer skins on the floor, and the wide swinging oil lamps of bronze suspended from the rafters. Down the wide staircase of brass from the sixth-floor landing came a flood of his children, Amnon, Dodiel, Adoniyahu, and the others, followed by wives, concubines, servants, slaves, guards.

Uri and Joab with his officers sat down in the lobby while David ran up, surrounded by his family, to see his own private rooms on the seventh floor, the harem for wives and concubines at the back or west side of the sixth floor, and on the fifth floor the huge dining room, the kitchens, the servant and slave quarters. Later, with Joab and Ahimelek, he visited the complex of council rooms, assembly hall, war room, treasury, recording room or scrollery, and guest rooms on the intermediate floors. His Kerethite and Pelethite bodyguards took up residence in the guardrooms and storerooms opening off the Great Lobby. When he had seen all and was returning downstairs to Uri and Joab and the others, Nathan the Prophet remarked quietly: "Adonai has given you a noble palace, my Lord David. His Ark sits outside your doors. I pray that holiness dwells under your roof, and that death never enters." David stopped a moment and looked sideways at the prophet. Nathan always had a reason for what he said and did. Then he thought better of what he was going to ask. He walked down the stairs in silence.

Uri, as military governor of Zion, remained in his own house, now opposite David's palace. His regiment of loyal Hittites occupied the Millo. The bulk of David's Kerethites and Pelethites were housed up the street toward the North Gate. Under Joab's personal supervision they served guard duty at the palace on rotation. As permanent house guests David kept

Nathan the Prophet, Ahimelek the Hittite, Hushai the Arkite, and Barzillai the Gileadite. Hushai found Jonathan's surviving son and grandson, Mephibosheth and Mikha, and they both came to reside at the palace. And, of course, there was "David's Angel," Malaki, forever sitting at the great double doors of the Cedar Palace—everybody's friend, everybody's mentor.

Daily activity at the palace was divided for David between his own quarters, where he lived and worked, and the harem section where wives, concubines, and children lived. The harem had its own life, its own meals, its own amusements, its own intrigues. When David came to Zion, he already had one son by each of his six wives, together with eight daughters. By Ahinoam he had Amnon and his sisters Riba and Hagar. By Abigail, Dodiel and his sister Hodesh. By Maaka, Absalom and his sister Tamar. By Haggith, Adoniyahu and his sister Shalheveth. By Abital, Shefatyahu and his sister Miriam. By Eglah, Ithream and his sisters Sherah and Zelofehad. Ahinoam would give him yet another son, Yivhar, in Zion. These children were all important to him.

Nobody ever reckoned the sons and daughters David had begotten by his concubines, the daughters of tribal chieftains chiefly in the southern desert but also among the east bank tribes. Common rumor put the number at roughly seventy children and forty concubines, who were separately housed.

With slaves and servants, the harem population came to about sixty, for each wife had a personal slave, each child had its own nurse, and other servants and slaves did the domestic chores. When he was at home, David had his midday meal each day with all his children and wives. Every week, he celebrated Shabbath seder with them all. Otherwise, until they had passed through puberty, the children remained with the harem.

But David took a lively interest in every detail about his children. He appointed one special tutor, Yehi-el ben Hakhmoni, for his sons. The daughters he left to the attention of wives, servants, and nurses. The children knew he was their father and the ultimate recourse for them in great as in little things. Dodiel, for instance, the son of Abigail, came to him one day in tears. The other children were teasing him because Dodi, the first part of his name, was also the slang term for "sweetheart." David changed Dodiel to Khileav on the spot. Everyone in the palace knew, however, that David's favorite child was Absalom. With his golden hair and blue eyes and beautiful body, he was a physical replica of David. David and everyone else spoiled him.

David's concubines were another and totally different class of women in his life. He brought twenty-one of them to Zion with him. He kept three as his personal body slaves, Afsaq, Balva, and Shunnamith. His Philistine concubine, Mishlag, supervised David's personal quarters with the help of Bithiyah, Yafi-el, Nara, Berotha, and Hodiyah. The others took care of the servants and slaves in the rest of the palace. While David tolerated male slaves, he abhorred male servants. All his servants had to be women, and David had slept with all of them at least once. They were all intensely loyal to him.

From the first days of his return after consolidating the southern, eastern, and northern borders of the land, he set out to organize its economic and military life. He did this knowing that the greatest threat of all—the Philistines to the west—had still to be erased. Yet even after many of David's regular scorchings, Philistia still showed no sign of any organized resistance. David's Luqqawatna raid was still paying dividends.

In the next two and a half years, David established his basic government. First he imposed total military control. Without that he would have remained a provincial princeling. When he looked at the land, he saw the topography—the plains, valleys, hills, mountains, rivers, trade routes—and not the traditional tribal boundaries. Over these contours he placed the template of his military organization. Once that was done, the days of the tribe were over. David controlled the economic life of his people.

At the northern end of the land, he had two main garrisons: one at Dan, west of the Jordan, and one east of the Jordan, in the valley between the mountains of Bashan and of Syria. Two more garrisons stood at Carmel, on the coast of the Great Sea, and at Megiddo, guarding the entrance to the Valley of Yezreel. From Yezreel southward there was a string of garrisons, at Eval Shekhem, Samaria, Shiloh, Bethel, Gibea, and down past Zion at Bethlehem, Hebron, Maon, Carmel of Judah, and Beer-sheva.

On his eastern flank but still west of the Jordan, David established only three main garrisons—running up north from Jericho, through Bethshan, and Kinnereth. Protection of his eastern flank was theoretically in the hands of his vassal states of Edom, Moab, Ammon, Gilead, and Bashan. But throughout David's reign and those of his successors, the east bank peoples would always mean trouble.

A Davidic garrison town implied much more than a resident force of soldiers. David distributed parcels of land around each garrison of his campaigns. He thereby redistributed the population out of native territories, liquidating the old tribal boundaries that had already been made militarily redundant. It was a highly imaginative policy that forced the Hebrews to think in terms of the kingdom rather than the tribe. And in each garrison there were foreign mercenaries. These were paid at a higher rate and owed allegiance and personal safety to David. Large numbers of Edomites and Hittites and Syrians—and later on, in his middle age, Philistines—were in this way seeded around the land.

The king's most grandiose fortress outside Zion was Megiddo. All the time he was formulating plans for wiping out the Philistines, David was also thinking of Megiddo's position at the head of the natural gateway to the central highlands and, indeed, to the heart of the kingdom of Judah. The door to Philistia opened on the coastal plain of Sharon; and Megiddo dominated Sharon. So at Megiddo he assembled the captured chariots, built stables for the horses, barracks for the drivers, and fortifications for the whole settlement. Megiddo in David's time and in the time of his successor was a prime garrison and arsenal of the Kingdom of Israel.

As a reward for his truly faithful services and because he was the most experienced commander of battle, Joab was made head of all armed forces. David's regular and conscript troops were divided into eight army corps.

Joab's most important assignment was protection of the trade routes. One separate division of David's army patrolled the routes between the garrisoned wayside stations. Early on, David divided the guarding of the routes into twenty-four sections. Attached to Joab as Overseer General of the Routes was a special camel-corps commander. He was appointed on a rotation basis out of a pool of twelve commanders. On his appointment, each one of these commanders brought his own contingent of four thousand mounted men to patrol the routes for a month. David attached supreme economic importance to the trade caravans and their safety.

While his national state was emerging, David let civil government mostly follow old tribal lines. Each tribe had a governor with the rank of prince. But the overall administration of the civil government remained in Zion under David's control. Around him and living with their families were all his ministers. He had a six-man Council of State: Ahitofel (economics), Joab (military), Yehoyada ben Benaya (caravan trade), Abiathar (religion), Jonathan, a maternal uncle of David (intelligence), Azmaveth Ben Adiel (treasury), Serayah (secretary), and Hushai the Arkite (foreign affairs).

As a consequence of this central organization and of David's presence in Zion, his chief councilors and the notables of the realm now poured into the city and with David's permission started to build their own houses down at its southern tip, near the Cedar Palace. The first and most notable of these men was Ahitofel, the most powerful nonmilitary man in the kingdom. His house was a little smaller than Commander Uri's but bigger than all the others. Ahitofel had long-range plans that did not include his remaining merely one of the king's ministers. And his plans envisaged a very close association between his house and the house of David.

As time went on, and the kingdom became consolidated, a wholly new population, Hebrews most of them, came to live in Zion. Most of them participated in the armed services or in David's government. For, bit by bit, the Hebrews came to regard Zion as the center of the land promised to Moses and the Hebrews long, long ago in the desert. And David, his wars, his loves, his friends, his actions, his comings and goings, became the focus of the entire population. As the affairs of the infant state began to progress and David's government bureaucracy grew, the whole tenor of social life changed. Once only a fortified garrison city, Zion slowly acquired the graces of a capital.

Within David's remaining thirty years of life, an entirely new class of people arose: moneyed, sophisticated, consciously superior to those outside the magic air of Zion. They were the first Hebrews who did not claim to be Reubenites or Ephraimites or Benjaminites. They were Zionists all. And from this new class was to arise the later Hierosolymite society—with its own style in dress and pronunciation, its ideal of male status and female beauty, its prejudices and pride, its myopia and wisdom, its learning and science—which lasted until the city was destroyed by the Romans almost a thousand years after David had captured it.

Of all the remarkable people who now clustered around David in Zion, none was destined to play a more intimate and fateful role in his life as king and as a man than Bathsheva, daughter of Ammiel, granddaughter of the "Gilohite demon" Ahitofel. If she escaped David's attention for the first five years of his reign in Zion, this was due as much to David's policy of not interfering in the private lives of his officials as to the well-thought-out plans of Ahitofel himself. When David took Zion, he was almost thirty-eight years old. Bathsheva was barely eighteen, too young, the clever Ahitofel believed, for the destiny he intended to fashion for her. She was kept by Ahitofel at Hebron, then moved to Zion, and became the wife of Uri the Hittite when David was forty-two. She started out with one tremendous advantage: her grandfather was the most important man in David's government.

Bathsheva had been born on her grandfather's farm at Giloh in southern Judah. But she had spent the major portion of her twenty-two years circulating in affluent Upper Hebron. Her father, Ammiel, was a man whose personal and family life centered on Ahitofel. Before David's arrival in Hebron, Ammiel, as sole heir to Ahitofel's wealth, worked for the Gilohite. When Ahitofel became David's minister of state, Ammiel became a warrior and distinguished himself in the fighting that led David to the kingship. As nearly always happens among the wealthy and prestigious, life among the Upper City Hebronites was free of many of the constraints imposed by the Law on the generality of Hebrews. The use of the veil by women and their education, the condemnation of homosexuality, the observance of liturgical restraints such as fasting and sustained prayer and tithing—these and many more rules were interpreted with great latitude.

Such was the type of society in which Bathsheva was reared. It was governed by fad and fashion, enlivened by rumor and bound by artificial conventions, strung on the hierarchy of wealth. She had never known a moment of hunger, fear, or constraint. Ahitofel saw in her the daughter he had never had; and, as the only child in the house, she reigned as queen. It was a house and a family which had very little love. Ammiel was the creature of his father. Her mother was neurotic, hated Ahitofel, and had never wanted a daughter anyway.

Ahitofel himself supervised her education. He employed Egyptian and Phenician teachers. And while her knowledge of the Covenant and her belief in Adonai may have been more conventional than well informed, she was a very accomplished young woman. As well as perfect Egyptian and Phenician— she had traveled to both countries by the age of eighteen—she spoke a Hebronite Hebrew with its distinctively languid drawl and softened consonants. She could play the harp, sing, and dance—all expertly. And Ahitofel made sure that she could ride camels, throw knives, and swim. And—marvel of marvels!—she had mastered the Phenician mode of writing. Ahitofel, who despised all other women and most men, went out of his way to include Bathsheva on business trips, to have her present at meetings and gatherings in his villa, and to talk incessantly with her about public and financial affairs.

As a young girl in her mid-teens, she stood out among her peers as taller than all and with physical proportions the others always envied—a high, narrow waist; full, upturned breasts; a gracefully rounded pelvis curving and swaying on legs that "glided on air," as Ahitofel once proudly remarked to some foreign guests he was entertaining. All Hebron knew of the feared Ahitofel's granddaughter. She was not very often visible in the streets, but on the odd occasions that she was, Hebronites went out of their way to catch a glimpse of this girl famed for her light hazel eyes, white skin, lustrous black hair, and her figure.

No one in the family at Giloh or Hebron could remember an ancestor who had the color of her eyes or the tint of her skin. And no one who ever met her could resist the personal charm and grace that clothed her. By the age of seventeen she was completely developed in body, and her mind was as adult as it ever would be. Succeeding years would only broaden her perceptions and teach her the lessons only life could teach. Men—those who were allowed to see her at close quarters— came away with the lasting impression that, for the brief time they were with her, they had been close to the personification of beauty itself.

Both Bathsheva's exterior and interior seemed beautiful. It was not, however, her physical charms so much as some resident luminescence, some quite tangible but invisible effulgence all around her, that captivated them. It seemed to onlookers that a hundred delicious secrets were locked in her, secrets that she would not really bother to communicate. When she entered a room, the effulgence was there. When she left, it departed with her.

Bathsheva saw her beauty and personal attractiveness in a very different light from those around her. "If you live with beauty," one desert poet sang, "you are its worshiper, or you are an animal. But if you yourself are beautiful, you only notice the animals and the worshipers."

Without Ahitofel, Bathsheva might have blossomed into a brainless beauty or, at best, a fine woman with a frustrated intelligence. But because of Ahitofel she became a highly sophisticated woman of great discrimination, adept at ignoring her effect on men while assessing how it affected their coolness and judgment.

More impressive was her openness. In spite of her privileged position and her careful schooling in the subtle hypocrisies practiced by the privileged to protect themselves from the commonality, she had no trace of snobbishness, was not haughty or cold or detached, found no work, nor any person, beneath her interest, spoke with a delicacy of expression which was straightforward yet without any hint of vulgarity.

The basic flaw in her character flowed from this combination of overwhelming personal beauty allied with privilege. Bathsheva was primarily interested only in power. It was the only element in life that excited her. Consequently she reserved her admiration and respect for her grandfather, Ahitofel, and a few like him, while for the young men who paraded in front of her she had nothing more than indulgently teasing smiles.

By the time David had returned from his military consolidation of the eastern and northern boundaries, Ahitofel had moved his entire family, including Bathsheva, to Zion and into his newly built house. Here Bathsheva would live for the next five years in the relative obscurity of a teenage girl in upper-class Hebrew society. Her father was usually off on the king's business. Her mother lived from morning until night in her harem quarters. Her grandfather she saw every day. She had permission to cross over into his part of the house whenever she liked. His study and bedroom were filled with curios, precious stones, and gold ornaments. The two, grandfather and granddaughter, had a perfect rapport. And Ahitofel continued to educate Bathsheva. He was banking on her for high stakes, and by the time she came to Zion, he had all his plans laid out. He wasted no time in restating them for her.

"My daughter," Ahitofel said to her one morning before he left the house, "I have spoken to your father and mother, and I am about to arrange a marriage for you. Your husband will be Commander Uri. Oh!"—as he saw her nose wrinkling in disapproval.

"It will be all right. It's all political. And very advisable, my dear." He was not using the ministerial voice that she knew so well. "The old lad wants only a housekeeper and a son. He won't bother you much." Then as her eyes reflected her puzzlement, he stalked over to the window, beckoning her. He looked down the street, pointing first to Uri's residence. "There's where your married home will be. But"—pointing to

David's Cedar Palace across the way—"there's where you will be someday."

"Grandfather," she said with a slight touch of smiling sarcasm, "seduction and fornication are such vulgar weapons."

He looked around sharply with an expression of mock surprise. "Oh, child! Come now! We're older and wiser than that, you and I. Nothing so crude!" He glanced back again at the Cedar Palace. "Oh, no! Something much cleverer, my dear. A deep plot!" he commented gently. "Rather, you will be a visiting cousin in the king's household. Anyway, women are only child factories for him." There was silence between them for a few moments as they both gazed over at the Cedar Palace. "You see, as I visualize it, you can influence the king. David fights. And David thinks. My best information is, he will only be interested in your brain. Besides, Uri is his best friend, and David is loyal to his friends." He meditated awhile. "And really," Ahitofel concluded reasonably, "the distance from Commander Uri's residence to that Cedar Palace is quite short."

She said nothing for a while. Finally she clapped her hands. "So you will arrange this marriage. And then we will see."

Ahitofel departed down the stairs. She watched him go. Halfway down a thought struck him. He stopped and looked back up at her, one eyebrow lifted in query. "I suppose . . . no, definitely not . . . anyway . . . it's worth saying now, just so you know my mind. Is there any danger you'll fall in love with him? With the king, I mean?" They looked at each other seriously for four or five seconds. She began to laugh. And Ahitofel laughed too, in relief.

"Such a happening," he said humorously as he took the last few steps to the lobby, "would start the fox for sure."

That day he had a special appointment with David's trusted Commander of Zion, Uri the Hittite. Uri, who had been quite a while assiduously searching for a wife, was introduced to Bathsheba at the beginning of her third year in Zion. Uri took one look at Bathsheba and immediately signed a betrothal contract with Ammiel. The betrothal would have taken place six months later and the formal marriage six months after that if the Philistine war had not begun again. As it was, Uri was wholly occupied in subduing Philistia over a period of almost twenty months.

David might have blithely continued his policy of regularly scorching the Philistine earth if it hadn't been for the watchful eye of his faithful friends in Tyre. As it was, he had just

returned from his autumn foray into Philistia—where he found
the same armed immobility—when a courier rode in from Tyre
with two pieces of news. Old Abibaal had died in his sleep
and been buried in the royal cemetery at Gubla in Phenicia.
His son, Hiram, David's friend, now reigned. Hiram wished
to renew for himself the treaty of friendship that had existed
between his father and David.

The second piece of news was ominous. The Phenician
traders who plied the sea lanes up around the curve of the coast
from Tyre to Anatolia, where Luqqawatna lay, reported the
overland movement of vast armed convoys traveling slowly but
obviously destined for Philistia. For the moment, the convoys
were gathering at an assembly point at the angle of the coast
where it turned south toward Phenicia. Hiram feared for Phenicia as well as for David. But the convoys were not coming
from Luqqawatna. They came from beyond, from the north.
David took only a few minutes with his councilors to decide
that he had to move immediately, but the planning took them
far into that night.

David put his finger on the key strategy. "Since Luqqawatna
no longer sustains Philistia, Gaza is the heart of our trouble.
If we eliminate it, the other four cities will fall to us like rotten
fruit. Gaza, therefore, we take first."

"Just in case, though," Joab suggested, "any of the other
four cities decided to come to Gaza's help, shouldn't we isolate
each one of them in advance of our attack?"

"Yes," David answered slowly, "for if all four attacked us
simultaneously while we were attacking Gaza, we couldn't
hope to win. They'd cut us to bits."

"Suppose the other four didn't—couldn't know that Gaza
was under attack—"

"That's it! Cut off their communications by courier and
carrier pigeon." Ahimelek was excited.

"Not yet enough," David commented. "How are we to be
sure that the duke of, say, Ekron won't decide to take on the
particular army corps we place in front of Ekron? Suppose he
routed that corps, then what?"

"There's no guarantee on God's earth that any of the four
dukes won't do just that," said Joab. "And I say—"

David interrupted him. "Yes! There is! There's Adonai on
Adonai's earth! There's Adonai's Ark. The Philistines will not
tackle any army that carries the Ark."

"But, David, there's only one Ark. There are four cities."

"Aye. But how many Philistines can recognize the real Ark?

There was a moment's silence, then a loud, appreciative laugh. "I'll get the Tyrian craftsmen to help us out," David continued. "But now, whatever we do, we cannot allow that convoy to arrive in Philistia." There were nods from everyone around the table. "Now, few outside in the city and among the tribes realize it, but at this moment we are walking on the sharp edge of the sword of death. This is a question of our supreme interest: the life and death of the kingdom! We therefore must bring everything we've got into this one struggle. For we win or we lose."

After the somber silence that followed, David outlined his plans. "I am going to leave only one regiment of Hittites here to defend Zion. Uri with the bulk of his Hittites will deal with the convoy. That land up there used to belong to the Hittites; the remaining Hittites will be friendly.

"Uri," he said, turning to him. "You will leave for Tyre within the week. Hiram will transport you and your men across the sea. Take that convoy from behind. In the meantime I will send instructions to Zoba and Damascus. The Syrians will block the coastal route southward. Between you, you and the Syrians should crush that convoy. Take no prisoners. Capture all the goods, but don't allow Zoba or the Syrians to have any of it. We cannot attack Philistia so long as that convoy exists."

Uri nodded ruefully, smiling a little. "There goes my betrothal!"

"Oh, by Adonai! Our Uri wants to go to bed!" David said jokingly. "And pray, who is the lass, Commander?"

"A daughter of Ammiel," Uri answered. "Bathsheba is her name."

"With a name like that"—Bathsheba's name meant "she who was sworn"—"the girl will wait for you forever, Uri," David said kindly. "But our matter cannot wait. We must leave within the week. Now as to our main problem. There is a short cut."

"The 'underground avenue'?" Joab broke in.

"Yes! My brother Ozem saw it. Clearly we cannot lay siege to Gaza in any ordinary way. It would take many, many months—even if we had that much time—and we haven't! We have to get in there by stealth. And I know only one way: the Iron Trail. But we don't know where the entrance is. That's one thing these jackals would never tell me. We know it's near Eilath; we must find out exactly where. Also the strength of the guard.

"The trail comes out in Gaza itself. There is an entire underground city beneath Gaza, and that's where the trail ends. Achish told me that much.

"Lastly, we know that Gaza and the other cities communicate by courier and by carrier pigeon. We have to know the regular times and routes of both couriers and pigeons for all cities, particularly for Gath and Ekron. You"—he turned to old Jonathan, his chief of intelligence—"must establish these for us, so that we can cut all communications when we need to.

"Now all this will take us well into the summer. We should plan to gather for the attack in September. All divisions of the army should be ready by July at the latest."

Before the end of the winter the first dispatches arrived from Uri. He had located the convoy assembly point and had established perfect liaison with David's Syrian allies. The convoy would obviously winter up north, but it would be moving with the first sign of spring. Uri's plan was to wait until very late in order to catch as much of the convoy as possible. The plan was approved by David in Zion. During those winter months, too, David sent secret messengers to Hiram with a special request: he wanted four replicas of the Ark of the Covenant, complete in every detail down to the figurines of the gold cherubim on its cover. Hiram sent six of his best craftsmen to Zion. There they worked in the privacy of Uri's barracks. In late March, the message of victory came from Uri: he had destroyed the convoy and captured its materiel. The Phenicians would transport it by sea to Tyre. From there it would go by caravan to Megiddo and the other northern garrison towns. He himself would march overland and be back in Zion by early June. David immediately sent him a message to proceed to Megiddo and station himself there to exercise and train the chariot corps. No word had as yet been received by David from Jonathan's spies concerning the Iron Trail. But by now he had an exact tally of Philistine courier and carrier-pigeon communications.

In late August the mustering order went out to the tribes for specific numbers of javelin men, lancers, swordsmen, slingshotmen, archers, camel riders, horsemen, mule and donkey riders. David also sent orders to Uri to leave Megiddo and come south along the plain of Sharon to Jaffa, some thirty miles north of Ashdod.

Early in September, David's grand campaign started. It lasted about two years. In scope and effect, it was the greatest of his reign and his era. He set out one afternoon with three of Joab's corps. They marched all night along prearranged routes. At one rest stop, near the Philistine border, each corps was joined by an oxcart carrying a replica of the Ark. By early morning light, one army corps sat in front of each of the three Philistine cities, Ekron, Ashkelon, and Ashdod. Not one Philistine soldier or citizen or courier would budge from his city as long as the Hebrew army sat there headed by what looked like the dreaded Ark of the Hebrew Covenant.

Abishai started marching a few hours later with his army corps. Just before he came in sight of Gath, he was joined by David and Joab, who brought him an oxcart bearing a fourth replica of the Ark. Abishai's station was in front of Gath. Simultaneously a squad of archers, placed, according to the findings of Jonathan's spies, beneath the normal routes of the carrier pigeons between all five Philistine cities, lay in readiness to shoot all the pigeons down. For the moment there could be no communication among the five fortress-cities.

Only one unnerving incident took place. As David approached Gath from the north, he was thinking particularly about Achish, when a shout from the advance scouts drew his eye to a small cloud of dust moving toward Gath from the west; it could be not more than a few horsemen at most.

"It's not soldiers. It's not that at all," David muttered. "It's something else. Come on, Joab!" he said, spurring his camel to a full gallop. "Let's ride ahead with a company. The others can follow."

The nearer the galloping men drew to Gath, the nearer that cloud of dust drew also to the city. David could see it streaking ahead faster than they were going. Eventually he could make out what it was: one lone chariot drawn by six horses carrying a chariot driver and one other man.

"It's an archer! Stop them. Anyone! It's a message from Gaza to Gath! Stop them!"

But the chariot was going at breakneck speed. It outstripped all pursuers. David and Joab watched in horror as it crashed into the outlying tents and men of Abishai's army drawn up in front of Gath, crushing everything in its path, its driver and occupant and horses miraculously escaping the javelins and arrows launched at them from every side. On it went at full speed and full tilt at the blank north wall of Gath, unremitting in speed, the driver whipping the six horses to a frenzy. At Abishai's camp, David and Joab reined in their camels.

"My God! They won't be able to stop in time!" Joab said.

"They don't want to stop in time, Joab," David said quietly and gravely. "Just watch now. And know what sort of men we're up against in this war."

The end of the unnerving episode came quickly. The chariot and the six horses continued toward the wall at unstoppable speed. Just before impact, the archer straightened, took a single arrow with a heavy padded shaft to it, strung his bow, and shot the arrow over the wall into Gath. Moments later, the first pair of horses ran at top speed into the wall, splitting their skulls and breastbones. The other four horses piled up after them in a horrible confusion of legs, bodies, harnessing, and blood-curdling neighing. The two occupants shot up from the chariot as though plucked by an invisible hand, and were hurled with a dull thud against the wall. Their bodies fell down on the thrashing limbs of the dying horses. The chariot was shattered like an eggshell.

"As Adonai lives!" Joab breathed, aghast. "But why?"

"Gaza had to get a message through. We have shut off all their communications. So these two men had to die. Dagon demanded it. They were glad to do it." He turned away and walked toward his tent. Joab caught up with him. "We've all the time in the world now, Joab," David threw back at him. "Let's get down and rest. Nothing will happen before midnight."

It was about one o'clock in the morning when Joab woke David. "There's a strange sound coming from Gath."

"Oh! They've started." He sat up and listened. It was the sound of many women's voices, of women and children. And up from the center of Gath, David and Joab could see the bright gleam of flames.

"What is it now?"

"They are burning their women and children," David answered. "They know Gath cannot be saved."

Gradually the flames at the center of Gath spread outward and upward. By then the wailing had stopped. The whole of the Hebrew army corps stood and watched as the dark bulk of Gath began to light up with leaping fires licking around the battlements, spitting through the narrow casement windows.

"What do the men do now?"

"Once the women and children are dead, then the men stand fully armed." David spoke dully, as if reciting a distasteful lesson. "At their posts. Without budging. Without crying. Holding shield and sword. Until they can stand no longer, they stand. Then they fall. Perhaps to their knees. Still holding their weapons. Perhaps on their backs. Perhaps on their face. But if you examine those bodies after it's over, you'll find the swords in the charred hands. The helmets on the skulls. The shields around bare bones. Just like that."

Now no sound could be heard but the crackling of the fires and the crashing of collapsing roofs. All stood watching Gath burn, no one speaking, their eyes stark, the night sky lit up, the smell of burning human flesh in their nostrils. After two hours, the flames started to falter. No one could have survived that inferno.

"Wake me at dawn," David said, and went off to rest. A somber Joab gave orders to bivouac for the remainder of the night.

As they rode back to Zion followed by the four army corps, Joab was curious. "What did they mean us to think?"

"Look around at the men. Have you talked with them today?"

"No."

"You'll find that the Philistines put fear into many. If my enemy shoves death down my throat even before I get to him, he already makes me taste it. And no one likes the smell of death. He smells his own mortality."

The rest of that winter passed uneventfully. In the spring, David made his annual early foray into Philistia and devastated the whole area. The Philistine fist was still bunched; the four Hebrew army corps stayed at their stations, a replica of the Ark facing each city. But the Philistines were surviving. David knew that essential food supplies were coming by sea to Ashkelon, Ashdod, and Gaza.

When the king returned to Zion, Jonathan was waiting for him with good news: they had found the entrance to the Iron Trail, and they also had an exact tally of the guards and a detailed description of the activity around the southern mouth of the trail.

At the end of May, David traveled to Tyre and met with Hiram. They worked out a plan to blockade all three Philistine ports, Ashdod, Ashkelon, and Gaza. To be effective, the blockade of Gaza would have to be put into operation simultaneously with a land attack. It would take Hiram all summer to assemble the necessary men-of-war. The campaign would begin in September.

"David, my friend," said Hiram, "you are now facing the problem of how to take a walled city. Now come with me."

He led the way down to the shipyards. As they entered, Hiram went on. "You've never seen a man-of-war out of the water, have you? Well, look at it. Look at it well!"

David walked the entire length from stern to bow. He stopped there, staring at the bronze battering ram attached to the keel.

"You'll never see it above water level," Hiram said, "but it's devastating beneath. Now come and see our newest design." He took him farther on and inside a warehouse that teemed with workmen and machines. "Here we test the strength of our rams," Hiram said, pointing to what looked like a tripod about fifteen feet high. Suspended from it was a metal battering ram with snub nose and widening body. A hemp hawser was attached to the wide end and went back to a windlass. About six feet beyond the tripod and suspended ram, they had constructed a wall of mortared stone blocks. "This ram is mostly iron, the first of its kind. We will have to build a ship specially to take it! Now watch!" He gave an order. The workmen drew the ram back by turning the windlass, until it remained poised at triple its length from the wall. Hiram looked around. "Ready?" he asked David. Then, "Let her go!" The rope was cut with a single blow of an ax. The ram leaped forward at the wall, battering into the mortared stones. It bounced and hit again, then came to rest. "Now," Hiram said, "come and examine the wall."

Where the ram had struck, the blocks had been shattered, the mortar smashed. Splits radiated around the wall from the gaping hole in its center.

"Can you imagine four of these at work on the gates or the walls of a city?"

David's reaction was typical. "How many have you ready?"

Hiram laughed. They left the warehouse and were passing down by the construction ships, talking as they went, when David's eyes fell on the three-tiered towers from which the Phenician builders constructed their high ships. "How high can you build one of these?" he asked.

"We have found that by pyramiding them we can build a manageable tower of up to sixty feet. Oh, I see what you're thinking. Yes, it would be a great attack tower for high walls. But the men on it would be exposed."

"Not if the tower were armored."

"True, true," Hiram said, reflecting. "Let's go and look at some plans."

When David returned to Zion a week later, he outlined his

ideas to his council. It was decided that several hundred men should be picked out and sent to Tyre at the end of August. Hiram would have four battering rams and six towers ready by then. The men would be trained on the spot in their use. The council put Ira in charge of the project.

Then, at a planning meeting with Joab and his commanders, David outlined the strategy of the use of ram and tower.

"The rams are useful only for breaking in gates and doors and for a weak part of a wall. And when in use, the men working the ram must be protected. The Kerethite phalanx will not be enough. It cannot withstand boiling oil or heavy boulders, and as you know, the Philistines use both. So we need to construct roofs for these rams that will withstand oil and boulders, and allow the men beneath to work the ram.

The towers are specifically for those parts of the walls where the enemy is strongest. We must avoid simply sending men charging at walls where the defending firepower is thickest."

"Unless we want them killed for sure," Uri said grimly.

"Exactly! These towers will be invaluable. But we need to train our archers to fire and hit from a moving platform. It's not easy. And we must have all this ready by September's end. We can thank God that the terrain around Gaza is level. Have you a good architect who can take charge of these new machines for us, Joab?"

"Oliab ben Matta, yes. He's the man."

When the meeting was ended, and they all stood up, Hushai the Arkite had a word with David. "No matter what you think will be the outcome of your siege of Ashkelon and those of Ashdod and Gaza, you have to think of the tribes. You depend on them for conscripts and supplies. You promised to take a wife from each one of them. My emissaries have drawn up a list of twelve selected from about two hundred candidates. You have to decide. Now! And I've spoken with Zadok and the other priests. They see no difficulty in shortening the ceremonies, or even in holding a joint ceremony for more than one wife. Privately, of course, and not in public—"

"Oh, Hushai, in private—for the love of God!"

"You've got to go over the list. I'll read a name and give you the reasons for its choice. Then you must select a date. Early September is my idea. Before you set out."

David sat down with a resigned air. "Let's hear the names." Hushai read out the names of David's proposed wives, adding the tribal commentary on each. "Laaga from Reuben...Dovmoreth from Simeon...Tovel from Dan

. . . Yophipanah from Naphthali . . . Helah from Gad
. . . Elihanna from Assher . . . Sara from Issachar . . . Naamith
from Zebulun . . . Hananel from Ephraim . . . Yashi from
Manasseh . . . Batya from Benjamin . . . Yehudiya from Judah . . ."

Hushai drew a deep breath. "Now remember, David, before
you say anything. I've checked. They're all virgins. Their health
is excellent. Teeth, hair, eyes, skin are all unblemished. None
of their families have any hereditary disease. All are under eighteen. Three are sixteen."

"You didn't use the word 'beautiful' once," David replied
morosely.

David thus became the possessor of twelve new wives, all of
whom he married before the siege of Gaza. Each of these new
marriages was political. Four of them would give him no children, and eight would give him one son each. That winter he
bedded all twelve, decided that he liked only four of them—actually, the four who never gave him any children, Laaga of Reuben, Dovmoreth of Simeon, Tovel of Dan, Yophipanah of Naphthali. These, he told Shunnamith, he would bed again. The others
became permanent members of his harem.

Winter was spent in preparation. David passed many hours
questioning the Pelethites who had lived in Gaza, and in going
over his own memories of what he had seen in the city. He sent
a special messenger to Hiram to garner further details from the
king of Tyre and his Phenicians. Under David's direction, they
constructed a model of Gaza out of baking clay—the kind used
for writing tablets.

From all available information, it seemed to David that the
weakest sides of Gaza were the east and north walls. Outside the
north wall lay the race track and the cemetery with the famous
grassy knoll of Dagon at its center. Outside the east wall stretched
the spacious exercise and parade grounds. About Gaza's port the
best estimates were pessimistic: the entrance was narrow; the
booms blocking the harbor were of wood reinforced with iron;
the fortifications were stout. The sea lanes outside could be
blockaded, but any attack from the sea on the port would be extremely hazardous.

"I think we have to take a gamble," David concluded at the
end of a marathon planning session. "We know that the Iron
Trail will take us inside the city—assuming that it is still
usable. If we can use it, then we can subvert the city from
within—assuming that they don't get us first. The best way
to assure complete inward surprise is to come at them from the
sea as well, and distract them from the underground route.

Moreover, if we take the port, there's nothing to keep us from the city itself."

Orders, therefore, went out in late December that a contingent of ten thousand desert fighting men would leave early in January and, by the second week in March, be in position to capture the southern end of the Iron Trail. The ten thousand would then enter the underground avenue and march to Gaza. Abishai's army corps would guard the mouth of the trail as a means of retreat and escape for the ten thousand, should the venture run into trouble. Two other armies, totaling about eighteen thousand men, would leave for Tyre at about the same time to board Hiram's troopships. At the end of February Hiram's men-of-war would blockade the Port of Gaza, and the ships bearing the eighteen thousand troops would anchor off Gaza about March fifteenth.

The ten thousand marching up the Iron Trail would reach Gaza by about March twentieth. They would occupy the port and signal the transports to enter. Before that, David's main army would have begun preliminary assaults on the east and north walls. David had one imperative instruction to commanders and men: when they entered Gaza, Duke Shekelath was his and his alone.

During February, signals started to come through from Kadesh-Barnea and from Hiram of Tyre. The strategy was working. The main armies departed for Philistia, entering through the southern desert. And a few days into March the last signal from Joab came, announcing his entry with the ten thousand into the maw of the Iron Trail. David departed immediately with the Kerethites and proceeded to join the patrols outside Gaza harbor. As March twentieth approached, the troopships moved in as close as safety allowed. There they waited.

On the night of the nineteenth, as David sat with the fleet offshore watching the lights of the Port of Gaza, the watchman in the crow's nest called the captain and pointed to a flat five-man scallop rowing furiously toward the fleet. David was alerted.

As the scallop approached the first line of men-of-war, the helmsman in the scallop cried out: "Peace, my brothers! Peace! And victory to my Lord David of Bethlehem!" No one attacked the scallop. It stopped at the first line. There was some exchange of words. Two Hebrews climbed down into the boat and it was rowed through the front line and headed for David's transport. When it came up, two of the Philistines left it and climbed aboard. They were unarmed. David, standing with his officers, examined them, speaking in Philistine.

"Who are you? Why have you come?"

One of the Philistines was spokesman. "I am Palganath. This is Maokh. We have come because we served under my Lord Achish, and we know from him that victory will belong to our Lord David. In exchange for our lives and that of our comrades, we will lift the booms at the harbor—"

"You two alone can't do that."

"We are not alone. My Lord Achish's entire company, one hundred and eighty men in all, is with us."

"Go on."

"We can do this tomorrow night. There is no moon. Furthermore, once you are inside, we can show you the covered entrance that leads to the five ducal palaces."

David then asked them to describe the defenses of Gaza, the disposition of troops, the number of defenders. His early estimates had not been wrong. Then he asked them a crucial question: "What guarantee can you give me that this is not a trap?"

The Philistines were nonplused. "None, my Lord David," they answered, reddening and looking at each other. "None! We haven't thought of that."

"And tell me: how was it possible for you to get out of Gaza harbor in safety, without being detected?"

"My Lord Achish's company has the midnight-to-dawn watch, my Lord David. Duke Shekelath wishes us to be the first to die, and he expects you to attack by night and from the harbor side."

"You speak about Lord Achish's company," David broke in harshly, "as if every man in it believed in Adonai—all true Hebrews! What sort of nonsense is that? Do you take us for fools? Joab, take these liars and—"

"My Lord David!" Palganath was almost shouting but there was no fear in his voice. "Kill us if you will—we do not believe in Adonai—we only know our Lord Achish is in prison—we wish to avenge him—we don't want to die." He fell silent, his eyes on David's face.

David stared for a long minute at the two men, at the lights of Gaza, and at the expressions on his officers' faces. He made up his mind. "Very well. Tomorrow. At midnight. Wave a lantern three times. In diagonal fashion. If we see no light, we do not come in."

"Are you sure, David?" Hushai asked him.

"No." His tone was level. "But I feel they are genuine. We will find out tomorrow."

For Joab and the ten thousand marching stealthily through the underground avenue, it had been a harrowing experience. The passageway had fallen into disrepair. The men grew to hate the smell of the pitch torches and oil lamps they carried for illumination. Most of the air holes had been blocked by sandstorms. They continually fought off tribes of desert rats. A few men lost their nerve and had to be killed. But every mile or so along the way, they found an enlargement in the passage, with a concealed trap door leading to the open air. It was thus that, as they approached the south wall of Gaza, they were able to check periodically on their objective.

However, although Joab thought they were beneath the outer walls, the passageway still wound on. After another fifty yards, Joab pricked up his ears. He halted the entire column and listened. It was the sound of marching feet. An alert was passed down the line. The front torches and lamps were extinguished. Joab and his officers stood there perspiring, swords, bows, and lances ready. He could see light flickering around a gradual curve about fifteen yards away. "String your bow! And at my signal, let fly, not before," he whispered to the others. He could now hear a low buzz of voices. "Get ready!" he said. The light grew brighter and brighter. He could now see the moving shadow of the first man before he appeared around that corner.

Joab lifted his javelin and took aim. "Through the throat," he said to himself. "Straight through his throat. Then a wild charge." The first figure came around the curve walking like a cat, tall, golden-haired, his left hand holding a lantern high, a huge sword in his right hand held ready to cut and thrust. It was very nearly a tragedy. Joab yelled out first in delight and then in horror, "Don't move! Don't fire! It's David! David!"

As he embraced Joab, David said: "Now I know that Adonai is with us. These"—indicating two tall Philistines—"are our friends. Palganath and Maokh, men of Achish. We wanted to find you, Joab, before you took a wrong turn and ended up in the city sewers. We will stay here until six o'clock. The guard at the port changes then, and the assault on the north and east walls will begin. We took the port during the night, almost without losing a man. Let's hope it goes well. We'll hit them from four directions: from within the palaces, from the port, and from the north and east walls." As they sat waiting for morning, Joab asked David about Achish. "All our friends know is that he's alive, in a cell beneath the temple of Dagon. Let's hope we get to him first."

The rest of the much-fabled story of how David took Gaza is told in the detailed chronicles of the kings of Judah. The general assault took place at six o'clock. The fighting went on for four days. The Philistines were finally reduced to little pockets of hardened warriors, each of which had to be taken individually and at great cost to Hebrew life.

The key to David's success was his secret entry into Gaza. When Shekelath saw the lumbering towers landing the Hebrews, he laughed outright. He knew all the tricks. But when he saw the body of Gaza attacked on its two most vulnerable sides, and found the port at his back completely in Hebrew hands, with men and supplies pouring up the Palm Avenue right into the city, he knew he was lost. The knell of death in his mind was the sudden shout, "David! David! David!" from the center courtyard of the five ducal palaces.

The moment he realized this, he put his aide-de-camp, Gonlan, in charge, and then he ran. He knew he was going to die. All he could think of now was Achish alive in that cell beneath the temple. Achish had to die with him. Achish was responsible.

Shekelath was sixty-one years old at this time, but a magnificent sixty-one, as slim and tough as a hardwood bow. He ran through the curved gallery, around the walls leading to the temple. Below in the courtyard he could see only a milling crowd of soldiers locked in deadly combat. He shot in through the door in the temple wall and down the stairs that ran down around the inner wall. At the bottom was Dagon's altar with its huge statue. To its left was the door to the cells. He could hear only the clatter of his own mailed feet on the way down. He hit the floor, swung to the left, and started for the door to the cells. He was halfway there when a voice rang out.

"Shekelath! My Lord Duke Shekelath!" He stopped, sword drawn. From behind the altar at the right hand side leaped David, the tip of his sword toward the ground, his legs apart, looking at Shekelath with burning eyes.

"My Lord Duke! You cannot go down there. It's guarded by Hebrews." Shekelath glanced over. Four husky Hebrews slipped out of the shadows. "That is to say, unless you kill me first," David went on. "Kill me! And you will certainly kill them." The voice was loud, taunting, contemptuous. The Philistine said nothing. He raised his eyes to the inscrutable face of Dagon's statue. For a few moments he was utterly still, his mind flooded with recollections of Dagon, of Luqqawatna, of his dead wife Solka, and their children, of the glory life had once promised him. Then he sprang into sudden ferocious life. His roar echoed around the temple.

"Solka! Dagon! Solka!" And he was transformed into a hurtling projectile shooting straight for the immobile David, his sword held steady and straight. Joab and the others saw it all fleetingly. The rushing body of the Philistine, his teeth bared, his outstretched arm, the gleaming sword, David's immobility until the last moment. Then the sudden snakelike upward flash of the sword of Goliath, which rang as it tore Shekelath's sword from his hand. It fell to the floor between the two men.

Shekelath had stopped. He looked at his sword. Then at David. Then at his sword again. Silence. "Pick it up, Shekelath!" the Hebrew said. Shekelath calculated. He bent down cautiously, stretching out his right hand. Slowly, agonizingly, his eyes watching David, his fingers closed over the haft steadily, stealing up the length of the haft and gripping it fully. In a bending position, holding the sword, he looked up at David. The Hebrew still maintained the same stance: the tip of Goliath's sword on the ground, David leaning on its haft. Shekelath tensed himself to leap. Again Joab saw the flash of Goliath's sword, heard Shekelath's scream of rage and pain, and then saw Shekelath falling back, staggering, leaving his hand and a portion of his wrist on the haft of his sword on the ground. He had not been able to lift it. He and David were not more than six feet from each other.

"Pick it up with your left hand, my Lord Duke." The voice was as hard as ever.

"You will kill me, Hebrew. But it's no use," Shekelath said defiantly.

"Kalkodon is gone! The mysteries of Dagon are finished!" David threw back tauntingly.

"We cannot be beaten! We will outlive your pygmy kingdom! Our Strong Ones will live on in other places, in every age. Thousands of years hence." Shekelath stood back, swaying, not letting the groan escape. He knew his left hand would be the next to go. And then? His legs. And then? He could not bear the thought of lying, a bleeding trunk on the ground, with this Hebrew pig leering at him. David saw his eyes and recognized his intent. He was ready for Shekelath as the Philistine sprang forward, his chest open for David's thrust, the roar of Philistia on his lips. But the Hebrew side-stepped and his sword cut down, taking off Shekelath's left arm. David faced Shekelath with one last stare.

"For them all, Shekelath! For all the Hebrews you did to death! For Achish!" He swung the sword back and, in one wide swath, cut the Philistine's legs off at the knees.

"All right! Guard the pig!" he yelled as he ran for the door leading to the cell. Shekelath had collapsed on the floor. Down below, it was not difficult to find Achish. He was alone on the stone floor surrounded by filth and dried blood. David handed the lamp to Joab and knelt down beside the miserable and unconscious remnant of Achish, his arms going around the emaciated trunk. At the sight of those dark-brown empty eye sockets, David's eyes filled with tears. He put his hand on Achish's forehead and murmured: "Achish! Achish! It's David. Wake up. Achish! You're safe, Achish!"

The mouth opened. Achish was trying to say something. David opened a flask and poured a few drops of liquor on the lips. He leaned down close to the mouth, and listened. He could hear only the air whistling in Achish's throat. He put his lips to Achish's ear again. "Achish, it's all right. We are all safe. Shekelath is finished. Gaza is ours."

He leaned down again, putting his ear to those lips, and heard the faint, agonizing syllables, "...David...David... Adonai...God...one...kiss...."

Joab had never seen David in such psychic pain. He stood up. There was no beauty in his eyes. "Bring the pig down now," was all David could say. They rolled Shekelath onto a cloak and brought him down to the cell. Lying on the ground, helpless, Shekelath saw David towering over him, his sword sheathed, his arms holding Achish across his chest.

"Cut out his tongue."

Joab knelt on Shekelath's chest, forced his mouth open with a sword haft, dug inside with his dagger, and hacked out the Philistine's tongue.

"Now chain him to the wall."

That done, the Hebrews left, David carrying Achish. He had his old friend well tended, but he survived only a few days, during which the final struggle for Gaza was fought. At the end of the first day, the ducal palaces and the outer areas were under David's control. But three more days were spent securing the city. The Philistines fought every inch of the way from house to house, from street to street. Underground, they had to be smoked out. And even Joab the killer was sick at heart when it was all over, so bloody was the inch-by-inch conquest of Gaza the Magnificent.

When it was finished, David had Achish's remains placed in a cedar war chest and buried out in the open countryside by a pool of fresh water. Achish would have liked such a burial place. And he had had his dearest wish—to meet with David before dying.

The temple of Dagon was stripped of its statue and altar, of its hangings and trophies. The door leading to the cells beneath the temple was blocked up, burying Shekelath alive. The temple was destined to become a camel stable, and, finally, demolished in the time of King Solomon.

David's total victory over the dreaded Philistines left him strangely empty and morose. Precisely now, when all power was within his grasp, he locked himself in his quarters in the Cedar Palace, buffeted by an army of gnawing doubts. Was this the "all," the total sum of happiness he had fought for and suffered for? Why did victory taste so bitter? Was it the pain of seeing Achish truncated and dying? What difference was there between serving Dagon and Adonai? In either case men died, women suffered, cities were burned, children were massacred. What reason had he now for going on?

As long as the king remained in seclusion, the whole of Zion remained strangely quiet. David did not know it, but his whole administration was in limbo. And it lasted almost three weeks. It was Malaki, sitting at the great double doors of the palace, who succeeded in breaking this mourning period by supplying David with the answers to his questions. He sent for David's wife Maaka and gave her instructions. At the beginning of the third week, David, closeted by himself on the seventh floor, heard the voices of children in the courtyard breaking the pall of silence. They were singing. He listened intently, because he recognized the melody as one of his own. Quickly he stood up, opened the window. The words sailed up:

> "Who is this
> that comes up out of the wilderness?
> Out of the wilderness
> Perfumed with the myrrh of war,
> Sweet with the frankincense of peace.
> Who is this?

He is my hero!
Attacked by the enemy,
Comforted by the angel.
He is my hero!
Surrounded by the heroes of Israel!
My hero! . . ."

He had composed that song for his triumphal entry into Hebron years before. He leaned over the balcony, a new excitement running through him. Below he could see the two golden-haired children, the seven-year-old Absalom hand-in-hand with the six-year-old Tamar, their faces uplifted to his windows, their blue eyes shining with hope, the two young voices ringing up to him, clear, untroubled, trusting, full of promise. ". . . Attacked by the enemy, / Comforted by the angel. . . ."

Inside himself he began to notice immediately a curious thing: all those doubts and questions ranged themselves, as it were, over on one side of his soul, and the promises of life, of grace and beauty, on the other side. The enemy. The angel. And he himself stood in between, with the choice to turn to either side. His eyes moistened as Tamar caught sight of him peering over the edge of the balcony. She nudged Absalom, pointed up at their father, and both began to wave to him as they finished the refrain. ". . . He is my hero! / Surrounded by the heroes of Israel. . . ."

David turned in panic and ran for the door, as if he had very little time left. He was halfway down the wide staircase when Absalom and Tamar rushed into his arms, hugging him, burying their faces in his shoulders, crying, and kissing him. He could not speak for a moment, but held them and caressed their heads. "My promises," they heard him whisper finally. "My future, my blessings from Adonai. I love you! I love you!"

With one child clinging to each hand, he walked down into the lobby. Maaka and Abigail were there, smiling. Haggith stood by herself with her young son, Adoniyahu, holding on to her skirts.

When David was almost out the door he heard Haggith hissing at Maaka and Abigail, "I know! I know what you're doing! It won't work!" And she flounced up the stairs, leading Adoniyahu.

"As if that half-witted ass of hers could be king after David," Abigail said calmly. David did not turn around. Everything was as he left it three weeks ago. With a broad smile, he stepped out into the sunlight and looked around.

"Why all the music from Commander Uri's house, Malaki?"

"Commander Uri's betrothal, my Lord!"

"Adonai! I forgot." He quickly entered the house. "Now run along, Absalom, Tamar. Run along!" Raising his voice: "Joab! Joab!" His henchman appeared from one of the back rooms. "Joab, we must send presents to Uri for—"

"Already done, David! Already done. But what about some food and wine? There's a lot to be decided. Ashkelon and Ashdod have already capitulated. Ekron will be ours soon. I have many men on the Syrian border. And Ahitofel is tearing his hair—"

"Yes. By all means, we must talk. By the way," David continued, throwing a conspiratorial glance over his shoulder, "the women are already crowning my successor!"

The
Spice of Wine

About a year after the destruction of the Philistines, David spoke privately with Nathan. He had become acutely conscious, he told Nathan, of the blessings of Adonai—his wives, children, many sons, great wealth. David's palace and city were blossoming with the signs of his people's new prosperity.

"Sit here beside me, Nathan. I have an idea. Here I am in my palace. Yet out there in my courtyard, the Ark of the Covenant stands with only leather curtains to shield it. It is not fitting, Nathan! I want to build a regular *heykal*, a temple, for Adonai and his Ark."

Nathan looked away and gazed out the window. "The Ark is safe, quite safe, where it is, my Lord David." His tone was a little bit patronizing, almost supercilious.

But David in his enthusiasm ignored that. He started again, sure he would win the other man's approval if he only knew his intentions. "Prophet! I have a mission from Adonai to make this people one compact body for his spirit. I want to start with a temple, *the* temple—"

"A temple can be reduced to rubbish—"

"Then establish permanent choirs of Levites to sing Adonai's praises all day—"

"Choristers can be killed. Singers can be seduced, corrupted—"

"To accompany a continuous series of whole burnt offerings of choice lambs and beeves—"

"Our enemies can loot all our lambs and beeves—"

"While the priests and scribes faithfully copy and study the Torah of Moses—"

"Books can be burned—"

"And write the history of my kingdom in royal chronicles—"

"History can be twisted into lies." Nathan cocked one skeptical eye at David.

David was almost white with anger, but he made one last attempt. "Yet now that I have founded this kingdom of Adonai's people, this *medinath yisrael*—"

"Foreigners, full of hate, can come and tear your kingdom apart limb from limb," Nathan bored on suavely, imperturbably. "You can be succeeded by an idiot son or by an unfaithful grandson or an apostate great-grandson. Or an earthquake can come and reduce your Zion, your fortresses, your roads, your ports to shambles. The grass can grow in your royal bedroom. And owls can hoot at night about the shattered chimneys of your villas." He paused and looked somberly at David for a moment. David was speechless with frustration.

"Forget it all, my King. Your kingdom is not the body Adonai wants you to fashion. And it won't house his spirit."

"Great god of thunder!" David swore irascibly, his voice rising hoarsely. He stood up, banging the table with his fist. "What then—what more must I do, before this Adonai, this faceless tyrant, this absent God, lets me die in peace and—"

"Oh, my Lord the King has quite a long time to go before he is gathered to his fathers." Nathan, unruffled, stayed in his chair, a small wry smile lurking at one corner of his mouth. David's lower jaw dropped. He stared at Nathan. "If my Lord will stop going up in smoke and sit down, we can face realities." David sat down sullenly, gathering his cloak around him and folding his arms across his chest.

"Lord David, the most stupid thing a king or a prophet can do is think he understands the intentions of Adonai. You heard Adonai's words from your father, who heard them from Shalama. Instead of battering Adonai's ears with prayers for understanding, you offer your own interpretation! That is exactly what Saul did about Agag the Amalekite, what Moses did when told to strike the rock and bring water out of it."

David, irritated and resentful, said nothing at first. Finally, he spoke. "Very well. Very well. So?"

"Leave the building of a temple to your sons. Yes, organize the singers in a choir—a good idea. And, yes, Serayah can busy himself copying chronicles as accurately as he will be allowed, but the present rate of daily sacrifices is quite sufficient. I don't know what Adonai meant—how you can provide a womb, or what body you are supposed to fashion, or what the spirit, the *neshami*, is that Adonai spoke of. Neither does my Lord the King. That's not the point."

"And the point?" David's voice was leaden, his tone sardonic.

"Start with what we know, Lord David. Your people—as you call them—this disparate, rambunctious, argumentative, opinionated mob. The greatest division among them concerns Adonai."

"What do you mean?" David's genuine interest was now aroused.

"You have a son you call Shefatyahu. You know what his northern relatives call him? Elishafat! Why? You remember hearing about old Eleazar, the keeper of the Ark at Kiryath-Yearim in Saul's time? You know what the Judahites called him? That's right—Azaryahu. And then there's one of the priests here. His mother called him Yedayahu. Know what the northerners call him? Elyada! And when he makes the priestly circuit in western Galilee, up there they call him Baalyada!"

"So?"

"So the northerners worship El, and the southerners worship Adonai—whose sacred name I won't pronounce; and some of the Galileans worship Baal. And God knows what they worship in the Negev and Jabesh-Gilead! Now we say: Adonai is One. Adonai is God. He has a name we may not pronounce. But tell me, O King, do Hebrews worship one and the same God? And worship him as the only real God?

"And your beloved Torah! Ah-ha! Does my Lord King know the different versions that exist? In one version, Adonai makes Adam from wet mud. In another he fashions him out of nothing. One version speaks of gods, another speaks of the sons of the gods, another speaks of one God. Some versions call him El, some Adonai, some something else."

"What has all this to do with the 'body' of Adonai?"

"I don't know. I know it has to do with the spirit, the life of Adonai."

There was silence between king and prophet for a few moments, both men reflecting. When David spoke, it was with a great sigh. He was obviously bewildered, discouraged.

"What finally does Adonai want from me? Why hasn't he appeared to me as he did to so many heroes of our people? Why this continual demand for more from me? Tell me, Nathan! Please."

"Only Adonai can tell you, Lord David. In the meantime, proceed with the choirs and chronicles. And commission Zadok and Serayah to write one official copy of the Law."

"Am I to forbid the use of El and Baal as names of Adonai?"

"No. Just be sure that all divine names in the Torah refer only to Adonai."

*   *   *

In the period of relative peace and consolidation that followed the campaign against Philistia, David was suddenly confronted with another great crisis, this one intensely personal. She even had a name—Bathsheva.

When Bathsheva was married to Uri six months after her betrothal, she entered his house as mistress of all his servants and possessions. Uri's demands on her from the beginning were slight. Ahitofel had made it clear to him that the marriage was mainly political. So only now and again did Uri call Bathsheva to his bed. Soon he omitted the call altogether, for he was sixty-one and, although vigorous, he had reached a point in life at which he did not desire any woman.

As for Bathsheva, she loved Uri's house and possessions. She was not sexually self-indulgent. It became immediately clear to Bathsheva that, after Uri, the most important and well-informed person in his household was Lassatha the Egyptian. Lassatha, now in her forties, supervised all Uri's servants and slaves, and reported directly to Bathsheva. Surprisingly, the Egyptian's beauty of body and face had not noticeably faded, and she still dressed with a ribbon holding her hair, a light, embroidered linen stole around her neck and shoulders, and inlaid wooden sandals. Time had rather completed the gracefulness and beauty which had blossomed for David years before.

From the start, Bathsheva detected that Lassatha had an enormous personal interest in her. And Lassatha, never servile but always at Bathsheva's service, made her mind clear to her mistress: "My Lord David is the loneliest man in the whole of Israel, Mistress Bathsheva. He has renounced the love of women, but he stills needs their advice and support."

"Does he bed them often?"

"Now only when he has to."

"What's the way to his mind, then?"

"Beauty, Mistress." She looked at Bathsheva. "On the right occasion."

"Well, let's find the right occasion."

It was their first conversation of substance about David. Never did Bathsheva realize that Lassatha's intention was to afford David the chance of celebrating love such as David and she had talked of so long before. Lassatha thought Bathsheva in her beauty and sophistication could be the woman to awaken him.

"Lassatha, do you know if he ever was loved by a woman—just for love's sake?"

"Yes . . . Mistress." Lassatha turned away. Bathsheva looked at her sharply.

The Egyptian dropped to her knees and sat back on her haunches. Her eyes were cast down. "I gave him love," she said simply. "He did not return it." She told Bathsheva about her first meeting with David when he was twelve, then his third visit to her when he was a fugitive. "He did not travel with me to the skies of love, Mistress. He merely held love's hand."

"You loved him?"

"Yes, Mistress."

"Still?"

"Yes, Mistress. And, Mistress Bathsheva"—for the first time since the dialogue had begun, Lassatha raised her eyes to look at the other woman—"it is going to hurt him. Please see that he doesn't suffer more than is necessary."

Bathsheva found it difficult to believe that one person could love another as much as Lassatha seemed to love David. Why, she hadn't so much as exchanged a word with him for years! She stared dumbfounded at Lassatha.

"I'm sorry, but I don't understand."

Lassatha suddenly realized that Bathsheva *could* not understand. She had never loved and did not believe in love. "Mistress," Lassatha continued, "there already are many people tearing at him. I only hope that my mistress will spare him any additional—"

"Don't worry, Lassatha," she answered not unkindly. "I want to be near him, not service him!" Lassatha rose, smiling, and Bathsheva immediately felt the pressure between them relax.

"How are we going to reach the king?" she asked, like a schoolgirl working out a plan for watering the ink.

"We will find an opportunity, Mistress," Lassatha said. "Surely!"

But almost two years were to pass before that opportunity came. Women were kept in such shuttered obscurity that a man might consort daily with his neighbor and yet never know of, much less see, either his neighbor's wife or his neighbor's female slaves. First there was the age-old Hebraic conviction that a woman's only importance was childbearing and child-rearing. Besides, the roughness of social life, and violence, made it safer for women to remain hidden. Held in such insular security, women tended to hatch—and execute—elaborate plots.

When David was in his forty-fourth year, messengers arrived one day late in October announcing the death some weeks earlier of old King Nahash of Ammon, David's ally and vassal. His successor was his son Hanun, just seventeen. David decided to send a delegation to make sure the transition went smoothly, because Ammon's position protecting two caravan routes was vital.

Three weeks later David was celebrating Shabbath with his entire harem when Joab and Uri interrupted him, angered and dismayed.

The delegation had been set upon the minute it entered Rabbath-Ammon. Hanun had had his men shave off one side, exactly half, of every Hebrew's hair and beard—pubic hair and all—and the corresponding half of each delegate's clothes was cut off. "Benayahu must have been quite a sight," Joab concluded, "with half his big arse hanging out. In fact, he doesn't look very well now."

Joab was right. David laughed, but not for long. Humiliating David's mission was merely young Hanun's insolent way of telling David that he was taking over the Ammon caravan routes himself. In addition, he had succeeded in enlisting the Syrians at Beth-Rehov and Zoba in his rebellion. "King Maaka has sent a thousand men and King Ishtov has sent twelve thousand to help Hanun," said Joab. "You're going to face an army of forty thousand or more up there. Our northern borders are in enemy hands."

David hastily assembled his council. "The real enemies are the Syrians," he told them. "Joab, you'll take fifty thousand and capture Medeba"—a fortress of Ammon—"Abishai will command with you. That will give us a base for operating against Syria. Send a message to Ishipelet to have the entire chariot corps here in five days. Jonathan, I want all the information you can get about what's going on in Zoba and beyond. This is trouble."

Joab invaded Ammon one week later and found very little opposition. He did not understand the tactic until he reached Medeba, where the Ammonites poured out of the city into battle formations. Simultaneously the Arameans from Syria had doubled behind him and were forming for battle on his rear. Joab split his forces, putting Abishai in charge of twenty-two thousand men facing the Ammonites. He turned the remaining twenty-eight thousand around and faced the Syrians. His instructions were characteristically laconic. "If the Arameans push me, help me. If the Ammonites push you, I'll help you. Fight to the death."

David was in his council room when the dispatches arrived telling him that Joab had taken Medeba, repulsing the Arameans, then turned to help Abishai to rout the Ammonites. Joab awaited instructions at Medeba. Almost coincidental with Joab's message came intelligence that Hadadezer, king of Zoba, had acquired some nineteen thousand Mesopotamian conscripts to add to a chariot corps of eleven hundred and a camel corps of seven hundred men. Shovakh, Hadadezer's general, was in overall command of the uprising. That very afternoon, David left Zion at the head of an army of thirty thousand infantry, seven thousand camel riders and horsemen, and Ishipelet's chariot corps of twelve hundred.

What amazed Joab and the other Hebrew commanders was the speed and decisiveness of David's moves. He insisted on forced marches and made straight for the Edrei Gap even though none of them was familiar with its topography. David was already there and in battle formation when Hadadezer arrived. The Hebrews' main force of infantry faced the Syrians in a long battle line at Helam. Behind them were the chariots and the cavalry. Behind them were two columns, with a wide avenue in between, of archers, javelin throwers, and macemen. The Syrians sent in the chariots to break that long Davidic line. Coming on the heels of the chariots was Hadadezer's infantry. David's line, on order, parted in the middle, allowing the chariots to rush through into the lethal avenue behind them. Then the long front line closed over the chariots as David's chariots and cavalry moved out on both flanks of his infantry to close on the onrushing Syrian infantry. It was the classic "double-anvil" tactic, and it worked to perfection.

The Syrian chariots were pounded to pieces by David's firepower in that long deadly avenue. Seven hundred chariots were captured and about two hundred destroyed. Only about two hundred escaped. The Syrian infantry was ground fine by David's cavalry and infantry. Shovakh was killed along with his major officers. The Mesopotamians lost nearly fifteen thousand and David executed the rest. Of the Syrians, nearly ninety-five hundred perished.

David marched on to Zoba, where he dictated new and harsher peace terms, and Ammon was now at his mercy. From the time of the outrage on David's mission to Hanun, the entire campaign had taken less than a month. The harsh winter rains were already falling when he brought his triumphant armies back into Zion.

When the rains ended, David sent Joab to capture Rabbath-Ammon, execute Hanun and the other conspirators, terrorize the ordinary populace, and extract a fat penalty from everybody. Against his inclination, David allowed the aging Uri to accompany Joab. The Hittite had once lived in Rabbath-Ammon and knew the terrain. Besides, Uri was getting bored in Zion. For some reason the dazzling Bathsheva failed to captivate him; and the acidulous Ahitofel, who seemed to visit her every day, greatly irritated him. He was glad to be out with the soldiers again.

Uri was back in ten days. Rabbath-Ammon was under heavy siege, and he had come to discuss with David the prosecution of that siege. Together they went over a plan of the city's defenses. The city was built on three rock plateaus all connected by black basalt walls. The highest plateau held the palace, main barracks, storehouses, and the residences of the chief Ammonites. Hanun and the defenders had concentrated their heaviest firepower on the highest of the three plateaus. Therefore Joab should first cut off the two lower portions of the city, and then concentrate on the third.

They discussed tactics in detail, and it was late at night when they finished. "Now go home to your wife for the night, Uri, and leave tomorrow morning at your ease."

"God forbid, Lord David! How could I be in bed with my wife while Israel's armies fight out in the fields?"

So Uri went out and spread his army blanket outside the great double doors of the Cedar Palace. Across the way, Lassatha was watching the midnight scene: Uri and his officers settling down for the night, Malaki chatting with them all, the lanterns finally extinguished, and the silence. She looked across at David's windows. He was still up. She turned away and walked over to Bathsheva's bedroom.

"My master, Commander Uri, will not be coming home, Mistress. He will probably depart at dawn. I think that we should be ready to put our plan into action tomorrow. We may not get another opportunity soon."

Bathsheva, who had been waiting for Uri's possible return to the house, nodded happily and handed Lassatha the hairbrush. "Brush my hair, Lassatha. It's time we prepared for bed.

"You must have loved him very much, Lassatha," Bathsheva

said as the Egyptian gathered and stroked, in an attempt to draw her into conversation. Lassatha ignored the remark.

"I was wondering," Bathsheva began again, "if it was usual for the king to entertain the wives of his notables alone, without their husbands?"

"Oh, yes, Mistress," Lassatha answered. "It's the king's privilege, and an honor for both the wife and the official. Mistress Ahodith, wife of Benayahu, Mistress Lala, wife of Barzillai, Mistress Hallelya, wife of Ahimelek—all those and many more have been with the king. There's no stigma attached to it. He did not touch them. Their husbands were highly honored by the king's graciousness. It's one of the things that makes David so loved."

"Well"—and Bathsheva tensed for this question—"what do I do now that puts me beyond all those fine ladies?" She spoke as though asking herself as much as Lassatha.

Lassatha chose to say nothing, but when she had finished and was about to leave, Bathsheva said from her bed: "Lassatha, do me a favor, take off your sandals and stole and head veil." Lassatha obeyed. "There!" Bathsheva said, looking at her. "Now walk over to the door and back. I want to look at you." Lassatha did so. Bathsheva watched with delight and genuine admiration, for she had not a trace of jealousy. That was an emotion she simply could not comprehend. Then she laughed out loud and clapped her hands at the demure intoxication, the natural blend of sensuality and grace that Lassatha could put into simply walking.

"Lassatha, you have just taught me more by that walk than I have learned in all my twenty-three years." Lassatha smiled. "Thank you, Lassatha. Good night, sleep well. And about tomorrow, you'll arrange it all? And you're sure he'll be interested enough to send for me?"

"Yes, my lady. Of that I am sure. But my heart hurts now. It would kill me if my Lord David were to be hurt."

"Don't worry," Bathsheva said, raising her voice reassuringly. "Don't worry, Lassatha, there's no chance at all of that, no chance at all."

David's siesta the following day lasted three hours longer than usual. He had been very tired from his long discussion with Uri, and since all the big decisions had been made, he was free to relax. The sun was already declining when he arose. It was a warm, sweet spring afternoon, which put David into high spirits. He teased Afsaq and Balva as they bathed him.

Afterward, as they massaged him with sweet-scented Abyssinian oil, he looked for a while at those dark faces absorbed in their work, then closed his eyes and surrendered completely to the hands that were drawing, pushing, patting, gently coaxing muscles and nerves into a tingling sense of well-being. At a certain moment, he knew his entire being was restored.

"May Adonai bless the mothers who gave birth to you! Both of you!" he said, sitting up with a broad, easy smile. "And I myself, the king, will give them shining blessings! Now ask Shunnamith to bring me some food, please."

Shunnamith brought the tray to the balcony. "The evening air is so balmy and the sun so golden, it would be an abomination not to eat outside. Besides, My Lord King will soon be closeted with Master Ahitofel and the others for hours."

David came out slowly, lazily, and sat at the table, facing east. It was his favorite view of the city and its surroundings—the hills and the desert, out over the Salt Sea and up to Moab, which had sheltered his family. David liked to sit here and eat in a leisurely fashion, one part of his mind thinking of immediate problems—in this case, the council of state to be held later in the evening—another part of him enjoying the copper-gold wash with which the sun was now drenching the earthen walls and battlements of Zion. Shunnamith cut the bread into bite-sized pieces, sliced the cheese, poured the wine. No words passed between them to break the sweet peace of the moment. Shunnamith glanced just once at Uri's balcony and, when she had finished her work, glided noiselessly from David's table.

The day was not quite spent. It was what David called "the tawny hours" before dusk. The sun was still strong enough to accent the hues and tones of the city buildings, but all sharpness of outline was melting. Soon each contour of building and hill would slip into a vague half-light, half-darkness. The streets below were almost empty.

David chewed some bread and cheese ruminatively, his eyes lingering on the copper-and-green radiance of the Salt Sea; then he lifted his eyes to look again at "the sweet mountains of Moab." He lifted the wine gourd and took a long draught. As he lowered the gourd, his eyes fell on Uri's roof garden. Five young girl servants, naked in the Egyptian fashion, were filling the marble bath Uri used when he was at home. David was about to lay the gourd on the table and turned to take some bread and cheese when his head was pulled around as if by some magnetic force.

Shunnamith, watching from behind the hanging door curtain

of David's room, saw the cheese drop from one hand, the wine gourd from the other, as David rose with the tense absorption of a hunter sighting his quarry.

What first caught David's eye was the way the young woman walked. She seemed to come surrounded by luminescence. The servants removed her robe and she stepped naked into the bath, scented, David imagined, with blue Egyptian rose water. One of the servants unloosed her hair. David watched fascinated as the servants, chattering and giggling, sat to one side while the woman proceeded to wash each breast, each nipple, each arm and hand. She knelt in the water and washed her waist and belly and groin. She lay back, the water coming up to her chin, lifted up one long, graceful leg, then the other. Neither she nor any of her girls betrayed any consciousness that they were being watched from the only place in that corner of the city that was higher than Uri's terrace.

David was utterly motionless, transfixed. It seemed to him that he had stumbled upon some secret and forbidden ritual, where nothing rough—nothing male—was allowed.

Everything on that terrace—the brown, sensuous bodies of the serving girls, the blue silk robe lying carelessly on a chair, the green marble of the bath, the red and yellow tiles of the roof—all focused his gaze on the woman bathing. Her skin was whiter than any he had ever seen, her hair was of deep and mysterious black, and, as she threw her head back to laugh, David saw in her eyes the same extraordinary translucence seen in the very best Hebron white wines.

After less than a quarter of an hour, during which David had made no discernible movement, the woman stood up, her body glistening, and faced in David's direction. He who had hacked and hewn so many bodies to death, and who had lain with literally hundreds of women, now found himself mesmerized, as if between the lift of her breasts and the delicately rounded triangle at the confluence of her thighs, some long-abandoned hope had suddenly rekindled. He gasped at the strength that was manifest in that single, vulnerable, glowing body—so different from the strength that had won him battles and made him a king, yet finally so much more powerful. Then the servants draped her blue silk robe around her and escorted her inside.

It was some moments before David came to himself. He noticed that the knuckles of his hands were white where they gripped the parapet. An inner panic seized him He might never see her again! Had he ever seen her before? He never interfered in the private lives of his officials, above all in that of Uri, his oldest friend, his trusted and faithful commander. But who in God's name was she? What was she doing here? He had never felt such an imperious need to know about a woman. He had to know right now. Tomorrow would be too late—centuries too late, a thousand years too late. His life would be empty. Or he would miss some revelation. A whole ganglion of jangling fears, hopes, nameless desires, painful velleities, obscure impulses, drummed through him in a series of tremors.

"Will there be anything else, my Lord King?" Shunnamith was back to take the tray, her face expressionless. He stared at her open-mouthed.

"Ah, no, no . . ." He flushed red. After a moment, he began again. "Girl," he said abstractedly, "do you know the servants in Master Uri's house?"

"Why, yes, my Lord King."

"Well, find out from them quietly who the woman is who was bathing on the roof just now." His voice was tremulous, out of control.

Shunnamith smiled. "But we all know her, my Lord King. That is Master Uri's latest wife, Bathsheva, daughter of Ammiel, granddaughter of Master Ahitofel."

"Master Ahitofel's . . . I see!" David's face relaxed and his voice regained its usual timbre. "Very good, girl. That will be all." The hurt and disappointment that flitted across David's face on hearing her answer cut sharply into Shunnamith. She truly loved her master.

David had suddenly lost interest in the council of state. He paced the balcony, then back into the room, then out again, then in again. His thoughts were tumultuous. My God! Uri's wife! My God! But he had to see her up close.

He was still pacing when Shunnamith called him to the council room. The others noticed his strained look and manner, but only Ahitofel made a remark about it.

"Worried about the troops, my Lord King?"

David shook his head. "Master Ahitofel, you are far too wise and knowledgeable to think that. No. It's just that here at home I feel at a loss. Perhaps I should be up with the others besieging Rabbath-Ammon." As he asked the half-question, he suddenly realized: She's his granddaughter! Good God in heaven! Is there something between them? What sort of power would that give Ahitofel over me?

"The demons let loose inside us are often more trying than

the enemies on the outside, Lord David," Ahitofel said with the air of one who knew.

"And how does one exorcise such demons, Master Ahitofel?"

"Always confront them, Lord David. Face up to what is real."

David's participation in the council that evening was desultory, his responses aimless. Ahitofel, Hushai, Ahimelek, Barzillai, all sensed that he was out of form. They broke up early at Ahitofel's suggestion.

David was happier to be alone. He sat motionless on his balcony, looking at the shuttered windows of Uri's house, calculating, reckoning everyone's position—Uri's, Bathsheva's, Ahitofel's, his own. He went over each detail of what had happened. Hour after hour the same question returned unanswered: Why had Uri's wife done what no wife in Zion ever did—bathe openly on the roof of her husband's house? If there was any answer, it was this: because she was Ahitofel's granddaughter. But at Ahitofel's suggestion? If so, why? Perhaps because she was as great a nonconformist as Ahitofel? Or was there perhaps a deliberate plot aimed at him? About four in the morning David stood up. He had made a decision, and he slept well.

The next day, Bathsheva was preparing to take her siesta when Lassatha entered.

"If you please, my lady. I have received a message for you from my Lord the King."

"Yes?" Bathsheva was annoyed by her own anticipation.

"My lady is invited to dine with the king tonight." Lassatha's eyes were lowered, her expression unreadable.

"Have the servants prepare my bath at five o'clock, Lassatha." As Bathsheva watched Lassatha go, she sensed something in the Egyptian that was so muted as to be obvious. "Lassatha! Lassatha!" The Egyptian stopped. "Things have gone well—have they not?"

Lassatha turned. In the shadow of the doorway, her eyes were darkened. There was no apparent change in her face. "Yes, my lady. Exactly as I said they would." She paused, obviously with something more to say. "My lady will remember what I added, the time that we talked..." Her voice sank to a whisper. Bathsheva looked at this woman who had already possessed David.

"Yes, Lassatha. I will remember. Do not worry."

"It's not worry, my lady. Rather—"

"Yes, yes, I know." Bathsheva cut her off. She knew that Lassatha loved David, and love that would sacrifice itself frightened Bathsheva.

In that delicious procrastination that some women find so precious before sallying forth for a special occasion, Bathsheva spent an entire extra hour straightening a line here, fixing a curl there. She had finally chosen, with Lassatha's help, a rose-colored silk gown held at the neck with a golden string. She put on lapis lazuli earrings set in white gold, a single gold Egyptian pendant around her neck, and some light rings with rubies and diamonds. She did not wear a veil. When at last she was satisfied, she rose and, accompanied by two maidservants and two bodyguards, walked over to the Cedar Palace. Malaki was sitting at one side of the double doors.

"Greetings, Lady Bathsheva," he said in the solemn voice he used for all such greetings. "Eat well and to the health of the king and your own health!" Bathsheva stopped and looked curiously at the empty sockets in that calm, distorted face.

Almost immediately David's house steward, the tall Nubian slave Kushai, bowed in front of her, his forehead almost touching the ground. With an eloquent gesture of long fingers, and without actually touching her, he drew her gently after him. She barely had time to take in her surroundings—the square, high-ceilinged lobby, its cedar rafters hung with long lamp chains, its walls decorated with the king's war trophies, the lion- and bearskin rugs on the wooden floor, a main staircase sweeping to the next floor. She had no sooner started up the stairs after Kushai than she saw David waiting at the top.

He wore a flowing house robe of his favorite deep blue, fastened with golden buckles at the shoulders and bordered with white rabbit fur. The royal headband gleamed on his forehead. It held the golden hair in place around his temples; the rest of it fell to his shoulders. Bathsheva had schooled herself a thousand times to think of this moment, and of what she would do and say. But she forgot every one of her planned reactions.

True, she noted everything—his hair, his face, his trimmed beard, his sandals peeking from under the hem of his robe. But once his eyes met hers, she was powerless to lower her gaze. For his eyes were not only far more blue than she had expected, but in the lamplight they were flecked with gold. His gaze was open, unwavering, and seemed to embrace her in its luminosity. Bathsheva could not read his look. And she had an inane desire to stroke his long eyelashes. Well before she reached the landing, her hands had begun to shake, yet she could barely keep from laughing out loud at her own reactions. This is idiotic, she thought.

But all her nervousness disappeared once she reached the landing. And instinctively she knew why: David was in complete control, but not through any boorish male assertiveness or self-absorption. There would be no such little games tonight, her instinct told her. This was no "little overlord" or "gaping peacock." This was a man. His right hand stretched out and took hers, his left hand touched her cheek lightly. The gesture was not even sensuous, but rather affectionately welcoming.

"They told me Ahitofel's granddaughter was beautiful," he said in the clipped tones of the Bethlehemites, "but you are as an angel of Adonai. It would take a poet—a great poet—to describe you."

On this first close look at Bathsheba, David knew infallibly that here was a person with whom he could have total understanding—provided her loyalties did not lie elsewhere. She was beautiful. Of that there could be no discussion. She was self-controlled, yet neither shy nor forward. There was no pretense. Clearly she had never used any part of herself for any unclean or ignoble purpose. There was a fascinating light in her eyes, and she evoked the feeling that every part of her held a resident sensuality, luxuriant and liquid. Bathsheba looked up into his eyes, smiling back at him and remembering Ahitofel's question: "Is there any danger you will fall in love with him?" What a fool Ahitofel was!

"I feel," David said pleasantly, "that you and I need not waste time pretending. This house is yours as my guest. Be at home!" They were still looking into each other's eyes. "Until they call us for dinner, let's sit on the south balcony." Bathsheba had not yet said a word. Yet he felt he had her total acquiescence, as if she had spoken a thousand sentences. They turned together, as though they had been doing it every evening for a year. Their bodies paired effortlessly.

He sat beside her on the balcony and, while she sipped some wine, took his harp and played and sang some ancient songs of the desert. Gazing out into the night, she acknowledged to herself that this was the first man she had ever met whose sensuality was so graphic and pervasive, and yet she had not the slightest feeling that he intended to bed her, or that he even felt like it. She had another fleeting and, this time, contemptuous recollection of her grandfather and his "deep plot" to have her as a "visiting cousin" at this king's household. And a voice shrieked within her: "I will not be a visiting cousin here. I will be this man's woman!" But outwardly she was calm.

"If a man is all brain, all calculation, Lord David," she mused out loud, thinking of her grandfather, "what is he really? How will he fare?"

David laughed. He had been asking himself the same question last night about the same man. "Insane, Bathsheva. And I daresay he will kill himself finally." They walked side by side to the dining room. "What do you wish the most at this moment?" David asked.

She stopped. "My Lord David, only one thing: that any moments we pass together could be as sweet and peaceful as those few minutes on your balcony just now."

He laughed, but later, when dinner was over and the servants had retired, and they were back on the balcony, he took up that point again. "When you spoke before dinner of sweet and peaceful moments, I'm sure you meant moments without probing, without questions asked or answers given. All my life, with perhaps one exception, no man or woman has ever simply been with me without demanding something."

"There is peace here, my Lord David. But, strangely, I find that although I arrived with one mind, I now have another. It is new to me. It is sweet. But I did not arrive here with that mind."

David stood up, smiling. "Your grandfather, Bathsheva, is a very powerful man—and, I may say, a loyal and wise and treasured councilor of mine. But between us there will always be a gap. Like all the others, he has hitched his caravan to my star. So be it. You know that. I know that. He knows that. Nobody is deceived. What you do not know is that I depend on Adonai. Don't ask me to explain him." His eyes strayed away from her. "Only lately have I realized that he is not like other gods." He turned and faced out into the night. "He has no particular territory, like Dagon in Philistia and Kemosh in Moab and Ra in Egypt. He is above and beyond all territories and lands. But he loves this land, and he loved me sufficiently to put it in my hands." He turned back again and faced her. "Don't misunderstand. I'm not religious. I can't stand the cant of priests. But unless a man acknowledges some superior hand in his life, he will be nothing more than an animal, in his purse, in his cups, and in his anger." David quoted the triple trial of a man according to Hebrew lore, *"Bekeeso, bekoso, uve-kaaso,"* hitting the hard "k's" harder for emphasis.

"Now Ahitofel regards all that as undiluted nonsense. And that is his right. But this means he does not, cannot believe in me. *Believe!* I say, *believe!*" His voice resonated on the word. "And so his heart is not with me. Only his brain. And"—he licked his lips—"his ambition.

"So he and I will look across the gap at each other. Respectfully, of course. We will circle each other, but always with that gap between us. Now you, Bathsheva, are you on his side of the gap?" He looked at her, smiling.

Bathsheva, eyes lowered, said nothing, betrayed nothing. After a long silence, David continued. "Last night I spent a long time thinking about what I saw from this balcony—your bathing yourself in the twilight. I concluded it could not have been by chance or by whim, but that you had meant for me to see you." Bathsheva's heart jumped with dismay. "So," David went on casually, "I asked myself: 'If the wife of Uri shows herself to me like that, she must want me to see her like that. Why?' I'm sure my clever little Shunnamith lent you her hand as well." He smiled. "But behind you all must have stood Ahitofel. I think I know what his intention was. It doesn't trouble me. What I do not know is your intention, Bathsheva."

She stood up beside him. "Lord David," she finally said, "it is already time to retire. And I am quite aware that the wife of Commander Uri should before long be back in her own house. But—" She broke off, biting her upper lip. "But," she began a second time, and a second time couldn't continue. He saw the gleam of tears.

"Don't cry, Bathsheva. It's not important." His words released her.

"Oh, no, my Lord David! It's such a relief finally to be able to cry and to have my tears understood and accepted. I'm not in pain at all." He was looking at the roundness of those hazel eyes, now washed in tears. Against the whiteness of her skin they seemed to reflect an inner flame. She had been shaken in her pride in herself, in the lure of a femininity that had never failed before.

He touched her cheek again, lightly, affectionately, and she suddenly realized that it was the quiet signature of his total acceptance of her, of his worship of her. It accepted her pride in herself. It said her body was beautiful and her soul precious; and that, over and above the desire of physical closeness, he saw in her some other value she yearned now to have for him, but which she had no chance of having unless she possessed him.

"I should have known when you touched me at the top of the stairs," she said, smiling through her tears.

"Let us relax a little, you and I," he said calmly. He took her hand and led her to his bedroom. They lay side by side, looking at the ceiling, his left arm cradling her neck.

"Whenever I have been approached by a man," Bathsheva volunteered, "I have always sensed through his soft words and the few liberties I, on occasion, permitted him, that if I consented, the real man would emerge rough and clawing. God! I couldn't even stand the smell of them. You see, I felt that their noblest words and accents concealed some unclean purpose." She turned her head on the pillow and looked at David's profile. "You seem so clean, David."

With infinite care, he withdrew his left hand, so as to lean on his elbow, while with his right hand he slowly stroked her hair, her face and neck, then her breasts. He slowly undid the strings that held her robe. She stood up and it dropped to the floor. She herself unwound the linen band holding her breasts. Naked, she lay down again. The act of undressing her body seemed to enable him to undress his own soul for her.

"When I was young and incapable of love, I was offered love, and, of course, I refused it. But then, when I became capable of love, nobody offered it. They offered me everything else—pleasure, release, debauchery, begetting and fathering. All I wanted. All I could manage. All day and all night and every day. But not love." David sighed.

"Love never came to me again—on the hands of a woman, anyway." A quick memory of Achish's suffering face flashed before him. He became silent, all his muscles relaxing.

"Was she beautiful?" Bathsheva wondered.

"Who? Oh, yes." This after a lapse. "Yes," he said again in a soft voice. "Indeed she was beautiful. It was Lassatha. You know, Uri's Lassatha. Your Lassatha, come to think of it. And, yes, she loved me. You know, when she stripped me naked, it seemed the most natural thing in the world."

"And the rest wasn't natural? Didn't come naturally?"

"What comes natural to a man is copulation, lechery, begetting, whoredom. He can call it what he likes. But that's it. Loving, celebrating love with another—that is exceptional."

"My lord speaks as an expert in the celebration of love." She teased him gently. "Is it better always to accept love and celebrate it, even if its future is black?"

In answer, he removed his royal headband and ring and laid them on a small table, opened the buckles on his shoulders, and let his robe fall softly on the carpet. The moonlight falling through the window lit up his hair and eyes.

"Bathsheva, I did not tell you the whole truth. I was offered love a second time. I was capable of it then. But I refused it—"

"David, it doesn't matter. All—"

"It does. You should know. Rather, I want to be sure you know. It's important—why I refused it then—it would have been love, but it was still too soon for me. Something inside me said: 'Don't give yourself! You can give yourself like this only once! Wait! Or it will have no meaning for you later! Your moment will come. Wait!' So I waited. I let her possess me, and I cried out as she took me." He stopped talking, searching her eyes, she searching his.

"But—" Bathsheva stumbled on her words. "She . . . she did love you, didn't she? That must be terrible, David, terrible. . . ."

"She said there was a penalty to pay, and that it would be terrible," David whispered. "I have lived with the threat of that penalty ever since."

She looked at him, eyes large with compassion. "And now, David? Now?"

"It's different now, Bathsheva. This time, you see. Our time. I know it."

"Beloved, I want all life and all life's meaning for you at this moment," she began, and then could not speak because he was close to her and her control was slipping. "Ah, my Lord David!" she said through tears of helplessness. A wholly new feeling started to invade her, widening her mind beyond the thoughts she had, expanding her emotions beyond the words coming to her lips. She was becoming uniquely conscious of her sensations, as her body responded to his hands and the touch of his limbs, and she felt her body slowly expanding upward.

"Stay with me, Bathsheva. Stay with me." She could barely hear his voice. His eyes never left her face.

"Beloved . . ." It was all she could say, for span after span of light and then blinding unconsciousness came over her in quick succession. And then the fear of the force let loose in her threw her limbs and body into a shaking, crying hope that this would never stop until all desire was fulfilled, and nothing more could ever be desired. He saw her head turn away weakly to one side, her eyes half-close, and he heard a tiny wail of weakness and surrender come from her slightly opened mouth. He was startled.

"Bathsheva!" he started in fear to appeal to her. But then, even though she lay utterly still except for the slightest fluttering of her eyelids, in some mysterious movement within her body she held him from the temptation of distraction. With gathering momentum, he felt himself rushing in her wake through some upward valley of effort. He became quickly aware that he was reaching a pitch he wanted more than anything else in the world but which he feared he could never reach and pass. She held him to her. He felt a cry of protest rising in his throat when he slipped over some invisible peak and found all his strength gone from him, all fear dissipated, all desire to struggle ceased. She heard him sobbing with happiness as he rested against her body, all separation or distinction between them left far behind.

"When did you know it would be like this?" Bathsheva asked in the calm that later reigned between them. "Or has it always been like this for David the Golden, with all women?" she teased.

"No, my lady," David said, sitting up. His features seemed to her for the first time to be completely naked, without any thought covering them. "No. Never before have I drunk the spice of wine—you remember the old Hebrew expression for love's sweetness. But when I saw you bathing yesterday, I knew. And you?"

Bathsheva gave a little rueful laugh. "Until this moment I have been with only one man. I was—am—married to him." David shivered. His memory flashed back to Raham instructing his class: "Every adulteress is to be stoned," he had announced. "To death!" Bathsheva did not notice his reaction.

"I do my duty by him," she continued, her mood changing abruptly. "And that, my Lord King," she said with a sidelong, mocking smile, "is something you men will never know. A woman can pretend so much, and a man expects so little really, unless she educates him. And it's easier to simulate than to educate. For most men, their triumph lies in power over the woman or over women. And they call that pleasure and ecstasy. But"—she lifted one eyebrow skeptically at him—"in doing one's duty, one gets love of a sort. Surely. But all women know it's not love itself."

"No. I don't suppose it is," he said slowly, idly searching the night. "But love itself, what is that?" he asked suddenly. "For a woman?" he added.

"Ecstasy—and I know you don't, can't know what that is."

"Ecstasy," David echoed the word. "When you turned your head away, at first I thought it was hurt, even death. I've heard dying men and women moan like that."

"It was all of those—in one sense. All of those. It was a death, I think. For the first time in my life, what I most deeply felt was the need to thank someone..." Her voice trailed off.

David pulled the coverlet over her gently, touching her forehead and hair. He could not look on the fairness of her skin without imagining a sharp, rough stone smashing its texture, drawing blood. He shuddered and drew on a robe. Although the air was warm, there was a chill on his soul.

On the balcony, he lost his self-control and wept as though the Great Sea itself could not contain his tears, his shoulders shaking, his eyes scalding, consumed with inner misery. Only the silent stars were witnesses to his breakdown.

"O God! O God!" he muttered to himself through his tears. "Why now? Why Uri's wife? O God! Why put the fruit within my reach and then take it away? O God!" His tears lessened a little as the excess of his sorrow ebbed momentarily. He stared out sightless over the city walls toward the hunched forms of Moab's mountains. Over there, in Mizpeh in the land of the flashing mirrors, he had seen Shoshanna, still young and beautiful, nursing the aged and cantankerous Jesse. There was another type of beauty in that devotion of Shoshanna, he thought. More human. More eternal. Fresh images of Uri the aging soldier and Bathsheva his young wife flashed across David's mind. And others, too: Raham and his terrible condemnation of adultery; Samuel telling him how Saul had failed the test, the *akeda;* Jonathan walking bravely into battle at Gilboa knowing that he was doomed because he was faithful. These were all knives in his heart.

"Adonai," he prayed softly, "I have failed one test. I shall not fail the next one. By the Covenant, Lord God of Israel, by all that is holy in this land of yours, I will send her away tomorrow. Spare me! Spare her! Spare Uri! Help us, Adonai! God of my fathers, help us! Help her to understand. Help me to believe, Adonai, my savior!"

But he felt no reassurance in his soul. He was alone. And he prayed until he slipped into an uneasy sleep.

David remembered for the rest of his life exactly where he was, with whom he was talking, what time it was when Shunnamith entered the council room and beckoned to him. Her face was bloodless, alarmed. It was five weeks after Bathsheba's visit. An afternoon of drizzling rain. Dispatches had come in from Joab about the siege of Rabbath-Ammon. Things were not going well.

"Lassatha from Commander Uri's house wishes to speak with my Lord David," Shunnamith said. David came out, irritated, pressed for time. But when his eyes met Lassatha's, he knew what her message was. Immediately he felt the tingle of cold sweat all over his body. There was a tiny point of constriction in his heart and a palpable shadow of pain on his face. Lassatha nodded. Bathsheba was pregnant.

"Tell her not to worry. I will take care of it," he said. She left hastily and he returned to the council room. "I have been thinking," he said to the dispatch officer. "Go back to Joab and tell him to send me Commander Uri. I need his opinion on the whole situation."

The next three days were full of private agony for David. It was the first time he had ever felt the jabbing finger of guilt. He found himself muttering Uri's name to himself again and again, as if he had just conducted a long conversation with the Hittite. His misery was only compounded by his recollection of Bathsheba and his desire for her. And once again he saw her bathing on the terrace. This time he felt a sharp pain in him, and he had to lie down, clutching his side, groaning in his helplessness. "My child... I want my child...."

When Uri arrived, he came straight to David. It took all David's self-control to face the grizzled old soldier, his friend and loyal subject, who now stood erect in front of him. Uri was now over sixty-five years old, David in his mid-forties. Everything about Uri now hurt—his armor, the dust of his journey, his fatigue from the long battle.

"Sit down, old friend," David said, and sent immediately for refreshment. "Now tell me, how does it really go up there?"

"We have captured the two lower plateaus, David, and the sectors of the city on them. We are waiting for starvation to weaken the last sector. Their firepower is heavy. Another two weeks—at most—if we keep up our daily attacks." When he finished relating the details, David bade him go home, refresh himself, and return in the morning. That evening David sent the Hittite's favorite food to Uri's house.

The following morning, Shunnamith brought David's food. She told David that Uri had spent the night wrapped up in his soldier's blanket outside the double doors of David's palace. Malaki, who also slept there, had told her. David was angry.

"What's the matter with him?" Shunnamith heard him say. After midday, he sent an invitation to Uri to dine with him that evening.

"Uri," David asked him during the meal, "why didn't you go home and enjoy some rest and pleasure last night?"

"My Lord David, all my comrades and men are in the field. Should I, the king's soldier, eat and drink and enjoy myself while they are in danger?" This was an unwritten law in the army of Israel: When a commander's army was in the field, he did not sleep at home. David had no answer to that. A feeling of desperation grew in him. The two men drank well into the night, until the Hittite was drunk and finally stumbled out of David's rooms singing to himself and swaying from side to side. Shunnamith watched the Hittite negotiate the doorway and the staircase, then lurch out through the double doors. David went to bed, sure that this time the Hittite would feel the need of his young wife.

Outside the great double doors, Uri was still standing, motionless, all traces of drunkenness gone from him. He was looking up at the windows of his house. They were still lit. Now and again Bathsheva or one of her slaves passed by a window. "Seer," he said to Malaki, "he doesn't know I know. Worse still, he doesn't know I love him so much it doesn't matter. He doesn't know." Malaki said nothing. "Seer," Uri said again, "is it wrong in the eyes of your Adonai to love your king unto your own death?"

Malaki could hear the tears in the Hittite's voice. "Master Uri, a man does what a man must do. Adonai will judge him."

"If only he had trusted me. A woman should not separate friends. If only he knew. He can have my wife, my head, my life..."

"He may well, Master Uri."

Uri settled down in his blanket. "Better that than deception," he said. Uri had loved David from the moment he saw his head, sleek as an otter's, emerge from the shaft of Siloam more than thirty years before. But though he knew what David was about—he had loyal servants, after all—and would accept it, his concept of loyalty forbade him to mention it to the king. It must come from David himself.

In the morning, David learned that Uri had again slept beside the other soldiers. He now felt desperate in the extreme. When Uri came, sober, to say goodbye, David handed him a letter for Joab. "Give that to Joab. It's my advice about the assaults on the walls of Rabbath-Ammon," he said.

"My Lord King, this I will deliver should it cost me my life—and anything else besides. I will do your will in all things." David turned away, unnerved, waving brusquely.

Outside, about to mount his camel, Uri spoke to Lassatha, whom he had sent for. "When I'm gone, that is, when I don't return"—he glanced up at David's windows—"be sure and tell him to take her." He looked down at Lassatha. "You and I, love him more than life itself." He started to mount. "And tell him to take her." He looked down at Lassath. "You and I, girl!" he said with a short laugh. "You and I! We love him!" He nodded several times. She could see the tears in his eyes. He gave one more look at David's windows. Then, straightening up, he rapped out his commands.

Joab read David's letter next evening in the camp outside Rabbath-Ammon. Uri stood there. Even the iron-hearted Joab had to turn away to hide his emotions. He put the letter in his belt and started to talk wildly about the next day's operations. He made no sense.

"Joab," Uri said abrasively, "stop clucking like a hen with an egg she can't lay. We're both too old for that." Joab stopped. He had his back to Uri. His hand went over to his sword. "No, Joab you old fool! That won't be necessary." A pause. Joab turned around. His eyes were full of pain. "We both know what must be done," Uri said.

Joab looked at Uri. "A woman," he said contemptuously. "Always a woman."

"Look! Tomorrow I'm going to lead the attack on the south wall of the city. Give me a company of those Edomite rabbits. They'll run at the first arrows." Joab said nothing. Uri persisted. "It's the only way, Joab. It's all over for me." He turned away, still talking as he left Joab's tent. "It's the last service I can render my friend."

The morning attack on the south wall was a disaster. Within minutes, Uri and the Edomite officers found themselves alone. The others had fled before the rain of arrows and javelins and rocks. When Joab recovered Uri's body two days later, he found it peppered with arrows. They buried it. The next dispatch rider brought the news to David in Zion, who received it calmly.

When the messenger was gone, he sent over one of his aides to announce the news to Bathsheva. All Zion then saw the signs of the usual forty days' mourning go up all over Uri's house. And the siege of Rabbath-Ammon went on. It was mid-May when Bathsheva's mourning was over. Still, the siege of

Rabbath-Ammon went on. In mid-October, Bathsheva was summoned to the Cedar Palace. The message was couched in official terms and said that "King David wishes to take Bathsheva to wife in honor of his faithful servant, Uri, who gave his life for the kingdom." She brought Lassatha and all her household with her to the palace. The wedding ceremony was private and quiet. That night was the first time since the previous March that they were alone.

David no longer thought of Uri. He now had to himself an image of beauty and happiness he had never imagined possible. And in spite of her pregnancy, the days and nights that followed were of unalloyed joy. In late November she gave birth to a son who was named Dodiyahu. David's ecstasy was complete. He spent hours looking at the child. He ordered a special cot to be made for it, special clothes to be woven for it. It was his love child, the acme of his celebration.

The beginning of another mood in the air started at Dodiyahus' circumcision. Nathan, of course, was present. When the ceremony was over, he said in an offhand manner, "My Lord King, there are one or two matters that must be discussed if my Lord King has a few moments..."

David led the prophet to a side room.

"My Lord King, a gross injustice has been done among your people and you have been so preoccupied that you don't know about it."

"By Adonai," David swore, "tell me, Nathan, and it will be corrected within the hour."

Nathan went on evenly. "A poor man—an ordinary laborer—worked for a rich landowner in Zion. He had a little lamb which he and his family treated as one of themselves. Now his patron, the rich man, seized that lamb one day and killed it—mind you, the rich man had flocks of his own, but you know men's greed, my Lord King—and he fed the flesh of the lamb to his guests—"

David was standing by now, his face livid. "Why wasn't I told about this? Give me the base man's name and he will be dead by sundown. Who is he, Master Nathan?"

Nathan looked at him grimly. "That is your story." David's mouth dropped open. He turned chalk white and sat down. He was not looking at Nathan now. One hand went over his heart.

But Nathan bored on: "Where did Adonai fail you that you did this? You can have anyone you like provided she is not married. You could have had Uri divorce her. But to kill Uri? For his own wife?

"There's more, my Lord David. Uri knew all your desire for her!" Nathan nodded at David. "He knew a week after your meeting. His servants were faithful and informed him of what had happened in his absence. He told Malaki, who told Lassatha. And then Uri chose to die rather than embarrass you."

Nathan stood up and went over to the window, hiding his face from David. He went on. "Adonai has instructed me to tell you the following: 'Now killing has entered your house. It will not stop there. Death makes death enter. You can't expel it. You slept with another man's wife in secret. Other men will sleep with your women in the sight of all Israel. Dodiyahu will die.'" Nathan choked on the words. "You will live, David," he added in a whisper, "but Dodiyahu will die." He did not look around at David but went toward the door. He heard a hoarse whisper from David.

"I have sinned . . . the penalty . . ."

"No, no, my Lord King. You will not die. That's your penalty. But others will, of your house . . ."

Some nights later David was lying beside Bathsheva when Dodiyahu started coughing. They called the servants and the doctors. The child developed convulsions and then a fever. David was frantic. He had the best doctors in the kingdom tend the child, offered sacrifices, fasted. After six days the child went into convulsions again. David lay on the floor crying and praying. About six o'clock, just as the sun went down, the child died, as Nathan had foretold.

The next nine months were like a dream for David. It was unreal. He rarely saw his councilors, leaving all matters of state in their hands and the siege of Rabbath-Ammon to Joab. He abandoned his harem. He refused to look back or look forward. He absorbed himself totally in Bathsheva. From morning until night and until the next morning. It was as if he knew that any joy remaining was going to be short. It was the first and only time that he would live with a woman, buried in her every mood, unable to leave her.

Never once did he realize that his life now hung from a great hook of illusions. Bathsheva's joy knew no bounds, for she became pregnant again. She was the king's wife. She had never imagined such sustained love cradled in privilege, with responsibility only to her love. And all the while their child was growing in her. She was surrounded on all sides by David and David's love. She too grasped it all, knowing deep inside her it could not last.

In late August, Bathsheva gave birth to another son. Shortly after his birth, Nathan walked in, called David aside, and spoke to him. "My Lord King, Adonai sent me to tell you he loves this child. He will bless him with peace and love. His name should be Yedidiyah, 'Yahweh has loved me.' Take good care of him. He will be a man of peace." David fell on Nathan's shoulders and wept for joy. At the circumcision he announced that the boy's royal name would be Solomon because, he said, "he will be a man of peace." But ever after, within the family, the child was called Yedidiyah.

David now started again to take up the reins of government. The siege of Rabbath-Ammon had to be finished soon. Dispatches from Joab informed him that they had cut off the water supplies to the Ammonite capital. The end was near. David, Joab wrote, should come and take the capital in the final assault, because "I have for so long been in charge of this siege, that if I now take the city, they will call it after me."

David arrived a week later. By that time all the outer defenses were smashed, and the city fell after two hours of well-directed assaults. David had decided to make an example of the Ammonites. Hanun, all his family, his advisers, all the nobles and rich merchants, and high and low army officers were summarily executed. Every Ammonite in the city was brought outside and made to lie face down on the rocky plateau. Then horses and mules dragged saws and iron axes over their bodies. Those who survived were made to stand in groups within brick kilns, where the heat and fumes killed off many more. Then those that were still alive were allowed to return to their homes. This treatment was meted out in every major city and town in Ammon. There would never again be a revolt in Ammon.

The booty in money and goods from Ammon was enormous. It enriched David's treasury, and his soldiers, beyond all expectations. David kept for himself the Ammonite crown: a finely worked tiara, made of solid gold encrusted with rubies and diamonds. His own goldsmiths encrusted it further with the six-pointed star. This was to be the crown of the kings of Judah.

In the middle years of David's kingship, a violent plague took a heavy toll of pregnant women and the elderly. It raged up and down the land for about six months, and then ceased as abruptly as it had started. David made up his mind that Hebrews needed to learn some of the medical science for which Egypt was renowned. He sent a delegation headed by Ahitofel and Hushai to the pharaonic court at No-Amon—Luxor—on the east bank of the Nile. As a result, an Egyptian named Sen-Hotep arrived in Zion, bringing with him a team of Egyptian doctors, dentists, surgeons, pharmacists, herbalists, and physical therapists. Sen-Hotep stayed some fifteen years before returning to Egypt. And the reports he drew up and sent regularly to his Pharaoh, Masaherta, in No-Amon, gave a detailed picture of the Davidic kingdom in its golden era.

Sen-Hotep was the son of a priest of Amon in No-Amon. He was trained in medicine and received his general education at the pharaonic schools of his native city. When he was sent to Zion he was just forty-one, already a distinguished civil servant, chief of internists at the city hospital, president of the Osirian Mysteries, and rector of the only religious academy in No-Amon. Within his own circle he was known as an expert in all the major religions of the area. His library included cuneiform tablets from Mesopotamia, goatskin parchments from the land of the Hebrews, copper scrolls from Philistia, and Phenician stone inscriptions, as well as a well-known collection of inscribed arrowheads and axheads.

That the Pharaoh Masaherta sent someone as valued as Sen-Hotep indicated to the Hebrews both the decline of pharaonic Egypt and the emergence of David and his kingdom. Egypt had been broken into two kingdoms, one ruled from Tanis in the Nile Delta, the other from No-Amon in Upper Egypt. As a result of this split, Egypt had become prey to the surrounding peoples. Upper Egypt found it increasingly difficult to maintain and develop its export-import trade. Tanis blocked Upper Egypt from the Great Sea. To the south, the Nubians constantly threatened, and on the east lay the pirate-ridden Red Sea. To the west were only the uncharted African jungles and deserts. An alliance with Zion that would provide direct access to the Great Sea seemed one solution. Masaherta seized David's request for medical help as the occasion to cement such an alliance.

Sen-Hotep was like any other Egyptian in his lack of desire to live in "the gloomy land of gray and brown mountains," as his countrymen called the land of David. As far as most Egyptians knew, Hebrews lived either in black goatskin tents or in ramshackle wooden huts. To leave No-Amon, a city six miles square with the most comfortable living conditions of its time, was hard indeed.

But Sen-Hotep was pleasantly surprised. During his fifteen years at Zion, he not only became a friend of David's but traveled extensively through Israel, and he was amazed at what he saw. The Egyptians thought of the land they called Canaan, once their vassal territory, as a squabbling melting pot of peoples—Hebrews, Amorites, Amalekites, Syrians, Jebusites, Phenicians, Geshurites, Philistines. Hebrews in particular they referred to as "Israel," but this term did not refer to the land. It was merely an ethnic designation. For in truth, the Hebrews had never in history possessed the land. "Israel" was the special name given by Adonai to Jacob, from whom all Hebrews mythologically derived their lineage.

Sen-Hotep quickly found that David's Hebrews used the term "Israel" to refer both to themselves and to their kingdom. By some alchemy of leadership, in twenty years—David was fifty-seven at the time of Sen-Hotep's arrival—this new king had created a nation.

At Kadesh-Barnea, the first Hebrew town Sen-Hotep entered, and all over the land, it was the same: everywhere that six-pointed star, everywhere the king's chariot patrols, and everywhere the same institutions for religion, justice, and commerce. Non-Hebrews—whether Nubians or Arameans or Edomites or whatever—did not live in independent walled cities and towns of their own, as they had before David's time. They had essentially the same legal protection as Hebrews, except that they could not celebrate their religion in public, could not move from place to place with the same freedom as Hebrews, and could not acquire more than a certain amount of land. But they enjoyed the security that David created. It was said, and with accuracy, that the king's highway patrols were never more than five miles apart from one another.

The only latent suggestions of ancient disunity, Sen-Hotep found, lay in the traditional enmity between the southern tribes, led by Judah, and the northern tribes. The Judahites, especially those of Hebron and Zion and Bethlehem, were, on the whole, ingrained monotheists: they believed there was only one God, Adonai. The northerners, on the other hand, were henotheists; they believed in one God, Adonai, but they also believed that other gods existed.

Culturally there were further differences. The Judahites regarded all northerners as country bumpkins—which they were. The northerners regarded the southerners as pompous upstarts—which they were inclined to be. Hadn't Abraham and Isaac and Jacob all been northerners? Hadn't the southerners nourished Sodom and Gomorrha, the sinful cities of the plain? And when, much later, the northern tribes did split from the south, they used Jacob's special name for Hebrews, "Israel."

The smug southerners were quite content to be called *yehudim*, the people of Judah, Judahites.

David, however, by a combination of religious and military domination, intermarriage, and economic success, held both south and north together. It was awhile before Sen-Hotep realized how the general unity was attained. There was a general shared disparagement and contumely for all other gods but the God of the Hebrews. Sen-Hotep heard everywhere the same triple assertion: "Our God is the only God. We are his people. David is the ruler of Adonai's land."

But the uniformity and prosperity went further. Except among the very poor, all ordinary and essential utensils—plows, sickles, harrows, scythes, hoes, chariots, axes, chisels, picks, hayforks, fire tripods, wheels, swords, spears, arrow tips, shields, helmets, body armor—were of the new wonder metal, iron. Furthermore, in spite of local products, there was throughout the land a certain uniformity of shape and standardization of size in ordinary household wares—jugs, jars, goblets, ladles, trays, plates, caldrons, pots, spoons, forks, knives. The sizes and styles used in Zion by the royal court had set the fashion in these matters as in much else. A new urban class had grown up in the cities and towns of Israel—partly military, partly administrative, partly merchant. While Sen-Hotep could see many traces of Egyptian imports, especially in women's hair styles, cosmetics, and dress, there had developed a distinctive leisure-class Hebrew manner of dressing, talking, eating, decorating, cooking, speaking, and general living. The norms and standards most ardently observed were "made in Zion" and stamped by the preference of David of Bethlehem.

From all he had heard about this one man's exploits—singlehanded combat against lions and bears, the slaying of giants, overseas invasion of the Philistine stronghold, his music, his angers, his loves, his military organization, and his wealth, the slightly built Sen-Hotep was fully prepared to see a god-king come out to greet him. Instead, the figure he saw descending the wide staircase in the Cedar Palace of Zion was unmistakably human. He was, however, totally different from anyone the Egyptian had ever met. His physique was powerful and displayed to advantage in full battle dress. The hair was still golden, now with streaks of silver in it. Sen-Hotep had never looked into a pair of eyes that shone with such independence and ease. He was completely won over.

As David descended the staircase he carried in his arms a

skinny young boy—it was Solomon—with a solemn face, raven-black hair, and his mother's hazel eyes. Walking on either side of David came his twenty-five-year-old son, Absalom, and Absalom's sister, Tamar. The boy was as tall and ruggedly built as his father, but Sen-Hotep noted a weakness he could not define in the youth's eyes and mouth. Both children were slim and, like David, golden-haired and blue-eyed. A young Egyptian slave, a scribe, preceded David to act as interpreter, but Sen-Hotep already spoke a moderately good Hebrew. David made him welcome, presented his children, and, after a drink of wine, had him escorted to his own quarters.

The next day, David was very frank with Sen-Hotep: "We need medical people here: doctors, dentists, midwives—I was delivered by an Egyptian midwife myself—nurses, therapists. We need some good pharmacologists and herbalists. In return, I believe we can serve some needs of the Pharaoh."

Sen-Hotep introduced the team of Egyptians he had brought with him, and he and David made plans for starting classes for Hebrews and establishing hospitals. That evening David invited the Egyptian to eat with him and his family in the massive dining hall of the palace. It took David a good twenty minutes to introduce all his children and wives, as each wife came forward with her children. Sen-Hotep was deeply impressed by Bathsheba when she advanced with her four sons, Solomon, Shimma, Nathan, and Shovav. Those five people with the same black hair and hazel eyes seemed in some mystic way to be one being.

Apart from the size of the dining hall—it ran the full length of the palace and was exactly half its width—Sen-Hotep was struck by two other things: the delicacy and sumptuousness of the food, and the obvious way the family grouped itself around David. A series of appetizers was served by the slaves: hard-boiled eggs in a special vegetable sauce, cooked carrots and cucumbers and beets, assorted olives and a goose liver pâté, all washed down with the "King's drink," white wine blended with honey and cloves. Then there was roast lamb, chicken casserole with prunes, pea purée garnished with lentils and artichokes, all followed by dates stuffed with almonds and rolled in honey, apples, oranges, melons, grapes, pears, berries, pomegranates. Thin bread and red Hebron wines were served throughout the meal.

At David's left sat Bathsheba, at his right, Solomon. The other tables were parallel to David's and seated all his sons and daughters and wives. Sen-Hotep noticed the dagger looks that some of the wives, whose names he had already forgotten, shot at Bathsheva. She, he noted, seemed to be either blissfully unaware of this or entirely indifferent. David himself dominated the entire room: each course began when he began it; he continually shouted out pleasantries and teasing remarks, and they were answered in lively, sometimes tart exchanges the Egyptian could not follow—his Hebrew was too weak. Laughter and talk filled the hall. At the end of the evening, as a special privilege, Sen-Hotep was invited to sit on the roof terrace of the palace and listen to David as he played his harp and sang. Bathsheva and Solomon were with him.

The Egyptian's main purpose was to see if Masaherta could benefit from David's economic "triangles," particularly his trade overseas and with Mesopotamia. Sen-Hotep traveled to Tyre and learned first-hand of the import-export arrangements between David and the Phenicians. The Egyptians were desperately in need of foreign markets, chiefly for their craftwork in metal and a whole list of luxury and "convenience" goods. They also needed credit facilities in Mesopotamia and Syria, as well as in the nations across the Great Sea. It had taken David more than ten years of peace to organize this economic advantage.

When the king concluded his agreements with Sen-Hotep, the Egyptian had agreed to invest sums with David that exceeded the normal half-yearly tax revenues of David's kingdom. Taking a Tyrian gold talent to weigh about fifty pounds of gold, David could expect Egyptian annual payment of his management fees to exceed twenty-five gold talents. And that was only the beginning. David would get a percentage of every price paid in any foreign market for Egyptian goods he transported.

Sen-Hotep was shown through the treasury and accountancy offices of the palace. The staff explained to him the method of recording all the loading and transport operations, of promissory notes, of banking deposits in the major cities with which David's government maintained commercial relations. When he handed back to Azmaveth one inventory of Damascus merchandise, Sen-Hotep remarked that the parchment was thicker but lighter than Egyptian papyrus.

"It's good goatskin," David answered, fingering the parchment. "Besides, we net an annual sum from the sale of that parchment here and abroad.

"Your papyrus is too expensive," he went on, "besides not being tough enough. Do you realize what would happen to papyrus when one of our drovers shoved it into his belt or a sea captain carried it pinned to his hair? Papyrus would not last. This"—he folded up the parchment—"can withstand rough handling."

That day on their way down the corridor from the treasury, they passed the Scrollery. Sen-Hotep could hear a sustained sibilant murmuring coming from inside.

"I call this my pigeon coop," David remarked, smiling. "One cannot read or copy without pronouncing the words out loud. So this buzzing goes on from cockcrow to sundown, six days a week.

"Come in a moment, Sen-Hotep," David invited. "Let me give you the answer to a question you've been asking me since your arrival here—what holds the Hebrews together?"

Sen-Hotep found himself in a long room. The walls were lined with shelves. Passing by them slowly, the Egyptian could see row after row of parchment scrolls, Egyptian papyri, and clay tablets. The floor of the Scrollery was occupied by narrow tables at which about thirty men sat working. Each man had an inkwell and a row of pens. In front of him was a clean scroll of parchment on which he was copying from some text on the table at his left. At the end of the room, perched on a high, wide desk piled with scrolls and tablets, sat a small man with a ferocious look permanently on his face. On either side of him two young boys stood. Now and again he handed a piece of parchment to one of them, whispered softly to him. The boy took the parchment to one of the copyists.

"This is Serayah, my master scribe," David introduced Sen-Hotep, tongue in cheek. Serayah scowled at David in an owlish fashion over the desk top, then looked at Sen-Hotep with an annoyed air. He greeted Sen-Hotep in perfect Egyptian. With a stare of almost childish annoyance at David, he excused himself and went back to his work. "He treats me like an outsider," David laughed. "Thinks I'm frivolous!"

"What are they doing, Sire?"

"We have a sacred book, the Law of Moses. It tells Hebrews the commandments and laws of Adonai. And it tells of Adonai's Covenant with the Hebrews. Here Serayah has already supervised the making of over one thousand copies of the Book of the Law. Each copy has been sent out and confided to the care of a scholar in each of our major cities, towns, and hamlets. Eventually every village will have one. You realize that the Law is read out loud and explained to the people each Shabbath. They cover the whole Book of the Law each year. We also instruct the scholars in how to explain the Law. The result is that all through the land, all Hebrews are hearing the same text, the same doctrine. It makes for unity and uniformity of mind.

"But let us go outside now," David suggested, "and get some fresh air."

Outside, in the small vegetable garden that David cultivated as a hobby, Sen-Hotep walked around with him as he tended his plants. "Our Moses left a Code of Law. He also left us a certain chronicle of events—how Adonai created the world from the beginning, with animals and man and plants. The Code of Law, of course, is very complete. But the chronicles themselves are confusing. People have added to them since the time of Moses."

David straightened up with a sigh and scraped the earth off his fingers and palms. "And then one day we raided the libraries of the Arameans, Ammorites and Syrians, and found that their scholars were well versed in the writing of the Assyrians and the Sumerians; and I myself discovered that those Assyrians and Sumerians had their own chronicles describing how the world was made—very like our Hebrew chronicles, except of course without a word about Adonai."

They were walking back toward the palace. "The Assyrians and Sumerians wrote about Gilgamesh, Gudea, Ea, Marduk, Tiamat, and a whole army of alien gods. I thought to myself, the Assyrians and Sumerians had bits and scraps which were lacking in the chronicles of Moses. So I put Nathan, Gad, Zadok, and Asher in charge of amalgamating those ancient chronicles with our own." By this time the two men were back on the seventh floor, seated on David's balcony overlooking the city.

"I detect," Sen-Hotep said delicately, "that you attach a great importance to the composition of this Book of the Law. But, then shouldn't you also include the other gods—even if you believe them to be false? False they are for you and in this land, but doesn't Baal rule in Phenicia, as Ra and Amon and Isis and Osiris in Egypt, and Hadad in Syria, and so on?"

"No," David said slowly. "Now I know there is only one God; Adonai. He made all things—men, animals, plants, the earth, the sky, the stars. All the rest, the gods and idols, are fictions."

"Sire," inquired Sen-Hotep, "what does this Adonai look like?"

"Adonai has neither face nor body. He's eternal. He is spirit.

You can't see him with your eyes or touch him with your hands or lips, or depict him in marble or paint."

"That's very like what we say about Osiris and Isis, Sire." Sen-Hotep warmed to his subject. "The most holy and pure Osiris cannot be known by men as long as they are in their bodies. They must be changed—usually by death, but also by the rites of the Osirian Mysteries—to another sphere of knowledge. There they can see Osiris and know him."

"What do you know him with?"

"We believe each man and woman, besides the body, has a *ka*, or double, and an *ikh*, a spirit, as well as a *bai*. The *ikh* flies off to enjoy the gods in the heavens. The *bai* visits the body in the tomb—if it has been mummified, and thus houses the *ka*. We know eternal beauty with the *ikh*."

David was silent for a long time. Eventually he answered, "About what happens when we die, we know little. Certainly only the pure can be with Adonai. But we do not need to wait for death. Adonai is present to us every day, in every place, in all our actions. No, no, my friend. It's different for us. Our God is with us here and now. He works through man's history. He has promised my people salvation. Through the Book of the Law."

"So you build the future of your people on a book?" Sen-Hotep concluded with a little smile.

"No, Sen-Hotep! On *the* Book. It will keep the soul of my people alive forever!"

As they rose, the Egyptian realized that the expression on David's face matched his own puzzlement of mind. When he was about to leave, he said brightly, "Is the King following some ancient prophecy blindly—as all of us do now and again?"

"No ancient prophecy, my friend." David smiled weakly, then became serious. "I am groping, Master Sen-Hotep. Groping." He finished the word almost in a whisper, then turned away.

The
Latchstring of the Eternal

▨▨▨ Ahitofel's plans had gone awry. They had been perfect in every detail but one. Bathsheva was married to the king. He had expected her to make him privy to David's intentions, thus permitting him to have even greater political and economic influence. But he had not reckoned on her genuinely falling in love with David. From the beginning, Bathsheva and David were in close collusion concerning Ahitofel. "Better I know what's going on in that twisted brain than that he plot in secret," was David's comment. It took Ahitofel about five years to realize that Bathsheva was no longer on his side.

With his usual prudence he had left his granddaughter alone for the first two years of her marriage to David. But he first became suspicious when Bathsheva's third son by David, Nathan, was born. During all his years at Hebron and in Zion, David had had at least one child per year from some wife or concubine. Rarely, however, did one of them conceive a second time, much less a third. Now, Ahitofel noted, no other wife of David's was bearing him children. Therefore only Bathsheva, he concluded, was enjoying the King's bed. It was time, then, to start cashing in on his investment. He chose a simple but profitable matter, the appointments of the Shekina Singers, the Doormen, and the Levites, the three most important classes of civil servants in the kingdom.

Shekina ("dwelling") was the fanciful name that David had given to the leather tent under which the Ark of the Covenant was sheltered in his palace courtyard. The Shekina Singers were a corps of musicians and singers trained in Zion. The best of them were stationed there to chant before the Ark. The others were distributed throughout the land. They insured a ritually correct performance of public chanting in honor of Adonai. The Doormen were appointed by David to attend to all important gates and doors in his kingdom: the gates of Zion, of the twelve royal cities, of the Cedar Palace, of the twelve entrances into the Shekina proper. The Levites were the official priests and scholars. They had forty-eight towns of their own. They were also distributed as resident scholars, officers of the law, and justices of the peace, in each city and town and village of any size. A special group offered sacrifices at the Shekina. Shekina Singers numbered close to two thousand. The Doormen were almost four thousand, the Levites about seventy-five hundred. The three groups created a network of royal control, influence, and intelligence throughout the land. They all collected regular fees from the people, plus a government allowance.

Every three years David rotated the occupants of the commanding positions in these classes. Ahitofel's plan was to give a list of select names to Bathsheva and have her suggest them to David. Not only would such appointees be in Ahitofel's pocket, they would enrich his pocket. Bathsheva appeared to be all sweetness and light with her grandfather. She accepted the task, reported back to Ahitofel later that she had done her part, and waited. When the appointments were announced, not one of Ahitofel's candidates had been named. To all her grandfather's complaints she answered simply and sadly: "This husband of mine is so difficult! Adonai help me to be patient with him!" Privately she and David shared a joke about the fate of Ahitofel's plan.

For a while longer Bathsheva played the same game with Ahitofel, sometimes obtaining what he wanted, sometimes grumbling about "the obstinacy of the king." And this could have gone on indefinitely, were it not for Bathsheva's own ambition. In the end she was too like her grandfather not to fall into the same trap as he. David, Ahitofel ceaselessly pointed out to her, was getting old. Her four sons were the youngest of David's eleven legitimate sons, the princes of the realm. His successor would of course be his firstborn, Amnon, son of Ahinoam. It was the Judahite custom. Besides, in David's eyes, the eighteen-year-old Amnon, son of a northern wife, would help reconcile the recalcitrant northern tribes, who were still far from won over to the idea of forming a single nation with the southerners.

"A pity that none of your four young princes will be king," Ahitofel remarked one day to Bathsheva as they sat in her quarters. Solomon, Shimma, Nathan, and Shovav were playing nearby. Bathsheva was sewing.

"Amnon is David's firstborn." She kept on sewing, and added, trying to sound uninterested, "If it weren't for him, Solomon would certainly be king."

"Yes! Our wise little Solomon!" Ahitofel commented glow-ingly, looking at the boy. "Our little king!" Bathsheva sighed. Ahitofel went on. "I see young Amnon keeps a lot of company with lovely Tamar." Grandfather and granddaughter looked quickly at each other to make sure they were thinking along the same lines.

Bathsheva gave a little laugh. "Yes! Sometimes I think Tamar's blue eyes and fair hair will entangle Amnon. That's what I think."

Ahitofel stood up languidly. "Perhaps even make him dizzy enough to fall off a high throne, eh? God knows!"

"Grandfather," she said evenly, "Absalom is very solicitous about his sister."

"Of course! Of course! A brother should be, my dear."

"But surely, grandfather, if Amnon gets dizzy and falls, Absalom as David's favorite will be king?"

"Once the eldest falls out of the line, daughter, the rule is: whomever the king chooses. And Absalom—well, Absalom has his own—er—weakness."

All David's sons and daughters by his first six wives were by now young adults. Seven princes and eight princesses, all with privileges and possessions of their own. Each of the princes, on entering the Covenant at age thirteen, was given his own house with his own slaves, servants, and animals. Each princess had her own slaves and servants in her own quarters at the palace. Each prince was also given an estate. Some, like Absalom, received land from his mother's family. Others received a grant from David. Amnon, Khileav, Absa-lom, Adoniyahu, Shefatyahu, Ithream, and Yivhar led a distinct and separate life of their own. They rode on specially bred royal mules and wore specially woven royal robes known to all of Zion. They visited each other's houses at Zion or in the country, and their sisters, Riba, Hagar, Hodesh, Tamar—Ab-salom's sister—Shalheveth, Miriam, Sherah, and Zelofehad were often with them. The princes and princesses, and the sons and daughters of David's brothers and sisters, formed a large yet close company.

Their mothers, who had their own quarters, continued to care for them—at this age, to guard their interests. These wives of David had more reason for disliking than liking one another: each one feared for her own future and her son's. Haggith, in particular, was known by all as "Mistress Spite." She thought of her son, Adoniyahu, as Adonai's gift to the nation, and of her daughter, Shalheveth, as a stirring beauty. Actually, Adoniyahu was weak-willed and dull, and Shalheveth was an ordinary girl. But what united Haggith with the other wives, with the exception of Abigail, was a common hatred of Bathsheva. They could not bear her continued beauty, her age—she was thirty-five, while they were all over fifty—and her position as David's favorite.

Abigail was too intelligent to be like the others. She knew that her son, Khileav, was a lout, that her daughter, Hodesh, would make a good marriage and bear healthy children. But Abigail had an aversion to Maaka and her two children, Absalom and Tamar. She also found Amnon a pompous, self-centered prig, and feared the time when he would be king. In her wisdom Abigail did not try to compete with Bathsheva; she cultivated her instead, and before long Bathsheva communicated to Abigail that she and Ahitofel were engaged in a small plot.

At first, events seemed to go the way of the conspirators. They all knew Amnon's weakness for the beautiful Tamar. Abigail persuaded her Khileav to throw a party for Amnon and Tamar, at which Tamar danced for them all until Amnon could barely keep his hands off her. Ahitofel had deliberately made a friend of Yonadav, the son of David's brother Shammai. And in time he suggested to young Yonadav that the future king of Israel should be allowed a little private fun. After a few more well-organized encounters, Amnon, already groaning with desire for Tamar, was ready to be taken: "I'd give ten golden talents for ten minutes alone with her," he told Yonadav. "I want to drown in her hair, to die between those legs!"

Yonadav replied, "It's simple! The thing about women is their compassion. You need to get her to pity you. Go home to bed. Send a messenger to Tamar. Tell her you're very ill and you wish her to come and bring you a favorite food. The rest is easy." Ahitofel reported to Bathsheva that Absalom had been invited to Giloh for the Shabbath. The coast was clear. Tamar would be alone.

All went well at first. Amnon was piteous. Tamar was beautiful. But when he propositioned her—she refused. She was not shocked or frightened. Rather, she wanted him to get permission from David to marry her. Tamar saw herself as Amnon's queen and had been plotting his seduction as earnestly as he had hers. And David could give the necessary permission. Amnon's answer, however, was to drag her forcibly to the bed, tear off her clothes, rape her several times, and sodomize her as well. When he had finished, he was disgusted with himself and with what she had become under his hands. At his orders a servant threw a cloak over her and led her outside. He had the door bolted from the inside.

Events still followed Ahitofel's plan. Absalom returned home to find Tamar sitting with her beautiful royal robe torn in mourning, ashes sprinkled on her head, her body unwashed and unkempt. He knew before he entered the house what had happened: Ahitofel had sent one of Abigail's trusted servants to tell him. The Gilohite arrived soon afterward to counsel brother and sister.

"You, Tamar, wash up and put on fresh clothes. You, Absalom, say nothing to Amnon for now. Make him your special friend. Make light of all this. The day will come, you know . . ." Absalom knew. He nodded. "And I," Ahitofel concluded, "will tell the king in private. This must be hushed up." Ahitofel saw to that.

The population of Zion had doubled and trebled since David had come to live there, and now it spilled over into the surrounding valleys and hills. Sen-Hotep, the Egyptian ambassador, came to the palace one day to tell David he had received an answer to an important request of David's.

"My royal master at No-Amon has answered that he can supply you with special architects to draw up the plans for your temple."

"Marvelous! Marvelous!" David exclaimed.

They both looked northward to the flat threshing floor. "That's where Amnon will build the temple," David said. "It belongs to a good Hittite, Araunah, but he'll sell it easily to me. Your architects must lay out the grandest, most impressive building they have ever designed. You Egyptians know how to build temples, but we Hebrews know how to worship in them!" The blue eyes twinkled. He walked back from the window and sat down. "Ah, me, Sen-Hotep. Life is good!" He took his harp and started strumming a favorite psalm of his own.

> "Adonai is my shepherd.
> I shall not want. . . ."

The Egyptian studied him, his eyes quietly taking in his mannerisms and his mood.

> *"He makes my bed in green pastures.*
> *He leads me to the bank of a quiet stream.*
> *And, even if I walk in the Valley of Shalmaveth,*
> *I will fear no harm...."*

"When did you compose that psalm, Sire?" Sen-Hotep asked.

"The morning after one terrible day." David laid aside his harp. "The Valley of Shalmaveth. It's north of Maon town in Judah. Shalmaveth had beautiful olive groves and tall pine trees. And an ever running stream of water. I wanted it—needed it." He took a sip of wine. "We had set up a meeting with the inhabitants. They came on their mules and camels adorned with silk and cloth-of-gold, smelling like Tyrian whores. But they had arranged a secret after-dinner entertainment—a squad of Edomite mercenaries to fall on me and to cut my throat.

"Well, entertainment there was. But not the kind they expected. Those Maonites took some wine and died instantly. A simple poison. I obtained it from the Pelethites. And the Edomites stole up on us that night, thinking we were asleep. They bled like pigs and screamed like jackals as they died." David sipped from his cup and laughed. "The next morning, looking on those green pine trees, olive groves, and fresh water, the words of this psalm came to me."

"Well, Sire." Sen-Hotep stood up. "I thank you. I will communicate with No-Amon, and give instructions for the architects to come to Zion—"

"To Jerusalem, Sen-Hotep! This is David's city where we stand. Zion, that is to say. But my capital is called Jerusalem, 'Foundation of Peace,' Jerusalem!"

"Jerusalem, Sire!" Sen-Hotep smiled and turned away. He had heard that same imperious tone of voice before, in No-Amon. Why did powerful men speak of themselves in the third person so easily? Power was seductive. The Egyptian architects would come in a few months. They, together with Phenician engineers, would draw up detailed drawings for the temple.

Two years after the rape of Tamar, Absalom and Ahitofel felt the time was ripe. Rumors had it that David was considering having Amnon anointed as his successor. Ahitofel whetted Absalom's appetite for vengeance by revealing portions of David's testament, by which Absalom would receive only a small share of power. "But be very careful, my boy," Ahitofel counseled. "Whatever you plan, make sure the king has no suspicions."

Absalom invited all the princes and princesses to a party celebrating the shearing time of his flocks at Baalhazor. He even invited David, but the king laughingly refused. An old man could not keep up with the young. So Absalom clattered off with the others, on their royal mules, decked out in their finest clothing. On the first evening, at the height of the carousing, when Amnon was blind drunk, Absalom's servants pounced upon him in front of the others and drove their swords through him, killing him then and there. The other children panicked, leaped on their mules, and headed back to Zion in utter fright.

But Absalom did not come back. Out of fear, he took refuge on his own estates at Geshur with his wife, three sons, and only daughter. David, out of love for Absalom, forbade any member of his army to pursue him. He merely wanted Absalom back. The whole palace, then all of Zion, and finally all the Hebrews learned what had happened. And some of the hotheads in the northern tribes discussed among themselves whether this was not the moment to throw off the yoke of David and the hated southerners. Absalom could be their king!

Absalom's absence and Amnon's death seriously affected David's health. In the two and a half years following, he stayed away from most of his usual companions, ate very sparingly, and wept for his sons. The daily administration of the kingdom suffered from his neglect. Things came to a head when smallpox carried off two of Absalom's sons, whom David loved dearly. Seeing the plague as an admonition from Adonai, the king sent Joab to bring Absalom back to Zion, but he would not allow the young man into the palace for yet another two years. And even when Absalom was eventually allowed into his father's presence, David made it clear that Solomon was now to succeed him on the throne. Ahitofel was delighted: his great-grandson would be king. Bathsheva now had more reason than ever before to influence the king according to her grandfather's wishes. Or so Ahitofel thought.

But to his surprise and chagrin, Bathsheva turned against him. For all she knew, Ahitofel might plot the assassination of David himself. And David she loved as her very life. Or Solomon might be next, if he refused to be Ahitofel's puppet. There was no trusting her grandfather. She admitted him just once more to her quarters, and, before he could say anything, she informed him that she had told David the whole sordid story from beginning to end. Ahitofel was beaten, but he had a choice. He could remain at his post, although David would surely take care that he died a violent death—and soon—for Ahitofel, not Absalom, had been the chief culprit in Amnon's assassination. Or he could retire to his family estates at Giloh. He had the king's guarantee that he would be allowed to live out the rest of his days in peace, honor, and prosperity.

Bathsheba was cold and contemptuous. "You, Grandfather, taught me never to trust those who betray others. You instructed me well."

Ahitofel wisely chose to retire. He never saw David's face again. But from Giloh he followed events at Zion and maintained his little band of paid informers at the court. He intended to avenge himself on both David and Bathsheba. But for the next few years Ahitofel plotted in secret.

About this time a visit from his very old and trusted friend Barzillai the Gileadite occasioned David's first realization of where his life was heading. Barzillai called on David in Zion for a deliberate reason. He was eighty-one and very infirm. And as he sat with Sen-Hotep and David, it became clear to David that the old man could not keep up an active life any longer.

"Why don't you come and be my house guest, Barzillai?"

"Lord David," he answered mournfully, "my mind wanders; I make mistakes in judgment. My memory is failing. Delicate food and fine wine doesn't interest me. I don't even find pleasure in the chants and dances of your boys and girls! My own wife has been dead for fifty years. Now why should the King desire to welcome such a useless man to his glittering court?

"Rather, Lord David, give me your special blessing and then let me go back to Rogelim. I'll die happily there, and they'll bury me beside my father and mother and wife."

"As you desire, old friend."

"One favor I would ask. Khimkham is my young steward. He has great promise. Give him his chance here in Zion. He's a good fighter, loyal and brave."

"Send him to me, Barzillai, by the next caravan. He'll have a long career at my court. I swear it!"

Both Barzillai and Sen-Hotep noted a change of mood in David almost from that moment. He suddenly became more tranquil, sweeter in tone, but more remote and reserved. Later, when Barzillai was gone and he was alone, David reflected on his own reactions. What amazed him was not that, like Barzillai, he was getting old. He found in himself a fresh and almost febrile desire for his old ambition. He desperately wanted Adonai to favor him as he had favored the great ones of Israel: to show him his eternal face.

Old age now settled in on him. It was a slow, gentle process in David's case. Each one of his last months and days splintered down until the husk of him, that great, robust humanity he had worn, was irreparably shattered. His physical being still fought every inch of the way, while its fear of imminent dissolution mounted. His moral being turned around and faced the inevitable—with great hopes, with great doubts. In the clash between physical refusal to be ended and moral consent to spiritual rebirth, David's death agony started remotely, in small things.

He stopped jousting with the young men. In summer, he did not feel like swimming. His sight and hearing became less acute. He woke mornings and sometimes his breath came laboriously, as if his lungs were brittle. Asayahu, his doctor, spoke about irrelevant things, like "vapors" and "night blasts" and the "phlegm of the marrow," and gave him ridiculous potions made of bitter herbs—David only pretended to swallow them.

It was the same with the first twinges of arthritis: he found suddenly one day that he could not hold and steady an arrow on the bowstring while drawing on a target. He had one of his men rub his wrist, hand, and fingers with hot oil the next morning. After a few more tries, he gave up. He now rarely galloped when riding and he found his appetite for food gradually diminishing. However, he still thought more sharply than many men around him who were twenty years younger. He could still work harder than any young person.

Again Absalom was the engine of Ahitofel's machination, and this time the "archangel" came within an ace of success. Shortly after David's sixty-third birthday. Absalom was noticed showily driving about in a new Egyptian chariot. "He has fifty runners who trot in front of him. You should see the entries he makes into the cities," Joab reported. But David made nothing of it. A son of his could and should enjoy his wealth and prestige as he wished.

But Joab persisted: "There's more to it than that, David. I smell trouble. And I don't like this friendship between Absalom and my cousin Amasa. Amasa is a vicious man." Joab's mother and Amasa's had been sisters.

"He's my cousin also," David retorted. "I know Amasa. He's loyal." David did not change his opinion, even when Absalom thundered into Zion with his chariot and runners. Joab shook his head in disbelief.

Absalom had never forgiven his father those two years in Zion when the whole of Israel knew he had to skulk in private, while even the filthiest beggar could see and speak to the king at his weekly public meeting. In addition, the idea of accepting Solomon as king was utterly repugnant to Absalom, and Solomon might even be instructed by a dying David to liquidate Absalom. It would not be the first such legacy. Moreover, Absalom found Solomon deceitful and double-faced. So from time to time Absalom secretly visited Ahitofel at Giloh, where he was cosseted with fine wines and delicately prepared food while Ahitofel played on his fears and ambitions.

"I think the people are fed up with this tyrannical old bandit," Ahitofel once remarked of David. "No one is safe nowadays. And they tell me that he is wandering in mind, too. He weeps and laughs by turns! And all this precisely at the moment that the people need and want a leader who understands them—who walks in their midst. And the taxes get heavier each year. I wonder if..." Absalom listened very carefully indeed to Ahitofel's suggestions, for Ahitofel knew what he was talking about.

In fact, a profound change had taken place in David's Zion, and Ahitofel shrewdly saw how to exploit it. Perched on its high crag, Zion was now an upper city housing the nobles, government administrators, priestly circles, and royal family. It was surrounded on all sides in the valleys around it by burgeoning suburbs. Zion had lost all semblance of the fortified citadel garrisoned by rough desert riders. In twenty years of peace and booming prosperity, it had become a sophisticated capital. Its streets were teeming with an arrogant leisure class, and its daily life was in the hands of men who had never known the earlier hardships. Besides, it had become cosmopolitan. Delicately clad Phenicians, perfumed and fastidious Egyptians, paunchy Syrian bankers, shinily dressed Moabites, quick-witted Greeks, and enormously tall Africans rubbed elbows with well-dressed Hebrew burghers, solemn-faced priests, and self-important lawyers. There were no longer any warriors bristling with weapons or any apparent need for them. The king and his court had become remote from the ordinary people.

David no longer held regular weekly public assemblies where any citizen could voice his complaints and needs. A horde of bureaucrats stood in the way. He himself was occupied with plans for the temple, affairs of government, the training of Solomon, the school of music he had founded, the writing of the royal chronicles as well as the copying and collation of the various versions of the Law, and a new highway from Zion to Bethlehem. Apart from all that, his sons and daughters, grandsons and granddaughters, nieces and nephews were all grown and full of their own problems, which they brought to him. Topping this caldron of concerns were the seething intrigues of his aging wives and his more recent concubines. He no longer seemed to know—or, what was far more dangerous, to care—about the concerns of citizenry.

Little by little the fragile unity he had forged by blood, iron, and charisma between the independent-minded northern tribes and Judah started to dissolve. The northerners never fitted in with the Judahites, anyway. They could never adapt to the courtly manners, sophisticated speech patterns, and subtleties that characterized the southerners. And the northerners failed to attain high positions of trust and wealth in the Davidic administration. They remained outsiders always. They worshipped Adonai, but they never abandoned their worship of the heathen gods.

A month after his talk with Ahitofel, Absalom began to frequent the streets outside the Cedar Palace and at the North Gate. He went on foot, wore no plumed headdress or embroidered hat. If someone out of reverence started to kneel and kiss his hand or cloak, Absalom would raise him up and embrace him, saying, "Do not kneel to me. I am your brother!" He satisfied complaints. He made loans of money or outright gifts. Gradually the word went around: "If you have a problem, Absalom will help you."

A year later, Absalom came to David. "When you held me at a distance and I was rotting in Geshur, Father, I made a vow to Adonai that, if you forgave me and accepted me back, I would offer a special sacrifice at Father Abraham's shrine at Mamre. I'd like to fulfill that vow, if you have no objections, and I'd like to take about two hundred guests and my cousin Amasa."

David was overjoyed with this piety. He gave his blessing, loaded Absalom with gifts, and stood watching his party from the staircase as they departed. Later, Bathsheva came to him shaking with fear.

"I don't like it, David. He is disloyal to you. I am afraid he will kill us all in our beds."

David flung his arms into the air. "My son finally asks forgiveness, and my beloved Bathsheva sees it as a plot." He stalked off.

The conspirators from Zion and Geshur awaited Absalom

at Hebron. Ahitofel was there, too. Absalom entered the Upper City in a triumph of cheers, and immediately sent out messengers to all twelve tribes: "When a trumpet sounds in your city, you will know that Absalom has been crowned king in Hebron." The bonfires of revolt had been carefully fanned by Absalom around the land in the preceding years. Now Absalom and Ahitofel were ready. At exactly the same time on the first day of the week, Absalom's agents blew trumpets in the various cities and towns, and the cry arose throughout the kingdom: "Absalom, our beloved protector, is king! Long live Absalom! Hebrews flock to Hebron!" The fires burst into flame and the whole land was ablaze. In the five days that followed, thousands of men from all over Israel, each one armed and asking the way to King Absalom's residence, streamed into Hebron while David's far-flung regiments languished in their encampments. At dawn of the day before the next Shabbath, Ahitofel and Absalom discussed their plans. The Gilohite was categorical: "March on Zion, Sire. Now! Catch the old fox in his bed, before he has a chance to take cover. Forget this Shabbath business."

Absalom agreed, and that afternoon he set out for Zion at the head of his new army. The enthusiasm was mighty.

In Zion, David's household had gathered as usual for the Shabbath meal, chatting and laughing while waiting for David to arrive. He came in with Nathan and they sat down amid the babel of voices.

"Solomon!" David boomed out. "Begin!"

The boy, now nineteen, stood up, laughing at his younger cousins, who were making faces at him.

"Why, my father, is this night more special than the other nights of the week?" Solomon's voice rang out. "Why are we gathered here?"

"Because Adonai on this night became the salvation of his people," David intoned. "For on this night, the enemies of Adonai's chosen sought to kill them—"

The door of the dining hall burst open. Joab strode in wearing full battle dress, his sword rattling in its scabbard, the metal studs in his boots hammering on the wooden floor.

"David. It's revolt. Absalom! He's had himself crowned and anointed at Mamre. He and his army left Hebron at about three o'clock. They'll be here in a matter of hours. Amasa is leading the troops, and Ahitofel is doing the thinking. The city is already rife with rumors."

The dining hall was suddenly as quiet as a grave.

"How many of them?" David asked. He was completely calm, as always in a grave crisis.

"At least fifteen thousand, maybe as many as twenty-five." Aside from the Kerethites and Pelethites and the city garrison of a few thousand, there were no Davidic regiments within twenty-five miles of Zion and no way to rally them in time. Ahitofel had planned his coup very carefully. David thought for about ten seconds. The drumming of his fingers on the table rattled deafeningly through the deathly silence of the dining hall.

"We'll have to make a run for it," he decided.

"All of us?" Joab asked.

"All. Except ten concubines, and a few others who can pretend they're with the revolt. We'll need some source of information."

Within an hour David and his whole family, with servants and retainers, were trailing in a long procession out the North Gate, preceded by the Kerethites and followed by the Pelethites. The citizens of Zion remained inside their homes, doors and windows barred. Malaki, seated on his platform outside the great double doors of the palace, listened to all the bustle in the courtyard.

"Are you sure you should stay, Malaki?" David asked him for the third time.

"Yes, Sire. Here I am useful to you."

"Remember! Talk only with Halpa"—Bathsheba's personal maid—"or Hushai."

David turned away and trotted his camel up the street. Outside the city he found the priests, Zadok and his son Ahimaaz and Abiathar and his son Jonathan. They were carrying the Ark. Hushai the Arkite stood beside them, his clothes rent in mourning, tears streaming down his face.

"Zadok," David called out, "turn back. The Ark belongs in Zion. Not with me. If Adonai favors me still, he will bring me back again to see it here again. If not, let him do to me as he likes. Blessed be the name of Adonai! But work with Malaki and Halpa and try to keep me informed. You too, Hushai. Stay here. What I need is eyes and ears in Zion. Station the young men, Ahimaaz and Jonathan, at the well of En-Rogel outside the walls. Get the information to them and they can do the rest. If necessary we'll go to Mahanayyim of Gilead. Now let us be off, in the name of God!"

He dismounted and walked barefoot up the Mount of Olives, humiliated, tears streaming down his face, full of confusion.

Was this betrayal by Absalom the punishment that Nathan had promised for the murder of Uri? But hadn't he repented of all that? Was it the end, then? Or could he defeat Absalom? How could he shield Absalom from danger in battle? His old fear of Adonai returned.

At the top of the Mount of Olives they met Ziva, the old servant of Saul who now served Mephibosheth, the grandson of Saul and the son of David's beloved friend Jonathan. The old man and his slaves led three donkeys loaded with two hundred bread loaves, hundreds of bunches of raisins, and dried fruits. One donkey carried a large jar of wine.

"Peace, Lord David," Ziva said. "You and your people need food for the journey."

"Where is Mephibosheth, Ziva?"

Ziva sighed uncomfortably. "In the city, Lord David. He actually hopes to be made king now!"

"If Adonai restores me, you shall receive all the land and the property that I gave to Mephibosheth," David promised.

He mounted his camel and they started down the other side, going in a northeasterly direction. But the humiliations were by no means finished. As he and his party followed a road leading them around the base of a steep hill near the town of Bahurim, they saw an old Saulite, Shimei, standing on the top of the hill. He had been waiting for David; news of his flight had preceded him.

"Murderer! Whelp of Satan! Apostate! Here is payment for all the blood of Saul's house that you shed. You murderer! You bandit!" Shimei shouted.

Abishai drew his sword.

"No, Abishai," David exclaimed. "You sons of Zeruiah know only the solution of the sword. Adonai must have told Shimei to curse me." So they passed around the hill, leaving Shimei to run around the top, pelting them with stones and mud, screaming obscenities.

They passed Bahurim and set up headquarters on the west bank of the Jordan, near the ford. The moment David's tents were pitched and his wives and children installed, Joab on David's command sent back messengers to tell Hushai, Malaki, and the priests where they were. "Now it all depends on Absalom—and Ahitofel," Joab grunted to Abishai.

"Don't leave me yet, old friend," David murmured to Sen-Hotep, when all the others had left him for the night and his body slaves had brought some refreshments. "I need your company." They sat together on the rugs covering the ground,

David leaning against one of the tent poles and staring out through the opening of the tent into the blackness of a starless night. Sen-Hotep shuddered and drew his cloak around him but said nothing. The other man's pain was palpable.

"I had begun"—David's voice was hoarse—"I had begun to believe Adonai had chosen me—formed me from my mother's womb . . ." His voice trailed off as if the opaque shadows outside had invaded the tent and choked his words. Then, in a barely audible voice: ". . . I have built in vain. It's all vanity and trash! I've spent my years and my strength for nothing."

"Perhaps," Sen-Hotep ventured in a quiet tone, "Adonai regards kings and kingdoms as of no consequence. Perhaps he—"

"Sen-Hotep! Look at me! Yesterday—no, this very midday, the great king! And this evening? Despised! Rejected by my people! Abandoned by the Mephibosheths! Abused by the Amasas! Muddied and stoned and jeered at by the Shimeis! Blamed for all the ills of the people! A man of sorrows and pain! My own son is about to pollute my concubines.

"I did wrong, surely, in the matter of Bathsheva. But didn't Adonai punish me enough? He took away my love child." Sen-Hotep could not break into the flow of David's pain. "Must I be tortured again?" He stopped to wipe away his tears.

"Do you know what Bathsheva said to me," he began again in a fresh outburst of misery, "when we ran upstairs to get a few belongings? 'David,' she said, 'let us take poison and have our bodies burned. This is the end. We can't get away. My grandfather, Ahitofel, surely must have covered all our escape routes.'

"I had to slap her face . . ." Sen-Hotep looked at David, speechless at the sight and sound of his anguish. The Hebrew said nothing for a while. Then, in a sort of tearful wonderment: "Then I screamed at her, 'Even if Adonai has your beauty disfigured and my beauty marred by the torturer's knife, still Adonai will save us.'"

"But the people! Your Hebrew—"

"*My* people! *My* people! The people of Adonai! Great Satan! They're cheering Absalom right now. Oh! *My* people!" He bowed his head and sobbed uncontrollably.

The Egyptian suddenly went rigid and wide-eyed, as if he had seen a menacing enemy appear out of thin air. He stood up stiffly and with great caution, his eyes on the king. David, sensing something, lifted his head and followed Sen-Hotep's movements, surprised at the abrupt change. Sen-Hotep stopped at the door of the tent and turned around.

"David of Bethlehem," he said in a mild, grave voice, "we are both old, and we can be frank with each other. We both have seen too many kings and princes and warriors and leaders come and go, seen too many good men—and bad ones, too—to be blind to a few facts. That your Adonai chose you to unite the tribes of Jacob, to restore peace, to give them the land for themselves—we know it and we can say it privately—it's all nothing! Nothing! A wisp of smoke!"

The Egyptian's voice changed. David now heard a note in. it he had never heard before, some echo of absolute authority. His tears dried up. "Be sure of one thing! One thing! Because of this I am sure. If the House of Israel has in truth a savior, if you, David, son of Jesse, are his holy and anointed one, Adonai will exalt you—always intended to exalt you—but far beyond the narrow confines of the Jordan and the Great Sea and the Bag of Sand and the Wheel of Galilee. You, my friend, will be Adonai's light for peoples you have not known and will never know. If Adonai does not intend this, there is no Adonai. There is no order or plan in men's lives. And our life is a cruel joke, what we Egyptians call the smile on the teeth of the crocodile. You see them all—before the teeth close round you! Good night, Sire! My homage to you." He touched his forehead and heart in the Egyptian fashion, and was gone.

David sat still, his head erect, his mouth open, hardly drawing a breath, looking out into the night. After a few minutes he stood up, went over to his saddlebags, and took out the Ephod. All its fourteen stones were dull, fireless. He gazed hopefully at the last stone in the first row, the bright-red fire garnet of Judah, and then lower down at the amber stone of Benjamin, the divine child. "Adonai," he prayed, "God of my fathers, of Abraham, of Isaac, of Jacob, hear my prayer from the depths." He ceased, and felt for one hanging instant that silence of poignant dependence when his heart missed a beat—young Abiathar's words to him at Adullam lit up across his mind: "one dreadful moment hanging on the precipice of silence." Then, like a divine smile, the fire garnet and the amber started glowing. Automatically he placed the thumb of his left hand on Judah's garnet and his ear finger on the amber, letting the palm of his hand rest lightly on the intermediate stones, the amethyst of Manasseh, the yellow serpentine of Dan, the dark-green malachite of Naphthali, the white carnelian of Assher. The bank of his hand rested on the red agate of

Ephraim, the yellow chrysolite of Issachar, and the green beryl of Zebulun. He placed the Satan finger of his right hand on the rusty-red sard of Reuben. The forefinger of his right hand fell on the blood-red carbuncle of Gad. He quickly read the letters spelled out by the remaining fingers. "The blood of battle will be spilled in Gilead across the Jordan." Beneath the thumb of his left hand, the amber of the divine child, Benjamin, became hot to his touch. "Adonai is with you!" the finger letters told him.

"And the child," David queried pleadingly, "will he be all right? Will he be my successor?" His deathly fear was that his beloved Absalom might die in the coming battle. The amber glowed again. "I, Adonai, will exalt him higher than any Hebrew who joins battle with my anointed," the finger letters spelled out. His fingers stopped. All the stones went dull and lifeless, except those beneath the heel of his left palm. David understood. "This is the Heel of Sheol, of Lord Maveth, of death..." He could remember the hushed tones of young Abiathar from years before.

At that moment Joab entered his tent. David rose and placed the Ephod in its leather bag, shrugging his shoulders. Of course death would visit the battlefield. Absalom, however, would be exalted. That was enough for him to know.

"Make everything ready for an early start tomorrow, Joab," he said. "We'll wait for a message from the city, but we'll be fighting on the east bank. And send messengers to the Gileadites and the Ammonites to tell them to receive us."

The forward patrols of Absalom's rebels came in sight of Zion about eight o'clock that evening. Its towers and battlements were obviously deserted and the North Gate stood open. The city was lit up as usual. The patrols waited until Absalom, preceded by his main column, arrived in his chariot, accompanied by Ahitofel and Amasa, by all the chieftains of the northern tribes, and by some few elders from Judah. They all stood for an instant looking at the silent city, its lights burning. A trap? It was possible. They could not easily believe that this magnificent prize was theirs for the taking. But Absalom broke the silence with a sudden whoop of triumph. He lashed his horses and drove his chariot at full gallop up the long ramp, in through the North Gate, and along the main street to the square in front of the Cedar Palace. Hushai the Arkite, Malaki, Zadok, and Abiathar stood in the courtyard with the slaves and servants. Up on the sixth floor, the faces of the ten concubines appeared apprehensive and pale at the windows.

"Long live the King! Long live Absalom the King!" The cries were as balm to Absalom's mind. He looked skeptically at Hushai.

"Why did you people not go into exile with David, your friend! Or wasn't he?" Absalom was enjoying himself tremendously.

Hushai answered for them all. "Whomever Adonai and this city and all the men of Israel choose, him we will revere as king and with him we will stay. Long live Absalom the King!" His cry was taken up by the others.

And Malaki intoned: "Blessed is he who comes in the name of Adonai!"

Even the suspicious Ahitofel was convinced. After all, the Ark of the Covenant was here. And the revolt had affected even David's intimate circle. Success beyond all expectation!

Absalom immediately took possession of the palace. Trumpeters ran through the streets of Zion announcing Absalom as king. He and Ahitofel held a strategy meeting with the elders, the chieftains, and Amasa.

"My advice is this," Ahitofel stated. "Sleep openly with those ten concubines David left behind. Why? Then all Israel will know that you have assumed all your father's privileges, and that you've broken with him utterly—that you mean what you say! And you must start at once. Tonight!" There were strong murmurs of assent around the table.

"Meanwhile, it is vitally urgent to finish off David. Immediately! He must not be allowed to escape! Give me twelve thousand fast riders to go after him. He is tired, discouraged. He has few fighters. We must get him—now—and it's all over. I'll give you this kingdom on the platter that carries his head. The people will run to you. Zion will be your bride, my Lord King!" Ahitofel smiled sardonically as the council room rang with cheers.

Something in what he said disturbed Absalom. "Bring me Hushai the Arkite," he commanded. They brought in Hushai. "Hushai, Ahitofel counsels us to go after David right away. What say you?"

It was Hushai's finest hour. He sat down slowly and stroked his beard. "A good idea, my Lord King. Excellent thinking, really." He bowed his head deferentially in Ahitofel's direction. "I'm in favor of dispatching the old man quickly. Now! Of course! Yet"—and here his voice took on a wary and grave tone—"it could be argued that Ahitofel may be wrong. I say *may* be wrong. I don't know. But I do know David. I have known David for years. He is ferocious and cunning when cornered. And all those men with him—Abishai, Joab, Ahimelek, the Kerethites and Pelethites—well, we all know that they shed blood as you and I breathe. Pursuit of them now may be a dangerous thing."

Ahitofel froze in his chair as Hushai went on: "I think David has laid a trap. He's master of the trap. How do you think he won this kingdom? He could have stayed here and held out for the time it would take his armies to reach Zion. He didn't. No, it's a trap. He'll cut the face off anyone who comes after him. And then? Then he'll come back. He'll castrate the men, rape the women, confiscate our possessions, and put our heads on pikes around the walls of Zion. No, my Lord King! I don't think we should move until you summon all the men of Israel from Dan to Beersheva. Assemble a huge army. Then we can fall on him like rain. If he skulks in a walled city, we can tie ropes around those walls and drag them down into the valley until they are nothing more than a pile of stones for his tomb! Numbers! That's what counts right now."

Suddenly the others had abandoned Ahitofel's plan and were loudly shouting out their agreement. In their hour of triumph they had forgotten David's cunning. Hushai had reminded them of it! Ahitofel sat back. These were people he could not manage. Too stupid. There was no point even in trying to persuade them that Hushai was a clever liar and a provocateur. And even if he could, there would soon be something else. He looked over at the weak sensuousness of Absalom's face. Yes, more problems there, too. It had to be now or never in getting David. Ahitofel saw with infinite clarity that it was all over for him, for Absalom, for all of them. Absalom would learn in due time. Meanwhile he, Ahitofel, had to escape the deluge. Ahitofel's eyes crossed once with Hushai's, and he saw there a look that spoke volumes. While Absalom and his men were setting up a black goatskin tent on the palace roof, Ahitofel very delicately, very politely rose and excused himself. He mounted his camel and rode off with his retinue.

By the next evening he was in Giloh. He spent a leisurely few days drawing up his will, selling off land and valuables. Then he gave some last instructions to his stewards, ordered all of them out of the room, and sat down alone to drink one last bottle of the finest red Hebron wine. After that, in the most deliberate fashion possible, he undid the long, tasseled cincture he wore around his house robe. He looped it around a rafter twice, tested its strength, made a noose for his neck, and tightened it as he stood on a table. Then he kicked the table out from under him.

Some minutes later, the stewards returned. He was quite lifeless. They cut him down, and buried the body beside his father's in the family tomb outside Giloh.

During the days that followed, all the land learned that every night David's son bedded one or more of David's concubines in that goatskin tent on the palace roof. The message was clear. If David couldn't prevent the violation of his own concubines in his own house, how could he protect the people of Israel?

Absalom was largely indifferent to Ahitofel's suicide. "He was getting old anyway," he commented. "And who could trust him?" He began recruiting, as Hushai had advised him. Inevitably he found that the vast majority of volunteers and conscripts came from the northern tribes. Only handfuls of Judahites rallied to Absalom's cause.

In Zion, Hushai eventually got an opportunity to speak briefly to Malaki, and told him Absalom's strategy. Malaki in turn told Bathsheva's maidservant Halpa. She, on the pretext of going to see her lover, went down to the well at En-Rogel outside the east wall in the Kidron Valley. There Ahimaaz and Jonathan had hidden.

Once they learned Absalom's plan, they rode off to find David, but halfway to Bahurim they heard hoofbeats behind them. Halpa must have been discovered. The two clattered into Bahurim and made for the house of a friend. He quickly hid them in a disused well shaft and had one of his servants stretch sacking over the mouth, then covered the sacking and the entire shaft with grain, so that it looked like a mound of grain. When Absalom's pursuers—five of them—arrived, they could find no trace of Ahimaaz and Jonathan, and went away muttering. Then Ahimaaz and Jonathan emerged and stealthily went on to where David was encamped.

When he was informed of Absalom's plan, David crossed the Jordan and led his party up to Mahanayyim, where Saul's son Ishbaal had taken refuge after the battle of Gilboa.

As David's party marched, Halpa was being tortured. When she finally broke down, she implicated Malaki, and Absalom, furious at the treachery, supervised the blind man's torture. But no matter how many glowing tips of the sword they thrust up under his nails, Malaki revealed nothing, did not even protest beyond a little groan. This enraged Absalom all the more, and he finally kicked the seer's head with his boot until the skull

burst and the brains spattered on the ground. The last words
heard from Malaki's beautiful mouth were as acid to Absalom's
ears: "David, our Lord King..." They shoveled his body onto
a blanket and threw it over the battlements into the cesspools of Hinnom.

Absalom, like his father, knew now that he had to move
fast. And what he actually set off was a bloody civil war
between the northerners and the southerners, between Judah
and the rest. The old division, not Absalom's ambition, was
the root issue.

Once he was safe in Mahanayyim, David's fortunes
changed. The Ammonite king, Shovi, Barzillai the Gileadite,
Malkhir of Lodebar, and others provisioned him. Secret messengers fanned out to Judah and Ephraim calling for volunteers.
The two army corps usually stationed at Carmel and Megiddo
arrived intact. By mid-June, David's forces were promising.

"Shouldn't we face them now, Joab?" he asked. The old
veteran disagreed. He wanted to wait until the autumn for a
larger number of warriors, but the matter was decided by Absalom. In July, Absalom and Amasa at the head of their army
were moving northward. They crossed the Jordan well north
of Mahanayyim and advanced down, obviously with intent to
attack. Reports indicated that they intended to pass through the
Forest of Ephraim. Absalom had twenty-two thousand infantry,
no chariots, and only a few hundred camelmen.

"Amasa is a fool," David said to his companions. "There's
only one way through that forest. It's narrow and winding, and
it leads into a trap. Here's how we do it. We will meet him
at the Azbar pasture—it's the only wide opening in the woods.
Ittai will hold the center in a spread-eagle fashion. He can hold
them for a while. Joab, you will flank on the left, Abishai on
the right. Station the archers at the entrance to Azbar. Send
the chariots the long way round. Tell them to keep out of sight
until all Absalom's men have entered the woods, then block
the entry. The Kerethites will stay here on guard. I shall stand
with Ittai at the center."

"Oh, no, you don't," Joab said stolidly, and the other two
shook their heads in agreement with Joab. "It's you they want,
David. We can die. Nobody cares. You can flee and fight
again. If you die, Israel is finished."

"All right, but let me give you one strict command. And
I will not condone any violation. When you catch up with my
son, do not kill him. Deal gently with the lad and take him
alive. For my sake! We'll punish him, but please remember

this one request!" He had raised his voice so that his army could hear him. "Spare my son!"

The three commanders moved their men up the three miles to the Forest of Ephraim. David sat down in Mahanayyim gateway, stationing a watchman on the roof of the tower. It was nine o'clock in the morning. At least once every hour he called to the watchman, asking if he could see anything. He needn't have worried about the outcome of the battle.

If Absalom had waited and developed sufficient forces to take David from the south as well as from the north, it would have made all the difference. As it was, his infantry marched straight into the Azbar pasture to find Ittai's men drawn up in a long, silent line, swords and lances pointing at the advancing army. Absalom could see no sign of any support troops to the left or right. The sun, already southwest, was shining in his eyes. Ittai's men had it at their backs. That line looked so thin, Absalom could not resist the attack. Amasa gave the signal and the northerners made one powerful thrust on Ittai's corps. As they spread out to cover the whole of that long line, the northerners found themselves attacked suddenly on the right and left by Joab and Abishai coming in from the flanking woods.

The struggle seesawed back and forth for about half an hour, and then it was decided. Ittai and his Pelethites pushed forward, driving the northerners back. They retreated, gradually finding themselves surrounded on all sides and bunched together, an easy target for the rain of arrows and javelins. Once they saw their retreat being cut off, several thousand broke ranks and started to run. But there was no easy way out. David's archers were waiting for them. Those who tried to climb into the woods on either side were trapped in ravines and impassable thickets. The few who got through found the chariots waiting for them at the northern edge of the forest. The slaughter was enormous.

Absalom dropped helmet, sword, and shield, and fled only when defeat was inevitable. But he made the mistake of driving his mule into the woods at the west of the Azbar pasture. In his headlong flight through the thickets, his long hair, streaming in the wind, caught in a low-hanging branch of a wild thorn tree and pulled him off his mount. He dangled a few feet off the ground, screaming in agony, unable to free himself, without sword or dagger to cut himself down. He might still have survived and been taken captive if an officer had not seen him and told Joab. Joab, in his fury, dashed into the thicket followed by another ten men. He stood calmly in front of Absalom and spat in the young man's face, then thrust three javelins through his heart. The ten others hacked his neck, body, and face with their swords.

When they got back to Azbar, they found that Amasa had been captured with his officers. "Blow the recall!" Joab ordered. It was over. They went and cut down Absalom's body, threw it into a lime pit, and piled stones on it.

The news of the victory reached David in stages. Joab deliberately sent a non-Hebrew, a Cushite named Kemta, to tell David that Absalom was dead and his army no more. No Hebrew should have to tell the great king that his beloved Absalom was already buried. No sooner had the Cushite set out through the Forest of Ephraim than Ahimaaz, Zadok's son, insisted on carrying the news of victory also. He ran through the flat valley west of the forest. David, sitting patiently in the gateway, heard the watchman call out.

"A man, Sire! A runner! Coming out of the forest!"

"Is he alone? No mob running after him?"

"Alone, yes, Sire."

"Then he has news. There's no defeat—yet."

"Sire! There's a second man. Running in from the valley."

"He also is bringing news."

"The second runner is faster, Sire. He'll be here first. It looks like Ahimaaz."

"A good man, Ahimaaz. His news will be good."

In a few minutes Ahimaaz arrived and bowed low. "A great victory, my Lord King! Adonai be praised! A great victory! Adonai has delivered the King from the rebels."

"The young lad—is he all right? Is he?"

Ahimaaz suddenly realized the import of what Joab had told him. He improvised. "When I left the battlefield, I could only hear great shouts, Sire."

"All right, Ahimaaz. Stand over there and rest yourself."

Almost immediately Kemta the Cushite arrived. David rushed over to him. "I bring good news, Lord King! Your enemies are dead!"

"My son—Absalom?"

Kemta did not hesitate. "May all the enemies of the king be as he is at this moment."

David staggered backward, his face drained, his left hand automatically tearing his robe from collar to waist. He bit his lip. His face flushed as he tried to suppress the hoarse cry of anger and pain that rose in his throat. He turned around and went upstairs to the guardroom over the gate, banged the door shut, dropped the bar into its sockets, and fell weeping and wailing to the floor. Ahimaaz and the others could hear a desolate voice coming from the throat of that strong man.

"My son, my son...Absalom...my son, my beautiful son...if only I could have died for you...Oh, Absalom, Absalom, my son, my son...."

The Cushite and the guards were paralyzed with fear. They could not bear the anguish of that terrible lament and moved out of earshot. Ahimaaz, still panting, dashed off to tell Joab.

Joab cast aside all restraint. When he arrived, he kicked the door of the guardroom down with his boots, walked in, and glared at the prostrate David.

"What are you doing?" he shouted. "Out there brave men have died to save you and your throne from that vicious fox who polluted your concubines, insulted your name, and then sought to kill you. Do you know that your brother Ozem is dead? That Eliab is bleeding to death, that Shammai has lost his right hand and one eye?"

David sat up, stunned and drowned in sorrow, hoping to hear some words of compassion and understanding from Joab. But all he saw was the bloodstained armor of a very angry man.

Joab stood aside and pointed to the doorway. "The men who survived are waiting for their king. Over nine thousand of their comrades are dead. For the love of God, old comrade, let us go. Let us go!" He put out his hand and helped David to his feet.

A period of great confusion followed among the Twelve Tribes. David craftily remained in Mahanayyim and let them stew. The administration of justice, the maintenance of ordinary law and order, the protection of the caravan routes, the safety of fairs and markets, the defense of outlying farms and hamlets that lay near the Bedouin-infested deserts, all were affected. A great fear hung over the land and people. In the south they said, "How can we not take back this man who saved us from the Philistines and made us prosperous?" But the north replied: "How can we bring him back when he killed our anointed king, Absalom?"

At the end of winter, David sent Zadok and Abiathar to talk to the elders of Judah about inviting him back to be their king. He sent other messengers to the northern tribes with the same proposition, promising even to replace Joab with Amasa as general of all the armed forces. Privately he told Joab of his offer to the northerners, but told him also that he had longer-range plans that he was not revealing. The Judahites were delighted. The northerners and the Absalomites accepted the compromise.

The day came at the beginning of spring when the elders, chieftains, and councilors arrived to escort David in honor back to Zion. His east bank allies, Barzillai, Shovi, and Malkhir, accompanied him down to the ford. From here on it was the men of Judah, of Ephraim, of Benjamin, and of all the Twelve Tribes. As they passed through Bahurim, Shimei, who had cursed and reviled David, rushed out and fell to the ground in front of David's camel, crying out for mercy. Joab wanted to kill him, but David demurred. "No one must die this day. We have had enough killing for now—" To Shimei he said, "I swear to you, Shimei, you shall be spared."

Within half a mile of Zion, he was met by Ziva and Mephibosheth.

"Why did you not flee with me, Mephibosheth?" David's words were blocks of ice. "Did you really expect Absalom to crown you king?"

Mephibosheth glanced at the warriors surrounding David. "I couldn't join you, Lord David. I'm lame, as you know. I had no mule. Ziva slandered me, saying that I wanted to be king."

David looked from one to the other. Which of them was lying, Ziva or Mephibosheth? "I don't believe either of you," he decided. "You and he will equally divide between you all the lands, slaves, and valuables I gave you out of reverence for the memory of Jonathan, your father. Now get out of my sight."

But even after David's return to Zion, the quarreling among the tribes did not stop. Many northerners would not accept David again. Inevitably there was a new revolt, this time led by a worthless adventurer from Benjamin, Sheva ben Bichri. He gathered a small army and proceeded to canvass the tribes for more. David sent Amasa into Judah to summon the Judahites. Joab and Abishai went after Sheva with the Kerethites and Pelethites. On their way they were met by Amasa coming up from Judah leading his new conscripts. When they met, and Amasa put out his hands to give Joab the traditional embrace, Joab ran his sword through Amasa's ribs and killed him instantly. Thus Joab became commander in chief again, and no one doubted that Joab had acted with the connivance of David.

They drove on and eventually cornered Sheva in a small walled town called Baalmaakha. The townspeople, seeing the huge army swarming around their poor walls, cut off Sheva's head and tossed it over the wall to Joab. He was satisfied. The danger was over. He sent the Judahite conscripts home and returned to Zion.

David was quite content with the results of the campaign and the death of Amasa. He could now attend to the reorganization of the palace and the court. The ten concubines violated by Absalom were locked up until death and became known as "David's widows," although more than half of them survived him. The prisoners taken at the battle of Ephraim Forest were made to empty the cesspool where Absalom had had Malaki's body flung. In the stench they sifted through all the filth and corpses until they found a decomposing body which had the unmistakable big head and small bones of the blind seer. They washed it clean and enclosed it in a triple coffin, and David had it buried with great honor outside the walls of Zion at the foot of a rocky hill called Golgotha.

The matter of the kingship and the succession was not yet resolved to David's satisfaction. He still feared the remaining Saulites, who did not lack for candidates. Saul's two sons by Rizpah the concubine, Armoni and Mephibosheth, were both alive, and his daughter Merab had borne five sons to Adriel the Meholathite. And then there was always the other Mephibosheth, Jonathan's son. David felt that Saul's sons and grandson were a direct threat. Now that David's kingship had been challenged from within, they had to go. But a certain decorum had to be observed in dispatching them.

On the pretext of satisfying Adonai's anger over some senseless murders that Saul had committed in the days of his madness, David delivered Rizpah's two sons and Merab's five sons into the hands of the murdered people's descendants. All seven were castrated and hanged by the neck until they were dead. Their bodies were exposed for public ridicule over several months. David then sent Ahimelek and Gad to help Rizpah transport the bodies. At the same time he sent for the bones of his beloved Jonathan and of Saul, who had both been buried in Jabesh-Gilead. He had an honorable and expensive tomb built near Saul's old fortress at Gibea, and there had the remains of all nine interred. To Rizpah he assigned some land, a comfortable little house, and a small government pension. But in that Gibea tomb he buried the last hopes of the remaining Saulite sympathizers. They would never again be a danger to him or his family. Neither Mephibosheth nor Mikha, Jonathan's son and grandson, could now constitute a threat to David.

* * *

People began only slowly to notice the great change in David. Absalom's revolt, its violent and bloody end, and its after-effects had distracted them all.

At first they saw the most obvious: in appearance, he had aged more swiftly in eighteen months than in the preceding twenty years. The beautiful sheen of his hair was gone. Only strands and flecks of gold shone in the old man's gray. The long eyelashes were still golden, and the eyes seemed bigger than ever, but their blue no longer scintillated. Like many of the others, he had become thin in exile, but his thinness was too gaunt, and the tone of his skin too bloodless; they reflected something more than the hardships of exile and war. Above all else, it was the tempo and quality of his movements that were different. The quicksilver charm of his reactions had gone forever. When alone, he shuffled rather than strode, and the touch of his hand was tremulous. His speech was still decisive, but slow. The smile was muted, the laughter muffled. All these signs became apparent within a year of his return to Zion.

During the year he gave only one clue about his inmost preoccupation. He had Nathan, Zadok, Sen-Hotep, Joab, Barzillai, Solomon, Adoniyahu and a few friends accompany him to the Egyptian cemetery outside the walls, where Hatich's bones lay. They brought them back to Zion, and David had them buried under the courtyard of Uri's former house. When the ceremony was over, Solomon started chatting and laughing with Adoniyahu, and David suddenly lost his temper. "How dare you violate her peace! Get out of here, I say!" That was all, but it was a clue to his state of mind.

As they walked back to the city, Sen-Hotep chided him mildly, without asking the reason for his irritability. "Come, come, Lord David! You must be annoyed at the mumbling of those priests at Hatich's funeral."

"Instead of all those long-winded prayers, they could have told us something of her lifelong service, her loyalty," David agreed. They walked on a little farther. "I don't know," he mused, "what good they're going to say of me—if anything—when I die. Do you realize"—he stood still, his eyes lifted to the sky—"almost everything important happened in the first fifty years of my life. I did it all in those years." He lowered his gaze and they walked on toward Zion. "And if I live the full threescore and ten, they'll say of me: 'Fifty years of great deeds, and twenty years of idleness!' Twenty years, Ugh!"

"Oh, I don't know about that," the Egyptian retorted. "There could be something more important than slaying giants, defeating Philistine dukes, or building a kingdom. There could be, don't you see?..."

"What could that be, Master Sen-Hotep—what?"

"If you don't know, how could I?" Sen-Hotep said, laughing quietly. "But, for instance, being a good and loyal servant of Adonai—like Hatich herself."

By this time they had reached the North Gate, and a chariot took them the rest of the way home. "Yes," David commented slowly, as they entered the Cedar Palace. "His servant. Adonai's servant. Sometimes an unmindful servant. Sometimes a victorious servant. Sometimes a suffering servant. But always Adonai's servant. Maybe it's greater than all other achievements."

"What you have created in this people, Lord David, in the time of peace in the kingdom, may be more long-lived than either the peace itself or the kingdom itself."

"Sen-Hotep, I love your race!" David said smilingly as they parted. "If Egyptian wisdom only infused our Hebrew service to Adonai, what beauty would be seen!"

"What beauty!" Sen-Hotep echoed with a grimace. The Egyptian had lived too long with both Egyptians and Hebrews to have any illusions.

The two people closest to him, Bathsheba and Sen-Hotep, realized before anyone else that David was failing. For the first few months after their return, Bathsheba and David shared the same bed as before, but she knew he had no desire for her. In the mornings he was already gone when she woke up. Night after night she braced herself to speak to him, but could never find the words.

One morning he came to her and said, "I have given orders. They will arrange a bedroom for you next door."

"David, please—" But the protest died on her lips when he looked at her mildly and lovingly.

"Don't be afraid, little one. You and Solomon are the most precious possessions I have." The stark realism of this—so far from the subtle word of intimacy she yearned for—made her cry bitter, lonely tears once he had left the room. But she had to admit to herself that he was right, she had feared for her future and Solomon's. The reinstated life of court and kingdom and family, all were painted backdrops. Officials, visitors, servants, wives, children, guests, all were playing parts, each saying his lines, while the central character was slowly departing.

When she spoke to Sen-Hotep, she found the Egyptian already fully aware of the change. "In Egypt," he commented, "where we study death and dying more avidly and deeply than living and life, we say that no one dies suddenly, especially an old man. The gods are too merciful. Some higher part of him consents to go over to the other side long before he faces death and those around him hear the rattle in his throat. When he stops breathing, something of him, the highest part of him, has already departed. What you are now realizing is that David has consented. Just be with him. He loves you. He loves all of us. Still. But he is now engaged in the greatest of all his undertakings."

In the three years that remained to him, his most important act was the purchase and preparation of the tableland north of Zion as a site for the temple. The purchase was marked by the unusual. In the spring following his return, he started to accumulate the gold and silver needed for building. His new finance minister, Ahitofel's replacement, was Somsomi, an Aramean from Zoba, popularly known as "Silver Tooth" because of the silver plating on the only tooth left in his mouth. For most people, Somsomi's inability to speak obscured his brilliant mind. He proposed that David take a census of Israel in order to equalize taxation and thus pay for public projects like the temple. David gave the order without thinking.

Joab was against it from the beginning. He saw it for the disaster it proved to be. "It will be extremely unpopular," he told David. The king could cajole the Judahites, but the northerners would balk. And he was right. The northern tribes had never submitted to a census before, and no sooner was it announced than they set about subverting it. They sent for Gad, the one prominent northerner who frequented David's court, and laid their plans. As for the Judahites, they had always conducted their own census before, falsifying figures and numbers. "There are more dead Judahites making fortunes than there are living Judahites on our rolls," Somsomi had complained bitterly.

Led by Joab, the census takers started at the Jordan, working their way up to the northern borders, then moving down the coastal area and the highlands as far as Beersheva. It took them nine months and twenty days exactly. The resulting official figures—102,000 men in the northern tribes, 94,000 in Judah—made David laugh derisively and annoyed Somsomi extremely. "Add another 102,000 at least to Judah," he told Somsomi. "I know my Judahites. And at least another 150,000 to the northerners." But the real trouble was yet to come. Some weeks later, Gad arrived in Zion covered with sackcloth and ashes and accompanied by a group of wailing northern Levites.

"Woe, my Lord King! Woe to us all! The word of Adonai is that you have sinned because, out of greed, you numbered the Hebrews. Adonai will punish this greed in one of three ways. You must pick one of them! Which shall it be: seven years of famine, flight before enemies, or a grave pestilence? Adonai will do to Israel according to the King's choice!"

"Take the pestilence, my Lord David," Nathan grated in David's ear. "There's one raging in Galilee at present, made to Gad's order. The seven years' famine means that they will withhold wheat and corn. The flight before your enemies is Gad's threat of revolt."

"We, O Seer of Adonai, choose the pestilence," David said solemnly. "And may Adonai spare all Hebrews. And we shall omit fifty percent of all taxes for the northern tribes this year."

Gad's face at once became ecstatic. He departed promising that Adonai would honor David's choice, and that he would pray for king and kingdom. Secretly David dispatched Sen-Hotep and a team of Egyptians to the north to examine the situation. It was, as Sen-Hotep reported back, ordinary poisoning resulting from the bad sewage system in most towns and villages. He made recommendations for eliminating the basic cause of the pestilence, which were carried out, and the deaths tapered off after a few months.

Now it was David's turn to use events for his advantage. He summoned his ministers and the elders of the northern tribes, with Gad. He told them that in a vision of the night he had seen the Angel of Adonai striking all the land, sword uplifted ready to strike thousands dead. Perhaps even the king! At that moment, David recounted, Adonai's voice came to him saying he would spare Zion. So the Angel remained hovering over that flat tableland just north of Zion.

"What do you counsel, Gad!"

Gad fell into the trap. "O King! On that tableland you must build an altar to Adonai. This is the word of Adonai!"

"Most assuredly, O man of God, but the land belongs to a heathen, to Araunah the Hittite, whom we have sworn to protect and honor. He and his family have used it as a threshing floor for generations. We must buy it from him before we build our sacred altar on it." No one there could dare refuse to contribute, although afterward many of the northerners reproached Gad in rough language for speaking up too fast. All the same, David received their gold and silver offerings to buy Araunah's land.

The purchase was ritually carried out. David and his retinue arrived there and Araunah bowed low in reverence. "Why should my Lord the King honor this nobody, this miserable man, with a visit!"

"I want to buy your threshing floor, Araunah."

Araunah's face took on a look of sheer horror. "By the life of the Great God, may I rot at the bottom of Hinnom and may my children and wife be beggars all the days of their lives, if I were to charge my Lord the King one wooden pin for this pigpen for which I paid dear to the Jebusite tyrants."

"I want to pay for it, Master Araunah, in order that all justice be fulfilled. What is the price?"

"But my Lord the King is like the Angel of Adonai, fair and shining and privileged. Why should he pay one smelly dog's eye for this unworthy weed patch for which in the far-off days of my beginnings among the Jebusites I paid with years of my sweat? Let my Lord take it. It is the gift of a humble and grateful heart." Araunah bowed down again.

"Your land is priceless, Master Araunah. But the elders and I offer you the miserly sum of four silver Tyrian talents."

Araunah fell flat on his belly on the ground, weeping and rolling around. "So help me Adonai! But this flea-ridden dungheap is not worth one hundredth of one Edomite button. Let my Lord the King do as he wills. Let him take the land."

"Ah, Master Araunah, we desire this land so much, the elders and I want to offer you double its price. Eight silver Tyrian talents, I pray you! Be kind and accept our poor money."

"Am I an unworthy heathen to accept eight royal talents for this bit of naked rock? And how can Araunah's children say afterward: 'You know, our grimy ancestor, Araunah, sold this rock for eight talents to Kind David?' Far be such a shameful thing from my Lord the King. Let him take the land. It is his. Simply his for the taking."

"Truly, Master Araunah, the wisdom and holiness of Adonai is with you. Now, tell us, I pray you: what price would your children be proud of?"

Still on the ground Araunah wept and groaned and tore his clothes. "As the Holy God lives, O King, there is no one like you in this land to read the hearts of ungrateful children and rescue an old man's last days and hours from the spittle and contempt of his ill-begotten children. Do as your own heart tells you, and have mercy on your servant."

"Will twenty stave off their hate, Master Araunah?"

Araunah only cried the louder, the tears coursing down his cheeks. "Oh, miserable cur that I am—"

"Thirty, Master Araunah?"

"Would that I had never been born to lie here so miserable before my Lord David who is like the Angel of Adonai."

"Forty, Master Araunah?"

"Ah! Ah!" His seizure reached its paroxysm. "O Angel of Adonai! O King of kings! I shall have to take my mangy oxen and threshing whips and chairs and baskets. I shall burn them! Yes! That's it! I shall burn them—all!—as a sacrifice of prayer and thanksgiving for my Lord the King. For without the threshing floor, what can I, poor dog, do with oxen and carts and threshing whips and chairs and baskets? Ah, me! Miserable exile that I am among the chosen ones of Adonai who have sworn on their sacred Covenant to protect me!"

"Fifty, Master Araunah, for the land and all you have on it!"

By this time the elders from the north were in visible commotion. But Araunah leaped up and ran to David, kissing the king's foot and the camel's side, laughing and crying, the tears rolling down his cheeks. "As the Great God lives, your name will be blessed forever, O King! And I and my family are your slaves for all our days!"

David traversed the entire terrain in the company of Sen-Hotep. "We'll have the men clear away those rocks and debris over on that western edge. And those willows must go." Sen-Hotep glanced at him. David shrugged. "I want no death tree around this place. I know you Egyptians do not believe in that sort of thing, but I'm a Hebrew."

"And those alders? Those hawthorn trees over there?" Sen-Hotep pointed to the eastern side of the rock floor.

"I want them both."

"Some other Hebrew idea, I suppose?"

"Yes! The alder's bark gives a marvelous red dye, its flowers an unbeatable green, and its twigs a luscious brown."

Sen-Hotep smiled. "Red for fire. Green for water. Brown for earth," he said slowly.

"You've listened carefully to Nathan or Gad," David growled.

"But isn't the alder the resurrection tree for you Hebrews? And isn't living man made up of fire, water, and earth?"

"That is what our fathers said," replied David.

The one problem David could not solve immediately was that the hill nearby made access from the city to the rock floor difficult and impractical.

It was on the occasion of his son Adoniyahu's marriage that a solution was suggested. Adoniyahu, his son by Haggith, was large of girth, prematurely bald, subject to unaccountable fits of blushing, and probably the clumsiest man in David's family. Now twenty-seven, with his head full of grandiose ideas of empire, Adoniyahu married Sassberri, an Ethiopian princess. His mother had arranged it. "A noble marriage of a true prince with a true princess," she said loftily.

Adoniyahu had slept in the same bed as his mother since he was born. And on the marriage night, when he approached the bridal suite, the hapless prince was set upon by the five enormous, dumb Nubian eunuchs Sassberri had brought with her. They stripped him naked and poured him into the famous "Ethiopian nightdress," a priceless garment made of treated deerskin and lined with sheep's wool. It was supposedly big enough to hold both husband and wife, and it had adjustable hooks to widen or narrow it. The garment was an heirloom passed down from father to son, mother to daughter.

The eunuchs quickly measured Adoniyahu's body size. They knew the princess's, since they bathed her three times a day. Having adjusted the garment, they carried him bodily to the bridal suite and laid him down on the bed. Sassberri then climbed in too. Nobody ever found out from Adoniyahu what happened, but Sassberri never conceived by him, and it was rumored that he was totally impotent. Certainly Sassberri was not barren. Later she left Adoniyahu, married one of David's nephews, and bore seventeen children, including three pairs of twins successively.

After Adoniyahu's wedding, and before the Ethiopian delegation of marriage guests departed, David talked with the vizier who had accompanied Sassberri, mentioning his plans for the temple and the awkward terrain between Zion and the threshing floor. The Ethiopian immediately began to speak of raised structures on spanning columns. "We have had to develop them, Sire," the vizier said, "because of the unevenness of our land. We even carry water great distances by this means." David called in his architects and engineers and had the vizier describe the viaducts in detail. Work was begun six weeks later on the first of them. It would be completed before David's death.

* * *

In the autumn of David's sixty-ninth year, he became subject to severe shivers and a general coldness in his limbs. His doctor, Asayahu, had his usual explanations about the "life bile," "the color of the blood," the influence of the full moon, the tides in the Nile. He had the king wrapped every third day in the still-warm pelt of a newly slaughtered sheep. The relief was temporary and, as David grumbled good-naturedly, the pelt made him smell like a ewe in heat. His body slaves had to pour a whole vial of Arabian perfume over him before he could stand the smell of himself.

David knew then something that Asayahu could not know: some force was ebbing out of his limbs; and what little remained seemed to be gathering into the center of him for a last show of resistance. Asayahu even recommended to David's family that they seek out a fresh, young, healthy woman for David. A virgin, Zadok added, while biting his lip in that well-known tic of his when the purity of the Law was uppermost in his mind. Thus, he explained, the king would not suffer any ritual uncleanness.

David laughed himself to sleep after this solemn discussion by his loving but foolish intimates. They actually went ahead with the plan. An official search party, loaded with gifts, escorted by a special detachment of David's own Kerethites, was organized to be sent out at the end of the winter to find the "King's handmaiden." Joab was to be in charge of the troops and Ittai was the chief official searcher. Along with them David decided to send two of his retired wives, Haggith and Abigail, to help Ittai make a final choice. Abigail took her son Khileav as her personal counselor. Haggith chose the weak-kneed Adoniyahu, mainly because he was so miserable at court.

Abigail needed a change of air anyway, and David had infinite trust in her good judgment. Haggith he just wanted out of his sight. She reminded him of painful things, and he knew she hated him. His choice of these two women was quite deliberate. As all knew, they loathed each other. Protocol, of course, would force them to behave in public as politely as the king's wives should, but each would vie with the other in satisfying the king and thus gaining his favor. As David realized, their sons also could not have been more opposed to each other. Adoniyahu could not stand the brutishness of Khileav, and Khileav spent his time poking fun at the effeminate Adoniyahu.

The popular joke in Zion was that Haggith took Adoniyahu

with her so that he would not kill himself with overexertion trying to overcome his perennial impotence with his still child-less wife. And David had a severe pain across his middle one evening from laughing as he listened to old Hushai retelling some of the ribald jokes told about Adoniyahu's pale face and shaking limbs after one night's enclosure in the "Ethiopian nightdress" with his wife. It was the first time that David had learned the reason for Adoniyahu's nickname, "Waddling Ass." Khileav was a horse of a different color. Nicknamed "the Beast," he was a wild boar of a man, his entire body from shoulders to toes covered in a mat of thick hair. At the age of twenty-eight he was still totally irresponsible, father of more illegitimate children than David's entire brood of legitimate ones. Khileav saw the whole expedition as a marvelous op-portunity to sleep with a different maiden every night.

Unintentionally, however, David had put two people in close proximity who each had a need for the other—for the other's talents, for the other's bad luck, for the other's evil: Haggith and Joab.

Joab was still resident in Zion, officially on the army payroll, quartered in the Millo barracks, and swordmaster for the new recruits in the king's special regiments. He still had his own house and land out at the edge of the wilderness near Tekoah, but David found it better not to let Joab live outside the city. Since the disastrous census of the previous year, Joab had never entered David's palace and David rarely spoke to him or even allowed Joab to see him. He had never forgiven him for the death of Absalom. "The Lord God of Israel will deal with Joab and all the sons of Zeruiah," was all David would reply to those who pleaded for his clemency. "But Joab will never stand in my presence again and find favor." Joab's greatest failing had probably been an excess of fidelity. If there was one su-preme hypocrisy in David's life, aside from his murder of Uri, it concerned Joab. The crimes Joab committed were, with few exceptions, acts actually sanctioned by David or efforts on Joab's part to protect David. Yet after David's death, and on David's explicit instructions, young Solomon as the new king would have Joab dragged away from the holy altar where he had sought sanctuary according to the Law, and have him cut down like a common criminal.

Perhaps Joab sensed this. Five years older than his cousin, he was not willing to bide his time until David died. Eventually, he cannily guessed, he would be assassinated by Solomon. Burned into his brain were David's last contemptuous words to him: "What is there between you and me, Joab, son of Zeruiah? Adonai will judge you for the innocent blood which you have spattered on your sword belt." What galled Joab was what galls every henchman in history. "In the old days I did his killing or we killed together. I raped for him or we raped together. Yes, and burned together, looted together, violated together, tortured together," Joab told his cronies, cursing. "And now I am unclean, and he has suddenly become holy."

Haggith came to need somebody like Joab both out of fear for her survival after David's death and from a flaming hatred of Bathsheba, the woman she blamed for her downfall. She still lived with her children, servants, and retainers in her own quarters in the palace. Since Absalom's death, David never saw her privately, and she wore the yellow veil of a retired royal wife. Once a week she went with others into David's long dining hall for the evening meal and the musical performances. She was also invited for special court ceremonies and for the glittering receptions David still gave from time to time for foreign dignitaries. Otherwise she was very much a prisoner in her own home, making occasional forays under armed escort into the marketplace or to visit some relative or friend. But David's spies and informers were everywhere. And like everyone else at court, Haggith knew that her every move was known to David and his intimates.

Besides, she knew from David's stare that never again would they have a friendly, much less a cozy, conversation together, never again would she lean laughingly on his breast and whisper with him tenderly. She knew that her son and family were to be excluded from any real honor and power forever—and would probably be liquidated by David's chosen successor, Solomon. She knew also that David deliberately hurt her at times by showering favors on Bathsheba in her presence. Bathsheba's persistent beauty in contrast with her own decline only heightened her hate for the "Gilohite whore" and spurred her revenge.

Her problem as well as her hope of triumph lay at one and the same time in Adoniyahu. For about a year and a half after the farce of his marriage to Sassberri, Adoniyahu had lived in Haggith's quarters, where Haggith was able to protect him from the scorn of the court and the contempt of the citizenry. Whenever he went out, it was in her company. The rest of the time he stayed within the palace compound. Haggith gave up the idea of having him trained as commander of David's elite corps. Benaya ben Yehoyada, David's overall commander of the elite corps, referred to him as "Princess Adoniyahu." Besides, the young prince could not hit a bull with a javelin at twelve paces.

Still, for better or worse, Haggith reposed all her hopes in Adoniyahu. And she had to have a plan. She proceeded to give several magnificent dinner parties for Adoniyahu to which she invited all the young men and women of his age, the sons and daughters of David's immediate circle and generation. She sent her steward, the one-eyed Malko, northward to recruit some big Galilean archers and lancers. He then went by Damascus and put fifty chariots on order in her name. The horses would come from Arabia. In the middle of all these preparations and plots, she was called in with the others to hear the announcement of the royal search party about to depart to find the "King's handmaiden."

The search party had been out less than twenty-four hours when Joab and Haggith found each other. At the first evening's encampment, Haggith sent for Joab as commander of the escorting troops, ostensibly to give him instructions for the nightly guard and food supplies for her part of the caravan. After going over the details, she looked up at the old fighter standing at attention by her couch.

"Will my Lord King's Lady have anything else to command?" Joab asked uncomfortably, after he registered her stare.

"That all depends," Haggith answered sharply, still looking straight at him, "on whether the son of Zeruiah is going to live a long or a short life."

"My lady?" Joab queried warily, his eyes watching her face intently. "May the Lord God of Israel and of our royal master, David, grant me a long life—" Joab started ritually.

"Oh, nonsense! In this tent you are not standing in the king's court," Haggith shot back at him. Then, contemptuously: "Is the son of Zeruiah a dog that can be drowned by a whelp of a boy"—a reference to the insulting language Goliath had used against David years before—"or a flea that my Lord Solomon can walk upon?"

Joab's eyes hardened. Head bowed, he looked up at her from beneath his eyebrows, the real sign of Joab's murderous anger. He said nothing. Haggith cocked her head to one side and laughed lightly. She knew the insult had gone home. Then, looking away from Joab and in a matter-of-fact tone, she continued.

"There is no one in the whole land of Israel who does not know that we are searching for a handmaiden who will bury our beloved king and lay his bones with his fathers'. And there is no one, even the fools in the tavern, my Lord Joab"—she threw him a foreboding glance—"who does not know that neither your life nor the life of your household nor the life of my son nor the life of my household will be worth two bleats of a she camel's foal the moment the king is gathered to his fathers and the Gilohite's son is king—"

"If indeed he does become king"—now it was Joab's turn to interrupt with words that slipped from him almost involuntarily, and Haggith looked at him, her eyes wide in surprise—"it will not be because those in danger did not know beforehand."

"Exactly! But now," she said, standing up and smiling, "it is late. Will my Lord Joab come back tomorrow? In the evening?"

While the search party was away, there was another change in David's life. Sen-Hotep, now tired and homesick for No-Amon and the sun of Egypt, came to David and asked his blessing on his retirement. David was shocked. It was another reminder to him that time was rushing them all to the gulf of eternity. He searched Sen-Hotep's face, trying to divine his thoughts.

"My friend, apart from Khimkham, you are the only one who gives me genuine peace." Khimkham had arrived in Zion from Gilead, and turned out to be a man of thirty-two years, already gray-haired, and profoundly wise. He had rapidly become an intimate and companion of the old king. "Of course I never talk with him as I do with you, but I know he understands me, Sen-Hotep." He looked out the window and was silent.

"There's only one area you've never touched on with me, David," Sen-Hotep remarked. "How you changed, why you changed, once you fled from Saul and Gibea."

David came hurriedly from the window and sat down, elbows on the table, his face in his hands. "What do you think I've been thinking about for the last year, Sen-Hotep, ever since we buried Hatich's bones? That's why I got so angry with poor Solomon that day. He was so like me at that age, so feckless, so inconsequential..."

He rubbed away the tears and glanced briefly at the Egyptian. "When I entered Saul's army—even after the killing at Elah—I was still the same as when I worked in the pastures at Beraka, good and gentle. Then something happened, I don't know what. Saul feared me—rightly so. I wanted to be king. And he really wanted to kill me. One thing led to another. I don't know . . . I think I found out good behavior was going to lead me to an early death, so I changed . . . I suppose I never was good in my youth for the right motives, only because it worked for me . . . and then," he said with a slightly bewildered and disgusted look, "I had to go down into the filth and work my way back . . . this time because I really decided it, not simply because I had to kill to survive. Have I answered your question?" He had a little smile for his friend.

"I have yet another," Sen-Hotep replied. "I came as near as any foreigner could to believing in your Adonai. What held me back was your law of blood," the Egyptian went on. "Your—I mean your Hebrew—fascination with blood vengeance—"

"But," David broke in, "it's the custom among us. And"— looking away over the rooftops of Zion—"doubtless Solomon will take care of a whole list of them for me after I have passed on—Shimei the Bahurimite, Mephibosheth, Joab—"

"Well, take Joab. You condemn him for killing many of your enemies, including Absalom. Wasn't their blood guilt the reason he killed them? And all for your sake? And didn't you even perhaps plan or help plan their deaths?"

"Perhaps . . . Yes, perhaps, but I am the king—"

"Oh!" Sen-Hotep had no response. He paused and reflected. "On second thought, I think I will stay here in Zion, with your permission. But there is one thing I would like to clear up. As you know, I will have nothing to do with the jackal-headed Anubis or the falcon-headed Horus, or the big-eared donkey-headed Seth or the baboon-headed Thoth or the crocodile-headed Sobek or the goose-headed Amon or with any animal-headed god. That's all piffle. What god there is must be higher, not lower, than human beings.

"But, David, your Adonai has never seemed loving or beautiful to me. He orders killings and persecutions. Whole tribes and nations. How could I, a sinner, a mortal, trust that sort of a god to receive me? What sort of a home is eternity with a god like that?"

"Beautiful and loving." David repeated the words several times to himself. "That's just it, Sen-Hotep," he said slowly. "Beautiful and loving. I want that when I die. Years ago, I wanted what I used to call my 'all.' Avidly! But I did not find it. In women or war or wealth. And now, even though I still live by our law of blood"—he shot Sen-Hotep a glance— "something has started talking inside me very quietly. I can't make out the words . . . but the sense is—beautiful and loving.

And I must go on listening and listening. For I am being drawn irrevocably to it. Years ago, I used to wake up to the silence of the predawn hours and feel happy. But now I wonder what I am going to wake up to when I die."

"Is that why you wanted the alders—the signs of resurrection—around you when you died?"

"I want resurrection," David admitted. "But I want—or, anyway, wanted something else before I died." There was a pathetic note of disappointment in David's voice.

"You remember," the king went on, "I decided to keep the hawthorn trees on the eastern edge of Araunah's floor? Well, when Adonai appeared to Moses, it was out of a burning hawthorn tree. We Hebrews have always called the hawthorn Adonai's tree, the tree of the first day of the week, when Adonai created light. Adonai appeared to all the great men of our race, all of them. None of them gave this race a kingdom. I and I alone—I, David of Bethlehem—I did! Why hasn't he appeared to me? Why? Why not to me?"

There was a deep silence between them for a few minutes. Sen-Hotep marveled at the faith in this Hebrew, who used hawthorn trees as bait for a god.

The search party was gone about three months. Khileav satisfied himself completely, although it practically beggared him to buy off the vengeful fathers, brothers, and fiancés of about sixty young girls whose virginity he violated. Adoniyahu stayed close to his mother. The troops were fêted and fed and honored everywhere they went. And, duly, after an exhaustive and exhausting search in the main towns and more prosperous hamlets of the kingdom, they eventually chose a buxom, healthy, outgoing fourteen-year-old Shunamite girl called Abishag.

Abishag was one of the newest generation in David's kingdom. Within David's secure borders, she had never known hunger or misery, the devastation of tribal warfare, or the waste of foreign invasion. Her father was a wealthy merchant from Carmel on the coast, and worked as an overseer in the king's fleet. Abishag had some Cretan blood in her from her mother's side, and David found her enormously pleasing. She was petite, large-breasted, brunette, with slightly almond-shaped gray eyes, their outer corners slanting upward beneath shapely eyebrows. At that age, she still had the plumpness and baby fat of youth. But she danced beautifully, played the harp and the flute, was clever at royal checkers, and invested a room with her laughter and gaiety the moment she entered it. Above all, she took to her task as the "King's handmaiden" with absolute devotion and enthusiasm.

But it was all no use. From the start, David told her clearly that he did not need her for making love. Ever since the death of Absalom he had abstained, not out of guilt, but because of what he had experienced in the guardroom over the gate of Mahanayyim the day they brought him the news of his son's death. However, Abishag did her best to at least provide him with heat, putting David to bed with hot-water bottles and charcoal panniers, wrapping herself around him until he fell asleep, and then sleeping close to him all night.

Still, David shivered and was cold in bed. He kept Abishag near him as a body servant and constant house companion, but he knew nothing could restore the heat to his body. David did not spend much time lamenting that; he was waiting for something much bigger.

One night early in summer, he woke up as he had not waked for twenty-five years. Somebody or something he had never met or seen before, he felt, had entered his bedroom. Abishag was sleeping soundly by his side, her breathing regular, deep, peaceful. He lifted his head quietly and glanced quickly around the room at all the familiar objects and corners. Everything in place. No one. He turned painfully on his back and stared out the window into the silent night, his mind racing around the possibilities: a robber? an assassin? a bad dream? But the more he concentrated, the fainter became that initial feeling. He gave up after a while. Perhaps it was some night sound from the city streets, or the sentries telling the hour. He had just turned over on his side, closed his eyes, and was about to try to sleep again, when he had the same sensation, this time a little more sharply.

He opened his eyes and lay waiting, listening, analyzing, as he had done hundreds of times in his guerrilla days. The liquids of caution distilled in him over those years of danger pooled coldly in his heart. And he was about to shout for the guards outside the door when it suddenly dawned on him that, although he was puzzled, he was without fear. He sensed no enemy near. Automatically, he relaxed. He had no fear!

After lying there quietly for about a quarter of an hour, he made up his mind that some new deepening of his wonder had taken place, much like what he had felt during his one boat trip, with Hiram of Tyre over the Great Sea to Luqqawatna. This time, though, as the first shafts of light fell across his window balcony, he opened his eyes fully. He was completely relaxed, with no desire to get out of bed, call for the servants or wake Abishag, and get going about the day's business. This struck him as something new. And he lay there sensing his body, moving his arms and legs ever so slightly and calculating his energy.

Then he remembered an incident of the previous evening. Abishag was trimming his toenails. Each nail she cut crackled like a bit of dried parchment, and the paring sprang away sharply. And not only his nails were dried up. Throughout his body there was this rigid and fragile brittleness.

But this morning, as he lay there sensing himself and discovering the world in the new day's light, he knew that now— and for a while past—that wonder returned each day like a dream, forcing its way into his eyes and ears with time's movement, with the sounds and smells and sights of everyday life. When Abishag awoke, she saw him lying there on his back, and she was immediately alarmed by the quiet tears she saw in his eyes. But he calmed her with a few words which she only half understood. "Mercy is his greatest gift... I'm all right, daughter... Just thinking. An old man is allowed his tears, isn't he? Don't worry now. Let's get on with the day."

As he arose and she dressed him, he closed his eyes and again relaxed, trying to feel his way back to where he had just seen time and eternity spatter each other with the gentle foam of life. There was no word in his native language either for eternity or for time. But in his own sensuous image, he felt that everyday he was groping for the latchstring in the door that opened out onto the eternal.

Abishag had become fast friends with Lassatha over the months, and it was the Egyptian who explained to the Shunamite what was really going on inside David. "He is being slowly drawn to eternity, Abishag. And the gods are kind— they let the chosen ones get acquainted slowly with the world of those who are gone from sight and touch. From now on let us watch him carefully. The end cannot be far off."

Abishag noted also that David spent longer and longer periods in the company of Sen-Hotep and young Khimkham, either at the palace or over on Araunah's threshing floor. Ostensibly the two men were helping him draw up the plans for the temple Solomon would build there after David's death. But David was clearly engaged in a fierce expectation. She overheard several of the conversations among the three.

"This temple built according to your plans," Khimkham said

one day in his graceful way, "will be the greatest monument to my Lord the King!" Sen-Hotep smiled quietly at David's reaction.

"No, no. It won't," David retorted a trifle sharply. "My greatest achievement is quite different. I see it now. I see that all I have accomplished by means of kingdom and glory, and wealth and women and battle, will all finally be reduced to dust. And so fast!"

"Well, then—" Sen-Hotep began.

"What I've done, if I've done anything worthwhile, is to provide a body for Adonai in this world. The people. The people! As long as Hebrews exist and are Hebrews, Adonai will have a physical presence among the sons of men.

"That persistent body of men and women and children— my Hebrews!—will be a perpetual sign that Adonai has not deserted his world. That men and women may still have hope. That salvation is still possible under these skies."

"It's a great thought," Sen-Hotep mused. "A great thought. I am trying to think of one such occasion in our long history down south—"

"There was at least one," David said insistently, a little grimly. "We were there once upon a time, we Hebrews, you remember?"

Sen-Hotep gave a wintry smile. "We Egyptians haven't yet realized what happened then," he remarked dryly. "We rewrite history too, my Lord David!" They both laughed the comfortable laugh of old men who have refused the barb of enmity, preferring the warmth of friendship.

Haggith's plan to place Adoniyahu on David's throne was truly her own. Having made her alliance with Joab during the search party's trip, she sent Adoniyahu and Joab to see Abiathar, the priest. For at least an air of legitimacy they needed a priest. They won Abiathar over, for he saw himself becoming the next high priest in Israel. Then surrounded by friends and well-wishers, he drove down to the well of En-Rogel, outside the east wall of Zion, one September day at noon. Adoniyahu was dressed like a peacock by his mother: silver britches, embroidered high-heeled shoes such as the Pharaohs wore, a scarlet tunic, and a quite ridiculous peaked cap adorned with ostrich plumes. "The people must see you clearly and know that you never look like anybody else," she told her son. She needn't have worried. Nobody in Zion had ever looked like Adoniyahu that day, nor ever would.

Abiathar sacrificed a sheep and gave his blessing to Adoniyahu as "the next king of Israel." Adoniyahu, under instructions from his mother, sat upon his mule and proclaimed in a loud voice: "I am now king! Go forth and announce my kingship to all my brother princes and to the Judahites and to all the tribes!" Then, in utter disregard of even the most elementary rules governing the actions of those who would steal a throne by a palace revolution, the party betook themselves to Adoniyahu's house to sit down to the most lavish feast ever given in Zion.

As they said in Israel afterward, "The best part of Adoniyahu's kingship was that feast." In fact, it was the *only* part. The plan went awry from then onward. Nathan wormed the news out of Abiathar, who could not keep his mouth shut. Nathan told Bathsheva and advised her to rush to David. She did so, and Nathan arrived shortly afterward to confirm her story. David started to laugh and then to weep with frustration. He knew now that he had to step aside in favor of Solomon right away. For after Adoniyahu it would be another one of the princes or some upstart.

His decision about how to deal with Adoniyahu was arrow-straight. He called Zadok, Nathan, and Benaya ben Yehoyada at once. Under his instructions and guarded by the Kerethites and Pelethites, they went down to the Gichon, the actual spring from which the Siloam stream and pool came. He sent Solomon there on his own royal mule, escorted by David's special warriors. At Gichon, Zadok anointed Solomon with a horn of the specially consecrated oil normally kept under lock and key beneath the Shekina near the Ark. The royal trumpeters on the walls of Zion blew the royal acclaim as the procession returned to Zion preceded by the Kerethites and followed by the Pelethites. All of Zion—except for Adoniyahu's carousing guests—came out and learned the news. The cry arose: "Adonai save Solomon! Adonai bless King Solomon! Long live our King. David will live forever!"

Solomon went straight to the palace and up to David's room, where David had lain down to rest. Sen-Hotep sat by the bedside and witnessed the conversation. Solomon received his father's blessing and instructions.

"Now, my son, an ounce of prevention is far better than a bloody cure. Kingship is a dangerous career. There is, for instance, Shimei the Bahurimite—you know what he did to me. Take care of him when I am gone. He is a Saulite. And others, too, like him—Mephibosheth, Joab, Adoniyahu, even

Ziva. But you know them all. Make sure they do not go to their fathers in peace." Solomon would make sure.

When Solomon—ceremonious, pompous, exaggeratedly deliberate as only a very self-important young man can be— departed, David looked at Sen-Hotep and raised his eyebrows in a query.

"As we said, old friend," the Egyptian commented dryly, "kings come, kings go, but—" He broke off, raising his right hand to complete his meaning. Then by way of conclusion: "The young man will do well. Don't worry." David slowly nodded a few times.

"I suppose," David rejoined a few minutes later, "he will be king, even a glorious king. But then he and the kingdom could be shaken and broken like a badly fired clay jar."

Sen-Hotep pursed his lips thoughtfully. "Didn't you once hear what your Adonai intended you to achieve in this world? What was it? *Gufleneshami,* 'a body for my spirit,' your Adonai said. Wasn't that it?"

David stirred and looked up at the ceiling. *"Guflene- shami . . . gufleneshami . . ."* He repeated that and other words to himself as if he were ruminating alone.

"Gufleneshami," Sen-Hotep interjected softly. David turned two glittering eyes on him. "Tell me, David, son of Jesse, when you fled from Absalom, did your spirit break?"

"No."

"Has anything ever broken your spirit—the sight of Goliath rushing at you, Saul's attempts to murder you, Shekelath's hate, the power of Dagon, the shame of your own sins, the famines and the pestilences of your time?"

"No."

"Still the flame of Adonai's life flickered in you? And nei- ther temple, nor the sweet voices of singers, nor royal chron- icles, nor anything else was of help or was needed?"

"No."

"Then what has Adonai been telling you? He speaks— you've told me again and again—by events because your Adonai is a god of history, you say. What has he been telling you?"

The blue eyes glittered at him. Both men were working their way along the outer cutting edge of the meaning that is possible in human words.

"Listen, my good friend." Sen-Hotep leaned forward, one hand reaching for David's shoulder. "A god who has no body, no seeable, touchable, smellable, audible presence, what do you think he would need among us men and women who finally only perceive truth in visible, seeable, touchable, smellable, audible beings like ourselves? Tell me."

"Some seeable, touchable, smellable, audible presence, I suppose..." David's voice trailed off as he looked away, thinking. "The body of a man or a woman or a—"

"A body, eh? A single body? Why only a single body? Why not three? Ten? Four hundred? Fifty thousand? Why not a whole tribe? An entire people? Hundreds of generations of an entire people? Why not?"

David looked back sharply, turning on his side, his eyes filled with meaning. He was stone-silent for some moments, his eyes blazing and holding Sen-Hotep's stare. "The people...the people...his people..." The words were said thickly, as if they meant something awesome for him. *"Gufleneshami..."* Then he straightened on the bed, his face turned upward. "Leave me now, Sen-Hotep. My head is bursting and my heart is sore. I'll think some more. And we'll talk again about this."

As the Egyptian left the room, he glanced back. Silent tears were pouring from David's closed eyes. "The sharpest salt in human tears comes from the peace of the gods and the sting of failure." Sen-Hotep remembered the old saying from the Theban Book of the Dead.

Meanwhile, none of the shouts and acclamations for Solomon had reached Adoniyahu's party. They were all so uproariously happy and boisterous in their celebration of both their new king and their own future careers in his administration that what went on in the streets totally escaped them. Only when Abiathar's son, Jonathan, rushed in white-faced and yelled out the news did utter panic break out. Tables were overturned, wine was spilled, food trampled upon, as they all ran for the door and their mules. But outside, ringing Adoniyahu's house, the Kerethites stood silently, swords drawn, lances pointing at the house, shields locked together, all in utter silence. The guests were arrested, put in chains, and thrown in the common prison to await punishment. Nathan, with special powers from Solomon, passed summary judgment and condemnation for high treason on each one individually, after which each one was taken out and garroted in the courtyard that afternoon. Joab escaped momentarily by sliding down a bedsheet converted hastily into a rope—a daring feat for a man of seventy-five, but Joab was in a great hurry to get to his home near Tekoah.

Adoniyahu mismanaged his own escape. He ran up the stairs to the roof of his house and fled by jumping wildly from roof to roof across Zion. Some of the inhabitants caught sight of that extraordinary figure in the silver britches, scarlet tunic, and plumed cap, and they took it to be a demon scattering temptations among the godly. Adoniyahu made directly for the principal altar near the Shekina and laid hold of its two ornamented ivory horns. The Law gave him immunity from arrest and seizure as long as he was there. He had to stay there hanging on to the horns for two days. Eventually, when the joke had gone far enough and all Zion had gone to see this treasonous idiot, Solomon sent him word by a slave that he could safely quit the horns and go home. "If you prove yourself a worthy man and loyal, not a hair of your head will be harmed."

After David's death, Solomon's executioners would eviscerate Adoniyahu. Joab, Abiathar, and about thirty other notables involved in the affair would also be done to death by Solomon's assassins.

Not until after David's death did either Sen-Hotep or Solomon learn about one of the acts of vengeance David had reserved to himself: the punishment of Doeg the Edomite, who, years before, had informed Saul about David's visit to the priests of Nov. The vengeance was terrible. Doeg was delivered into David's hands shortly after the city of Jebus was captured. David had him scourged with whips, castrated, and confined to the iron mines at Ezion-Geber. Fifteen years later, on one of his periodic visits to the mines, David descended the mine shaft with Joab and cut off Doeg's head himself. Such acts of vengeance were sacred in David's eyes.

David died the following January, on the eighteenth. The day before his death he had a lively discussion with Sen-Hotep. They had been out on the threshing floor with Khimkham for one of the usual surveying visits—this time concerning the location of the Holy of Holies and the High Altar at the center of the future temple.

"Sometimes, Lord David," Sen-Hotep began, "I have a queer feeling. It seems to me you are planning each minute detail of this temple, yet you do not really pin your hopes for the permanence of your people on this magnificent structure nor on the sacrifices and songs of praise that will fill its days." Khimkham felt that Sen-Hotep's words went too near the bone.

He looked timidly at David, expecting an outburst. But there was none.

"Absolutely correct, my friend," the king replied. "A temple will be built. For all I know, several temples will be built. But Hebrews' belief and their search for holiness will go on independently of any temple, any sacrifice, any halleluya songs."

That evening the three ate together quietly, and then Khimkham retired, leaving David and Sen-Hotep to their usual nightly talk.

"I cannot imagine the spirit of a people lasting without a visible structure to house it," Sen-Hotep offered.

"I can." David's voice was very calm and confident. "Don't you see, no structure is permanent. But spirit can be. No matter what happens to my people, they will keep this spirit."

"No matter what happens?" Sen-Hotep frowned.

"No matter what! They may be flattened between layers of cold-minded heathens and stone-hearted aliens. Belief and the search for holiness may be gone out of style among men. May even weaken, as it did among the northerners when I was a boy. What I have been trying to do—for a long time without knowing it—was to make sure that this belief and that search for holiness shape and mold my people in a form indestructible by others." David became excited now by his own thoughts.

"I want them to have a terrible need to meet the eternal within this world, to leap straight into the intimacy of Adonai, their creator. Where others edge away, startled, afraid, tentative, I want them to plunge ahead recklessly in a faith peculiar to them. A faith that will set them apart. Quicken them! Enliven them! Strangers will recognize that belief on their faces. Heathen strangers will see that search in their eyes. Conquerors will smell that untouchable holiness in the odor of their bodies when they burn them and of their blood when they shed it in hate."

Sen-Hotep was quiet for a while. At length he stood up, stretched himself, and walked over to the window. "Looks like bad weather is coming. A storm."

"Yes, it's been brewing for hours."

The Egyptian turned, smiling. "The old bones, eh? You felt it in your bones!" David said nothing but merely returned the smile.

During the small hours of the morning, a thunderstorm lashed the land with great careening sheets of rain driven by mad west winds over Zion and Araunah's threshing floor, and off into the east over Moab. When Sen-Hotep got up that morning shortly after sunrise, he almost went back to bed. Though the fury of the storm had abated, the sky in the west was packed with long, low banks rolling over each other darkly to climb up toward the vault of heaven.

The rain was still falling heavily. One look, and he shuddered with all his Egyptian sensibilities. He had never got used to the weather in this country. He wouldn't leave the house today, he decided. Surely David would stay in, too.

In the palace, David had been awake all night listening tranquilly to the thunder and gazing at the sudden, cracked smile of yellow-blue lightning zigzagging through the rain. When the blustering voice of the wind had quietened, Abishag heard him get up twice and go over to the window. The third time, when he came back, she asked him if everything was all right.

"I was just wondering why Adonai is riding his chariot so thunderously tonight." He closed his eyes then and fell asleep. It was about five o'clock.

Abishag woke him about three hours later for his breakfast. He sat up in bed, drank the heated wine, and nibbled tentatively at some fruit. But he had no great appetite, and pushed the food aside. When Abishag returned, she found him standing over at the open windows, a cloak thrown over his nightclothes. He was peering at the sky, humming a slow tune to himself. He heard her step.

"Abishag?"

"My Lord!" she sang out in greeting, then added gaily, "How many times did Adonai ride his chariot across the heavens last night?"

He looked around at her with great hollow eyes and a glint of a smile in them. "Oh, no, girl! I was mistaken. He wasn't riding his chariot. That storm was his signature!" He looked out again. "That was Adonai's signature."

Without turning around, he gave his instructions for the day. "Send a messenger to Sen-Hotep and tell him I'll meet him downstairs—just before noon. He'll grumble, of course. Ask Khimkham to come and see me when I'm dressed. And make sure the chariot is ready to take us to the threshing floor. And there are some more lines of poetry for Solomon there on the table. Make sure he gets them. He will know what to do with them."

Khimkham and he worked over the plans for the temple for a couple of hours. As usual, Abishag heard the old man squabbling with his young help: "... I tell you, the main door must look east. East! . . . Egyptian tile wears badly in this climate . . ." It was the same every morning. They argued and disputed walls and doors and terracing and cornicing. All the shouting and banging on the table was part of the pleasure, for when they emerged they were always in a good humor. This noon she heard them come ambling out of David's room. Then silence. She tiptoed to the door and craned around the jamb.

The two men were standing in front of Bathsheva's door. David was looking in at his wife. It was siesta hour, and Bathsheva was fast asleep. She lay on her side, her head cradled on her arm, her black hair loose and falling down over the coverlet. Abishag was curious. She padded down the corridor to David's side. Bathsheva stirred slightly at that moment, and David's eyes brightened in an almost childlike way, as if he hoped she was going to wake up and see him. When she was still again, the brightness left his eyes. "Be sure and tell her I came to say goodbye," he whispered to Abishag.

Down in the lobby Sen-Hotep was waiting. "Oh-ho! That's a wan smile," David chided him good-naturedly. All three laughed.

Outside, about to step into the chariot, David stopped. He was thinking to himself: Malaki should be here in his place at the double doors . . . just to see . . . But out loud he said nothing, merely mumbling to himself as old men do.

As they drove across the new viaduct that led onto the threshing floor, David talked about his poetry. "I decided yesterday to pull all my poems out of the Book of Ha-Yashar. They're better than anything in that book. I'll knit all my own into one song. About love. And this song will be the greatest of all songs! The song of songs! I've talked with Solomon about it."

By this time they had arrived. "Adonai himself prepared this table mountain for the temple," David remarked as they helped him from the chariot. The sky in the west was overcast. Due southwest the sun was peering wanly through scurrying clouds. David seemed unaware of the weather. He seemed to be still thinking of his poetry. "Did I recite my latest poem for you, Sen-Hotep?" He spoke from memory:

> "By night, upon my bed,
> I yearned for him whom my soul loves.
> I yearned, but could not find him.

"I will rise now,
And go about the city streets,
And in the broad land
I will seek him whom my soul loves.
I yearned, but could not find him.

"My beloved spoke to me:
Rise up! My fair one!
Come away with me.
For, look!
The storm is past.
The rain is over again.

"And I answered:
Let me see your face!
Let me hear your voice!
For your voice is sweetness.
And your face is beauty.
Many waters cannot quench love.

"If a man gave all the wealth of his house,
Just to obtain that love,
The price would be as nothing!"

"I've written it down for Solomon. He'll take care of it."
David walked out into the center of the threshing floor with
the other two. "Now let's see those plans again."

Sen-Hotep and Khimkham remembered every detail of what
happened then. By this time the clouds had completely obscured
the sun. Khimkham went back to the chariot and fetched the
pitch torches. They spread the plans out between them and
worked with this light for about an hour on the problem of the
east portico. Fortunately, the rain had stopped. David tried to
read some notes on the plans. He grumbled about the bad light.
Sen-Hotep reminded him of his own prediction of more rain.
David went on talking. He told them to hold the plans and stay
where they were. He walked over to the east end of the threshing
floor to the spot where the portico would be built. He was
facing east, his back to them, when they heard him groan. He
staggered a little. They dropped everything and ran over to
him. He was hunched down, holding his chest with both hands,
his face gray with pain, his breathing stentorian and labored.

"Adonai! But there's a bear squeezing my chest," he said.
"Help me sit down, will you. I'll be all right."

He sat down on Sen-Hotep's cloak, still breathing pain. They knelt on either side of him.

"David," the Egyptian began.

"No! I've had this before. It's easing up now." After a minute or two the pain did ease off and he began to breathe more easily, still sitting there in the gathering darkness that, in their preoccupation, none of them noticed for a few long minutes.

Then Khimkham brought over the torches and stood them in cracks of the rock flooring, and Sen-Hotep said, "Let me run now and get the chariot, David. We should get you back to the palace."

"No, no. This is where I'm supposed to be. I'm all right, I tell you. I'm all right!"

But he was not. In a few minutes the hands clutched the chest again and he groaned in pain, his face taut. They laid him down gently on his back, pillowing his head with Khimkham's cloak. It was at this moment that they began to notice for the first time that the wind was crying more and more shrilly. They could hear warning choruses from the crows in the oak trees standing to the north of the floor. But their main concentration was on David. He held on to a hand of each man with a viselike grip and looked out over Moab. He said only a few words. One about Bathsheva: "Tell her I loved her." The other about Malaki: "Bury me up at Golgotha beside his grave. I want to be where he is."

As soon as the agony passed, they felt the grip loosening. The face relaxed. He opened his eyes and looked up at the sky. The two men read the message: it was the end.

"Khimkham," Sen-Hotep said, "now! Take the chariot and fetch help."

"No," David said weakly. "No, no! Stay with me. No help can help now. Stay."

"Let me get Nathan—"

"Nathan can care only for the living."

"I'll get Solomon—"

"Neither." His breathing was difficult. "The lad sees me alive or he sees me dead. Not in between—not fitting."

"Well, then, Bathsheva should be—"

"No—no—I want her to sleep nights—no bad dreams— she's suffered enough—anyway, I've said goodbye." After this he said nothing. The pain was returning in sharp bites, making it more and more impossible to draw air into his lungs.

"We'd better get help," Khimkham said, glancing up at the sky.

"No. Not now—he's leaving us."

David was calm, his face eased of gross pain. But the breathing was faint and weak. He still held on to their hands on either side of him. Sen-Hotep glanced back at Zion. No lights were visible except at the North Gate tower. The whole city was still as death, people, dogs, birds, animals cowering in silence. In the peculiar half-light, half-darkness of the storm, striations of light and shade were passing perpendicularly across Zion's walls and towers.

They continued kneeling and watching David. Through the pain he could recognize them, hear their murmurs of helpless distress. And though he could no longer speak, he could see their faces on either side as they bent over him, the tears shining in their eyes. Looking out between them toward the east, he could see the hawthorn trees. They were utterly different from every other day. A lovely and blinding light was breaking all around them, washing them in gold. He wished he could tell Sen-Hotep and Khimkham about that holy fire burning, self-contained, all-absorbing. But then he couldn't see them any longer, although he could still feel the rock beneath his back and the warmth of their hands. David wished they could see the wonderful light of Adonai's presence. It seemed to grow stronger, according as the blackness of his pain started to engulf his whole body from head to toe, slashing him loose from his roots in the visible world.

That light blotted all else out, as it grew brighter and brighter, no longer enveloping merely the hawthorn trees, but suffusing his eyes and mind with the beginning of a freedom he had always desired. After what seemed an infinitely long time—in reality, only a few fleeting seconds—that lambent brilliance exploded noiselessly around him, lighting up every corner and cranny of his being. In that self-translucence he heard a voice he had always expected: "David, David." And he knew as unshakably as Samuel had known in his own day that this was his Adonai at last calling him by his name. The ultimate tenderness of that voice saying his name, calling him away, released his spirit from all desire to live on in the body.

The Egyptian and the young Hebrew saw his lips moving but they could not hear his last cries: "My Adonai!...My Adonai!..." They felt only a pittance of power left in those once powerful fingers now clinging limply to their hands. Nor could they know what David's beloved Adonai allowed his chosen one to see in the moment-long foresight of death. David no longer had the words to describe, and they, crouched on that barren, storm-lashed rock table, had no supernal light in their eyes to foresee, either the magnificent temple Solomon would build where his father now lay in his last agony, or its successor, the temple of Herod, whose pinnacles would tower in tempting glory, or the dull gray Antonia fortress the Romans would build a thousand years later on the northwest corner of that rock table, or, a little distance beyond the Antonia, the three Roman crosses erected on Golgotha at the eve of one Pesach, or the mosaicked Mosque of Omar with its shining gold dome that Muslims would build sixteen hundred years later, or the long lines of men, women, and children standing and bowing and praying in front of a huge, weather-beaten wall.

At the palace in Zion, Abishag and Lassatha stared from the roof. At first they could see only the flickering eyes of the torches out on the table mountain. Then they realized that one body lay supine on the rock floor. Almost simultaneously they screamed and ran down the stairs from floor to floor, down the main staircase, through the Great Lobby, and out into the street toward the North Gate. People dashed out of their houses and started after them.

The Egyptian had just closed David's eyelids, and Khimkham was weeping bitterly, when the lights of the sun started to return. During David's dying moments the clouds had been driven away by a brisk wind. Some blue sky could already be seen. From Zion, the two men heard a growing volume of noise—trumpets and cries and hooves and the sound of running feet. They looked. Already the long ramp and the viaduct were full of people and riders streaking toward the threshing floor. As the first figures crossed the edge of the floor, in the forefront they could recognize Lassatha, mouth open, hair streaming, eyes staring wildly, hands stretched out. From her they could hear the cry that echoed all the way from the threshing floor to the Cedar Palace in Zion: "David! David! David!"